Chain of Gold

THE ELDEST CURSES
With Wesley Chu

The Red Scrolls of Magic

The Shadowhunter's Codex
With Joshua Lewis

The Bane Chronicles
With Sarah Rees Brennan
and Maureen Johnson

Tales from the Shadowhunter Academy
With Sarah Rees Brennan, Maureen Johnson,
and Robin Wasserman

Ghosts of the Shadow Market
With Sarah Rees Brennan, Maureen Johnson,
Kelly Link, and Robin Wasserman

THE LAST HOURS

BOOK ONE

Chain of Gold
CASSANDRA CLARE

WALKER
BOOKS

This is a work of fiction. Names, characters, places and incidents
are either the product of the author's imagination or, if real, used
fictitiously. All statements, activities, stunts, descriptions, information
and material of any other kind contained herein are included for
entertainment purposes only and should not be relied on for
accuracy or replicated as they may result in injury.

Fi rst published in Great Britain 2020 by Walker Books Ltd
87 Vauxhall Walk, London SE11 5HJ

Text © 2020 Cassandra Clare, LLC

Jacket photo-illustration © 2020 Cliff Nielsen

Frontispi ece Cassandra Jean © 2019 Cassandra Clare, LLC

The right of Cassandra Clare to be identified as the author of this
work has been asserted by her in accordance with the
Copyright, Designs and Patents Act 1988

This book has been typeset in Dolly and Plantin

Printed and bound in Great Britain by Clays Ltd, Elcograf S.p.A.

British Library Cataloguing in Publication Data:
a catalogue record for this book is
available from the British Library

ISBN 978-1-4063-5809-4
ISBN 978-1-4063-9200-5 (Export/Airside PB)
ISBN 978-1-4063-9738-3 (Exclusive)
ISBN 978-1-4063-9737-6 (Illumicrate)
ISBN 978-1-4063-9736-9 (Fairyloot)

www.walker.co.uk

MIX
Paper from
responsible sources
FSC® C020471

For Clary (the real one)

Chain of Gold

PART ONE

– ❈ –

That was a memorable day to me, for it made great changes in me. But, it is the same with any life. Imagine one selected day struck out of it, and think how different its course would have been. Pause you who read this, and think for a moment of the long chain of iron or gold, of thorns or flowers, that would never have bound you, but for the formation of the first link on one memorable day.
—Charles Dickens, *Great Expectations*

Days Past: 1897

Lucie Herondale was ten years old when she first met the boy in the forest.

Growing up in London, Lucie had never imagined a place like Brocelind. The forest surrounded Herondale Manor on all sides, its trees bent together at the tops like cautious whisperers: dark green in the summer, burnished gold in the fall. The carpeting of moss underfoot was so green and soft that her father told her it was a pillow for faeries at night, and that the white stars of the flowers that grew only in the hidden country of Idris made bracelets and rings for their delicate hands.

James, of course, told her that faeries didn't have pillows, they slept underground and they stole away naughty little girls in their sleep. Lucie stepped on his foot, which meant that Papa swept her up and carried her back to the house before a fight could erupt. James came from the ancient and noble line of Herondale, but that didn't mean he was above pulling his little sister's plaits if the need arose.

Late one night the brightness of the moon woke Lucie. It was pouring into her room like milk, laying white bars of light over her bed and across the polished wood floor.

She slipped out of bed and climbed through the window, dropping lightly to the flower bed underneath. It was a summer night and she was warm in her nightdress.

The edge of the forest, just past the stables where their horses were kept, seemed to glow. She flitted toward it like a small ghost. Her slippered feet barely disturbed the moss as she slid in between the trees.

She amused herself at first by making chains of flowers and hanging them from branches. After that she pretended she was Snow White fleeing from the huntsman. She would run through the tangled trees and then turn dramatically and gasp, putting the back of her hand to her forehead. "You will never slay *me*," she said. "For I am of royal blood and will one day be queen and twice as powerful as my stepmother. And I shall cut off her head."

It was possible, she thought later, that she had not remembered the story of Snow White entirely correctly.

Still, it was very enjoyable, and it was on her fourth or fifth sprint through the woods that she realized she was lost. She could no longer see the familiar shape of Herondale Manor through the trees.

She spun around in a panic. The forest no longer seemed magical. Instead the trees loomed above like threatening ghosts. She thought she could hear the chatter of unearthly voices through the rustle of leaves. The clouds had come out and covered the moon. She was alone in the dark.

Lucie was brave, but she was only ten. She gave a little sob and began to run in what she thought was the right direction. But the forest only grew darker, the thorns more tangled. One caught at her nightdress and ripped a long tear in the fabric. She stumbled—

And fell. It felt like Alice's fall into Wonderland, though it was much shorter than that. She tumbled head over heels and hit a layer of hard-packed dirt.

With a whimper, she sat up. She was lying at the bottom of

a circular hole that had been dug into the earth. The sides were smooth and rose several feet above the reach of her arms.

She tried digging her hands into the dirt that rose on every side of her and climbing up it the way she might shinny up a tree. But the earth was soft and crumbled away in her fingers. After the fifth time she'd tumbled from the side of the pit, she spied something white gleaming from the sheer side of the dirt wall. Hoping it was a root she could climb up, she bounded toward it and reached to grasp it. . . .

Soil fell away from it. It wasn't a root at all but a white bone, and not an animal's . . .

"Don't scream," said a voice above her. "It'll bring them."

She threw her head back and stared. Leaning down over the side of the pit was a boy. Older than her brother, James—maybe even sixteen years old. He had a lovely melancholy face and straight black hair without a hint of curl. The ends of his hair almost touched the collar of his shirt.

"Bring who?" Lucie put her fists on her hips.

"The faeries," he said. "This is one of their pit traps. They usually use them to catch animals, but they'd be very pleased to find a little girl instead."

Lucie gasped. "You mean they'd eat me?"

He laughed. "Unlikely, though you could find yourself serving faerie gentry in the Land Under the Hill for the rest of your life. Never to see your family again."

He wiggled his eyebrows at her.

"Don't try to scare me," she said.

"I assure you, I speak only the perfect truth," he said. "Even the imperfect truth is beneath me."

"Don't be silly, either," she said. "I am Lucie Herondale. My father is Will Herondale and a very important person. If you rescue me, you will be rewarded."

"A Herondale?" he said. "Just my luck." He sighed and wriggled closer to the edge of the pit, reaching his arm down. A scar gleamed on the back of his right hand—a bad one, as if he had burned himself. "Up you go."

She grasped his wrist with both her hands and he hauled her up with surprising strength. A moment later they were both standing. Lucie could see more of him now. He was older than she'd thought, and formally dressed in white and black. The moon was out again and she could see that his eyes were the color of the green moss on the forest floor.

"Thank you," she said, rather primly. She brushed at her nightdress. It was quite ruined with dirt.

"Come along, now," he said, his voice gentle. "Don't be frightened. What shall we talk about? Do you like stories?"

"I love stories," said Lucie. "When I grow up, I am going to be a famous writer."

"That sounds wonderful," said the boy. There was something wistful about his tone.

They walked together through the paths under the trees. He seemed to know where he was going, as if the forest was very familiar to him. He must be a changeling, Lucie thought wisely. He knew a great deal about faeries, but was clearly not one of them: he had warned her about being stolen away by the Fair Folk, which must be what had happened to him. She would not mention it and make him feel awkward; it must be dreadful to be a changeling, and to be taken far away from your family. Instead she engaged him in a discussion about princesses in fairy tales, and which one was the best. It hardly seemed any time at all before they were back in the garden of Herondale Manor.

"I imagine this princess can make her own way back into the castle from here," he said with a bow.

"Oh, yes," said Lucie, eyeing her window. "Do you think they'll know I was gone?"

He laughed and turned to go. She called after him when he reached the gates.

"What's your name?" she said. "I told you mine. What's yours?"

He hesitated for a moment. He was all white and black in the night, like an illustration from one of her books. He swept a bow, low and graceful, the kind knights had once made.

"You will never slay *me*," he said. "For I am of royal blood and will one day be twice as powerful as the queen. And I shall cut off her head."

Lucie gave an outraged gasp. Had he been listening to her, in the woods, playing her game? How dare he make fun of her! She raised a fist, meaning to shake it at him, but he had already vanished into the night, leaving only the sound of his laughter behind.

It would be six years before she saw him again.

1

BETTER ANGELS

The shadows of our own desires stand between us and
our better angels, and thus their brightness is eclipsed.
—Charles Dickens, *Barnaby Rudge*

James Herondale was in the middle of fighting a demon when he was suddenly pulled into Hell.

It wasn't the first time it had happened, and it wouldn't be the last. Moments earlier he had been kneeling at the edge of a slanted roof in central London, a slim throwing knife in each hand, thinking about how disgusting the detritus that collected in the city was. In addition to dirt, empty gin bottles, and animal bones, there was definitely a dead bird wedged into the rain gutter just below his left knee.

How glamorous the life of a Shadowhunter was, indeed. It *sounded* good, he thought, gazing down at the empty alley below him: a narrow space choked with rubbish, lit dimly by the half-moon overhead. A special race of warriors, descended from an angel, gifted with powers that allowed them to wield weapons of shining *adamas* and to bear the black Marks of holy runes on their bodies—runes that made them stronger, faster, more deadly than any mundane human; runes that made them burn brightly in the dark. No one ever mentioned things like accidentally kneeling on a dead bird while waiting for a demon to turn up.

A yell echoed down the alley. A sound James knew well: Matthew Fairchild's voice. He launched himself off the roof without a moment's hesitation. Matthew Fairchild was his *parabatai*—his blood brother and warrior partner. James was sworn to protect him, not that it mattered: he would have given his life for Matthew's, vows or not.

Movement flashed at the end of the alley, where it curved behind a narrow row of houses. James spun as a demon emerged from the shadows, roaring. It had a ribbed gray body, a curving, sharp beak lined with hooked teeth, and splayed paw-like feet from which ragged claws protruded. *A Deumas demon*, James thought grimly. He definitely remembered reading about Deumas demons in one of the old books his uncle Jem had given him. They were meant to be notable in some way. Extremely vicious, perhaps, or unusually dangerous? That would be typical, wouldn't it—all these months of not running across any infernal activity at all, and he and his friends happened on one of the most dangerous demons out there.

Speaking of which—where *were* his friends?

The Deumas roared again and lurched toward James, drool spilling from its mouth in long strings of greenish slime.

James swung his arm back, ready to throw his first knife. The demon's eyes fixed on him for a moment. They were coruscating, green and black, filled with a hate that turned suddenly into something else.

Something like recognition. But demons, at least the lesser kind, didn't recognize people. They were vicious animals driven by pure greed and hatred. As James hesitated in surprise, the ground under him seemed to lurch. He had only a moment to think, *Oh no, not now*, before the world went gray and silent. The buildings around him had turned to ragged shadow, the sky a black cave speared with white lightning.

He closed his right hand around his knife—not the handle, but the blade. The jolt of pain was like a slap to the face, snapping him out of a stupor. The world came rushing back at him in all its noise and color. He barely had time to register that the Deumas was in midair, claws extended toward him, when a swirl of cords whipped through the sky, entangling the demon's leg and yanking it backward.

Thomas! James thought, and indeed, his massively tall friend had appeared behind the Deumas, armed with his *bolas*. Behind him was Christopher, armed with a bow, and Matthew, a seraph blade blazing in his hand.

The Deumas hit the ground with another roar, just as James let both his knives fly. One plunged into the demon's throat, the other into its forehead. Its eyes rolled back, it spasmed, and James suddenly remembered what it was he'd read about Deumas demons.

"Matthew—" he began, just as the creature burst apart, showering Thomas, Christopher, and Matthew in ichor and burnt bits of what could only be described as goo.

Messy, James recalled belatedly. Deumas demons were notably messy. Most demons vanished when they died. Not Deumas demons.

They exploded.

"How—wha—?" Christopher stuttered, at a clear loss for words. Slime dripped off his pointed nose and gold-rimmed spectacles. "But how . . . ?"

"Do you mean how is it possible that we finally tracked down the last demon in London and it was also the most disgusting?" James was surprised by how normal his voice sounded: he was already shaking off the shock of his glimpse into the shadow realm. At least his clothes were untouched: the demon seemed to have exploded mostly over the other end of the alley. "Ours is not to question why, Christopher."

James had a feeling his friends were gazing at him resentfully. Thomas rolled his eyes. He was scrubbing at himself with a handkerchief that was also half-burnt and covered in ichor, so it was doing little good.

Matthew's seraph blade had begun to sputter. Seraph blades, infused with the energy of angels, were often a Shadowhunter's most trusted weapon and best defense against demons, but it was still possible to drown one in enough ichor. "This is an outrage," Matthew said, tossing the extinguished blade aside. "Do you know how much I spent on this waistcoat?"

"No one told you to go out patrolling for demons dressed like an extra from *The Importance of Being Earnest*," said James, tossing him a clean handkerchief. As he did, he felt his hand sting. There was a bloody cut across his palm from the blade of the knife. He closed his hand into a fist to prevent his companions from seeing it.

"I don't think he's dressed like an extra," said Thomas, who had turned his attention to cleaning off Christopher.

"Thank you," said Matthew with a slight bow.

"I think he's dressed like a main character." Thomas grinned. He had one of the kindest faces James had ever known, and gentle hazel eyes. None of which meant he didn't enjoy mocking his friends.

Matthew mopped at his dull gold hair with James's handkerchief. "This is the first time in a year that we've patrolled and actually found a demon, so I'd supposed that my waistcoat would probably survive the evening. It's not as if any of you are wearing gear either."

It was true that Shadowhunters usually hunted in gear, a sort of flexible armor made of a tough, leatherlike black material resistant to ichor, blades, and the like, but a lack of reliable demonic presence on the streets had made them all a bit lax about rules.

"Stop scrubbing at me, Thomas," said Christopher, windmilling his arms. "We should go back to the Devil and clean up there."

There was a murmur of assent among the group. As they picked their sticky way back to the main street, James considered the fact that Matthew was right. James's father, Will, had often told him about the patrols he used to do with his *parabatai*, Jem Carstairs—now James's uncle Jem—back when they had battled demons nearly every night.

James and other young Shadowhunters still faithfully patrolled the streets of London, seeking out demons that might harm the mundane population, but in the last few years demon appearances had been few and far between. It was a good thing—of course it was a good thing—but still. It was decidedly odd. Demon activity was still normal as far as the rest of the world was concerned, so what made London special?

There were plenty of mundanes out and about on the streets of the city, though the hour was late. None glanced at the bedraggled group of Shadowhunters as they made their way down Fleet Street; their glamour runes made them invisible to all eyes not gifted with the Sight.

It was always strange to be surrounded by a humanity that did not see you, James thought. Fleet Street was home to the newspaper offices and law courts of London, and everywhere were brightly lit pubs, with print workers and barristers and law clerks, who kept late hours, drinking into the dawn light. The Strand nearby had spilled the contents of its music halls and theaters, and well-dressed groups of young people, laughing and boisterous, chased the last omnibuses of the night.

The bobbies were out working their beats too, and those denizens of London unfortunate enough to have no homes to go to crouched muttering around cellar vents that sent up drifts of warm air—even in August the nights could be damp and chilly. As they passed a group of such huddled figures, one looked up, and James caught a glimpse of the pale skin and glittering eyes of a vampire.

He looked away. Downworlders weren't his business unless they were breaking Clave Law. And he was tired, despite his energy Marks: it always drained him to be dragged into that other world of gray light and black ragged shadows. It was something that had been happening to him for years: a remnant, he knew, of his mother's warlock blood.

Warlocks were the offspring of humans and demons: capable of using magic but not of bearing runes or using *adamas*, the clear crystalline metal from which steles and seraph blades were carved. They were one of the four branches of Downworlders, along with vampires, werewolves, and the fey. James's mother, Tessa Herondale, was such a warlock, but her mother had been not just human but a Shadowhunter. Tessa herself had once possessed the power to shape-shift and take on the appearance of anyone, living or dead: a power no other warlock had. She was unusual in one other way as well: warlocks could not have children. Tessa was an exception. Everyone had wondered what this would mean for James and his sister, Lucie, the first-ever known grandchildren of a demon and a human being.

For many years, it appeared to have meant nothing. Both James and Lucie could bear Marks and seemed to have the abilities of any other Shadowhunter. They could both see ghosts—like the Institute's chatty phantom-in-residence, Jessamine—but that was not uncommon in the Herondale family. It seemed they might both be blessedly normal, or at least as normal as a Shadowhunter could be. Even the Clave—the governing body of all Shadowhunters—had seemed to forget about them.

Then, when James was thirteen, he first traveled into the shadow realm. One moment he had been standing on green grass: the next, charred earth. A similarly scorched sky arced above him. Twisted trees emerged from the ground, ragged claws grasping at the air. He had seen such places in woodcuts in old books. He knew what he was looking at: a demon world. A Hell dimension.

Moments later he had been jerked back to earth, but his life had never been the same again. For years the fear had been there that he might at any moment hurtle back into shadow. It was as if an invisible rope connected him to a world of demons, and at any moment the rope could be pulled taut, snatching him out of his familiar environment and into a place of fire and ash.

For the last few years, with his uncle Jem's help, he'd thought he had it under control. Though it had been only a few seconds, tonight had shaken him, and he was relieved when the Devil Tavern appeared before them.

The Devil made its home at No. 2 Fleet Street, next to a respectable-looking print shop. Unlike the shop, it was glamoured so that no mundanes could see it or hear the raucous noises of debauchery that poured from the windows and the open doors. It was half-timbered in the Tudor style, the old wood ratty and splintering, kept from falling down by warlocks' spells. Behind the bar, werewolf owner Ernie pulled pints: the crowd was a mix of pixies and vampires and lycanthropes and warlocks.

The usual welcome for Shadowhunters in a place like this would have been a cold one, but the patrons of the Devil Tavern were used to the boys. They greeted James, Christopher, Matthew, and Thomas with yells of welcome and mockery. James stayed in the pub to collect drinks from Polly, the barmaid, while the others tramped upstairs to their rooms, shedding ichor on the steps as they went.

Polly was a werewolf, and had taken the boys under her wing when James had first rented out the attic rooms three years ago, wanting a private bolt-hole he and his friends could retreat to where their parents wouldn't be hovering. She was the one who'd first taken to calling them the Merry Thieves, after Robin Hood and his men. James suspected he was Robin of Locksley and Matthew was Will Scarlett. Thomas was definitely Little John.

Polly chuckled. "Almost didn't recognize the lot of you when you tramped in here covered in whatever-you-call-it."

"Ichor," said James, accepting a bottle of hock. "It's demon blood."

Polly wrinkled her nose, draping several worn-looking dish-cloths over his shoulder. She handed him an extra one, which he pressed against the cut on his hand. It had stopped bleeding but still throbbed. "Blimey."

"It's been ages since we've even seen a demon in London," said James. "We may not have been as swift with our reaction time as we ought."

"I reckon they're all too scared to show their faces," said Polly companionably, turning away to fetch a glass of gin for Pickles, the resident kelpie.

"Scared?" James echoed, pausing. "Scared of what?"

Polly started. "Oh, nothing, nothing," she said, and hurried away to the other end of the bar. With a frown, James made his way upstairs. The ways of Downworlders were sometimes mysterious.

Two flights of creaking steps led to a wooden door on which a line had been carved years ago: *It matters not how a man dies, but how he lives. S.J.*

James shouldered the door open and found Matthew and Thomas already sprawled around a circular table in the middle of a wood-paneled room. Several windows, their glass bumpy and pocked with age, looked out upon Fleet Street, lit by intermittent streetlamps, and the Royal Courts of Justice across the way, dimly sketched against the cloudy night.

The room was a fond and familiar place, with worn walls, a collection of ragged furniture, and a low fire burning in the grate. Over the fireplace was a marble bust of Apollo, his nose chipped off long ago. The walls were lined with occult books written by mundane magicians: the library at the Institute didn't allow such things, but James collected them. He was fascinated by the idea of those who had not been born to the world of magic and shadows and yet yearned for them so strongly that they had learned how to pry open the gates.

Both Thomas and Matthew were free of ichor, wearing wrinkled but clean clothes, their hair—Thomas's sandy brown and Matthew's dark gold—still damp. "James!" Matthew cheered upon seeing his friend. His eyes were suspiciously bright; there was already a half-drunk bottle of brandy on the table. "Is that a bottle of cheap spirits I see before me?"

James set the wine down on the table just as Christopher emerged from the small bedroom at the far end of the attic space. The bedroom had been there before they had taken over the space: there was still a bed in it, but none of the Merry Thieves used it for anything besides washing up and storing weapons and changes of clothes.

"James," Christopher said, looking pleased. "I thought you'd gone home."

"Why on earth would I go home?" James took a seat beside Matthew and tossed Polly's dish towels onto the table.

"No idea," said Christopher cheerfully, pulling up a chair. "But you might have. People do odd things all the time. We had a cook who went to do the shopping and was found two weeks later in Regent's Park. She'd become a zookeeper."

Thomas raised his eyebrows. James and the rest of the group were never sure whether to entirely believe Christopher's stories. Not that he was a liar, but when it came to anything that wasn't beakers and test tubes, he tended to be paying only a fraction of attention.

Christopher was the son of James's aunt Cecily and uncle Gabriel. He had the fine bone structure of his parents, dark brown hair, and eyes that could only be described as the color of lilacs.

"Wasted on a boy!" Cecily said often, with a martyred sigh. Christopher ought to have been popular with girls, but the thick spectacles he wore obscured most of his face, and he had gunpowder perpetually embedded under his fingernails. Most Shadowhunters regarded mundane guns with suspicion or disinterest—the application of runes to metal or bullets prevented gunpowder from igniting, and non-runed weapons were useless against demons. Christopher, however, was obsessed with the idea that he could adapt incendiary weapons to Nephilim purposes. James had to admit that the idea of mounting a cannon on the roof of the Institute had a certain appeal.

"Your hand," Matthew said suddenly, leaning forward and fixing his green eyes on James. "What happened?"

"Just a cut," James said, opening his hand. The wound was a long diagonal slice across his palm. As Matthew took James's hand, the silver bracelet that James always wore on his right wrist clinked against the hock bottle on the table. "You should have told me," Matthew said, reaching into his waistcoat for his stele. "I would have fixed you up in the alley."

"I forgot," James said.

Thomas, who was running his finger around the rim of his own glass without drinking, said, "Did something happen?"

Thomas was annoyingly perceptive. "It was very quick," James said, with some reluctance.

"Many things that are 'very quick' are also very bad," said Matthew, setting the point of his stele to James's skin. "Guillotines come down very quickly, for instance. When Christopher's experiments explode, they often explode very quickly."

"Clearly, I have neither exploded nor been guillotined," said James. "I—went into the shadow realm."

Matthew's head jerked up, though his hand remained steady as the *iratze*, a healing rune, took shape on James's skin. James could feel the pain in his hand begin to subside. "I thought all that business had stopped," Matthew said. "I thought Jem had helped you."

"He did help me. It's been a year since the last time." James shook his head. "I suppose it was too much to hope it was gone forever."

"Doesn't it usually happen when you're upset?" said Thomas. "Was it the demon attacking?"

"No," James said quickly. "No, I can't imagine—no." James had been almost looking forward to the fight. It had been a frustrating summer, the first one in over a decade that he hadn't spent with his family in Idris.

Idris was located in central Europe. Warded all around, it was an unspoiled country, hidden from mundane eyes and mundane inventions: a place without railroads, factories, or coal smoke. James knew why his family couldn't go this year, but he had his own reasons for wishing he were there instead of London. Patrolling had been one of his few distractions.

"Demons don't bother our boy," said Matthew, finishing the healing rune. This close to his *parabatai*, James could smell the familiar scent of Matthew's soap mixed with alcohol. "It must have been something else."

"You ought to talk to your uncle, then, Jamie," said Thomas.

James shook his head. He didn't want to bother Uncle Jem about what felt now like a moment-long flicker. "It was nothing. I was surprised by the demon; I grabbed at the blade by accident. I'm sure that's what caused it."

"Did you turn into a shadow?" said Matthew, putting his stele away. Sometimes, when James was pulled into the shadow realm, his friends reported that they could see him blurring around the edges. On some occasions, he'd turned entirely into a dark shadow—James-shaped, but transparent and incorporeal.

A few times—a very few times—he'd been able to turn himself

into a shadow to pass through something solid. But he didn't wish to speak about those times.

Christopher looked up from his notebook. "Speaking of the demon—"

"Which we weren't," Matthew pointed out.

"—what kind was it again?" Christopher asked, biting the end of his pen. He often wrote down details of their demon-fighting expeditions. He claimed it helped him in his research. "The one that exploded, I mean."

"As opposed to the one that didn't?" said James.

Thomas, who had an excellent memory for detail, said: "It was a Deumas, Christopher. Odd it was here; they're not usually found in cities."

"I saved some of its ichor," said Christopher, producing from somewhere on his person a corked test tube full of a greenish substance. "I caution all of you not to drink any of it."

"I can assure you we had no plans to do any such thing, you daft boot," said Thomas.

Matthew shuddered. "Enough talk of ichor. Let's toast again to Thomas being home!"

Thomas protested. James raised his glass and toasted with Matthew. Christopher was about to clink his test tube against James's glass when Matthew, muttering imprecations, confiscated it and handed Christopher a glass of hock instead.

Thomas, despite his objections, looked pleased. Most Shadowhunters went on a sort of grand tour when they turned eighteen, leaving their home Institute for one abroad; Thomas had only just returned from nine months in Madrid a few weeks ago. The point of the travel was to learn new customs and broaden one's horizons: Thomas had certainly broadened, though mostly in the physical sense.

Though the oldest of their group, Thomas had been slight in

stature. When James, Matthew, and Christopher arrived at the dock to meet his ship from Spain, they combed through the crowds, nearly failing to recognize their friend in the muscular young man descending the gangplank. Thomas was the tallest of them now, tanned as if he'd grown up on a farm instead of in London. He could wield a broadsword in one hand, and in Spain he had adopted a new weapon, the *bolas*, made of stout ropes and weights that whirled over his head. Matthew often said it was like being comrades with a friendly giant.

"When you're entirely done, I do have some news," Thomas said, tipping his chair back. "You know that old manor in Chiswick that once belonged to my grandfather? Used to be called Lightwood House? It was given to my aunt Tatiana by the Clave some years ago, but she's never used it—preferred to stay in Idris at the manor with my cousin, er . . ."

"Gertrude," said Christopher helpfully.

"Grace," James said. "Her name is Grace."

She was Christopher's cousin too, though James knew they had never met her.

"Yes, Grace," agreed Thomas. "Aunt Tatiana's always kept them both in splendid isolation in Idris—no vistors and all that—but apparently she's decided to move back to London, so my parents are all in a dither about it."

James's heart gave a slow, hard thump. "Grace," he began, and saw Matthew shoot him a quick sideways glance. "Grace—is moving to London?"

"Seems Tatiana wants to bring her out in society." Thomas looked puzzled. "I suppose you've met her, in Idris? Doesn't your house there adjoin Blackthorn Manor?"

James nodded mechanically. He could feel the weight of the bracelet around his right wrist, though he had worn it now for so many years that usually he was unconscious of its presence.

"I usually see her every summer," he said. "Not this summer, of course."

Not this summer. He hadn't been able to argue with his parents when they'd said the Herondale family would be spending this summer in London. Hadn't been able to mention the reason he wanted to return to Idris. After all, as far as they were aware, he barely even knew Grace. The sickness, the horror that gripped him at the thought that he would not see her for another year was nothing he could explain.

It was a secret he had carried since he was thirteen. In his mind, he could see the tall gates rising before Blackthorn Manor, and his own hands in front of him—a child's hands, without scars, cutting industriously away at the thorny vines. He could see the Long Hall in the manor, and the curtains blowing across the windows, and hear music. He could see Grace in her ivory dress.

Matthew was watching him with thoughtful green eyes that were no longer dancing. Matthew, alone of all James's friends, knew that there was a connection between James and Grace Blackthorn.

"London is being positively swarmed by new arrivals," Matthew remarked. "The Carstairs family will be with us soon, won't they?"

James nodded. "Lucie is wild with excitement to see Cordelia."

Matthew poured more wine into his glass. "Can't blame them for being tired of rusticating in Devon—what's that house of theirs called? Cirenworth? I gather they arrive in a day or two—"

Thomas upset his drink. James's drink and Christopher's test tube went with it. Thomas was still growing accustomed to occupying so much space in the world, and he sometimes proved clumsy.

"*All* of the Carstairs family are coming, did you say?" said Thomas.

"Not Elias Carstairs," said Matthew. Elias was Cordelia's father. "But Cordelia, and of course . . ." He trailed off meaningfully.

"Oh, bloody hell," said Christopher. "Alastair Carstairs." He looked vaguely ill. "I'm not remembering incorrectly? He's an awful pill?"

"'Awful pill' seems a kind way of putting it," said James. Thomas was mopping up his drink; James looked at him with concern. Thomas had been a shy, small boy at school, and Alastair a rotten bully. "We can avoid Alastair, Tom. There's no reason for us to spend time with him, and I can't imagine he'll be yearning for our society either."

Thomas spluttered, but not in response to what James had said. The contents of Christopher's spilled test tube had turned a violent puce and begun to eat through the table. They all leaped up to grab for Polly's dish towels. Thomas hurled a pitcher of water at the table, which drenched Christopher, and Matthew doubled over laughing.

"I say," said Christopher, mopping wet hair out of his eyes. "I do think that worked, Tom. The acid has been neutralized."

Thomas was shaking his head. "Someone should neutralize you, you mopstick—"

Matthew collapsed in hysterics.

In the midst of the chaos, James could not help feeling very far away from it all. For so many years, in so many hundreds of secret letters between London and Idris, he and Grace had sworn to each other that one day they would be together; that one day when they were adults, they would marry, whether their parents wished it or not, and live together in London. It had always been their dream.

So why hadn't she told him she was coming?

"Oh, look! The Royal Albert Hall!" Cordelia cried, pressing her nose against the window of the carriage. It was a brilliant day, bright sunlight streaming down over London, making the sparkling white row houses of South Kensington glow like rows of ivory soldiers in an expensive chess set. "London really does have marvelous architecture."

"A shrewd observation," drawled her older brother, Alastair, who was ostentatiously reading a book on sums in the corner of the carriage, as if to announce that he couldn't be bothered to glance out the window. "I'm sure no one has ever commented on London's buildings before."

Cordelia glared at him, but he didn't look up. Couldn't he tell she was just trying to raise everyone's spirits? Their mother, Sona, was leaning exhaustedly against the side of the carriage, violet hollows under her eyes, her normally radiant brown skin sallow. Cordelia had been worried about her for weeks now, ever since the news about Father had come to Devon from Idris. "The point, Alastair, is that now we're here to live, not visit. We'll meet people, we can entertain visitors, we needn't stay in the Institute—even though I would like to be near Lucie—"

"And James," said Alastair, without looking up from his book.

Cordelia gritted her teeth.

"Children." Cordelia's mother glanced at them reprovingly. Alastair looked resentful—he was one month shy of his nineteenth birthday and, in his mind at least, certainly not a child. "This is serious business. As you well know, we are not in London to amuse ourselves. We are in London on behalf of our family."

Cordelia exchanged a less hostile look with her brother. She knew he was worried about Sona too, though he never would have admitted it. She wondered for the millionth time how much he knew about the situation with Father. She knew both that it was more than she did, and that he would never speak to her of it.

She felt a little thump of excitement as their carriage pulled up at 102 Cornwall Gardens, one of a row of grand white Victorian houses with the number painted in austere black on the rightmost pillar. There were several figures standing atop the front steps,

beneath the portico. Cordelia instantly recognized Lucie Herondale, a little taller now than she had been the last time Cordelia had
seen her. Her light brown hair was caught up under her hat, and her
pale blue jacket and skirt matched her eyes.

Beside her stood two figures. One was Lucie's mother, Tessa
Herondale, the famous—among Shadowhunters, at any rate—wife
of Will Herondale, who ran the London Institute. She looked only a
little older than her daughter. Tessa was immortal, a warlock and a
shape-shifter, and she did not age.

Next to Tessa was James.

Cordelia remembered, once, when she'd been a small girl,
reaching to pet a swan in the pond by her house. The bird had
launched itself at her, barreling into her midsection and knocking
her down. For several minutes she had lain on the grass, choking
and trying to get her breath back, terrified she'd never suck air into
her lungs again.

She supposed it was not the most romantic thing in the world
to say that every time she saw James Herondale she felt as if she'd
been attacked by a waterfowl, but it was true.

He was beautiful, so beautiful that she forgot to breathe when
she looked at him. He had wild, tumbled black hair that looked as if
it would be soft to touch, and his long, dark lashes fringed eyes the
color of honey or amber. Now that he was seventeen, he had grown
out of his gawky younger self and was sleek and lovely all over, perfectly put together, like a marvelous bit of architecture.

"Oof!" Her feet hit the ground and she nearly stumbled. Somehow she'd wrenched the carriage door open and was now standing
on the pavement—well, wobbling really, as she struggled to keep
her balance on legs that had gone to sleep after hours of disuse.

James was there instantly, his hand on her arm, steadying her.
"Daisy?" he said. "Are you all right?"

His nickname for her. He hadn't forgotten.

"Just clumsy." She looked around ruefully. "I was hoping for a more gracious arrival."

"Nothing to worry about." He smiled, and her heart turned over. "The pavements of South Kensington are vicious. I've been attacked by them more than once myself."

Make a clever response, she told herself. *Say something witty.*

But he had already turned away, inclining his head toward Alastair. James and Alastair had not liked each other at school, Cordelia knew, though her mother did not. Sona thought Alastair had been very popular.

"I see you're here, Alastair." James's voice was curiously flat. "And you look—"

He eyed Alastair's bright yellow-white hair with some astonishment. Cordelia waited for him to continue, with great hope that he would say *you look like a turnip*, but he didn't.

"You look well," he finished.

The boys looked at each other in silence as Lucie raced down the steps and threw her arms around Cordelia. "I am so very, very delighted to see you!" she said, in her breathless way. For Lucie, everything was always very, very, very something, be it beautiful or exciting or horrid. "Darling Cordelia, we shall have so much fun—"

"Lucie, Cordelia and her family have come to London so that you and Cordelia can train together," said Tessa in her gentle voice. "It will be a great deal of work and responsibility."

Cordelia glanced down at her shoes. Tessa was being kind in repeating the story that the Carstairs had come to London in a hurry because of Cordelia and Lucie needing to be *parabatai*, but that wasn't the truth.

"Well, you must remember being sixteen yourself, Mrs. Herondale," said Sona. "Young girls adore dances and dresses. I certainly did when I was their age, and I imagine you did as well."

Cordelia knew this was entirely not true about her mother but kept her mouth shut. Tessa arched her eyebrows. "I do recall attending a vampire frolic once. And some sort of party at Benedict Lightwood's house, before he got demon pox and turned into a worm, of course—"

"Mother!" Lucie said, scandalized.

"Well, he did turn into a worm," said James. "Really more of a vicious, giant serpent. It was entirely one of the most interesting parts of history class."

Tessa was saved further comment by the arrival of the removers' vans carrying the Carstairs' belongings. Several large men leaped down from one of the vans and went to pull back the canvas covering the various furniture pieces, which had been fastidiously roped down.

One of the men assisted Risa, Sona's lady's maid and cook, down from the first of the vans. Risa had worked for the Jahanshah family when Sona was in her teens and had been with her ever since. She was a mundane who had the Sight, and thus a valuable companion for a Shadowhunter. Risa spoke only Persian; Cordelia wondered whether the men in the van had tried to make conversation with her. Risa understood English perfectly, but she liked her silence.

"Please thank Cecily Lightwood for me, for the loan of her domestic help," Cordelia's mother was saying to Tessa.

"Oh, indeed! They will come on Tuesdays and Thursdays to do the rough, until you can find suitable servants of your own," Tessa replied.

"The rough" was everything Risa—who cooked, shopped, and helped Sona and Cordelia with their clothes—would not be expected to do, like scrubbing the floors or caring for the horses. The idea that the Carstairs were planning to hire their own servants soon was another polite fiction, Cordelia knew. When they left Devon, Sona had let all the servants go, save for Risa, as they were trying to conserve as much money as possible while Elias Carstairs was awaiting trial.

A large shape on one of the vans caught Cordelia's eye. "Mama!" she exclaimed. "You brought the piano?"

Her mother shrugged. "I like a bit of music about." She gestured imperiously toward the workmen. "Cordelia, it's going to be messy and noisy. Perhaps if you and Lucie would go take a turn about the neighborhood? And Alastair, you stay here and help direct the servants."

Cordelia was delighted at the prospect of time alone with Lucie. Alastair meanwhile looked caught between sourness at having to remain behind with his mother, and pomposity at being trusted with the responsibilities of the man of the house.

Tessa Herondale looked amused. "James, go with the girls. Perhaps Kensington Gardens? It's a short walk and a lovely day."

"Kensington Gardens does seem safe," James said gravely.

Lucie rolled her eyes and seized Cordelia's hand. "Come along, then," she said, and pulled her down the steps and onto the pavement.

James, with his long legs, matched them easily. "There's no need to bolt, Lucie," he said. "Mother isn't going to haul you back and demand that you drag a piano into the house."

Cordelia cast a sideways look at him. The wind was ruffling his black hair. Even her own mother's hair was not so dark: it had undertones of red and gold. James's hair was like spilled ink.

He smiled at her easily, as if he hadn't just caught her staring at him. Then again, he was doubtless used to being stared at when with other Shadowhunters. Not just because of his looks, but for other reasons as well.

Lucie squeezed her arm. "I'm so happy you're here," she declared. "I never thought it would really happen."

"Why not?" said James. "The Law demands you train together

before you can become *parabatai*, and besides, Father adores Daisy, and he does make the rules. . . ."

"Your father adores any Carstairs," said Cordelia. "I'm not sure it's to my particular credit. He may even like Alastair."

"I think he has convinced himself Alastair has hidden depths," said James.

"So does quicksand," said Cordelia.

James laughed.

"That's quite enough," said Lucie, reaching over to smack James on the shoulder with a gloved hand. "Daisy is my friend, and you're monopolizing her. Do go off somewhere else."

They were walking up Queen's Gate toward Kensington Road, the clatter of omnibus traffic all around them. Cordelia imagined James wandering off into the crowd, where surely he would find something more interesting to do, or perhaps be kidnapped by a beautiful heiress who would fall in love with him instantly. These sort of things happened in London.

"I will walk ten paces behind you like a train-bearer," said James. "But I must keep you within sight, otherwise Mother will kill me, and then I will miss tomorrow's ball and Matthew will kill me, and I will be dead twice."

Cordelia smiled, but James was already dropping back as promised. He ambled along behind them, giving the girls space to talk; Cordelia tried to hide her disappointment at the lack of his presence. She lived in London now, after all, and sightings of James were no longer rare glimpses but would hopefully become part of her everyday life.

She glanced back at him; he had already taken out a book and was reading it while walking and whistling under his breath.

"What ball did he mean?" she asked, turning to Lucie. They passed under the black wrought-iron gates of Kensington Park and into leafy shade. The public garden was full of nannies pushing babies in prams and young couples walking together under the trees. Two little girls were making daisy chains, and a boy in a blue sailor suit was running along with a hoop, shrieking with laughter. He ran to a tall man, who picked him up and swung him into the air as he laughed. Cordelia squeezed her eyes shut for a moment, thinking of her own father, of the way he had tossed her into the air when she was very small, making her laugh and laugh even as he caught her on her way down.

"The one tomorrow night," Lucie said, linking her arm with Cordelia's. "We're throwing it to welcome you to London. All the Enclave will be there, and there will be dancing, and Mother will have a chance to show off the new ballroom. And I will have a chance to show off you."

Cordelia felt a chill go over her—part excitement, part fear. The Enclave was the official name for the Shadowhunters of London: every city had an Enclave, who answered to their local Institute as well as the superior authority of the Clave and the Consul. She knew it was foolish, but the thought of so many people prickled her skin with anxiety. The life she had lived with her family—constantly traveling save when they were at Cirenworth in Devon—had been devoid of crowds.

And yet this was what she had to do—what they had all come to London to do. She thought of her mother.

It was not a ball, she told herself. It was the first skirmish in a war.

She lowered her voice. "Will everyone there—does everyone know about my father?"

"Oh, no. Very few people have heard any details, and those are being quite closemouthed about it." Lucie eyed her speculatively. "Would you be willing—if you told me what happened, I swear I would not share it with a soul, not even James."

Cordelia's chest hurt, as it always did when she thought about her father. But she must tell this to Lucie nevertheless, and she would need to tell it to others, too. She would not be able to help her father unless she was straightforward in demanding what she wanted. "About a month ago, my father went to Idris," she said. "It was all very secret, but a nest of Kravyād demons had been discovered just outside the border of Idris."

"Really?" said Lucie. "They're nasty ones, aren't they? Man-eaters?"

Cordelia nodded. "They had wiped out nearly a whole pack of werewolves. It was the wolves, actually, who brought the news to Alicante. The Consul put together an expeditionary force of Nephilim and called in my father because of his expertise with rare demons. Along with two of the Downworlders, he helped plan the expedition to slay the Kravyāds."

"That sounds very exciting," said Lucie. "And how wonderful, to be working with Downworlders like that."

"It ought to have been," said Cordelia. She glanced back; James was a good distance away, still reading. He couldn't possibly hear them. "The expedition went wrong. The Kravyād demons had gone—and the Nephilim had trespassed onto land that a vampire clan believed was theirs. There was a fight—a bad one."

Lucie paled. "By the Angel. Was anyone killed?"

"Several Nephilim were injured," said Cordelia. "And the vampire clan believed that we—that the Shadowhunters—had allied with the werewolves to attack them. It was a terrible mess, something that could have undone the Accords."

Lucie looked horrified. Cordelia didn't blame her. The Accords were a peace agreement between Shadowhunters and Downworlders that helped maintain order. If they were broken, bloody chaos could ensue.

"The Clave launched an investigation," Cordelia said. "All right and proper. We thought my father was meant to be a witness, but he was arrested instead. They are blaming him for the expedition having gone wrong. But it was not his fault. He couldn't have known—"

She closed her eyes. "It nearly killed him, having let down the Clave so badly. He will have to live with the guilt all his life. But none of us expected them to end the investigation and arrest him instead." Her hands were shaking; she laced them tightly together. "He sent me one note, but nothing after that: they forbid it. He is being held under house arrest in Alicante until his trial can take place."

"A *trial?*" said Lucie. "Just for him? But there were others in charge of the expedition as well, weren't there?"

"There *were* others, but my father is being made the scapegoat. Everything has been blamed on him. My mother wanted to go to Idris to see him, but he forbid it," Cordelia added. "He said we must go to London instead—that if he is convicted, the shame that will fall on our family will be immense, and that we must move quickly to stave it off."

"That would be very unfair!" Lucie's eyes flashed. "Everyone knows Shadowhunting is a dangerous job. Surely it will be determined after your father is questioned that he did the best he could."

"Perhaps," Cordelia said, in a low voice. "But they need someone to blame—and he is right that we have few friends among Shadowhunters. We have moved so much because Baba was ill, never living long in one place—Paris, Bombay, Morocco—"

"I always thought it was very glamorous."

"We were trying to find a climate that might be best for his health," said Cordelia, "but now my mother feels she knows few allies. That is why we are here, in London. She hopes we can make friends quickly, so that if my father faces imprisonment, we will have some to stand by our side and defend us."

"There is always Uncle Jem. He *is* your cousin," Lucie suggested. "And Silent Brothers are held in high esteem by the Clave."

Lucie's uncle Jem was James Carstairs, known to the majority of Nephilim as Brother Zachariah. Silent Brothers were the doctors and archivists of the Nephilim: mute, long-lived, and powerful, they inhabited the Silent City, a mausoleum belowground with a thousand entrances all over the world.

The oddest thing about them to Cordelia was that—like their counterparts, the Iron Sisters, who carved weapons and steles out of *adamas*—they chose to be what they were: Jem had been an ordinary Shadowhunter once, the *parabatai* of Lucie's father, Will. When he had become a Silent Brother, powerful runes had silenced him and scarred him, and shut his eyes forever. The Silent Brothers did not age physically, but neither did they have children, or wives, or homes. It seemed an awfully lonely life. Cordelia had certainly seen Brother Zachariah—Jem—on important occasions, but she did not feel she knew him as James and Lucie did. Her father had never been comfortable in the presence of a Silent Brother and had done his lifelong best to prevent Jem from visiting their family.

If only Elias had thought differently, Jem might now be an ally. As it was, Cordelia had no idea how to begin to approach him.

"Your father will not be convicted," said Lucie, squeezing Cordelia's hand. "I will speak to my parents—"

"No, Lucie." Cordelia shook her head. "Everyone knows how close our families are. They won't think your mother and father are impartial." She exhaled. "I am going to go to the Consul myself. Directly. She may not realize they are trying to make this scandal with the Downworlders go away by blaming my father. It is easier to point the finger at one person than to admit everyone made mistakes."

Lucie nodded. "Aunt Charlotte is so kind, I can't imagine she won't help."

Aunt Charlotte was Charlotte Fairchild, the first woman ever to be elected Consul. She was also the mother of James's *parabatai*, Matthew, and an old family friend of the Herondales.

A Consul had enormous power, and when Cordelia had first heard of her father's imprisonment, she'd thought immediately of

Charlotte. But the Consul wasn't free to do whatever she wanted, Sona had explained. There were groups within the Clave, powerful factions always pressuring her to do this or do that, and she couldn't risk angering them. It would only make things worse for their family if they went to the Consul.

Privately Cordelia thought her mother was wrong—wasn't that what power *was*, the ability to risk angering people? What was the point of being a female Consul if you still had to fret about keeping people happy? Her mother was too cautious, too fearful. Sona believed the only possible way out of their current situation was for Cordelia to marry someone influential: someone who could salvage their family name if Elias went to prison.

But Cordelia would not mention that to Lucie. She had no intention of mentioning it to anyone. She could barely bring herself to think about it: she was not against the idea of marrying, but it had to be to the right person and it had to be for love. It would not be as part of a bargain to reduce her family's shame when her father had done nothing wrong. She would solve this with cleverness and bravery—not with the sale of herself as a bride.

"I know, it absolutely is awful right now," said Lucie, and Cordelia had the feeling she'd missed several moments of Lucie talking, "but I just know it will be over soon and your father will be back safely. And meanwhile you'll be in London and you can train with me and—Oh!" Lucie took her arm out of Cordelia's and dipped into her handbag. "I almost forgot. I have another installment of *The Beautiful Cordelia* for you to read."

Cordelia smiled and tried to put the situation with her father out of her mind. *The Beautiful Cordelia* was a novel that Lucie had begun when she was twelve. It had been intended to cheer Cordelia up during an extended stay in Switzerland. It chronicled the adventures of a young woman named Cordelia, devastatingly beautiful to all who beheld her, and the handsome man who adored her, Lord

Hawke. Sadly they had been parted when the beautiful Cordelia had been kidnapped by pirates, and ever since then she had been trying to find her way back to him, though her journey was complicated by many adventures as well as so many other attractive men—who always fell in love with her and desired marriage—that the real Cordelia had lost count.

Every month, faithfully, for four years, Lucie had mailed Cordelia a new chapter and Cordelia had curled up with her fictional counterpart's romantic adventures and lost herself in fantasy for a while.

"Wonderful," she said, taking the sheets of paper. "I can hardly wait to see if Cordelia escapes from the wicked Bandit King!"

"Well, as it turns out, the Bandit King isn't entirely wicked. You see, he's the youngest son of a duke who's always been—sorry," Lucie ended meekly at Cordelia's glare. "I forgot how you hate to be told the story before you read it."

"I do." Cordelia knocked her friend in the arm with the rolled-up manuscript. "But thank you, darling, I shall read it directly I have a moment." She glanced over her shoulder. "Is it—I mean, I wish to chat alone with you, too, but are we being dreadfully rude asking your brother to walk behind us?"

"Not a bit," Lucie assured her. "Look at him. He's quite distracted, reading."

And he was. Though James seemed entirely caught up in whatever he was perusing, he nevertheless skirted oncoming passersby, the occasional rock or fallen branch, and once even a small boy holding a hoop, with admirable grace. Cordelia suspected that if she had tried such a trick, she would have crashed into a tree.

"You're so lucky," Cordelia said, still looking over her shoulder at James.

"Why on earth?" Lucie looked at her with wide eyes. Where James's eyes were amber, Lucie's were pale blue, a few shades lighter than her father's.

Cordelia's head snapped back around. "Oh, because—" *Because you get to spend time with James every day?* She doubted Lucie thought that was any special gift; one didn't, when it was one's family. "He's such a good older brother. If I'd asked Alastair to walk ten paces behind me in a park, he would have made sure to stick by my side the entire time just to be annoying."

"Pfft!" Lucie exclaimed. "Of course I adore Jamie, but he's been dreadful lately, ever since he fell in love."

She might as well have dropped an incendiary device on Cordelia's head. Everything seemed to fly apart around her. "He what?"

"Fell in love," Lucie repeated, with the look of someone enjoying imparting a bit of gossip. "Oh, he won't say with who, of course, because it's Jamie and he never tells us anything. But Father's diagnosed him and he says it's definitely love."

"You make it sound like consumption." Cordelia's head was whirling with dismay. James in love? With who?

"Well, it is a bit, isn't it? He gets all pale and moody and stares off out of windows like Keats."

"Did Keats stare out of windows?" Sometimes keeping up with Lucie was difficult.

Lucie plowed on, undeterred by the question of whether England's foremost Romantic poet had or had not stared out of windows. "He won't say anything to anyone but Matthew, and Matthew is a tomb where James is concerned. I heard a bit of their conversation this morning by accident, though—"

"Accident?" Cordelia raised an eyebrow.

"I may have been hiding beneath a table," said Lucie, with dignity. "But it was only because I had lost an earring and was looking for it."

Cordelia suppressed a smile. "Go on."

"He is definitely in love, and Matthew thinks he is being foolish. It is a girl who does not live in London, but she is about to arrive here for an extended stay. Matthew does not approve of her—" Lucie broke off suddenly and clutched at Cordelia's wrist. "Oh!"

"Ouch! Lucie—"

"A lovely young lady about to arrive in London! Oh, I am a goose! Of course it's clear who he meant!"

"Is it?" Cordelia said. They were nearing the famous Long Water; she could see the sun sparkling off the surface.

"He meant you," Lucie breathed. "Oh, how lovely! Imagine if you got married! We could be sisters in truth!"

"Lucie!" Cordelia dropped her voice to a whisper. "We've no proof he meant me."

"Well, he'd be mad not to be in love with you," said Lucie. "You're terribly pretty, and just as Matthew said, you've just arrived in London for an extended stay. Who else could it be? The Enclave simply isn't that large. No, it must be you."

"I don't know—"

Lucie's eyes rounded. "Is it that you don't care for him? Well, you can't be expected to, yet. I mean you've known him all your life, so I imagine he isn't that impressive, but I am quite sure you could get used to his face. He doesn't snore or make rude jokes. Really, he isn't bad at all," she added judiciously. "Just consider it? Dance one dance with him tomorrow. You do have a dress, don't you? You must have a lovely dress, if he is to be properly stunned by you."

"I do have a dress," Cordelia hastened to reassure her, though she knew it was far from lovely.

"Once you have stunned him," Lucie went on, "he will propose. Then we shall decide whether you will accept and if you do, if you will have a long engagement. It might be better if you did, so that we can complete our *parabatai* training."

"Lucie, you are making me dizzy!" Cordelia said, and cast a worried look over her shoulder. Had James heard any of what they had said? No, it didn't seem so: he was still wandering along, reading.

A betraying hope swelled in her heart, and for a moment she allowed herself to imagine being engaged to James, being welcomed into Lucie's family. Lucie, her sister in the eyes of the law now, carrying a sheaf of flowers at her wedding. Their friends—they would certainly have friends—exclaiming, *Oh, you two make a perfect couple*—

She frowned suddenly. "Why does Matthew not approve of me?" she asked, and then cleared her throat. "I mean, if I was the girl they were talking about, which I am sure I was not."

Lucie waved her hand airily. "He did not think the girl in question cared for James. But as we have already ascertained, you can fall in love with him quite easily, if you put a bit of effort into it. Matthew is overly protective of Jamie, but he is nothing to fear. He may not like many people, but he's very kind to the ones he does like."

Cordelia thought of Matthew, James's *parabatai*. Matthew had hardly left James's side since they had both been in school in Idris, and she had met him now and then at social events. Matthew was all gold hair and smiles, but she suspected there might be a lion under the kitty cat if hurting James was involved.

But she would never hurt James. She loved him. She had loved him all her life.

And tomorrow she would get the chance to tell him so. She had no doubt that would give her the confidence to approach the Consul and present her father's case for leniency, perhaps with James by her side.

Cordelia raised her chin. Yes, after the ball tomorrow, her life would be very different.

DAYS PAST:
IDRIS, 1899

Every year for as long as James could remember, he and his family had gone to Idris to spend the summer at Herondale Manor. It was a large edifice of golden-yellow stone, its gardens sloping down to the enchanted green space of Brocelind Forest, a high wall separating it from the manor of the Blackthorn family next door.

James and Lucie would spend the days playing on the outskirts of the dark forest, swimming and fishing in the nearby river, and riding horses over the green fields. Sometimes they would try to peep over the wall of the Blackthorn house, but the walls were choked with thorny vines. Razor-tipped briars wrapped around the gates as if Blackthorn Manor had been long abandoned and overgrown, and though they knew that Tatiana Blackthorn lived there, they had only seen her carriage going in and out from a distance, the doors and windows firmly shut.

James had once asked his parents why they never socialized with the woman who lived next door, especially since Tatiana was related to James's uncles, Gideon and Gabriel Lightwood. Tessa explained diplomatically that there had been bad blood between their families since Tatiana's father had been cursed and they'd been unable to save him. Her father and her husband had died that day, and her son, Jesse, had died in the years since. She blamed Will and her brothers for her losses. "People become locked in bitterness sometimes," Tessa said, "and they wish to find someone, anyone, to blame for their grief. It is a shame, for Will and your uncles would have helped her if they could."

James had not given much more thought to Tatiana: a strange woman who hated his father unreasonably was not someone he wished to know. Then, the summer James turned thirteen years old, a message came from London to tell Will that Edmund and Linette Herondale, James's grandparents, had died of influenza.

If Will had not been so distracted by his loss, perhaps things would have gone differently.

But he was, and they didn't.

The night after they learned of Linette's and Edmund's deaths, Will had been sitting on the floor in the drawing room, Tessa in the overstuffed armchair behind him, and Lucie and James had been stretched upon the fireplace rug. Will's back had been against Tessa's legs as he stared unseeing into the fire. They had all heard the front doors open; Will had looked up when Jem came in, and Jem, in his Silent Brother robes, went over to Will and sat down beside him. He drew Will's head against his shoulder, and Will held the front of Jem's robes in his fists and he cried. Tessa bowed her head over both of them, and the three were united in adult grief, a sphere James could not yet touch. It was the first time it had ever occurred to James that his father might cry about anything.

Lucie and James escaped to the kitchen. That was where Tatiana Blackthorn found them—sitting at a table while their cook, Bridget, fed them pudding for dinner—when she arrived to ask James to cut the briars.

She looked like a gray crow, out of place in their bright kitchen.

Her dress was worn serge, ragged at the hems and cuffs, and a dirty hat with a beady-eyed stuffed bird on it was tilted sideways on her head. Her hair was gray, her skin was gray, and her eyes were dull green, as if misery and anger had sucked all the color out of her.

"Boy," she said, looking at James. "My manor gates are stuck fast by overgrowth. I need someone to cut the briars. Will you do it?"

Maybe if things had been different, if James had not already been feeling restless with the desire to help his father but no idea how to do so, he might have said no. He might have wondered why Mrs. Blackthorn didn't simply ask whoever had been doing the briar cutting for her all these years, or why she suddenly needed this task accomplished in the evening.

But he didn't. He stood up from the table and followed Tatiana out into the falling night. Sunset had begun, and the trees of Brocelind Forest seemed to flame at the tops as she strode across the grounds between their two houses, up to the front gates of Blackthorn Manor. They were black and twisted iron, with an arch at the top that spelled out words in Latin: LEX MALLA, LEX NULLA.

A bad law is no law.

She bent down among the drifting leaves and stood up, holding an enormous knife. It had clearly once been sharp, but now the blade was such a dark brown with rust it looked almost black. For a moment James had the fantasy that Tatiana Blackthorn had brought him here to kill him. She would cut out his heart and leave him lying where his blood ran out across the ground.

Instead she shoved the knife into his hands. "There you go, boy," she said. "Take your time."

He thought for a moment that she smiled, but it might have been a trick of the light. She was gone in a rustle of dry grass, leaving James standing before the gates, rusty blade in hand, like Sleeping Beauty's least successful suitor. With a sigh, he began to cut.

Or at least, he began to try. The dull blade sliced nothing, and the briars were as thick as the bars on the gates. More than once he was stuck sharply by the wicked points of the thorns.

His aching arms soon felt like lead, and his white shirt was spotted with blood. This was ridiculous, he told himself. Surely this went beyond the obligation to help a neighbor. Surely his parents would understand if he tossed the knife aside and went home. Surely—

A pair of hands, white as lilies, suddenly fluttered between the vines. "Herondale boy," whispered a voice. "Let me help you."

He stared in astonishment as a few of the vines fell away. A moment later a girl's face appeared in the gap, pale and small. "Herondale boy," she said again. "Have you a voice?"

"Yes, and a name," he said. "It's James."

Her face disappeared from the gap in the vines. There was a rattling sound, and a moment later a pair of briar cutters—perhaps not entirely new but certainly serviceable—emerged beneath the gates. James bent to seize them.

He was straightening up when he heard his name called: it was his mother's voice.

"I must go," he said. "But thank you, Grace. You are Grace, aren't you? Grace Blackthorn?"

He heard what sounded like a gasp, and she appeared again at the gap in the vines. "Oh, do please come back," Grace said. "If you come back tomorrow night, I shall sneak down to the gates here and talk with you while you cut. It has been so long since I spoke with anyone but Mama."

Her hand reached out through the bars, and he saw red lines on her skin where the thorns had torn her—James raised his own hand and for a moment, their fingers brushed. "I promise," he found himself saying. "I will come back."

2

ASHES OF ROSES

Though one were fair as roses,
His beauty clouds and closes;
And well though love reposes,
In the end it is not well.
—Algernon Charles Swinburne,
"The Garden of Proserpine"

"Matthew," said James. "Matthew, I know you're under there.
Come out, or I swear on the Angel I will pith you like a frog."

James was lying atop the billiard table in the Institute's games
room, glaring down over the side.

The ball had been going on for at least half an hour, and no
one had been able to find Matthew. James was the one who'd
guessed his *parabatai* was hiding in here: it was one of their favorite rooms, comfortable and handsomely decorated by Tessa. It
was papered up to the dado rail with gray and black stripes, and
painted gray above that. There were framed portraits and family
trees on the walls, and a gathering of comfortable, well-worn
sofas and wing chairs. A beautifully polished chess set glowed
like a jewel box atop a Dunhill cigar humidor. There was also the

massive billiard table that Matthew was currently hiding under.

There was a clatter, and Matthew's blond head appeared beneath the table. He blinked green eyes up at James. "Jamie, Jamie," he said, with mock sorrow. "Why must you chivvy a fellow so? I was peacefully napping."

"Well, wake up. You're needed in the ballroom to make up the numbers," said James. "There are a shocking number of girls out there."

"Damn the ballroom," said Matthew, scooting out from under the table. He was splendidly turned out in dove gray, with a pale green carnation in his buttonhole. In one hand he clutched a cut-glass decanter. "Bother the dancing. I intend to remain in here and get thoroughly foxed." He glanced at the decanter and then hopefully up at James. "You can join me if you want."

"That's my father's port," said James. It was strong stuff, he knew, and very sweet. "You'll be vilely ill in the morning."

"*Carpe decanter,*" said Matthew. "It's good port. I've always admired your father, you know. Planned to be like him one day. Though I once knew a warlock who had three arms. He could duel with one hand, shuffle a deck of cards with the next, and untie a lady's corset with the third, all at the same time. Now there was a chap to emulate."

"You're *already* foxed," said James disapprovingly, and reached down to seize the decanter out of Matthew's hand. Matthew was too quick for him, though, and swung it out of reach while rising up to clasp James's arm. He yanked him off the table, and in a moment they were rolling on the carpet like puppies, Matthew laughing uncontrollably, James trying to wrestle the bottle away from him.

"Get—off—me!" Matthew wheezed, and let go. James fell backward with such force that the top of the decanter flew off. Port splashed over his clothes.

"Now look what you've done!" he lamented, using his pocket

handkerchief to do what he could to mop up the scarlet stain spreading across his shirtfront. "I smell like a brewer and I look like a butcher."

"Piffle," said Matthew. "None of the girls care about your clothes anyhow. They're all too busy gazing into your great big golden eyes." He widened his eyes at James until he looked as if he were going mad. Then he crossed them.

James just frowned. His eyes were large, black-fringed, and the color of pale gold tea, but he'd been tormented too many times at school about his unusual eyes to find any pleasure in their uniqueness.

Matthew held out his hands. "Pax," he said wheedlingly. "Let it be peace between us. You can pour the rest of the port on my head."

James's mouth curved up into a smile. It was impossible to stay angry with Matthew. It was almost impossible to *get* angry at Matthew. "Come with me to the ballroom and make up the numbers and we can call it peace."

Matthew rose obediently—however much he'd drunk, he was always steady on his feet. He helped James up with a firm hand and straightened his jacket to cover the wine stain. "Do you want any of the port *in* you, or do you only want to wear it?" He offered James the decanter.

James shook his head. His nerves were already frayed, and though the port would soothe them, it would also muddle his thoughts. He wanted to remain sharp—in case. She might not come tonight, he knew. But then again, she might. It had been six months since her last letter, but now she was in London. He needed to be prepared for anything.

Matthew sighed as he set the bottle on the mantel. "You know what they say," he said, as he and James left the room and began to wend their way back toward the party. "Drink, and you will sleep; sleep, and you will not sin; do not sin, and you will be saved; therefore, drink and be saved."

"Matthew, you could sin in your sleep," said a languorous voice.

"Anna," said Matthew, sagging against James's shoulder. "Have you been sent to fetch us?"

Lounging against the wall was James's cousin Anna Lightwood, gorgeously dressed in fitted trousers and a pin-striped shirt. She had the Herondale blue eyes, always disconcerting for James to see, as it felt a bit as if his father were looking at him. "If by 'fetch,' you mean 'drag you back to the ballroom by any means possible,'" Anna said. "There are girls who need someone to dance with them and tell them they look pretty, and I cannot do it all on my own."

The musicians in the ballroom suddenly struck up a tune—a lively waltz.

"Crikey, not waltzing," said Matthew, in despair. "I loathe waltzing."

He began to back away. Anna seized him by the back of the coat. "Oh, no, you don't," she said, and firmly herded both of them toward the ballroom.

"Stop looking at yourself," said Alastair, in a weary tone. "Why are women always *looking* at themselves? And why are you frowning?"

Cordelia glared into the pier glass at the reflection of her brother. They were all waiting outside the grand ballroom at the Institute, Alastair looking perfect in immaculate black and white, his blond hair slicked back with pomade, hands gloved in kidskin.

Because Mother dresses me, but she lets you wear whatever you like, she thought, but didn't say it, since their mother was standing right there. Sona was determined to dress Cordelia in the height of fashion, even if the height of fashion didn't suit her daughter at all. For tonight she'd chosen a dress for Cordelia of pale lilac edged with glittering bugle beads. Her hair was swept up into a waterfall of curls, and her swan-bill corset was making her breathless.

Cordelia was of the opinion that she looked awful. Pastels were all the rage in the fashion papers, but those papers expected girls to be blond, small-bosomed, and pale-skinned. Cordelia was decidedly none of those things. Pastels washed her out, and even the corset couldn't flatten her chest. Nor was her dark red hair thin and fine: it was thick and long like her mother's, reaching to her waist when brushed out. It looked ridiculous in tiny curls.

"Because I have to wear a corset, Alastair," she snapped. "I was checking to see if I'd turned plum-colored."

"You'd match your dress if you did," Alastair noted. Cordelia couldn't help but wish her father were there; he always told her she looked beautiful.

"Children," said their mother reprovingly. Cordelia had the feeling she would address them as "children" even when they were old and gray and sniping at one another from Bath chairs. "Cordelia, corsets not only create a womanly shape, they show that a lady is finely bred and of delicate sensibilities. Alastair, leave your sister alone. This is a very important evening for all of us, and we must be mindful to make a good impression."

Cordelia could sense her mother's unease that she was the only woman in the room wearing a *roosari* over her hair, her worry that she lacked the knowledge of who the powerful people in the room were, when she would have known it immediately in the salons of the Tehran Institute.

Things would all be different after tonight, Cordelia told herself again. It didn't matter whether her dress was hideous on her: what mattered was that she charm the influential Shadowhunters in the room who could effect an introduction to the Consul for her. She would make Charlotte understand—she would make them all understand—that her father might be a poor strategist, but it was no reason for him to be in jail. She would make them understand that the Carstairs family had nothing to hide.

She would make her mother smile.

The ballroom doors opened and there was Tessa Herondale in rose chiffon, with small roses in her hair. Cordelia doubted *she* needed to wear a corset. She was already quite ethereal-looking. It was hard to believe she was the woman who had taken down an army of metal monsters.

"Thank you for waiting," she said. "I did want to bring you in all together and make the introductions. Everyone is just dying to meet you. Come, come!"

She led them into the ballroom. Cordelia had a faint memory of playing here with Lucie when it had been quite deserted. Now it was full of light and music.

Gone were the heavily brocaded walls of years ago and the massive velvet hangings. Everything was airy and bright, the walls lined with pale wooden benches padded with gold-and-white-striped cushions. A frieze of golden birds darting among trees ran above the curtains—if you looked closely, you could see that they were herons. Hung on the walls was an assortment of ornamental weapons—swords in jeweled scabbards, bows carved of ivory and jade, daggers with pommels in the shapes of sunbursts and angel wings.

Most of the floor had been cleared for dancing, but there was a sideboard laden with glasses and pitchers of iced lemonade. A few tables draped in white were scattered around the room. Older married ladies and some younger ones who didn't have dancing partners clustered at the walls, busying themselves with gossip.

Cordelia's gaze instantly searched out Lucie and James. She found Lucie at once, dancing with a young man with sandy hair, but she scanned the room for James's tousled dark hair in vain. He did not seem to be here.

Not that there was time to dwell on it. Tessa was an expert hostess. Cordelia and her family were whisked from group to group, the introductions made, their virtues and values enumerated. She was introduced to a dark-haired girl a few years older than herself, who looked entirely at ease in a pale green dress trimmed with lace. "Barbara Lightwood," said Tessa, and Cordelia perked up as they curtsied to each other. The Lightwoods were cousins of James and Lucie's, and a powerful family in their own right.

Her mother fell immediately into conversation with Barbara's parents, Gideon and Sophie Lightwood. Cordelia fixed her gaze on Barbara. Would she be interested in hearing about her father? Probably not. She was looking out at the dance floor with a smile on her face.

"Who's the boy dancing with Lucie?" Cordelia asked, which provoked a surprising burst of laughter from Barbara.

"That's my brother, Thomas," she said. "And not tripping over his own feet, for a change!"

Cordelia took another look at the sandy-haired boy laughing with Lucie. Thomas was very tall and broad-shouldered, intimidatingly so. Did Lucie fancy him? If she'd mentioned him in her letters, it was only as one of her brother's friends.

Alastair, who had been standing at the edge of the group looking bored—truthfully, Cordelia had nearly forgotten he was there—suddenly brightened. "Charles!" he said, sounding pleased. He smoothed down the front of his waistcoat. "If you'll excuse me, I must go pay my respects. We haven't seen each other in an age."

He vanished between the tables without waiting for permission. Cordelia's mother sighed. "Boys," she said. "So vexing."

Sophie smiled at her daughter, and Cordelia noticed for the first time the vicious scar that slashed across her cheek. There was something about her vivaciousness, the way she moved and spoke, that caused one not to see it at first. "Girls have their moments," she observed. "You should have seen Barbara and her sister, Eugenia, when they were children. Absolute horrors!"

Barbara laughed. Cordelia envied her, to have such an easy rapport with her mother. A moment later a brown-haired boy approached and invited Barbara to dance; she was whisked away, and Tessa steered Sona and Cordelia to the next table, where Lucie's uncle Gabriel Lightwood sat beside a beautiful woman with long dark hair and blue eyes—his wife, Cecily. Will Herondale was leaning against the edge of their table, arms folded, smiling.

Will looked over as they approached, and his face softened when he saw Tessa, and behind her, Cordelia. In him, Cordelia could see a bit of what James would become when he was grown.

"Cordelia Carstairs," he said, after greeting her mother. "How pretty you've become."

Cordelia beamed. If Will thought she was pretty, perhaps his son thought so too. Of course, due to Will's prejudice toward all things Carstairs, he probably thought Alastair was perfect and also pretty.

"I hear you have come to London to be *parabatai* with our Lucie," said Cecily. She looked nearly as young as Tessa, though since she wasn't an immortal warlock, one wondered how she managed it. "I am pleased—it is high time more girls became *parabatai*. It has been a state monopolized by men for far too long."

"Well, the first *parabatai* were male," Will pointed out, in a manner that made Cordelia wonder if Cecily had once found him insufferable, as she found Alastair.

"Times are changing, Will," said Cecily with a smile. "It's the modern age. We have electric lights, motorcars . . ."

"Mundanes have electric lights," said Will. "*We* have witchlight."

"And motorcars are a fad," said Gabriel Lightwood. "They won't last."

Cordelia bit her lip. This was not at all how she wanted the evening to go. She was meant to be charming people and influencing them, but instead she felt like a child banished to the perimeter of adult conversation about motorcars. It was with extreme relief that she saw Lucie abandon Thomas on the dance floor and race over to her. They hugged, and Cordelia exclaimed over Lucie's pretty blue lace dress, while Lucie stared in horror at Cordelia's lilac nightmare.

"May I take Cordelia to meet the other girls?" she said to Sona, smiling her most charming smile.

"Of course." Sona looked pleased. It was, after all, what she had brought Cordelia here for, wasn't it? To meet the sons and daughters of influential Shadowhunters? Though really, Cordelia knew, more the sons than the daughters.

Lucie took Cordelia's hand and drew her over to the refreshment table, where a group of girls in colorful dresses had gathered. In the avalanche of introductions, Cordelia caught only a few of their names: Catherine Townsend, Rosamund Wentworth, and Ariadne Bridgestock, who must be related to the Inquisitor. She was a tall, lovely-looking girl a few years older than the others, with brown skin a shade darker than Cordelia's own.

"What a pretty dress," Ariadne said to Cordelia, her voice warm. Her own gown was of flattering wine-colored silk. "I believe that's the shade they call 'ashes of roses.' Very popular in Paris."

"Oh, yes," Cordelia said eagerly. She'd known so few girls growing up—just Lucie, really—so how *did* one impress them and charm them? It was desperately important. "I did get this dress in Paris, as a matter of fact. On Rue de la Paix. Jeanne Paquin made it herself."

She saw Lucie's eyes widen in concern. Rosamund's lips tightened. "How fortunate you are," she said coolly. "Most of us here in the poky little London Enclave rarely get to travel abroad. You must think us *so* dull."

"Oh," said Cordelia, realizing she had put her foot in it. "No, not at all—"

"*My* mother has always said Shadowhunters aren't meant to have much of an interest in fashion," said Catherine. "She says it's mundane."

"Since you've spoken of Matthew's clothes admiringly so often," said Ariadne tartly, "should we assume that rule is only for girls?"

"Ariadne, really—" Rosamund began, and broke off with a laugh. "Speak of the devils," she said. "*Look* who's just come in."

She was looking toward the far doors of the ballroom, through which two boys had just spilled. Cordelia saw James first, as she always did. He was tall, beautiful, smiling: a painter's vision in black and white with tousled ebony hair.

She heard Lucie groan as the girls whispered among themselves: she caught James's name in the whispers, and then a second name in the same breath: *Matthew Fairchild*.

Of course. James's *parabatai*. It had been years since Cordelia had seen him. She remembered a slim blond boy. Now he was a well-built young man, his hair darkened to bronze, with a face like a dissipated angel.

"They are *so handsome*," said Catherine, sounding almost pained. "Don't you think so, Ariadne?"

"Oh—yes," Ariadne said hastily. "I suppose."

"She only has eyes for Charles," said Rosamund. Ariadne turned red, and the girls went off into gales of laughter. All but Lucie, who rolled her eyes.

"They're just *boys*," she said.

"James is your brother," said Catherine. "You cannot be objective, Lucie! He is *gorgeous*."

Cordelia had begun to feel a certain dismay. James, it seemed, was not her discovery alone. He and Matthew had stopped to laugh with Barbara and her dance partner; James had an arm slung over Matthew's shoulder and was smiling. He was so beautiful it was like an arrow in the heart to look at him. Of course she was not the only one to have noticed. Surely James could have his pick of girls.

"Matthew isn't bad-looking either," said Rosamund. "But so *scandalous*."

"Indeed," Catherine added, eyes sparkling. "You must be careful of him, Miss Carstairs. He has a *reputation*."

Lucie began to turn an angry shade of pink.

"We should guess who James will ask to dance first," said a fair-haired girl in a pink dress. "Surely you, Rosamund; you are looking so lovely tonight. Who could resist you?"

"Ah, yes, who will be graced by my brother's attentions?" drawled Lucie. "When he was six, he threw up in his own shoe."

The others girls pointedly ignored her as the music began once more. Someone who appeared to be Rosamund's brother came to claim the fair-haired girl for a dance; Charles left Alastair and came across the room to take Ariadne's hand and whisk her onto the floor. Will and Tessa were in each other's arms, as were both sets of Lucie's aunts and uncles.

A moment later Matthew Fairchild approached the table. He was suddenly startlingly close to Cordelia. She could see that his eyes were not dark, as she had thought, but a deep shade of green like forest moss. He bowed slightly to Lucie. "Might I have this dance?"

Lucie cast a glance back at the other girls that Cordelia could read as clearly as words on a page. *She* was not concerned about Matthew's reputation, the look said. Head held high, Lucie sailed out onto the dance floor with the Consul's second son.

Which was commendable of her, Cordelia thought, but it did leave Cordelia alone with a group of girls she was not sure liked her. She could hear a few of them whispering that she seemed terribly pleased with herself, and she thought she caught her father's name, too, and the word "trial"—

Cordelia stiffened her spine. She had made a mistake in mentioning Paris; she would not compound it by seeming weak. She gazed out upon the dance floor, a smile glued to her lips. She caught sight of her brother, now in conversation with Thomas Lightwood. The two boys sat casually on a rout-seat together, as if they were exchanging confidences. Even Alastair was doing a better job of charming the influential than she was.

Not far from them, leaning against a wall, was a girl dressed in the height of fashion—men's fashion. Tall and almost painfully slender, she had dark, dark hair like Will and James did. Hers was cut short and smoothed down with pomade, the edges finger-combed into careful curls. Her hands were long, ink-and-tobacco-stained and beautiful to look at, like the hands on a statue. She was smoking a cheroot, the smoke drifting up past her face, which was unusual: fine-boned and sharp edged.

Anna, Cordelia realized. This was Anna Lightwood, Lucie's cousin. She was certainly the most intimidating person in the room.

"Oh, my," said Catherine, as the music rose. "It's a waltz."

Cordelia glanced down. She knew how to dance: her mother had engaged an expert instructor to teach her the quadrille and the lancer, the stately minuet and the cotillion. But the waltz was a seductive dance, one where you could feel your partner's body against yours, scandalous when it had first become popular. She'd never learned it.

She very much wanted to dance it with James. But he probably didn't even wish to dance at all; he probably wanted to talk with his friends, as any young man would. She heard another spate of giggles and whispers, and Catherine's voice saying, "Isn't she that girl whose father—"

"Daisy? Would you like to dance?"

There was only one boy who called her that. She looked up, incredulous, to see James standing in front of her.

His beautiful hair was disorderly, as it always was, and more charming for that: a lock of it fell over his forehead, and his lashes were thick and dark over his pale gold eyes. His cheekbones arched like wings.

The group of girls had fallen into a stunned silence. Cordelia felt as if she might be floating.

"I don't," she faltered, having no idea what she was saying, "quite know how to waltz."

"Then I shall teach you," James said, and a moment later they had whirled out onto the dance floor.

"Thank goodness you were free," James said with frank cheerfulness as they moved among the other couples, searching for a space. "I was afraid I'd have to ask Catherine to dance, and all she talks about is how scandalous Matthew is."

"Glad to be of service," said Cordelia, a bit breathless. "But I truly can't waltz."

"Oh, neither can I." He grinned and spun to face her. She was so close to him, and they were *touching*, his hand on her forearm. "At least not well. Shall we agree to try not to mash each other's toes?"

"I can try," Cordelia said, then gave a small squeak as he drew her into his arms. The room swam for a moment. This was James, *her* James, and he was holding her, his hand on her shoulder blade. He took her other hand and placed it firmly on his arm.

And then they were off, and she was doing her best to follow. She had learned that much at least: how to be led in a dance, how to respond to your partner's hinted movements. James danced well—nothing surprising there, given how graceful he was—and he made it easy to follow him.

"Not bad," James said. He blew at the lock of hair dangling over his forehead, but that only made it fall farther into his eyes. He grinned ruefully as Cordelia forced herself through sheer exercise of will not to reach up and push it back. "Still, always embarrassing when your parents dance better than you do."

"Humph," Cordelia said. "Speak for yourself." She caught sight of Lucie dancing with Matthew a few feet away. Lucie was laughing. "Maybe Catherine is in love with Matthew," she suggested. "Maybe he holds a dark fascination for her."

"That would be exciting. And I assure you, nothing exciting

has happened to the London Enclave in a very long time."

Dancing with James was its own reward, of course, but it occurred to Cordelia that it might also be useful. "I was just thinking how very many people there are in the Enclave, and how little I know of them. I know you and Lucie, of course. . . ."

"Shall I give you a bit of the tour of the rest of them?" he asked, as they executed a complicated turn. "Perhaps a few pointers on who everyone is will make you feel more at home?"

She smiled. "It would, thank you."

"Over there," he said, and indicated Ariadne and Charles, dancing together. Her wine-colored dress glowed under the lights. "Charles you know, and with him is Ariadne Bridgestock, his fiancée."

"I didn't know they were engaged!"

James's eyes crinkled at the corners. "You know Charles is nearly assured of the position of Consul when his mother steps down after her third term. Ariadne's father is the Inquisitor, a very advantageous political alliance for Charles . . . though I'm sure he loves her as well."

James didn't sound as if he entirely believed that, though to Cordelia's eyes, Charles was gazing down at his fiancée quite adoringly. She hoped James hadn't become cynical. The James she remembered was anything but cynical.

"And that must be Anna," she said. It could not have been anyone else than the cousin Lucie had described in her letters: beautiful, fearless, always dressed in the finest clothes Jermyn Street had to offer. She stood laughing as she spoke with her father, Gabriel, near the door to the withdrawing room.

"Anna indeed," said James. "And there is her brother, Christopher, dancing with Rosamund Wentworth."

Cordelia moved her gaze to a slim boy in glasses she recognized from photographs. Christopher, she knew, was one of James's close friends, along with Matthew and Thomas. He was glumly dancing with a furious-looking Rosamund.

"Alas, Christopher is far more at home with beakers and test tubes than he is with female company," said James. "Let's just hope he doesn't pitch poor Rosamund into the refreshment table."

"Is he in love with her?"

"Lord, no, barely knows her," said James. "Besides Charles and Ariadne, Barbara Lightwood has an understanding with Oliver Hayward. And Anna is always breaking someone's heart. Beyond that, I'm not sure I can think of any romances brewing in our set. Though having you and Alastair here might bring us some excitement, Daisy."

"I didn't realize you remembered that old nickname."

"What, *Daisy*?" He was holding her close as they danced: she could feel the heat of him all up and down her front, making her prickle all over. "Of course I remember it. I gave it to you. I hope you don't intend me to stop using it."

"Of course not. I like it." She forced herself not to move her gaze from his. Goodness, his eyes were startling up close. They were the color of golden syrup, almost shocking against the black of his pupils. She had heard the whispers, knew people found his eyes odd and alien, a sign of his difference. She thought they were the color of fire and gold, the way she imagined the heart of the sun. "Though I don't think it suits me. Daisy sounds like a pretty little girl in hair ribbons."

"Well," he said. "You are at least one of those things."

And he smiled. It was a sweet smile, the kind she was used to from James, but there was an edge to it, a hint of something more—did he mean she was pretty, or a little girl? Or did he just mean she was a girl? What *did* he mean? Goodness, flirting was vexing, Cordelia thought.

Wait, was James Herondale *flirting* with her?

"A number of us are having a picnic in Regent's Park tomorrow," he said, and Cordelia felt her body tighten. Was he about to ask her to accompany him somewhere? She would have preferred a private ride or walk in the park, but she would accept a group outing. In truth, she would have accepted a visit to Hades. "On the chance that Lucie hasn't already mentioned it to you—"

He broke off: suddenly he was looking past her, at someone who had just come into the room. Cordelia followed his gaze and saw a tall woman, thin as a scarecrow in the black of mundane mourning, with gray-streaked hair dressed in the style of decades ago. Tessa was hurrying toward her, a concerned look on her face. Will was following.

As Tessa reached her, the woman stepped aside, revealing the girl who had been standing behind her. A girl dressed all in ivory, with a soft waterfall of white-gold curls gathered back from her face. The girl moved forward gracefully to greet Tessa and Will, and as she did so, James dropped Cordelia's hands.

They were no longer dancing. James turned away from Cordelia without a word and strode across the room toward the newcomers. She stood, frozen in confusion, as James bent to kiss the hand of the stunningly beautiful girl who had just walked into the room. Titters rose on the dance floor. Lucie had stepped back from Matthew, her eyes wide. Alastair and Thomas both turned to look at Cordelia with expressions of surprise.

At any moment, Cordelia knew, her mother would notice that she was drifting in the middle of the dance floor like an abandoned tugboat and charge toward her, and then Cordelia would die. She would die of the humiliation. Cordelia was scanning the room for the nearest exit, ready to flee, when a hand grasped her arm. She was spun around and into an expert grip: a moment later she was dancing again, her feet automatically following her partner's.

"That's right." It was Matthew Fairchild. Fair hair, spicy cologne, a blur of a smile. His hands were gentle as he swept her back into the waltz. "Just—try to smile, and no one will notice anything happened. James and I are practically interchangeable in the public consciousness anyway."

"James—left," Cordelia said, in shock.

"I know," said Matthew. "Very bad form. One should not leave a lady on the dance floor unless something is actually on fire. I'll have a word."

"A word," Cordelia echoed. She was beginning to feel less stunned and more angry. "A *word*?"

"Several words, if it will make you feel better?"

"Who is she?" Cordelia said. She almost didn't want to ask, but it was better to know the truth. It was always better to know the truth.

"Her name is Grace Blackthorn," said Matthew quietly. "She is the ward of Tatiana Blackthorn, and they have just come to London. Apparently she grew up in some hole in the country in Idris—that's how James knows her. They used to cross paths in the summers."

It is a girl who does not live in London, but she is about to arrive here for an extended stay.

Cordelia felt sick to her stomach. To think she had thought that Lucie was talking about *her*. That James could have felt those feelings about *her*.

"You look ill," Matthew observed. "Is it my dancing? Is it me personally?"

Cordelia drew herself up. She was Cordelia Carstairs, daughter of Elias and Sona, one of a long line of Shadowhunters. She was the inheritor of the famous sword Cortana, which had been passed down through the Carstairs family for generations. She was in London to save her father. She would *not* fall apart in public.

"Perhaps I'm nervous," she said. "Lucie did say you didn't like many people."

Matthew gave a sharp, startled laugh, before schooling his face back into a look of lazy amusement. "Did she? Lucie's a chatterbox."

"But not a liar," she said.

"Well, fear not. I do not dislike you. I hardly know you," said Matthew. "I do know your brother. He made my life miserable at school, and Christopher's, and James's."

Cordelia looked over at James and Grace reluctantly. They made a stunning picture, his dark hair and her fair icicle beauty. Like ashes and silver. How, how, *how* could Cordelia ever have thought someone like James Herondale would be interested in someone like her?

"Alastair and I are very different," Cordelia said. She didn't want to say more than that. It felt disloyal to Alastair. "I like Oscar Wilde, for instance, and he does not."

The corner of Matthew's mouth curled up. "I see you go directly for the soft underbelly, Cordelia Carstairs. Have you really read Oscar's work?"

"Just *Dorian Gray*," Cordelia confessed. "It gave me nightmares."

"I should like to have a portrait in the attic," Matthew mused, "that would show all my sins, while I stayed young and beautiful. And not only for sinning purposes—imagine being able to try out new fashions on it. I could paint the portrait's hair blue and see how it looks."

"You don't need a portrait. You *are* young and beautiful," Cordelia pointed out.

"Men are not beautiful. Men are handsome," objected Matthew.

"Thomas is handsome. *You* are beautiful," said Cordelia, feeling the imp of the perverse stealing over her. Matthew was looking stubborn. "James is beautiful too," she added.

"He was a very unprepossessing child," said Matthew. "Scowly, and he hadn't grown into his nose."

"He's grown into everything now," Cordelia said.

Matthew laughed, again as if he was surprised to be doing it. "That was a very shocking observation, Cordelia Carstairs. I am shocked." But his eyes were dancing. "Did James tell you about tomorrow?"

"He did say there was some sort of excursion—a picnic, I think. I am not sure if I am invited, though."

"Of course you're invited. I'm inviting you."

"Oh. Can you do that?"

"I think you'll find I can do whatever I want, and I usually do."

"Because the Consul is your mother?" Cordelia said.

He raised an eyebrow.

"I've always hoped to meet her," Cordelia said. "Is she here tonight?"

"No, she's in Idris," he said, with a gracious half shrug. "She left a few days ago. It's unusual for the Consul to live in London—she's rarely here. The Clave requires her."

"Oh," said Cordelia, struggling to hide her disappointment. "How long will she be—"

Matthew spun her in a surprising twirl that left the other dancers looking at them in puzzlement. "You will come to the picnic tomorrow, won't you?" he said. "It will keep Lucie amused while James moons after Grace. You want Lucie to be happy, don't you?"

"Of course I do—" Cordelia began, and then, glancing around, realized that she had not seen Lucie in some time. No matter how she craned her head and searched among the dancers, she did not see her friend's blue dress, or the glint of her brown hair. Puzzled, she turned to Matthew. "But where is she? Where did Lucie go?"

3

This Living Hand

This living hand, now warm and capable
Of earnest grasping, would, if it were cold
And in the icy silence of the tomb,
So haunt thy days and chill thy dreaming nights
That thou would wish thine own heart dry of blood
So in my veins red life might stream again.
—John Keats, "This Living Hand"

It was a bit like the moment in a dream where one realized one was dreaming, only in reverse. When Lucie saw the boy from the forest come into the ballroom, she assumed she was dreaming, and only when her parents began to hurry over toward him and his two companions did she realize that she wasn't.

In a daze, she pushed through the crowd toward the ballroom doors. As she neared her parents, she recognized the woman they were speaking to, her taffeta dress stretched across bony arms and shoulders, her oversize hat covered with lace, tulle, and a memorable stuffed bird. Tatiana Blackthorn.

Lucie had always been a bit frightened of Tatiana, especially when she had come to their house, demanding that James cut the thorns from her gates. She remembered her as a sort of towering skeleton, but with the passage of years, it seemed that Tatiana had shrunk: still tall, but no longer a giant.

And there beside her was Grace. Lucie recalled her as a determinedly poised child, but she was quite different now. Cold and lovely and statuesque.

But Lucie barely spared them a glance. She was staring at the boy who had come in with them. The changeling boy she had last seen in Brocelind Forest.

He had not altered at all. His hair was still a black spill over his forehead, his eyes the same eerie green. He wore the same clothes he had in the forest: dark trousers and an ivory shirt whose sleeves had been rolled up above his elbows. It was very odd attire for a ball.

He was watching as Tessa and Will greeted Tatiana and Grace, Will bending to kiss Grace's satin-gloved hand. Oddly, neither of them greeted the boy. As Lucie neared them, her brows drew down into a frown. They were speaking to each other, ignoring him entirely, talking *through* him as if he weren't there. How could they be so rude?

Lucie hurried forward, her mouth opening, her gaze fixed on the boy, *her* boy, her boy from the forest. He raised his head and saw her looking, and to her astonishment, a look of horror passed over his face.

She stopped dead. She could see James making his way through the crowd toward them somewhere in the distance, but the boy was already stepping away from Tatiana and Grace, moving toward Lucie. *Speeding* toward her, actually, like a runaway horse on Rotten Row.

No one else seemed to see him. No one turned to look at either of them, even when he seized hold of Lucie's wrist and drew her after him out of the room.

*   *   *

"Would you do me the honor of this dance?" said James.

He was conscious of the presence of his parents, and of Tatiana Blackthorn, observing everything with her poison-green eyes. He was conscious of the music, continuing around them, and conscious of his own heartbeat, loud as thunder in his ears. He was conscious of all those things, but they seemed distant, as if trapped behind a wall of glass. The only thing that was real in the room was Grace.

James's parents looked on with concern etched on their faces. He felt a sense of guilt that they must be wondering, now, why he had rushed over to Grace: as far as they knew, he was barely acquainted with her. But the guilt, too, felt distant. They didn't know what he did. They didn't know how important this was.

"Well, go on, Grace," Tatiana said, a beaky smile spreading across her thin face. "Dance with the gentleman."

Without looking up, Grace put her hand lightly in James's. They made their way out onto the floor. Touching Grace was like touching *adamas* for the first time: sparks rocketed through James as he drew her toward him, placing one hand on her shoulder and the other at her waist. She had always been graceful when they had danced, as children, in the overgrown garden of her house in Idris. But she felt different in his arms now.

"Why did you not tell me you were coming?" he said in a low voice.

She finally raised her face and he was struck by a jolt of recognition: Grace might hold herself with near-silent poise, but she *felt* with an absolute intensity. She was like a fire blazing in the heart of a glacier. "You didn't come to Idris," she said. "I waited—I expected you—but you never came."

"I wrote to you," he said. "I told you we weren't coming this summer."

"Mama found the letter," she said. "First she hid it from me. I thought you had forgotten—at last I found it in her room. She was dreadfully angry. I told her again we only had a friendship, but—" She shook her head. James was conscious that everyone in the room was staring at them. Even Anna was looking at them curiously through the cheroot smoke that wreathed her like mist off the Thames. "She wouldn't say what was in it, she just smiled as the days went by and you didn't come. And I was so frightened. When we are not together, when we are not with one another, the bond between us weakens. I feel it. Don't you?"

He shook his head. "Love must be able to survive distance," he said, as gently as he could.

"You don't understand, James. You have a life here in London, and friends, and I have nothing." Her voice shook with the strength of her feeling.

"Grace. Don't say that." But he thought of the overgrown house full of stopped clocks and rotted food. He had sworn he would help her escape from that.

She slid her hand down his arm. He felt her fingers circle his wrist, below the silver bracelet. *Loyalty Binds Me.* "I should have trusted you would have written to me," she whispered. "That you thought of me. I thought about you each night."

Each night. He knew she meant it innocently, but he felt himself tense. It had been so long since he had last kissed her. He could not remember what it had been like, not exactly, but he knew it had shattered him. "I think of you every day," he said. "And now that you are here . . ."

"I never thought it would happen. I never thought I would see London," she said. "The streets, the carriages, the buildings, it's all so wonderful. The people . . ." She looked around the room. There was a look in her eyes, avid, almost hungry. "I cannot wait to know them all."

"There is an outing tomorrow," James said. "A group going to Regent's Park. Would your mother allow you to come?"

Grace's eyes gleamed. "I think she will," she said. "She had said she wants me to meet people here in London, and oh—I should like to know your *parabatai*, Matthew. And Thomas and Christopher that you've spoken so much of. I—I should like your friends to like me."

"Of course," he murmured, and drew her closer against him. She was light and slim, not nearly as soft and warm as Daisy—

Daisy. Raziel, he'd been dancing with Daisy just a few minutes ago. He couldn't remember excusing himself. Couldn't remember leaving her.

He looked away from Grace for the first time and searched the floor for Cordelia. He found her in moments—she was easy to spot. No one else had hair that color, a deep dark red, like fire shining through blood. She was dancing with Matthew, he saw to his surprise. Matthew's arms were around her, and she was smiling.

Relief went through him. So he hadn't done her any harm. That was good. He liked Cordelia. He had been glad to see her there among the usual group of girls, knowing he could ask her to dance and she would make no wrong assumptions about his intentions: they were family friends.

The music stopped. It was a pause for refreshments. Couples began to flood off the dance floor—James smiled to himself as he saw Jessamine, the Institute's resident ghost, drifting above the head of Rosamund Wentworth as Rosamund gossiped with her friends. Jessamine loved overhearing gossip, even though she'd been dead for a quarter century.

Cordelia flashed past as she hurried away from Matthew; she was glancing around, as if searching for someone. Her brother, perhaps? But Alastair seemed to be deep in conversation with Thomas. Very puzzling, that—James was positive Thomas hadn't liked Alastair much at school.

"My mother is summoning me back," Grace said. "I had better go."

Tatiana was indeed beckoning from the sidelines. James touched Grace's hand lightly with his own. He knew they could not hold hands, as Barbara and Oliver were doing. They could not show any affection openly.

Not now. But someday.

"Tomorrow, in the park," he said. "We will find a time to talk."

She nodded and turned away, hurrying toward Tatiana, who stood alone by the ballroom doors. James watched her go: it had been years of summers, he thought, but Grace was still a mystery.

"She's very pretty," said a familiar voice behind him. He turned and saw Anna leaning against the wall. She had the uncanny ability to disappear from one spot and appear in another, like a moving point of light.

James leaned against the wall next to Anna. He had spent many dances this way, draped against the William Morris wallpaper with his acerbic cousin. Too much dancing always made him feel as if he were being disloyal to Grace. "Is she?"

"I assumed that was why you bolted across the room like Oscar spotting a biscuit." Oscar was Matthew's golden retriever, well known for loyalty if not intelligence. "Bad form, James. Abandoning that nice Cordelia Carstairs."

"I hope you know me well enough to know that I don't simply bolt at every pretty girl I see," said James, nettled. "Maybe she reminded me of a long-lost aunt."

"My mother *is* your aunt, and you've never been that enthused to see her." Anna smiled, her blue eyes sparking. "So how do you know Grace Blackthorn?"

James glanced over at Grace, who was being introduced to Charles Fairchild. Poor Grace. She wouldn't find Charles the least bit interesting. James liked Matthew's older brother well enough, and they were practically family, but he had only one interest—Shadowhunter politics.

Grace was nodding and smiling politely. James wondered if he ought to rescue her. The world of Alicante and its dramas and policies couldn't be further from Grace's experience.

"And now you're thinking you ought to rescue her from Charles," said Anna, running her fingers through her pomaded hair. "I can't blame you."

"Do you not like Charles?" James was slightly surprised. Anna viewed the world with amused tolerance. She rarely went so far as to particularly like anyone, and it was even more rare for her to *dislike* them.

"I cannot admire all his decisions," said Anna, clearly choosing her words with care. James wondered what decisions she meant. "Go ahead, then, Jamie—rescue her."

James got only a few steps before the world around him shifted and changed. Anna vanished, as did all the music and laughter: gray, formless nothing swirled around him. He could hear only the sound of his own heartbeat. The floor seemed to tilt under him like the deck of a sinking ship.

NO, he cried out silently, but there was nothing he could do to stop it: the shadows were rising all around him as the universe went gray.

The boy drew Lucie down the hall and through the first open door, taking them into the games room. He didn't move to shut the door, only went to light the witchlight on the mantel, so Lucie shut it herself, and turned the key for good measure.

Then she spun around and stared accusingly. "What on earth are you doing here?" she demanded.

The boy smiled. He looked, puzzlingly, no older than Lucie remembered him—sixteen, seventeen perhaps. Still slender, and under real light and not a forest moon he was terribly, shockingly pale, with that cast of bruised sickliness to him: his green eyes fever-bright and shadowed.

"I *was* invited," he said.

"You can't have been," Lucie said, putting her hands on her hips. The witchlight had flared up, and she could see that the room was in some disarray: someone had knocked over a decanter, and the billiard table was crosswise. "You are a forest-dwelling faerie changeling."

At that, he laughed. He had the same smile she remembered. "Is that what you thought?"

"You told me about faerie traps!" she said. "You appeared from the forest and vanished back into it—"

"I am no faerie, nor a changeling," he said. "Shadowhunters know about faerie traps too."

"But you have no runes," she said.

He glanced down at himself—his arms, revealed from the elbows down, his hands. Every Shadowhunter was Marked with a Voyance rune on the back of their dominant hand when they turned ten years old, to help them master the Sight. But the only mark on the back of his hand was the old burn scar she had noticed in the forest. "No," he said. "I don't."

"You didn't say you were a Shadowhunter." She leaned back against the billiard table. "You never told me what you were."

"I never thought it would matter," he said. "I thought by the time you were old enough to ask questions and demand answers, you wouldn't be able to see me anymore."

Lucie felt as if a cold hand had been placed on her back. "Why wouldn't I be able to see you?"

"Think about it, Lucie," he said gently. "Did it seem like anyone else in the ballroom could see me? Did anyone greet me or acknowledge me, even your father?"

She said nothing.

"Children can see me sometimes," he said. "Not many others. Not people as old as you."

"Well, thank you *very* much." Lucie was indignant. "I'm hardly ancient."

"No." A smile hovered around his soft mouth. "No, you're not."

"But you said you were invited." Lucie was not inclined to drop the comment. "How could that be, if no one can see you, though why that should be—"

"All the Blackthorns were invited," he said. "The invitation was addressed to Tatiana Blackthorn and Family. I am family. I am Jesse Blackthorn."

"But he's dead," Lucie said, without thinking. She met his gaze with her own. "So you're a ghost?"

"Well," he said. "Yes."

"That's why you said 'even your father,'" said Lucie. "Because he can see ghosts. All the Herondales can. My brother, my father— they should be able to see you too."

"I am no ordinary ghost, and if you can see me, you are no ordinary girl," said Jesse. Now that he'd told her who he was, the resemblance was unmistakable. He had Tatiana's height, and Gabriel's handsome, angular features. Though the crow-dark hair must have come from his father. Blackthorn blood and Lightwood blood, blended.

"But I can touch you," said Lucie. "I touched you in the forest. You lifted me out of the pit. One cannot touch a ghost."

He shrugged. "Think of me as on the threshold of a door. I am unable to take a step outside the door, and I know I can never be allowed back in, to live again. But the door has not closed behind me."

"Your mother and your sister—can they see you?"

He perched on the billiard table with a sigh, as if resigning himself to settling into a long conversation. Lucie could not believe it.

To see her forest changeling again, and then to find out he was not a changeling but an odd kind of ghost no one else could see. It was quite a lot to be getting on with.

"They can see me," he said. "Perhaps because they were there when I died. My mother worried I would vanish on them when we moved to Chiswick House, but that doesn't seem to have happened."

"You could have told me your name."

"You were a little girl. I believed you wouldn't always be able to see me. I thought it would be kinder not to tell you who I was, when our families are enemies." Jesse spoke as if the enmity was a fact, as though there were a bloodstained feud between the Blackthorns and the Herondales as there was between the Montagues and Capulets. But it was Tatiana Blackthorn who hated them: they had never hated her.

"Why did you drag me out of the ballroom?" Lucie demanded.

"No one else can see me save my family. I don't understand how *you* can; it's never happened before. I didn't want everyone to think you were mad. And besides . . ."

Jesse jerked upright. A shadow passed over his face, and Lucie felt a chill at her very bones; for a moment his eyes seemed too large for his face, too liquid, all the wrong shape. She thought she could see darkness in them, and the form of something moving. He turned his eerie gaze on her. "Stay in this room," he said, grasping her wrist below the bell of her sleeve. She gasped; his hands were ice-cold.

"There is death here," he said, and vanished.

The gray world surrounded James. He had forgotten the cold that came when the shadows rose up. Forgotten the way he could still see the real world, as if through a thin scrim of dust: the ballroom was all around him, but it had turned to black and white like a photograph. The Nephilim on the dance floor had become shadows, stretched and elongated like figures from a nightmare.

He staggered back a step as trees seemed to explode up through the ground, sending roots twining along the polished wood floor. He knew enough not to scream: there was no one to hear him. He was alone in a world that was not real. Scorched earth and sky flickered in and out of his vision, even as the shadow figures twirled around him, unheeding. He recognized a face, a gesture here and there—he thought he saw Cordelia's bright hair, Ariadne Bridgestock in her wine-colored dress, his cousin Barbara as she reached up toward her dancing partner—just as a curling tendril of root wound its way around her ankle and drew her down.

Lightning seemed to fork behind his vision, and suddenly he was back in the ordinary ballroom, the world teeming with sound and light. There was a firm grip on his shoulders. "Jamie, Jamie, Jamie," said an urgent voice, and James—his heart trying to beat its way out of his chest—tried to focus on what was in front of him.

Matthew. Behind him were other Shadowhunters: James could hear their laughter and chatter, like the background dialogue of characters in a play.

"Jamie, breathe," Matthew said, and his voice was the only steady thing in a world turning upside down. The horror of this happening in front of a crowd of people—

"Did they see me?" James breathed. "Did they see me turn?"

"You didn't," Matthew said, "or at least, only a very little bit—perhaps just a bit fuzzy round the edges—"

"It's not funny," James said through his teeth, but Matthew's humor acted like a slap of cold water. His heart was starting to slow down. "You mean—I didn't turn into a shadow?"

Matthew shook his head, letting his hands slide from James's shoulders. "No."

"Then how did you know to come to me?"

"I felt it," Matthew said. "That you had gone to—that place." He shuddered slightly and reached into his waistcoat, drawing out a flask monogrammed with his initials. James could smell the sharp, biting scent of whiskey as he unscrewed the top. "What happened?" Matthew asked. "I thought you were just talking to Anna."

In the distance, James could see that Thomas and Christopher had caught sight of him with Matthew. They were both looking over with curiosity. He and Matthew must look as if they were speaking very intently, James realized. "It was your brother's fault," he said.

"I am perfectly prepared to think everything is Charles's fault," said Matthew, his voice steadier now. "But in this case—"

He broke off as a yell echoed through the room.

Cordelia couldn't understand why she was so worried about Lucie. Several withdrawing rooms had been opened up, and Lucie could have wandered off to any of those, or returned to her own bedroom. She could really be anywhere in the Institute. Matthew had told her not to worry before he'd hurried off somewhere, but Cordelia couldn't shake her sense of unease.

"For pity's sake!" someone called, interrupting her thoughts. It was a man's voice, low and baritone. "Someone come help her!"

Cordelia glanced about: everyone seemed to be looking surprised and chattering to each other. In the distance she could see a loose circle of people standing around whatever was going on. She picked up her skirts and began to push her way through the crowd.

She could feel her hair coming out of its carefully arranged curls and spilling down over her shoulders. Her mother would be furious, but *really*. Why didn't people *move*? They were Shadowhunters. What on earth were they doing standing around like sticks while someone was in distress?

She wriggled through a small knot of onlookers and there, on the floor, was a young man holding Barbara Lightwood's limp body in his arms. Oliver Hayward, Cordelia realized. Barbara's suitor. "We were dancing," he was saying, looking bewildered, "and she just collapsed—"

Cordelia dropped to her knees. Barbara Lightwood was ghastly white, her hair dark with sweat at her temples. She was breathing in short, erratic bursts. In times like this, all shyness deserted Cordelia: she could only think of what to do next. "She needs air," she said. "Her corset is probably tormenting her. Has anyone a knife?"

Anna Lightwood pushed through the crowd and moved forward, kneeling down opposite Cordelia with fluid grace. "I have a dagger," she said, drawing a sheathed blade from her waistcoat. "What needs to be done?"

"We need to cut her corset off," Cordelia said. "She has had a shock, and she needs to breathe."

"You might leave that to me," said Anna. She had an extraordinary husky voice, honey and sandpaper. She reached to lift Barbara out of Oliver's lap, then ran the dagger down the back of her dress, delicately separating the fabric and then the thicker material of the corset underneath. As it sagged free of Barbara's body, Anna glanced up and said absently, "Ari—your wrapper—"

Ariadne Bridgestock swiftly drew her silk wrapper from her shoulders and handed it to Anna, who swaddled Barbara in it to keep her decent. Barbara was already beginning to breathe more regularly, the color in her cheeks returning. Anna looked at Cordelia over Barbara's head, a considering look in her blue eyes.

"What on earth?" Sophie Lightwood had made her way through the circle of onlookers, her husband, Gideon, just behind her. "Barbara!" She turned to Oliver, who stood nearby, looking utterly distressed. "Did she fall?"

"She just collapsed," repeated Oliver. "We were dancing, and she fainted—"

Barbara's eyelids fluttered. She sat up in her cousin's arms, blinking up at her mother. Her cheeks flushed bright red. "I'm—I'm all right," she said. "I'm all right now. I had a spell, a silly dizzy spell."

Cordelia rose to her feet as more guests joined the loose circle of bystanders surrounding Barbara. Gideon and Sophie helped their daughter to her feet, and Thomas, appearing from the crowd, offered his sister a worn-looking handkerchief. She took it with a wobbly smile and dabbed at her lip.

It came away stained with blood.

"I bit my lip," Barbara said hastily. "I fell, and bit my lip. That's all."

"We need a stele," Thomas said. "James?"

Cordelia hadn't realized James was there. She turned and saw him standing just behind her.

The sight of him startled her. Years ago, he'd had the scalding fever: she was reminded of the way he'd looked then, pale and sick. "My stele," he said roughly. "Inside my breast pocket. Barbara needs a healing rune."

For a moment Cordelia wondered why he couldn't fetch it himself, but his hands were clenched at his sides, hard as stones. She reached out and fumbled nervously at his chest. Silk and cloth under her hand, and the beat of his heart. She seized hold of the slim, pen-shaped object in his pocket and held it out to Thomas, who took it with a look of surprised thanks. She hadn't really looked at Thomas before—he had bright hazel eyes, like his mother's, framed by thick brown lashes.

"*James.*" Lucie had slipped between James and Cordelia and was tugging at her brother's sleeve. "Jamie. Did you—"

He shook his head. "Not now, Luce."

Lucie looked worried. The three of them watched in a silent group as Thomas finished the healing rune on his sister's arm, and

Barbara exclaimed again that she was just fine and had only had a dizzy spell. "I forgot to eat today," she said to her mother, as Sophie put her arm around her. "That's all it is."

"Nevertheless, we had better get you home," Sophie said, glancing around. "Will—can you have the carriage brought around?"

The crowd had begun to scatter; clearly there was nothing more of interest to see here. The Lightwood family were headed to the door, Barbara on Thomas's arm, when they paused. A pigeon-chested man with a black handlebar mustache had rushed up to Gideon and was speaking to him excitedly.

"What's the Inquisitor saying to Uncle Gideon?" Lucie asked curiously. James and Matthew only shook their heads. After a few moments, Gideon nodded and followed the man—the Inquisitor, Cordelia supposed—to where Charles stood speaking to Grace Blackthorn. Her face was turned up to his, her eyes bright and interested. Cordelia remembered all the lessons her mother had given her in how to appear interested in conversation at social events: Grace seemed to have already absorbed them all after only being in society for a short time.

Charles turned reluctantly away from Grace and fell into discussion with Gideon Lightwood. The Inquisitor was moving through the crowd, stopping to speak to several Shadowhunters as he went. Most seemed to be about Charles's age: Cordelia guessed he was somewhere in his twenties.

"Looks like the party's over," said Alastair, appearing out of the crowd holding a cigar. He was gesturing with it, though Cordelia knew that if he ever started puffing tobacco, Sona would murder him. "Apparently there was a Shax demon attack in Seven Dials."

"A demon attack?" James said, with some surprise. "On mundanes?"

Alastair smirked. "Yes, you know, the sort of thing we're meant to prevent. Angelic mandate and all that."

Matthew's face had turned to stone; Lucie was looking at him anxiously. James's eyes narrowed.

"Charles is going with Gideon Lightwood and Inquisitor Bridgestock to see what's going on," Alastair said. "I offered to go with them, but I don't know the streets of London well enough yet. Charles will get me acquainted with the city and I will soon be a gift to any patrol."

"*You*, a gift," Matthew said, his eyes glittering. "Imagine."

He walked away. Alastair watched him go with one eyebrow raised. "Moody, isn't he?" he said, to no one in particular.

"No," said James shortly. His jaw was set, as if he was barely tolerating Alastair's presence. Cordelia thought back to the time Alastair had been at the Academy and wished she knew what had happened there.

Alastair looked as if he was about to speak again, but Sona appeared out of the crowd, arriving like a docking steamship. Her *roosari* quivered as her gaze fell upon Alastair, and then Cordelia. "Children," she said, as Alastair hastily slid his cigar into his pocket. "I believe we should take our leave."

Rumors of the attack were clearly spreading through the ballroom, breaking up the dance. The musicians had stopped playing, and quite a few of the girls in pastel dresses were being bundled into wrappers and gloves by anxious parents. Will and Tessa were now at the center of a crowd, bidding them good night. Nearby Charles was tucking a wrapper fondly about Ariadne's shoulders as Gideon and the Inquisitor waited for him by the doors.

A moment later Will and Tessa had joined Cordelia and the others. As Sona thanked them for a delightful evening, Cordelia's attention was arrested by the Fairchilds. Matthew was standing beside a thin man with faded ginger hair who was confined to a Bath chair. Matthew leaned over the back of it, saying something to make the older man smile: Cordelia realized this must be Henry

Fairchild, Matthew's father. She had nearly forgotten he was a veteran of the Clockwork War, in which he had lost the use of his legs.

"Oh, dear," Tessa was saying. "We will try again, Mrs. Carstairs, truly. You deserve a real welcome to the London Enclave."

Sona smiled. "I am sure if we put our heads together, we can think of something."

"Thank you for rushing to help Barbara, Cordelia," said Tessa. "You will make quite an excellent *parabatai* for Lucie."

Cordelia looked over at Lucie, who smiled at her. It was a slightly shaky smile. There were shadows in Lucie's eyes, as if something was bothering her. When she didn't reply to Tessa, James moved a step closer to his sister, as though to put a barrier between her and further attention. "Cordelia was a great help to Barbara," he said. "She was the one who had the idea to cut her corset away."

Sona looked slightly horrified. "Cordelia has a tendency to throw herself into every situation headlong," she said to Tessa and Will. "I'm sure you understand."

"Oh, we do," said Will. "We're always speaking very sternly to our children about that very thing. 'If you don't throw yourself into situations headlong, James and Lucie, you can expect bread and water for supper again.'"

Alastair choked on a laugh. Sona stared at Will as if he were a lizard with feathers. "Good night, Mr. Herondale," she said, turning both herself and her offspring toward the door. "This has certainly been a most interesting evening."

It was long past midnight. Tessa Herondale sat in front of the mirror in the bedroom she had shared with her husband for twenty-three years, and brushed her hair. The windows were closed, but soft summer air seeped in under the sill.

She recognized Will's step in the hallway before he came into the bedroom. More than twenty years of marriage did that.

He shut the door behind him and came to lean against one of the bedposts, watching her at the vanity table. He had shrugged off his jacket and undone his tie. His dark hair was mussed, and in the slightly blurred mirror, he looked no different to Tessa than he had when he was seventeen.

She quirked a smile at him.

"What is it?" he said.

"You're posing," she said. "It makes me want to paint a portrait of you. I'd call it *Gentleman, Dissipated*."

"You can't paint a line, Tess," he said, and came over to her, putting his hands on her shoulders. Now that he was close up, she could see the silver in his dark hair. "Much less capture my glorious handsomeness, which, I hardly need to point out, has only grown with age."

She didn't disagree—he was as handsome as ever, his eyes still the same startling blue—but there was no need to encourage Will. Instead she reached up and tugged on one of the more silvered locks of his hair. "I'm well aware of that. I saw Penelope Mayhew flirting with you tonight. Shamelessly!"

He bent his head to kiss her neck. "I hadn't noticed."

She smiled at him in the mirror. "I take it from your insouciant manner that all went well in Seven Dials. Did you hear from Gideon? Or"—she made a face—"Bridgestock?"

"Charles, actually. It was a nest of Shax demons. Quite a few more than they've been used to dealing with lately, but nothing they couldn't manage. Charles was very insistent that there was nothing to worry about." Will rolled his eyes. "I have a feeling he was fretting in case I suggested the picnic at Regent's Park lake tomorrow be canceled. All the young ones are going."

There was a very faint lilt at the end of Will's speech, which sometimes came when he was tired. The faintest remnants of an accent, sanded away by time and distance. Still, when he was exhausted or grieved, it came back, and his voice would roll softly like the green hills of Wales.

"Do you worry?" he said, meeting her eyes in the mirror. "I do, sometimes. About Lucie and James."

She set down her hairbrush and turned around, concerned. "Worry about the children? Why?"

"All this—" He waved his hand vaguely. "The boating parties, the regattas and cricket matches and fairs and dances, it's so . . . mundane."

"You're worried they're turning into mundanes? Really, Will, that's a bit prejudiced of you."

"No, I'm not worried about that. It's just that—it's been years since there's been anything but minimal demonic activity in London. The children have grown up training, but barely needing to patrol."

Tessa rose from her chair, her hair tumbling down her back. It was one of the oddities of being a warlock: her hair had stopped growing when she stopped aging, rather unexpectedly, at nineteen. It remained the same length, halfway to her waist.

"Isn't that good?" she said. "We don't want our children in danger from demons, do we?"

Will sat down on the bed, kicking off his shoes. "We don't want them unprepared, either," he said. "I remember what we had to do when we were their age. I don't know if they could face the same thing. Picnics don't ready you for war."

"Will." Tessa sank down beside him on the bed. "There is no war."

She knew why he worried. For them, there had been war, and loss. Tessa's brother, Nate. Thomas Tanner. Agatha Grant. Jessamine Lovelace, their friend, who now guarded the London Institute in ghostly form. And Jem, who they had both lost and kept.

"I know." Will reached out to stroke her hair. "Tess, Tess. Do you think when you stopped growing older, you stopped aging in your heart? You never became cynical and fearful? Is it old age catching up with me, that I am so fretful and disquieted over nothing?"

She seized him by the chin, turning his face to hers. "You are not old," she said fiercely. "Even when you are eighty, you will be my beautiful Will."

She kissed him. He made a pleased, startled noise, and his arms came up about her. "My Tess," he said. "My lovely wife."

"There is nothing to be afraid of," she said, drawing her lips across his cheek. His hands tightened in her hair. "We have been through so much. We deserve this happiness."

"There are others who deserve happiness who have not gotten it."

"I know." A sob caught in her throat; they were both talking about the same person, and she did not know if the tears she held back were for him or for Will and herself. "I know." She kissed his eyes as he laid her back onto the pillows, his hand finding the knot holding her dressing gown closed. His lean body pressed hers into the mattress. Her fingers found their way into his hair, twining among the thick curls. "I love you," she gasped as the dressing gown fell away. "I love you, Will."

He did not answer, but his lips on hers said more than any words.

Standing on the roof of the Institute, James watched Charles Fairchild's carriage as it rattled out of the Institute's courtyard, under the great black iron gates.

James often came to the roof when he could not sleep, and tonight insomnia had descended with a vengeance. He could not stop thinking of what he had seen in the ballroom—and the night before last, in the dark alley near the Devil Tavern.

The shadow realm. That was what he had always called it in his head, that black and gray place that opened up in front of him sometimes like a vision of Hell. He had first seen it when he was thirteen, and the visions had come repeatedly after that, usually when he lost control of his emotions. The world would go gray, and later those who had been with him—his family or friends—would report that his body had turned half-transparent, like gray smoke.

Once when he had done it on purpose, at Grace's request, he had nearly been unable to come back. The horror of that experience had left him with screaming nightmares. His parents, at their wits' end, had sought out help from Uncle Jem. James had woken up one morning with Jem sitting at the foot of his bed in an armchair, gazing at him through closed eyelids.

So, Jem had said. *You know, of course, that our universe contains many worlds.*

James had nodded.

Think of the universe then as like a honeycomb, each of its chambers a different realm. So some chambers lie next to one another. I believe that the walls between our own world and this world that you are seeing, this world of shadows, have grown thin. You see this realm and you find yourself drawn into it.

"Is it dangerous?" James said.

It could be. Demon realms are unstable places, and this power of yours is not something we know much about. It is possible that you could be drawn into the shadow realm and find yourself unable to come back.

James had been silent for a moment. Finally he said, "So more is at stake than just my sleeping through the night."

Potentially much more, agreed Jem. *You must build a fortress of control around yourself. You must come to know this power, so that you may master it.*

"Was this how it was for my mother?" James had said quietly. "Before she learned to control her shape-shifting?"

Your mother had brutal teachers. They held her against her will and forced her to Change. It must have been terrifying, and painful. James was silent. *You know that your mother has not used her power since the end of the Clockwork War. Since then the act of shape-shifting has been . . . difficult for her. Painful. She has chosen not to do it.*

"Is this all because of my grandfather?" James had demanded. "My mother's demon father? Is this his gift to us? I would have been perfectly satisfied with a new pair of socks on my birthday."

The question of your grandfather's identity, Jem had said, *is one that I've concerned myself with since before you were born. It may well cast some light on your power, and your mother's as well. But that identity has been well hidden—so well hidden as to be suspicious in itself. Beyond the fact that he was a Greater Demon, I have no other insight yet to share.*

As far as James could tell, Jem made no progress over the next year in determining his grandfather's identity, or at least no progress worth sharing. But in that year, James learned to prevent himself from being drawn into the shadow realm, under Jem's instruction. On a cold night in winter, with a bitter wind blowing, Jem took him to the top of Hampstead Heath, and he resisted the pull even when shivering so hard his teeth seemed to shake. They sparred in the training room, Jem surprisingly spry for a Silent Brother, and talked through the feelings that triggered the power— how to control them and breathe through them, even in the middle of a fight. On one memorable occasion, Jem borrowed Matthew's dog, Oscar Wilde, riled him up, and released him on an unsuspecting James during breakfast.

James thought some of Jem's training ideas were deliberate pranks—Silent Brothers had the best poker faces he could imagine, after all. His father assured him that it wasn't in Jem's nature, and that however odd the training, he was sure it was intended sincerely. And James had to admit that the strange regimen did seem to work.

Gradually his sleep became more restful, his mind less constantly watchful. The shadow realm receded from the corners of his vision, and he felt its influence retreat from him, a weight he'd had no awareness of until it lifted. Soon he was losing himself to shadow less and less. It had not happened even once in this past year, until two nights previously, when they'd fought the Deumas demon.

He had thought it might not happen again at all, until tonight.

Nobody had noticed, he told himself now. Well, perhaps Matthew, but that was the bond of *parabatai*: to some extent, Matthew could feel what James felt. Still, Matthew could not see what he saw. He had not seen the dancers turn sinister, the blasted room, or Barbara being pulled down into shadow.

And a few moments later, Barbara had collapsed.

James did not know what to think of it. The visions he saw in the shadow realm had never been echoed in the real world: they were sights of horror, but not of premonition. And Barbara was well—it was only a dizzy spell, she'd said—so perhaps it was a coincidence?

And yet. He distrusted coincidence. He wanted to talk to Jem. Jem was the one he confided in about the world of shadows: Jem was a Silent Brother, a keeper of all the wisdom the Shadowhunters had accrued through the ages. Jem would know what to do.

He took a box of matches from his pocket. It was a rather unusual item, the cover printed with a sketch of Hermes, the messenger god of the Greeks. Jem had given it to him some months ago, with strict instructions as to its use.

James struck one of the matches against the iron rail that ran around the roof. As it burned, he thought unexpectedly of one more person who he suspected had noticed something odd about his behavior: Cordelia. It was in the way she'd looked at him when he'd come up to her and asked her to take his stele.

It wasn't as if Cordelia didn't know about his world of shadows.

Their families were close, and she had been with him when he had had the scalding fever at Cirenworth and had passed in and out of the shadow realm. He thought perhaps she had even read out loud to him then. It was difficult to recall: he had been very ill at the time.

The match had burned down to his fingertips: he flicked the burnt stub aside and tipped his head back to look at the moon, a milky crescent in the sky. He was glad Cordelia was in London, he realized. Not just for Lucie, but for himself. It was odd, he thought—almost as if he had forgotten what a steady light her presence could be when the world went dark.

Days Past:
Cirenworth Hall, 1900

After James was expelled from school at Shadowhunter Academy, his parents sent him to Cirenworth Hall to decide what he wanted to do with the rest of his life.

Cirenworth Hall was a rambling Jacobean pile in Devon that Elias Carstairs had fallen in love with in 1895 and bought on the spot, intending it as a place his family could return to in between their long travels.

James liked *being* there, because he liked the Carstairs family— well, other than Alastair, who was luckily spending the summer with Augustus Pounceby in Idris. But on this particular trip, rain had fallen without surcease. It had begun even before they left London, a gray spattering that had deepened during the ride to a steady, regular thrum, and then had settled in for a long residency over Cirenworth that showed no sign of ending. London in heavy rain was a bleak enough affair, but Cirenworth brought things to a new low of marshy wetness that led James to wonder why anyone had bothered to settle Britain at all.

At least it was not for long. His parents had a series of boring political meetings scheduled in Alicante, so he and Lucie were spending a little less than a month at Cirenworth. Afterward, they'd all return to Herondale Manor together, where the Carstairs would visit them in turn later in the season and where, James hoped, it would be a fine and clear summer.

The worst part was that everybody was carefully giving him so much *room*. He had the understanding that it was expected he desired *room* in which to *feel* things. This left him spending most days reading in the parlor while Lucie and Cordelia trained, drew in sketchbooks, put on Wellington boots and stomped out to the blackberry bushes to collect blackberries in the pouring rain, brewed and drank literally thousands of cups of tea, engaged in spirited swordplay in rooms definitely not built for swordplay, at one point caught some kind of small, loud bird and kept it in a cage for a few days, and allowed James so much space that he began to fear he was invisible.

He yearned for the quiet of Idris. Once they were at Herondale Manor, he could wander the woods by himself for hours and nobody would question it. (Except Grace, perhaps: What would he tell her? Would she have heard anything? He didn't think she and her mother heard a lot of gossip.)

He would never have responded to Cordelia's kindness with anything but kindness in return, but eventually Lucie became so obsequiously friendly that one afternoon James burst out, "You don't have to be so *careful* when you talk to me, you know. I'm all right."

"I know," Lucie said, startled. "I know you're all right."

"Sorry," he said. Lucie gave him a sympathetic look. "I'm going to do some training tomorrow, I think," he added.

"All right," she said. She hesitated, as though she was trying to decide whether to speak.

"Lucie," James said heavily. "It's me. Just say it."

"Well . . . it's only . . . do you want Cordelia and me there?"

"Yes," he said. "You should come. That would be . . . that would be good."

She smiled, and he smiled back, and he felt like maybe everything would someday, not today, but someday, be all right.

Then the next day he went to train with Lucie and Cordelia. Cordelia had brought with her the Carstairs' famous sword, Cortana, which James had long wanted to admire up close. He didn't get a chance, though, because ten minutes into their first exercise, he collapsed in a sudden spasm of unbearable pain.

The girls cried out and ran to him. He had crumpled like a puppet with its strings cut, and only the years of training he'd already put in kept him from accidentally falling onto his own blade. By the time he realized where he was and what had happened, he was on the floor.

The look on Lucie's face as she touched his forehead did not reassure him.

"By the Angel," she exclaimed, "you're burning up."

Cordelia was already racing toward the door, calling, *"Mâmân!"* in alarm. Her image wavered and faded as James closed his eyes.

Scalding fever, Sona and Elias declared. They'd seen it before. It was a disease unique to Shadowhunters. Most got it as infants, when it was very mild. Once it passed, you could never catch it again. Before James was even up from the floor of the training room, Sona was barking orders, her heavy skirts gripped in both hands. James was carried to his bedroom, Lucie dragged away to her own quarters, and messages dispatched to Will and Tessa, and the Silent Brothers.

Feverish, James lay in his bed and watched the light fade outside. As the night came on, he began to shiver. He wrapped himself in all the blankets available but shook like a leaf. He waited for the

Silent Brothers to come—until they had checked him, nobody else could be in the room.

It was Brother Enoch who came, not Uncle Jem, to James's disappointment. *Yes, it is almost certainly scalding fever,* he said. *Everyone who has not had it before will need to depart the house. I will go to tell them.*

Lucie had not had it before. James didn't know about anyone else. He waited a long time for Enoch to come back, but he must have fallen asleep, because all of a sudden there was morning light casting silvery stripes on the wall, and the sound of a door, and footsteps, and then Cordelia was there.

James rarely saw Cordelia without Lucie. This was not how he would have chosen to present himself for one of their rare moments alone. He was half under his covers, shifting around restlessly, unable to get comfortable. His face was flushed with fever and his nightshirt clung to him, wet with sweat.

He took a breath to speak and broke into a pained cough. "Water?"

Cordelia hurried to pour him a glass from the carafe on the nightstand. She tried to press it into his hand, but he couldn't grip it. She slid her hand behind his neck, warm against his skin, supporting him as she held the glass to his lips.

He flopped back on the pillows, his eyes closed. "Please tell me you've had scalding fever before."

"Yes. My mother has too," she said. "And the mundane servants are immune. Everyone else has gone. You should have some more water."

"Is that the treatment?"

"No," said Cordelia, "the treatment is a grayish concoction made by Brother Enoch, and I suggest you hold your nose when you try to get it down. It will help with the fever, but apparently there's nothing else for it but time. I brought books," she added. "They're over on top of the chest of drawers. I . . . I could read to you."

James flinched at the light but forced himself to look at Cordelia. Tendrils of her deep red hair curled against her cheekbones. They reminded him of the curlicues cut into the surface of his Uncle Jem's beautiful violin.

He flicked his eyes over to the chest of drawers where, indeed, a surprisingly tall pile of books rested that had not been there before. She gave an apologetic smile. "I wasn't sure what you might like, so I just took things from all over the house. There's a copy of *A Tale of Two Cities* with the second half missing, so maybe it's only a tale of one city. And a collection of poetry by Byron, but it's a bit nibbled around the edges, I think by mice, so it might be theirs. Otherwise it's Persian literature. There aren't even Shadowhunter books around. Oh, except one copy of a book on demons. I think it's called *Demons, Demons, Demons.*"

James let his eyes close again but allowed himself a smile. "I've read that one," he said. "My father is a great admirer of it. You probably don't even have the newest version, which adds a fourth 'Demons.'"

"As ever, the London Institute's library puts ours to shame," said Cordelia, and then Sona came in and stopped short, surprised to see her.

"Cordelia," she said with what James hoped was mock surprise. "Really? Alone in a boy's bedroom?"

"*Mâmân*, he can barely sit up, and I am a trained warrior who wields a mythical sword."

"Mmm," said Sona, and waved her out. She descended on James with, she explained, her own remedies from home: pastes and poultices of frankincense, of marigold and *haoma*.

"I'd like it," James said, "if Cordelia would come back and read to me later. If she wants to."

"Mmm," said Sona again, dabbing his brow with a compress.

* * *

Cordelia did come back, and she did read to James. And then she returned again and read again, and again. He was too fevered to track the passage of time. Sometimes it was dark outside and sometimes light. When he was awake, he ate what he could, and drank a little water, and forced down some of Enoch's loathsome potion. Sometimes his fever would break for a time, and then he would grow overwarm and sweat through his clothes; sometimes it was as though a bitter cold wind tore through his body and no number of blankets or logs in the fireplace would help. Through it all was Cordelia, quietly reading, occasionally reaching out to wipe his brow or refill his water glass.

She read him the poems of Nizami, and especially the story of Layla and Majnun, one she clearly loved and had known since she was very small. Her cheeks grew unexpectedly red at the more romantic parts: the poor boy falling in love with the beautiful Layla on first sight, wandering mad in the desert when they were separated.

"'That heart's delight, one single glance his nerves to frenzy wrought, one single glance bewildered every thought. He gazed upon her, and as he gazed, love conquered both. They never dreamed to part.'"

She glanced at James and then quickly glanced away. James started. Had he been staring? He was not entirely aware of his own behavior.

"'The killing witchery that lies, in her black, delicious eyes. And when her cheek the moon revealed, a thousand hearts were won: no pride, no shield, could check her power. Layla, she was called.'"

"Layla," he murmured to himself, but he didn't think Cordelia had heard. He closed his eyes.

* * *

Only once—that he knew of—did he tumble into the shadow realm. He was awake, shaking with fever, his hair matted to his head with cold sweat, agitated. He saw Cordelia's eyes widen in alarm as the change came over him. She leaped to her feet and he thought, *She means to go for help; she is frightened, frightened of me.*

He reached for her, and the shadow that was his hand caught hers, darkness against flesh. He wondered how his touch felt to her. His whole body was tensed, like a horse shying from thunder. The room smelled of lightning.

"James, you must hold on. You must. Don't go anywhere," Cordelia said. "Stay with me."

"So cold," he managed to add, shaking. "Can't get warm. Can't ever get warm."

In his body, he would have squinted his eyes shut, trying to still his trembling. As a shadow, it was as though his eyes were open wide and he could do nothing to close them. He saw Cordelia cast about the room for something, anything to help. It was no use, he knew; the fire was already roaring, he was already wrapped in blankets, there was a hot-water bottle at his feet. Nevertheless, a bitter, raw wind tore through him.

Cordelia made a noise of frustration, then furrowed her brow in determination. The thought drifted through James's mind, far behind the endless howling wind, that she looked beautiful. It was not the thought he might have chosen, and he did not have time to think about it now.

But then Cordelia carefully laid herself down on the bed next to him. He was under mountains of blankets and she was atop them, of course. But her presence began to force back the cold. Instead of feeling the agony of being whipped raw by ice, his awareness turned to the length of her body, warm and solid, all along his own. Through the many layers between them he could still feel her pressed against his side: her leg shifting into a comfortable position, her hip against his. He was looking up at the ceiling and she was on her side, but her face was very close. Her hair smelled like jasmine and woodsmoke. She put her arm over his chest and pulled herself as close as she could.

It took a strenuous effort, but he turned his head to the side, to look at her. He found her eyes open, luminous and deep, gazing at him. Her breathing was very steady.

"'I sought not fire, yet is my heart all flame. Layla, this love is not of earth.'"

He shuddered and felt himself come back to this world fully, felt his body return to the space he occupied. Cordelia didn't take her eyes off him, but she released her lower lip from between her teeth, her body slackening in relief.

James was still cold, but not nearly as cold as he had been. Cordelia reached up and pushed a lock of his hair out of his eyes. He shuddered again, but not because of cold, and let his eyes close, and when he awoke again it was morning, and she was gone.

It was only another day or so before James's fever broke for good. And only another day after that, Brother Enoch deemed him no longer contagious and his parents arrived with Lucie. And then he was well enough to get up, and then he was leaving Cirenworth for Idris and the familiar comforts of Herondale Manor. The weather there, his father reported, was fine.

Once he was out of bed, James and Cordelia returned to their ordinary, cordial way. Neither of them mentioned the time they had shared during James's illness. No doubt, James thought, Cordelia had simply cared for him with the kindness and generosity she showed to everyone she liked. They did not embrace when they said goodbye. (Lucie clung to Cordelia like a limpet, despite Cordelia's reassurances that she and her family would be at Herondale Manor themselves later that same summer.) As he stepped into the Portal, James waved to Cordelia, and she, amicably, waved back.

In the night, for a long time to come, James thought of jasmine and woodsmoke, the press of her arm, fathomless dark eyes gazing into his.

"'*The secret path he eager chose, where Layla's distant mansion rose; he kissed the door. A thousand wings increased his pace, whence, his fond devotions paid, a thousand thorns his course delayed. No rest he found by day or night—Layla, forever, in his sight.*'"

4

HALF SICK OF SHADOWS

Or when the moon was overhead
Came two young lovers lately wed;
"I am half sick of shadows,"
said The Lady of Shalott.
—Alfred, Lord Tennyson,
"The Lady of Shalott"

The next day proved bright and beautiful. Regent's Park seemed to shine in the late afternoon sunlight, from the York Gate to the green lawn stretching down to the lake. By the time Cordelia and Alastair arrived, the east bank was already crowded with young Shadowhunters. Colorful woven blankets of bright cerise and sky-blue cotton had been thrown over the grass, and little groups were seated around picnic hampers and crowded down by the lakeside.

Some of the younger set were floating miniature boats on the water, and the white sails of them made the lake look thick with swans. The older girls were in pastel day dresses or skirts with high-necked blouses, the young men in knit sweaters and plus fours. Some were decked out in mundane rowing gear—jackets and trousers in white linen, though white, for Shadowhunters, was traditionally the color of mourning and usually avoided.

Scandalous! Cordelia thought with dark amusement as she and Alastair neared the crowd. It was different from the night before: that had been a gathering of the Enclave, Shadowhunters from the oldest to youngest. These were people her age. Not perhaps the ones who could be most helpful to her father—but everyone here had parents, some of whom were quite influential. Many had older brothers or sisters. The ball might not have gone as Cordelia had wished, but today, she was determined to make her mark.

She recognized Rosamund Wentworth and some of the other girls from the party, deep in conversation. The same anxiety began to rise in her that had risen at the ball: How was one supposed to break into social groups? Make them want you as part of them?

She'd spent the morning with Risa and the Lightwoods' cook, helping to prepare the vastest, most spectacular picnic basket she thought anyone had ever seen. Taking the rolled-up blanket from under her arm, she spread it out deliberately close to the lake, just before the spot where the grass turned into sand and gravel.

She would put herself right in the middle of the view, she thought, plonking herself down and gesturing for Alastair to join her. Cordelia watched Alastair as he dropped the heavy picnic basket with a muttered curse, then flopped down beside her.

He wore a striped jacket of gray linen, pale against his brown skin. His dark eyes roamed restlessly over the crowd. "I cannot recall," he said, "why we agreed to this."

"We cannot spend our lives hiding in our house, Alastair. We must make friends," said Cordelia. "Recall that we are meant to be ingratiating ourselves."

He made a face at her as she began unpacking the picnic hamper, setting out freshly cut flowers, cold chicken, game pies, fruit, butter in a jam pot, three types of marmalade, white and brown bread, potted crab, and salmon mayonnaise.

Alastair raised his eyebrows.

"People like to eat," Cordelia said.

Alastair looked as if he was about to argue, then brightened and scrambled to his feet. "I see some of the boys from the Academy," he said. "Piers and Thoby are down by the water. I'll just go ingratiate myself, shall I?"

"Alastair," Cordelia protested, but he was already gone, leaving her alone on the thick plaid picnic blanket. She put her chin in the air, setting out the rest of the food—strawberries, cream, lemon tartlets, and stone ginger beer. She wished Lucie were here, but since she hadn't arrived yet, Cordelia would have to stick it out on her own.

You are a Shadowhunter, she reminded herself. One of a long line of Persian Shadowhunters. The Jahanshah family had fought demons for longer than people like Rosamund Wentworth could imagine. Sona claimed they had the blood of the famous hero Rostam in them. Cordelia could manage a picnic.

"Cordelia Carstairs?" Cordelia glanced up to see Anna standing above her, elegant as ever in a pale linen shirt and buff trousers. "May I join you?"

"Of course!" Delighted, Cordelia made space. She knew Anna was a topic of legend and admiration: she did as she liked, dressed as she liked, and lived where she liked. Her clothes were as spectacular as the stories about her. If Anna chose to sit with her, Cordelia could not be seen as dull.

Anna sank gracefully to her knees, reaching into the basket to retrieve a bottle of ginger beer. "I suppose," she said, "we have not been officially introduced. But after the drama of last evening, I feel as if I know you."

"After hearing about you from Lucie for so many years, I feel as if I know *you.*"

"I see you have ranged your food about you like a fortress," Anna said. "Very wise. I think of each social occasion as a battle to be entered, myself. And I always wear my armor." She crossed her legs at the ankle, showing her knee-high boots to advantage.

"And I always bring my sword." Cordelia tapped the hilt of Cortana, currently half-concealed beneath a fold of blanket.

"Ah, the famous Cortana." Anna's eyes sparkled. "A sword that bears no runes, yet can kill demons, they say. Is that true?"

Cordelia nodded proudly. "My father slew the great demon Yanluo with it. They say the blade of Cortana can cut through anything."

"That sounds very useful." Anna touched the hilt lightly and withdrew her hand. "How are you finding London?"

"Honestly? It is overwhelming. I have spent most of my life traveling, and in London I only know James and Lucie."

Anna smiled like a sphinx. "But you brought enough food to provision an army." She cocked her head to the side. "I'd like to invite you to tea at my flat, Cordelia Carstairs. There are some matters we should discuss."

Cordelia was stunned. What could glamorous Anna Lightwood possibly have to discuss with her? The thought crossed her mind that perhaps it had to do with her father, but before she could ask, Anna's face lit up and she began waving at two approaching figures.

Cordelia turned to see Anna's brother Christopher and Thomas Lightwood picking their way along the edge of the lake. Thomas towered over Christopher, who appeared to be chatting to him amiably, the sun glinting off his spectacles.

Anna's smile took on a curl at the edges. "Christopher! Thomas! Over here!"

Cordelia plastered on a bright smile as they came closer. "Do come say hello," she said. "I've lemon tartlets, and ginger beer, if you like."

The boys glanced at each other. A moment later they were

settling onto the blanket, Christopher nearly upsetting the picnic basket. Thomas was more careful with his long arms and legs, as if nervous he might knock something over. He wasn't beautiful like James, but he would certainly suit a lot of girls. As for Christopher, his fine-boned resemblance to Anna was even clearer up close.

"I see why you called for our help," Thomas said, his hazel eyes sparkling as he took in the picnic spread. "It would be staggeringly difficult for you to consume all this by yourselves. Best to call in the reserves."

Christopher snagged a lemon tart. "Thomas used to be able to clear out our larder in an hour—and the eating contests he had with Lucie, I shudder to report them."

"I may have heard a bit about that," said Cordelia. *Thomas adores ginger beer,* Lucie had told her once, *and Christopher is obsessed with lemon tarts.* She hid a smile. "I know we've met before on occasion, but now that I'm officially in London, I hope that we'll become friends."

"Absolutely certainly," said Christopher, "especially if there will be more lemon tarts in the offing."

"I doubt she carries them everywhere with her, Kit," said Thomas, "stuffed into her hats and whatnot."

"I keep them in my weapons belt instead of seraph blades," said Cordelia, and both boys laughed.

"How is Barbara, Thomas?" asked Anna, as she picked up an apple. "Is she well after last night?"

"She seems quite recovered," Thomas said, gesturing to where Barbara was walking down by the lake with Oliver. She was twirling a bright blue parasol and chatting animatedly. Thomas bit into a meat pie.

"If you were a truly dedicated brother, you would be at her side," Anna said. "I would hope that if I collapsed, Christopher would weep inconsolably and be incapable of consuming meat pies."

"Barbara doesn't want me near her," Thomas said, unperturbed. "She's hoping Oliver will propose."

"Is she?" said Anna, her dark eyebrows winging upward in amusement.

"Alastair!" Cordelia called. "Do come eat! The food is vanishing!"

But her brother—who was not, Cordelia noticed, chatting with boys from the Academy, but was standing alone by the lakeside—only cast her a glance that indicated that she was tiresome.

"Ah," said Thomas, in a slightly too casual voice. "Alastair is here."

"Yes," said Cordelia. "He's the man of our house at the moment, since my father is in Idris."

Christopher had produced a small black notebook and was scribbling in it. Anna was gazing down at the lake, where several of the young ladies—Rosamund, Ariadne, and Catherine among them—had decided to take a turn. "He has my sympathy," said Thomas, with an easy smile. "My father is often in Idris as well, with the Consul—"

I know, Cordelia thought, but before she could ask him anything, she heard Lucie calling her name. She looked up to see her future *parabatai* heading toward them, holding a straw hat in place with one hand and a basket in the other. Behind her was James, his hands in the pockets of his pin-striped trousers. He wore no hat, and the wind tugged at his already tousled black hair.

"Oh, lovely!" Lucie said, upon seeing Cordelia's mountain of food. "We can combine our winnings. Let's see what you have."

Anna and Christopher made space as Lucie dropped to her knees and began unpacking yet more food—cheese and jam tarts, sandwiches and lemonade. James sat down by Christopher, glancing idly at his notebook. He said something in a low voice, and Thomas and Christopher laughed.

Cordelia felt her breath catch in her throat. She hadn't really spoken to James since they'd danced the night before. Unless one counted him asking her to remove his stele from his jacket. She remembered the way his hands had been fisted at his sides. He seemed a different person now.

"What did it turn out to be, last night?" she said to Lucie. "The demon business in Seven Dials."

James glanced over at her. His smile was easy—too easy, Cordelia thought. As if he were an actor on a stage, told to look as if he were enjoying himself. "Shax demons all up and down Monmouth Street. They had to call on Ragnor Fell to help glamour the place so the mundanes wouldn't notice what was going on."

Thomas frowned. "It's odd," he said, "after so long, we encountered that demon the other night, and now yesterday—"

"You encountered a demon?" Lucie demanded. "When was that?"

"Er," said Thomas, his hazel eyes darting around. "I may have been wrong. It may not have been a demon. It may have been a textbook about demons."

"Thomas," said Lucie. "You are the most dreadful liar. I want to know what happened."

"You can always get the truth out of Matthew," said James. "You can wheedle anything out of him, you know that, Luce." He glanced around the lake. "Where is Matthew? Isn't he meant to be coming?"

He looked over at Cordelia, and she felt a sudden rush of anger. She'd been quiet—now that she'd managed to lure all these people to her Picnic Blanket of Machinations, how was she meant to bring up her father? But James's words brought back the night before in a sharp flash of memory. He was asking her if she knew where Matthew was because she'd danced with Matthew, and she'd danced with Matthew because James had abandoned her and Matthew had stepped in.

Cordelia rose to her feet, nearly knocking over a bottle of ginger beer. She took a deep breath, brushed off her blue serge skirt, and said, "James, I'd like to speak with you in private for a moment, if you don't mind."

Everyone looked astonished, even Lucie; James only nodded.

"Lead the way," he said.

There was a small Italian folly near the lake, complete with white pillars. Cordelia led James away from the crowd of picnickers in silence, passing a few groups of strolling mundanes; now she climbed the few steps of the folly to its central pavilion, turned, and faced him.

"Last night," she said, "you were most appallingly rude to me, and I would like an apology."

He looked up at her. So this was what it would be like to be taller than James, she thought. She didn't mind it. His expression was calm, unreadable even. It wasn't an unfriendly look, but it was entirely closed off, letting no one in. It was an expression she had seen on James's face before: she had always thought of it privately as the Mask.

She raised an eyebrow. "You're not going to apologize?"

Maybe it wasn't better to be taller than him, she thought. When he looked up at her, he had to do it through his eyelashes, which were thick and black as the silk fringes on a scarf. "I am trying to think of the best way to do it. What I did—leaving you on the dance floor—was unforgivable. I am trying to think of a reason you ought to forgive me anyway, because if you did not, it would break my heart."

She cleared her throat. "That is a decent start."

His smile was faint, but real, breaking through the Mask. "You've always had a charitable nature, Daisy."

She pointed her finger at him. "Don't you Daisy me," she said. "Have you taken the time to understand what it is to be a girl in such a situation? A girl cannot ask a gentleman to dance; she is at the mercy of the choice of the opposite sex. She cannot even refuse a dance if it is asked of her. To have a boy walk away from her on the dance floor is humiliating. To have it happen when one is wearing a truly frightful gown, even more so. They will all be discussing what is wrong with me."

"Wrong with you?" he repeated. "There is nothing wrong with you. Everything you say is true, and I am a fool for not having thought of it before. All I can do is swear to you that you will never lack at any social event in future, someone to stand up with or dance attendance on you. You might not credit it, having met Thomas and Christopher and Matthew, but they are quite popular. We can make you the toast of the season."

"Really?" she said. "Thomas and Christopher and Matthew are *popular?*"

He laughed. "Yes, and I can make you a further promise as well. If I offend you again, *I* will wear a truly frightful gown to the next significant social gathering."

"Very well." She put her hand out. "We can shake on it like gentlemen do."

He stepped forward to shake her hand. His warm fingers curled around hers. His lips, slightly curved, looked incredibly soft. He appeared to be searching her face with his gaze; she wondered what he was looking for.

"James," she said.

"Yes?"

"Rather than you wearing a frightful dress," she said, "perhaps there is another way you could help me."

"Anything." He had not let go of her hand.

"You could tell me which of the young men of the Enclave are eligible," she said. "If I had need of—of marrying, which of them are kind, and would not be terrible company."

He looked stunned. "You cannot get married—"

"Why not?" She drew her hand back from his. "Do you think I would be an undesirable match?"

He had gone a strange color; she had no idea why until she looked behind her and realized that a carriage had just drawn up near the folly.

The carriage's doors were painted with the four Cs of the Shadowhunter government: Clave, Council, Covenant, Consul. Matthew was in the box seat, reins in hand, the wind blowing through his blond curls.

Behind him, laughing, was Matthew's brother, Charles, and beside him, Grace, in a straw bonnet and a blue dress trimmed in matching Cluny lace.

Cordelia glanced back at James and saw something in his eyes flicker—a sort of dark light behind the irises. He was watching Charles help Grace down from the carriage. Matthew was scrambling out of his driver's seat, leaving the reins loose, casting about for his friends.

"What is it between you and Grace Blackthorn?" Cordelia said quietly. "Do you have an understanding?"

"Understanding" was something of a broad term. It could mean a secret engagement, or as little as a declaration of serious romantic interest. But it seemed to fit as well as anything else.

The odd light was still in James's eyes, darkening their gold to smoked glass. "There are those close to me I would give up my life for," he said. "You know that."

The names were unspoken but Cordelia knew them: Lucie, Will, Tessa, Christopher, Matthew, Thomas. Jem Carstairs.

"Grace is one of them," said James. "We are neighbors in Idris. I have seen her every summer for years. We love one another— but it is a secret. Neither my parents nor her mother are aware of our bond." He lifted his wrist, the bracelet there gleaming for a moment in the sun. "She gave me this when we were thirteen. It is a promise between us." There was an odd distance in his voice, as if he were reciting a story he had heard, rather than recalling a memory. Shyness, perhaps, at revealing something so intimate?

"I see," said Cordelia. She looked over at the carriage. Ariadne had come up to Charles and they were greeting each other; Grace had turned and was gazing toward the folly.

"I had thought we would not go to Idris this year," James said. "I wrote to Grace to tell her, but her mother kept the letter from her. We were each left wondering at the silence of the other. I only discovered she had come to London yesterday, at the ball."

Cordelia felt numb. Well, of course he had run off, then. Every summer he had seen Grace save this one; how he must have missed her. She had always known James possessed a life she knew little of with his friends in London, but she had not realized how very much she didn't know him. He might as well be a stranger. A stranger in love with someone else. And she, Cordelia, the interloper.

"I am glad we are friends again," Cordelia said. "Now you must wish to speak to Grace alone. Just signal her to join you here—everyone is distracted. You will be quite unnoticed."

James began to speak, but Cordelia had already turned and made her way back toward the lake and the picnickers. She could not bear to pause and listen to him thank her for going away.

Lucie didn't blame Cordelia for wanting to tell James off; he'd been terribly rude the night before. Even if a girl was just your friend, you shouldn't leave her in the middle of a dance. Besides, it gave the Rosamund Wentworths of the world too much scope for nasty gossip. She reminded herself to tell Cordelia about what had happened to Eugenia Lightwood as soon as they were alone.

In fact, there was a great deal she wished to discuss with

Cordelia when they were alone. *Last night I met a ghost that no one else could see. The ghost of a boy who is dead, but not quite dead.*

She had opened her mouth a few times to mention Jesse to James or her parents, then decided against it. For a reason she couldn't quite understand, it felt private, like a secret she had been charged with. It was hardly Jesse's fault she could see him, and he *had* saved her all those years ago in Brocelind. She remembered telling him that when she grew up, she wanted to be a writer. *That sounds wonderful*, he had said in a wistful tone. At the time she'd believed he was stricken with envy about her glorious future career. It was only now that it occurred to her he might have been talking about growing up.

"I see Cordelia is returning," said Anna. She was leaning back on her elbows, the sunshine bright on her dark hair. "But without James. Interesting."

Anna, like Lucie, found everything about human behavior interesting. Sometimes Lucie thought Anna ought to be a writer too. Her memoirs would be sure to be scandalous.

Cordelia was indeed making her way back toward them, stepping carefully between the brightly colored picnic blankets. She sank down beside Lucie, fanning herself with her straw bonnet. She was wearing another ghastly pastel dress, Lucie noticed. She wished Sona would let Cordelia dress as she wished.

"Did James get what he deserved?" Lucie asked. "Did you keelhaul him?"

Cordelia's smile was bright. "He is thoroughly abashed, I assure you. But we are good friends again."

"Where is he, then?" Thomas inquired. His shirtsleeves were rolled up, and Lucie could just glimpse the edge of the colored ink design on his left forearm. It was unusual for Shadowhunters to get tattoos, as their skin was so often Marked by runes, but Thomas had done just that in Spain. "Did you bury his body in the park somewhere?"

"He went to speak to Grace Blackthorn," said Cordelia, selecting a bottle of lemonade. Lucie glanced at her sharply—she herself had only realized the night before that the girl James was in love with was Grace, not Daisy. She hoped she hadn't put silly thoughts into Cordelia's head by rattling on in the park about how James might be in love with her.

Cordelia certainly didn't seem bothered, and she'd brushed off the whole idea in Kensington Gardens. She probably thought of James as a cousin. It was certainly a setback to Lucie's hopes. It would have been delightful to have Daisy as a sister-in-law, and she could not imagine that Grace would be delightful in the same way. She couldn't recall ever having seen her smile or laugh, and she would be unlikely to be charmed by Will's songs about demon pox.

"I didn't realize she was here." Christopher helped himself to a sixth lemon tart.

"She is," Matthew said, appearing out of the thicket of parasols and picnickers. He slid gracefully into a sitting position beside Anna, who glanced at him and winked. Matthew and Anna were especially close: they enjoyed many of the same things, like fashionable clothes, disreputable salons, shocking art, and scandalous plays. "Apparently, Charles promised last night to bring her here in our carriage. We had to detour out to Chiswick to fetch her."

"Did you get a look at Lightwood—at Chiswick House?" asked Thomas. "I hear it's in utter disrepair."

Matthew shook his head. "Grace was waiting for us at the front gates when we arrived. I did think it a bit odd."

Chiswick House had once belonged to Benedict Lightwood and was meant to pass to his sons, Gabriel and Gideon. Everything changed after Benedict's disgrace, and in the end the newly named Chiswick House had been given to Tatiana, even though she had married a Blackthorn.

Tatiana had famously let the place fall to pieces—perhaps

because after Jesse had died, she had not felt there was anyone of Blackthorn blood to whom the house could be left. Grace was Tatiana's adopted ward, not her daughter by blood. When Tatiana died, the house would pass back into the hands of the Clave, who might even return it to the Lightwoods. Tatiana would probably rather burn it down than have that happen.

Jesse had said that both his mother and sister could see him. How strange that must be, for him and for them. She recalled the night before: Jesse saying that death was in the ballroom. But it hadn't been, she thought. There had been a demon occurrence in the city, but it had been handled easily.

But what if he had not meant death was there last night? What if he had meant that a greater danger surrounded them all?

Lucie shivered and glanced down toward the lake, where everything was comfortingly ordinary—Charles and Ariadne chatting with Barbara and Oliver; Alastair skipping stones across the lake with Augustus Pounceby. Rosamund and Piers Wentworth looking smug about something. Catherine Townsend sailing a small boat with remarkable skill.

She heard Cordelia, beside her, murmur to Matthew about how it seemed as if it might rain. A few dark clouds scudded across the sky, casting shadows across the silvery surface of the water. She caught her breath. She was imagining things, surely—the reflections of the clouds could not be getting thicker, and darker.

"Cordelia," she whispered. "Do you have Cortana?"

Cordelia looked puzzled. "Yes, of course. Under the blanket."

"Reach for it." Lucie rose to her feet, aware of Cordelia drawing her shining gold blade without another question. She was about to call out when the lake water burst apart as a demon broke the surface.

*　*　*

"That was Cordelia Carstairs," said Grace. She had approached James when he signaled, but had paused a few feet away, her expression troubled.

James had rarely seen her in the sunlight; she reminded him of a pale, night-blooming flower easily singed by the sun. Her hat shaded her eyes, and her ivory kidskin boots were planted in the long grass. He had always wondered that Tatiana bothered to make sure Grace had well-made and fashionable clothes when she cared about so little else.

"Yes?" James said. It wasn't like Grace to be jealous, and he wasn't sure that she was. She looked worried, but that could be many things. "You know the Carstairs have long been my friends." He held out his hand, the silver bracelet on his wrist sparking in the sun. "Grace. You are far away, and we have been far away from each other long enough."

She took a step toward him and said, "Do you remember when you told me all about Cordelia? That summer after you had the scalding fever?"

He shook his head, puzzled. He remembered the fever, of course, and Cordelia's voice through the dizziness. She had been kind to him, though he did not recall telling Grace about it. "No," he said. "Not specifically, but I have always told you everything, so it would hardly be surprising."

"Not just that she was with you when you were ill," Grace said. "But about *her*. About Cordelia."

"About Cordelia?" He lowered his hand, recalling Brocelind Forest, the light filtering down through the green leaves, the way he and Grace had rested in the grass and told each other everything. "I do not think I know that much about her," he said, realizing with an odd pang that it was true. He supposed he could tell Grace that Cordelia had asked him to help her find an eligible man, but for some reason, he did not want to. "She and her family have always been reticent. Lucie knows her much better than I do. I do remember a time. . . ."

"What is it?" Grace had come close to him. He could smell her perfume as she looked up at him: it was always the same scent of violets. "What do you remember?"

"Lucie fell from the side of a cliff once," he said slowly. It was an oddly dim memory. There had been a field of daisies—Cordelia had been very brave—it was how she had gotten her nickname. *Daisy.* "In France. Cordelia was with her. It would have been a bad fall, but Cordelia caught her wrist and held on to her for hours until we found them. I'll always be grateful to her for saving my sister."

It seemed to James that Grace relaxed slightly, though he could not have guessed why. "I'm sorry to have interrupted you with your friend," she said. "It's just been so long since we've been alone."

A strange pang of something like unease went through James. "You had wanted to meet Matthew and Christopher and Thomas," he said. "I could take you. . . ."

She shook her head, and he was struck as always by her beauty. It was cold and perfect—no, she was not cold, he reminded himself. She held herself tightly closed, for she had been hurt badly by the loss of her parents, by Tatiana's whims and cruelty. But that was not the same as coldness. There was color in her cheeks now, and her eyes glittered fiercely.

"I want you to kiss me," she said.

He never thought of saying no.

The sun was bright as he reached for her, so bright it hurt his eyes. He drew her toward him: she was small and cool and slight, delicate as a bird. Her hat slipped from her head as she tilted her face up toward his. He felt the rustle of lace against his hands as they circled her waist, and the cool, soft press of her lips against his.

The sun was a burning needle transfixing them both to the spot. Her chest rose and fell against his; she was trembling as if she were cold. Her hands gripped his shoulders. For a moment, he only felt: their lips against each other's, the taste of her like sugar pastilles on his tongue.

His eyes began to burn, though they were closed. He felt breathless and sick, as if he'd dived under salt water and come up for air too late. Something was wrong. With a choked gasp of nausea, he broke away from Grace.

Her hand went to her mouth. There was a look on her face he had not expected—a look of undeniable panic.

"Grace—" he began, when the air was suddenly cut through by the sound of screams, coming from the lake. And not just one person screaming, as Oliver had called out last night, but multiple voices, crying out in fear.

James caught hold of Grace and pushed her toward the folly. She had no idea how to fight—had never been trained. She was still looking at him in horror. "Stay here," he demanded, and bolted toward the lake.

Cordelia didn't see it happen. By the time she had unsheathed Cortana, the demon had sprung from the water and directly onto Piers Wentworth. He went down with a howl of pain, kicking and thrashing.

There was instantly a melee. Shadowhunters were screaming—some had leaped for Piers, including Alastair and Rosamund, and were trying to peel the creature from his body. Charles had shoved Ariadne behind him—she looked exasperated—and was shouting for everyone to get away from the lake. Barbara was screaming, words that sounded like "What is it? What is it?"

But Cordelia could think of only one thing: Alastair. She raced toward the shore. She could see Alastair's bright hair among the scrum of people. As she neared them, she saw Piers lying motionless by the water's edge: the rim of the water was scarlet, and more scarlet was billowing into the lake. Rosamund was on her knees beside him, screaming. The demon had vanished, though Cordelia had not seen anyone kill it.

Alastair had backed away from Piers; Ariadne was on her knees next to the fallen boy, her dress in the blood and sand. As Cordelia drew near to her brother, she saw that there was blood on him, too. She reached him among the chaos, breathless.

"Alastair—"

There was a stunned look on his face. Her voice shook him awake: he caught at her free arm and pulled her toward the grass. "Cordelia, get back—"

She looked around wildly. Shadowhunters were running everywhere, knocking over hampers and trampling picnic food underfoot. "What happened, Alastair? What was it?"

He shook his head, his expression bleak. "I have absolutely no idea."

James raced down the slope of the green hill toward the lake. The sky had darkened, stained everywhere with clouds: in the distance he could see mundanes hurrying away from the park, wary of approaching rain. The water of the lake had turned from silver to gray, rippled with strong wind. A small crowd had formed at the lake's edge. The picnic had been abandoned: bottles and hampers had been kicked over, and everywhere Shadowhunters were seizing up weapons. James caught sight of Matthew and Lucie among the throng: Matthew was handing Lucie an unlit seraph blade from his own belt. He thought he caught sight of Cordelia's red hair, close to the lakeside, just as Barbara came racing up to him.

Her eyes were wide and terrified; Oliver was racing behind her, determined to catch her up. She reached James first. "Jamie—Jamie—"

She caught at his sleeve. "It was a demon. I saw it attack Piers."

"Piers is hurt?" James craned his neck to see better. He had never liked Piers Wentworth, but that didn't mean he wanted anything to happen to him.

"Barbara." Oliver reached them, out of breath from lack of training. "Darling. Demons cannot withstand sunlight. You know that."

Barbara ignored her suitor. "James," she whispered, dropping her voice. "You can see things other people can't, sometimes. Did you see anything last night?"

He looked at her in surprise. How did she know he'd fallen briefly into the shadow realm? "Barbara, I don't—"

"I did," she whispered. "I saw—shapes—ragged black shapes—and I saw something catch hold of me and drag me down."

James's heart began to pound.

"I saw one again, just now—it leaped on Piers, and it disappeared, but it was there—"

Oliver shot James an irritable look. "Barbara, don't overexcite yourself," he began, just as Matthew appeared, making a beeline for James. Behind Matthew, the crowd was parting: James could see Anna with Ariadne and Thomas, all kneeling around the body of Piers on the ground. Thomas had torn off his jacket and pressed it against Piers's throat; even from here, James could see the blood.

"Where's Charles?" James said, as Matthew approached: Charles was, after all, the closest thing to the Consul that they had here.

"Went to put up wards to keep the mundanes away," Matthew said. The wind was rising, skirling the leaves on the ground into minor cyclones. "Right now, someone needs to get Piers to the infirmary."

"Piers is alive?" James asked.

"Yes, but it doesn't look good," said Matthew, raising his voice to be heard over the wind. "They're putting *iratzes* on him, but they're not working."

James met Matthew's gaze with his own. There were only a few kinds of wounds that healing runes couldn't help. Wounds infected by demon poison were among them.

"I told you," Barbara cried. "The demon clawed at his throat—" She broke off, staring toward the far edge of the grassy area, where trees bordered the lake.

James followed her gaze and stiffened in horror. The park was a gray landscape through which the wind rushed: the lake was black, and the boats on it twisted and sagged strangely. Clouds the color of bruises scudded across a steel-colored sky. The only brightness he could see was a clear golden light in the distance, but it was trapped among the crowd of Nephilim like a firefly trapped in a jar; he couldn't identify what it was.

The boughs of the trees whipped back and forth in the rising wind. They were full of shapes—ragged and black, just as Barbara had said. Clawed shadows torn from a greater darkness. How many, James couldn't tell. Dozens, at least.

Matthew was staring, his face white. *He can see what I see*, James realized. *He can see them too.*

Springing down from the trees, the demons rushed at them.

The demons raced like hellhounds across the grass, leaping and surging, utterly silent. Their skin was rough and corrugated, the color of onyx; their eyes flaming black. They tore through the park under the dark, cloud-blackened sky.

Beside Cordelia, Alastair ripped a seraph blade from the pocket of his jacket and held it up. "*Micah!*" he cried—every seraph blade needed to be given an angel's name to be activated.

The low gleam of the blade became a bonfire. There was a sudden riot of illumination as seraph blades blazed up everywhere; Cordelia could hear the names of angels being called, but the

Shadowhunters' voices were slow with astonishment. It had been a long time of relative peace, and no one expected demonic activity during the day.

Yet it was here. The demons surged like a wave and crashed down upon the Nephilim.

Cordelia had never expected to find herself in the middle of a battle. To slay a few demons here and there on patrol was something she had hoped for, but this—this was chaos. Two demons with feral, doglike faces flung themselves at Charles and Ariadne; he stepped in front of her and was knocked aside. Cordelia heard someone call out Charles's name: a moment later the second demon was upon Ariadne. Its jaws closed on her shoulder and it began to drag her body across the grass as she kicked and struggled.

Cordelia started toward her, but a shadow rose up in front of her, a black shadow with dripping jaws and eyes like red coals. There was no room in her to scream. Her sword whirled in a blazing arc. Gold sliced across shadow: ichor spilled, and she nearly stumbled. She whirled to see that Anna had raced to Ariadne's side, a long silver dagger in her hand. She plunged it into the attacking demon's back, and it vanished in a spray of ichor.

More demons surged forward. Anna cast a helpless look at Ariadne lying in the bloodstained grass and turned back with a cry; she was soon joined by others—Thomas, his *bolas* sailing through the air, and Barbara and Lucie, armed with seraph blades.

A demon lunged for Alastair: Cordelia brought Cortana down in a great curving arc, severing its head.

Alastair looked peevish. "Really," he said. "I could have done that on my own."

Cordelia considered killing Alastair, but there was no time—someone was screaming. It was Rosamund Wentworth, who had refused to move from her brother's side. She crouched over his bleeding body as a demon snapped its jaws at her.

James raced toward her across the grass, seraph blade blazing at his side. He sprang into the air, landed on the demon's back, and thrust his seraph blade into its neck. Ichor spilled as the demon vanished. Cordelia saw him spin around, his eyes searching the grass and finding Matthew. Matthew, who had a curved blade in his hand, stood by Lucie, as if he meant to drive off any demon who came near her.

James ran toward Matthew and his sister, just as another scream tore the air.

It was Barbara. One of the shadow demons pounced, slamming Oliver to the ground and closing its jaws around Barbara's leg. She cried out in agony and collapsed.

A second later James was there; he flung himself at the creature on top of Barbara, knocking it to the side. They rolled over and over, the Shadowhunter and the demon, as screams tore through the crowd of assembled Shadowhunters.

Matthew dived forward, executing a perfect midair flip, and kicked out. His boot connected with the demon, knocking it free from James. Matthew landed as James sprang up, seizing a dagger from his belt. He flung it, and it sank into the demon's side; spitting and hissing, the demon vanished.

And there was silence.

Cordelia didn't know if the demons had been defeated, or if they had scurried away in retreat or victory. Perhaps they had done all they had meant to do in the way of damage. There was no way of knowing. Frozen in shock, battered and bloody, the group of Shadowhunters who had come to Regent's Park for an afternoon picnic stared at each other across the bloody grass.

The picnic area was in shreds: patches of grass burned with ichor, hampers and blankets scattered and destroyed. But none of that mattered. What mattered were the three still figures that lay in the grass, unmoving. Piers Wentworth, his shirt drenched in blood, his sister sobbing at his side. Barbara Lightwood, being lifted into Thomas's arms—Oliver had his stele out and was drawing healing rune after healing rune on her dangling arm. And Ariadne, crumpled in a heap, her pink dress stained with red. Charles knelt with her, but her head was in Anna's lap. Dark blood trickled from the corner of her mouth.

The demons might have gone, but they had left devastation behind.

5

FALLEN WITH THE NIGHT

The gas-lamps gleam in a golden line;
The ruby lights of the hansoms shine,
Glance, and flicker like fire-flies bright;
The wind has fallen with the night,
And once again the town seems fair
Thwart the mist that hangs i' the air.
—Amy Levy, "A March Day in London"

Cordelia leaned close to Lucie as they jolted through the streets in the Institute's carriage, surrounded by the blurred traffic of omnibuses, motorcars, and pedestrians. Advertisements whirled past. THE HORSESHOE HOTEL. THREE-GUINEA STOUT. NEW PALACE STEAMERS. Signs advertising tailors and fishmongers, hair tonic and cheap printing. A world incredibly distant from the one Cordelia had just left behind in Regent's Park. A world where small things mattered.

Matthew was sitting across from them on the upholstered carriage seat, gripping the seat cushions with his fists. His hair stuck out madly. Blood and ichor stained his linen jacket and silk tie.

The moment the demons had gone, James had taken off on

Balios, one of his father's horses, hoping to reach the Institute and prepare them for the arrival of the wounded. Charles had bolted off with Ariadne in the Consul's carriage, leaving Matthew to cadge a ride with Lucie and Cordelia.

Alastair had returned to Kensington to tell Sona what had happened. Cordelia was half-glad for the ichor burns on her hands: she had told him she would need treatment in the Institute infirmary, and besides, she could potentially stay to offer help and assistance. After all, they had to be mindful of the impression they were making on the Enclave.

"*Now?*" he had demanded, dark eyes snapping. "At this moment, you're worried about the impression we're making in London?"

"It's important, Alastair," she'd replied. "It's for Father."

Alastair hadn't protested further. Cordelia had been a little surprised; she knew he thought her scheming was pointless. They had argued about it at Cirenworth, and she'd told him she couldn't comprehend why he wouldn't stand behind their father with her, why he seemed to feel that there was no hope when they hadn't yet tried everything. He'd only told her she didn't understand.

"I still don't see how it's possible," said Lucie. "Demons *don't* come out during the day. They simply don't."

"I've heard of them appearing under thick cloud cover before," said Cordelia. "If no sunlight could get through—"

Matthew gave a hoarse laugh. "That was no natural storm. Yet I have never heard of demons who could control the weather, either."

He drew a silver flask from his waistcoat pocket. Lucie shot him a sharp look before glancing away.

"Did you see the wounds?" she asked. "I have never seen anything like it. Barbara's skin was turning black at the edges where she was bitten—"

"You have never seen anything like it because there never has been anything like this," said Matthew. "Demons who bring their own night with them? Who attack us when we are vulnerable because we believe we cannot be assailed?"

"Matthew," said Cordelia sharply. "Stop frightening Lucie when we do not even know what we are dealing with yet."

He took a swig from the flask as the carriage rattled through Ludgate Circus and onto Fleet Street. Cordelia could smell the sharp, sweet perfume of the alcohol, familiar as childhood. "Lucie doesn't get frightened, do you, Luce?"

Lucie crossed her arms over her chest. "I am frightened for Barbara and Ariadne, and for Piers," she said. "Are you not concerned? Barbara is our family, and Ariadne one of the kindest people I know."

"There is no special protection in this world for kind people," Matthew began, and broke off as Cordelia glared at him. He took another swig from his flask and bared his teeth. "Yes, I'm being a beast. I know that perfectly well."

"Then stop doing it," said Cordelia. "My father always said that to panic before you have all the facts was to fight the enemy's battle for him."

"But who *is* the enemy?" said Lucie. "Demons, I suppose, but demons usually attack without strategy or method. These demons avoided every mundane in the park and went straight for us."

"Demons aren't always random in their actions," Cordelia said. "Perhaps a warlock who has summoned a pack of demons is responsible, or even a Greater Demon amusing themselves. Ordinary demons are like animals, but if I understand it rightly, Greater Demons can be quite like people."

They had reached the Institute. Matthew shot her a swift, surprised look as the carriage rolled under the gate with its Latin motto: PULVIS ET UMBRA SUMUS.

We are dust and shadows.

As they came to a sliding stop in the courtyard, Matthew

reached to throw the carriage door open. He leaped down and turned to help Cordelia and Lucie after him. The courtyard was already full of carriages—Cordelia recognized the symbol of the Inquisitor's family, an arched bridge, on one of them. She could also see Balios, his reins tied to a post near the front steps. His flanks were foamy with sweat; James must have ridden hell-for-leather through the streets.

As another carriage began to rattle under the gate, Matthew glared at his flask, which was apparently empty. "I think I'll take a walk," he said. "I shall return shortly."

"*Matthew!*" Lucie looked horrified. "But the infirmary—and Thomas needs us—"

"I don't like illness," Matthew said shortly, and walked away, clearly choosing his steps very carefully. Cordelia wondered what had been in the flask. Something quite strong, she guessed.

Lucie looked furious. "How *can* he—"

She broke off as the new carriage came to a stop and Gabriel and Cecily Lightwood spilled out. Gabriel looked harried; Cecily, beside him, was carrying a very small boy—dark-haired and blue-eyed. Cordelia guessed he was Alexander, Lucie's youngest cousin.

"Lucie!" Cecily cried, hurrying toward her niece. Cordelia hung back with a feeling of awkwardness. It was a sharp reminder of how far away from all this she had grown up. Not just geographically, but also socially. Alastair had at least had time at the Academy. This world, Lucie and James's world, was a world of family and friends who loved each other, but did not know her at all.

"But I don't understand," Cecily was saying. "I know what Anna's message said, but a demon attack in *broad daylight*? It makes no sense at all. Could it not have been something else?"

"Perhaps, Aunt Cecily, but these creatures left the sort of wounds that demons leave," said Lucie. "And their blood was ichor."

Gabriel put a hand on Lucie's shoulder. "Half the Enclave has been dispatched to the park to help those who are still there and determine what occurred. It is most likely a freak occurrence, Luce. Horrible, but unlikely to ever happen again."

"And Jem—Brother Zachariah will be here with the other Silent Brothers," said Cecily, glancing up at the Institute. "They will heal Barbara and the others. I know they will."

Brother Zachariah. Jem.

Of course he would be here, Cordelia realized. Jem Carstairs was a dedicated Silent Brother, and loyal to the London Institute. *I could talk to him,* she thought. *About my father.*

Jem was here to heal, she knew. But her father needed help as much as anyone, and there were other Silent Brothers in the Institute.

Looking from Gabriel to Cecily, she said, "Would you mind if I accompanied you to the infirmary? If there are bandages there, I could wrap my hands—"

Lucie looked remorseful. "Daisy! Your hands! I should have given you a dozen *iratzes*, a hundred *iratzes*. It is only that you were so brave about your injuries—"

Oh, dear. Cordelia hadn't meant to make Lucie feel guilty. "Truly, it only hurts a little—"

Cecily smiled at her. "Spoken like a true Carstairs. Jem would never admit when he was in pain either." She kissed the top of Alexander's head as he fussed to be put down. "Come, Lucie, let us get your future *parabatai* to the infirmary."

James had never seen the infirmary like this before. Of course he'd heard stories from his mother and father about the aftermath of the Clockwork War, the dead and the wounded, but during his lifetime there had rarely ever been more than one or two patients in the sickroom. Thomas had once ended up there for a week when he'd fallen out of a tree and broken his leg. They'd stayed up nights playing cards and eating Bridget's jam tarts. James had been disappointed when the healing runes finally worked and Thomas went home.

The scene was very different now. The room was already crowded: there were many Shadowhunters who had been burned by ichor or who had cuts and bruises. An impromptu nursing station had been set up at the counter, where Tessa and Will—with help from the Silent Brothers—were dealing out bandages and healing runes to whoever needed them.

The three more seriously injured Shadowhunters had been placed in beds at the end of the room, where a screen partially shielded them from the chaos in the rest of the infirmary. James could not help looking, though, especially at Thomas—the rest of the Lightwoods had not arrived yet, and Thomas sat silently by Barbara's side. James had tried to sit with him, but Thomas had said he would rather be alone with Barbara. He was holding his sister's hand as Uncle Jem tended to her: she lay still, her only movement her breathing.

Brother Shadrach, Brother Enoch, and Jem had arrived only moments after James had brought the news of the attack to the Institute. Shadrach leaned over Piers, treating him with a tincture meant to replace some of his lost blood. Brother Enoch crouched by Ariadne, his aspect grim. Inquisitor Bridgestock and his wife were huddled not far from their daughter, exchanging fearful looks. They had been a childless couple before they had adopted orphaned Ariadne from the Bombay Institute, and they had always treated her like a precious treasure. Charles slumped in a chair nearby: like Barbara, Ariadne was motionless save for her shallow breathing. One could see the tracery of her veins beneath the skin of her wrists and temples.

James was still filthy with grass, dirt, and sweat; nevertheless, he stayed behind the counter, cutting and rolling bandages.

If Thomas would not have him, he would help in any other way he could. He could hear snippets of conversation floating above the hushed stir of voices:

"*It was demons, Townsend. Or at least, it was either demons or some creature we've never seen before—*"

"*These are the marks of demon attacks, of claws and teeth. There is no wound that a Downworlder can inflict that is immune to healing runes, but these are. We must find what poison is in their bodies and work to cure that—*"

"*But daylight—*"

"*Who is still at the park? Does anyone have a list of names of those who attended the picnic? We must be certain not a one was left behind—*"

James thought of Grace. He wished he'd been able to speak to her after the attack, but Balios, though nearly twenty-eight, was the fastest horse in the park by far, and only James could ride him—James or Lucie, and Lucie had wanted to remain with Cordelia.

In the end, it had been Christopher, looking more frightened than he had during the demon battle, who had offered to take Grace back to Chiswick in his carriage—Charles, of course, having already rushed to the Institute with Ariadne. James could not help but dread Tatiana's reaction to the attack. It seemed entirely within her usual behavior to decide London was too dangerous and drag Grace back to Idris.

James. The voice was silent, an echo in his head. He knew who it was instantly, of course. Only Silent Brothers spoke this way, and he would never mistake Jem for anyone else.

James, might I have a word with you?

James glanced up to see Jem, tall and dark in his parchment-colored robes, leaving the infirmary. Setting the bandages down, he slipped out the door and into the corridor outside. He followed his uncle to the music room, neither of them speaking as they went.

The corridors of the Institute had been redesigned by Tessa some years ago, the dark Victorian wallpaper gone in favor of light paint and true stone. Elegant carved sconces emerged from the walls at spaced intervals. Each was in the shape of the symbol of a Shadowhunter family: Carstairs, Ke, Herondale, Wrayburn, Starkweather, Lightwood, Blackthorn, Monteverde, Rosales, Bellefleur. It was James's mother's way of saying that they were all Shadowhunters together, all with an equal place in the Institute.

Not that the Clave had always treated his mother as if *she* were equal, James thought. He pushed the thought away; the whispers about his mother, himself, and Lucie always made his blood boil.

The music room was rarely used—Lucie was not musical at all, and James had played the piano for a few years and then abandoned it. Golden sunlight poured through the windows, illuminating dancing trails of dust motes. A grand piano loomed in the corner, half-covered by a white drop cloth.

Jem's violin had pride of place—a Stradivarius carved of mellow wood, it rested in an open case atop a high table. James had seen his father come into this room just to touch the violin sometimes, a faraway look in his eyes. He wondered if he would do the same with Matthew's belongings if one day, he lost his *parabatai*.

He pushed the thought away. Matthew was like food, sleep, breathing; doing without him would not be possible.

I got your message, Jem said. *The one you sent last night.*

James started. "I had nearly forgotten." He could see himself in a gold-framed mirror on the wall: there was grass in his hair, and a bloody scratch on his cheek. He looked like an escapee from Bedlam. "I'm not sure it matters now."

It might, Jem said. He seemed tense, if one could ever describe a Silent Brother as tense. *Barbara was still conscious when I arrived here. She whispered to me of you—*

"Of me?" James was startled.

She said, *"James must be protected."* Did you turn into a shadow at the lake?

"No," James said. "I saw the shadow realm last night—and again today—but I did not become a shadow myself. I was able to control it."

Jem relaxed minutely. *James,* he said. *You know that I have been trying to discover which Greater Demon your grandfather was. Your ability—*

"It's not an ability," James said. "It's a curse."

It is not a curse. Jem's tone was sharp. *It is not a curse any more than the magic warlocks do is a curse, or the ability your mother has is a curse.*

"You have always said it is dangerous," said James.

Some gifts are dangerous. And it is a gift, though it may come from the bloodline of fallen angels.

"A gift I cannot use for anything," James said. "Last night at the party, when I slipped into darkness—I saw Barbara pulled to the ground by a shadow. Then today at the lake she was dragged to earth by a demon with its teeth in her leg." He set his jaw. "I don't know what it means. Nor did the visions help me, or allow me to help Barbara or the others." He hesitated. "Perhaps if we went back to the lessons—we could learn more about the shadow realm, whether it is perhaps trying to give me some sort of sign—"

It would be wise for us to continue the lessons, yes, Jem said. *But we cannot begin now. The poison consuming those who were attacked is like nothing I have ever seen, nor do the other Brothers know it. We must bend all our will now to finding the cure.*

The door opened, and Will stuck his head into the music room. He looked weary, his shirtsleeves rolled to the elbow, his shirt stained with tinctures and salve. Still, he smiled when he saw James and Jem. "Is everything all right?"

"Uncle Jem was worried about me," said James. "But I am quite well."

Will came up to his son and pulled him into a quick, rough

hug. He said, "I am glad to hear it, Jamie *bach*. Gideon and Sophie have arrived, and to see them with Barbara—" He kissed the top of James's head. "It does not bear thinking of."

I should return to the infirmary, said Jem. *There is much still for me to do.*

Will nodded, releasing James. "I know Gideon and Sophie would feel better if you were the one tending Barbara. Not to insult Brother Shadrach, who I'm sure is an excellent and well-respected member of the Brotherhood."

Jem shook his head, which was as close as he got to smiling, and the three of them left the music room. To James's surprise, Thomas was waiting in the corridor outside, looking hollow-eyed.

Will exchanged a quick glance with James and left his son alone with Thomas. It was good, James thought, to have a father who understood the significance of friendship.

Thomas spoke as soon as the adults were out of earshot. "My parents are here," he said, in a low voice. "James, I need something to do. Something that might help my sister. I think I might go mad otherwise."

"Of course—we all must help Barbara," said James. "Thomas, in the park, Barbara saw the demons before everyone else. She was the one who warned me."

"She had perfect Sight even before she got her Voyance rune," Thomas said. "Perhaps because my mother was a Sighted mundane before she became a Shadowhunter. We've never been sure— Barbara wasn't terribly interested in testing her abilities—but she always had unusually keen senses."

"It is almost as if she could glimpse my shadow realm," James murmured, remembering what Barbara had said: that she had been able to see ragged black shapes at the ball, that she had felt herself drawn down. An idea had begun to take shape in his mind. He wondered if he should go back and speak of it to Jem, but no—Jem would never let him do it. He would think it was too dangerous. Reckless, even.

But James was feeling reckless, and from the look of it, Thomas was too. "We need to round up Matthew and Christopher," James said. "I have an idea of what we can do."

Some of the color came back to Thomas's face. "Christopher has just returned from Chiswick," he said. "I saw him in the entry hall. But as for Matthew . . ."

Cordelia had determined to make herself useful in the infirmary. It was the only way she could be sure she wouldn't be tossed out on her ear. After all, none of the wounded were her relatives or even her friends. And she wasn't likely to be making many new friends at this rate.

Lucie had been recruited for duty as well. Dozens of labeled jars and pots had been taken down from the cupboards behind the marble-topped counter where Tessa was presiding over the dispensing of ingredients for tinctures and potions. Cordelia's own hands had been slathered in salve and wrapped in bandages; they looked like white paws as she handled the mortar and pestle she'd been given.

The front of the infirmary was taken up with those who had scratches, sprains, and burns. The tinctures and salves were mostly for them: Lucie was busy handing them out, her cheerful flow of chatter audible above the low hum of other conversation. A screen had been pulled in front of the far end of the room, and Cordelia was almost glad for it: it was too awful to see Sophie and Gideon Lightwood break down by Barbara's bedside, or even Rosamund sitting silently by her brother. Cordelia was sorry she had ever harbored uncharitable thoughts toward the Wentworths. No one deserved this.

"It's all right." Tessa's voice was gentle. James's mother was busy finely chopping mugwort into a bowl; she cast a sympathetic glance at Cordelia. "I have seen the Silent Brothers bring people back from much worse."

Cordelia shook her head. "I have not. I suppose I have been very sheltered."

"We all have been, for a time," said Tessa. "The natural state of Shadowhunters is battle. When it is always ongoing, there is no time to stop and think that it is not an ideal condition for happiness. Shadowhunters are not suited to a halcyon state, yet we have had that time for the past decade or so. Perhaps we had begun to think ourselves invincible."

"People are only invincible in books," said Cordelia.

"I think you will find most of the time, not even then," said Tessa. "But at least we can always pick up a book and read it anew. Stories offer a thousand fresh starts."

It was true, Cordelia thought. She had read the story of Layla and Majnun a thousand times, and each time the beginning was a thrill, even though she knew—and dreaded—the end.

"The only equivalent in real life is memory," Tessa said, looking up as Will Herondale came into the room, followed by Cousin Jem. "But memories can be bitter as well as sweet."

Will smiled at his wife—James's parents always looked at each other with such love, it was nearly painful to see—before heading toward the small group of Lightwoods gathered around Barbara. Cordelia heard them greet him, and Sophie's worried tones, but her gaze was on Jem. He had come toward the counter and was reaching for several jars of mixed herbs. It was now or never.

"Cousin Jem," Cordelia whispered. "I need to speak with you."

Jem glanced up in surprise. Cordelia tried not to start; it was always strange to see a Silent Brother this close. She remembered all the times her mother had suggested her father go to the Basilias, the Shadowhunter hospital in Alicante, to cure his lingering illness. Elias had always insisted he did not wish to go anywhere

where he would be surrounded by Silent Brothers. They rattled his nerves, he claimed; most of them were like creatures of ice and blood. Ivory robes marked in red, skin drained of color, scarred with red runes. Most were without hair and worse, had their eyes sewn shut, their sockets sunken and hollow.

Jem did not look like that. His face was young and very still, like the face of a knight from the Crusades carved on a marble tomb. His hair was a tangle of black and white threads. His eyes were permanently shut, as if in prayer.

Are you all right, Cordelia? asked Jem's voice in her mind.

Tessa immediately moved to shield the two of them from the gaze of the rest of the sickroom. Cordelia tried to appear as if she were absolutely fascinated with her mortar and pestle, energetically mashing together feverfew and goldenseal.

"Please," she whispered. "Have you seen Baba—my father—in Idris? How is he? When can he come home?"

There was a long pause.

I have seen him, said Cousin Jem.

For a moment, Cordelia let herself remember her father, truly remember him. Her father had taught her to fight. Her father had his faults, but he was never cruel, and when he did pay Cordelia some mind, his attention made her feel ten feet tall. It often felt as though Alastair and Sona were made of different stuff than Cordelia, glass or metal with edges that could cut, but Elias was the one who was like her.

Memories can be bitter as well as sweet.

She murmured, "You are a Silent Brother. I know my father was not always welcoming to you—"

Never think I am resentful of the distance he kept, said Jem. *I would do anything I could for you and our family.*

"He wrote me a note, asking me to believe in him. He says he is not responsible for what happened. Can't you make the Clave believe him too?"

There was a long pause. *I cannot assure the Clave of what I do not know myself*, said Jem.

"They must ask him what happened," said Cordelia. "They *must* try the Mortal Sword. Will they?"

Jem hesitated. Cordelia saw that Lucie was approaching them, just as she realized she had mashed the herbs in the mortar into green sludge.

"Daisy," Lucie said in a low voice. This struck Cordelia as alarming. Lucie could rarely be convinced to whisper about anything. "Could you come with me a moment? I very much need your assistance."

"Of course," Cordelia said, a bit hesitantly. "It is only that—"

She turned toward Jem, hoping to get his answer to her question. But he had already vanished into the crowded sickroom.

"Where are we going?" Cordelia whispered, as they hurried along the corridors of the Institute. "Lucie. You cannot simply abduct me, you know."

"Nonsense," said Lucie. "If I wished to abduct you, you can be sure that I would do it quite expertly, no doubt beneath the veil of silence and darkness." They had reached the vestibule; Lucie took down a cloak from a peg on the wall and handed another to Cordelia. "Besides, I told my father I was taking you home in the carriage because you faint at the sight of blood."

"*Lucie!*" Cordelia followed her friend out into the courtyard. The sun had only just set, and the evening was brushed with a steel-blue patina. The yard was crowded with carriages, each bearing the crest of a Shadowhunter family.

"Not every bit of a good story is true," said Lucie. Her cheeks were bright pink. The air had become chill; Cordelia pulled her cloak around her. "It's the story that's important."

"I don't want to go home, though," Cordelia pointed out, as she and Lucie wove their way through the crowd of carriages. She squinted. "Is someone *singing* inside the Baybrook carriage?"

Lucie waved a dismissive hand. "Of course you're not going home. You're coming with me on an adventure." She waved at something half-hidden behind the Wentworth carriage. "Bridget!"

It was indeed Bridget, her graying red hair wound into a chignon, having clearly just finished readying the Institute's brougham and a fresh horse—Balios's brother Xanthos. The two were a matched pair. Cordelia had heard a great deal about them growing up. Lucie went instantly to pat Xanthos's soft, white-speckled nose; Cordelia tried to smile at Bridget, who was eyeing them both suspiciously.

"Carriage all ready for you, Miss Baggage," Bridget said to Lucie. "Try to not get in trouble. It fusses your parents."

"I'm just taking Cordelia home," Lucie said, blinking innocently. Bridget wandered off, muttering about finding certain people stuck in certain trees while sneaking out of certain windows. Lucie bent to whisper something in Xanthos's ear before gesturing for Cordelia to join her in the carriage. "It's all glamoured," she explained, as the brougham rattled under the open gate and into the streets of London. "It would just upset the mundanes to see a carriage racing about with no driver."

"So the horse knows where to take us?" Cordelia settled back against the upholstered bench seat. "But it's *not* to Cornwall Gardens?"

Lucie shook her head. "Balios and Xanthos are special horses. And we're going to Chiswick House."

Cordelia stared. "Chiswick House? We're going to see Grace and Tatiana? Oh, Lucie, I don't know—"

Lucie held up a hand. "There could be a time—a short time—during which you may have to distract them. But it is not a social call. I am on a mission."

Cordelia did not think Grace seemed the sort of person who could be easily distracted. "I shan't," she said firmly. "Not unless you tell me what this mission is."

Lucie was silent a moment, her face small and pale in the shadows of the carriage. "You know I can see ghosts," she said, and hesitated.

Cordelia blinked. It was the last thing she'd expected Lucie to say. Ghosts were something all Shadowhunters knew existed, and when ghosts wanted to be seen, most Nephilim could see them. But the Herondales had a special ability: Will, James, and Lucie could all see ghosts that *didn't* want to be seen. "Yes, but what—?"

"A ghost told me—" Lucie broke off for a moment. "Jessamine told me there is a ghost at Chiswick House that might know about these daylight demons," she said at last. "Daisy, I have to do something for Barbara and the others. I cannot just sit about passing out tinctures. If there is anything I can do to help, I must do it."

"Of course—but why not tell your father or your mother? They would surely understand."

"I do not wish to raise hopes that may come to nothing," said Lucie. "Besides, they might feel they needed to tell some of the others, and I—I have been told that being sought out by ghosts is not an appealing trait in a young woman."

Cordelia caught at Lucie's hand with her own bandaged one. "Tell me who said that to you. I will kill them."

Lucie sniffled and then laughed. "You needn't kill anyone. Just come with me to Chiswick, and I will be perfectly satisfied."

"We must bar the doors," said James. "They don't lock, and we can't be interrupted." He frowned. "Matthew, can you stand?"

The ballroom had been closed up after the ball; it was rarely used except for social functions. The room was warm and close as James, Christopher, and Thomas threw off their jackets and stripped down to shirtsleeves. Most were still wearing the same weapons belts they'd had on in the park: James had added several new daggers to his own.

Only Matthew was unarmed. Blinking and disheveled, he found his way to a plushly upholstered chair and fell into it. "I am quite all right," he said, waving an airy hand. "Please continue with your plan." He squinted. "What *was* your plan?"

"I'll tell you in a moment," James said. He was quite sure none of them were going to like it. "Thomas?"

Thomas nodded, seized hold of a heavy sideboard, and began to shove it in front of the ballroom doors. Christopher looked worriedly at Matthew. "Perhaps some water?" he said.

"I'm *quite* all right," Matthew repeated.

"I found you drinking from a flask and singing 'Elsie from Chelsea' in the Baybrooks' carriage," said Thomas darkly.

"It was private there," said Matthew. "And well-upholstered."

"At least it wasn't the Bridgestocks' carriage, because they have already experienced enough tragedy today. Nothing bad has happened to the Baybrooks," said Christopher, with great sincerity.

"Nothing until now," said James. "Christopher—was everything all right, dropping off Miss Blackthorn?"

He tried not to sound as if he were too invested in the answer. Matthew raised an eyebrow but said nothing.

"Oh, perfectly," said Christopher. "I told her all about culturing bacteria, and she was so fascinated that she never spoke a word!"

James had gone to pile chairs in front of the doors to the withdrawing room. He hoped Grace had not expired from boredom. "Did you have to tell Mrs. Blackthorn what had happened at the park? She can't have been pleased."

Christopher shook his head. "I confess I didn't see her. Miss Blackthorn asked that I drop her at the gates, not the front door."

"She probably doesn't want anyone to see the state of the place," said Matthew, yawning. "The gates alone are festooned in rust."

James eyed him. "Thomas," he said, in a low voice. "Maybe a healing rune?"

Thomas nodded and approached Matthew cautiously, as one might approach a stray cat on the street. Some time ago James had discovered that healing runes sobered Matthew up: not entirely, but enough.

"Push up your sleeve, then, there's a good fellow," Thomas said, seating himself on the arm of Matthew's chair. "Let's wake you up and James can tell us whatever mad thing he has planned."

Done with the chairs, James cast a glance around the room, dusted off his hands, and said, "We'd better check the locks on all the windows. Just to be sure."

"It seems somehow blasphemous to use Marks to rid oneself of the effects of alcohol," Matthew added, as Thomas put his stele away. The Mark in question gleamed, new-made, on Matthew's wrist. He looked already more clear-eyed, and less as if he were about to fall asleep or be sick.

"I've seen you use your stele to part your hair," said James dryly, as he began to examine the window locks.

"The Angel gave me this hair," replied Matthew. "It's one of the Shadowhunters' gifts. Like the Mortal Sword."

"Now *that* is blasphemy," said Thomas. Christopher had joined James in checking the window fastenings, though James desperately wished he could open one and get some air into the room.

"A thing of beauty is a joy forever, Thomas," said Matthew. "James, why are we locking all the windows? Are we afraid of over-curious pigeons?"

James slammed a bolt home and turned to look at the others. "I have spent the past four years of my life trying to train myself not to do what I'm about to do. I don't wish to even consider the possibility of being interrupted."

"By a pigeon?" said Matthew, but the look in his eyes was sympathetic, despite his lightly mocking words. "Jamie, what are we doing here?"

James took a deep breath. "I am going to deliberately send myself into the shadow realm," he said.

The Merry Thieves exploded in a chorus of protest. Matthew stood up, his eyes glittering. "Certainly not," he said. "The danger—"

"I do not think there will be danger," said James. "I have been in and out of the shadow realm many times in my life. It has been ages since I fell accidentally into that world. Yet in the past week, I have seen it three times, once just before the attack today. I cannot think that is a coincidence. If I can use this ability to help Barbara, Ariadne, all of us—you must let me do it."

"Bloody hell." Matthew rubbed at his eyes. "If we don't help you here, you'll just try to do this after we're all gone, won't you?"

"Clearly," said James. He tapped the daggers at his waist. "I'm armed, at least."

Matthew twisted the signet ring on his finger, marked with MF. It had been a gift from James when they had become *parabatai*, and he tended to fiddle with it only when distressed. "Very well, James. As you wish."

James cleared his throat. "All right. Let's get on with it."

He was met with the gaze of six expectant eyes.

"Well?" Thomas said hopefully, after a long pause. "Go on into the shadow realm, then."

James concentrated. He stared at the blank floor and tried to conjure up images in his mind of the shadow realm. The scorched gray sky and dimmed sun. He imagined the ballroom wrong, the windows set oddly into the walls, the chandeliers melting and sagging.

He opened his eyes and yelled. A pair of eyes was staring directly into his, so close that he could make out the details inside the green irises, the faint splotches of brown and black. *"Matthew!"*

"I really don't think staring at him is going to help, Matthew," said Thomas, and Matthew took a reluctant step back from his *parabatai*. "Jamie, is there anything that might help you begin the process? We've all seen you do it. . . . You start to get shadowy, and turn a bit blurry around the edges."

"When I go into the shadow realm, the realness of my presence here begins to fade," James said. He did not mention that in the past, he had "faded" enough in this world to pass through a solid wall. He did not intend to do it again. "But it is not what drives me into the shadow realm. More of a side effect of being there."

"Often it happens when you are upset or shocked," said Christopher. "I suppose we could try upsetting or shocking you."

"Given everything that's happened, that shouldn't be too hard," said James.

"Nonsense," said Matthew, hopping up on a nearby occasional table. It was quite frail-looking, with thin gold-painted wooden legs, and James eyed it worriedly. "The last time I saw you shocked was when that Iblis demon was sending Christopher love letters."

"I have a dark charm," said Christopher sadly.

"Please recall that I am the pale neurasthenic one and you are the stern heroic one," Matthew said to James. "It is very tedious when you mix up our roles. We will have to think of something quite impressive to startle you."

"So what is my role?" said Christopher.

"Mad inventor, of course," said Matthew promptly. "And Thomas is the one with a good heart."

"Lord, I sound dull," said Thomas. "Look, James, come here for a second."

James moved toward Thomas, who seemed to have decided on something: in moments like this, he looked very like his mother, with her brilliant hazel eyes and ferocious mouth.

A fist came sailing out of the air and landed squarely in James's solar plexus. He went flying backward, hitting the floor with a gasp. His head swam.

Matthew dropped down by his side, as James heaved himself up onto his elbows, gasping. The pain wasn't bad but the feeling of trying to catch his breath was sickening.

"Thomas!" Matthew yelled. "What were you trying to—?"

"I was trying to surprise him!" Thomas yelled back. "This is important, Matthew!" He darted a worried look at James, belying his angry words. "You don't mind, do you, Jamie?"

"It's all right," James said breathlessly. "Only it didn't work. If I turned into a shadow every time something hit me, I couldn't patrol." He stared up at the ceiling, which had mirrors on it. He could see himself lying splayed on the parquet, hair very black against the white, Matthew kneeling over him like a squire over the body of a dead knight.

He could see Christopher and Thomas in the mirror as well, or at least the tops of their heads. Christopher was reaching up to pull something down from the wall. Thomas had his arms crossed.

Matthew jumped to his feet with the agility of a fox and held out a hand to help James up after him. James had only just regained his footing when an arrow shot past his head. One of the windows shattered, and Matthew threw himself against James. They tumbled to the floor again, knocking the breath out of James for the second time in five minutes.

He rolled into a sitting position, shouldering Matthew aside, to find Thomas goggling at Christopher, who was clutching one of the bows that had been hanging on the wall.

"In case anyone was wondering if those were *purely* ornamental," said James, getting to his feet, "they are not."

"In the name of a million bloody angels, Christopher, what the hell did you just do?" Matthew demanded, leaping up after James. "Did you try to kill James?"

Christopher lowered the bow. James thought he could hear noises in the Institute: doors slamming in the distance and running feet. *Bloody hell.*

"I was not trying to kill James," said Christopher in an injured tone. "I was hoping the shock of the arrow flying past would startle him into the shadow realm. Pity it didn't work. We must think of a new plan to grievously alarm James at once."

"Christopher!" James exclaimed. "I cannot believe you would say that! I also cannot believe you would shoot at me."

"It had a seventy-two percent chance of working, in perfect laboratory conditions—"

"We are not in perfect laboratory conditions!" James shouted. "We are in the ballroom of my house!"

At that moment, the doors of the ballroom rattled. "What's going on?" It was Will's voice. "James, are you in there?"

"Bloody hell. My father," James said, casting about. "Look, all of you—get out through the windows. Well, the broken one anyway. I'll take the blame. I'll say *I* shot the window out."

"In the ballroom?" Thomas said practically. "Why would you do such a rattle-headed thing?"

"I'm capable of anything!" James made a grab for Christopher's bow; Christopher ran around behind Thomas as if his friend were a maypole. "Come on, Kit, give it over—"

Thomas rolled his eyes. "He's going to say, 'Because I'm a Herondale,' isn't he?"

The pounding on the door increased. James turned his fiercest glare on the others. "I *am* a Herondale," he said. "And I am telling you to get out of my Institute so the only one who gets punished here is me."

"Answer me, James!" Will shouted. "Why have you blocked this door? I demand to know what's going on!"

"James isn't here!" Matthew called, moving closer to him. "Go away!"

James looked at Matthew, puzzled. "Really?"

"I heard breaking glass!" Will called.

"I was practicing fighting moves!" Matthew answered.

"In the ballroom?"

"We're trying to distract Thomas! It's been a very emotional day!" Matthew shouted back.

"*What?*" Will's voice was incredulous.

"Don't you blame this on me!" Thomas whispered.

"James." Matthew put his hands on James's shoulders and turned James toward him. Now that the window of the ballroom was shattered, cooler air came in, lifting Matthew's sweat-dampened hair off his forehead. His eyes were intent, black in the dimness, fixed on James. James found himself startling at the seriousness of Matthew's gaze. "If you're going to do this, you need to do it now."

"I know," James said. "Math—help me."

It was an old nickname for Matthew, given to him by Will, after the Welsh king Math ap Mathonwy—the keeper of all wisdom and knower of all things. Will always said Matthew had been born knowing too much. There was a dark awareness in his gaze now as he leaned in toward James's ear.

"Jamie," he whispered. "I'm sorry to have to do this." He swallowed. "You are cursed. A child of demons. It is why you can see the shadow realm. You are seeing the place you belong."

James jerked back, staring at Matthew. Matthew, who smelled of brandy and familiarity. Matthew, who could be cruel but never to James.

James's vision began to slide into grayness.

Matthew went white. "James," he said. "I didn't mean it—"

But James could no longer feel Matthew's hands on his shoulders. He could no longer feel the ballroom floor under his feet. The doors of the ballroom were beginning to crack open, but he could no longer hear them.

The world had gone monochrome. James saw broken black walls, a splintered floor, and dust that glittered like dull jewels scattered across the place where Barbara had fallen. He bent to reach for it as the universe jerked beneath his feet and he was thrust forward into nothingness.

Days Past:
Idris, 1900

James was just over the scalding fever, reunited with his family in the bright meadows and cool forests of Idris. And yet he felt uneasy as he opened the windows in his bedroom at Herondale Manor, bringing fresh air to the room for the first time in months. Perhaps it was how quickly one traveled, through Portals. He had only just been waving goodbye to Cordelia and her parents, and feeling about Cordelia in a manner that he could not possibly put into words, it was so excellent and strange and perplexing. He could have used several days at sea, or aboard a train, to gaze out at the landscape and feel complicated things. Instead, ten minutes after being at Cirenworth, he was pulling protective sheets off furniture and lighting witchlights, and his father was loudly proclaiming the healing quality of the Idris air.

James was unpacking his things when his mother came into the bedroom, sorting through correspondence. She held out a small envelope. "One for you," she said, and left him in privacy with the letter.

James didn't recognize the handwriting. It was in a refined

feminine hand. He briefly thought, *But I don't know anybody in Idris to send me a letter,* and then realized: *Grace.*

He sat on the bed to read it. All it said was, *Meet me at our Place. Tomorrow, dusk. Yrs, GB.*

He felt a bit guilty; he had not thought of Grace in a time. He wondered if she had done anything this past year and, with a start, realized it was plausible that she had gone nowhere and talked to nobody. Tatiana Blackthorn was notorious for avoiding all Shadowhunter society, and especially with the Herondales not in residence, she had very few neighbors, and those some distance away.

By the Angel, he thought. *Am I Grace's only friend?*

"I have no one else, no," Grace said.

They sat together on the forest floor, James leaning against a high looping oak root and Grace upon a stone. Grace's look of sorrow turned quickly back to her usual calm composure.

"I have no news to report since our last meeting, I fear," she said. "But you look as though you have battled against something. More than tired."

"Oh!" said James. "Well, that is one thing that has happened to me since I last saw you. I'm just getting over scalding fever, I'm afraid."

Grace mock-flinched away, then laughed. "No, I've had it, don't worry. My poor James! I do hope you weren't lonely."

"I was lucky there," said James. He felt a slight twinge in the pit of his stomach, for no reason he understood. "Cordelia and her mother had both had it, so they could stay. They took good care of me. Cordelia especially. It really made the situation much more tolerable. Much less bad. Than it could have been. If she had not been there."

Even James understood that he was rambling a bit. Grace only nodded.

* * *

The next day James woke late, to find his parents already out and his sister perched on one of the overstuffed armchairs in the parlor, scribbling furiously into a notebook.

"Do you want to do something?" he asked Lucie.

Without looking up, she said, "I *am* doing something. I'm writing."

"What are you writing about?"

"Well, if you don't leave me alone, I'll write about *you*."

So, with nothing else to do, he walked to Blackthorn Manor.

The manor looked, to his eyes, identical to how it had appeared the first time he'd gone there a year ago, to cut the briars from the gates. The house itself was closed and silent, like a giant bat curled into itself to sleep through the day, until the darkness gave it leave to unfurl its wings again. If anything, the briars were longer than they had been when he first began his work last year, the thorns more numerous, longer and sharper. The first half of the motto above the gates was obscured, and all that could be read now was LEX NULLA.

He walked the perimeter, around the stone wall, through the uncut underbrush. He felt silly. He hadn't brought a book or a sword or anything to do. When he came again to the front gates, though, Grace was waiting behind them.

"I could see you through my bedroom window," Grace said, without preamble. "You looked lost."

"Good morning," James said, and Grace smiled at his manners. "Do you think your mother would want me to trim the briars up again?"

An awkward silence fell. Then Grace said, "I cannot imagine that my mother would *mind* if the vines were to be cleaned up. If I fetched you shears, and you cut them back from the gates, I would keep you company."

"That seems a fine bargain," said James with a grin.

"I cannot promise to make enough idle conversation to fill the time, of course," Grace added. "I could read to you, if you like."

"No! No, thank you," he said quickly. Grace looked surprised, so James added, "I would rather hear about your life."

"My life is this house," she said.

"Then," he said, "tell me about the house."

So she did. James never told his parents where he was going. He would simply leave the house in the afternoon, trim the vines and overgrowth outside the walls of the manor, and talk with Grace for two hours or so, before growing tired and thirsty, begging Grace's pardon, and sauntering home.

Grace told him of the manor's grandeur and the layers of dust and neglect that had overtaken it: "Sometimes I feel I live in a giant cobweb, but my mother doesn't trust anyone to come and clean, and the place is too big for any two people to keep up." She told him of the twisting thorns carved into the oak banister, the coat of arms above the mantel, the frightening metal statue lurking on the second floor. Her descriptions sounded dreadful to James, like the house was a carcass, once a beautiful living thing, rotting away.

The thought made him shiver, but when he returned home, the feeling faded; at night he still fell asleep to his memory of Cordelia's voice, low and steady in his ear.

Lucie announced she planned to read to James from her work in progress, *Secret Princess Lucie Is Rescued from Her Terrible Family*. James listened with a carefully arranged look of interest, even though he was subjected to endless tales of Cruel Prince James and his many awful deeds.

"I think that Cruel Prince James has been somewhat boxed in by his name," James offered at one point. Lucie informed him that she wasn't looking for critique at this stage in the creative process.

"Secret Princess Lucie only wishes to be kind, but Cruel Prince James is driven to cruelty because he simply cannot stand to see Princess Lucie best him again and again, in every domain," said Lucie.

"I'm going to go now," said James.

Lucie closed the notebook and looked at James. "What's she like, Grace Blackthorn? You see her sometimes when you're over there cutting the briars, don't you?"

"I suppose." James was caught off guard. "She's . . . sad. She's terribly lonely, I think. All she knows is her mother and their creepy house."

"How awful for her."

"Yes, it is awful. She is truly to be pitied."

"Indeed," said Lucie.

At their spot in the forest, James told Grace about the friends he'd made: Matthew (who Grace knew was the Consul's son), and Thomas and Christopher, who he referred to as "your cousins," to no reaction from Grace. She only said, shyly, "I must say that I am a little glad that they are not here with you in Idris. Oh, I am sure you would be having a grander time if they were! But then we would not have all this time together, and I would miss it."

James worried about Grace. It would not do for him to be her only friend; there was only so often he could see her. He thought of Cordelia's visit later in the summer and whether there would be any possibility that they could meet, given that his friendship with Grace must remain a secret.

Now Grace appeared to hesitate. "Would I offend you if I asked what happened to you at Shadowhunter Academy? I have heard only rumors."

James told her about his strange power of passing into shadow, it having been revealed before a good portion of the Academy, and his expulsion. "It is a hardly a secret," he said, wondering why it felt like a great confession. "It is because of my mother being a sort of warlock. Everyone knows it, yet still they mutter and point."

"It often seems to me," she said, "that warlocks are great partners to us in fighting demons, and they are themselves partly demonic. I do not see why others must fuss so."

"Shadowhunters don't like difference," James said. "They always see evil in it. But here, I have told you a secret and now you must tell me one."

Grace smiled. "I have no secrets."

"Not true. Where do you come from, Grace Blackthorn? Do you remember your parents?"

"Yes," she said. "I was eight when they—they were killed by demons. I would have been left by myself had it not been for Mama."

That did explain why Grace had only a single rune, on her left hand. The Voyance rune was the first Mark Shadowhunters received when they were children. Tatiana had clearly not welcomed the idea of Grace continuing her Shadowhunter education further.

"You would have been taken in by an Institute," said James. "Shadowhunters don't abandon their own."

"I suppose," said Grace, "but I wouldn't have had a family. And now I do. A mother, and a family name, and a home." She did not look entirely happy about it. "I do wish I had been able to keep something of my parents', though."

James was startled. "Do you truly possess nothing of theirs?"

"There is one thing," she said. "My mother had a silver bracelet she wore. Mama says it is very valuable, and she keeps it in a box in her study. She says she will let me wear it when I am older, but every year I ask, and every year I am not yet old enough."

"Can you not retrieve it from its box?"

"The box is locked up tight," she said. "My mother is fond of locks. All over the house I find drawers, cupboards, boxes that won't budge without the right keys.... I cannot imagine that Mama remembers what key goes to what lock. There are so many of each." Her expression changed in a subtle way. "But enough of this sorrowful subject! I have heard from my mother that the Carstairs family will be visiting you later this summer. No doubt you will spend all your time with them, once they get here."

"No," James said, "I expect Cordelia will want to spend all her time with Lucie—they're to be *parabatai* someday. Of course, Lucie is also writing her book, so there may well be times when I really *should* spend time with Cordelia, as a good host. I mean, whatever she likes. Obviously, if she wanted to spend every day with me, that would be all right—"

He stopped, realizing that he had become entirely crazed sometime in the past ten seconds. Grace was being very polite about it. "I'm so sorry," he said. "I did not mean to suggest—"

Grace laughed lightly. "Nonsense! I know you mean well, James. You're just in love with Cordelia."

James was horrified. "I am fond of her, that is all. We are friends, as you and I are."

"Oh?" Grace said. "And if she arrives here in Idris and tells you she has met the most *wonderful* man and they have had a whirlwind romance and now they are promised to each other? You would only congratulate her like you would any of your friends?"

"I would tell her she was too young to get married," James said stiffly. The truth was that when he thought of Cordelia marrying someone else, it felt like being kicked in the heart. With a start, he realized that in his vague imaginings of the future

Cordelia had always been there, a steady, welcome presence, a warm light in the dark of the unknown.

"Cruel Prince James strode into the chamber, his cape flashing behind him and his terrible, terrible mustache askew with rage," Lucie narrated the moment James walked through the door.

"Does it need be said twice that it's terrible?" James said.

"He required a hot beverage to soothe his throat, parched from barking out his wicked commands all day. Tea, he thought, yes, tea and *revenge*."

"I'll just go put the kettle on," James sighed.

"What a strange sort of friendship we have," Grace said. They were back at Blackthorn Manor, James clipping away at the briars along the high stone wall, and Grace on the other side, ambling along with him. He caught glimpses of her every once in a while as they walked, through gaps in the stone. "It's a pity you can't turn into a shadow and come join me, on my side of the wall."

James stopping clipping. "I hadn't thought of that." *Maybe I could.* He put down the shears in the grass and looked at his hands. He did not know what to do. He thought hard of nothingness, of the gray of the shadow realm. With a start, he stumbled forward through the wall.

He recovered himself. He was still a shadow, though he was not in the shadow realm: he stood very clearly inside the garden walls of Blackthorn Manor. There was overgrown grass everywhere—and Grace, staring at him.

Can you come back? she was mouthing, or possibly saying out loud, and James, with a huge effort, did. Back in his physical form, he clenched and unclenched his fists.

"That was amazing," Grace said. "I imagine you'd get used to the feeling, if you practiced."

Maybe. "Do you think I could leave by the gate?"

Grace laughed. At the gate, as he departed, she reached for his arm. "Wait. James. I was thinking. If some night you find yourself unable to sleep, and you find yourself cast into shadow . . . Perhaps you could come here, and walk through the briars and into the house, and into Mama's study, and dip your shadowed hand through the top of the right box, and retrieve my bracelet for me."

James felt a surge of warmth toward Grace. He had feared she might be horrified by his presence as a shadow, but not only did she accept him, she presented an opportunity for his power to be used to help. He felt for some reason that he owed her, though he could not have said why. "I could. I will."

"Leave me a sign, if you do it," Grace said, "and the next night I will meet you in the forest. You would be a true friend to me if you could do this."

"I can," said James. "I will."

6

No More of Mirth

All within is dark as night:
In the windows is no light;
And no murmur at the door,
So frequent on its hinge before.

Close the door; the shutters close;
Or through the windows we shall see
The nakedness and vacancy
Of the dark deserted house.

Come away: no more of mirth
Is here or merry-making sound.
The house was builded of the earth,
And shall fall again to ground.
—Alfred, Lord Tennyson,
"The Deserted House"

"This cannot be where they live," Lucie whispered, half in amazement, half in horror.

Her mother had described Chiswick House to her once. What it had been like years ago, when Tessa had attended a ball there disguised as Jessamine. Her parents couldn't talk about the ball, in fact, without shooting each other fond, syrupy looks. It was quite disgusting.

Uncle Gabriel had described the house, too, in a much more exciting and suitable story about the way that he, Aunt Cecily, Uncle Jem, Lucie's parents, and Uncle Gideon had dispatched the evil Benedict Lightwood, who had turned into a demonic worm and marauded through the Lightwood gardens. It was a story with a great deal of blood and excitement, and it had been very clear—to Lucie at least—that the gardens had been glorious. The manor house itself had been glorious: white stone, spreading green lawns down to the Thames. Gorgeous Greek follies seeming to float above the ground. There had been Italian gardens, and moonlight-washed balconies, and tall, proud pillars, a famous reproduction of the Venus de' Medici from the Uffizi Galleries in Florence, a magnificent avenue of cedars sweeping up to the house. . . .

"My mother said she heard it had fallen into disrepair, but I did not expect this," Cordelia whispered back. Her gaze, like Lucie's, was glued to the outside of the massive gates that closed off the property. Latin words were etched across the top of the ironwork.

ULTIMA FORSAN. *The end is closer than you think.*

They sent a shiver down Lucie's spine. She put her hand to her waist, where her weapons belt rested. Bridget had left seraph blades, belts, and steles in the carriage for them, and they had Marked themselves carefully with various runes—Strength, Stealth, Night Vision. One never could be too careful in a possibly haunted place.

Lucie only wished they had been able to change into gear. They were still wearing their dresses from the picnic, torn and bloodstained.

"There is disrepair and then there's disaster," Lucie said, reaching for her stele. "How can Grace bear to live here?"

"I suppose she finds other things to make her happy," Cordelia said in a subdued voice as Lucie scratched an Open rune on the gates and they swung open, scattering a powder of red rust.

They stepped forward onto the broken stones and overgrowth of what had once been a gorgeous avenue lined with potted cypress and cedar trees. The rot of dying cedar filled the air now and tickled the back of Lucie's throat. The trees overhead had grown into each other, their branches tangling, bending, and snapping. Dead branches littered the ground.

As they came out from the avenue and into the broad circular drive in front of the house, Lucie was struck by the destroyed beauty of the manor. A double set of stairs, wonderfully constructed, led up to a broad entryway: blackened vines twisted their way around fluted columns. If she cast her gaze up she could see the balconies her mother had spoken of—but they had been taken over by clusters of thorns.

"Like Sleeping Beauty's castle," Lucie murmured.

"I was just thinking that!" said Cordelia. "Did you ever read the older fairy tales? I remember them being much more frightening. There was one where Sleeping Beauty's palace was ringed all around with sharp briars, and the bodies of the princes who tried to get through hung on the thorns when they died, and their bones whitened in the sun."

"Delightful!" said Lucie. "I shall be sure to include that in a book."

"Not in *The Beautiful Cordelia*, you won't," said Cordelia, moving up to inspect the house more closely. "Lucie, there isn't a single light on, not a single bit of illumination. Maybe they are not home?"

"Look—there," Lucie said, and pointed. "I saw a light, darting across one of the windows. If you do not want to knock on the door, you need not. I admit, it is quite alarming here."

Cordelia squared her shoulders. "I am not alarmed."

Lucie hid a smile. "Then I am going to seek a ghost while you distract the inhabitants. We will meet back at the gates in a quarter hour."

Cordelia nodded and began to climb the cracked marble steps to the front door. The sound of her knocking faded as Lucie slipped around the house to the back, where the grass sloped down toward the dark water of the river. She found herself looking up at the stone wall of the manor, cracked with age and veined through with a million thick and twisting vines.

Lucie took a running jump and seized the vines. She began to climb quickly, hand over hand, the way she had always climbed the rope in the training room, hoping to find an open window she could climb through. To her delight, halfway up the wall she realized she had reached a balcony. Even better.

Lucie pulled herself up and over the balcony railing and tumbled onto the ground. She leaped up before any of the thorny briars could penetrate her cloak and give her a nasty scratch. She felt terribly pleased with herself—she wondered if her father would have been proud if he'd known how handily she'd climbed the wall.

Probably not, she had to conclude. Probably he simply would have been murderous that she was here at all. Parents really were unable to see what their children could accomplish, alas. Lucie reached for the handle of the cracked French doors, their glass smeared with black dirt and greenish rot. She pushed inward—

The door flew open, showing a massive, empty ballroom beyond. Well, nearly empty. Jesse Blackthorn stood in front of her, his green eyes blazing with rage.

"What in Raziel's name are you doing here?" he hissed.

The shadow realm was piercingly cold. James had never felt the chill before: he had always stood somehow apart from the dark place, but now he was *within*. It was no longer silent, either. He could hear wind blowing, and a distant sound like shattering glass.

All around him there was blowing dust. Perhaps this place had once been an ocean and had dried up, blowing away with the harsh wind. Certainly there seemed nothing in front of him but an endless sea of sand.

He turned, wondering if he could see any path back to the ballroom. To his surprise, he saw instead the skyline of London—the dome of St. Paul's, the crenellations of the Tower of London, and the familiar arches of Tower Bridge. Tower Bridge itself seemed to glow, eerily red. James coughed; there was dust in his mouth, bitter as salt.

Bitter as salt. He knelt down and scooped a handful of the bone-colored dirt of this world into his hand. He had never been able to touch anything here before. But the dirt was solid, dusty, like any other dirt. He slid a handful into his trouser pocket and rose to his feet as the vision of London faded.

There was only darkness around him now, lit by a faint, eerie glow whose source he could not see. Trackless waste led in all directions. He tried to push down his rising terror, the part of him that said he would die here, in utter darkness: frozen to the spot with no path to follow.

And then he saw it. A tiny flicker of golden firefly light in the distance.

He moved toward it, slowly at first, and then faster, as the light became a blaze. The cold began to vanish, and the scent of living things surrounded him—roots and leaves and flowers—as he stepped back into the world again.

Cordelia had almost given up knocking when the front doors of Chiswick House finally swung open. Grace stood on the threshold.

Much to Cordelia's surprise, she was alone. Ladies did not open their own front doors—servants performed that task. But then, what ordinary human being, even one with the Sight, would be willing to work in such a place? No wonder Grace had insisted she be picked up and dropped off at the gates.

Grace was wearing the same dress she'd worn to the picnic earlier, though the hem was torn and it was stained with grass. Not that Cordelia minded. There was something humanizing about Grace exhibiting even small imperfections.

Grace carried a fiery torch in her right hand; behind her, the foyer of the house was dark. There was a dank smell in the air. Grace stared at Cordelia, her expression caught between blankness and surprise.

"Miss Carstairs," she said finally. She did not invite Cordelia in, or ask her why she was there. Having acknowledged Cordelia's presence, she seemed content to remain as they were.

Cordelia cleared her throat. "Miss Blackthorn," she said. *Was* this a distraction? Somewhere Lucie was creeping about, seeking a ghost. Cordelia had rather thought Tatiana would come to the door too, but she would have to make do with Grace. "I came to see if you were all right after today's events," said Cordelia. "As a fellow newcomer to London, I know it can be difficult—"

"I am quite all right," Grace said. Cordelia had the unnerving feeling that behind Grace's blank expression, she was sizing Cordelia up.

"We are not so dissimilar, you and I," Cordelia said. "Both of us traveled a long way to get here—"

"Actually, there's a Portal in the greenhouse at Blackthorn Manor," said Grace coldly. "It leads to the garden here. So it was a short journey."

"Ah. Well, that is different, but neither of us know the Enclave well, or the young people in this city aside from Lucie and James.

We are simply trying to make our lives here as best they can be—"

The torchlight cast strange shadows on Grace's countenance. "We are not alike," she said, without any anger. "I have obligations you cannot understand."

"Obligations?" The word startled Cordelia. "You cannot mean—" *James. You cannot mean James.* An understanding with a man might be considered an obligation, but only if the relationship was unwanted. Since Grace had entered into hers with James secretly, without her mother's knowledge, surely it must be what she desired?

Grace gave a tight smile. "Did you come because you find the situation amusing?"

"I don't know what you mean."

With a sigh, Grace began to turn away. Cordelia reached out to catch at her sleeve. Grace gave a low cry of pain and snatched her arm away.

"I don't—" Cordelia stared; she had touched Grace only lightly. "Are you hurt? Can I help?"

Grace shook her head violently as a dark shadow loomed up behind her. It was Tatiana Blackthorn.

Tatiana was the same age as Cecily Lightwood but looked years older, the lines of hatred and anger cut into her face like knife marks. She wore a stained fuchsia dress, her gray-brown hair loose and cascading. She looked at Cordelia with loathing.

"Just like your cousin," she sneered. "No sense of propriety at all." She took hold of the door. "Get off my property," she finished, and slammed it loudly in Cordelia's face.

Cordelia was making her way back toward the gates when she heard the noise.

She had supposed there was nothing to do but wait for Lucie in the carriage—Tatiana had ordered her off the property, after all.

Really, she was most peculiar. There had been a glittering hatred in her eyes when she'd mentioned Jem that unnerved Cordelia. How could you hate people for so long? Especially when you were blaming them for something that, while terrible, had not been their fault? Benedict Lightwood had become a monster by the time Will, Jem, and the others had slain him. Many choices were not easy— they were near impossible, and there was no point hating people who were forced to make them.

The noise interrupted her thoughts: it was like the hissing of angry voices. It seemed to be coming from the greenhouse in the front gardens: a wood-and-glass structure with a cupola on the roof. Its windows were dark, no doubt as filthy as the rest of the house was. But why would there be anyone *in* there? It was night, and no one lived at the manor save Grace and Tatiana.

Cordelia hesitated, then unwrapped the bandages on her hands. To her relief, the salve had mostly healed her burns. She wiggled her unbound fingers and drew Cortana from its sheath before creeping to the door of the greenhouse.

To her surprise, the door swung open without the creak of rusty hinges. It seemed that alone among the artifacts of the gardens— the overgrown follies, the sunken pit of thorns and brush that had once been a small amphitheater—the greenhouse was still in use.

She moved inside, into a world of deep shadows and the heavy smell of rotting greenery. It was quite dark, only the little moonlight shimmering through the dirty glass illuminating the space.

She slipped her witchlight out of her pocket with her free hand. It had been given to her on her thirteenth birthday by Alastair—a cool, round piece of *adamas* carved by the Iron Sisters, alive with the promise of light inside it.

She closed her hand around the stone, and it flared into life. She kept the light under control, not wanting the greenhouse to glow like a torch, betraying her presence. The light was a dim yellow, illuminating a path that led between rows of what had once been potted orange trees.

The roof rose high above, disappearing into shadow. Shapes flitted back and forth in the heights—bats, Cordelia suspected. She didn't mind bats. There were plenty in the countryside.

She was less enthusiastic about spiders. Thick silvery webs wound between the trees. She made a face as she moved down the path, which was at least well-trod. Someone had been here recently. She could see the prints of heeled shoes in the packed dirt.

The webs were empty, though. They hung shimmering like the lace of an abandoned wedding dress, vacant of spiders or even the bodies of trapped bugs. *Strange,* Cordelia thought, glancing about. It was easy to imagine how this place had once been beautiful, the woodwork painted white, the glass letting in glimpses of blue sky. There were few flowers left now, though she spied the purplish petals and darkly budded berries of nightshade plants scattered beneath the shadow of a single great tree that still rose, stark and leafless, against a far wall.

Naughty, Cordelia thought. It was frowned on for Shadow-hunters to grow plants like nightshade, which provided key ingredients in dark magic spells. There were plants she didn't recognize as well—something like a fleshy white tulip, and something else a bit like a red Venus flytrap. None looked as if they had been culti-vated recently: weeds grew up and around everything. A gardener's nightmare.

The heavy scent in the air had intensified—like foliage that had been left to rot, a dying garden. Cordelia peered ahead of her, and saw thickening darkness and a twitch of movement—

She ducked just as a dark talon whipped by over her head. *Demon!* screamed a silent voice inside her head. The stink in the air, half-covered by the smell of rotting leaves—the lack of birds or even spiders inside the greenhouse—of course.

There was movement in the darkness—Cordelia caught sight of a great misshapen face looming over hers, bleached and fanged and bony, before the demon hissed and reared back from the light.

Cordelia turned to run but a curling tentacle whipped around her ankle, tightening like a noose. She was jerked off her feet, hitting the ground hard. Her witchlight went flying. Cordelia screamed as she was dragged into the shadows.

Lucie drew herself up to her full height—which was not very impressive; in all her family, she was the shortest. "I think it should be clear," she said. "I am creeping about, spying."

Jesse's eyes flashed. "Oh, for—" He stepped back. "Come inside, quickly."

Lucie did as he asked and found herself standing inside a vast room. Jesse stood in front of her, in the same clothes he had worn at the ball and before that, in the forest. One rarely saw a gentleman without a jacket, and certainly not in his shirtsleeves unless he was your brother or some other family member. She would not have noticed his state of undress when she was so young, but she was very conscious of it now. A metal disc—a locket perhaps—winked in the hollow of his throat, its surface etched with a circlet of thorns.

"You're mad to come here," he said. "It's dangerous."

Lucie looked around. The size of the room, the roof vaulting overhead, only served to make it feel more deserted. Moonlight shone in through a broken window. The walls had once been dark blue but were nearly black now, with a fine grime of dirt. Massive tangles of shimmering fabric, now occluded with dust, hung from the ceiling, swaying in the breeze from the broken windows. She moved toward the center of the room, where a huge crystal chandelier hung. It looked as if it had once been fashioned into the shape of a glittering spider, but the years had taken its crystals and scattered them on the floor like hardened teardrops.

She bent down to pick one up—a false diamond, but still beautiful, all glimmer and dust. "This was the ballroom," she said in a soft voice.

"It still is," said Jesse, and she whirled to face him. He was standing in an entirely different place than he had been before, though she hadn't heard him move. He was all black and white—the only color on him was the silver Blackthorn ring on his scarred right hand and his green eyes.

"Oh, it is rotted away now. It gives my mother pleasure to let time take this place, to let the years wither and destroy the pride of the Lightwoods."

"Will she ever stop hating them?"

"It isn't just the Lightwoods she hates," said Jesse. "She hates everyone she holds responsible for the death of my father. Her brothers, your father and mother, Jem Carstairs. And beyond even that, the Clave. She holds them responsible for what happened to me."

"What *did* happen to you?" Lucie asked, slipping the broken crystal into the pocket of her cloak.

Jesse was prowling about the room: he looked like a black cat in the dimness, long and lithe, with shaggy dark hair. Lucie turned to watch him as he faded in and out of the shadows. The chandelier swung, its remaining crystals sending glittering bolts of light through the room, scattering sparks in the darkness. For a moment, Lucie thought she saw a young man in the shadows—a young man with pale blond hair and a hard twist to his unforgiving mouth. There was something familiar about him. . . .

"How long have you been able to see the dead?" Jesse asked.

Lucie blinked and the blond boy vanished. "Most Herondales can see ghosts," she said. "I've always been able to see Jessamine. So can James. I hadn't thought of it as anything special."

Jesse had moved to stand under the chandelier. For someone so calm, he had a surprising amount of restlessness. "No one but my mother and sister have seen me since . . . since you saw me in Brocelind six years ago."

Lucie frowned. "You are a ghost, but not like any other ghost. Even my father and brother can't see you. It's so odd. Are you buried?"

"It's very forward to ask a gentleman if he's buried," said Jesse.

"How old are you?" Lucie was undeterred.

Jesse sighed and looked up at the chandelier. "I have two ages," he said. "I am twenty-four. And I am seventeen."

"No one has two ages."

"I do," he said, unruffled. "When I was seventeen, I died. But my mother had—prepared."

Lucie licked her dry lips. "What do you mean, prepared?"

He gestured at himself. "This, what you are looking at, is a manifestation of my soul. After my death, my mother told the Silent Brothers she would never give them my remains, that she refused to allow them to touch me again, to burn my body to ashes. I do not know if they questioned what she did then, but I know she brought a warlock into the room in the hours after I died, to preserve and to safeguard my physical body. My soul was cut free to wander between the real world and the spirit realm. Thus I do not age, I do not breathe, and I live only during the nights."

"Which you spend haunting ballrooms and wandering about the forest?"

He gave her a dark look. "Usually I spend my time reading. Both the manor house in Idris and Chiswick House have well-stocked libraries. I've even read my grandfather Benedict's unpublished papers. They were hidden in the chimney. Horrid stuff—he was obsessed with demons. Socializing with them, crossbreeding them—"

"Ugh," said Lucie, waving a quelling hand. Benedict Lightwood's peculiarities were well known. "What do you do during the day?"

He smiled faintly. "I vanish."

"Really? Vanish where?"

"You have a great deal of questions."

"Yes," said Lucie. "In fact, I came here to ask you a question. What did you mean last night when you said, 'There is death here'? Nothing happened at the ball."

"But today it did," said Jesse. "Grace told me."

Lucie tried to imagine Grace and Jesse sitting in this shadowy room, exchanging the news of their days:

I saw a demon attack in Regent's Park during the daytime.

Did you, now? Well, I didn't do much, as you know, I'm still dead.

She cleared her throat. "So you can see the future?"

Jesse paused. He looked made out of moonlight and cobwebs, shadows at his temples, in the hollow of his throat, at his wrists. "Before I reveal anything else," he said, "you must swear you will tell no one about me—not your brother, not Cordelia, not your parents. Understood?"

"A secret?" Lucie loved and hated secrets. She was always honored to be entrusted with one, and then was immediately tempted to tell it. "Why must it be a secret? Many know I can see ghosts."

"But as you have so perspicaciously noted, I am not an ordinary ghost," said Jesse. "I am kept in this state by necromantic magic and the Clave forbids such things. Should they find out, they would search for my body and burn it, and I would be dead in truth. And forever."

Lucie swallowed. "So you still hope—you think you might return? To full life?"

Jesse leaned back against the wall, his arms folded. "You have not promised."

"I give my word. I will tell no one about you. Now explain what you meant last night with your warning."

She had thought he might smirk or say something mocking,

but he looked very serious. "Being what I am puts me between two worlds," he said. "I belong here and yet I don't. Sometimes I can glimpse other things that do not quite belong. Other ghosts, of course—and demons. There was a sinister presence in that ballroom, and I believe it is the same one that returned today."

"But why?" Lucie whispered.

Jesse shook his head. "That, I do not know."

"Will they return—?" Lucie began. There was a flare of light. Jesse turned, surprised, toward the back wall of the house: the French doors had lit up, glowing a startling white.

Lucie darted to one of the windows and looked out. She could see the gardens clearly in all their tangled darkness. A small distance away was the greenhouse, and it was glimmering like a star.

Witchlight.

A moment later the light had winked out. Cold fear clawed at Lucie's chest. "Daisy," she breathed, and tore the doors open. Tumbling out onto the balcony without another look at Jesse, she flung herself at the wall and began to climb down.

Cordelia scrabbled at the ground with her free hand, her fingers sinking into the dirt as she was hauled into the shadows. The demon tentacle wrapped around her leg was agonizing—it felt as if a million small teeth were biting into her skin—but more horrifying was the heat on the back of her neck, the breath of whatever was hovering over her—

Something caught her hand. *Lucie,* she thought. She shrieked as she came to a sudden stop, the painful cord around her leg tightening, jerking her body sideways. She reached up to clutch the hand that had caught hers, and saw who it belonged to.

The greenhouse was dim, but she knew him instantly. A shock of black hair, pale gold eyes, the face she had memorized. James.

He wasn't wearing gear. He was in trousers and shirtsleeves, and his face was pale with shock. Still, he was gripping her wrist firmly, hauling her toward the door, as the cord around her leg tried to drag her farther into the greenhouse. If she did not move fast, she would be torn in two.

Using James's grip as an anchor, Cordelia twisted around to free Cortana—it had been trapped beneath her—and surged downward with the blade in her hand. She slashed the sword through the tentacle holding her.

Cortana sparked gold as it cut through demon flesh. There was a deep, rumbling cry, and suddenly Cordelia was free, sliding toward James in a welter of ichor and her own blood.

The pain lanced through her like fire as he hauled her to her feet. There was nothing elegant about it, nothing of a gentleman helping a lady. This was the urgency of battle, hands grasping and yanking in desperation. She fell against James, who caught at her. Her witchlight pulsed dimly in the dirt where she had dropped it.

"What the blazes, Daisy—?" James began.

She whirled, pulling out of his grasp to snatch up the witchlight. In its renewed glow, she realized that what she had thought was a massive tree rising against the far wall of the greenhouse was something very different.

It was a demon, but not like any she had seen before. From a distance it almost seemed a butterfly or moth, pinned to the wall, wings outspread. A second, closer look revealed that its wings were membranous extensions, shot through with pulsing red veins. Where the wings joined together, they rose into a sort of central stalk, crowned by three heads. Each head was like a wolf's, but with black, insectile eyes.

Extending from the bottom of the stalk was a knot of long tentacles, like the limbs of a squid. Clustered with membranous seedpods, they hit the floor of the greenhouse and stretched out along the dirt like roots. They wound between the trees and the potted plants, they choked the bases of flowering bushes, they reached across the floor toward Cordelia and James.

The one that Cordelia had severed lay on the ground, pulsing slow freshets of ichor. Not swiftly, but inexorably, the others slipped after it.

She dropped her witchlight into her pocket. If she was going to need to fight, she wanted both hands free.

James had apparently had a similar thought: he slid a dagger from his weapons belt and sighted along his arm, his eyes narrowed. "Daisy," he said without looking at her. "Run."

Did he actually mean to face the thing down with a throwing blade? It would be suicide. Cordelia seized his free arm and bolted, yanking James after her. Too startled to hang back, he followed. She glanced back once and saw the boiling rush of black talons behind them, causing her to put on a frantic burst of speed. Good Raziel, how enormous was this greenhouse?

She tore past the last of the potted orange trees and came up short. She could see the door at last, but her heart sank: it was wrapped around with black talons, curving along the walls, their tips pressing against the door, holding it shut. Her hand tightened on James's wrist.

"Is that the door?" he whispered. She shot him a look of surprise— how could he not know? Hadn't he come in the same way she had?

"Yes," she said. "I have a seraph blade, but only one—we could try—"

James hurled the dagger, the runes along its blade shining. He moved so fast it was like a blur: one moment he was holding the blade and the next it had plunged into the demon's membranous wing, shattering the glass behind it. Shrieking, the demon began to pull itself away from the wall.

James swore and drew two more blades: they were arcs of silver spinning from his hands. The demon screeched, a high and horrible noise, as the knives plunged into its torso. The creature spasmed—it seemed almost to be crumbling, its leathery seedpods pattering to the ground like rain. It gave a last choking hiss and vanished.

No longer held closed, the greenhouse door swung wide. Amid the shattered glass and the stench of demon blood, James ducked swiftly through the door, pulling Cordelia with him; together they tumbled out into the night.

They raced away from the greenhouse, through overgrown grass and tangled weeds. When they were some distance away, in a clearing near the entrance to what had once been the Italian gardens, James came up short.

Cordelia nearly stumbled into him. She was dizzy, her vision blurring. The pain in her leg had returned. She slid Cortana into its sheath at her back and sank to the ground.

They were in a small hollow of overgrowth; the greenhouse was a great dark star in the distance, capping a rise of garden. Dark trees leaned together overhead, their branches knotted. The air was clean and cool.

James went down on his knees, facing her in the grass. "Daisy, let me see."

She nodded. James placed his hands lightly on her ankle, above her low leather boots, and began to raise the hem of her dress. The trim of her petticoat was soaked through with blood, and Cordelia couldn't hold back a small noise as her ankle was bared.

The skin looked as if it had been torn with a serrated knife. The top of her boot was drenched in blood.

"It looks bad," James said gently, "but it's just a cut to the skin. There's no poison." He drew his stele from his belt. With infinite care, he touched the tip to her calf—the horror, Cordelia thought, that her mother would have experienced at the idea of a boy touching her daughter's leg—and traced the outlines of a healing rune.

It felt as if someone had poured cool water over her ankle. She watched as the injured flesh began to knit itself back together, slashed skin sealing up as if weeks of healing had been compressed into seconds.

"You look as if you've never seen what an *iratze* can do," James said, a small quirk to the corner of his mouth. "Have you not been injured before?"

"Not this badly," said Cordelia. "I know I should have—you must be thinking what a baby I've been. And that demon—ugh—I should *never* have let it knock me off my feet—"

"Stop that," James said firmly. "Everyone gets pummeled by a demon now and again; if they didn't, we wouldn't need healing runes." He smiled, that rare lovely smile that cut through the Mask and lit up his face. "I was thinking that you reminded me a bit of Catherine Earnshaw from *Wuthering Heights*. My mother has a favorite passage about how she was bitten by a bulldog: *'She did not yell out—no! she would have scorned to do it, if she had been spitted on the horns of a mad cow.'*"

Cordelia had not read *Wuthering Heights* in years, but she felt herself smile. Incredible that James could make her smile after what they'd just been through. "That was impressive," she said. "To dispatch such a sizable demon with only throwing knives."

James threw his head back with a low laugh. "Give the credit to Christopher," he said. "He made these blades for me—he's spent years working on ways of developing new substances that can bear even the strongest runes. Most metals would shatter. It does mean there's hell to pay whenever I lose one, though," he added, looking ruefully at the greenhouse.

"Oh, no," Cordelia said firmly. "You *can't* go back in there."

"I wouldn't leave you," he said simply, melting her heart. "Daisy, if I tell you something, will you promise not to tell anyone else?"

She could not have said no when he called her Daisy.

"You know that I can turn into a shadow," he said. "That at first, I had little control over the change."

She nodded; she would never forget the way he had reached out for her when he had the scalding fever, the way she had tried to hold his hand but it had turned into vapor.

"For years I have worked with your cousin Jem to learn to control it—the change, the visions." He bit at his lower lip. "And yet tonight I entered the shadow realm under my own will. Once inside, it brought me here."

"I don't understand," Cordelia said. "Why here of all places?"

His eyes searched hers. "I saw a light within the shadows," he said. "I followed it. I believe it was the light of Cortana."

She fought the urge to reach back and touch the blade just to make sure it was still there. "It is a special sword," she admitted. "My father always said that we did not know the extent of what it could do."

"When I landed in the greenhouse, I'd no idea where I was," he said. "I was choking on dust. White-gray dust, like burnt bones. I brought a handful of the stuff back from the other world—" He reached into his trouser pocket and brought out a pinch of what looked like ash. "I am going to bring it to Henry and Christopher. Perhaps they can test what is in it. I have never been able to bring anything back from the shadow realm before; perhaps it happened because I went into the realm willingly."

"Do you think it's because I was fighting the demon—with Cortana—that you were drawn to this place?" she said. "Whatever kind of demon it was—"

James glanced again at the greenhouse. "It was a Cerberus demon. And it's probably been here for years."

"I've seen pictures of Cerberus demons before." Cordelia

wobbled to her feet. James rose and put his arm around her to steady her. She tensed at his nearness. "They don't look like that."

"Benedict Lightwood was a great enthusiast for demons," said James. "When they cleared this place out after he died, they found a dozen Cerberus demons. They're watchdog creatures; he'd placed them here to protect his family and property. I suppose they missed the one in the greenhouse."

Cordelia moved away from James slightly, though it was the last thing she wanted to do. "And you think over the years, it changed? Became more a part of the place?"

"Have you read *On the Origin of Species*?" asked James. "It is all about how animals adapt to their environments through generations. Demons don't have generations—they don't die, unless we kill them. This one adapted to its surroundings."

"Do you think there are more around?" The raw pain in Cordelia's ankle had faded to a manageable ache as she twisted around, looking up and down the garden for Lucie. "We could be in danger. Lucie—"

James went white. "Lucie?"

Cordelia's heart skipped a beat. *By the Angel.* "Lucie and I came here together."

"Of all the foolish—" Suddenly he was worried. She could see it in his face, his eyes. "Why?"

"Lucie wanted to make sure Grace was all right, and she asked me to come with her," lied Cordelia. "In fact, she went into the house, where Grace and Tatiana are. Rather foolishly, I wandered off to see the gardens. . . ."

An odd look of utter shock passed across James's face, as if he had just remembered something terribly important.

"Grace," he said.

"I know you might wish to go see her," said Cordelia. "But I must warn you that Tatiana is in a very bad mood."

James continued to look silently stunned. There was a rustle of noise and Lucie burst out of the overgrowth.

"Cordelia!" she gasped, her face lighting with relief. "And Jamie!" Her face wrinkled up; she came to a dead stop. "Oh, dear. Jamie. What are you doing here?"

"As if you have a perfectly reasonable excuse for lurching about someone else's property in the dead of night?" James said, transforming from a worried young man into a towering older brother in a matter of seconds. "Papa and Mam are going to murder you."

"Only if you tell them." Lucie's eyes flashed. "How else are they going to find out?"

"Of course they will," said James darkly. "The existence of a Cerberus demon in the greenhouse could hardly—"

Lucie's eyes rounded. "A what in the where?"

"Cerberus demon in the greenhouse," James repeated, "where, incidentally, you sent your future *parabatai* completely alone—"

"Oh, no, it's all right, I went in on my own," Cordelia said, and started. "I was going to move the carriage from the gates. If Tatiana looks out a window and sees it, she'll be furious."

"We'd better go," Lucie said. "James, will you be coming with us or going back the way you came?" She squinted. "What *is* the way you came?"

"Never you mind," said James, with his crooked smile. "Go take the carriage. I'll follow along shortly and see you both at home."

"I imagine James is staying because he wants to see Grace," Lucie said in a low voice as she and Cordelia hurried back along the overgrown pathways of the Chiswick House gardens. They ducked through the gates and found the carriage exactly where it had been before, Xanthos seeming to stand guard. "Moon around under her window or whatever. I hope Tatiana doesn't bite off his head."

"She certainly doesn't seem to *want* visitors," said Cordelia as they clambered into the carriage. "I felt rather bad for Grace."

"James used to feel pity for her," said Lucie as the carriage started to move. "Then it seems that somehow he fell in love with her. Which is very odd, really. I've always thought of pity as the opposite of love—"

She broke off, her face going white. Light was visible through the tangled branches of trees. Figures were hurrying across the road, toward the manor house.

"It's Papa," Lucie said, in a grim tone, as if she'd just seen another Cerberus demon. "In fact, it's *everyone*."

Cordelia stared. The road was suddenly full of witchlight. It shone upon the dark gates of the house, upon the rows of beech trees on either side of the road, upon the ragged outline of the manor itself. Lucie might have exaggerated slightly in saying everyone was there, but certainly a large group of Shadowhunters on foot was bearing down on the Blackthorns' residence. Cordelia could see familiar faces—Gabriel and Cecily Lightwood, Charles Fairchild's red hair—and of course, Will Herondale.

"What are they doing here?" she wondered. "Should we go back—warn James to make himself scarce?"

But the carriage had already begun speeding up, Xanthos trotting them quickly away while the last of the Enclave members poured through the gates.

As the house receded in the distance, Lucie shook her head, looking grim. "He wouldn't thank us for it," she said. She sighed. "He'd just be angry we let ourselves get in trouble too—besides, James is a boy; he won't be in the same sort of hot water if they do catch him wandering about the place. If they found us, you'd be in awful trouble with your mother. It isn't in the least fair, but it's the truth."

* * *

Moonlight filtered into the greenhouse through shattered glass panes. The Nephilim were long gone, having made their examination of the place and their demands of the mistress of the house. It was finally quiet.

The seedpods the Cerberus demon had dropped in its death throes began to shake and tremble, like eggs about to hatch. Their leathery casings split as thorn-sharp teeth tore them open from within. Covered with a sticky film and hissing like cockroaches, the newborn demons tumbled to the packed-earth floor of the greenhouse, each no bigger than a child's hand.

But they would not remain that size for long.

Days Past:
Idris, 1900

Deciding to sneak into Blackthorn Manor as a shadow was one thing, but actually going through with it was another. For days after Grace asked him, James made excuses to himself about why tonight could not be the night: his father up too late to not notice his leaving; weather too foul to roam around outside; moon too bright to give him sufficient cover of darkness.

Then one night James awoke from agitated dreams and found himself flushed and breathless, as though he'd been fleeing something monstrous. The linens of his bed were thrown off. He stood and paced his bedchamber for a time, unable to think of sleep. Then he pulled on trousers and shirt and climbed out of his window.

He had been thinking of Cordelia, not Grace, but he found himself at the wall around Blackthorn Manor nonetheless. Unable to turn back, having come this far, he willed himself into shadow. Quickly enough he found himself through the wall and across the grounds and into the entrance hall.

He hadn't been prepared for the state of Blackthorn Manor in the middle of the night, its deadly hush, its aura of menace like an opened tomb. Thick silver dust trailed along the edges of banisters and furniture and tangled into cobwebs in every corner. At the edge of his vision was a gray blur: he knew it was the border of the shadow realm. He knew he was courting that world by turning his flesh to shadow.

But he had made a promise.

James could see ghosts, and there were no ghosts here. But this place felt haunted regardless. The shadows seemed to listen intently to his footfalls. Most strange of all, every clock in the house that he passed was stopped at exactly the same hour of twenty to nine.

James went up the stairs. At the end of a long corridor before a turret wall stood a ghastly suit of armor, easily twice as tall as a human. Thankfully, it was only a decoration: fashioned from steel and copper, it resembled nothing so much as a massive human skeleton, with a chest piece in the shape of a rib cage and a helmet and mask that formed a leering skull. It stopped him short, and he stood staring at it until it came to him what it must be: one of Axel Mortmain's famous clockwork creatures, an empty shell that had once housed a demon. The very monsters that his own parents had defeated when they were only barely older than he was now.

Grace had told him that Tatiana had left the house untouched all these years, but that was not entirely true: she had installed this mechanical creature's corpse in its gallery. Why? What did it mean to her? Was it admiration of Mortmain, who had nearly destroyed the Shadowhunters?

James hated to turn his back on the thing, but he moved on, and quickly found the door to Tatiana's study. The room was piled with boxes and crates, stacks of yellowed pages and decaying books. On the wall was a portrait of a boy, about the same age as James, shining green eyes dominating his gaunt face. James knew who it must be, though he had never seen him: Jesse Blackthorn.

There was a metal box set on the low wrought-iron table below the portrait of the dead boy, carved all over with the winding vines that the Blackthorns used to decorate seemingly everything. The lock was built into the lid, presenting a simple keyhole in the smooth surface.

Without looking directly at the box, he lowered his hand to its lid; he felt his body flash into and out of shadow in irregular jerks and for an awful moment saw that other land, the blighted place of twisted trees.

James thrust his ethereal hand through the lid into the box, closed it around a cold serpent of metal, and withdrew it. It was Grace's mother's bracelet, just as she had described.

He fled from the room, from the manor itself. The moonlight through the dusty windows of the hallways wavered and writhed like a mass of silver snakes.

Out of the manor grounds and nearly home, James became aware that he remained a shadow. He stopped where he was, a nondescript stretch of road lined on both sides with dense trees and foliage, neither Blackthorn nor Herondale home visible. The sky was dark, the moon a bright sliver. Gray shimmered at the edge of his vision as he closed his eyes and willed himself to become solid again.

Nothing happened.

He was not, at the moment, a being who breathed, but he felt himself breathe anyway, hard and shaky. When he had become a shadow during his scalding fever, it had only been for moments. It had not been much longer at Shadowhunter Academy. But he had not made the change on purpose, either time.

Oddly, his mind turned to Cordelia, to her voice reaching through the fever, through the shadows. He fell to his knees, his hands making no mark in the dirt of the road. He closed his eyes. *Let me come back. Let me come back.*

Do not leave me alone in these shadows.

He felt a jolt, as if he had fallen and hit the ground hard: his eyes flew open. He was no longer a shadow. He staggered to his feet, gasping in the cold, clear air. The gray had gone from the edge of his vision.

"Well," he said out loud to nobody, "never again. That's easily done. Never again."

The next night Grace was waiting for him under the shade of a yew tree, just inside the entrance to Brocelind Forest. Without a word he placed the bracelet in her hand.

She turned it thoughtfully over and over between her pale fingers, and he saw the moonlight strike across the engraving laid within the curve of metal.

LOYAULTÉ ME LIE. James knew the meaning. It had been the maxim of a long-dead king of England. *Loyalty Binds Me.*

"It was the motto of the Cartwrights," Grace said, her voice very soft. "I was Grace Cartwright once." A smile touched her lips, faint as winter moonlight. "As I waited for you, I realized how foolish I had been to ask for this. I can't wear it without my mother seeing. I do not even dare keep it in my room lest she find it." Grace turned to him. "Would *you* wear it?" she asked. "As my friend. As my only real friend, truly. Then when I see you, I will be reminded of who I am."

"Of course," he said, his heart breaking for her. "Of course I will."

"Hold out your arm," she whispered, barely loud enough to be heard, and he did.

He told himself later that he would never forget her fingers on his skin, the way the whole of Brocelind Forest, perhaps all of Idris, gave a great sigh, as Grace gently closed the bracelet on his wrist.

He looked down at Grace. How had he never noticed before that her eyes were almost the precise color of silver, like the bracelet itself?

He wore it through the summer, into the next year and the year after. He had, even now, still not taken it off.

7

FALL OF SONGS

Bright is the ring of words
When the right man rings them,
Fair the fall of songs
When the singer sings them.
—Robert Louis Stevenson,
"Bright Is the Ring of Words"

"You have to understand," said Charles, his eyes glittering earnestly. "The Enclave is extremely annoyed with you, James. Some of them I would even say are angry."

It was the morning after his odd visit to Chiswick; James was sitting in the chair in front of his father's desk. Tessa had never redecorated the Institute's office and it still had a dark Victorian feel to it, with pine-colored wallpaper and Aubusson rugs on the floors. The chair his father sat in was heavy mahogany, the armrests chipped and scratched. Charles Fairchild leaned against the wall near the door, which he had shut and locked after the three of them. His red hair gleamed like a dull old penny in the witchlight.

Lucie had been swept away by Tessa after breakfast to help in the infirmary. The Silent Brothers had put Barbara, Piers, and

Ariadne into deep, unwavering enchanted sleep: they had hopes that their bodies would resist the poison while they rested. One could sense the shadow in the house, the sickroom atmosphere, along with the thick tension in this room.

"That seems like it must be very upsetting for the Enclave, then," said James. "Bad for their dyspepsia."

He was trying not to glare at Charles but was losing the battle. He'd slept badly the night before after returning to the Institute with his father. It would have been one thing if his father had been angry, but it was clear Will had been more worried than anything else, and James's insistence that he'd merely gone for a walk and ended up in Chiswick didn't help matters.

"You need to take this seriously, James," said Charles. "It was necessary to use a Tracking rune to find you—"

"I wouldn't say it was *necessary*," said James. "I was not in need of help, nor was I lost."

"James," his father said calmly. "You *disappeared*."

"I should have told you I was going out," said James. "But— demons attacked us in daylight yesterday. We still have three Shadowhunters in the infirmary, and no cure for their condition. Why is the Enclave focused on me?"

Red flared in Charles's face. "The Enclave is meeting to discuss the situation with the demons today. But we're Shadowhunters—life doesn't simply stop because of a demon attack. According to Tatiana, you went to her house last night and demanded to see Grace, and when she said no, you smashed her greenhouse to pieces—"

Will threw up his hands. "Why would James vandalize a random outbuilding because he couldn't see a girl? It's ridiculous, Charles, and you know it."

James half closed his eyes. He didn't want to look directly at his father and see Will's distress: his tie askew and his jacket rumpled and his face showing the evidence of a sleepless night. "I told you,

Charles. I never spoke to Mrs. Blackthorn or Grace, either. And there was a Cerberus demon in that greenhouse."

"Maybe so," said Charles. He was beginning to remind James of a dog that refused to give up a shoe it was gnawing on. "But you would never have been in a position to see it had you not already been on the grounds of Chiswick House and broken into the greenhouse."

"I didn't break into the greenhouse," said James, which was technically true.

"Then tell me what you did do!" Charles pounded his right fist into the palm of his other hand. "If what Tatiana is saying isn't true, then why don't you tell me what did happen?"

I went into the shadow realm to see if I could find a connection to the demon attacks. I followed a light I believe was Cortana and discovered myself in the greenhouse, where Cordelia Carstairs was already being attacked by a tentacle.

No. No one would believe him. And they would think he was mad, and he would be getting Cordelia and Matthew and Lucie and Thomas and Christopher into trouble as well.

Silent, James gritted his teeth.

Charles sighed. "You leave us to assume the worst, James."

"That he's a senseless vandal? Honestly, Charles," said Will. "You know how Tatiana feels about our family."

"I killed a demon in that greenhouse," James said evenly. "I did what I was supposed to do. Yet I am the one the Enclave is blaming, rather than the Shadowhunter keeping a demon on the grounds of her house."

It was Will's turn to sigh. "Jamie, we know that Benedict kept Cerberus demons."

"The one that was there—and I do believe you when you say it was there—cannot be blamed on Tatiana," said Charles. "The rest of the property has been searched, and there were no more. It was your bad luck to stumble across this one."

"That greenhouse is full of dark magic plants," said James. "Surely someone noticed that."

"It is," Charles admitted, "but given the severity of her complaints, James, no one is going to note the presence of a few belladonna bushes in her shrubbery. You still wouldn't have run across the demon if you hadn't been trespassing already."

"Tell Tatiana we'll pay for the repairs to the greenhouse," said Will wearily. "I must say all this seems a vast overreaction, Charles. James happened to be there, he ran into a demon, and things took their natural course. Would you rather he'd let it loose to devour the neighborhood?"

Charles cleared his throat. "Let us stick to practicalities." Sometimes James had a hard time remembering that Charles was a Shadowhunter, and not one of the thousands of bowler-hatted, sack-suited bankers who flooded down Fleet Street every morning on their way to offices in the City. "I have had a long conversation with Bridgestock this morning—"

Will said something rude in Welsh.

"However you may feel about him, he remains the Inquisitor," said Charles. "And at the moment, with my mother in Idris dealing with the Elias Carstairs situation, I represent her interests here in London. When the Inquisitor speaks, I must hear him out."

James started. He had not connected Charlotte's trip to Idris with the situation affecting Cordelia's father. He supposed he should have: he recalled overhearing his sister and Cordelia in Kensington Gardens, Cordelia saying her father had made a mistake. The tremble in her voice.

"No punishment is being recommended for James at this point," Charles went on. "But James—I suggest you avoid Chiswick House, and avoid Tatiana Blackthorn and her daughter entirely."

James went still. The hands of the grandfather clock were blades, sweeping slowly around the face, cutting time.

"Let me apologize to her," James said; the silver bracelet felt as if it were burning on his wrist. He didn't know if he meant Tatiana or Grace.

"Now, James," Charles said. "You should not try to make a young woman choose between you and her family. It is not kind. Grace told me herself that if she were to marry a man not of her mother's choosing, she would be disowned—"

"You barely know her," James snapped. "One carriage ride—"

"I know her better than you think," said Charles, with a flash of schoolboy superiority.

"Are you two talking about the same girl?" said Will, his eyebrows rising. "Grace Blackthorn? I don't see—"

"It's nothing. Nothing." James could stand it no longer. He rose, buttoning his jacket. "I must be off," he said. "There's an orangery in Kensington Gardens that needs smashing. Ladies, lock up your outbuildings. James Herondale is in town and he has been slighted in love!"

Charles looked pained. "*James*," he said, but James had already swept past him and out of the room, slamming the door behind him.

Cordelia plucked nervously at the fabric of her visiting gown. Quite surprisingly, an official invitation to tea from Anna Lightwood—on monogrammed stationery, no less—had arrived by penny post that morning. Cordelia was shocked that after everything that had happened, Anna had remembered her desultory offer. Still, she had seized at the opportunity to get out of the house like a drowning man seizing a rope.

She'd barely been able to sleep after getting home the night before. Curled under her coverlet, she couldn't help thinking of Cousin Jem and her father, and helplessly of James, the way he'd been gentle with her ankle, the look on his face when he'd talked about the shadow realm that only he could see. She couldn't think of a way to help him, any more than she could help her father. She wondered if not being able to help the people you loved was the worst feeling in the world.

Then at lunch, her mother and Alastair had occupied themselves by trading the latest gossip—Raziel knew where they'd found it out—that James had been discovered wandering about Tatiana Blackthorn's gardens, having merrily smashed in all her windows and terrified her and her daughter by racing drunkenly about her lawn. Even Risa looked amused as she refilled the teapot.

Cordelia was horrified. "That is *not* what happened!"

"And how would *you* know?" said Alastair, sounding a bit as if he knew exactly why she did. But he couldn't have guessed, could he? Cordelia couldn't be sure; Alastair often seemed as if he knew a great deal more than he was letting on. She thought longingly of the distant past when the two of them had been able to settle their differences by hitting each other over the head with toy teakettles.

So, thank goodness for tea with Anna, even if she had nothing decent to wear. Cordelia cast a last glance at herself in the pier glass between the vestibule windows. While her apple-green princess dress with pink embroidery was fashionable and pretty, all the flounces made her resemble an old-fashioned lamp, and her face above the lace collar looked jaundiced. With a sigh, Cordelia caught up her gloves and reticule from the hall table and headed toward the door.

"Cordelia!" Sona hurried toward her, the heels of her boots click-clicking on the parquet floor. "Where are you going?"

"To take tea with Anna Lightwood," said Cordelia. "She invited me yesterday."

"That's what your brother said, but I didn't credit it. I want you to make friends, Layla." Sona rarely used Cordelia's pet name—given to her by Sona, after the heroine of the poem they both loved—unless she was worried. "You know that I do. But I am not sure you should visit Miss Lightwood."

Cordelia felt her back stiffen. Alastair had come to observe the conversation between his sister and mother. He was leaning against the doorway to the breakfast room, smirking. "I accepted the invitation," she said. "I will go."

"At the ball the other night, I overheard much talk about Anna Lightwood," said Sona, "and none of it was complimentary. There are those in the Enclave who see her as improper and brash. We have come here to make friends and form alliances, not to alienate the powerful. Are you certain she is the best choice for a social call?"

"She seems proper enough." Cordelia reached for her new straw hat, decorated with a silk posy and ribbons.

Alastair spoke from the doorway. "There may be those in the older generation who disapprove of Anna, but in our set she is one of the most popular Shadowhunters in London. It would be unwise for Cordelia to turn down her invitation."

"Really?" Sona looked curious. "Can that be true?"

"It is." Alastair pushed back a lock of his pale hair. Cordelia could remember when his hair had been black as a crow's wing, before he had started dying it. "Anna's uncle is the head of the Institute. Her godmother is the Consul. Without a question, the most prominent families to know in London are the Herondales, the Lightwoods, and the Fairchilds, and Anna is tied to all of them."

"Very well," said Sona, after a pause. "But Alastair, you go with her. Pay a short call and observe the proprieties. Afterward, if you like, the two of you can go shopping in Leadenhall Market."

Cordelia half expected a protest from Alastair, but he only shrugged. "As you say, Mother," he said, brushing past Cordelia on his way to the door. He was already dressed to go out, Cordelia thought with mingled surprise and amusement, in a deep gray flannel coat that suited his dark eyes. The shape of his weapons belt was just visible beneath the line of his coat; the Enclave had suggested that all Shadowhunters arm themselves as a precaution when going out, even in daylight. Cordelia herself had Cortana strapped to her back, glamoured so that it would be invisible to mundanes.

Perhaps Alastair really did know more than he was letting on.

The late afternoon sun shone brightly on Grosvenor Square as Matthew's father, Henry, answered the door at the Consul's house.

James ceased what he suspected might have been overly loud knocking as the door swung open. Henry smiled when he saw James: he had a plain but kindly face, ginger hair that had faded to brown streaked with gray, and a hint of Matthew's grin.

"Come in, come in, James," he said, rolling backward. He had been terribly injured twenty-five years ago in the Battle of Cadair Idris, and he had never walked again. He had taken a standard Bath chair for invalids and bent his inventive spirit upon it—it was fitted now with a smaller version of the wheels one might find on an automobile. A curved appendage with an electric light hung over one of Henry's shoulders. Over the other shoulder, a clawed attachment allowed him to reach for objects placed high overhead. A shelf beneath the seat carried books.

Christopher adored his godfather and spent hours in Henry's laboratory, working on all sorts of inventions as well as improvements to the Bath chair. Some had been very useful, like the steam-powered elevator they had installed so that Henry could easily reach his cellar laboratory; others, like Henry and Christopher's attempt to create a demon-repelling ointment, had not.

Henry had a kind spirit and had welcomed James as Matthew's *parabatai* even before the two of them had gone through the ceremony in the Silent City. "Matthew's in the back garden," he said now, his eyes crinkling at the corners. "He said something about reading a book surrounded by the uncritical beauties of nature."

James had to concede this did sound like Matthew. "Is he alone?"

"Unless you count Oscar." Oscar Wilde was Matthew's dog, who James had found wandering on the streets of London and presented to Matthew. The dog adored Matthew uncritically, much like the beauties of nature.

James cleared his throat. "There was something I found—an odd sort of dirt—I wondered if you could take a look at it for me? You know, in your laboratory."

Most people would have treated this as a strange request. Not Henry Fairchild. His eyes lit up. "Indeed! Give it here."

James passed over the small vial of dirt he had filled from the contents of his pocket the night before.

"I shall take a look at this as soon as possible. I am leaving soon to see Charlotte in Idris, but I shan't be gone too long." Henry winked at James and rolled away toward the lift that would take him to the laboratory.

James made his way past the drawing room, dining room, kitchen—where he bowed to the cook, who waved a spoon at him, in greeting or threat he wasn't sure—and out through the back door, which led to the garden. He and Matthew had spent hours training there: it was a welcoming square green space with a massive London plane tree at its center. Matthew was standing in its shade, reading a book. He was absorbed enough that he didn't hear the door shut, or notice James coming toward him across the grass until James had nearly reached him.

He looked up, and his green eyes widened. "James," he said, and the word sounded like an exhale of relief. He quickly schooled his face into a frown. "I don't know whether to embrace you as a brother or strike you down as a foe."

"I vote the first one," said James.

"I suppose it isn't really fair to be angry about last night,"

Matthew mused. "I imagine you have little control over what happens when you go into the shadow realm. But—once your father had finished shouting at us all in Welsh for breaking his window and letting you leave—the news came through that they'd tracked you to Chiswick House, and I did *wonder*."

"Wonder what?" James perched himself on the arm of a white garden bench.

"Whether you'd used the shadow realm to go and see Grace," said Matthew. "I mean, what else is there in Chiswick? Nothing interesting."

"I didn't go there voluntarily," said James.

"Then tell me what happened," said Matthew, tucking his novel into the crook of a tree. "Actually, wait." He held up a hand just as James had started to speak. "Wait—wait—"

"I shall murder you if this keeps up," said James.

Matthew grinned, and there was the sound of barking. Boisterous hellos bounced off the garden walls. Thomas and Christopher, having paused to greet a tail-wagging Oscar, were running down the back steps of the house. "James!" Christopher called as they got closer. "What happened last night? Where'd you disappear to?"

"There you go, James," Matthew said smugly. "Now you don't have to tell the story more than once."

"Yes, what happened to you last night?" said Thomas. "You just vanished, you know. Matthew was about to rip the Institute apart brick by brick to see if you'd fallen into the crypt when your father tracked you to Chiswick."

"Why Chiswick?" Christopher wondered aloud. "Nothing interesting happens there."

"It has now," said Matthew cheerfully.

Before the conversation could degenerate further, James explained how he had gone into the world of shadows, how he had followed a light and found himself in the greenhouse. He described the warped Cerberus demon and how he had killed it. When he got to the part about Lucie and Cordelia, Matthew began to look less cheerful.

"What on earth were they doing there?" he said.

"They'd gone to check on Miss Blackthorn and see if she was all right," said James, who wasn't sure he believed this particular story himself. Lucie had had her bright-eyed storytelling face on. As for Cordelia—he realized with a slight jolt that he doubted he'd be able to tell if she was lying to him or not. He didn't know her that well, though he felt as if he ought to.

"Seems dangerous to be out and about at night after those attacks," said Matthew. "Lucie—the girls shouldn't be taking such risks."

"As if you're going to stop going out at night," Thomas pointed out. He and Christopher had sprawled on the grass while James was talking. Matthew was leaning against the plane tree, absently stroking Oscar's head. "Here's my question: Why Lightwood—I mean, Chiswick House? Why the *greenhouse?*"

"No idea," said James, keeping his thoughts about Cortana to himself; they were too vague and would only confuse things. "Perhaps because the demon was there?"

"Demons do like to take up residence in ruins, especially those where there are remnants of black magic," said Christopher. "And we all know what Grandfather Benedict was up to in that house. It's why he turned into a worm."

"Ah," said Matthew, "fond family memories."

"Well, the Clave agrees with you," said James. "They believe the demon has been there since Benedict's time. And while it seems entirely unconnected to the attacks, I do feel we have been seeing an unusual number of demons lately in rather unusual places."

"'Demons in unusual places' was Benedict's motto," said Matthew, tossing a stick for Oscar. "How do we know what the Clave thinks? Charles has been remarkably tight-lipped."

"Not to me," said James. "He came to see me this morning."

Thomas's expression darkened. "Don't tell me he believes all that poppycock about you going to see Miss Blackthorn and being refused—?"

"He does believe it," said James, not wanting to hear the story again. He was already annoyed at himself for having let Charles get to him where Grace was concerned; of course Charles knew nothing significant about her. "Or at least, I was unable to give him another, better explanation. I cannot say I was wandering about the shadow realm. Better, I suppose, that they think I am a lunatic in love."

"But you barely know Miss Blackthorn," said Christopher, nibbling a piece of grass.

James's eyes met Matthew's. Matthew was looking at him with sympathy, but there was a clear statement in his green eyes. *It's time.*

"I do know Grace," said James. "And I do love her." He explained about the summers in Idris, Blackthorn Manor next door, and the hours he'd spent with Grace in Brocelind, painting pictures in words for her of London, the great city she had never seen. He explained that Tatiana Blackthorn loathed him, and spoke of Charles's admonition that he stay away from the Blackthorns. By the time he was done, the first stars were beginning to come out in the darkening sky.

Christopher was the first to speak. "I didn't know that you were in love with someone, James. I'm sorry. I should have been paying attention."

"I didn't know either," said Thomas, "and I *have* been paying attention."

James said, "I am sorry I didn't tell you before. Grace has always worried that her mother would find out and be furious. Even Lucie does not know."

Though, he realized, Cordelia did. It had not even seemed strange to tell her.

Thomas was frowning. "My aunt Tatiana is mad. My father has often said so, that his sister was driven to madness by what happened to her father and her husband. She blames our parents for their deaths."

"But James has never done anything to her," said Christopher, his eyebrows knitting together.

"He's a Herondale," said Thomas. "That's enough."

"That's ridiculous," Christopher said. "It is as if one was bitten by a duck and years later one shot a completely different duck and ate it for dinner, and called that revenge."

"Please do not use metaphors, Christopher," said Matthew. "It gives me the pip."

"This is bad enough without mentioning ducks," said James. He had never fancied ducks since one had bitten him in Hyde Park as a small child. "I'm sorry, Thomas. I feel as if I have failed in helping Barbara."

"No," Thomas said quickly. "We have only just started. I was thinking—perhaps you and I and Matthew should go to the Devil Tavern and look through the book collection. There are volumes there that the Clave will never find combing through the Institute's library. We could see if there is any mention of these daylight demon creatures."

"What about Christopher?" said Matthew.

Christopher held up a vial filled with a red substance. "I managed to acquire some blood that the Silent Brothers had taken from one of the patients last night," he said proudly. "I intend to mix modern science and Shadowhunter magic to attempt to create an antidote for the demon poison. Henry has said I can use his laboratory while he is in Idris."

Thomas squinted. "That had better not be my sister's blood."

"It's Piers's," said Christopher, "though for the sake of pure science, it should not matter."

"And yet we are all relieved," said James. "Matthew and I can go to Fleet Street—perhaps Thomas should help Christopher in the lab?"

Thomas sighed. "I always end up helping Christopher in the lab."

"It is because you are remarkably good at dodging explosions," said James, "and also, you can curse in Spanish."

"How does that help?" said Thomas.

"It doesn't," said James, "but Christopher likes it. Now—"

"*James!*" It was Henry, calling from the house.

James sprinted away. Oscar had fallen asleep in the grass, his paws sticking up into the air.

There was a short silence. Matthew took his book from the tree and brushed off the cover.

"Grace," Thomas said finally. "What is she like? I don't think we've exchanged two words."

"Very shy," said Matthew. "Very quiet, looks painfully frightened a great deal of the time, yet always admired at social events."

"That's odd," said Thomas.

"Not really," said Christopher. "Men like the idea of a woman they can rescue."

Both Matthew and Thomas looked at him in amazement. He shrugged.

"I heard my mother say it once," he said. "Seems true in this case."

"Do you think she's in love with James?" said Thomas. "Because he seems gone on her. I hope it's not unrequited."

"She had better love him back," said Matthew. "He deserves it."

"We don't always love people who deserve it," said Thomas quietly.

"Maybe not," said Matthew. "But often we don't love those who don't deserve it, and very right, too." His fingers gripped the book he held so tightly that they had gone pale.

Thomas put his finger to his lips. James had returned, carrying a letter. The address had been written in a decidedly feminine hand: *J. H., care of Matthew Fairchild. URGENT.*

"Someone sent you a letter here?" said Thomas curiously. "Is it from Grace?"

James, who had already scanned the first few lines, nodded. "She didn't want to risk getting me in hot water with the Enclave. She knew I'd either be here, or Matthew would find me and deliver the message." He was quite sure his friends had been talking about him while he was gone, but he didn't mind it: his relief at seeing Grace's writing felt like a palpable thing. The loops and scrolls of her hand were as familiar to him as the forest outside Herondale Manor.

"So what does she say?" said Matthew. "She adores your face and yearns to run her fingers through your messy raven hair?"

"She wants me to meet her tonight, at ten," James said. He slipped the letter into his pocket, his mind racing. "I had better go. I have no way to get a message back to her, and I'll have to walk—the streets are entirely snarled up with traffic."

"You can't walk all the way to Chiswick—" Thomas protested.

James shook his head. "Of course not. She proposed a spot in London—a place Matthew and I used to do balancing exercises. I've described it to her before."

"Still." Matthew looked hesitant. "Is it wise? My brother is an idiot, but if the Enclave wants you to stay away from the Black-thorns—"

"I must," said James, not wanting to explain; he knew his friends, and they would insist on coming with him if he did. Better to leave now and let them think his concern was a purely romantic one. He bent to rub Oscar's head and said, "Thomas, Christopher, you handle the laboratory work. Matthew, I will find you when I return from meeting Grace, and we will go to the Devil."

"I am always going to the devil," said Matthew, a glint in his eye. "I shall be at the tavern by midnight. Join me there when you can."

James excused himself and hurried from the house. The letter in his pocket seemed to beat against his chest like a second heart. Over and over he saw the last line Grace had written:

I shall wait there, and pray that you come. Help me, James. I am in danger.

Alastair dropped Cordelia off at Anna's house with a perfunctory pat on the head and a promise to return just before nine o'clock. Since their mother usually served dinner at nine this seemed to Cordelia to be cutting it rather close, but he rattled off in the carriage before she could even ask him where he was going. She couldn't say she was entirely surprised.

With a sigh, Cordelia turned to face Percy Street, a small side street near Tottenham Court Road. It was made up of long rows of houses of red brick that all looked very much the same. Each had sash windows, white-painted doors, brick chimneys, a shallow set of steps, and a fence about the servants' entrance made of black wrought iron.

On the stairs in front of No. 30, a girl sat crying. She was a very fashionable girl, in a walking dress of blue foulard with lace trimmings and acres of flounces about the skirt. She wore a headband trimmed with silk roses, and they wobbled as she cried.

Cordelia checked the address she had written down, hoping it would have changed. Alas, definitely No. 30. She sighed, squared her shoulders, and approached.

"Pardon me," she said, as she reached the steps. The girl was blocking them completely; there was no way to politely edge past. "I'm here to see Anna Lightwood?"

The girl's head jerked up. She was very pretty: blond and

rosy-cheeked, though she'd been crying. "Who are you, then?" she demanded.

"I, ah . . ." Cordelia peered more closely at the girl. Definitely a mundane: no Marks, no glamour. "I'm her cousin?" It wasn't quite true, but it seemed the right thing to say.

"Oh." Some of the suspicion went out of the girl's face. "I—I am here because—well, because it's just too, too awful—"

"Might I inquire as to the problem?" Cordelia asked, though she rather dreaded finding out what it was, as it seemed the sort of thing where she might have to come up with a solution.

"Anna," the girl wept. "I loved her—I love her still! I would have given it all up for her, all of it, polite society and all its rules, just to be with her, but she has thrown me out like a dog on the street!"

"Now, Evangeline," drawled a voice, and Cordelia looked up to see Anna leaning out of an upstairs window. She was wearing a man's dressing gown in rich purple-and-gold brocade, and her hair was a cap of loose, short waves. "You can't say you've been thrown out like a dog when you've got your mama, two footmen, and a butler coming for you." She waved. "Hello, Cordelia."

"Oh, dear," said Cordelia, and patted Evangeline gently on the shoulder.

"Besides, Evangeline," said Anna. "You're to be married Wednesday. To a baronet."

"I don't want him!" Evangeline sprang to her feet. "I want you!"

"No," said Anna. "You want a baronet. Not to live in my messy little flat. Now go on, Evangeline, there's a good girl."

Evangeline burst into a fresh spate of tears. "I thought I was the one," she wept. "After all the other girls—I thought they didn't mean anything—"

"They didn't," Anna said cheerfully. "And neither did you. Do come up, Cordelia, the water's already boiled."

Evangeline let out a wail that made Cordelia jump back in fear for her life. She leaped to her feet, her blond curls flying. "I shall not stand for this!" she announced. "I'm coming back in!"

Anna looked alarmed. "Cordelia, please stop her, my landlady hates fusses—"

There was the sound of hoofbeats pounding along the road, growing rapidly louder. A light carriage drawn by two matched grays hurtled up the street; a Junoesque woman in a flared skirt and redingote perched upon the driver's box seat. She pulled up briskly in front of the house and turned a furious face toward No. 30.

"Evangeline!" she roared. "Get into the carriage this instant!"

The fire went out of Evangeline. "Yes, Mama," she squeaked, and darted into the carriage.

The plumes on Evangeline's mother's hat trembled as she gazed sternly at Anna, perched in her sash window, examining an unlit cigar. "You!" she shouted. "You are a disgrace! Breaking girls' hearts like that! An absolute disgrace, sir! If it were but a century ago, I should slap a glove in your face, decidedly!"

Anna burst out laughing. The door of the carriage slammed, and the horses broke into a gallop. The carriage wheels squealed as the conveyance rocketed around the corner and was soon out of sight.

Anna glanced down at Cordelia pleasantly. "Do come up," she said. "I am on the second floor and will leave that door open for you."

Feeling as if she had been winged by a typhoon, Cordelia made her way up the stairs and into a slightly shabby entryway. A lamp glowed in an alcove halfway up the inside steps. The rug was threadbare and the banister rail so splintered she feared to touch it, and she nearly tripped up the last three shallow steps.

Anna's door was, as she had said, wide open. The flat inside was much pleasanter than Cordelia had imagined, given the state of the hallway. Softly colored old Victorian wallpaper in dark green and gold, a haphazard scatter of furniture that didn't match but looked glorious anyway, like warring armies who had found a peculiarly harmonious peace. There was a fearsomely large sofa of worn, deep gold velvet, some winged armchairs with tweedy pillows, a Turkish rug, and a Tiffany lamp of a dozen colors of glass. The mantel of the fireplace was decorated with a multitude of knives that had been stuck into it at odd angles, each with a jeweled, glittering hilt; atop a small table by the bedroom door was a large, vibrantly colored stuffed snake with two heads.

"I see that you're examining Percival," said Anna, gesturing at the serpent. "Spectacular, isn't he?"

She stood in front of the sash window, looking out as the sun sank behind the rooftops of London. Her dressing gown fell open about her long body, and beneath it Cordelia could see that she was wearing dark trousers and a sheer white gentleman's shirt. It was unbuttoned to below her clavicle; her skin was only a shade darker than the whiteness of the shirt, and her hair, curling at the back of her neck, was the same black as James's. Herondale black, the color of the wing of a crow.

"He's certainly brightly colored," said Cordelia.

"He was a love gift. I never do court dull girls." Anna turned to look at Cordelia, the dressing gown sweeping around her like wings. Her features were not what Cordelia would ever have called pretty—she was striking, stunning, even. "Pretty" seemed too small and imprecise a word for Anna.

"Did that woman call you 'sir'?" said Cordelia curiously. "Did she think you were a man?"

"Possibly." Anna flicked her cigar into the fireplace. "Best to let people believe what they want to believe, in my experience."

She threw herself onto the sofa. No braces held up her trousers, but unlike the men for whom they were tailored, she had hips, and the trousers hung from them, clinging close to her slight curves.

"Poor Evangeline," said Cordelia, undoing the strap that held

Cortana and leaning her sword against the wall. Settling her skirts about her, she sat down in one of the armchairs.

Anna sighed. "This is not the first time I have tried to break it off with her," she said. "The last few times I was gentler, but as her wedding day drew near, I felt one must be cruel to be kind. I had never wanted her life ruined." She leaned forward, her focus on Cordelia. "Now, Cordelia Carstairs—tell me all your secrets."

"I think I'd better not," said Cordelia. "I don't know you very well."

Anna laughed. "Are you always so straightforward? Why did you come to tea if you didn't want to gossip?"

"I didn't say I didn't want to gossip. Just not about myself."

Anna's smiled deepened. "You're a vexing little thing," she said, though she didn't sound vexed. "Oh! The kettle."

She leaped up in a swirl of glimmering brocade and busied herself in the small kitchen. It had brightly painted walls and a small window that looked out onto the brick facade of the building opposite.

"Well, then, if you want to gossip but you don't want to tell me about yourself, why don't you tell me about your brother? Is he as awful as he used to be at school?"

"Did you go to school with Alastair?" Cordelia was surprised; surely Alastair would have mentioned it.

"No, James and Matthew and the rest of the Merry Thieves did, and Matthew says he was a miserable blighter and gave them all the pip. No offense meant. I admit, Thomas never says a bad word about him. Sugar? I haven't any milk."

"No sugar," said Cordelia, and Anna whirled back into the parlor with tea in a chipped cup and saucer. She handed it to Cordelia, who balanced it awkwardly on her knees.

"Alastair is rather awful," she admitted, "but I don't think he means to be."

"Do you think he's in love?" Anna said. "People can be awful when they're in love."

"I don't know who he'd be in love with," Cordelia said. "He's hardly had time to fall in love with anyone, since we've just arrived in London, and I doubt everything that's happened has put anyone in a falling-in-love mood—"

"What did your father do, exactly?" Anna said.

"What?" Cordelia nearly spilled her tea.

"Well, we all know he did something dreadful," said Anna. "And that your mother's come here to try to ingratiate herself back into Shadowhunter society. I hope everyone won't be too stiff-necked about it. I quite like your mother. She reminds me of a queen out of a fairy tale, or a peri from *Lalla Rookh*. You're half-Persian, aren't you?"

"Yes," Cordelia said, a little warily.

"Then why is your brother so blond?" Anna asked. "And you so redheaded—I thought Persians were darker-haired."

Cordelia set her cup down. "There are all sorts of Persians, and we all look different," she said. "You wouldn't expect everyone in England to look alike, would you? Why should it be different for us? My father is British and very fair, and my mother's hair was red when she was a little girl. Then it darkened, and as for Alastair—he dyes his hair."

"He does?" Anna's eyebrows, graceful swooping curves, went up. "Why?"

"Because he hates that his hair and skin and eyes are dark," said Cordelia. "He always has. We have a country house in Devon, and people used to stare when we went into the village."

Anna's eyebrows had ceased swooping and taken on a decidedly menacing look. "People are—" She broke off with a sigh and a word Cordelia didn't know. "Now I rather feel sympathy toward your brother, and that was the last thing I wanted. Quick, ask me a question."

"Why did you want to get to know me?" Cordelia said. "I'm

younger than you, and you must know loads more interesting people."

Anna rose, and her silk robe fluttered. "I must get changed," she said, vanishing into the bedroom. She closed the door, but the walls were thin: Cordelia could hear her perfectly well when she spoke again. "Well, at first, it was because you're a new girl in our set, and I was wondering if you were good enough for our Jamie or our Matthew."

"Good enough for them in what sense?"

"Well, marriage of course," said Anna. "Anything else would be scandalous."

Cordelia sputtered. She heard Anna laugh. She had a soft, rich laugh, like melting butter.

"You are too much fun to tease," she said. "I meant good enough to know their secrets—and Christopher's and Tom's as well. They are my special favorites, those four, you must have noticed. And, well, the current crop of girls in London is rather dire—of course, Lucie's a delight, but she'll never look at any of the boys as anything but brothers."

"Seems sensible," Cordelia murmured, "especially in James's case."

"They need a muse," said Anna. "Someone to be inspired by. Someone to know their secrets. Would you like to be a muse?"

"No," said Cordelia. "I would like to be a hero."

Anna poked her head out of the door and looked at Cordelia for a long time from under her dark lashes. Then she smiled. "I suspected as much," she said, vanishing back into the bedroom. The door banged shut. "That's *really* why I asked you here."

Cordelia's head was spinning. "What do you mean?"

"We are in danger," called Anna. "All of us, and the Clave will not see it. I am afraid if steps are not taken, it will be too late for Barbara and Piers and—and Ariadne." There was a slight tremor in her voice. "I need your help."

"But what can I—" Cordelia began, and broke off as she heard the downstairs front door bang open.

"Anna!" A deep male voice echoed up the stairwell. It was soon joined by the tread of running feet, and Matthew Fairchild burst into Anna's parlor.

8

No Strange Land

But (when so sad thou canst not sadder)
Cry;—and upon thy so sore loss
Shall shine the traffic of Jacob's ladder
Pitched betwixt Heaven and Charing Cross.
—Francis Thompson, "In No Strange Land"

Matthew wore a brocade waistcoat, and a new silk hat was clutched in his hand, though his head was bare, his curls tousled. Shimmering stones glittered in his tiepin and at his cuffs, and his signet ring gleamed on his hand. "Anna, you won't believe—" He broke off as he saw Cordelia. "What are you doing here?"

Cordelia was not sure such a rude question deserved an answer. "Having tea."

His gaze scanned the room. His eyes were a most peculiar color, clear green in some lights, darker in others. "I don't see Anna," he said, sounding astonished and a little suspicious, as if he suspected Cordelia of having hidden Anna in the teapot.

"She's in her bedroom," said Cordelia, as coolly as she could manage.

"Alone?" Matthew inquired.

"Matthew!" called Anna from the bedroom. "Don't be awful."

Matthew went to lean against Anna's bedroom door, turning his head to speak to her through the crack. It was clear he didn't care whether Cordelia overheard him. "I have already had a maddening day," he said. "James has been slandered by Tatiana Blackthorn and my rotten older brother is backing her up to the hilt; James has gone off to rendezvous with Grace. I am here to get squiffy and try to forget what a foolish thing my *parabatai* is doing." He glanced at his watch. "Also, I have to be at Fleet Street by midnight."

Anna reemerged, looking spectacular in a black velvet coat, matching trousers, and a white silk shirt tied at the collar. A monocle dangled around her neck and her boots were shimmering black. Between her and Matthew it was hard to say who looked the more as if they had wandered out of an illustration in *Punch* regarding the glamorous youth of today.

"A dreadful tale," Anna said. "Shall we go?"

"Certainly," said Matthew. "Cordelia, it was lovely, if surprising, to see you."

"There is no need to say farewell," Anna said, drawing on a pair of white gloves. "Cordelia will be coming with us. That was why I invited her here in the first place."

"I thought you wanted to have tea!" objected Cordelia.

"No one ever just wants to have tea," said Anna. "Tea is always an excuse for a clandestine agenda."

"Anna, Cordelia is a proper young lady," said Matthew. "She may not wish to risk her reputation by sallying out with Downworlders and reprobates."

"Cordelia wants to be a hero," said Anna. "One cannot do that by staying at home stitching samplers." Her eyes gleamed. "I was at the Enclave meeting today; you were not. I know how the Enclave has decided to handle our current situation, and I do not think it will help those who are stricken, or prevent the attack at the lake from happening again."

When Matthew spoke, the brashness had gone out of his voice. "I thought Barbara was getting better. Thomas said—"

"The Silent Brothers have put all the wounded to sleep," said Cordelia, who had heard this from Alastair. "They hope that they will heal, but . . ."

"Hope is not a solution," said Anna. "The Clave insists this was a random demon attack, which took place not in daylight but under cloud cover. They have set patrols in Regent's Park."

"It was not random," said Cordelia. "There were mundanes in the park, too—none were attacked."

"And the demons came before the cloud cover did," said Matthew. "When Piers fell screaming, the sun was still visible."

"You begin to see the problem," said Anna. "Several Enclave members made those points, among them my parents, but the majority prefer to think of this as the sort of problem they have faced before. Not something new."

"And you think it's something new," said Cordelia.

"I am sure of it," said Anna. "And when a new supernatural threat enters London, who are the first to know of it? *Downworlders.* We should be asking questions in Downworld. There was a time when the Clave had connections with High Warlocks, with the leaders of the vampire and werewolf clans. With the Queen of the Seelie Court." She shook her head in frustration. "I know Uncle Will and Aunt Tessa have done all they can, but these alliances have been left to fray and now Shadowhunters can only imagine relying on themselves."

"I see," said Matthew, whose eyes had begun to sparkle. "We shall be going to the Hell Ruelle, then."

"Matthew and I occasionally attend an artistic salon in a building owned by the High Warlock of London," said Anna. "Malcolm Fade."

"Malcolm Fade?" Cordelia had heard of him. High Warlocks of cities were sometimes elected. Sometimes they simply claimed the title. Malcolm Fade had appeared in London somewhere around the turn of the century and announced that he would be High Warlock as Ragnor Fell was stepping down and no one had seen Magnus Bane recently.

Lucie had been electrified, especially when he came to pay a call on the Institute and chat with Will and Tessa. She said he had hair the color of salt and eyes the color of violets and she had been in love with him for almost a week, her letters full of nothing else.

"Every Downworlder who is anyone will be there," said Anna. "It is time for us to do what we do best."

"Drink?" said Matthew.

"Be charming," said Anna. "Ask questions. See what we can learn." She held out a gloved hand. "Come, come. Get up. Is the carriage downstairs, Matthew?"

"At your service," said Matthew. "Are you quite sure you want to come, Cordelia? It will be scandalous."

Cordelia didn't bother to reply, just retrieved Cortana as they left the flat. It was dark outside; the air was chilly and dank. A carriage with the Consul's coat of arms painted across the door waited for them at the curb. Someone had left a pile of roses with the heads snipped off on the front steps. Evangeline, or a different girl?

"So what kind of salon is this, exactly?" Cordelia inquired, as the carriage door swung open and Matthew helped her inside. One of the Consul's servants, a middle-aged man with brown hair, sat impassively up front in the box seat.

She had heard of salons, of course—gatherings where the great and the famous and the noble came together to appreciate art and poetry. It was rumored that more daring things happened at salons as well, in the shadows and the dark gardens, couples gathering to tryst where no one could see them.

Anna and Matthew scrambled up after her, Anna disdaining Matthew's helping hand. "An exclusive one," said Anna, settling back on the velvet bench seat. "Some of the most famous Downworlders in the world attend."

The carriage set off at a clip.

Anna said, "Some you may have heard of; some you may not. Some with reputations they don't deserve—and some with reputations they more than do."

"I never thought of Downworlders as being interested in painting and poetry," said Cordelia. "But I suppose there is no reason they shouldn't be, is there? It's just those aren't things that Shadowhunters do. We don't create like that."

"We can," Matthew said. "We are simply told we shouldn't. Do not confuse conditioning with a native inability."

"Do you create, Matthew?" asked Cordelia, looking at him sharply. "Do you draw, or paint, or pen poetry?"

"Lucie writes," said Matthew, his eyes like dark water. "I thought she wrote for you, sometimes."

"Lucie worries," said Cordelia. "She doesn't say so, but I know she worries, that all her writing will come to nothing, because she is a Shadowhunter and that must come first." She hesitated. "What does it mean, 'Hell Ruelle'?"

Anna's eyes gleamed. She said, "Official academic gatherings in Paris have always been controlled by men, but salons are a world ruled by women. One famous noble lady seated her artistic guests in her *ruelle*—the space between her bed, any lady's bed, really, and the wall. A *scandalous* spot. Informally, an artistic gathering presided over by a woman came to be known as a 'ruelle.'"

"But you said Malcolm Fade ran this one, I thought."

"He owns the building," said Anna. "As for who runs it, you will see soon enough."

Cordelia did not like having to wait to find things out. She sighed and glanced at the window. "Where are we going?"

"Berwick Street," said Anna, and dropped a wink. "In Soho."

Cordelia didn't know much of London, but she did know that Soho was where bohemians roamed. Dissolute writers and starving artists, penniless socialists and aspiring musicians, rubbed shoulders with a mix of shopkeepers, tradesmen, aristocrats who had fallen down in the world, and ladies who were no better than they should be.

It had always sounded wildly exciting, and exactly the sort of place her mother would never let her go.

"Soho," she breathed, as the carriage rattled down a narrow, dark street on whose pavement the stalls of a public market had been set up. Naphtha beacons illuminated the faces of stall owners chatting and haggling with customers over chipped china plates and mugs and secondhand clothes. Gentlemen—well, they weren't gentlemen, most likely, Cordelia thought—tried on overcoats and jackets in the street, their wives fingering the material and exclaiming on the fit. Boswell's butcher had thrown its doors open and was selling cuts of meat—"Whatever will spoil before tomorrow, darling," Anna said, noting Cordelia's curious stare—by gaslight, and there were bakers and grocers doing the same. They passed a tea shop and then the Blue Posts pub, its windows alive with light.

"Here," said Anna, and the carriage stopped. They scrambled out and found themselves at the corner of Berwick and a small alley called Tyler's Court, leading away from the main thoroughfare. The air was full of the sound of people laughing and shouting, and the smell of roasting nuts.

After a brief, whispered conference with Matthew, Anna disappeared down the alley, her tall, black-clad form melding almost immediately with the shadows. Cordelia was left alone with Matthew. He had his hat tipped down over one eye and was regarding her thoughtfully.

Cordelia glanced about at the shop signs. She could see the silhouettes of women lounging in doorways. She thought of her mother's voice saying, *A fallen woman, you know.* As if the girl in question had merely overbalanced. Cordelia tried to imagine it. Kissing men for money, doing more than just kissing. . . .

"What are you thinking?" Matthew asked.

Cordelia wrenched her gaze away from a woman with rouged cheeks smiling up at a man in ill-fitting laborer's clothes. "What's a lapidary?" she asked, not because she actually wanted to know, but because the sign opposite her said A. JONES, LAPIDARY and Matthew was making her nervous.

"A lapidary phrase is one that is worth carving into stone," said Matthew, "and preserving forever—a wise saying such as 'we are dust and shadows,' or alternately, any words that come out of my mouth."

Cordelia pointed at the sign. "They sell phrases there?"

"They sell objects with phrases carved into them," Matthew said. "For instance, if you wished words of love to be etched into your wedding band. Or words of regret and sorrow on your grave. For my own headstone, I was hoping for something a bit grand."

"You surprise me," said Cordelia. "I am all astonishment."

Matthew threw his arms up in the air, his face glowing in the naphtha beacons. "Perhaps a simple 'O grave, where is thy victory? O Death, where is thy sting?' But does that truly capture the light I brought to the lives of friends and acquaintances, the sorrow they will feel when it is extinguished? Perhaps:

> 'Shed not for him the bitter tear
> Nor give the heart to vain regret;
> 'Tis but the casket that lies here,
> The gem that filled it sparkles yet.'"

Matthew's voice had risen; applause rose from the crowd out-side the Blue Posts when he was finished. He lowered his arms just as Anna emerged from the alley.

"Do stop babbling rot, Matthew," she said. "Now come along, the both of you, they're expecting us."

> It was deep night, the forest deep and dark. The beauti-ful Cordelia, astride her white palfrey, galloped along the twisting road that gleamed white in the moon's graceful light. Her shining scarlet hair blew behind her, and her radiantly beautiful face was set with steely determination.
>
> Suddenly she cried out. A black stallion had appeared, blocking the road ahead of her. She pulled back on the reins, skidding to a halt with a gasp.
>
> It was him! The man from the inn! She recognized his handsome face, his radiant green eyes. Her head swam. What could he possibly be doing out here in the midst of the night, wearing very tight breeches?
>
> "My word," he said, his voice heavy with sarcasm. "I was warned that the ladies in this neighborhood were fast, but I didn't think that was meant to be taken literally."
>
> Cordelia gasped. The nerve of him! "Pray, remove yourself from my path, sir! For I have an urgent errand this night, upon whose completion many lives depend!"

Lucie reached the end of her sentence—and her typewriter ribbon—and clapped her hands together in delight. *Pray, remove yourself from my path, sir!* Cordelia had such spirit! And sparks were about to fly between her and the handsome highwayman, who was in reality a duke's son, convicted of a crime he hadn't committed and forced to make his living on the roads. It was all so romantic—

"Miss Herondale?" said a soft voice behind her.

Lucie, seated at her desk by the window, turned in surprise. She had forgotten to kindle the witchlight in her room as dusk had fallen, and for a moment all she could see was a male figure in dark clothes, standing smack in the center of her bedroom.

She shrieked. When nothing happened, she shrieked again, lifted the neat stack of completed pages that she'd set aside, and hurled it at the figure in the middle of her room.

He leaped aside nimbly, but not nimbly enough. The manuscript struck him and exploded into a white cloud of paper.

Lucie reached toward the lamp on her desk. In the sudden illumination she saw him clearly: black hair, as pin-straight as her brother's was wild and untidy. Green eyes looked out at her beneath dark lashes.

"So this is what people mean when they say the pages just flew by," said Jesse dryly, as the last of the papers settled to his feet. "Was that necessary?"

"Was it necessary to invade my bedroom?" Lucie demanded, her hands on her hips. She could feel her heart pounding, and was a little surprised at herself. It wasn't as if seeing ghosts was that rare an occurrence for her. Jessamine drifted in and out of Lucie's bedroom frequently: she loved to look at Lucie's clothes when she took them out of the wardrobe and to give her unwanted fashion advice. Lucie had been almost ten years old before she'd realized—when Rosamund and Piers Wentworth had laughed at her—that most girls didn't have a pestering ghost friend.

Jesse had picked up a page and was looking at it critically. "Too many uses of the word 'radiant,'" he said. "At least three times on the same page. Also 'golden' and 'shining.'"

"I don't recall asking your advice," Lucie said, rising to her feet. Thank goodness she had changed for dinner and wasn't still sitting about in her dressing gown. She did sometimes forget to get dressed when deep into a story, the words flying from her fingers. "What was the last book you read?"

"*Great Expectations*," he said promptly. "I told you, I read a great deal."

He sat down on the edge of Lucie's bed—and immediately leaped back up, blushing. Lucie took her hands off her hips, amused.

"A ghost with a sense of propriety. That *is* funny."

He looked at her darkly. He really did have a most arresting face, she thought. His black hair and green eyes made a wintry contrast against his pale skin. As a writer, one had to pay attention to these things. Descriptions were very important.

"There is actually a purpose in my coming here," he said.

"Other than mocking and humiliating me? I'm so glad!"

Jesse ignored this. "My sister and your brother have arranged a secret rendezvous tonight—"

"Oh, by the Angel." It was Lucie's turn to sit down heavily on the edge of her bed. "That's dreadfully awkward."

Before Jesse could say another word, the bedroom door jerked open and Lucie's father stood on the threshold, looking alarmed.

"Lucie?" he said. "Did you call out? I thought I heard you."

Lucie tensed, but the expression in her father's blue eyes didn't change—mild worry mixed with curious puzzlement. He really couldn't see Jesse.

Jesse looked at her and, very irritatingly, shrugged as if to say, *I told you so.*

"No, Papa," she said. "Everything is all right."

He looked at the manuscript pages scattered all over the rug. "Spot of writer's block, Lulu?"

Jesse raised an eyebrow. *Lulu?* he mouthed.

Lucie considered whether it was possible to die of humiliation. She did not dare look at Jesse. She stared straight at her father instead. He still looked worried. "Is something wrong, Papa?"

Will shook his head. Lucie could not remember when the white threads at his temples had appeared, salting the black of his hair. "Long ago," he said, "I was the one warning the Clave that something terrible was coming. A threat we did not know how to face. Now I *am* the Clave, and I still cannot convince those around me that more steps should be taken than simply setting patrols in a park."

"Is that really all they are doing?"

"Your mother believes the answer is to be found in the library," Will said, running his fingers distractedly through his hair. The backs of her father's hands were scarred from a demon attack that had happened years ago, when Lucie was a child. "Your uncle Jem believes the warlocks may have some useful knowledge hidden in their Spiral Labyrinth."

"And what do you believe?" said Lucie.

"I believe there are always those who stay vigilant and seek the truth rather than easy answers," he said, with a smile that Lucie could tell was more for her than for himself. "In the meantime, I shall be with your mother in the library. We are still under the A section of the *Unusual Demons* book. Who knew there was a worm-like creature called the Aaardshak common in Sri Lanka?"

"Cordelia, perhaps," said Lucie. "She has been everywhere." She frowned. "Is it selfishly awful to worry that all this business will delay our becoming *parabatai*? I feel I will be a better Shadow-hunter when it is done. Were you not one, after you became *parabatai* with Uncle Jem?"

"A better Shadowhunter and a better man," said Will. "All the best of me, I learned from Jem and your mother. All I want for you and Cordelia is to have what I had, a friendship that shall shape all your days. And never to be parted."

Lucie knew her parents had done great deeds that had become famous Nephilim stories, but they had suffered too much. Lucie had long ago decided that living in a story would be terribly uncomfortable. Far better to write them, and control the tale so it was never too sad or too scary, only just enough to be intriguing.

Will sighed. "Get some sleep, *fy nghariad bach*. Hopefully our infirmary dwellers will be better tomorrow."

The door clicked shut behind her father, and Lucie gazed around her shadowed room. Where was her ghost?

"Well, that was interesting," said Jesse in a thoughtful voice.

Lucie spun around and glared at Jesse, who was sitting on the windowsill, all pale skin and dark eyebrows like slashes in his face. He did not reflect against the glass panes. They were black and empty behind him.

"You're just lucky I didn't tell him you were here," she said. "He would have believed me. And if he thought there was a boy in his daughter's room, he would have figured out how to tear him limb from limb, even if he couldn't see him."

Jesse didn't seem particularly concerned. "What did he call you? When he was leaving the room?"

"*Fy nghariad bach*. It means 'my darling' in Welsh. 'My little darling.'"

She gazed at him challengingly, but he didn't seem inclined to mock her. "My mother speaks often of your father," he said. "I did not think he would be like that."

"Like what?"

His gaze slid away from hers. "My own father died before I was born. I thought perhaps I would see him when I died, but I have not. The dead go somewhere far away. I cannot follow them."

"Why not?" Lucie had once asked Jessamine what happened after one died: Jessamine had replied that she did not know, that the limbo ghosts inhabited was not the land of death.

"I am held here," said Jesse. "When the sun rises, I go into darkness. I am not conscious again until the night. If there is an afterlife, I have never seen it."

"But you can speak to your sister and mother," said Lucie. "They must know how odd all this is. But they keep it a secret? Has Grace ever told James?"

"She has not," said Jesse. "The Blackthorns are used to keeping secrets. It is only by accident that I discovered Grace was meeting your brother tonight. I saw her writing to James, though she didn't know I was there."

"Oh, yes—the secret rendezvous," Lucie said. "Are you worried that Grace will be ruined?"

It was distressingly easy for a young lady to be "ruined"—her reputation destroyed if she was found alone with a gentleman. The mother always hoped the gentleman would do the right thing and marry the lady rather than doom her to a life of a shame, even if he didn't love her, but it was far from a sure thing. And if he didn't, one could be sure no other man would go near her. She would never marry.

Lucie thought of Eugenia.

"Nothing so trivial," said Jesse. "You know the stories of my grandfather, I am sure?"

Lucie raised an eyebrow. "The one who turned into a great worm because of demon pox, and was slain by my father and uncles?"

"I feared your parents would not have considered it the kind of tale suitable for a young lady's ears," said Jesse. "I see that was an idle concern."

"They tell it every Christmas," said Lucie smugly.

Jesse stood up. Lucie could not help but glance at the mirror over the vanity, where she could see the reflection of her own face, but not Jesse. A girl in an empty room, talking to herself. "Grandfather Benedict dabbled in a great deal of black magic," he said. "And his relationship with demons—" He shuddered. "When he died, he left a Cerberus demon behind in the greenhouse. Its mandate is to protect our family."

"The demon James saw in the greenhouse? But he killed it. And when the Enclave searched the grounds, they found nothing."

"The Cerberus had been bred with a certain demonic plant," said Jesse. "When slain, it drops pods that at first look harmless. After some hours, they hatch and become new Cerberus demons. By now they would be full grown."

Lucie felt a chill. "What do you fear?"

"Grace left the house without my mother's knowledge—indeed, against her express orders. The newborn Cerberus demons would have sensed it. My grandfather instilled them with the mandate to protect our family. They will go forth to find Grace and retrieve her," said Jesse.

"But how can you be sure? Why would the new demons inherit the mandate of the old?"

"I read it in my grandfather's papers," Jesse said. "He hoped to create an obedient demon that would give birth to new demons when slain—ones that would remember all their progenitor knew. Believe me, I never thought his plan would actually *work*. Grandfather was mad as a hatter. But by the time I became aware of what was going on, it was too late."

"But . . . ," Lucie spluttered. "Will they harm Grace?"

"No. They regard her as a Blackthorn. But if Herondale—if your brother is with her, they will regard him as an enemy. He killed their progenitor in the greenhouse. They will attack him, and it will be no easy task to fend off a group of Cerberus demons alone."

Not only would James be alone, Lucie was not even sure he was armed. "What does your mother know of this? Surely she could not have wanted a demon on her property—"

"My mother resents Shadowhunters, and not without reason. I think she has always felt protected by the presence of the Cerberus in the greenhouse." Jesse sighed. "To be honest, I am not even sure she knows about the new demons. I only worked out what had happened when I saw them leaving the manor, and as a ghost, I could not stop them." His voice was full of frustration. "I have not even been able to find my mother to warn her what is going on."

Shaking her head, Lucie fell to her knees in front of the trunk at the foot of her bed that held her weaponry. She threw it open. Dust puffed up: inside were stacks of daggers, seraph blades, knives, chains, darts, and other such items, all wrapped daintily in folded velvet.

Noiselessly, Jesse appeared beside her. "Cerberus demons are not small. You might wish to bring a few more foot soldiers."

"I was planning on that," said Lucie, taking a small axe out of her trunk. "What will you do in the meantime?"

"Try to track down my mother and send her after Grace. She can tell the Cerberus demons to stand down; they'll listen to her. Do you have any idea where James and Grace are meeting?"

Lucie yanked a satchel that held several daggers and seraph blades out of the trunk and looped it over her shoulder. "You mean you don't know?"

"No; I did not see all of the letter," said Jesse. "Do you think you can find them?"

"I'm certainly going to try." Lucie rose, axe in hand. "Let me tell you something, Jesse Blackthorn. Your mother may have reason to be resentful of Shadowhunters, but if her ridiculous demons hurt my brother, I will have no pity. I shall beat her to death with her own stupid hat."

And with that, she flung open her bedroom window, crawled out onto the ledge, and dropped noiselessly into the night.

9

DEADLY WINE

No growth of moor or coppice,
No heather-flower or vine,
But bloomless buds of poppies,
Green grapes of Proserpine,
Pale beds of blowing rushes
Where no leaf blooms or blushes
Save this whereout she crushes
For dead men deadly wine.
—Algernon Charles Swinburne,
"The Garden of Proserpine"

Cordelia and Matthew went only a short way down the alley before a door rose up in front of them. It shimmered in the side of a worn-looking wall, and Cordelia suspected that to mundanes, the opening would not be visible at all.

Inside was a narrow hallway whose walls were heavy red cloth tapestries hanging from ceiling to floor, obscuring whatever was behind them. At the end of the hall was another door, also painted red.

"When this place is not home to the salon, it is a gaming house," Matthew whispered to Cordelia as they approached the door. "There is even a trapdoor in the roof, so that if they are raided by police, the gamesters can escape over the eaves."

The door was flung suddenly open. Lounging in the space it revealed was a tall man in an iron-gray jacket and trousers. In the dimness, his hair appeared utterly white. Cordelia thought he must be in his sixties at least, but as they approached she realized his face was young and sharp, his eyes dark purple.

This must be Malcolm Fade, High Warlock of London. Most warlocks had a mark that set them apart, a physical sign of their demon blood: blue skin, horns, claws made of stone. Malcolm's eyes were certainly an unearthly shade, like amethysts.

"Three of you this time?" he said to Anna.

She nodded. "Three."

"We try to limit the number of Shadowhunters in the salon," said Malcolm. "I prefer Nephilim to feel outnumbered among Downworlders, as it is so often the other way around." A woman's voice called from behind him: Malcolm didn't turn, but smiled. "You do enliven the place, though, as Hypatia reminds me." He thrust the door wide and stood aside to allow them to enter. "Come in. Are you armed? Never mind, of course you are. You're Shadowhunters."

Anna passed through the doorway and then Matthew, Cordelia last. As she stepped by Malcolm, he peered down into her face. "There's no Blackthorn blood in your family, is there?" he asked suddenly.

"No—none, I don't think," said Cordelia, surprised.

"Good." He ushered them past. Inside, the salon was a series of interconnected rooms, decorated in blazing jewel tones of red and green, blue and gold. They moved down a bronze-painted corridor and into an octagonal room full of Downworlders. Chatter and laughter rose up about them like a tide.

Cordelia felt her heart flutter a bit—there was something about this night that felt dangerous, and not because she was in a room full of Downworlders. The fact that none of them were making any attempt to hide it did make it seem somehow less worrisome. Vampires stalked by proudly, their faces gleaming in the electric light; werewolves prowled the shadows in elegant evening dress. There was music coming from a string quartet standing on a raised cherrywood stage in the center of the room. Cordelia glimpsed a handsome violin player with the gold-green eyes of a werewolf, and a clarinetist with auburn curls, his calves ending in the hard hooves of a goat.

The walls were a deep blue, and massive gilt-framed paintings hung upon them, depicting scenes from mythology. At least, Cordelia thought they were scenes from mythology. Usually when people were naked in paintings, she found, it was because the painter believed that the Greeks and Romans had no need or use for clothing. Which Cordelia found puzzling, especially when the subjects were engaged in activities such as fighting minotaurs or wrestling serpents. Any Shadowhunter knew that in a battle, gear that covered your body was crucial.

"I simply cannot see why one would wish to picnic in the nude," Cordelia said. "There would be ants in dreadful places."

Anna laughed. "Cordelia, you are a breath of fresh air," she said, as a woman with dark hair bore down on them, carrying a silver salver. Her black hair was wrapped around an ivory comb hung about with silk peonies, and her embroidered gown was deep crimson. Glittering on the salver were crystal glasses filled with sparkling liquid.

"Champagne?" she said, and as she smiled, the glimmer of fang teeth appeared against her lower lip. A vampire.

"Thank you, Lily," said Anna, taking a glass. Matthew did the same, and after a moment's hesitation, Cordelia followed. She had never had champagne, nor anything like it—according to her mother, ladies drank only sweet liquors like sherry and ratafia.

Matthew downed his champagne in one swallow, placed the empty glass back on Lily's tray, and took another. Cordelia lifted her glass as a dapper warlock with a ring of quills around his neck passed by arm in arm with a blond vampire in a garnet-red frock. She was lovely, and pale as new snow: Cordelia thought of the mundane women who paid to have their faces enameled white to preserve their youth and keep their fashionable pallor.

They ought to just become vampires, she thought. It would be less expensive.

"What's that little smile of yours?" Matthew inquired. "You look as if you're about to laugh."

Cordelia took a sip of champagne—it tasted like airy bubbles—and regarded him archly. "What of it?"

"Most girls would be afraid," he said. "I mean, not Anna. Or Lucie. But most."

"I don't frighten easily," said Cordelia.

"I'm beginning to sense that." He glanced over at Anna and Lily: the vampire girl was laughing, her head close to Anna's. "Anna can seduce anyone," Matthew said to Cordelia, in a low voice. "Anyone at all. It's her talent."

"Not my only talent, I hope," said Anna, looking up as Malcolm Fade reappeared. He gestured to Lily with a dismissive wave; Lily flounced off in a swirl of silk.

"Hypatia wishes to see you, Anna," said Malcolm. "She has a friend visiting from out of town who has requested to meet you."

Anna gave a curling smile. "And this friend is visiting from where?"

"The seaside," said Malcolm. "Do come, you know how Hypatia gets."

Anna dropped a wink to Cordelia and Matthew and turned to follow Malcolm down a passageway papered with damask wallpaper. They were quickly out of view.

"She's so beautiful," said Cordelia. "Anna, I mean."

"Anna has a quality." Matthew raised a thoughtful eyebrow. "The French would call it *jolie laide.*"

Cordelia knew French well enough to frown. "Pretty-ugly? She's not ugly!"

"It doesn't mean that," Matthew said. "It means unusually pretty. Oddly beautiful. It denotes having a face with character." His gaze traveled from the top of her hair to the tips of her shoes. "Like you have."

He reached out to snag a glass of champagne off a passing tray as the handsome werewolf from the string quartet went by with a smile. Somehow Matthew had drunk the one he had and discarded it with impressive speed and discretion. He took a swallow of the new one and met Cordelia's eyes over the rim.

Cordelia was not entirely sure how she felt about being called "pretty-ugly," but there were more important issues at hand. She didn't know when she would again be alone with Matthew. She said, "Do you remember how I asked you about your mother at the ball?"

"I always enjoy thinking about my mother at these sorts of parties," he said.

She took another swallow of champagne and tried to restrain a hiccup. "Your mother is the Consul," she continued.

"I had noticed that, yes."

"And she is currently in Idris, where they are preparing to try my father."

His eyes narrowed. "I thought—" He shook his head. A group of vampire ballerinas glanced over at them and giggled. "Never mind. I think too much and I drink too much. That is always my problem."

"There is something I don't understand," said Cordelia. "Why haven't they tried my father with the Mortal Sword yet? Then they would have proof he's innocent."

Matthew looked faintly surprised. "Indeed. It makes little sense to possess a magical object that forces the holder to tell the truth if you aren't going to use it in criminal trials."

The word "criminal" still shook Cordelia to the bone. "We have very little information, but my brother does have school friends in Idris. He has heard they do not plan to use the Mortal Sword in the trial. Do you think you could convince your mother that they must?"

Matthew had procured another drink, possibly from a potted plant. He was watching her over the rim of the glass. Cordelia wondered how many people had seen Matthew grinning over a drink and failed to spot him watching them with those dark green eyes. "You are very upset about this, aren't you?" he said.

"It is my family," she said. "If my father is found guilty, we will not just lose him, we will be as the Lightwoods were after Benedict's death. Everything we have will be stripped from us. Our name will be disgraced."

"Do you care that much? About disgrace?"

"No," said Cordelia. "But my mother and brother do, and I do not know if they would survive."

Matthew set his glass down on a marquetry side table. "All right," he said. "I will write to my mother in Idris."

The relief was almost painful. "Thank you," said Cordelia. "But have her write back to Lucie, please, at the Institute. I don't want my mother to see the reply before I do, in case she says no."

Matthew frowned. "My mother would not—" He broke off, looking past her to where Lily waved from the other end of the room. "That is Anna's signal," he said. "We must go."

Cordelia felt a slight thrill of unease. "Go where?"

"Into the heart of it all," said Matthew, gesturing toward the damask-papered corridor Anna had disappeared down before. "Brace yourself. Warlocks can be as tricky as faeries if they set their minds to it."

Curious, Cordelia followed Matthew down the hall. Paper lanterns lit the way. At the very end of the passage was a cabinet of carved ebony, an array of curios spread out under glass. Matthew gave the glass a playful tap.

The cabinet swung inward.

Within was a golden grotto. The whole room gleamed, from the painted ceiling to the floor where the carpet shone as if it were flaxen tissue paper. There were giltwood tables holding all manner of treasures: clockwork birds inlaid with lapis and gold, gauntlets and blades of delicate faerie workmanship, a polished wooden box decorated with the symbol of an *ourobouros*—a serpent biting its own tail—and an apple carved from a single ruby. At the very end of the room was a four-poster bed the size of Cordelia's whole bedroom at home, inlaid with copper and brass, covered in dozens of cloth-of-gold cushions. Seated upon the edge of the bed as if it were a throne was a woman, a sleek warlock who seemed artfully shaped from enchanted materials: her skin mahogany, her hair bronze, her dress a shimmering gold.

Cordelia hesitated upon the threshold. There were other people in the room besides the warlock woman: Malcolm Fade himself, and Anna Lightwood, lounging alone on a conversation settee of walnut wood and gilt velvet, her long legs hooked over the slender wooden arms.

Malcolm Fade smiled. "Welcome, little Shadowhunters. Few of your kind ever see the inner chambers of Hypatia Vex."

"Is she welcome, I wonder?" asked Hypatia, with a catlike smile. "Let her approach."

Cordelia and Matthew advanced together, Cordelia moving cautiously around the rococo chairs and tables, gleaming with gilt and pearls. Close up, the pupils of Hypatia Vex's eyes were the shape of stars: her warlock mark. "I cannot say I care for the idea of so many Nephilim infesting my salon. Are you interesting, Cordelia Carstairs?"

Cordelia hesitated.

"If you have to think about it," said Hypatia, "then you're not."

"That hardly makes sense," said Cordelia. "Surely if you do not think, you cannot be interesting."

Hypatia blinked, creating the effect of stars turning off and on like lamps. Then she smiled. "I suppose you may stay a moment."

"Good work, Cordelia," said Anna, swinging her legs off the edge of the settee. "Arabella, how are the drinks coming on?"

Cordelia turned to realize a faerie woman with tumbling blue and green hair was also in the room. She was standing in an alcove, partially hidden: before her was a sideboard where she was mixing drinks. Her hands waved in midair like fronds in water, unstoppering decanters and crystal vials full of red liquid, and busily pouring them into a variety of goblets and flutes.

Cordelia's eyes narrowed.

"Just ready, darling!" Arabella said, and walked over to distribute drinks. Matthew accepted a drink with alacrity. Cordelia noticed that Arabella walked with a rocking, unsteady gait, as if she were a sailor unaccustomed to treading on the land.

When Arabella gave Anna her drink, Anna pulled Arabella into her lap. Arabella giggled, kicking up her French heels. Her legs were shockingly bare, and covered in a faint iridescent pattern of scales. They flashed in the golden light like a rainbow.

A *mermaid*. So this was Hypatia's "friend from the seaside." They were a type of faerie rarely seen out of water, since their human legs caused them pain to walk on.

Arabella noticed Cordelia's gaze and shrugged, shoulders moving fluidly beneath her heavy masses of blue and green hair. "I have not been on land for many years. The last time I visited this ugly city, the Downworlders and Shadowhunters were trying to form the Accords. I was not much impressed with Nephilim then, and I have not been fond of Shadowhunters since. Still, exceptions can be made."

Before the Accords were formed. This woman had not been on the land for more than thirty years.

Arabella leaned into Anna as she spoke, and Anna's scarred fingers drifted nimbly through the waves of the mermaid's hair. Tiny fish, small as sparks from a fire and bright blue, stirred when disturbed and leaped from strand to strand, chasing Anna's movements.

"My lovely, your hair is like a beautiful stream," murmured Anna. "Because there are fish in it."

Apparently Anna could seduce multiple people in one evening. Arabella blushed and bounced up to gather more drinks from the sideboard.

"We know why Anna brought *you*, Matthew," said Malcolm. "You are amusing. But is there a reason this young Carstairs girl is accompanying you tonight?"

"Because we need your help," said Cordelia.

Everyone in the room laughed. Malcolm smiled and raised his empty glass to Cordelia as if she had made a particularly good joke; Arabella was still at the sideboard, sprinkling flowers into two flutes of wine and humming.

Anna and Matthew looked pained.

"Magnus Bane would help them," said Hypatia, the stars in her eyes sparkling. "That is why they have come. Magnus has made them believe a warlock will always help them."

"Magnus is not here," said Malcolm. His gaze was distant. "I bear you no ill will, child, but I loved a Shadowhunter once and it brought me only sorrow."

"She became an Iron Sister, and broke his heart," said Hypatia.

"Oh," said Cordelia, surprised. The Iron Sisters were even more secretive than the Silent Brothers. Stern and removed, they shaped *adamas* into runed weapons for the Nephilim from their hidden fortress. They had done so for a thousand years. Like the Silent Brothers, they did not marry, and held the responsibility of placing protective spells on Shadowhunter babies when they were born. No one not of their sisterhood was allowed in the Adamant Citadel. Only women could choose to be Iron Sisters, though it seemed as lonely to Cordelia as Silent Brotherhood. "That seems very sad."

"Indeed," said Malcolm. "Our kind and yours are best apart, whatever Bane might say."

"I have not met Bane," said Hypatia, tapping her golden fingernails together. "Before he last left London he helped the Nephilim, but do they recall his graciousness, or do they only expect help at the first sign of trouble? I let you come to my salon because you amuse me, Matthew Fairchild. Because you are a child—a silly and beautiful child, who touches the fire because it is lovely, and forgets that it will burn him. Do not presume that means you can ask for favors."

"It might be amusing for you to find out what it is they want," suggested Anna.

"As if you don't already know," said Hypatia, but the look she gave Anna was a fond one, and Anna smiled.

"What if we did something for you?" Cordelia said. Arabella was making the rounds, setting her flower-bedecked drinks in front of the warlocks. Malcolm lifted his and eyed it as if he were hoping to find solace at the bottom. Hastily, Cordelia said, "What if I saved your lives?"

This time they didn't laugh. They simply stared. "Charming," Hypatia said. "But we are not in any danger."

"I disagree," said Cordelia.

She drew Cortana. Every glittering light in the room caught fire along the blade.

Cordelia struck Hypatia's crystal flute with a sweep of her blade. The flute exploded, sending glass and wine in all directions. Arabella gave an indignant scream and Cordelia swung the sword to point directly at her.

"It's a pity," Cordelia said. "I've never met a mermaid before. I wish you hadn't turned out to be a poisoner."

Matthew, who had already drained his glass, set it down on the table with a loud thump. *"Poison?"*

"Only for the warlocks," said Cordelia. "It was them she was trying to kill."

Hypatia sounded outraged. "May I ask where you came to this wild conclusion?"

"My mother knows a great deal about medicinal plants, and she shared her knowledge with me," said Cordelia. "There is a plant cultivated by the mermaids, an underwater variety of deadly night-shade, which they will not sell even at the Shadow Markets. One taste is death. I saw her sprinkle those blossoms in your cups."

Malcolm Fade waved a hand over his own cup. Purple sparks woke and danced in his glass. The red wine stain on the carpet unfurled like a flower and turned to purple smoke. Hypatia looked at the broken flute as if it had turned into a rat.

"I was a child in Cornwall long ago, where *Atropa belladonna* grows wild," said Malcolm quietly. "I am an expert in the uses of deadly nightshade, and I have seen its cousin deadly nightsea before. Miss Carstairs is right. She *has* saved our lives."

"Seize the mermaid," Hypatia said between her teeth.

Anna was already up and out of her chair, dagger in hand, her movements light as a cat's. Arabella was fumbling in her bodice, her teeth bared, but Anna caught at her wrist, twisting it hard. An item fell from Arabella's fingers and rolled upon the golden carpet: it was the horn of a sea creature, sharpened to a deadly point.

"Let me end my life," Arabella hissed, writhing, but Anna continued to hold her prisoner with an arm about her neck. Runes flared along Anna's bare, slender arm; the dagger in her other hand glimmered like diamonds. "Let me die with honor as sea people do."

"Honor? There is no honor in poison. It is a coward's trick," said Hypatia. "You intended to poison me and Malcolm Fade. And to what end? What power do you seek?"

"She seeks revenge," said Malcolm. "I have heard of you, Arabella. You considered yourself insulted by the Nephilim years ago. It must have been a much greater matter than any of us realized, for when Hypatia told you they were here tonight you sought to pay them back." His eyes narrowed. "Hypatia and I would have been dead—warlocks poisoned by Shadowhunters, you would claim. Every Downworlder in London would have been after Nephilim blood."

Her face like stone, Hypatia picked up a small golden bell and shook it; the ringing echoed through the room. A blue-skinned faerie girl with foxgloves in her hair popped her head in through the door. "You rang, mistress?"

Hypatia's mouth was a tight line. "Hyacinth. Have the guards take this mermaid away and put her in the wine cellar."

"Please reconsider putting a poisoner in the wine cellar," said Matthew. "I beg of you, for the sake of my future visits."

Hypatia waved a hand. "Put her in the Whispering Room, then. She shouldn't be able to cause any trouble there; we'll take her to the Spiral Labyrinth shortly."

"And then?" said Cordelia as two trolls wearing coats with gold braid entered, detached Arabella from Anna's grip, and escorted the hissing mermaid out of the room. "What happens to her?"

"A trial," said Hypatia. "A Downworlder matter of no interest to you. It will be fair. Downworlders are always fair."

"Then you should have little issue with offering Cordelia assistance," said Anna, brushing dust from her cuffs. "As she saved your life."

"Anna is right," said Malcolm. "A debt is a debt. What is it you wish for help with, Nephilim?"

Cordelia let Matthew tell the tale; the picnic, James's vision of the shadow realm, the demons who came in daylight, the wounded Shadowhunters, and the poison the Silent Brothers could not cure.

"Your friend saw a shadow land nobody else can see?" said Hypatia. "Is he the child of the shape-changing warlock girl, and the Shadowhunter mad enough to marry her? I knew that would be trouble."

Matthew looked furious. Cordelia said, "He can indeed see what others cannot. It is a rare talent."

"So this is a kind of demon that comes in daylight," said Malcolm. "And transmits a poison your scholars have never seen before."

"If such demons were free in London, it would not be good for anyone," said Anna.

"Of course, all demons come from other worlds," said Hypatia. "But if you think that as the children of demons we are intimately familiar with their geography and those who dwell in them, you are quite mistaken."

"We are not insulting you, Miss Vex," said Cordelia. "But you have your ear to the ground of Downworld. Nothing happens in it that you do not know. If there was other word of these strange demons . . ."

"There is not," Hypatia said firmly. "All discussion has been about the lack of demons in London, in fact, and how strange it is."

"Ragnor called it 'the calm before the storm,' but he is a doom-sayer at the best of times," said Malcolm.

"Well, they seem to be returning," said Anna. "A cluster of Shax demons appeared in Seven Dials just the other day."

"And Deumas demons were encountered in the City," Matthew added. "Nasty, messy sorts of creatures."

Hypatia and Malcolm exchanged a look. Demons were everyone's problem, Downworlders and Shadowhunters alike. A single attack against Shadowhunters by unknown creatures was one thing, but Shax and Deumas demons were indiscriminate killers.

"There was a rumor," said Malcolm, "though it was only a rumor, mind, that some sort of powerful individual—a warlock, perhaps—put out the word among the demon groups that London was to be avoided."

"Since when have demons ever listened to anyone?" inquired Anna.

Malcolm shrugged. "As I said, a rumor. Besides, in such a situation, it seems wise to leave well enough alone."

"The time for leaving well enough alone has passed," said Cordelia. "These sunlight demons may be a harbinger of worse to come for us all; surely we should work together to discover if that is the case?"

"I detest it when Shadowhunters make sense." Hypatia sighed. "Ragnor Fell is back in London, and he has often worked with Shadowhunters in the past. He knows a great deal about demon worlds, having made himself a student of dimensional magic. If there is a dimension that breeds demons who can withstand sunlight, he would know about it."

"It does seem a place to start. How do we find him?" said Matthew.

"I will send him an urgent message," said Hypatia. "He will contact you." She sank back into her chair. "Now go," she said, closing her starry eyes. "I find myself weary of angels."

There seemed little else to say. Matthew, Anna, and Cordelia made their way back through the main room of the salon, where a vampire was reciting poetry about blood. In moments they had reached Berwick Street and the outside world: Cordelia inhaled lungfuls of cool night air. It tasted of dirt and city.

"Nephilim!" It was the blue-skinned faerie girl Hypatia had called Hyacinth. She looked around at the city in distaste before handing Matthew a velvet-wrapped bundle. "Fade wished you to have this," she said. "He is grateful for what you all did. What *did* you do?" she added curiously. "I've never heard of a warlock being grateful before."

Anna winked at her. "I'll tell you the story in a moment."

Cordelia and Matthew looked at Anna in surprise. Hyacinth blushed and giggled her way back down the alley.

"I'm going to linger a bit longer," Anna said, with a catlike stretch. "You two can take the carriage; I'll make my own way home."

Matthew pulled back a corner of the velvet. Folded gently within were perhaps a half-dozen blades of fine and careful faerie workmanship.

Matthew whistled. "A real gift." He looked at Cordelia with admiration, his bronze hair gleaming in the naphtha light. "I would never have guessed Arabella was engaged in poisoning."

"I told you earlier," said Anna, gesturing for the carriage. "I never do court dull girls."

Days Past:
Paris, 1902

"You must go to Paris," Matthew had said to Thomas the day before Thomas left for Madrid. He, James, and Matthew were sprawled in their chairs in the Devil Tavern, waiting for Christopher. "If you are finally getting to flee this dull island for someplace cultured, you must go to Paris first."

"It's not on the way to Spain," Thomas had said. "And that will be plenty of excitement for me."

"Nonsense," said Matthew. "Only Paris is like Paris. And you must stay in my absolutely favorite digs, the Hotel d'Alsace. On the Left Bank. Everyone calls it L'Hotel."

"Doesn't that just mean 'the hotel' in French?" James had said, barely looking up from his book.

"That's because it's the hotel where anybody who is anybody stays."

"I'm not anybody," Thomas had protested.

"Oscar Wilde stayed there," said James. "When Matthew says 'anybody,' that's usually who he means."

"Not *only* Oscar Wilde," Matthew had said. "But yes, Oscar Wilde. He died there."

"I trust you'll have a more pleasant time," said James.

Thomas really had intended to confine his travels to Spain, but Matthew's words had stuck with him, and when the head of the Madrid Institute had suggested that Thomas take two weeks off to see a bit more of the world, Thomas had recalled Matthew's promises that the whole world would be changed in his eyes after he had beheld the City of Lights.

L'Hotel felt like being in someone's home, albeit someone a bit scruffy. It was in the sixth arrondissement, which on the whole had a friendly but slightly shabby feeling. It was full of mundanes who were attending the Sorbonne nearby, and Thomas found it easy to feel part of the crowd as he strode the neighborhood streets at sunset, thinking about where to dine. He declined to check in with the Paris Institute, saw only a bare handful of Downworlders, and set out to enjoy himself.

Unfortunately, Thomas had grown used to being in easy reach of his closest friends, and even the Madrid Institute was a lively place where company was always close at hand. The solitude quickly began to wear on him. Here he knew no one and spoke essentially none of the language. Whole days passed where his only conversation was with a waiter, or a museum employee, or the desk clerk at L'Hotel.

He grew lonely, and in his loneliness he grew bored. He dutifully went to the Louvre and had thoughts about what he saw, but nobody to share them with. He wrote them down in a notebook and wondered if he would ever look at it again. He counted the days until he returned to Spain, wondering how to tell Matthew that the city itself was not enough of a companion to satisfy him.

And then, unaccountably, he saw someone he knew.

Not a friend. Alastair Carstairs was definitely not a friend. But more than an acquaintance, surely. They'd been at the Academy together. Where Carstairs had been, not to put too fine a point on it, awful. He had been one of the "mean boys," the ones who played cruel and dangerous pranks. The ones who identified any other boy's quality that stood out and made sure to hammer it down with the force of their contempt and their laughter. In Thomas's case, that had been his size. He was short for his age, and narrow-shouldered, and he looked younger than he was.

Of course, that had been years ago. Thomas now towered above most people. In fact, he only spotted Alastair because he could see over the heads of the crowd between them.

Matthew had directed Thomas to Librairie Galignani, on the Rue de Rivoli, as a must-visit location—"It's the oldest English-language bookshop on the whole continent!" Thomas lingered over books of poetry, allowing himself to take a long time to decide what to buy. And then Alastair appeared.

Thomas hadn't decided yet whether to acknowledge Alastair, but he wasn't given much choice. Alastair was staring directly at him. As Thomas watched, Alastair's face went through a series of expressions: mild recognition, confusion, shock, exasperation, long-suffering forbearance.

Thomas gave him a little wave.

Alastair pushed his way through the people between them. "By the Angel, Lightwood," he said. "You've become gigantic."

Thomas raised his eyebrows. A few other people nearby did as well.

"This is your revenge, I suppose," Alastair went on, as if Thomas had done this to him personally, "for all the times I called you 'wee little Thomas' or 'half pint' or—I can't remember, I'm sure I had something cutting and witty to say."

"What are you doing in Paris?" Thomas said.

"What are *you* doing in Paris?" Alastair said back in a superior tone, as though he'd caught Thomas at something.

"I'm on holiday from my travel year in Spain."

Alastair nodded. A silence fell. Thomas began to panic. They were not friends. What Thomas knew about Alastair was mostly negative. He did not know what his duties were here.

He was thinking of ways to politely excuse himself, perhaps by fleeing the bookstore and returning some hours later, when Alastair spoke up. "Do you want to come to the Louvre, then? I'm going over there after this."

Thomas could have said, *I've been already, thanks,* or *Actually, I have a pressing lunch engagement,* but he didn't. He had been alone for days. He said, "All right."

So they went. It was crowded, and Alastair was grumpy about it, but he didn't take it out on Thomas. He didn't belittle the art. He didn't speak in rapturous tones, either; to Thomas's surprise, Alastair seemed content to place himself before a work of art and simply behold it for a long moment, letting it wash over his senses. His face was serious, his brow wrinkled, but Thomas was sure that it was the most content he had ever seen Alastair.

For his part, Thomas had visited this very museum and had assembled a number of, he thought, insightful observations about a number of pieces. He shared a few of these with Alastair, tentatively. He waited for Alastair to scoff, but Alastair just acknowledged Thomas's comments with a nod. Thomas had no reason to like Alastair, had in fact every reason to dislike Alastair, but in these small moments standing next to one another in the presence of a beautiful object, he was glad Alastair was there, and Alastair's acknowledgment of him, however small, made him feel better than he had since he'd arrived in Paris.

Maybe he had changed, Thomas thought. Maybe everyone grew up sooner or later. Maybe he had not even been that bad in the first place.

He thought back to his time at the Academy and decided that, no, Alastair had definitely been terrible in the first place. But he seemed calmer now, more thoughtful.

After they left the museum, Thomas and Alastair went for a walk along the Seine. Alastair wanted to know all about Madrid, and Thomas was even able to rise some stories from Alastair about his time in Damascus, and Morocco, and Paris itself. Having grown up in Idris and London, Thomas felt that Alastair must be very worldly. And yet he wondered if so much relocation would make a person lonely.

The Eiffel Tower rose in front of them, and Alastair gestured at it. "Have you been up there yet?"

"I have," Thomas answered. "The view is stunning."

"What do you think of the view from here?" Alastair asked.

Thomas had the distinct feeling that a trap was being laid for him, but he wasn't sure why, or how to avoid stepping into it. "I think it's a fascinating structure," he said. "There's nothing like it."

Alastair gave a mirthless chuckle. "Indeed there isn't. In fact, many Parisians are horrified by it. They find it ugly, hideous even, and they call it 'Eiffel's folly.'"

Thomas looked up at the tower again. The sun was sinking, burnishing the metal with an orange-pink glow. For a moment it put him in mind of the soaring *adamas* towers that protected the Shadowhunter capital of Alicante, the way they caught the light of the setting sun and held it a little longer than one expected. "It isn't ugly," he said. "It's just unusual."

Alastair looked satisfied. "Quite right. Gustave Eiffel is a genius, and I feel certain he shall one day be appreciated. Sometimes you have to stand back and let people do what they are good at, even if it seems like madness at the time."

They had dinner together at a bistro nearby, which Thomas thought was fairly decent, but Alastair described as "indifferent." They talked late into the night; they closed down the restaurant while everyone else left and they were still talking: about books, travel, music, history. Thomas told Alastair that he planned to get a tattoo of a compass rose on the inside of his arm. He hadn't told anyone else that, and Alastair seemed curious.

"Where on your arm?" he asked, and when Thomas showed him, Alastair ran his fingers over the spot, unselfconsciously, his fingertips tracing a path from the sensitive skin of Thomas's inner wrist to the crook of his elbow.

Thomas sat stunned and shivering, though he was hot all over. Alastair didn't seem to notice, only took his hand back and asked the waiter for the bill, which he paid. Alastair refused to tell Thomas where he was staying, but he told Thomas to meet him at a certain address the next afternoon, for a surprise.

Fifteen minutes after the meeting time, Thomas decided that Alastair was not coming, and was probably somewhere laughing about it, but Alastair did in fact appear, and even apologized for his lateness. He led Thomas to the doors of the Théâtre Robert-Houdin.

"I know we're supposed to avoid mundane things," said Alastair, "but you must see this. It's a film. A moving picture! This one is the latest. It's called *Le Voyage dans la Lune*."

Even Thomas could translate this, and for seventeen minutes they marveled together at what the mundanes had done—made pictures move, like a theater but in images projected onto a screen. There was a narrator who, Thomas supposed, told the story, but he couldn't follow it at all. He enjoyed it anyway, watching these mundanes in their strange costumes climb into a large metal box like an artillery shell, go to the moon, and be chased away by strange creatures already living there.

"Do you think it's real?" he said to Alastair as they walked out, blinking in the sudden light of the daytime.

"What? No, don't be stupid," Alastair said, pushing a lock of dark hair behind his ears. People always fussed over blond hair, like Matthew's, as if it were special, but privately Thomas thought dark hair and eyes were much more striking. "It's like a play, or a magic trick. That's what mundanes do; they can't do magic, so they play tricks that look like magic, but it isn't really."

Alastair said goodbye to him at the end of the lane; he said he was leaving Paris the next day, but he continued to refuse to tell Thomas why he was there or where he was going or why he was leaving the next day. Thomas supposed that they weren't, after all, friends, though he had enjoyed the time they'd spent together. He wasn't fully sure what a friend was, if it wasn't someone you enjoyed spending time with.

The whole trip had seemed disconnected and dreamlike. Alastair had come from nowhere and now returned to nowhere, and Thomas had no idea when they would next see each other, or how they would act when they did. Were they now friends? Had they been friends these past few days?

"I return to Spain in a couple of days myself," Thomas said.

Alastair gave a little chuckle. "It's odd that you came here from Madrid. Like taking a vacation from a vacation."

"I suppose," said Thomas. Then he frowned. "No, it isn't odd. A travel year isn't a vacation. It's an assignment to a post. Do you have to snipe at everything?"

Alastair looked startled. "I'm sorry," he said after a long moment. "I don't mean anything by it."

He seemed worried in that moment, and human and vulnerable in a way that made Thomas want to—well, he wasn't sure what he wanted to do, but he stuck out his hand to Alastair, who stared at it for a moment, then slowly took it.

His hand was warm and calloused against Thomas's, and Thomas remembered the feel of Alastair's fingers on the inside of his arm and tried not to change expression. They shook.

Alastair had not asked Thomas about his friends or his family. Thomas hadn't asked Alastair, either. For these days it had been as though nobody else existed in the entire world.

"Well," Thomas said. "Goodbye, Carstairs."

"Goodbye, Lightwood. Try not to get any taller. You're starting to be off-putting in the other direction."

Thomas watched Alastair walk away and waited for him to turn around one last time, but Alastair never looked back as he turned the corner and disappeared.

10

LOYALTY BINDS

Close, side by side, from morn till night,
Kissing and dalliance their delight,
Whilst thou from human solace flying
With unrequited love art dying.
—Nizami Ganjavi, *Layla and Majnun*

The proprietor would not let Lucie up to the Merry Thieves' private rooms at the Devil Tavern, so she was reduced to sending a message through Polly, the werewolf barmaid. She sat in an uncomfortable wooden chair and fumed as a mixture of Downworlders and magicians stared at her curiously: a small, bonneted girl with Nephilim runes, clutching an axe. In the corner, a kelpie who seemed to be marinating in a tank of gin gave her a beady look.

"Drain of pale?" inquired a wild-haired vampire, offering her a half-drunk bottle of gin.

"She doesn't drink." It was Thomas, glowering. The vampire shrank back. Christopher appeared at Thomas's shoulder, blinking.

"I knew you'd be here," said Lucie triumphantly.

"We very nearly weren't," said Christopher. "We decided to use the laboratory upstairs instead of at Grosvenor Square since

Matthew and James weren't going to be here to be bothered or blown up—"

Thomas shushed him. "Christopher, enough. Lucie, what's going on? Did something happen?"

After dragging the two of them outside, Lucie did her best to explain the situation without mentioning Jesse. She blamed Jessamine instead, and a gossip network between ghosts that she had invented on the spot. Fortunately, neither Christopher nor Thomas was the suspicious type.

"We need Matthew, and he's bloody gone off to Anna's," said Thomas, after telling her the little they knew—the letter that had come for James at Matthew's house, his determination to meet Grace, the time of the meeting set for ten o'clock. "He'll know where James has gone. James said it was where the two of them used to practice balance."

"But what if we're too late?" said Christopher, vibrating with anxiety.

Lucie checked the clock that hung before the church of St. Dunstan-in-the-West, across the dark line of Fleet Street. They were quite near the Institute here. She could see its distinctive spire rising above the roofs of London. "Nine o'clock," she said. "One of you must have a carriage. We'll go to Anna's."

Which was how they found themselves a quarter of an hour later on Percy Street, Thomas helping Lucie down from his family's Victoria. The street was empty of pedestrians, though there were lights on in many windows. Lucie made out a shape sitting on Anna's stairs in the dark. She felt no surprise—ladies were always making cakes of themselves on Anna's doorstep.

Then Lucie made out broad shoulders on the silhouette and realized that the person on Anna's doorstep was a man.

He bolted upright, and the light from the arc lamps fell on him. On Percy Street, the streetlights were older and less reliable, their fierce yellow burn stripping the world down to harsh lines. Lucie saw bright hair and a scowling face.

"*Alastair?*" Thomas sounded astonished.

Christopher groaned as Alastair Carstairs raced down the street toward them, a whirlwind in an unbuttoned town coat. Beneath the coat his waistcoat was disarranged, and one side of his high wing-tip collar was askew.

"You've lost your hat, Alastair," said Lucie.

Alastair said, "I have lost my *sister!*"

Lucie went cold. "What do you mean? Has something happened to Cordelia?"

"I don't bloody know, do I?" said Alastair. "I let her go take tea with Anna Lightwood and now I return to pick her up at the agreed-upon time and they are both *gone.* I should never have left her alone with—"

"Be very careful what you say about Anna," said Christopher. Lucie thought she ought to have found it funny: Christopher, who was never angry, speaking in those icy tones to Alastair. But somehow, it was not funny at all.

Alastair advanced upon Christopher dangerously, but Thomas caught his arm as he went by. Lucie watched with great satisfaction as Alastair was brought to a complete standstill, without Thomas having to exert any particular effort. The muscles of Alastair's arm tensed beneath his coat sleeve as he strained against Thomas's grip. Alastair was tall enough, and looked strong enough, but he couldn't make any headway.

"Steady, Alastair," said Thomas. "I know you are worried about your sister. We are worried about James. Better we discuss setting matters right than brawl in public."

Alastair tilted his chin to meet Thomas's eyes, the line of his jaw a hard slash. "Let me loose," he snarled. "And cease constantly addressing me by my first name. You are not a scrubby schoolboy trailing after me any longer."

Thomas, his cheeks flaming red, whipped his hand back as if he'd been burned.

"Stop it!" Lucie snapped. Thomas had only been trying to be kind. "Matthew is most likely with Anna and Cordelia. He can chaperone—"

Alastair's expression went flat. "You think I would be relieved to hear she's with *Matthew*? You think I don't know a drunk when I see one? Believe me, I do. If he puts Cordelia in harm's way—"

There was the sudden and welcome rattle of wheels on stony road. They all whirled to see the Consul's carriage rolling up to Anna's house. The carriage door opened and disgorged Cordelia and Matthew, who was holding a rolled-up piece of velvet.

The two of them froze at the sight of the visitors. "What are you doing here?" Matthew said. "Has something happened to Barbara and the others?"

"No," Thomas said hastily. "Nothing like that. But it is urgent. James is in danger."

James walked through the night from the King's Road toward the Thames. Matthew had often taken him on impromptu tours of Chelsea, past Queen Anne–style buildings with their grand sweeps of stone steps and terra-cotta panels turning gold in the sunshine, pointing out the residences of famous poets and artists who had lived scandalous lives. Now the lit windows of the houses shone dimly through a heavy mist, which grew heavier as James approached the river.

The riverside at Chelsea Embankment was a promenade under plane trees heavy with leaves, visible only as dark clouds above James's head, their wet trunks illuminated by the ghostly globes of the cast-iron lampposts that lined the river's edge. The Thames, beyond the river wall, was barely distinguishable in the thick fog:

only the sound of a petrol-powered police boat chugging past and the gleams of a bobby's lantern on its wake betrayed the river's presence.

James was early. He started walking slowly toward the arch of Battersea Bridge, trying to quell his impatience and worry. *Grace.* He recalled their kiss in the park, the inchoate agony that had risen up inside him. As if he were being stabbed through with a needle. A premonition of demons, perhaps, the unknown danger so close, the shadow realm just touching this one. It was hard to know, but then it was hard to know anything that had to do with Grace. There were times when he thought of her that he felt such pain that all his bones seemed strung on a single wire, and he imagined that if the wire was pulled taut, it would kill him.

"How much is love meant to hurt?" he had asked his father once.

"Oh, terribly," his father had said with a smile. "But we suffer for love because love is worth it."

Suddenly she was there, as if she had appeared between one moment and another, standing beneath an ornate triple-headed lamppost at the near end of the bridge: a small, misty figure in the fog, dressed as she always was in light colors, her face a pale moon in the lamplight. James broke into a run, and she dashed down the steps of the bridge toward where he stood on the embankment.

When they reached each other, she threw her arms around him. Her hands were cool against the back of his neck, and he felt dizzy and assailed by memories: the crumbling walls of Blackthorn Manor, the shadows in the forest where they'd sat and talked together, her hand fastening the silver bracelet around his wrist. . . .

James drew away enough to look down into her face. "What happened?" he said. "Your letter said you were in danger."

She dropped a hand now to circle his wrist, her fingers sliding over the band of metal as if to make sure it was still there. Her fingers pressed against his pulse point. "Mama is mad with rage. I don't know what she will do. She told Charles—"

"I know what she told Charles," he said. "Please tell me you were not worried about *me*, Grace."

"You came to the house to see me," she said. "Did you know that Cordelia was there?"

He hesitated. How could he say that he hadn't come to the house to see her? That there had been a moment—a terrible moment—when Cordelia had mentioned that Grace was in the house, and he'd realized he had not thought of her? How was it possible to feel such agony when someone's name was mentioned, yet forget them in duress? He recalled Jem having told him that stress could do terrible things to one's mind. Surely that was all it was.

"I didn't know until I arrived and saw her and Lucie," he said. "I gather they wanted to see that you were all right. When I came, I heard the noises in the greenhouse, and—" He broke off with a shrug. He hated lying to Grace. "I saw the demon."

"You were being brave, I know, but Mama does not see it that way. She thinks you came only to humiliate her and remind the world of her father's misdeeds."

James badly wanted to kick a lamppost. "Let me talk to her. We could sit down, all of us, my father and you and your mother—"

"James!" Grace looked almost furious for a moment. "What my mother would do to me if I even suggested such a thing—" She shook her head. "No. She watches everything I do. I was barely able to get out tonight. I had thought that coming to London might soften her toward you, but she has become harder than ever. She says the last time Herondales were at Chiswick House, her father and husband died. She says she will not let you destroy us."

Tatiana is utterly mad, James thought helplessly. He had not realized it had gone so much beyond spite. "Grace, what are you saying?"

"She says she will bring me back to Idris. That she was wrong to let me attend parties and events that you and your sister would be at, and the Lightwoods—she says that I will be corrupted and ruined. She will lock me away, James, for the next two years. I will not see you, not be able to write to you—"

"That is the danger you meant," he said softly. He understood. Such loneliness would seem like danger to Grace. It would seem like death. "Then come to us at the Institute," he said. "The Institute is *there* to provide sanctuary to Nephilim in distress. My parents are kind people. We would protect you from her—"

Grace shook her head hard enough to dislodge her small, flower-trimmed hat. "My mother would only petition to have the Clave return me to her, and they would do it as I am not eighteen yet."

"You don't know that. My parents have influence within the Clave—"

"If you truly love me," she said, her gray eyes flaring, "then you will marry me. Now. We must elope. If we were mundanes, we could run to Gretna Green and marry, and nothing could tear us apart. I would belong to you, and not to her."

James was stunned. "But we are not mundanes. Their marriage ceremony would not be considered valid by the Clave. Marry me in a Shadowhunter ceremony, Grace. You don't need her permission—"

"We cannot do that," Grace protested. "We cannot remain in the Shadowhunter world where my mother can reach us. We must escape her influence, her ability to punish us. We must be married in Gretna and if needs be, we will let our Marks be stripped."

"Let our Marks be stripped?" James went cold all over. Having your Marks stripped was the most severe punishment a Shadowhunter could endure. It meant exile and becoming a mundane.

He tried to imagine never seeing his parents again, or Lucie, or Christopher or Thomas. Having the bond that tied him to Matthew severed, like having his right hand sliced off. Becoming a mundane and losing everything that made him a Shadowhunter. "Grace, *no*. That isn't the answer."

"It isn't the answer for *you*," she said coolly, "for you have always been a Shadowhunter. I have never been trained, never borne but a few Marks. I know nothing of the history, I have no warrior partner nor friends—I might as well have been raised a mundane!"

"In other words," said James, "you would be losing nothing, and I would be losing everything."

Grace stepped out of James's arms. Pain took her place, the ache of being without her. It was physical, inexpressible, and unexplainable. It was simply what it was: when she was not there, he felt it like a wound.

"You would not be losing *me*," said Grace.

"I don't want to lose you," he said, as steadily as he could through the pain. "But we have only to wait a little while and we can be together without also losing everything else."

"You don't *understand*," Grace cried. "You can't. You don't know—"

"Then *tell me*. What is it? What don't I know?"

Her voice was hoarse. "I must have you do this for me, James," she said. "I must. It is so important. More than you can know. Only say you will. Only say it."

It seemed almost as if she were begging him to say it even if he did not mean it, but what would be the point of that? No. She must want him to mean it. To be willing to do it: risk the end of the only life he knew, risk never seeing any of those he loved again. He closed his eyes and saw, against the backs of his eyelids, the faces of his parents. His sister. Jem. Thomas. Christopher. Matthew. Matthew, who he would be damaging in a way that might never be repaired.

He struggled to say the words, to shape them. When he finally spoke, his voice was as hoarse as if he had been screaming. "No. I cannot do it."

He saw her flinch back. "This is because you did not come to Idris," she said, her lips trembling. "At the beginning of this summer. You—you forgot me."

"I could never have forgotten you. Not after weeks, or months, or years, Grace."

"Any man would marry me," she went on. "Any man would do this if I asked him. But not you. You have to be different." Her mouth twisted. "You are made of different stuff than other men."

James flung up a hand in protest. "Grace, I *do* want to marry you—"

"Not enough." She took a step back from him—then her eyes widened suddenly, and she screamed. James's body moved faster than thought. He flung himself at Grace and they both hit the pavement hard. Grace gasped and pressed herself against the river wall as a demon shot past them, a hairbreadth away.

And it *was* a demon. A dark, twisted shape like a mangled tree root, eyeless and noseless but with thorn-sharp brown teeth, its body coated with black slime. It had no wings, but long, bent legs like a frog's: it sprang at them again, and this time James yanked a blade from his belt and flung it. Runes flashed across the blade like fire as it sailed through the air and struck, nearly blowing apart the demon's chest. Ichor splattered, and it vanished back to its own dimension.

Grace had scrambled to her feet; he pulled her up the steps and onto the bridge, for a better vantage point. "A Cerberus demon," she said, blinking. "But it was dead—the one in the greenhouse was dead—that's why I thought I could leave—" She sucked in her breath. "Oh, God. There are more of them coming."

She thrust out her hands as if she could push them away. They were coming, indeed: dark shapes were appearing through the fog from the middle of the bridge, crawling and leaping like hellish frog-monsters, slithering and slipping across the wet road. As one hopped toward them, it shot out a long, black, sticky tongue, snatched up an unfortunate pigeon, and deposited the bird into its fanged mouth.

James fired off throwing knives: one, two, three times. Every time, a demon fell. He pressed a knife into Grace's hand, his eyes entreating her—she backed up against the railing of the bridge, the blade gripped in her shaking hand. A demon reached for her and she stabbed out; it made an eerie howling sound as black-red ichor streamed from its shoulder. It hopped away from her, hissing, and lunged again. She ducked. James flung a knife and destroyed the thing, but he knew he was nearly out of blades. When they were gone, he would have only one weapon left: a seraph blade.

It would not be enough to protect himself and Grace. Nor could they run. The demons would easily catch them.

Two creatures dived for them. James hurled his last blade, dispatching one Cerberus demon in a rain of ichor. The other fell beside it, cloven in two by a dainty throwing axe.

James froze. He knew that axe.

Whirling, he saw Lucie running full tilt toward him from the road. And she was not alone.

Cordelia was there, Cortana gleaming in her hand. Matthew was beside her, armed with Indian *chalikars*: circular throwing knives edged with razor-sharp steel. Then came Christopher with two crackling seraph blades and Thomas, wielding his *bolas*. One flick of the ropes, and one twist of Thomas's powerful arm, and a demon sailed clear off the bridge and into the river.

Alastair Carstairs was also with them. As James stared, he leaped onto the iron railing of the bridge, balancing just as James and Matthew had once done in practice. A long-bladed spear was in his hand. Two sweeps sliced one of the creatures in half. It exploded into nothingness, splattering Alastair with ichor, which struck James as a positive development on two fronts. Alastair leaped down from the railing with a disgusted noise, and charged into the fray.

As the Shadowhunters spread out around them, a cry rose from the demons—a thick, clogged sound. If a corpse rotting in the dirt had a sound, James thought, that was what it would have been. He sprang backward, swung around, and delivered a spinning kick to an oncoming demon. There was a blur of gold, and the demon vanished; James looked up to see Cordelia standing over him, Cortana in her hand. Its blade was smeared with demon blood.

There was no time to thank her. Another demon lunged; James seized his seraph blade. "*Zerachiel!*" he cried, and the blade became a wand of fire.

His friends were in the thick of battle—save Grace, who had backed away, clutching the dagger. James spared a bitter thought for Tatiana, who had never been willing to let Grace train to fight, before spinning to fend off a reaching demon. Before he could, a crackling seraph blade sliced sideways into the creature's flesh. It hopped back, hissing like a pot on the boil, leaving James with a clear line of sight to Christopher. He stood holding the seraph blade, which sputtered like a frying potato.

"Christopher," said James, "what *is* that thing?"

"A seraph blade! I have tried to enhance it with electricity!"

"Does that work?"

"Not at all," confessed Christopher, just as a demon flew shrieking at his face. He stabbed it, but his seraph blade leaped with an erratic line of fire. Lucie and Thomas were both there before the demon could touch Christopher, Lucie's axe and Thomas's *bolas* almost meeting in the creature's flesh. It winked out of existence, but another took its place immediately, rising above them like a menacing cloud.

Abandoning the seraph blade, Christopher seized a dagger from the inside of his waistcoat and stabbed it into the creature. It staggered back, just at the moment that a long spear soared through the fog and slammed into it. It folded like a letter and vanished, leaving a smear of ichor behind.

James looked over wildly and saw Alastair Carstairs, holding a matching spear in his left hand and looking thoughtfully at the spot from which the demon had just vanished.

"You're carrying spears?" James demanded.

"I never leave the house without my spears!" cried Alastair, causing them all to stare, even Grace.

James had questions, but no chance to ask them. He heard his sister shout, and he dashed forward only to find Lucie and Cordelia fighting back-to-back, a dagger in Lucie's hand and Cortana in Cordelia's. Cortana formed a wide golden sweep, and every creature who managed to sneak past Cordelia's guard, Lucie stabbed. Matthew stood atop the railing, hurling one *chalikar* after another to provide cover for the girls.

A demon loomed suddenly behind Thomas, whose *bolas* was wrapped around another demon: possibly around its throat, though with these creatures it was hard to tell.

"*Lightwood!*" shouted Alastair. "Behind you!"

James knew it was Alastair, because nobody else would be such a fool as to shout that in the middle of a fight. Of course Christopher turned, and of course Thomas, who the shout was aimed at, did not. James dived for Thomas, rolling on the ground to reach him faster, just as the demon lunged. Its teeth and claws raked Thomas's arm, drawing blood. There was no room for Thomas to use his *bolas*. He yelled and punched the demon: it staggered and James, rising to his feet, stabbed it through the back.

But there was no time to rest: more demons had come. Matthew leaped down from the railing and ran toward them. He threw himself to the ground and slid the last few feet across the wet pavement—a great sacrifice for Matthew, who loved his clothes—hurling a *chalikar* into the mass of demons. One went down, but there seemed a dozen others. Alastair was hurling spears with deadly accuracy, Cordelia was laying about her with Cortana like a warrior goddess. They were all fighting well, and yet—

The largest demon rose up in front of James. Without a second's hesitation, he plunged his seraph blade into the creature. Ichor splashed black against his hand, spattering the ground at his feet. The demon gurgled and seemed to crumple, its froglike legs giving out under it. James raised his blade to dispatch it, just as it looked up at him with its deadly black eyes.

He saw himself reflected in those eyes as if they were mirrors. He saw his own black hair, his pale face, the gold of his pupils. He saw the same expression he had seen on the face of the Deumas in the alleyway near Fleet Street.

Recognition.

"*Herondale boy,*" the demon said, in a voice like the last hiss of dying fire in a grate. "*I know you. I know all about you. The blood of demons burns in your veins. Why would you slay those who worship your mother's father? Why destroy your own kind?*"

James froze. He could see several of the others twist to look over at him: Matthew looked furious, the others horrified. Lucie had her hand over her mouth. Alastair, who stood the closest to him, was staring with wide dark eyes.

James exhaled a shuddering breath. "I am not your kind," he said.

"*You do not know what you are.*"

Enough, James thought. *This is enough.* "If you worship my grandfather," he said savagely, "then *go*, in his name. Not back to Chiswick House—back to the dimension you came from."

The demon hesitated, and as it did, all the other demons went still. Every figure at the riverside was turned toward James.

"We will go, then, as you say, to show that we honor your blood," said the demon. "But there is one condition. If you or your friends speak a word of what happened here, tonight, to any member of the Clave, we will return. And your families will pay in blood and death for your betrayal."

"Don't you dare—!" James began.

The demon grinned. "In the name of Hell's most cunning prince," it said, in a voice so low only James could hear it.

Then it vanished—they all vanished. As quickly as the world had exploded into motion and noise, it went still again. James could hear the river, the harsh breath of Alastair nearby, the pounding of his own heart.

He dropped his still-burning blade to the ground. He saw Lucie and Cordelia lower their weapons. Thomas and Matthew staggered to their feet; there was a cut along Matthew's face, and Thomas's shirt was torn, his arm bleeding badly.

They were all staring at James. He felt numb.

He had known his grandfather was a Greater Demon. But Princes of Hell were another matter. They were fallen angels. As powerful as Raziel, but evil and rotten to the core.

Hell's most cunning prince. He couldn't help but look at Lucie, but it was clear she hadn't heard the demon's final words: she was smiling and saying something to Cordelia.

Demons lied. Why should Lucie have to torment herself over a possible untruth? His mind raced ahead: he had to talk to Uncle Jem again, as soon as possible. Jem was the one who had been looking for their grandfather. Jem would know what to do.

It was Christopher who broke the silence. "What just happened?"

"Demons vanished," said Matthew, dabbing blood from his face. "The leader seemed to feel it was an old friend of James's grandfather."

"Oh, the demony grandfather?" said Christopher.

"Yes, obviously the demony one, Christopher," said James.

"The other one's Welsh," said Thomas, as if this explained things. He directed this statement in Alastair and Cordelia's direction.

"No need to explain about Herondale," said Alastair, with an unpleasant smile. "I imagine this happens to him fairly often."

Cordelia stepped on his foot.

Grace had emerged from the shadows. She walked toward the rest of the group, her hands clasped in front of her, her face white and stiff. "I'm sorry, I don't know how to fight—"

"It's all right," James said, "it's all right, we'll get you trained properly—"

"James! Grace!" It was Lucie. She gestured toward the road; a second later James heard jingling, and saw an old-fashioned pony trap emerging from the fog, drawn by two scrawny brown horses. Sitting in the trap was Tatiana Blackthorn.

She pulled up short and leaped down from the carriage. As always, she presented a bizarre appearance: she was wearing a costume with full skirts and fussy lace, a dress from another age made for a much younger and plumper girl. On her head was a hat piled high with false fruit and stuffed birds. It trembled with her rage as she raked the group with her furious gaze, which came to rest on her daughter.

"Grace," she snapped. "Get into the trap. Now."

Grace turned to James; her face was white. In a low voice, he said, "You do not need to do as she says. Come back to the Institute with me. I beg of you."

Grace's face was still tearstained, but her expression had closed like a bank vault. "James. I cannot. Walk me to the carriage, please."

James hesitated.

"Please," she said. "I mean what I say."

Reluctantly, James held out his arm for Grace to take. He saw Tatiana's lips tighten into a thin line. James waited for her to snap, but she stayed silent: she had clearly not expected so many Shadowhunters there. And so many from the families she hated—Herondales, Lightwoods, Carstairs . . . she would wish to be gone as soon as possible, James suspected.

She glared daggers at James as he walked to the carriage, supporting Grace on his arm. He helped her in, and she sank back against the seat, her eyes closing wearily. James wished he could say something to her about the argument they'd had earlier. He and Grace had never argued before. He wanted to beg her not to go back to Chiswick House, but he suspected it would only make things worse for her if he did.

"I will write to you tomorrow," he began.

"No," Grace said through white lips. "No. I require some time, James. I will write to you."

"That's enough," hissed Tatiana, shooing James away from the carriage. "Leave my daughter alone, Herondale. I don't need you luring her into trouble—"

"The only trouble we encountered was *your* family's Cerberus demons," said James in a low, furious tone. "I suggest you cease with your threats, unless you wish me to tell the Clave about them."

He couldn't tell anyone, of course, given the demon's threat, but Tatiana didn't know that. Not that it mattered. A low chuckle bubbled its way up from her throat. "*My* demons?" she echoed. "And where are they now, Herondale?"

"Dead," James said shortly. "We killed them."

"How impressive," she said. "Tattle away, boy. I'll tell the Clave Grace raised the demons herself. I'll tell them she's deep in black magic studies up to her pretty little ears. I'll turn her loose and throw her back on their mercy with her reputation stained forever. I'll ruin her life, if you want to play that game." She jabbed a finger toward his chest. "You *care*, Herondale. That is your weakness."

James stepped back in revulsion as Tatiana clambered into the trap. A moment later it was rattling off down the road, the ponies snorting and the reins jangling.

There was a long and awkward silence as the group of Shadow-hunters watched the Blackthorn carriage vanish into the fog.

"Well," said Alastair at last. "I think it's time for Cordelia and I to be going."

"I cannot go yet," said Cordelia. She held out her arm and saw her brother's eyes widen. A long, bloody cut ran from her elbow to her wrist. She had barely felt it during the battle, but it was beginning to sting. "I need a healing rune. If I return home like this, Mother will faint."

"Several of us are wounded," said Christopher. "Unless we want to explain what happened here, and it seems that would be a bad idea, we should probably apply *iratzes*." He turned to Thomas. "I will do yours."

"Please don't," said Thomas. Christopher did not always have the best of luck with runes.

"Oh, bloody hell, I'll do it," said Alastair, and stomped heavily over to Thomas's side. Thomas watched in what seemed to be shock as Alastair produced a stele and began to draw on the bare skin of his arm where his shirt had been torn.

Beside Cordelia, Lucie produced her stele with a flourish. "Our first healing rune!" she announced, putting the tip of the stele to Cordelia's wrist. "A historic moment for a pair of soon-to-be-famous *parabatai*."

"I hate to seem ungrateful for the assistance," said James. "But what on earth brought you all here? How did you know what was going to happen?"

"I heard about the Cerberus from Jess—Jessamine," said Lucie, putting the finishing touches on Cordelia's rune. They were both leaning against the low wall that ran along the Embankment. "Ghosts, they gossip." She repeated for James the story she'd told the rest of them on the way to Chelsea, finishing with: "So, it seems the demon you killed in the greenhouse had time to multiply, and the new demons came looking for Grace when she left Chiswick."

"There were certainly a lot of them," said Cordelia. "Much worse than just the one in the greenhouse."

"Perhaps they all had secret assignations with Grace," said Lucie.

Alastair snorted. "That Blackthorn woman must be mad, letting Cerberus demons run wild in her shrubberies," he said, putting his stele away. Thomas touched his own arm with a sort of wondering look; his wound was already beginning to close up. Alastair might be snappish, but he was handy with a stele.

James and Matthew had sat down on the ground so James could properly steady Matthew's face with his hand. He drew an *iratze* lightly on his cheek while Matthew squirmed and complained. "It's hard to say how much she knew," James said. "I'm sure she was aware of the original demon in the greenhouse, but likely not its vengeful progeny."

"She knew enough to come here," Christopher pointed out. "Though she may just have been following Grace."

James looked thoughtful; Cordelia could not help but wonder what Tatiana had said to him by the pony trap. He had looked stunned, as if she had hit him in the face.

"They disappeared because you told them to, didn't they?" Cordelia said.

"So it seems." James was examining Matthew's cheek, apparently considering his rune work. Satisfied, he sat back. Matthew produced a flask from his pocket with a relieved air, unscrewed the top, and took a long drink. "They went back to whatever dimension

Cerberus demons hail from. In the name of my grandfather."

He sounded bitter.

"How nice for you to be related to such an important sort of demon," said Alastair dryly.

"If it actually cared that James was related to an 'important' demon, it should have said something to me, too," said Lucie. "I *am* his sister. I do not appreciate being overlooked."

James smiled—which, Cordelia suspected, had been Lucie's aim. He had a perfectly lethal dimple that flashed when he smiled. Such things should be illegal.

"They're loyal to the Blackthorn family, in their horrid sort of way," said Lucie thoughtfully. "That's why they wanted us not to say anything about what happened tonight."

"Ah," said Alastair. "Because the Clave wouldn't look too kindly on the Blackthorns breeding a pack of Cerberus demons and letting them chase after Herondale, even though he is very irritating."

"I told you, Benedict Lightwood's the one that bred them," Lucie said crossly.

"Unpleasant as all that was," Matthew said, "there is something comforting about fighting the ordinary kind of demon under cover of darkness, rather than poisonous ones that appear during the day."

"Oh!" said Cordelia. "That reminds me. We should tell them what Hypatia said, Matthew. That we could speak to Ragnor Fell about the demons in the park."

Everyone started to sputter questions. Matthew held up a hand. "Yes, we spoke to Hypatia Vex at the Hell Ruelle. She said she would send Ragnor a message. It is hardly a sure thing."

"Perhaps, but Anna was right," said Cordelia. "We must speak to more Downworlders regardless. There was much talk of Magnus Bane—"

"Ah, Magnus Bane," said Matthew. "My personal hero."

"Indeed, you once described him as 'Oscar Wilde if he had magic powers,'" said James.

"Magnus Bane threw a party in Spain I attended," said Thomas. "It was a little difficult, since I did not know a soul. I got rather drunk."

Matthew lowered the flask with a grin. "Is that when you got *your tattoo?*"

Lucie clapped her hands. "The boys joke about the tattoo Thomas got in Spain, but Thomas will never let me see it. Isn't that the meanest thing you ever heard, Cordelia? I am a *writer*. I believe I should have the experience of studying a tattoo at close quarters."

"I believe you shouldn't," said Thomas, with conviction.

"Is the problem that it is in an unmentionable place?" asked Lucie.

"No, Lucie," said Thomas, with a hunted air.

"I'd like to see it," said Alastair, in a surprisingly quiet voice.

Thomas hesitated, then unbuttoned the shirtsleeve of his unwounded arm, and rolled it up to his elbow. Everyone leaned forward. Against the pale skin on the inside of Thomas's muscular arm was a gray-and-black tracery of a compass. North, south, east, and west were delineated by blades like the points of daggers, and at the heart of the compass, unfurling dark petals, was a rose.

Cordelia had thought a tattoo would be rather more like their Marks, but it reminded her of something else instead. It was ink, the way books and poems were made of ink, telling a permanent story.

Lucy applauded. Alastair made an odd sort of noise. He was looking away, as if the sight of Thomas bothered him.

"I think it is lovely, Thomas," Cordelia said. "North points up your arm, along the vein that runs to your heart."

"So does that mean you're close friends with Magnus Bane, Thomas?" said Lucie. "Can you reach out to him for help?"

"He never even made an appearance at the party," said Thomas, rolling his sleeve down. "But reaching out to Ragnor Fell is a good idea."

"As long as he will keep all this to himself," said Christopher, pushing his spectacles up the bridge of his nose. "We cannot tell any Shadowhunters what happened here tonight. We all heard what that demon said."

There was a murmur of assent, broken by Alastair. "Cordelia and I must depart," he said. "As for your little secrets, you cannot trust demons. It does not matter what they claim."

Cordelia knew that tone in his voice. "Alastair, you must promise to keep everything that happened here tonight to yourself."

"Why should I promise?" Alastair demanded.

"Because even if demons are liars, the risk is too great," said Cordelia, a little desperately. "The demon said it would target our families if any of us spoke of what happened tonight. Think of Mother and Father."

Alastair looked mutinous.

"If you do not promise," Cordelia added, "I will not go home with you. I will stay out all night and be utterly ruined. I will have to marry Thomas or Christopher."

"What ho," said Christopher, looking surprised. Thomas smiled.

"If you have any concern for our family, you must promise," Cordelia said. "Please, Alastair."

There was a murmur all around; Lucie looked worried. James was looking at Cordelia with an expression she could not decipher.

Alastair's eyes narrowed. "Very well, I promise," he muttered. "Now come away at once. We have much to discuss when we return home."

It was nearing midnight when the five of them—Lucie, James, Matthew, Thomas, and Christopher—finally returned to the

Institute. Lucie regarded the bright-lit windows curiously as they spilled into the courtyard. It was unusual at this hour for all the lamps to be on.

James lifted a finger to his lips before pushing open the wide front doors—they opened to the touch of any Shadowhunter's hand—and led the way inside and up the stairs.

The first-floor hallway shimmered with witchlights. The door of the parlor stood open, and the sound of a Welsh song rang out into the corridor.

Nid wy'n gofyn bywyd moethus,
Aur y byd na'i berlau mân:
Gofyn wyf am galon hapus,
Calon onest, calon lân.

James and Lucie exchanged a worried look. If Will was singing, that meant he was in a sociable mood and would seize them the moment he saw them and begin reminiscing about Wales and ducks.

"Perhaps," said James in a whisper, "we should all swiftly exit and ascend to an upper chamber using a window and a grappling hook."

Tessa appeared in the doorway of the drawing room. At the sight of all five of them, she raised her eyebrows. Lucie and James exchanged a glance: too late for the grappling hook.

Lucie stepped forward and slid an arm around her mother's waist. "Sorry, Mam, we had a late picnic down by the river. Are we in trouble?"

Tessa smiled. "You are all scamps, but I hope you enjoyed your-selves. We can discuss this later. Your father has a guest. Go in and introduce yourselves. I'll just pop up to the infirmary and be back."

James led their expedition into the parlor, Thomas, Matthew, and Christopher all murmuring their greetings to Tessa as they passed. In the parlor, sitting upon two matched gray velvet wing-backed chairs, were Will and a tall green warlock with horns curling in his snowy hair. He wore a dour expression.

Will made the introductions. "Ragnor Fell, my beloved son and daughter. Also a disgraceful pack of home invaders. I think you all know Ragnor Fell, the former High Warlock of London?"

"He taught us in the Academy," Christopher said.

Ragnor Fell glared at him. "By the name of Lilith," he drawled. "Hide the breakables. Hide the whole house. Christopher Lightwood is here."

"Christopher is often here," said James. "The house remains mostly intact."

Will grinned. "Mr. Fell is here on a social call," he said. "Isn't that nice?"

Will had tried to make clear that the Institute's doors were open to Downworlders, but few had ever taken him up on that hospitality. Will and Henry talked often of Magnus Bane, but Bane had been in America Lucie's whole life.

"Mr. Fell expressed a keen interest in Welsh music, so I sang a few songs," said Will. "Also, we had a few glasses of port. We've been enjoying ourselves."

"I have been here for hours," said Ragnor, in a dolorous voice. "There have been many songs."

"I know you enjoyed them," said Will. His eyes were sparkling. Far above them, Lucie heard an odd sound: as if something in the house had tipped over and crashed. Perhaps a lamp.

"I do feel as if I have been to Wales and back," said Ragnor. His eyes lit on Matthew. "The Consul's son," he said. "I remember you. Your mother is a kind woman—has she quite gotten over her illness?"

"That was some years ago," Matthew said. He attempted a smile and failed; Lucie bit her lip. Few knew that Charlotte had been quite ill when Matthew was fifteen, and she had lost a baby she was carrying. Poor Matthew, to be so reminded.

Matthew walked over to the mantel and poured himself a glass of sherry with slightly trembling hands. Lucie saw Will's eyes follow Matthew, but before he could speak, the parlor door opened and Tessa appeared, carrying a lighted taper. Her face was in shadow.

"Will, *bach*," she said in a low voice. "Come with me for a moment; I have something to ask you."

Will sprang to his feet with alacrity. He always did when Tessa was the one who called him away. Lucie knew the love her parents shared was an extraordinary one. It was the kind of love she tried to capture in the pages of her own writing, but she could never find the right words.

As soon as the door shut behind Lucie's parents, Ragnor Fell wheeled on James.

"I see this generation of Shadowhunters has no more sense than the last," he said sharply. "Why are you gallivanting around London town at this time of night when I need to speak with you?"

"What, and interrupt your social call?" said James, grinning. "Father said you were listening to Welsh songs for hours."

"Yes, more's the pity." Ragnor made an impatient gesture. "My friend Hypatia let me know that some young Shadowhunters came to her salon tonight asking questions about unusual demons and hinting at a dire future for us all. She mentioned *your* name." He stabbed a finger in Matthew's direction. "She said she owed you lot some sort of debt and asked if I could help."

"Will you?" Thomas spoke for the first time since they had entered the parlor. "My sister is one of the wounded."

Ragnor looked astonished. "Thomas Lightwood? Lord, you're huge. What *have* the Nephilim been feeding you?"

"I grew a little," Thomas said, impatient. "Can you help Barbara?

The Silent Brothers have put all those injured to sleep, but so far there is no cure."

Thomas gripped the wooden back of a chair, carved to represent crossed seraph blades. His skin was tanned, but he held the chair so hard his hands were white. Ragnor Fell surveyed the room, his pale eyebrows raised.

"The scarcity of demons in London over the past years has not escaped my notice," he said. "I have also heard the rumors that a powerful warlock is behind this absence."

"Do you believe it?" said Lucie.

"No. If we warlocks could easily keep demons out of our cities, we would do it. But it would not require a powerful warlock so much as a corrupt one to play with this kind of magic."

"What do you mean?" said James. "Surely keeping demons away is a good thing, not a bad one."

Ragnor nodded his shaggy head slowly. "One would think," he said. "And yet what we are seeing here is that someone has cleared the minor demons out of London in order to make a path for those even more dangerous." Ragnor hesitated. "Among warlocks, my name is often invoked when dimensional magic is spoken of—the most difficult and unstable kind of magic, the kind that involves other worlds than ours. I have made myself a student of it, and none knows more than I. Demons cannot appear in daylight. It is a rule of nature. And yet. Are there ways to bring demons into this world that would make them impervious to it?"

"Yes?" Lucie hazarded.

Ragnor glared. "Don't expect me to tell you what they are," he said. "Only that they are forbidden by the Spiral Labyrinth, for they involve complex dimensional magic that presents a danger to the fabric of the world itself." He shook his white mane of hair. "I do not have solid information, only rumors and guesses. I would not betray one of my own kind to a member of the Clave unless I knew for certain that they were guilty of a crime, for the Clave would arrest them first and examine the evidence later. But you . . . you are children. Not yet in the Clave. If you were to look into this . . ."

"We won't tell Father anything you don't want us to," James promised. "We won't tell anyone. We swear it on Raziel's name."

"Except Cordelia," said Lucie hurriedly. "She is to be my *parabatai*. I cannot hide things from her. But we will not tell anyone else, and certainly not a single adult."

There was a murmur as the others promised along with her. To swear something, for a Shadowhunter, was a serious thing; to swear on the name of the Angel was even more serious.

Ragnor turned to James. "Few warlocks could perform this magic, and even fewer would be willing. In fact, I can think of only one so corrupt. Emmanuel Gast. Word among the warlocks is, if the price is high enough, there is no work too low for him. I do not know if the rumor is true, but I do know his address."

Ragnor went to the writing desk in the corner of the room and scratched the address down upon a sheet of paper. Lucie stared at the Waterman's gold-embossed fountain pen in Ragnor Fell's heavy hands, an extra joint on each finger making the shadow of his hand upon the page seem almost a claw.

"Thank you," said James, when the warlock was done.

"I don't suppose I need to ask you not to tell Gast who sent you," he said, straightening up from the desk. "If I find out you did, I shall turn you all into a matched set of teacups. As for me, I am going to Capri. My nerves are in a state. If London is to be devoured by demons, I do not wish to be present for the event. Good luck to you all."

This seemed an odd attitude for a former High Warlock, but Lucie kept her mouth shut as Fell made his way to the door. She thought he might leave without another word, but he lingered a moment.

"I do not entirely know how to treat you Herondales," he admitted. "A warlock has never had a child before. I cannot help but wonder: What will you become?"

He looked steadily at James, and then at Lucie. The fire crackled in the grate, but neither of them spoke. Lucie thought of the demon at the bridge, telling James it would honor his blood. Her blood.

Ragnor shrugged.

"So be it," he said, and left.

Lucie dashed over to the writing desk and seized the piece of paper in her hands, then spun around smiling. Thomas and James returned her smile; Thomas with hope, James with weariness. Matthew was gazing bleakly at the glass in his hand.

Then the door opened, and Will and Tessa came in.

Lucie, worried for an instant they had heard some betraying hint of Ragnor Fell's information, tucked the paper quickly into the pocket of her walking dress. Then she caught sight of their faces, and everything else was forgotten.

It was like the end of summer in Idris. One day she and James would be playing in the forest among the green trees and mossy dells of flowers. Then would come an almost imperceptible change in the air and she would know: there would be frost tomorrow.

Thomas backed up, his face turning white beneath his tan. His shoulder struck Matthew's and the glass fell from Matthew's hands. It shattered at their feet, scattering shards across the hearth.

There would be no more waiting for frost, Lucie thought. It was here.

"Thomas, we are so sorry," said Tessa, reaching out her hands. "Your parents are on their way. Barbara has died."

11

TALISMANS AND SPELLS

Knowledge is proud that he has learn'd so much;
Wisdom is humble that he knows no more.
Books are not seldom talismans and spells.
—William Cowper,
"The Task, Book VI: Winter Walk at Noon"

"The *tahdig* is cold." Sona towered in the doorway of the town house, her arms crossed as she glared at her two children. "Risa set supper out more than two hours ago. *Where* have you been?"

"We went to the infirmary at the Institute," lied Alastair, his eyes wide and innocent. He truly was the son of a Persian mother with a temper, Cordelia thought with some amusement. She had patted down her hair and skirts in the carriage as much as she was able, but she was well aware she looked a fright. "We thought we would bring flowers, to show our concern as part of the London community."

Some of the anger went out of Sona's face. "Those poor children in the sickroom," she said. She stood back and ushered them inside. "Come in, then. And take your shoes off before you get mud on the rugs!"

Supper was a swift affair of cold *tahdig* and *khoresh bademjan*. By the end of it, Sona had been convinced that the idea of helping out at the infirmary had been hers. "You are a good boy, Alastair *joon*," she said, kissing him on top of his head as she rose from the table. "And you, too, Cordelia. Though you should not have picked the flowers yourself. Your dress is ruined. So much mud!" She shook her head.

"Good," said Cordelia. "It's a horrid dress."

Sona looked hurt. "When I was your age—" she began. This, Cordelia knew, presaged a story about how when Sona had been a girl, she had been perfectly obedient to her parents, a dutiful Shadowhunter, and had always kept her clothes in pristine condition.

Alastair tossed his napkin onto the table. "Our Layla looks exhausted," he said. "Helping the ill is very tiring. I'll see her upstairs."

There were three floors to the town house, the upper floor given over to Alastair's and Cordelia's bedrooms and a small study. Diamond-paned windows looked over the dark sky above Kensington. Alastair paused at the top of the stairs and leaned against the damask wallpaper. "Let's never talk to those terrible people ever again," he said.

He was twirling one of his Chinese spears between his fingers, its leaf-shaped blade catching the light that seeped up from downstairs. Alastair had a collection of spears, some of which folded up and could be kept in his pockets, several of which were secured in his coat lining.

"I like them," Cordelia said crossly. "All of them."

She could hear her mother singing to herself in her bedroom; a long time ago, Alastair himself had often sung and played the piano. Once they had been a musical family. Once things had been very different. Tonight had reminded Cordelia of when she and her brother were children, and co-conspirators as isolated siblings often were. Of the time before Alastair went to school, and came back so very hard to reach.

"Really?" Alastair inquired. "Which one do you find so agreeable? If it's Herondale, he will never like you better than Miss Blackthorn, and if it's Fairchild, he will never like you better than the bottle."

Cordelia's lips tightened. "Whether you like them or not, they are influential people, and I'd prefer to think you're keeping our father's well-being foremost in your mind."

Alastair snorted. "Your plan is to save Father by making people *like* you?"

"Clearly you have never thought making people like you was important, Alastair, but I am not like that."

Alastair looked startled, but recovered quickly. "You should think less about making people like you, and more about making them *owe* you."

"Alastair—"

But someone was rapping on the door downstairs. The sound rang in the silence. Whoever was outside knocked three times in quick succession, then stopped.

Alastair's expression changed. "We've spoken of this enough. Good night, Cordelia."

Not Layla anymore. *Cordelia.* His expression was stern as he turned to hasten downstairs.

Cordelia reached out and grasped his coat. "Who could be visiting so late? Do you think it is bad news?"

Alastair started, seeming astonished that Cordelia was still present, and his coat slipped through her fingers.

"I know who it is. I will manage the situation. Go to bed at once, Cordelia," Alastair ordered, not meeting her eyes. "If Mother catches you out of bed, there will be the devil to pay and no pitch hot."

He dashed down the steps.

Cordelia leaned over the banister. Two floors down, she could see the encaustic tiles of their hall, the newly painted surfaces portraying yellow starbursts shining through a maze of swords. She saw her brother open the door, and saw the shadow cast on the swords and stars as their visitor walked in. The man removed his hat. With some surprise, Cordelia recognized Charles Fairchild.

Alastair glanced around worriedly, but it seemed clear that both their mother and Risa had gone to sleep. He took Charles's hat and coat, and they headed together toward the drawing room.

Cordelia's heart was pounding. Charles Fairchild. Charles, who had told James not to venture near Grace. Charles, who Matthew clearly did not trust—but who Alastair clearly did.

Alastair had promised her he would not tell James's secrets. He had *promised*.

But he had not wanted to make the promise. Cordelia bit her lip, swore under her breath, and started down the steps. The stairs in their new home were oak, painted gray with a yellow runner up the center and a wrought-iron railing painted gray as well. Cordelia wrestled with her conscience as she ran down them lightly, her stockinged feet making no sound.

There was a back entrance to the drawing room. Cordelia slipped through the dining room, where the plates were still on the table, and down a servants' corridor. At the end of the hall was the door to the drawing room, already slightly ajar. She pressed herself up against it, peering through the crack—she could just see Charles, warming his hands at the fire crackling in the white plaster grate.

His red hair looked dark in the low light, and very orderly. As Cordelia watched, Alastair stepped closer to Charles: now she could see her brother fully. He was running his fingers through his tangled hair in a hopeless attempt to make it lie flat.

"Alastair." Charles turned so his back was to the fire. "Why are you looking a state? What happened?"

"I went to find you earlier today," Alastair said. There was a sulky note in his voice that surprised Cordelia. "My sister was with Anna—I went to your house, and even to your club. Where were you?"

"I was at the Institute, of course. My fiancée remains ill, unless you've forgotten."

"I would be very unlikely," said Alastair coldly, "to forget your fiancée."

In the shadows, Cordelia blinked in confusion. Did Alastair not like Ariadne? She did not recall him mentioning her before.

"Alastair," said Charles, in a warning tone. "We've discussed this."

"You said it would be temporary. A temporary political engagement. But I have spoken with Ariadne, Charles. She very much believes this marriage will happen."

Alastair had been standing close to Charles, so close their shadows touched. Now he turned his back on Charles and walked over to the bookcases. Cordelia tried to move back and nearly stepped on her dress. Fortunately, Alastair stopped before he could have seen her and stared at the books blankly. Cordelia had rarely seen such misery on his face.

"This is not fair to her, Charles," said Alastair. "Or to me."

"Ariadne does not care what I do. Her interests lie elsewhere." Charles paused for the briefest of moments. "She will gratify her parents with a good match, and I will find it useful to be connected to the Inquisitor. If I become Consul, I could do so much good for the Clave, as well as for you. My mother is too sentimental, but I can make our people strong again. It is what I have wanted all my life. You understand. I told you all my hopes in Paris."

Alastair closed his eyes, as if the word "Paris" pained him. "Yes," he said. "But you said—I thought—"

"What did I say? I would not make any false promises. You know how it must be. We are both men of the world."

"I know," said Alastair, opening his eyes. He turned to look at Charles. "It is only that—I love you."

Cordelia inhaled sharply. *Oh, Alastair.*

Alastair's voice cracked as he spoke. Charles's voice cracked too, but his was not the sound of something breaking. It was the sound of a whip.

"You absolutely cannot say that," Charles said. "Not where someone might hear you. You know it, Alastair."

"No one can hear us," said Alastair. "And I have loved you since Paris. I thought you loved me."

Charles said nothing. And for a moment, all Cordelia could think was that she hated Charles Fairchild for hurting her brother. Then she saw the infinitesimal tremble of Charles's hand as he put it in his pocket, and she realized that Charles might be scared too.

Charles took a deep breath and crossed the carpeted floor to Alastair's side. Cordelia could see them both very clearly. Too clearly, perhaps, she thought, as Charles took his hands from his pockets and put them on her brother's shoulders. Alastair's lips parted slightly.

"I do," Charles said. "You know I do."

His hands slid up into Alastair's hair. He was still wearing gloves, his fingers dark against Alastair's pale hair; he drew Alastair in toward him, and their lips met. Alastair made a soft sound, like surrender. He slid an arm around Charles's neck and pulled him down onto the sofa.

They stretched out together, Charles atop Alastair. It was Alastair's turn to bury his hands in Charles's hair, to press against Charles's body and fumble with his waistcoat. Charles's hands were flat against Alastair's chest, and he was kissing Alastair hungrily, over and over—

Cordelia squeezed her eyes shut. This was her brother's life, his business, his very *private* business. Oh, dear, she hadn't come for this *at all*. She could hear soft moans, could hear Alastair whispering to Charles in Persian, endearments she could never have imagined her brother uttering.

There was a gasp. She would risk it, she decided. She would flee, and hopefully they would be too intent on each other to hear her.

Then she heard Charles say, "Alastair. I cannot—I cannot." There was a thumping sound, and Cordelia opened her eyes to see Alastair sitting disheveled on the couch, and Charles standing, straightening his waistcoat. Alastair's jacket was thrown over the back of the sofa. "Not now."

Alastair no longer played music, but he still had a musician's hands. Cordelia watched as those hands lifted, twisted together in a brief instant of pain, and stilled.

"What is wrong, Charles?" he said, his voice husky and rough. "If this is not what you came for, then why are you here?"

"I thought you had accepted the situation with Ariadne," said Charles. "I would not leave you, Alastair. We would still be—what we are. And I thought that you would agree to marry too."

"That I would marry?" Alastair sprang to his feet. "I have told you over and over, Charles, even if I did not have you, I would never marry some poor woman and deceive her as to my love and regard. I have convinced my mother I can be of better use to the family in politics—"

"You will find it difficult to succeed in politics without a wife," said Charles. "And you do not need to deceive a woman."

"Ariadne is an unusual case," said Alastair. "If she did not prefer women, she would be unlikely to be willing to marry you."

Charles stood very still, his eyes fixed on Alastair's face. "And if it were not Ariadne?"

Alastair looked bewildered. "Speak sense, Charles. What do you mean?"

Charles shook his head as if he were clearing away cobwebs. "Nothing," he said. "I am—unsettled. Much has happened this night, all of it bad."

Cordelia tensed. What did he mean? He couldn't possibly know about their encounter with the demons at Battersea Bridge. Had someone else fallen ill?

Charles spoke in a heavy voice. "Barbara Lightwood has died."

Cordelia felt as if she had been punched in the stomach. She heard Alastair as if from a distance, sounding stunned, "Thomas's sister is dead?"

"I wouldn't have expected you to care," said Charles. "I thought you hated those fellows."

"No," said Alastair, surprising Cordelia. "But—Ariadne is all right?"

"She lives still," said Charles. "But Raziel alone knows what will happen. To any of them."

Alastair sat back down. "Perhaps we should leave London. It may not be safe here for Cordelia, for my mother—"

Cordelia felt a jolt of surprise that her brother had thought of her.

Alastair put his head in his hands. *"Nemidoonam,"* he whispered. Charles looked blank, but Cordelia understood him: *I don't know. I don't know what to do.*

"We are Shadowhunters," said Charles, and Cordelia wondered— did he not worry about Matthew falling ill? About Henry? "We do not run, or spend our time in mourning. This is the time to fight and win. The Enclave will need a leader, and with my mother in Idris, now is the time for me to show them my best qualities." He touched Alastair lightly on the shoulder. Alastair looked up, and Cordelia closed her eyes. There was something too personal about the way Alastair looked at Charles, all his defensiveness stripped away.

"I must go," Charles said. "But do not forget, Alastair, that whatever I do, it is with the thought of you ever in my mind."

"Throw that back over here, Alexander," Lucie said in a low voice.

"That" was a small red rubber ball. Lucie's young cousin scooted along the marble floor of the library, but the ball bounced out of his reach and into Lucie's lap.

Alexander looked mutinous. "Not fair," he said. He was tired and fussy, as he had been awake for many hours past his usual bedtime. Lucie wasn't sure what time it was exactly—she was sure many hours had passed since she had learned of Barbara's death—but it all seemed strangely like a bad dream, timeless and imprecise.

Lucie glanced up and frowned. "Jessamine. Don't take the child's ball from him."

"I just want to be included," Jessamine said. She was drifting among the stacks, where Lucie had taken Alexander to amuse him while his parents and hers huddled in conversation. At some point Jessamine had appeared, sensitive to the unsettled feeling inside the Institute. She bobbed near Lucie, her long blond hair unbound and floating.

"Perhaps it is better for them to leave London," Tessa was saying. She and Will sat with Lucie's aunt Cecily and uncle Gabriel at a long table in the center of the big room. Green banker's lamps cast a soft glow over the room. "It will be good for Sophie and Gideon to join Henry and Charlotte in Idris, for they are always a comforting presence. And surely being here at the moment will only remind them of Barbara."

Lucie had seen her uncle Gideon and aunt Sophie only briefly when they had arrived to view Barbara's body and collect Thomas. Both had seemed hollowed out, like puppets in the shapes of her uncle and aunt, going through the motions of what was necessary. Still, they had tried to comfort Oliver, who sat sobbing beside Barbara's still body. She had thrashed and cried out at the last, it seemed, just before Tessa had arrived to find her dead: she had clawed Oliver's hands, and blood stained the white cuffs of his shirt and mixed with his tears.

Oliver, devastated, was to return to York and his parents; Gideon and Sophie, it seemed, were headed to Idris, where Eugenia had collapsed on hearing the news of her sister's death and was not well enough to travel by Portal. Thomas, though, would not be going with them. He had insisted on remaining in London, and would be staying with Cecily and Gabriel at their home in Bedford Square.

"We will take the best possible care of Thomas," said Cecily. "Christopher will be so delighted to have him with us. But I cannot help but wonder if Thomas will regret not going to Idris. Surely it will be painful to be parted from his family at such a time."

"You are also his family," said Will. "Christopher and Thomas are like brothers, Cecy."

"I don't think he'll regret it," said Gabriel. He was a kind uncle, but his aquiline features—like Anna's and Christopher's—made him look sterner than he was. "Thomas is much like Gideon. The type who must have something to do when tragedy strikes. Christopher wishes for his help in working on an antidote—"

"But Kit is just a boy," said Cecily. "He should hardly be expected to accomplish something so monumental."

"There is nothing to say that Christopher and Thomas's efforts will be in vain," said Will. "We must all recall there was a time when the Clave doubted us and doubted Henry, and we prevailed."

"Poor Sophie," said Jessamine unexpectedly. "She was always such a kind girl. Except for that time she hit me over the head with a mirror and tied me to my bed."

Lucie did not inquire further. Jessamine's stories usually ran the gamut from rambling to alarming. Instead she pulled Alexander into her lap and rested her chin atop his head.

"It seems to be the lot of the living to have tragedy visited upon them," Jessamine mused.

Lucie did not point out that the alternative seemed worse. Jessamine never seemed to wish she was alive; she seemed content in her role as ghost guardian. *So different from Jesse,* Lucie thought.

Jesse, who had asked her to keep him a secret, so that his odd half-life would not be discovered and ended by the Clave. Jesse, who seemed to badly want to live.

"We were all very brave then," said Tessa. "I wonder sometimes if it is easier to be brave when one is young, before one knows truly how much there is to lose."

Cecily murmured something in response; Lucie hugged Alexander, who was half-asleep in her arms, tightly. He was a comfort, despite being three years old and fussy. She felt somewhere in the core of her heart the truth of what her mother had just said. And one *should* put truth in books, she thought, but this would never be the sort of thing she put in the pages of *The Beautiful Cordelia*. Books were about experiencing joy. This was the raw and awful stuff of life.

It was much too terrible.

James was sitting at his writing desk, trying to read, but his eyes were skipping over the words on the page. He kept thinking of Barbara. He had not been extremely close with his cousin—the difference in age between them meant she regarded him indulgently as a child, as she did Thomas—but she had been there all his life, kind and cheerful, without her sister's sharp tongue, always expecting the ready best of everyone. He had never lived in a world without Barbara in it.

Lucie was in the library, he knew, absorbing the company of others. But James had always found solace in books. Admittedly not the kind of book he was reading currently, though.

He had been surprised how very little material there was in the library on the Princes of Hell. They were not the kind of demons Shadowhunters *fought*—in the mythology about them, they were the mirrors of angels like Raziel. Their interests seemed to go beyond humanity, who were like ants to them. Their battles were with angels and the rulers of realms—other worlds than Earth, dimensions the princes seemed to collect like chess pieces. They could not be killed, though sometimes they were able to wound each other in a manner that left the injured party weakened for years.

There were nine of them in total. There was Sammael, the first to loose demons upon the Earth. Azazel, the forger of weapons who fell from grace when he gifted humans with the instruments of violence. Belial, who "did not walk among men," was described as the prince of necromancers and warlocks, and a thief of realms. Mammon, the prince of greed and wealth, could be bribed with money and riches. Astaroth, who tempted men to bear false witness, and who took advantage of the grieving. Asmodeus, the demon of lust and rumored general of Hell's army. Belphegor, the prince of sloth and, strangely, tricksters and snake-oil salesmen. Leviathan, the demon of envy, chaos, and the sea, who was monstrous and rarely summoned. And lastly, of course, there was Lucifer, the leader of the archangels, the most beautiful of any prince, the leader of the rebellion against Heaven.

It seemed impossible to James any of them could be his grandfather. It was like having a mountain for a grandfather, or an exploding star. Nothing evil was more powerful than the Princes of Hell, save perhaps Lilith, the mother of demons.

He sighed and set the book down, trying to push back an intrusive thought of Grace. He did not like the way they had parted at the riverbank: she had said she would need time, and he knew he must give her that. Still, the thought of her burned inside his stomach, as if he had swallowed a match tip.

A knock on the door pulled him from his reverie. He set his book down, rising to his feet. His muscles ached.

"Come in," he called.

It was his father, but Will was not alone: Uncle Jem was with him, a noiseless presence in his drifting parchment robes. His hood was down, as it often was when he was inside the Institute. Will had told James many years ago that when Jem had first become a Silent Brother, he had not liked people to see his scars. It was strange to think of Uncle Jem having such feelings.

"Someone's here to see you," Will said, moving aside to let Jem pass into the room. He glanced from his son to his old *parabatai*. James knew that under the songs and jokes, the careful deflection, his father was a man who felt things deeply. He himself was like his father in that way: they both loved intensely, and could be intensely hurt.

If it bothered Will that James and Jem had secrets he did not know and could not share, he did not show it. James had been miserable until Jem had shown him how to control the shadow power. All Will had ever cared about was that after his lessons with Jem, James seemed happier.

Will's blue eyes were deeply shadowed; James knew he and Tessa had been up for hours, first in the sickroom and then in the library. James and Lucie had stayed with Thomas as long as they could, until he had returned to Christopher's house, silent with grief and exhaustion. Afterward, Lucie had gone off to the library to look after Alexander, but James had returned to his room. He had always been the sort who bore his pains privately.

Will ruffled James's hair and said something about being needed elsewhere before slipping out of the room. When he was gone, James sat back down at his desk and glanced up at his uncle Jem.

You sent for me? Jem said.

"Yes. I need to tell you something. Or perhaps ask you something. I am not sure which."

Is this about Barbara? Or the others? asked Jem. *We do not know why she died, James. We think the poison reached her heart. Piers and Ariadne remain in a stable condition, but the Brothers' need to find a cure has become even more desperate.*

James thought of the blood Christopher had taken from the infirmary, the laboratory in the house on Grosvenor Square. He knew Christopher was doing all he could to find a cure for the demon poison, but he couldn't help but hope Henry would come back from Idris soon to lend aid. Not to mention there was the matter of the dirt James had found in the shadow realm. . . .

"I sent the message to you before I knew about Barbara," James said, dragging his thoughts back to the present. "I feel foolish now. My problems do not measure up to those—"

Tell me why you sent for me, said Jem. I will be the judge of whether or not it was important.

James hesitated. "I cannot tell you all of it," he said, "for reasons I cannot explain entirely. Only know that I encountered a demon, who told me that my grandfather was a Prince of Hell." He glanced up at his uncle's face. "Did you know that?"

The white streak in Jem's hair danced as he shook his head. *As I've been searching for your grandfather's name, I've heard a great many stories from different sources. There was one, a warlock woman, who told me he was a Prince of Hell. But there were also others who named different demons. Since I did not know who to trust, I thought it better not to burden your family until I was sure of the truth.*

"Perhaps a clue could be found in the shadow realm," said James. "I'm seeing it more and more, just as there seem to be more demons in London. If there's some connection—"

Did the demons at the lake speak to you? Mention your grandfather? James shook his head.

I assume the demon who identified your grandfather was the Cerberus demon in the greenhouse in Chiswick, said Jem. James didn't contradict him; it was close enough. *It could be that this demon, having been bound to Benedict and Tatiana, had heard your name and said to you whatever it felt could hurt you most. Demons are deceptive. It might not be the truth.*

"But what does it mean if it is true?" James whispered. "If I am descended from a Prince of Hell?"

It means nothing about who you are, said Jem. *Look at your mother, your sister. Would you claim some flaw in them? You are your mother and father's son, James. That is what matters. What has always mattered.*

"You are being kind," said James. "Kinder than the Clave would be, if it turns out to be true."

Jem took James's face in his hands. His touch was cool, as always, and his face was young and old at the same time. How could he look no older than James and at the same time, ageless?

If you saw humanity as I can see it, Uncle Jem said. *There is very little brightness and warmth in the world for me. There are only four flames, in the whole world, that burn fiercely enough for me to feel something like the person I was. Your mother, your father, Lucie, and you. You love, and tremble, and burn. Do not let those who cannot see the truth tell you who you are. You are the flame that cannot be put out. You are the star that cannot be lost. You are who you have always been, and that is enough and more than enough. Anyone who looks at you and sees darkness is blind.*

He let go of James abruptly, as if he had said too much.

It is not enough, is it? Jem said, his silent tone somehow resigned. *The uncertainty has been planted. You feel you must know.*

"Yes," James said. "I am sorry."

Very well, said Jem. *I will call on an old friend, on one condition. You do not mention this again, to anyone, until we hear from him.*

James hesitated. He was keeping so many secrets already—secrets for Grace, the secret of the attack in Chelsea, the secret of Emmanuel Gast. Before he could reply, though, the sound of clattering wheels echoed from outside; there was a crash, and James heard the front doors of the Institute fly open.

He raced to the window. Jem was beside him instantly, noiseless as a ghost.

Several carriages had drawn up in the courtyard: in the cool light of the moon, James could make out the coats of arms of the Baybrooks and Greenmantles, but not the others. He heard shouting—Will and Gabriel were racing down the front steps. The door of the Greenmantle carriage flew open and two women clambered out, supporting the body of a man between them. His white shirtfront was soaked in blood and his head hung at an angle, like a broken doll's.

Beside James, his uncle had gone rigid. There was a faraway look on his face; James knew he could speak inside his mind to the other Silent Brothers, gathering information from them. *It's happened*, Jem said. *There's been another attack.*

The light of late morning was yellow as butter. It hurt Cordelia's eyes as she paced the swords-and-stars tiles of the vestibule at Cornwall Gardens. Sona and Alastair were both fast asleep. Risa was in the kitchen, humming to herself as she made *nân-e barbari*, a flatbread that was her specialty.

Cordelia had not been able to sleep at all. Between her desperate worry over her father, the news about Barbara, and her new concern for Alastair, she had not been able to lie down, much less close her eyes.

Poor Thomas, she thought. And poor Barbara, who had been so happy dancing with Oliver, walking with him in Regent's Park.

Shadowhunters knew death. They accepted that death came: in battle, by knife or tooth or sword. But for a strange poison to steal away life while one slept, like a ghost or a thief, was not part of Shadowhunter life. It felt wrong, like a boot put on backward. Just as it felt to imagine losing her father to the injustice of the Clave.

The sound of a knock on the front door nearly sent Cordelia sailing into the air. The Lightwoods' housemaid had the morning off.

Cordelia glanced toward the kitchen, but Risa must not have heard the knock. There was nobody to open the door but her. Cordelia braced herself and flung it open wide.

James Herondale stood on the front step. She caught her breath. She had never seen him in gear before, and its darkness made his hair look more black, his eyes the burning gold of a lion's eyes. Around his upper left arm was a white silk band of mourning.

He met her gaze without flinching. His black hair continually looked tousled, as if he were caught in a storm no one else could see. "Daisy," he said. "I have—very bad news."

She could pretend she didn't know, but suddenly she couldn't bear it. "Barbara," she whispered. "I know. I'm so sorry, James. Charles came by last night, he's friends with Alastair and—"

"I feel I ought to have known they were friends—they were both in Paris at the same time, weren't they?" James ran a hand through his tangled hair. "But why would Charles have come by so late to see your brother? He couldn't have known about the attack yet—"

"Attack?" Cordelia stiffened. "What attack?"

"There was a small gathering at the Baybrooks' last night. When the visitors left, they were savaged by a group of the same demons that attacked us in the park."

Cordelia's mind raced. "Was anyone killed?"

"Randolph Townsend," said James. "I didn't know him well, but I saw them bring his body in. Vespasia Greenmantle and Gerald Highsmith were wounded and poisoned." James ran his hands through the already wild crown of his black hair.

"Is the Clave admitting now that this is not a problem limited to Regent's Park?"

"Yes," said James bitterly, "and they are going to set more patrols, in a wider area, though my parents are begging them to call in warlocks and the Spiral Labyrinth. The attack was at night, at least, so they are less panicked, but—I am not sure they should be.

This was a group of adult Shadowhunters. They were armed. Everyone has been since the picnic. But according to the Baybrooks, they were cut down in an instant. Only Randolph had a chance to raise a seraph blade before the demons were sinking teeth into their flesh."

"Did the demons vanish suddenly, the same way they did at the lake?"

"Apparently the Baybrooks said they were gone nearly as quickly as they appeared."

"It seems to me," said Cordelia, "that they are not simply seeking to kill. They seek to bite. To sicken."

James frowned. "But Randolph was killed."

"He was the only one fighting back," said Cordelia. "It seems to me they are *willing* to kill—Barbara or Piers could easily have died of blood loss—but their directive is to spread this—this infection."

"So you think someone is controlling them," said James. "Good. So do I. Hopefully we can find out who from Gast."

"Gast?" echoed Cordelia.

His eyes sparked a dark gold. "One good thing happened last night. It seems your trip to the Hell Ruelle was successful. Hypatia Vex sent Ragnor Fell to assist us with the name of a warlock who may have summoned these demons. Emmanuel Gast." He glanced up toward the windows of her house. "Ragnor did insist that we keep the information a secret."

"Another secret," said Cordelia. "There do seem to be so many now. And poor Thomas—does he know—?"

"About Gast? Yes. Ragnor came just before we found out about Barbara." Pain flashed across James's face. "Thomas blames himself for her death, though there is nothing he could have done."

James looked exhausted, Cordelia realized. He had come far out of his way to tell her this news, so that she did not have to hear it from people who didn't know Thomas or care about him or his friends.

He must be desperate to leave, she thought. She couldn't keep him here talking when he no doubt wished to be with his family, or with Grace.

"It was kind of you to come and tell me," she said, leaning against the doorway. "I would ask you in for tea, but I know you must be eager to return to your family."

"Actually, I am not returning to the Institute. I have made a plan with Matthew and Lucie to confront Gast in his flat. I'll be meeting them there. I came to see if you would join us."

Surprised, Cordelia said, "Oh, did Lucie ask you to fetch me along?"

James hesitated. "Yes. She did."

"Anything for my future *parabatai,* of course," Cordelia said. And she did mean it. She wanted badly to see Lucie, and even more to have something useful to do. Some way to help. All night she had been thinking of Barbara, who she had known so little, but who had been so young, and seemed so kind.

"I doubt this warlock will be happy to see us," said James. "Bring your gear and Cortana; we must be ready to fight."

Emmanuel Gast lived in a flat above a handkerchief manufacturer's, near the junction between Cheapside and Friday Street. Matthew pointed up Friday Street as they went past. "There used to be a pub up that street called the Mermaid Tavern, where Shakespeare used to drink."

In Lucie's opinion as a writer, this was *not* an artistically inspiring avenue. On each side of the street were dingy brown buildings with narrow leaded windows and grubby Dutch gables. Awnings hanging outside several buildings were dyed a mottled brown too, not by design but with the dust of the streets and the smog of the city. Cheapside was one of the busiest thoroughfares in London, crowds surging from the fishmongers' stalls all the way to the white bell tower of St. Mary-le-Bow.

She wrinkled her nose. "I don't think much of Shakespeare's taste."

Matthew smiled, though he looked as tired as Lucie felt. He wore dark gear just as she did, a white mourning band around his wrist and a white flower in his buttonhole. He had been making jokes all morning, and Lucie had been trying as best she could to keep up. It was hard not to let her mind wander to thoughts of Barbara, of the now even more crowded infirmary at the Institute. Of when the next attack might come, and who might be hurt or killed in it.

"Luce." Matthew touched her arm lightly. They were glamoured, and the crowds moved around them, parting like a river forking around a central island. Newsboys hawking the *Evening Standard* darted up and down the streets: Matthew had greeted one earlier, explaining to Lucie that he was an Irregular, one of the many Downworlder street urchins who ran errands out of the Devil Tavern. "There is something rather odd I wanted to talk to you about. Charles—well, Charles is always odd, but Charles and Grace—"

"James! Cordelia!" Lucie rose up on her toes, waving through the crowds. Her brother and Cordelia had alighted from their carriage some distance away and were walking toward them. They were clearly deep in conversation, their heads bent together as if they were exchanging secrets.

Lucie sank back down on her heels, a little puzzled. She rarely saw James lost in conversation with anyone other than his three closest friends.

"Interesting," said Matthew, his green eyes narrowed. He raised a hand and waved, and this time James saw them. He and Cordelia darted through the crowds to catch them at the corner. Lucie stared a little: Cordelia looked so very different out of the awful clothes her mother made her wear. She was in gear: a long tunic over boots and trousers, her red hair caught back in a braid, and a leather satchel over one shoulder. She looked even younger and prettier than she had at the Institute ball.

"It's a boardinghouse," said Matthew as soon as Cordelia and James were within earshot. "We've already been inside. The landlady said our friend Emmanuel Gast was 'away from home for an indefinite period.'"

"Matthew was unable to charm her," said Lucie. "The woman is a block of concrete in human form. We did manage to find out the flat's the one on the third floor, though."

A smile crept over James's face. One of the things he enjoyed most about patrolling was clambering around rooftops. "Then we go up the side of the building."

"I was afraid of this," Matthew muttered as they followed James into a narrow, rubbish-choked alley. "My boots are new."

"Stiffen your sinews, Matthew," said James. "And cry God for Harry, England, and Saint George!"

"Shakespeare," said Cordelia. "*Henry V.*"

"Well spotted," said James, and produced a grappling hook. He threaded the end of a rope through and stood back to throw it. His aim, as always, was excellent: the grappling hook sank into the lintel of a third-floor window; the rope unfurled down the side of the building. "Once more unto the breach," he announced, and began to climb.

James was followed up the rope by Cordelia, then Lucie, and Matthew last, still cursing the dirt on his boots. Lucie was halfway to the window when she heard a yell. Glancing down, she saw that Matthew was on his hands and knees in the alley. He must have fallen from the rope.

"Are you all right?" she asked in a loud whisper.

When he stood up, his hands were shaking. He deliberately avoided Lucie's gaze as he caught at the rope. "I told you," he said. "New boots."

Lucie began to climb the rope again. James had reached the window: balanced on the lintel, he glanced around and kicked the window in; the whole thing collapsed inward, sash, glass, and all. He vanished inside, followed by Cordelia. Lucie and Matthew climbed in after them.

The flat was dim and filled with a stench as of rotting waste. There was brown wallpaper, smeared with grease. Pictures torn from magazines were stuck to the walls. There was very little light, though Lucie could see a humped old sofa and a stained Turkish rug. A tall bookshelf was lined with shabby-looking tomes; James eyed them curiously.

"I think Ragnor was right," he said. "There's a real concentration on the study of dimensional magic here."

"No stealing the books and bringing them back to the Devil Tavern," said Matthew. "It would not be the first time your book kleptomania has gotten us in trouble."

James held his hands up innocently and went to search beneath some of the furniture. Cordelia followed his lead and peeked behind the cheap wooden frame of a small oil painting showing Queen Elizabeth, all scarlet hair and white powder, making a most unpleasant face.

"Look at these." There was dust in James's hair, and he was frowning. "I wonder if they're some kind of weapon?"

He indicated what looked like a heap of broken pieces of wood, scattered over the floor behind the sofa. "They're awfully dusty," said Cordelia. "As if no one's touched them in ages."

James bent to pick one up, frowning, just as Matthew glanced over. He'd been searching a small, shabby desk covered with loose papers. He held up a messy sketch. "James, look here."

James squinted. "It's a box. Surrounded by scrawls."

"It's not a box," Matthew told him helpfully. "It's a drawing of a box."

"Thank you, Matthew," James said dryly. He tilted his head to the side. "There's something familiar about it."

"Does it remind you of boxes you have been acquainted with before?" said Matthew. "Look at the scrawls a bit more closely. Don't they remind you of runes?"

James took the paper from his *parabatai*. "Yes," he said, sounding a bit surprised, "very much so—not runes that we use, but still awfully close—"

Cordelia, who had knelt down to look at the shards of wood, said, "These do have runes carved into them—our kind of runes—but they also look as if they've been part-eaten by a sort of acid."

"And look at those scratches on the wood," said James, joining her. He glanced at Gast's sketch, and then back at the shards. "It's as if—"

Lucie half heard Matthew say something in response, but she was already taking advantage of their distraction to slip through a half-open door into the flat's small bedroom.

Her hand flew to her mouth. She gagged and bit down hard on her own thumb, the pain cutting through the nausea like a knife.

The room was nearly bare save for an iron-posted bed, a single window, and what remained of Emmanuel Gast lying ruined on the bare floorboards. Flesh and bone had been carved apart, ribs cracked open to show a collapsed red cavern. Blood had sunk in black grooves into the wooden floor. The most human-looking part of him left were his hands, his arms outflung with the hands turned palm up as if he were begging for mercy he had not received.

He had been dead a long time. The stench was putrid.

Lucie took a step back. The door behind her swung suddenly shut, slamming closed with a force that vibrated the wall. She dropped her hand, tasting blood in her mouth as the *thing* on the floor heaved and a black shadow spilled upward between jagged white ribs.

It was a ghost. This ghost was no Jessamine, or Jesse Blackthorn, who looked solid and human. There was an awful shimmer in the air around it, as if with his violent end a space had been torn in the world. It—*he*—was ragged at the edges, his face skull-pale in a nest of straggling brown hair. She could see the patterned wallpaper through his transparent body.

The ghost of Emmanuel Gast blinked watery blue eyes at her. "Why have you summoned me, fool?" it demanded, in a voice like the hiss of steam escaping from a pipe.

"I did *not* summon you," said Lucie. "I had no idea you were even dead, until this very disgusting moment." She glared.

"Why have you dragged me back to this place of agony?" Gast hissed. "What do you want, Shadowhunter?"

Lucie reached for the knob of the door behind her and rattled it, but it was stuck. She could faintly hear the voices of the others in the parlor, calling her name.

She took a deep breath, almost choking on the fetid air. Even though he was dead, Gast was still their only tenuous connection to the demons that had killed Barbara.

She drew herself up to her full height. "Did you summon the demons? The ones that have been attacking Nephilim in broad daylight?"

The ghost was silent. Lucie could see where its throat had been slit, its spine showing through the slashed hole in its neck. Whoever had murdered Emmanuel Gast had wanted to make very sure he was dead.

"Answer me!" Lucie cried.

To Lucie's amazement, the warlock's flickering outlines resolved into a more solid shape. The ghost's eyes smoldered with a red anger, but it spoke, its voice hollow. "I am the one who raised it. I, Emmanuel Gast, the most scorned of warlocks. Years ago the Spiral Labyrinth turned against me. They cast me out of warlock society. My golden reward was taken from me. I have been forced to take the lowliest of hires to feed and clothe myself. Yet all this time I studied. I learned. I was wiser than they thought."

Wise? Lucie wondered. From the look of things, Gast's recent decisions had been anything but wise.

"I see the way you look at me." Blood dripped from the ghost's wounds, a silent patter of black stains on the bare floor. "You scorn me for raising such a demon—a death-dealer, the poisoner of life. But the gold. I needed it. And the demon will kill only Shadowhunters."

"Someone paid you to do this," Lucie whispered. "Who? Who did it?"

The ghost hissed. "What are you? You are a Shadowhunter, but not a Shadowhunter. You drag me back from the brink?" It reached out a hand, insubstantial, curling into a claw. "What is this monstrous power . . . ?"

"Monstrous?" Lucie snapped. "What's monstrous is that you summoned these creatures into this world, knowing the damage they would do—"

"You know nothing of me," said Gast. "I went to the bridge to raise the demon. I brought it into this world and then I captured it, kept it where it would be safe, a gift for the one who gave me gold. But when I returned here, I was betrayed. I could not stop it. My blood and my life ran out over the floor as my killer tore the demon from its hiding place."

Lucie could stand no more. "Who did this? Who hired you?"

For an instant Lucie believed Gast would simply vanish away into the shadows and the London smoke. He began to tremble, like a butterfly transfixed with a pin but not yet dead. "I will not tell—"

"You *will!*" Lucie shouted, her hand outthrust, and she felt something go through her, like electricity through a wire, like the feeling of a rune burning on her skin—

The ghost threw its head back and roared, revealing Gast's

warlock mark—multiple rows of teeth, like a shark. Something hit the door behind Lucie; she stepped aside just in time for James to burst into the room in a cloud of plaster dust: he had smashed the door off its hinges. Cordelia spilled in next, her satchel over her shoulder, and Matthew came after her. The latter two stood blinking in horror at the corpse on the floor.

Lucie glanced at James. He nodded: he could see the ghost as well, in the way all Herondales could. It was a perfectly ordinary ghost sighting, Lucie told herself. This ghost was not Jesse.

"The one who hired me came to me masked, face wrapped around in cloth and wearing layers of cloaks." Emmanuel Gast answered her slowly, almost reluctantly. "I know not if they were man or woman, old or young."

"What more do you know?" James demanded, and the ghost writhed. "Who is controlling the demons now?"

"Someone more powerful than you puny Nephilim," snarled the ghost. "Someone who tore down my wards, ripped my body apart—" His voice rose to a wail. "I shall not think on it! I shall not relive my death! Truly you are monsters, despite your angel blood."

Lucie could not bear it a moment longer. "Go!" she shouted. "Leave us!"

The ghost winked out of existence, between one breath and the next. Cordelia was already over by the bed, dragging the dirty coverlet off, throwing it over what remained of Gast. The air reeked; Lucie was choking. James reached for her.

"I have to get outside," she whispered, turning away from her brother. "I must breathe."

She pushed past her friends and into the living room. The door to the flat was not locked. Lucie clutched at the banister as she stumbled down the narrow steps and outside into the street.

Cockney voices floated around her, men in round hats passing by with packages under their arms. She struggled to catch her breath. Ghosts had never frightened her—they were the restless dead, grieving and disquieted, rarely seen. But there had been something different about Gast.

A coat settled on Lucie's shoulders, bottle green superfine, and warm, smelling of expensive cologne. Lucie glanced up to see Matthew's face hovering above hers, sunlight making his hair brilliant. He looked serious for once as he carefully buttoned the coat closed around her. His hands, usually swift and bright with rings, flying through the air when he talked, were moving with great deliberation over such a small task. She heard him draw in a slow breath.

"Luce," he said. "What happened in there? Are you all right?"

She shivered. "I'm all right," she said. "I've rarely seen a ghost in such—such a condition."

"Lucie!" James and Cordelia joined them on the street. Cordelia caught at Lucie's hand and squeezed it. James ruffled his sister's hair.

"Gast did not die easily," he said. "Good work, Lucie. I know that can't have been pleasant."

He called me a monster. But she didn't say it out loud. "Did you find anything in the flat after I went into the bedroom?" she asked.

James nodded. "We took a few things—sketches, and Cordelia has the wood shards in her satchel."

"That reminds me," said Matthew, relieving Cordelia of her bag. He approached the grubby-faced newsboy he'd pointed out to Lucie earlier and engaged in a spirited discussion with him, eventually proffering the satchel.

"Is Matthew selling my satchel to a newsboy?" Cordelia said curiously.

James smiled crookedly. "I see we'd better explain the Irregulars to you, lest you think we spend our time leading London's children into depravity and crime."

Matthew returned, the wind tousling his dark gold hair. "I told

Neddy to take the bag to Christopher," he said. "It may be that identifying what those shards are will help." He glanced at Cordelia,
who looked slightly puzzled. "I doubt Christopher has left Tom's
side since last night—perhaps this will provide a distraction for
them both."

"Perhaps," Lucie said. "If we can return to the Institute, I would
like to write down what Gast said, that I might remember each
detail."

It was only half of what she really thought. She had lied to the
others about Jessamine being part of a ghost gossip network. Jessamine never left the Institute, and avoided the company of other
ghosts. But Lucie knew not all spirits were like that. Many wandered. She wanted suddenly to know if another ghost might know
of the death of Emmanuel Gast. She wanted to talk to Jesse.

12

THE END OF IT

She loves me all that she can,
And her ways to my ways resign;
But she was not made for any man,
And she never will be all mine.
—Edna St. Vincent Millay,
"Witch-Wife"

As the carriage rolled under the Institute's gates, James saw his parents standing in the courtyard. His father was in a cutaway morning coat and a blue sapphire tiepin that Tessa had given him for their twentieth anniversary. Tessa herself wore a formal day dress. They were clearly prepared to go out.

"And where have you been?" Will demanded, as James clambered out of the carriage. The others leaped down behind him, the girls, being in gear, needing no help to dismount. "You stole our carriage."

James wished he could tell his father the truth, but that would be breaking their sworn promise to Ragnor.

"It's only the second-best carriage," James protested.

"Remember when Papa stole Uncle Gabriel's carriage?

It's a proud family tradition," said Lucie, as the group of them approached the Institute steps.

"I did not raise you to be horse thieves and scallywags," said Will. "And I recall very clearly that I told you—"

"Thank you for letting them borrow the carriage to come and get me," said Cordelia. Her eyes were wide, and she looked entirely innocent. James felt an amused stab of surprise: she was an interestingly skillful liar. At least his parents wouldn't wonder why they were all in gear: as James and Lucie had left the house earlier, Will had said to them that for years he'd trusted them to patrol in the darkness, but now they must arm themselves at all times, treating day as if it were night. He'd also advised James to bring Matthew with him, which James had been planning to do anyway. "I had very much wanted to come to the Institute and see what I could do to help."

Will softened immediately. "Of course. You are always welcome here, Cordelia. Though we are, as you can see, going out—Charles has invoked the Consul's authority and called a meeting in Grosvenor Square to discuss last night's attack. Only for high-level Enclave members, apparently."

Matthew grimaced. "By the Angel, that sounds awful. I hope it's all right for me to stay here tonight."

Tessa smiled. "We already made up one of the spare rooms for you."

"As I have known Charles since he was born, I have a difficult time taking him seriously as an authority figure," said Will thoughtfully. "I suppose if he says anything I don't like, I can request that he be spanked."

"Oh, yes, please," said Matthew. "It would do him a world of good."

"Will—" began Tessa in exasperation, just as Bridget emerged from the front doors. She appeared to be carrying an enormous medieval spear: its haft was worn, its long iron point spotted with rust. She clambered into the driver's seat of the carriage and sat grimly, clearly awaiting Tessa and Will.

"I do hope you're going to glamour that carriage," said James. "People will think the Romans have returned to reconquer the British Isles."

Tessa and Will climbed into the carriage. As Bridget gathered up the reins, Tessa leaned out the window. "Uncle Jem is in the infirmary with several other Silent Brothers, looking after the ill," she called. "Please try not to cause them any trouble, and see to it that they have whatever they need."

James nodded as the carriage rolled out of the courtyard. He knew there would be guards around the Institute as well; he had seen a few of them, marked out clearly in their black gear, outside the gates as they approached. His parents had been through too much to ever leave the Institute unguarded.

He glanced at his sister, wondering if she was thinking the same. She stood looking up at the higher levels of the Institute—perhaps at the sickroom? He was used to a Lucie in motion, not a Lucie who stood pale and withdrawn, clearly lost in thought.

"Come along then, Luce," he said. "Let's get inside."

She frowned at him. "No need to use your worried voice. I'm perfectly all right, James."

He threw an arm around her shoulder. "It's not every day you see a warlock scattered liberally around his own bedroom," he said. "You might as well take a little time to recover. Raziel knows none of us have had much time to recover from anything lately."

In fact, James thought, as the four of them approached the Institute, he had barely had a moment all day to think of Grace. His mother always said the cure for worry was to throw yourself into activity, and he had certainly done that, but he could not leave things this way with Grace forever. He had not realized how bad the situation with Tatiana actually was. Surely Grace would reach out, and together they would remove her to a place of safety.

Surely it would happen soon.

"So, Jessamine," said Lucie. "Can ghosts lie?"

They were all in Lucie's room: Matthew and James had settled Lucie on the settee and wrapped her in blankets, despite her complaints that she was fine and needed no assistance. James had insisted that he hadn't liked how pale she'd looked when she'd come out of Gast's flat.

Cordelia was next to Lucie on the sofa, while James and Matthew occupied the two armchairs as only young men did: legs and armed sprawled everywhere, gear jackets tossed casually on the bed, muddy boots mussing up the carpet. Both were gazing up at Jessamine, though only James could see her.

"Certainly not!" Jessamine looked shifty. "Ghosts are completely honest. I keep telling you, it was mice who knocked your silver mirror behind the desk and broke it."

"It appears clear that if ghosts are liars, they are terrible liars," said James.

Matthew sighed. "It is very strange to see you conversing with the invisible."

"Humph," said Jessamine. She wobbled a bit and firmed up, her outlines clearing as she drifted down toward the floor. Shadowhunters, having the Sight, could generally see ghosts who wanted to be seen, but Lucie knew it was an effort for Jessamine to make herself visible to all eyes.

"Oh!" said Cordelia. "It's very nice to meet you, Jessamine. Lucie speaks of you often."

Jessamine beamed.

"You are a very attractive ghost," said Matthew, tapping his ringed fingers against his chest. "I do hope Lucie and James have mentioned as much."

"They have not," Jessamine noted.

"Very remiss," said Matthew, his eyes sparkling.

"You are not at all like Henry," said Jessamine, eyeing Matthew speculatively. "He was forever setting things on fire, and not a compliment to be heard."

"Jessamine," Lucie said. "This is important! Do tell us, can ghosts lie? Not you, of course, my dear."

"Ghosts *can* lie," Jessamine conceded. "But there are certain forms of necromancy that can compel them to tell the truth, and even to allow the living to control them." She shuddered. "That is why necromancy is so dreadful and forbidden."

"*That's* why?" Cordelia sounded doubtful. Turning to Lucie, she said, "Are you worried Gast's ghost might have been lying?"

Lucie hesitated. Part of her *hoped* he had been lying, since he had claimed the demon was only meant to kill Shadowhunters. It was a frightening thought. "I just don't want us to go off on a wild-goose chase. Gast was insistent that someone extraordinarily powerful hired him to summon these demons. We need to find out who that was."

"We also need to know what kind of demons these are," said Cordelia. "We cannot go to the Enclave just to report that Gast raised a bunch of poisonous demons: we already know these demons bear poison. We do not know why their poison is so deadly, or what Gast did so they can appear in daylight."

"This all seems very dull," said Jessamine. "If you don't need me, I'll be going." She vanished with a sigh of relief, no doubt at no longer having to keep herself in visible form.

Lucie reached up to pull down one of her writing notebooks from the edge of the desk. Perhaps it was time to begin recording their thoughts. "There is another odd thing. We know Gast raised multiple demons, but he kept referring to one demon. He said he raised *it*, not *them*."

"Perhaps the demon had offspring," James suggested. "Some demons have dozens of spawn, like spiders—"

From outside Lucie's window came the rattle of wheels and the neighing of horses. A moment later there was the sound of cries from the courtyard. James and Lucie both rushed to the window.

A driverless carriage had drawn up before the Institute's front steps. Lucie recognized the arms on the side instantly: the four Cs of the Consul. It was Charles Fairchild's carriage.

The carriage door flew open and Grace tumbled out, her hair streaming over her shoulders, her dress stained with blood. She was screaming.

Beside Lucie, James's body tensed like iron.

The front doors of the Institute burst open and Brother Enoch came rushing down the steps. He reached into the carriage behind Grace and lifted out the twitching body of a woman, clad in a stained fuchsia dress. Her arm was bloody, wrapped in a makeshift bandage.

Tatiana Blackthorn.

Cordelia and Matthew had joined them at the window. Cordelia had her hand over her mouth. "By the Angel," said Matthew. "Another attack."

Lucie turned to tell James to hurry to Grace, but there was no need to say it. He was already gone.

James burst into the infirmary to find a scene of horror. Screens had been put up between the beds along the west wall where the sick lay in their poisoned sleep. James could see only their silhouettes—dark shapes hunched under covers, still as corpses. At the far end of the room two beds had been pushed together: Tatiana had been carried across the room, and blood smeared the floor in a trail leading to where she lay sprawled crosswise upon them, her body jerking and twisting. Her shoulder had been torn, and her arm; her hat had come off, and the thin tufts of her graying hair were matted to her skull.

Brother Enoch was bending over Tatiana, dripping dark blue fluid from a beaker into her open mouth as she gasped for air. James thought wildly of a baby bird being fed by its mother. Jem stood by, holding bandages soaked in antiseptic. Grace knelt in the shadows by the foot of her mother's bed, her hands gripping each other tightly.

James approached, passing the beds in which the other patients lay in their restless drugged states. Ariadne, Vespasia, and Gerald might have been only sleeping, had it not been for the dark maps of black veins beneath their skin. They seemed to grow more visible by the day.

Hello, James.

It was Jem's voice, gentle in his mind. James wished he had something to tell his uncle, other than the frustrating threads of a mystery that refused to knit itself together. But Jem was already searching out the identity of James's grandfather. He couldn't burden Jem with more questions that might have no answers.

Will she live? he asked silently, indicating Tatiana.

Jem's voice was unusually strained. *If she dies, it will not be because of these injuries you see here.*

The poison. *Death-dealer, poisoner of life,* Gast had said. But what in the Angel's name had he raised?

"James." A hand caught at his arm; he looked down to see Grace, her face ashen, her lips deadly white. She was gripping his arm with both hands. "Take me out of here."

He turned slightly to shield them both from view. "Where shall I take you? What do you need?"

Her hands trembled, shaking his arm. "I need to talk to you, James. Take me somewhere we can be alone."

"James has been gone for an absolute age," Lucie said. She had been scribbling in her notebook, but had begun to look worried. "Would you go and look for him, Cordelia?"

Cordelia did not want to go look for James. She'd seen the look on his face when Grace tumbled out of Charles's carriage in the courtyard. The longing that had turned so quickly to fear for Grace; the quick unconscious way he'd touched the bracelet on his wrist. He hated Tatiana, she knew, and with good reason. But he would have done anything to protect her to spare Grace pain.

She wondered what it would be like, to be loved like that. Even alongside her sadness, there was a strange admiration in her for the way that James loved Grace, the all-encompassingness of it.

That didn't mean she wanted to barge in on James and his lady love. But Lucie had asked, and Cordelia could see no reason to refuse. She smiled weakly. "I'm not sure I'm meant to leave you alone with a man," she said. "Seems scandalous."

Lucie chuckled. "Matthew's not a man. We used to hit each other with soup ladles as children."

Cordelia rather expected Matthew to laugh too, but instead he looked away, suddenly occupied with a spot of dirt on his sleeve. With a silent sigh, Cordelia ruffled Lucie's hair and went out into the corridor.

She was still learning her way around the Institute. The symbols for Shadowhunter families were everywhere and as Cordelia passed them, witchlight touched the shapes of wings and the curves of towers. Cordelia found a set of stone steps and headed down it, only to jump in surprise as Anna Lightwood stepped out from beneath a marble frieze of an angel poised over a green hill. The dragon of Wales was pictured in the background.

Anna was in trousers and a jacket of sharp French tailoring. Her blue eyes were the exact color of Will's, darker than Lucie's: they matched her waistcoat, and the lapis head of her walking stick.

"Have you seen James?" Cordelia demanded without preamble.

"No," said Anna shortly. "No clue as to his whereabouts, I'm afraid."

Cordelia frowned, not because of James, but because of Anna's expression. "Anna? What's wrong?"

Anna scowled. "I had come here to horsewhip Charles, but it appears that he is elsewhere."

"Charles Fairchild?" Cordelia echoed blankly. "I believe he's at home—he called a gathering at his house for high-ranking Enclave members. You could go horsewhip him there, but it would make for a very strange meeting."

"High-ranking Enclave members?" Anna rolled her eyes. "Well, no wonder I don't know about it. So I suppose I'll have to wait until later to puncture him like the pustulant boil he is." Anna began to pace within the small confines of the stairwell. "Charles," she said. "Bloody Charles, everything in service of his ambitions—" She whirled, slamming her walking stick against a stair. "He has done a dreadful, dreadful thing. I need to go to the infirmary. She shouldn't be alone. I must see her."

"See who?" Cordelia was bewildered.

"Ariadne," said Anna. "Cordelia—would you accompany me to the sickroom?"

Cordelia looked at Anna in surprise. Elegant, composed Anna. Though at the moment her hair was mussed, her cheeks flushed. She looked younger than she usually did.

"Of course," Cordelia said.

Fortunately, Anna knew the way to the infirmary: they did not speak as they climbed the stairs, both lost in thought. The infirmary itself was much quieter than it had been the last time Cordelia was there. She did not recognize most of those who lay still and feverish in the beds. At the back of the room, a large screen had been pulled out to shield the patient there: Tatiana Blackthorn, presumably. Cordelia could see the silhouettes of Brother Enoch and Jem cast against the screen as they moved around Tatiana's bed.

Anna's attention was focused on a single patient. Ariadne Bridgestock lay quietly against the white pillows. Her eyes were shut, and her rich brown skin was ashen, stretching tightly over the branching black veins beneath her skin. Beside her bed was a small table on which lay a roll of bandages and several stoppered jars of different-colored potions.

Anna slipped in between the screens surrounding Ariadne's cot, and Cordelia followed, feeling slightly awkward. Was she intruding? But Anna looked up, as if to assure herself that Cordelia was there, before she knelt down at the side of Ariadne's bed, laying her walking stick on the floor.

Anna's bowed shoulders looked strangely vulnerable. One of her hands dangled at her side: she reached out the other, fingers moving slowly across the white linen sheets, until she was almost touching Ariadne's hand.

She did not take it. At the last moment, Anna's fingers curled and dropped to rest, beside Ariadne but not quite touching. In a low and steady voice, Anna said, "Ariadne. When you wake up—and you will wake up—I want you to remember this. It was never a sign of your worth that Charles Fairchild wanted to marry you. It is a measure of his lack of worth that he chose to break it off in such a manner."

"He broke it off?" Cordelia whispered. She was stunned. The breaking off of a promised engagement was a serious matter, undertaken usually only when one of the parties in question had committed some kind of serious crime or been caught in an affair. For Charles to break his promise to Ariadne while she lay unconscious was appalling. People would assume he had found out something dreadful about Ariadne. When she awoke, she might be ruined.

Anna did not reply to Cordelia. She only raised her head and looked at Ariadne's face, a long look like a touch.

"Please don't die," she said, in a low voice, and rose to her feet. Catching up her walking stick, she strode from the infirmary, leaving Cordelia staring after her in surprise.

Lucie set her notebook aside. Matthew was drawing circles in the air with a forefinger and frowning lazily, as if he were a pasha looking over his court and finding them to be ill-mannered and unprepared for inspection.

"How are you, Luce?" he said. He had moved to sit beside her on the settee. "Tell the truth."

"How are *you*, Matthew?" Lucie retorted. "Tell the truth."

"I am not the one who saw the ghost of Gast," said Matthew, and grinned. "Sounds like an unfinished Dickens novel, doesn't it? *The Ghost of Gast.*"

"I am not the one who nearly tumbled off a rope I should easily have been able to climb," said Lucie quietly.

Matthew's eyes narrowed. They were extraordinary eyes, so dark you could only tell they were green if you stood close to him. And Lucie had, many times. They were close now, close enough that she could see the slight scruff of golden hair along his jawline, and the shadows under his eyes.

"That reminds me," he said, and rolled up his sleeve. There was a long graze along his forearm. "I could use an *iratze*." He aimed a winning smile at her. All Matthew's smiles were winning. "Here," he added, and held out his stele to her. "Use mine."

She reached to take it from him, and for a moment, his hand

closed gently around hers. "Lucie," he said softly, and she almost closed her eyes, remembering how he had put his coat around her in the street, the warmth of his touch, the faint scent of him, brandy and dry leaves.

But mostly brandy.

She looked down at their entwined hands, his more scarred than hers. The rings on his fingers. He began to turn her hand over in his, as if he meant to kiss her palm.

"You are a Shadowhunter, Matthew," she said. "You should be able to scale a wall."

He sat back. "And I am," he said. "My new boots were slippery."

"It wasn't your boots," said Lucie. "You were drunk. You're drunk now, too. Matthew, you're drunk most of the time."

He released her hand as if she had struck him. There was confusion in his eyes, and visible hurt as well. "I am not—"

"Yes, you are. You think I can't recognize it?"

Matthew's mouth hardened into a narrow line. "Drink makes me amusing."

"It does not amuse me to watch you hurt yourself," she said. "You are like a brother to me, Math—"

He flinched. "Am I? No one else has such complaints about what I do, or my desire for fortification."

"Many are afraid to mention it," said Lucie. "Others, like my brother and my parents, do not see what they do not want to see. But I see, and I am worried."

His lip curled at the corner. "Worried about me? I'm flattered."

"I am worried," said Lucie, "that you will get my brother killed."

Matthew did not move. He remained as still as if he had been turned to stone by the Gorgon in the old stories. The Gorgon was a demon, Lucie's father had told her, though in those days there were no Shadowhunters. Instead gods and demigods had walked on the earth, and miracles had showered down from the heavens like leaves from a tree in autumn. But there was no miracle here. Only the fact that she might as well have stabbed Matthew in the heart.

"You are his *parabatai*," said Lucie, her voice shaking slightly. "He trusts you—to be at his back in battle, to be his shield and sword, and if you are not yourself—"

Matthew stood up, nearly upending the chair. His eyes were dark with fury. "If it were anyone else but you, Lucie, saying these things to me—"

"Then what?" Lucie also rose to her feet. She barely reached Matthew's shoulder, but she glared at him anyway. She had always given as good as she got in the soup ladle battles of their childhood. "What would you do?"

He slammed his way out of her room without replying.

In the end, James brought Grace to the drawing room.

It was quiet in there, and deserted: there was a fire on, and he helped her into a chair close to it, bending to draw off her gloves. He wanted to kiss her bare hands—so vulnerable, so familiar from their days and nights in the woods—but he stepped back and left her alone to warm herself by the flames. It was not a cold day, but shock could make one shiver down to one's bones.

The light from the flames danced over the William Morris wallpaper and the deep colors of the Axminster rugs that covered the wooden floor. At last Grace rose to her feet and began to pace up and down in front of the fire. She had pulled the last pins from her hair, and it streamed over her shoulders like icy water.

"Grace?" Now, in this room, with only the sound of the ticking clock breaking the silence, James hesitated, as he had not had time or pause to do in the infirmary. "Can you speak of what happened? Where was the attack? How did you escape?"

"Mama was attacked at the manor," said Grace, her voice flat. "I do not know how it happened. I found her unconscious at the bottom of the front steps. The wounds in her shoulder and arm were the wounds of teeth."

"I am so sorry."

"You don't have to say that," said Grace. She had begun to pace again. "There are things you don't know, James. And things I must do, now that she is sick. Before she wakes."

"I am glad you think she will recover," said James, coming close to her. He was not sure if he should reach to touch her, even as she stopped pacing and raised her eyes to his. He did not think he had seen Grace like this before. "It is important to have hope."

"It is certainty. My mother will not die," said Grace. "All these years she has lived on bitterness, and her bitterness will keep her alive now. It is stronger than death." She reached to caress his face. He closed his eyes as her fingertips traced the contour of his cheekbone, light as the touch of a dragonfly's wing.

"James," she said. "Oh, James. Open your eyes. Let me look at you while you still love me."

His eyes flew open. "I have loved you for years. I will always love you."

"No," said Grace, dropping her hand. There was a great weariness on her face, in her movements. "You will hate me soon."

"I could never hate you," James said.

"I am getting married," she said.

It was the sort of shock so immense one hardly felt it. *She's made some kind of mistake,* James thought. *She's confused. I will fix this.*

"I will be marrying Charles," she went on. "Charles Fairchild. We have been spending quite a bit of time together since I came to London, though I know you have not noticed it."

A pulse had started to pound behind James's eyes, in time with the ticking of the grandfather clock. "This is madness, Grace. You asked *me* to marry you last night."

"And you said no. You were very clear." She gave a slight shrug. "*Charles* said yes."

"*Charles* is engaged to Ariadne Bridgestock."

"That engagement is broken. Charles told Inquisitor Bridgestock he was ending it this morning. Ariadne did not love Charles; she will not care whether they marry or not."

"Really? Did you ask her?" James demanded fiercely, and Grace flinched. "None of this makes sense, Grace. You've been in London less than a week—"

Her eyes glittered. "I can get a great deal accomplished in less than a week."

"Apparently. Including harming Ariadne Bridgestock, who has never done anything to you. Charles is a cold person. He has a cold heart. But I would have expected better from *you* than to be a party to something like this."

Grace flushed. "You think Ariadne is desperate? She is beautiful and rich, and Charles is prepared to tell everyone *she* broke it off with *him*."

"While she was unconscious?"

"Clearly, he will say it was before she fell ill," Grace snapped.

"And if she dies, how convenient for you," said James, pain like a white flare behind his eyes.

"I told you that you would hate me," said Grace, and there was something almost savage in her expression. "I tell you, she does not want Charles, and if she dies, yes, she will need him even less than she does now!" She gasped for breath. "You cannot see it. I am more desperate than Ariadne could ever be."

"I cannot see what you will not tell me," said James in a low voice. "If you are desperate, let me help you—"

"I *offered* you the chance to help me," she said. "I asked you to marry me, but you would not have it. Everything you have here, it is all more important to you than I am."

"That's not true—"

She laughed sharply. "To love me, James, you must love me above all other things. We will forever be my mother's target if we marry—and then our children will be—and how could that be worth it to you? I already know it is not. When I asked you to marry me last night, it was only a test. I wished to see if you loved me enough. Enough to do anything to protect me. You do not."

"And Charles does?" James's voice was low. "You barely know him."

"It doesn't matter. Charles has power. He will be the Consul. He does not need to love me." She faced him across the worn pattern of the carpet. "I must do this now, before my mother wakes. She would forbid it. But if she wakes and it is done, she will not go against the Clave and Consul. Don't you see? It is impossible between us, James."

"It is only impossible if you make it so," said James.

Grace drew her shawl around her shoulders as if she were cold. "You do not love me enough," she said. "You will realize that soon and be grateful I have done this." She held her hand out. "Please return my bracelet to me."

It was like the lash of a whip. Slowly James reached for the clasp of the silver circlet. It had rested there so long that when he removed it, he saw a strip of paler flesh circling his wrist, like the pallor left behind when a wedding ring was removed. "Grace," he said, holding it out to her. "You don't need to do this."

She took the bracelet from him, leaving his wrist feeling unnaturally bare. "What we had was the dream of children," she said. "It will fade like snow in summer. You will forget."

His head felt as if his skull were cracking; he could barely breathe. He heard his own voice as if it came from a long distance away. "I am a Herondale. We love but once."

"That is only a story."

"Haven't you heard?" James said bitterly. "All the stories are true."

He flung the door open, desperate to get away from her. As he raced down the hall, the faces of strangers flew by in a blur; he heard his own name called and then he was down the stairs and in the entryway, seizing up his coat. The sky was cloudy overhead and shadows had gathered thickly in the courtyard, resting among the branches of the trees like ravens.

"Jamie—"

Matthew appeared out of the dimness, his hair bright in the dark entryway, his expression concerned. "Jamie, what's wrong?"

"Grace is marrying Charles," said James. "Let it be, Math. I need to be alone."

Before Matthew could say a word, James threw open the doors and fled, vanishing beneath the arched gates that marked the entrance to the Institute, the words carved on them gleaming in the dull sunlight.

We are dust and shadows.

Matthew swore, his fingers fumbling at the buttons of his coat. James had just vanished into the shadows outside the Institute without a single weapon on him, but Matthew was sure he could catch him up. He knew James's haunts as well as James knew them himself: all the places in the city James might seek out when he was upset.

His hands were shaking too badly to get the buttons right, though. He swore again and reached for the flask in his waistcoat. Just a nip to steady his hands and put him to rights—

"Was James—did he seem all right?" said a voice behind him.

Matthew turned, dropping his hand. Grace stood at the foot of the steps, a gray shawl like a spider's web wrapped around her thin shoulders. Matthew knew she was thought strikingly beautiful by most, but she had always seemed like the shadow of a shadow to him, lacking vibrancy and color.

"Of course he isn't all right," Matthew said. "Neither am I. You're marrying Charles, and none of us wants that."

She pulled the shawl tighter about herself. "You don't understand. We all do what we must. I am doing what I have to do."

"James has loved you, sincerely, since he was a child," said Matthew. "And now you tear his heart to pieces? And for what? Charles will never feel half of what James feels for you."

"Feelings," she said with contempt. "That is all men think women want, isn't it? Sympathy—sentiment—nonsense. I have never felt any tenderness for anything or anyone living—"

"Have you truly never felt anything for anyone?" Matthew demanded, half-angry and half-curious.

She was silent for a long moment. "My brother," she said at last, with a peculiar half smile. "But then, he is not now living."

"So you never cared for James at all," he said, full realization dawning slowly. "Has James disappointed you in some way? Or were you just tired of him before you even came to London? All the time you've spent with Charles, all the bloody carriage rides, all the whispering in corners—Lord, you planned this like a military campaign, didn't you? If the first regiment falls, always have a replacement at the ready." He laughed bitterly. "I told myself I was a fool for being suspicious that you were going behind James's back. I didn't imagine half the truth."

She looked paler than usual. "You would not be wise to spread such rumors. Let it be, Matthew."

"I cannot." He started in on his coat again; oddly his hands were steady, as if anger had flattened his nerves. "Charles is a bastard, but even he doesn't deserve—"

"Matthew," she said, coming closer and laying her hand on his elbow. He paused in surprise, looking at her face, upturned to his. He could see that the shape of it was indeed lovely, almost doll-like in its perfection.

She stroked her hand down his sleeve. He told himself he should pull back from her, but his feet seemed rooted to the floor. It was as if he were being drawn toward her, though he hated her at the same time.

"You feel something for me now, don't you?" said Grace. "Kiss me. I demand that you do."

As if in a dream, Matthew reached for her. He grasped Grace's slim waist in his hands. He pressed his hungry mouth against her lips and kissed her, and kissed her. She tasted of sweet tea and oblivion. He felt nothing, no desire, no yearning, only an empty desperate compulsion. He kissed her mouth and her cheek and she turned in his arms, still holding his wrist, her body against his—

And then she stepped back, releasing him. It was like waking from a dream.

He flinched back in horror, stumbling away from Grace. There was nothing timid in that glance, nothing of the girl with her face downcast at the ball. The color of her eyes had turned to steel.

"You—" he began, and broke off. He couldn't say what he wanted to say: *You made me do that.* It was ludicrous, a bizarre abdication of personal responsibility for an even more bizarre act.

When she spoke, her voice held no emotion. Her lips were red where he had kissed her; he felt like being sick. "If you get in my way after this, if you do anything to impede my marriage to Charles, I will tell James you kissed me. And I will tell your brother, too."

"As if they do not already know I am a terrible person," he said, with a bravado he did not feel.

"Oh, Matthew." Her voice was cold as she turned away from him. "You have no idea what terrible people are like."

13

BLUE RUIN

Twenty bridges from Tower to Kew
Wanted to know what the river knew,
For they were young, and the Thames was old,
And this is the tale that the River told.
—Rudyard Kipling, "The River's Tale"

James sat on the edge of a stone bastion atop Blackfriars Bridge, his legs dangling over the edge. The dark-jade water of the Thames flowed by below. Small rowboats and lighters chugged alongside river barges, distinguished by their characteristic red-brown sails, like splotches of blood against the cloud-darkened sky. Aboard them, men in flat caps yelled to each other through the river spray.

To the north, the dome of St. Paul's glowed against a backdrop of thunderclouds; on the other side of the river, the Bankside Power Station puffed black smoke into the sky.

The rhythmic slap of the tidal river against the granite piers of the bridge was as familiar to James as a lullaby. Blackfriars was a special place in his family: it figured in quite a few of his parents' stories. He usually found it comforting here. The river rolled on, regardless of the turmoil in the lives of the people who crossed the bridge or boated across the water. They could leave no real mark on the river, as their troubles left no real mark on time.

Now it was not comforting. Now he did not feel as if he could breathe. The pain he felt was physical, as if sharp steel rods had been slid through his ribs, stopping his heart.

"James?"

James glanced up. Matthew was walking toward him, his topcoat open. He was hatless, fair hair tangling in the breeze off the river, scented with coal and salt.

"I've been looking for you all over the City," Matthew said, swinging himself up on the stone bastion beside James. James fought the urge to tell him to be careful. It was a long fall to the river, but Matthew's hands were steady as he braced himself. "Tell me what happened."

James couldn't explain it—the choking feeling, the dizziness. He recalled his father saying that love was pain, but this felt other than pain. It felt as if he had been deprived of air almost to the point of death and now was gasping and choking on it, trying desperately to get enough into his lungs. He couldn't find words, couldn't do anything but lean over and put his head down on Matthew's shoulder.

"Jamie, Jamie," Matthew said, and his hand came up to press itself strongly against James's back, between his shoulder blades. "Don't."

James kept his face pressed into the tweed of Matthew's coat. It smelled like brandy and the Penhaligon's cologne Matthew nicked from Charles. James knew his body was bent in a somewhat awkward way, his hand gripping Matthew's shirtfront and his face jammed into his shoulder, but there was something about the comfort of your *parabatai*—no one else could give it to you, not mother or sister or father or lover. It was a transcendence of all that.

People were wont to dismiss Matthew—because of his clothes,

because of his jokes, because of the way he took nothing seriously. They assumed he was liable to break, to give way when things became difficult. But he wasn't. He was holding James up now, as he always had—and making it look easy, as he always had.

"I suppose there are a lot of useless things I could tell you," he said in a low voice, as James drew back. "That it was probably better this happened sooner, and that it is better to have loved and lost than never to have loved at all, and all that. But it's all rot, isn't it?"

"Most likely," said James. He was aware his hands were shaking in a way that reminded him of something. He couldn't quite recall what. He was having trouble focusing, ideas skittering about like mice diving away from an approaching cat. "I thought my life would be one thing. Now it seems it is to be entirely different."

Matthew screwed up his face in a way parents often found adorable. James thought it made him look like Oscar. "Believe me," he said. "I do know how that feels."

James was slightly surprised to hear it. He'd walked in on Matthew in compromising positions before with girls and boys, but he'd never thought Matthew's heart was engaged with any of them.

There was Lucie, of course. But James suspected that Matthew did not love her, either, beyond the remnants of a childhood infatuation. Somewhere along the way, James sensed, Matthew had lost faith in most things. It would be easy for him to keep his faith in Lucie, but faith alone was not love.

James reached his hand into Matthew's coat. Matthew grumbled but didn't slap his hand away as James unbuttoned the inside pocket and drew out his *parabatai*'s silver flask.

"Are you sure?" said Matthew. "The last time you were feeling heartbroken, you took shots at a chandelier with a mundane gun and nearly drowned yourself in the Serpentine."

"I wasn't *trying* to drown myself," James pointed out. "Besides, Magnus Bane saved me."

"Don't mention that," said Matthew, as James uncapped the flask. "You know how angry I am about that. I idolize Magnus Bane, you had one chance to meet him, and you embarrassed us all."

"I'm quite sure I never mentioned any of you to him," said James, and tipped the flask back. He choked. It was blue ruin: the cheapest, harshest kind of gin. It went down like lightning. He coughed and thrust the flask away.

"Even worse," said Matthew. "How sharper than the serpent's tooth it is to have an ungrateful *parabatai*."

"I'm fairly sure that isn't the original Shakespeare," James said. "It was a good thing Bane was there," he added. "I was in a bad state. I barely recall it. I know it was because of Grace—she had written to me to say we should cut off contact with each other. I couldn't understand it. I went out to drink, to forget—" He broke off, shaking his head. "The next day she wrote to me again to apologize. She said she had only been frightened. I wonder now if it would have been better had things ended then."

"We do not get to choose when in our lives we feel pain," said Matthew. "It comes when it comes, and we try to remember, even though we cannot imagine a day when it will release its hold on us, that all pain fades. All misery passes. Humanity is drawn to light, not darkness."

The sky was full of London's black smoke. Matthew was a pale mark against the storm-dark sky; the bright fabric of his waistcoat shone, as did his fair hair. "Math," James said. "I know you never liked Grace."

Matthew sighed. "It doesn't matter what I think of her. It never did."

"You knew she didn't love me," James said. He still felt dizzy.

"No. I feared it. It is not the same. Even then, I could never have guessed what she would do. Charles will never make her happy."

"She asked me to marry her last night—to run away and marry her in secret," said James. "I said no. Today, she told me it had been a test. It was as if she had decided that our love was already a broken and ruined thing, and was trying to prove it." He took a ragged breath. "But I cannot imagine loving her more than I have—more than I do."

Matthew's fingers whitened where he grasped the flask. After a long moment, he spoke with some difficulty. "You cannot torment yourself," he said. "If it had not been that test, it would have been another. This is not an issue of love, but of ambition. She wishes to be the Consul's wife. Love has no place in this plan."

James tried to focus on Matthew's face. It wasn't as easy as it ought to have been. Lights danced behind his eyelids when he closed them, and his hands were still shaking. Surely this could not be from one sip of blue ruin. He knew he wasn't drunk, but a feeling of detachment was still there. As if nothing he did now mattered. "Tell me, Matthew," he said. "Tell me the name of the shadow that is always hanging over you. I can become a shadow. I could fight it for you."

Matthew squeezed his eyes shut, as if in pain. "Oh, Jamie," he sighed. "What if I said there is no shadow?"

"I would not believe you," said James. "I know what I feel in my own heart."

"James," said Matthew. "You're starting to slide off the bridge."

"Good." James closed his eyes. "Maybe I'll be able to sleep tonight."

Matthew leaped down, just in time to catch James as he slumped backward off the wall.

James knelt upon the roof of the Institute. He knew that he was dreaming, yet at the same time it felt impossible that what was happening to him was not real: he could see London laid out before him as clearly as a painting, see its roads and alleys and boulevards, see the stars hanging high above the city, pale white as the pearly teeth of a child's doll. He could see himself, as from a distance, see the black of his hair, and the deeper black of the wings that rose from his back.

He saw himself struggle with the weight of the wings. They were jagged and dark, with overlapping layers of feathers that shaded from deep black to gray. He realized then—they were not his wings: a monster knelt on his back, a creature whose face he could not see. A humped, misshapen thing, in pale gray rags, its sharp talons dug deep into his back.

He felt the pain. It was as fierce as fire, burning through his skin; he staggered to his feet, twisting and turning as if he could hurl the creature off him. Light blazed up all around him—pale gold light, the same light he had seen when he had passed into the shadow realm and then into the Chiswick greenhouse.

The light of Cortana.

He saw her there, the blade in her hand, her hair like fire. She cut at the creature on James's back, and with a searing pain it tore away from him, Cortana sunk deep into its body. It fell away, tumbling down the steep incline of the roof.

James's shirt was rags, soaked in blood. He could feel more blood trickling between his shoulder blades. Cordelia ran to him. She whispered his name: James, James, as if no one had ever spoken it before.

All about them the sky bloomed with brilliant lights. He could no longer see Cordelia. The lights formed into shapes and patterns—he had seen them before, the scrawls on the paper in Gast's flat. The knowledge of what they were tickled at the edge of his brain. He called out for Cordelia, but she was gone, like the dream he'd known she was.

When James woke in the morning, he was lying in his own bed. He was fully dressed, though someone had taken off his jacket and shoes and set them on a chair. In a velvet wing-backed chair nearby Matthew was dozing, his cheek propped on his hand.

Matthew always looked quite different when he was asleep. The constant motion that was such a distraction when he was awake vanished, and he became one of those paintings he loved: a Frederic Leighton, perhaps. Leighton was famous for painting children in their innocence, and when Matthew slept, he looked as if sorrow had never touched him.

As if he knew he was being watched, he stirred and sat up, focusing on James. "You're awake." He began to grin. "How's your head? Ringing like a bell?"

James sat up slowly. He had been with Matthew on many mornings when his *parabatai* was complaining of a bad head, or aches and misery and the need to swallow a glass of raw egg and pepper before he could face the day. But James felt nothing like that. Nothing hurt or ached. "No, but—how do I look?"

"Ghastly," Matthew reported happily. "Like you saw the ghost of Old Mol and your hair's still sticking up."

James stared down at his own hands, turning them over. His bare wrist still looked odd, the bracelet's absence like a glaring wound. But there was no actual pain, either physical or mental.

"On the other hand," Matthew said, his eyes diabolically alight, "I can't say your parents were too pleased when I carried you in last night. . . ."

James bolted out of bed. His clothes were as rumpled as if he'd slept under a bridge. "You carried me? My parents were here?"

"They had indeed come back from their meeting with my brother," said Matthew, "who was, apparently, very boring, which I could have told them."

"MATTHEW," James said.

Matthew held his hands up innocently. "I said nothing to them, but apparently Charles told them of his engagement to Grace at the meeting, and they deduced you were trying to drown your sorrows. I told them that you'd only had a sip of gin and they decried you as a lightweight."

"Dear God." James staggered to the washroom. Thankfully there was water in the pitcher, and a bar of sandalwood soap. He scrubbed himself down hastily and rinsed his hair. Feeling less revolting, he went into the dressing room, threw on new clothes, and returned to the bedroom, where Matthew sat on the foot of his bed with his legs crossed. He handed James a mug of tea without a word—exactly the way he liked it: strong and sugared, with no milk.

"Where did you produce that from?" James wondered aloud, accepting the mug.

Matthew hopped to his feet. "Come along," he said. "Food has been laid on in the breakfast room. Let us sample some of Bridget's delicious eggs and I'll explain."

James eyed his *parabatai* with suspicion. Bridget's eggs were famously awful. "Explain what?"

Matthew made a hushing gesture. Rolling his eyes, James slid his feet into shoes and followed Matthew through the winding corridors to the breakfast room, where food was still laid out. A silver urn with now-cold coffee in it, plates of veal chops, and James's least favorite, kedgeree. He settled at the table with a plate of mushrooms and toast. His mind felt surprisingly clear, as if he had come out of a strange fog. Even the toast and mushrooms tasted different.

He frowned. "Something's happened," he said, realizing how quiet it was. Only the sound of clocks ticking in the Institute. The corridors had been devoid of people. He stood and went to the window, which looked out over the courtyard. It was empty of carriages. His grip tightened on the sill. "Matthew, has anyone—"

"No," Matthew said quickly. "No, Jamie, no one else has died. The Enclave decided to move the wounded to the Silent City. They were too ill to be Portaled there, so your parents are helping with the task, as are Christopher's. Even Charles has loaned our carriage."

"And Grace?" said James. Her name felt odd in his mouth, as if it had acquired a new sound. He remembered the sick pain he had felt the day before, propelling him out into the dark. A feeling as if his chest were cracking apart, his bones splintering. He did not feel it now. He remembered the pain, but intellectually, not physically. It would surely come back, he thought. He should brace himself while he could.

"The Pouncebys have taken her in," said Matthew. "They are in Highgate, near the entrance to the Silent City. She will be able to visit her mother." He paused. "She will be all right, James."

"Yes, I trust she will," said James. "And Lucie? Does she know what's going on?"

Matthew looked surprised. "Yes, but—did you hear what I said of Grace?"

Before James could answer, Lucie came into the dining room. She was in training clothes—a soft belted tunic over leggings and boots—and she carried a handful of letters with her. The post must just have come. She dropped the correspondence into the mail salver on the bureau and came toward James with a worried look. "Jamie! Oh, thank goodness. Mother told me about Charles and Grace, but I have kept the news entirely to myself. Are you all right? Is your soul harrowed?"

"Cruel Prince James is quite all right, thank you," he said. Rather oddly, he noticed, Matthew had slid around behind Lucie and appeared to be poking at the mail. "Where have you been, Luce?"

"Up in the training room with Cordelia," she said. "Alastair went with Charles to help move some of the sick, and she stayed back with me. We thought perhaps we ought to be a bit more prepared, you know, in case you have another secret assignation that ends in a demon attack."

"I don't think that's likely," James said, and saw Matthew give him yet another peculiar look.

"James," said Lucie severely. "You do not need to pretend to be brave, as Lord Wingrave was when his hand was rejected in marriage."

James wondered if this was someone he was supposed to know. "Who on earth's that?"

"He's in *The Beautiful Cordelia*," Lucie said. "I swear I read that bit out loud last Christmas. Papa was very impressed."

Matthew whirled around, his hands behind his back. "Ah, Lucie," he said a little too loudly. "You have been training, I see, like a great warrior of England. Like Boadicea, who defeated the Romans. Sit down! Let me make you a honey sandwich."

Lucie looked hesitant, then seemed to shrug and accept the gesture. "You are a mad person, Matthew," she said. "But I do adore honey sandwiches." She flopped down in a chair and reached for the teapot. "I suppose Charles and Grace haven't announced their engagement formally yet, but that would be awfully rude of them with Ariadne so ill. I am surprised the Inquisitor hasn't tried to get Charles arrested."

As Matthew crossed the room to get the honey pot from the sideboard, he pressed something flat and papery into James's hand. "I know it's addressed to Lucie," he said in a low voice. "But it's for Cordelia. Take it to her."

One did not ask questions when one's *parabatai* made a request. "It seems I have forgotten to put on socks," James announced. Lucie stared at him as if he'd lost his wits. He edged toward the door, trying to prevent Lucie from seeing his feet. "I shall return in a moment."

James took the stairs toward the upper floors two at a time. He felt lighter than he had in months, as if he had put down a massive burden he hadn't even known he was carrying. As he reached the third-floor landing, he examined the object that Matthew had handed him: a letter, addressed in the Consul's unmistakable handwriting, to Lucie Herondale.

The door of the training room was open. It was a large room, which had been made larger a few years ago when they had joined it up with the rest of the attic. The floor was polished wood covered in tatami mats, and flexible ropes dangled from the raftered beams overhead, knotted at various lengths to make for easier climbing. Witchlight torches lit the room, and cloudy sunlight poured in through the windows high above.

Cordelia stood at the north end of the room in front of a large silvered mirror, Cortana gleaming gold in her hand. She wore training clothes she must have borrowed from Lucie: they were tight and short on her, her ankles visible beneath the hems of the trousers.

She turned, moving with the sword as if they danced together. Her light brown skin gleamed in the witchlight, sheened with sweat at her collarbones, her throat. Her hair had come free from its pins. It tumbled down her back like a waterfall of autumn leaves. Together she and Cortana were a poem written in fire and blood.

He must have made a noise, for she turned to look at him, eyes wide, her chest rising and falling with quick breaths. A jolt went through him. Something like a memory—Cordelia lying beside him, her hair soft against the side of his neck, the warmth of her hip against his—

He tried to shake the thought from his head; nothing like that had ever happened in his life. A fragment of his dream the night before, perhaps?

He drew the letter from his pocket and held it out to her. "Daisy," he said. "I have something for you."

Many years of practice had acquainted Cordelia well with solo training. Her father had always said that a living partner was necessary to learn certain aspects of sword art—how could you learn to turn a blade at close quarters, for instance, if you had no opposing sword to press yours against? Alastair had retorted that Shadowhunter training was somewhat unique: you were rarely fighting another opponent with a sword, after all, and far more often a peculiarly shaped monster.

Cordelia had giggled, and Elias had rolled his eyes and relented. After all, they moved around so often for Elias's health that neither Cordelia nor Alastair had regular training partners except each other, and they did not match in height or weight. So when Lucie had gone off to procure herself a cup of tea, Cordelia had fallen into the old patterns of practicing her footwork—lunging with Cortana in hand, practicing sequences of actions over and over until they were as natural to her as walking downstairs. She raised Cortana, turned, spun, and lunged—only to nearly lose her balance in surprise as James walked through the open door of the training room.

She stared at him for a moment, caught off guard. Something about him seemed different. His clothes were ordinary—morning coat, gray trousers—and his hair was the usual dark tangle. There were slight shadows under his eyes, which was unsurprising for someone who had been out late.

She slid Cortana into the sheath at her back as James drew a letter from his pocket and offered it to her with a smile; she could see Lucie's name scrawled across the front.

"How did you know this was for me?" she asked. Her hands were shaking as she took the letter from him and began to open it.

"Matthew told me," he said. "I believe he is distracting Lucie in the dining room, though who knows how long that will last."

"It's all right, you know—I trust Lucie," Cordelia said. "If I hadn't been prepared for her to read the letter I wouldn't have had it sent here."

"I know," said James. "But it is *your* letter. Why shouldn't you read it first? In fact, if you'd like me to leave, I can."

"No," Cordelia said, dropping her gaze to scan Charlotte's scrawled lines. "No—do please stay."

Dear Lucie,

I hope this letter finds you well, and dear Cordelia
also. I am afraid that I only have a little bit of news,
as the situation with Elias Carstairs has been put on
hold while the current emergency is dealt with. We
did indeed attempt to try Elias by the Mortal Sword,
but unfortunately doing so did not shed any light on
the situation, as Elias has no memory of the events of
the night of the battle. It is a very complicated matter.
Please give Cordelia my best wishes. I look forward to
returning to London and seeing you soon.
Love,
Charlotte

Cordelia sat down hard on the windowsill. "I don't understand," she whispered. "Why wouldn't he remember?"

James crinkled his eyebrows. "What do you mean? What's happened?"

"You know my father is soon to be on trial," she said slowly. "In Idris."

"Yes," he said. "I have not wanted to pry. I have not even asked Lucie for details, though I was curious." He sat down beside her on the windowsill. "I will not lie," he said. "I have heard whispers. But I put little stock in whispers. There have been enough about me and my family, and enough of them untrue, for me to prefer my own judgment to that of others." He laid his hand over hers. "If you want to share the truth with me, I would be glad to hear it, but it is your choice, Daisy."

His fingers were warm and calloused, rough with scars. James seemed different, Cordelia thought again. More—present. As if he were here in the moment, not holding the world at arm's length.

The whole story came pouring out of her: her father's illness over the past years, necessitating their many moves from place to place, his agreeing to help with the expedition, the disaster that had followed, his arrest, their journey to London, the upcoming trial, Cordelia's attempts to find a way to save her family. "Matthew was kind enough to arrange for me to get this letter, but it is another dead end. I don't know how to help my father."

James looked thoughtful. "Daisy, I'm so sorry. This is something that your friends should be helping you with, and I am one of them."

"There is nothing anyone can do," Cordelia said. For the first time, she felt hopeless about her father.

"Not necessarily," said James. "Considering who my *parabatai*'s mother is, I hear more about the legal processes of the Clave than I might prefer. I can tell you that if this is going to be a trial with no Mortal Sword, it will have to rely on testimony and character witnesses."

"Character witnesses? But my father knows so few people," Cordelia said. "We have always been moving—never even at Cirenworth for long stretches of time—"

"I've heard many stories about your father," James went on. "Mostly from Jem. After Jem's parents were killed by the demon Yanluo, it was Elias who tracked the demon down with Ke Yiwen and slew it, saving countless lives. Your father may have been weary and sick these last few years, but before that he was a hero, and the Clave needs to be reminded of that."

Hope began to return to Cordelia's heart. "My father rarely talks about his life before our family. Do you think you could help me find out the names of some of these witnesses? Though," she added hastily, "I understand if you can't. I know Grace will need you now, with her mother ill."

James hesitated. "I no longer have an understanding with Grace."

"What?"

He had drawn his hands back; they were trembling. She realized with a slight shock that the metal cuff was no longer on his wrist. Grace must have taken it back. "You are the first person I've told, aside from Matthew. Last night—"

Christopher exploded into the room like a small cyclone. He was hatless and wore a frock coat that looked as if it had probably belonged to his father, made of herringbone with several holes burned into the cuffs. "Here you are," he said, as if they had betrayed him by not being in a more easily discovered location. "I have come with news."

James rose to his feet. "What is it, Kit?"

"Those wooden shards you sent me," said Christopher. "Thomas and I were able to analyze them using the laboratory in the tavern."

"The wooden shards? The ones we thought might be weapons?" said Cordelia.

Christopher nodded. "The peculiar thing is that the acid that had burned the wood was the blood of some sort of demon, and there was demonic residue on the wood, but only on one side of each shard."

James's eyes widened. "Say that again."

"Only on one side of each shard," said Christopher obediently. "As if it had been placed there deliberately."

"No." James reached into his pocket and drew out a folded paper. Cordelia recognized it as the sketch he and Matthew had found at Gast's. He held it out to Cordelia. "I meant to ask you before," he said, urgency underlining his tone. "I thought when I first glanced at this that they were runes—I don't know what on earth was in my head. Some of these are alchemical symbols, but the others are clearly Old Persian writing, probably from the Achaemenid era."

Cordelia took the paper from James. She had not been able to look at the paper closely before, but James was right—below the odd symbols was a name in Old Persian. The cuneiform writing *did* look a bit like runes, but she recognized it immediately; her mother had insisted she and Alastair know at least a little of the language of Darius the Great. *"Merthykhuwar,"* she said slowly. "It is a name for a kind of demon that existed in Persia long ago. Shadowhunters call it the Mandikhor."

"Even mundanes have a word for it," James said. "'Manticore.'" He glanced over at Christopher. "I know what the shards are now," he said. "How could I not have seen it before? They're the remains of a Pyxis box."

"A Pyxis?" Cordelia was startled. Long ago, Shadowhunters had developed wooden containers called Pyxis boxes to trap the essence of demons they hunted; after the Clockwork War, when Axel Mortmain had used a Pyxis box to transfer demon souls into clockwork monsters, they had been abandoned as a tool by the Nephilim. No one had used them for years.

"I've seen a Pyxis before, at the Academy," James said. "If a demon had been trapped in a Pyxis and burst out, that would explain why there was demon residue only on one side of the wood—the inside. And the markings on the shards resemble the alchemical symbols that were carved on Pyxis boxes—"

The sound of running footsteps in the hall interrupted him. The door flew open again; this time it was Matthew and Lucie, both looking harried. Christopher, who had seized a seraph blade from his belt, lowered it in relief. "Thank Raziel," he said. "I thought it was a demon attacking."

Matthew gave Christopher a dark look. "Put that away," he said. "I don't fancy being stabbed; I am far too young and beautiful to die."

"I see you have been waylaid on your way to find socks, James," said Lucie. "Bridget came and told us Christopher was here. What's going on? Has anything happened?"

"Quite a lot of things, actually," said Christopher. "We can discuss it all at the Devil Tavern. Thomas is waiting there, and I do not want to leave him alone."

The Devil Tavern was a half-timbered building on Fleet Street with vast glittering windowpanes that seemed to divide light, leaving the interior of the pub darkly shaded. There were very few people inside, only a few men hunched over tankards of ale, but a grizzled werewolf barkeep and his wide-eyed barmaid watched Lucie, Cordelia, James, Christopher, and Matthew cross the room and ascend the steps, their gazes curious.

Cordelia was unsurprised to see that the walls of the Merry Thieves' rooms were crowded with fascinating-looking books. There was an antique-looking dartboard in which several throwing daggers were embedded, its embossed red-and-black surface showing the marks of many more. There was a corner with sheets of metal fixed to the walls and a sturdy steel-topped worktable, upon which sat a set of shiny brass scales and a somewhat battered-looking wooden beer crate filled with glass test tubes, retorts, and other chemistry paraphernalia. A mobile laboratory for Christopher, Cordelia assumed.

A low horsehair sofa was placed directly across from a fireplace whose mantel boasted a bust of Apollo, below which was carved a verse about wine. Thomas sat upon the sofa, a book in his hand. His broad shoulders were hunched, his eyes shadowed with exhaustion. Still, his face lit up when he saw his friends.

"Tom," said James. He went and sank down next to his friend on the worn sofa, placing a hand on his shoulder. He glanced up and saw the others still hesitant. He gestured for them to join him and Thomas. It was always James, Cordelia thought as they drew up chairs. Always James keeping the group together, noticing when they needed each other.

Thomas set down the book he'd been holding; Cordelia was startled to see it was a book of Sufi poetry, the verses of Hafiz and Ibn al-Farid, written out in Persian and Arabic. "Cordelia," he said. He sounded weary, as if his voice had been slowed by grief. "Lucie. I'm glad to see you."

"Welcome to our sanctum, ladies," said Matthew, unscrewing the cap of his flask. "Christopher salvaged quite a bit of this furniture for us. Like King Arthur and his knights, we prefer to sit at a round table that we all might be equal."

"Also," Christopher added, taking a book down from the shelves and handing it to James, "it was the only table my mother was willing to spare."

"I couldn't go to Idris," Thomas said rather suddenly, as if someone had demanded of him why he was still in London. "I wish to see Eugenia, but I need to stay here. I need to help Kit find the cure for this demon disease or poison or whatever this is. What happened to my sister cannot happen to someone else."

"Sometimes grief and worry must take the form of action," said Cordelia. "Sometimes it is unbearable to sit and wait."

Thomas shot her a grateful look. "Exactly that," he said. "So—Christopher told you all about the shards?"

"Yes," Christopher interjected, "and James realized the shards are from a Pyxis."

"A Pyxis?" Thomas echoed. "But they were destroyed after the Clockwork War. They're unsafe—remember what happened at school."

"*Most* Pyxides were destroyed after the Clockwork War," said James. "In Gast's flat, though, I found a drawing. It looked rather like a sketch of an ordinary box—he wasn't a very good artist—"

"Ah, the drawing with the wobbly runes around it?" Matthew said.

"They weren't runes," James said. "They were alchemical symbols—the kind you'd carve onto a Pyxis box."

"Oh!" said Lucie. "The markings on the shards. They were alchemical symbols too. Of course."

"That wasn't all," said James. "On the paper Gast had scrawled a word in Old Persian. Cordelia was able to translate it."

He looked at her expectantly.

"It was a demon's name," Cordelia said. *"Merthykhuwar."* She frowned. Such demons had featured in old stories from her childhood; she had always thought of them as near-mythical, like dragons. "In modern Persian it would be *Mardykhor.* But Shadowhunters—Shadowhunters call it a Mandikhor. They are said to be viciously poisonous."

"You think Gast summoned up a Mandikhor demon?" Matthew asked. "But aren't they meant to be extinct? And what've they got to do with Pyxis boxes?"

James flipped open the book Christopher had handed him and slid a pair of small gilt reading glasses onto his nose. Something in Cordelia's chest tightened, as if she had snagged a small piece of her heart, like a piece of cloth on a thorn. She looked away from the sight of James and his adorable spectacles. She had to find someone else to feel this way about. Or someone to feel a different way about. Anything, so she could stop feeling like this.

She tried not to think about what he had said in the training room. *I no longer have an understanding with Grace.* But why? What could have happened between them, and happened so quickly?

"'The Mandikhor is both here and there, both one and many,'" James quoted. "See, one of the nastiest things about the Mandikhor is that it can split itself into many pieces, each of which is both its own separate demon and a part of the original creature. That's why they're best captured in Pyxis boxes. The Mandikhor is difficult to kill—partly because it can produce an endless stream of smaller demons; you'd find yourself not even being able to get near it. But with a Pyxis, if you use the box to capture the Mandikhor, the smaller demons will disappear." He looked up from the book. "I started to guess it was a Pyxis when Christopher told me about the shards. Cordelia's translation confirmed it. I knew Gast must have summoned up one of the few demons he would need a Pyxis to capture. In this case, a Mandikhor."

"It doesn't look anything like those creatures that attacked us at the park," said Christopher, peering over James's shoulder. The book was illustrated, but Cordelia didn't need to see it: she knew what a Mandikhor looked like. Scorpion tail, lion body, triple row of jaws dripping poison.

"I am fairly sure those were the Khora," offered Cordelia. "The smaller demons that split from the Mandikhor. They do not resemble it. And that must be why Gast referred to the demon in the singular—he *did* raise one demon. It split into smaller demons later."

"So someone hired Gast to raise a Mandikhor and trap it in a Pyxis," said Lucie. "But when he returned to his flat with the demon caged in the box, they ambushed and killed him—and set the creature free."

"Gast is not the mind behind this," James agreed. "He was a tool, useful only for building a Pyxis and summoning the demon. Someone else is directing its movements and attacks."

"Not *just* summoning the demon," said Lucie. "Remember what Ragnor said—Gast summoned it in such a way, using dimensional magic, that it is protected from sunlight."

They all exchanged glances. Cordelia knew what the others were thinking—who could have hired Gast? Was there no motive save to spread bloodshed, contagion, and death?

Thomas ran a hand through his thick hair. "If the demon were trapped and killed, what of those who are poisoned? Would they get better?"

James shook his head. "The sick will not be healed. We still need an antidote for that. But the demons will be gone, and that is quite a start." He set the book down. "The Enclave has been searching for these demons with no success—how would they have guessed they were seeking the offspring of an extinct creature? But now that we know it is a Mandikhor . . ."

"In the stories of *Merthykhuwar* demons, they make their homes in between spaces," Cordelia said slowly. "For instance, the border between two countries, or the middle of a bridge. Somewhere that is neither here nor there."

James drew off his spectacles; he was biting his lip thoughtfully. "When I went into the shadow realm, from the ballroom," he said, "I saw—among others things—Tower Bridge. A strange red light poured from it. I think—"

Matthew sat up straight. "We know Gast raised the demon from a bridge," he said. "A place between, as Cordelia said. Perhaps it still resides there."

"So if we were to go to Tower Bridge, with a Pyxis, it's possible that we could recapture the Mandikhor?" said Lucie. "And then the Khora would disappear—just as if it had died?"

"Yes, but we'd have to get a Pyxis first," said Christopher practically. "That would be difficult."

"But perhaps not impossible," said Matthew. He was tapping his fingers restlessly against the arm of his chair, his hair and necktie disheveled. "If most were destroyed after the Clockwork War . . ."

"A few remain," said James. "Unfortunately, they're in Idris."

"I was afraid you were going to say that," muttered Matthew, reaching for his flask again. "I think it will be noticed by the Clave if we disappear from London and turn up in Idris, rooting around the Gard like treasure hunters."

James gave him an exasperated look. "The only Pyxides in the *Clave's* possession are in Idris. There are a few others. We just need to find one. There's a certain shop in Limehouse—"

"Wait," said Cordelia suddenly. "A box covered in alchemical symbols—the *ourobouros* is an alchemical symbol, isn't it? Matthew, didn't we see a box with a serpent design on it? In the Hell Ruelle?"

Matthew started. "Yes," he said. "In the chamber of Hypatia Vex. A wooden box with an *ourobouros* symbol burned into the sides. It makes sense; Hypatia is an inveterate collector."

"Excellent," said Christopher. "We'll just tell her we need it, then."

"Go ahead, if you fancy being turned into a china cabinet," said James. "Hypatia does not like Shadowhunters." He looked thoughtful. "Good catch, though, Daisy. There must be some way for us to get to it."

"We could rob the Hell Ruelle," said Thomas.

"And wear masks," said Lucie eagerly. "Like highwaymen."

"Only a fool would rob Hypatia Vex," said Matthew. "And let it not be said that Matthew Fairchild is a fool. At least, let it not be said in my hearing. I would find it very hurtful."

"I think Christopher is right," said Cordelia. "We should ask Hypatia."

Christopher looked stunned and gratified in equal measure. "We should?"

"Well, not us," said Cordelia. "It is true she does not like most Shadowhunters. But there is certainly at least one she likes very much."

"Daisy, darling, I'm delighted to see you," Anna declared. "Though it is entirely bad form to appear unannounced at teatime. There simply won't be enough cake for everybody. The girls will have cake and the boys nothing. There is no other fair way to do it."

The flat on Percy Street remained a cheerful oasis of chaos.

Perhaps it was even more chaotic than it had been on Cordelia's last visit. A lace-edged ribbon that Cordelia suspected came from a lady's corset adorned one of the knives stuck in Anna's mantelpiece, swinging jauntily from a jeweled hilt. Anna's gold-covered sofa and mismatched chairs were all filled with people. Thomas, too tall for the chairs, was stretched out on the hearth rug with his boots balanced on the coal bucket. On her small table, Anna had laid out, with the air of a magnificent hostess, a fruitcake she called barmbrack, and a Victoria sponge she'd purchased from a pastry cook's.

"That is unjust desserts," said James.

"The world is unjust, my love," Anna told him. She sat upon the arm of the high wing-backed chair where Christopher was sitting, swinging one booted foot in front of her, and idly reached down to stroke Thomas's hair. The fine strands slipped through her long, scarred fingers. "Of course I would offer *you* cake, dear cousin, if I thought it would ease your heart."

Thomas gave her a fond but tired look. "I think in this case, assistance would be better than cake."

"By all means," said Anna. "Tell me what's going on."

As James explained that they required a Pyxis—though not precisely why, implying it was related to the demon attacks— Cordelia looked back and forth between the two cousins, James and Anna. In many ways, the two of them looked more like brother and sister than James and Lucie, or Anna and Christopher. They shared the same crow-black hair, like Will's and Cecily's, and the same chiseled, angular faces. They both wore their intelligence like armor—sharp minds and sharp retorts protecting what softness might lie beneath.

"And so," James finished, "we thought, perhaps tonight at the Hell Ruelle—"

Anna flicked an eyebrow upward. "Ah yes, about that. Let me be perfectly clear what you are asking: You want me to seduce a warlock in order to procure you a tragically outmoded box in which to, no doubt, house a dangerous demon?" Anna surveyed the room. "How did you decide on this plan? And why in Raziel's name haven't you told anyone else about it?"

"Because we are guessing?" hazarded Matthew.

"Because we cannot," said Lucie stiffly. "We have sworn a vow to protect the source who gave us the information our *guesses* are based on. We cannot even tell you, dear Anna. You must simply trust us that this is for a good reason."

Anna threw her hands up. "All right. You are off your heads, every one of you."

James's mouth tugged upward at the corner. "Don't you think you could do it?"

"Humph." Anna toyed with her watch so the chain caught the light and glittered. "I could do it. But it goes entirely against my code. It is against my strict policy to seduce anybody twice."

"I didn't know you'd seduced Hypatia once," said Matthew.

Anna waved an impatient hand. "Ages ago. How do you think I got invited to the Hell Ruelle in the first place? Honestly, Matthew."

"How did you leave things with Hypatia?" said Lucie. "Was her heart broken? In that case, she might want . . . revenge."

Anna rolled her eyes. "Wait here a moment, my dear novelist. In fact, all of you wait here, except Cordelia. You come with me, Daisy."

She swung up from her place on the arm of Christopher's chair and strode across the room, bounding up a couple of steps and disappearing behind a wooden door. Cordelia stood, smoothed the frills of her gown, wiggled her eyebrows at Lucie, and marched into the infamous bedchamber of Anna Lightwood.

It was surprisingly ordinary. If Cordelia had hoped for scandalous etchings or tearstained love letters pinned to the walls, there were none. Instead there were cigars laid out with bottles of cologne on a battered walnut desk, and a kingfisher-blue waistcoat slung carelessly over a japanned screen. The bed was unmade, the sheets a tangle of silk.

As Cordelia closed the door carefully after her, Anna glanced up, tossing her a grin and a brightly colored bundle. Cordelia caught it reflexively. It was a long bolt of cloth: a royal-blue silk.

"What's this?" asked Cordelia.

Anna leaned against one of her bedposts, her hands in her pockets. "Indulge me. Hold it up against yourself."

Cordelia did as she was told. Perhaps Anna was having a dress made for a paramour? And using Cordelia as a model?

"Yes," Anna murmured. "The shade quite suits your coloring. As would a claret, I think, or a deep gold or saffron. None of these insipid pastels all the girls are wearing."

Cordelia smoothed a hand down the fabric. "I didn't think you liked dresses."

Anna shrugged, a brief lilt of her shoulders. "Wearing them myself was like having my soul in a prison of petticoats, but I deeply appreciate a beautiful woman in a gown that matches her. In fact, one of my favorite paramours—a lady who entertained me for almost two weeks—was a *belle* who you might know from the mundane fashion papers."

"Is this for her? Is it—" Cordelia began, delighted.

Anna laughed. "I'll never tell. Now put it down and come along. I've got what I came for."

She held up a small black-bound memorandum book. Cordelia hadn't even seen her retrieve it. They strode out of the bedroom, Anna waving the book over her head in triumph. "This," she announced, "will hold the answers to all our questions."

The occupants of the parlor looked up. Lucie, Christopher, and Matthew were squabbling over cake—though, Cordelia saw, a piece had been set on a plate for Thomas already and rested in his lap. James was looking into the cold grate of the fireplace, his expression distant.

Matthew looked up, his eyes fever-bright. "Is this your list of conquests?"

"Of course not," Anna declared. "It's a memorandum book ... about my conquests. That is an important but meaningful distinction."

Cordelia sank back onto the sofa beside Lucie, who had succeeded in acquiring a piece of Victoria sponge. Matthew leaned against the frame of the sofa beside her; James was looking over at Anna now, his eyes the color of sunlight through pale yellow leaves.

Anna flipped through the book. There were many pages, and many names written in a bold, sprawling hand.

"Hmm, let me see. Katherine, Alicia, Virginia—a very promising writer, you should look out for her work, James—Mariane, Virna, Eugenia—"

"Not my sister Eugenia?" Thomas nearly upended his cake.

"Oh, probably not," Anna said. "Laura, Lily . . . ah, Hypatia. Well, it was a brief encounter, and I suppose you might say she seduced me. . . ."

"Well, that hardly seems fair," said James. "Like someone solving a case before Sherlock Holmes. If I were you I would feel challenged, as if to a duel."

Matthew chuckled. Anna gave James a dark look. "I know what you're trying to do," she said.

"Is it working?" said James.

"Possibly," said Anna, regarding the book. Cordelia couldn't help but wonder: Was Ariadne's name in there? Was she considered a conquest now, or something—someone—else?

"I appreciate the scientific rigor with which you've approached this project, Anna," said Christopher, who had gotten jam on his sleeve. "Though I don't think I could manage to collect that many names and also pursue science. Much too time-consuming."

Anna laughed. "How many names would you want to collect, then?"

Christopher tilted his head, a brief frown of concentration crossing his face, and did not reply.

"I would only want one," said Thomas.

Cordelia thought of the delicate tracery of the compass rose on Thomas's arm, and wondered if he had any special person in mind.

"Too late for me to only have one," declared Matthew airily. "At least I can hope for several names in a carefully but enthusiastically selected list."

"Nobody's ever tried to seduce me at all," Lucie announced in a brooding fashion. "There's no need to look at me like that, James. I wouldn't say yes, but I could immortalize the experience in my novel."

"It would be a very short novel, before we got hold of the black-guard and killed him," said James.

There was a chorus of laughter and argument. The afternoon sun was sinking in the sky, its rays catching the jeweled hilts of the knives in Anna's mantelpiece. They cast shimmering rainbow patterns on the gold-and-green walls. The light illuminated Anna's shabby-bright flat, making something in Cordelia's heart ache. It was such a homey place, in a way that her big cold house in Kensington was not.

"What about you, Cordelia?" said Lucie.

"One," said Cordelia. "That's everyone's dream, isn't it, really? Instead of many who give you little pieces of themselves—one who gives you everything."

Anna laughed. "Searching for the one is what leads to all the misery in this world," she said. "Searching for many is what leads to all the fun."

Cordelia met James's eyes, half by accident. She saw the worry in his—there had been something brittle in Anna's laugh. "Then this should be fun," Cordelia said quickly. "Seducing Hypatia. After all, what are rules for if not to be broken?"

"You make an excellent point," said Matthew, finagling a piece of cake from Lucie's plate. She slapped at his hand.

"And getting this Pyxis might help quite a few people," said Cordelia. "It could have helped Barbara. It could still help Ariadne."

The blue of Anna's eyes darkened. "Oh, very well. Let's try it. Might be a lark. However."

"However what?" said Christopher. "If you haven't got the proper clothes, I could lend you my new waistcoat. It's orange."

Anna shuddered. "Orange is not the color of seduction, Christopher. Orange is the color of despair, and pumpkins. Regardless, I have all the clothes I need. However"—she held up a finger, the nail clipped quite short—"the Hell Ruelle is not assembled every night. The next salon is tomorrow."

"Then we will go tomorrow," said James.

"We cannot possibly all go to the Hell Ruelle," said Anna. "Hypatia wouldn't like it if we all show up in a gaggle. A gaggle is not dignified."

"It makes sense for me to go," said Matthew. "They know me there."

"I should go as well," said James. "It is possible my shadow power might be useful. I have utilized it before to—to acquire certain things."

Everyone looked puzzled, but James's expression was not one that suggested a request for clarification would be welcome.

Anna smiled her slow, scotch-and-honey smile. "And Cordelia as well, of course," she said. "A beautiful girl is always a distraction, and we will need to be very distracting indeed."

James and Matthew both glanced at Cordelia. *I will not blush,* she told herself fiercely. *I will not.* She had a suspicion she looked as if she might be choking.

"Bother," said Lucie. "I can already tell I'm going to be left out."

Anna turned toward her. "Lucie, you are very much needed. At the Institute. You see, there is a meeting of all the Enclave tomorrow night, and I had planned to attend. Apparently there is some significant news."

Lucie looked puzzled. Enclave meetings were restricted to Clave members who were eighteen and older. Only Anna and Thomas qualified.

"I can attend," said Thomas, with some reluctance. "Though I am not keen on sitting in a room full of people looking at me bloody pityingly."

They all looked at him in surprise; Thomas rarely swore.

"I was not thinking of attendance," said Anna. "They may moderate what they have to say if you are there. Better to spy on them."

"Oh, spying," said Lucie. "Perfect. They'll be meeting in the library; I know which room is over it. We can spy on them from overhead. Christopher shall be able to analyze what they say from a scientific perspective, and Thomas can recall it all with his excellent memory."

She beamed, and Cordelia found herself wanting to smile. Hidden in Lucie's practicality was a great kindness, she knew—Thomas had lost his sister and was desperate for something to do, some action to take. Lucie was giving him just that.

Thomas seemed to understand as well. He smiled at Lucie—the first smile Cordelia had seen on his face since Barbara's death. "Espionage it is," he said. "At last, something to look forward to."

14

AMONG LIONS

She dropped her glove, to prove his love, then looked at him and smiled;
He bowed, and in a moment leaped among the lions wild:
The leap was quick, return was quick, he has regained his place,
Then threw the glove, but not with love, right in the lady's face.
"By God!" said Francis, "rightly done!" and he rose from where he sat:
"Not love," quoth he, "but vanity, sets love a task like that."
—Leigh Hunt, "The Glove and the Lions"

James insisted on walking Cordelia home, though it was a dis-
tance from Percy Street to Kensington. Anna had whisked Matthew
away on a secret errand, and Thomas, Christopher, and Lucie had
returned to the Devil Tavern to research the working of Pyxis boxes.
Cordelia had wished she could stay with them, but she knew the
limits of her mother's patience. Sona would be wondering where
she was.

It was getting on toward twilight, the shade thickening under
the trees on Cromwell Road. Only a few horse-drawn carriages
clipped by in the blue light. It felt almost as if they had the city
to themselves; they weren't glamoured, but still no one cast them
more than glances of idle curiosity as they passed by the great brick

pile of the Natural History Museum. They were probably looking at James, Cordelia thought: like his father, he drew glances without trying. In the darkening light, his eyes reminded her of the eyes of tigers she had seen in Rajasthan, golden and watchful.

"It was clever of you to think of Anna," said James. Cordelia looked at him in some surprise; they had been chatting rather desultorily about their educations: Cordelia had been taught by Sona and an ever-changing group of tutors. James had gone to Shadowhunter Academy for only a few months; he'd met Thomas, Matthew, and Christopher there, and they'd promptly blown up a wing of the school. They'd all been expelled, save Thomas, who hadn't wanted to stay at the Academy without his friends and returned to London willingly at the end of the school year. For the past three years the Merry Thieves had been taught by Henry Fairchild and Sophie Lightwood. "I was grateful to have you with us today."

"The calming presence of a feminine hand?" Cordelia teased. "Lucie could do that."

James laughed. There was a graceful lightness to his walk that she had not noticed when she had first come to London. As if he had laid down something heavy he had been carrying, though that made little sense in the circumstances. "Lucie wouldn't want to bother. Familiarity breeds contempt, I fear, and to us we are her ridiculous brother and his ridiculous friends. I worry sometimes—"

He broke off. The wind caught the edges of his black morning coat. They flew like wings at his sides.

"You worry about Lucie?" asked Cordelia, a little puzzled.

"It's not that," James said. "I suppose I worry we all tumble into our roles too easily—Christopher the scientist, Thomas the kind one, Matthew the libertine. And I—I don't know what I am, exactly."

"You are the leader," said Cordelia.

He looked amused. "Am I?"

"The four of you are tightly knit," said Cordelia. "Anyone could see that. And none of you is so simple. Thomas is more than just kind, and Christopher more than beakers and test tubes, Matthew more than wit and waistcoats. Each of you follows his own star—but you are the thread that binds all four together. You are the one who sees what everyone needs, if anyone requires extra care from their friends, or even to be left alone. Some groups of friends drift apart, but you would never let that happen."

James's amusement had gone. There was a little roughness in his voice when he said, "So I am the one who cares the most, is that it?"

"You have a great power of caring in you," Cordelia said, and for a moment, it was a relief to say those words, to say what she had always thought about James. Even when she had watched him loving Grace, and felt the pain of it, she had thought, too, of what it would mean to be loved by someone with such a capacity for loving. "It is your strength."

James looked away.

"Is something wrong?" she asked.

"That night at Battersea Bridge," he said. They had reached Cordelia's house but remained on the pavement, in the shadow of a beech tree. "Grace asked me if I would run away with her. Cut my ties with my family, marry her in Scotland, and start over as mundanes."

"But—but your parents, and Lucie—" Cordelia's thoughts went immediately to her friend. How shattered Lucie would have been to lose her brother like that. As if he had died, but worse almost, because he would have chosen to have left them.

"Yes," said James. "And my *parabatai*. All my friends." His tiger eyes glittered in the dark. "I refused. I failed her. I failed to love as I should have. I am not sure caring could be my strength."

"That was not love she asked for," said Cordelia, suddenly

furious. "That is not love. That is a test. And love should not be tested like that." She paused. "I am sorry," she said. "I should not—I cannot understand Grace, so I should not judge her. But surely that is not the reason your understanding has ended?"

"I am not sure I do know the real reason," James said, locking his hands behind his back. "But I know it is final. She took back her bracelet. And she is marrying Charles."

Cordelia froze. She must have heard wrong. *"Charles?"*

"Matthew's older brother," said James, looking surprised, as if he thought perhaps she had forgotten.

"No," Cordelia breathed. "She cannot. They *cannot.*"

Somehow James was still explaining, saying something about Ariadne, about engagements being called off, but Cordelia's mind was full of Alastair. Alastair and Charles in the library—Alastair in agony over Charles's engagement. Alastair saying that at least it was Ariadne—he could not possibly have known of *this.*

Oh, Alastair.

"Are you all right?" James took a step toward her, his expression worried. "You look very pale."

I ought to go home, she was about to say. James had moved closer to her; she could smell the scent of him, of sandalwood soap and a mixture of leather and ink. She felt the brush of his hand against her cheek, his thumb softly tracing her cheekbone.

"Cordelia!" Both James and Cordelia turned, startled: Sona was standing on the threshold of the house, candlelight burning behind her. A silk *roosari* covered her dark hair and she was beaming. "Cordelia *joon*, do come inside before you catch cold. And Mr. Herondale, it was kind of you to escort Cordelia home. You are truly a gentleman."

Cordelia looked at her mother in surprise. She hadn't expected Sona to be in such a good mood.

James's eyebrow flicked upward, black as the wing of a crow, if the wing of the crow had a faintly sardonic air. "It's a pleasure to escort Daisy anywhere."

"Daisy," Sona repeated. "Such a charming pet name. Of course, you were children together, and now you are reunited and quite grown-up. It's all so delightful."

Ah. Cordelia realized what was going on with her mother. James was eligible—very eligible. As the son of the head of the London Institute, he might be expected to wield significant influence in the future, or even to become the head of an Institute himself, a job that paid far more than the salary provided by the Clave to a typical Shadowhunter.

Besides, he was charming when he was not wearing the Mask, and that sort of thing had an effect on mothers. At Sona's urging, she and James climbed the steps to the front door of the house: warm light spilled out from the vestibule, along with the smell of Risa's cooking.

Sona was still exclaiming over James. "Delightful," she said again. "Might I offer you refreshment, James? Tea, perhaps?"

Cordelia was seized by the impulse to flee the scene, but the Angel alone knew what her mother would say to James then. Besides, she could not flee—Alastair should hear this news from her, rather than from gossip or a stranger.

James smiled. It was the sort of smile that could lay waste to a good portion of England. "I remember the tea you made me at Cirenworth," he said. "It tasted of flowers."

Sona brightened. "Yes. A spoonful of rosewater, that's the secret to good *chai*."

"You had a beautiful samovar as well, I recall," said James. "Brass and gold."

Sona was beaming like a lighthouse. "It was my mother's," she said. "Alas, it is still among the things we have not unpacked, but my mother's tea set—"

"James has to go," Cordelia said firmly, and steered James back down the steps. "James, say goodbye."

James bid Sona a quick goodbye; Cordelia hoped he didn't notice the clear look of disappointment on her mother's face. She released her grip on his jacket as Sona went back inside.

"I had no idea your mother liked me so much," said James. "I should come round more often when I am in need of feeling appreciated."

Cordelia made an exasperated sound. "I fear my mother might be equally enthused over any eligible bachelor who pretended an interest in tea. That is why I told you to find me one, remember?"

She had made her voice light and joking, but the smile left James's face anyway. "Right," he said. "When all this business is over . . ."

"Yes, yes," Cordelia said, starting back up the stairs.

"I really do like tea!" James shouted from the bottom of the steps. "In fact, I love it! I LOVE TEA!"

"Good for you, mate!" yelled the driver of a passing hansom cab.

Despite everything, Cordelia could not stop herself from smiling. She went inside and shut the door; when she turned, her mother was standing directly behind her, still looking delighted. "He is handsome, isn't he?" said Sona. "I never would have thought it. He was such an awkward boy."

"*Mâmân*," Cordelia protested. "James is just a friend."

"Why have such a handsome friend? It seems a waste," said Sona. "Also, I do not think he regards you as only a friend. The way he looks at you—"

Cordelia threw her hands up. "I need to speak with Alastair about—about training," she said, and escaped at speed.

The door to Alastair's room was open. Cordelia stood a moment in the hallway, looking at her brother: he was seated at his satinwood writing desk, mundane newspapers strewn in front of him. He rubbed at his eyes as he read, weariness evident in the set of his shoulders.

"Any interesting news?" she asked, leaning against the door-frame. She knew better than to actually enter without an invitation; Alastair kept his room neat as a pin, from the polish on the walnut wardrobe to the spot-free set of blue armchairs by the window.

"Charles says that a rash of demon attacks can often be accompanied by a spike in what the mundanes report as crime," said Alastair, flicking aside the page he was reading with a newsprint-stained finger. "I can't say I'm seeing anything here, though. Nary a single juicy murder or the like."

"I was actually hoping to speak with you about Charles," said Cordelia.

Alastair flicked his gaze up at her. People often remarked that the two of them had the same black eyes, the iris only a shade lighter than the pupil. A strange effect considering Sona's eyes were light brown and Elias's blue. "About Charles?"

She nodded.

"Well, come inside then, and shut the door," he said, leaning back in his chair.

Cordelia did as requested. Alastair's room was bigger than hers, furnished in dark gentleman's colors: green walls, a muted Persian rug. Alastair had a collection of daggers, and he had brought quite a few of them with him from Cirenworth. They were the only beautiful things Cordelia remembered Alastair ever paying special attention to: one had a sheath of blue-and-white enamel, another was inlaid with golden designs of dragons, kylins, and birds. A *pishqabz* carved of a single piece of ivory hung above the washstand, near it a *khanjar* whose blade bore an inscription in Persian: *I wanted so much to have a gleaming dagger, that each of my ribs became a dagger.*

Cordelia settled herself in a blue armchair. Alastair turned a little to look at her; his fingers tapped out a rhythm on the newsprint. "What about Charles?" he said.

"I know he has become engaged again," she said. "To Grace Blackthorn."

Alastair's restless hands stopped moving. "Yes," he said. "Pity for your friend James."

So he knows, Cordelia thought. Charles must have told him. "So—are you all right?" she asked.

Alastair's black eyes were fathomless. "What do you mean?"

Cordelia couldn't bear it any longer. "I heard you and Charles talking in the library," she said. "I heard you say you loved him. I won't tell anybody else, I promise. You know I always keep my word. It doesn't make the least bit of difference to me, Alastair."

Alastair was silent.

"I wouldn't have said anything, but—for Charles to become engaged again, after he knew how unhappy you were about Ariadne—Alastair, I don't want anyone to be cruel to you. I want you to be with someone who will make you happy."

Alastair's eyes glittered. "He's not cruel. You don't know him. He and Grace have an understanding. He explained it to me. Everything Charles does is so he and I can be together." There was something mechanical about the words, as if they had been rehearsed.

"But you don't wish to be someone's secret," said Cordelia. "You said—"

"How do you know what I said? How could you possibly have overheard us without going out of your way to do so? You were upstairs, we were downstairs—unless you followed me," Alastair finished slowly. "You were eavesdropping. Why?"

"I was afraid," Cordelia said, in a low voice. "I thought you were going to tell Charles—what I had made you promise not to say."

"About that demon creature at the bridge?" he said incredulously. "About your little friends and their little schemes and secrets? I gave you my word."

"I know," she said, close to crying, "and I should have trusted you, Alastair. I'm sorry. I didn't mean to overhear such things. I know they're private. I only wanted to tell you I loved you just the same. It makes no difference to me."

She thought the reassurance might help, but instead Alastair's mouth wrenched out of shape with sudden violence.

"Really," he said coldly. "Well, it makes a difference to me to have a sister who is a sneak and a spy. Get out of my room, Cordelia. Now."

"Jesse," Lucie whispered. "Jesse, where are you?"

She sat on the floor by the cast-iron fireplace in the Institute drawing room. She had come home from the Devil Tavern once night had begun to fall in earnest. Both Thomas and Christopher had been distracted and preoccupied, anyway, and she wasn't sure how much real Pyxis research was getting done. Christopher had had some kind of realization about the antidote he was working on and vanished into the steel-lined corner of the tavern room, where he had banged about trying to distill something in a retort.

But that wasn't the real reason she had wanted to leave. Night had a new importance now. Night meant she could talk to Jesse.

"Jesse Blackthorn," she said now, feeling a little ridiculous. "Please come here. I want to speak with you."

She glanced about the room, as if Jesse might be hiding under a sofa. This was their family room, where the Herondales often gathered in the evenings. Tessa had kept some of the older decorations here—a gilt-framed mirror still hung over the fireplace—and the furniture was comfortably shabby, from the flowered armchairs by the fireplace to the big old desk, scarred with years of marks from the nibs of pens. The walls were papered in light damask, and well-thumbed books lined the walls.

Tessa would read aloud from a new book, and the others would sprawl around the fire; sometimes they would exchange gossip, or Will and Tessa would tell familiar stories from the past. It was a place Lucie associated with great comfort, and afternoons spent scribbling away at the desk. So it was perhaps doubly unnerving when Jesse appeared, evolving out of the shadows in his white shirtsleeves, his face pale under his dark hair.

"You came!" she said, not bothering to hide her astonishment. "I really didn't know if that was going to work."

"I don't suppose you ever wondered if now was a convenient time for *me*," he said.

"What could you possibly have been doing?" she wondered aloud.

Jesse made an unghostlike snorting sound and seated himself on the rickety desk. The weight of a live person would likely have tipped it over, but he was not a live person. "You wanted to speak with me. So speak."

She told him hastily about Emmanuel Gast, how she had found the ghost and what he had said to her. As he listened, Jesse played with the gold locket around his throat.

"I am sorry to disappoint you, but I have heard nothing of this warlock. Still, it is clear these are dark doings," he said, when she was done. "Why put yourself in the middle of this? Why not let your parents solve these mysteries?"

"Barbara was my cousin," she said. "I cannot do nothing."

"You do not need to do this."

"Perhaps being dead has made you forget how perilous life is," said Lucie. "I do not think James, or Cordelia, or any of us have chosen to be the ones to solve this mystery. It has chosen us. I am not going to bring danger to my parents, either, when there is nothing they can do."

"I am not sure there is anything anyone can do," said Jesse. "There is deliberate evil at work here. A desire to destroy Shadowhunters and to hurt them. It will not be ended soon."

Lucie sucked in her breath.

"Luce?" The door opened. It was James. Lucie started, and Jesse vanished—not the way Jessamine sometimes disappeared, with a wake of trailing smoke, but simply snapping out of existence between one second and the next. "What are you doing in here?"

"Why shouldn't I be in the drawing room?" she said, knowing she sounded disagreeable. She felt immediately guilty—he hadn't known she was in the middle of trying to interrogate a ghost.

James tossed his jacket over a flowered armchair and sat down beside her, picking up a poker from the rack of fireplace instruments.

"I'm sorry about Grace," she said. "Matthew told Thomas and Christopher."

James sighed, moving the coals in the fire about restlessly. "Probably better that he did. It isn't as if I wish to announce the news to everyone."

"If Grace doesn't want you, she is a terrible idiot," Lucie said. "And if she wants to marry Charles, she is even more of a terrible idiot, so she is a terrible idiot twice over."

James went still, his hand motionless on the poker. The sparks flew upward. "I thought I would feel incredible grief," he said at last. "Instead I am not sure what I feel. Everything is sharper and clearer, colors and textures are different. Perhaps that *is* grief. Perhaps it is just that I don't know how such loss should feel."

"Charles will be sorry he married her," said Lucie, with conviction. "She will devil him until the day he dies." She made a face. "Wait. She'll be Matthew's sister, won't she? Think of the awkward dinner parties."

"About Matthew." James set the poker down. "Luce. You know that Matthew has feelings for you, and you don't return those feelings."

Lucie blinked. She hadn't expected the conversation to take this turn, though it was not the first time they'd discussed the matter. "I cannot feel something that I don't feel."

"I'm not saying that you should. You don't owe your feelings to anyone."

"Besides, it is a fancy," Lucie said. "He does not *really* care for me. In fact, I think—"

She broke off. It was a theory she had developed, seeing the way Matthew's gaze had been drifting the past few days. But she was not ready to share it.

"I don't disagree." James's voice was low. "But I fear that Matthew is in pain for reasons even I do not understand."

Lucie hesitated. She knew what she ought to say about the way Matthew had chosen to address his pain, but she could not bear to say the words to her brother. A moment later she was spared the choice as footsteps sounded in the hall. Her mother and father came in, both bright-eyed from the brisk wind outside. Tessa stopped to set her gloves on a small Moroccan table by the door, while Will swept over to kiss Lucie and ruffle James's hair.

"Gracious," said James, his tone light. "What is the meaning of all this unbridled affection?"

"We were with your aunt Cecily and uncle Gabriel," said Tessa, and Lucie realized her mother's eyes were a bit *too* bright. Tessa took a seat on the sofa. "My poor loves. All our hearts are shattered for Sophie and Gideon."

Will sighed. "I remember when Gideon and Gabriel could barely stand each other. Now Gabriel is there each day for his brother. I am glad you and James have each other, Luce."

"I suppose the good news is that there have been no new attacks today," said Tessa. "We must hold to that. This dreadfulness could end at any time."

Will sat down beside his wife and pulled her into his lap. "I am going to kiss your mother now," he announced. "Flee if you will, children. If not, we could play Ludo when the romance is over."

"The romance is never over," said James glumly.

Tessa laughed and put up her face to be kissed. James looked exasperated, but Lucie was not paying attention: she could not help but hear Jesse's voice in her head.

There is deliberate evil at work here. A desire to destroy Shadowhunters and to hurt them. It will not be ended soon.

She shivered.

In the morning, a grand package festooned with ribbons arrived at 102 Cornwall Gardens. It was addressed to Cordelia, and Sona followed Risa as the maid carried it up to Cordelia's room.

"A gift!" Sona said, as Risa deposited the box on Cordelia's bed. Sona was entirely breathless. Cordelia looked at her with concern—her mother was usually quite energetic, so a few flights of stairs should not have winded her. "Perhaps it is from a gentleman?"

Cordelia, who had been seated at the vanity table brushing out her hair, sighed. She had cried half the night, horribly aware that she had embarrassed her brother. She certainly didn't feel she deserved a gift, or an excursion to the Hell Ruelle in the evening, for that matter. "It's probably from Lucie—"

Her mother already had the wrappings off and the box open. Risa had stepped back, plainly finding Sona's excitement alarming. As Sona tore through a delicate layer of paper, she gasped aloud. "Oh, Layla!"

Curiosity getting the better of her, Cordelia came to join her mother at the side of the bed. She gaped. Out of the box had tumbled a dozen dresses: day dresses and tea gowns alongside gorgeous evening wear, all in rich colors: kingfisher-blue lace, cotton in cinnamon and wine, silks in Prussian green, claret, and burgundy, shimmering gold and dark rose.

Sona held up a silk dress the color of bronze, with a soft chiffon edging at the bodice and the hem. "It's so lovely," she said, almost reluctantly. "They're from James, aren't they?"

Despite her surprise, Cordelia knew exactly who they were from. She had seen the small card signed A tucked among the tea gowns. But if believing they were from James meant her mother would allow her to wear them, she would let her mother think what she liked.

"It's very kind of him," she said. "Don't you think? I can wear it tonight—there's a gathering at the Institute."

Sona smiled in delight, the smile like a weight on Cordelia's heart. The dresses were so very extravagant: her mother would surely believe now that James's imaginary romantic intentions toward Cordelia were serious indeed. It was a sort of irony, she thought, that for once both she and her mother wanted the same thing. And that neither of them was going to get it.

Anna fetched Cordelia at precisely nine o'clock that night, in a black carriage that resembled dark leather. Cordelia hurried out the door, bundled in her coat despite the warmness of the evening. She clambered into the carriage, ignoring her mother calling after her that she should bring gloves, too, or possibly a muff.

The interior of the carriage shone with brass fittings and red velvet bench seats. Anna had her long legs carelessly crossed before her. She was dressed in elegant black menswear, her shirtfront starched and white. There was an amethyst pin, the color of her brother's eyes, winking in her cravat, and her coat fit sleekly along her narrow shoulders. She seemed entirely composed. Cordelia envied her confidence.

"Thank you," Cordelia said breathlessly, as the carriage began to move. "The dresses are absolutely lovely—you didn't have to—"

Anna waved her thanks away. "It cost me nothing. A werewolf seamstress owed me a favor, and Matthew helped me pick out fabric." She raised an eyebrow. "So, which one did you decide to wear?"

Cordelia removed her coat to show the shimmering bronze gown beneath. The silk was cool and heavy against her skin, like the touch of water; the chiffon at the hem caressed her legs and ankles. It was practical, too—her mother had helped her cunningly conceal Cortana in a sheath on her back that ran below the material of her dress.

Anna chuckled approvingly. "Deep colors are the right ones for you, Cordelia. Claret red, kingfisher blue, emerald green. Sleek lines and simplicity, none of this silly frou-frou everyone's wearing."

The carriage had turned toward the West End. There was something exciting about moving toward the heart of London, away from Kensington's greenery, into the crowds and the life that pulsed through them. "Do we have a plan?" Cordelia said, gazing out the window at Piccadilly Circus. "What we're going to do when we get there?"

"I will seduce," said Anna. "You will distract, or at the least, not get in my way."

Cordelia smiled. She leaned against the window as Anna pointed out landmarks to her: the statue of Eros in the center of the roundabout, and the Criterion Restaurant, where Arthur Conan Doyle had set the first meeting of Holmes and Watson. Soon they were rolling into Soho with its narrower streets. Fog hung like spider's webs stretched between the buildings. The carriage rattled past an Algerian coffee vendor, the window crammed with the shining brass and tin of coffee cans. Nearby was a shop for light fittings with a shiny new black-and-gold facade on which the words W. SITCH & CO. were inscribed, and past it a collection of market stalls. In the dark, narrow street, oil flares blazed like warning fires, and the cloth hangings protecting the stall fronts flew in the wind.

The carriage came to a stop at last in front of Tyler's Court. The air was full of smoke and shadow and the chatter of voices speaking a dozen different languages. James and Matthew lounged against the stone walls. They both wore fitted black evening coats.

Matthew had added a bottle-green tie and velvet trousers to his ensemble. James had his collar turned up against the wind, his face pale between his black hair and the fine black material of his suit.

Anna threw open the door of the carriage and hopped out, leaving the door open behind her. Cordelia tried to follow, only to find that it was less than easy to move in her new dress. She inched across the bench seat, squeaking slightly, and half tumbled out the carriage door.

Arms braced her before she hit the pavement. James had caught her by the waist. Her hair brushed his cheek and she inhaled his cologne: cedarwood, like the forests in Lebanon.

He set her on her heels, his hands still on her hips. She could feel the imprint of the Herondale ring he wore against her side. He was staring, and Cordelia realized with a jolt that she had left her coat in the carriage. She was standing in front of Matthew and James in her new dress, with nothing else to cover her.

She could not help but be conscious of how closely the dress clung to her body. The fabric over her hips was so tight that she hadn't been able to wear a petticoat beneath it, only her combination and a light corset. Anyone could see the shape of her waist, the swell of her bosom, and even the silk draped across the curve of her stomach. The narrow sleeves slipped down her shoulders, uncovering the tops of her breasts; the weight and softness of the material was like a caress. She felt elegant in a way she never had before, and a little wild.

"Cordelia," said Matthew. He looked slightly stunned, as if he'd walked into a wall. "You look different."

"Different?" Anna scoffed. "She looks stunning."

James hadn't moved. He was looking at Cordelia, and his eyes had darkened, from the color of a tiger's eyes to something richer and deeper. Something like the gold of Cortana when it flashed in the air. He exhaled and let her go, stepping back. Cordelia could feel her heart beating in her throat, a sharp pulse, as if she had drunk too much of her mother's strong tea.

"We had better go in," James said, and Cordelia saw Anna smile sideways, a catlike smile, before she led them into the narrow court.

The faerie at the door recognized Anna and Matthew and let them all pass through into the Hell Ruelle with only a lift of her lavender eyebrows. They found themselves in the Ruelle's dazzling series of interconnected rooms. As they followed Anna, who strode along with purpose, Cordelia realized what she had not before: that the rooms spread out from a central large chamber like the arms of a starfish. The ceilings in the passages were low, but every room was illuminated by electric light, brilliant and harsher than witchlight.

They found Hypatia Vex holding court in the central chamber. The decor of the octagonal room had been changed. The walls were now hung with paintings of bacchanals: naked dancers encircled with streaming ribbons, demons with eyes painted red and foreheads garlanded with flowers, their bodies lacquered gold like James's eyes. Behind Hypatia Vex hung a massive triptych of a dark-haired woman holding a black owl with golden eyes.

The stage in the center of the room was empty now, though chairs and couches had been arranged around it. They were full of Downworlders. Cordelia recognized the vampire girl Lily, jeweled combs in her black hair, sipping blood from a crystal glass. She winked at Anna, but Anna was focused on Hypatia, who was seated on an intricately carved oak settee, upholstered in red-and-green jacquard fabric. She was wearing another shimmering gown, this one black silk that made it seem as if the luxurious curves of her body had been dipped into ink.

Nor was she alone. Next to her was a handsome werewolf with green-gold eyes. Cordelia had seen him the last time they had come here. He had been the violin player in the string quartet. Now there was no music and he was focused on Hypatia, his body turned toward hers attentively, his long fingers playing gently with a strap of her gown.

Anna's blue eyes narrowed.

"Anna," said James in his low voice. "You may have your work cut out for you."

"That's Claude Kellington," said Matthew. "He's the master of entertainment here. In charge of the stage."

Anna turned to them, her eyes bright. "Matthew," she said. "Distract him."

Matthew winked and strode over to the settee. Lily glanced over at him as he passed her, possibly sizing him up as a potential snack. He was very handsome, Cordelia thought; she didn't know why she didn't respond to him as she did to James. But then, she didn't respond to anyone as she did to James.

Raising an eyebrow, Kellington rose and followed Matthew back into the crowd. Cordelia and James exchanged a look as Matthew wove toward them, the werewolf in tow.

"Please don't tell me the three of you have some sort of act," said Kellington as he drew near, and Cordelia realized with a jolt of surprise that Anna had slipped away, silent as a cat. "No one wants to see singing and dancing Shadowhunters."

"I was hoping my *parabatai* and I might recite some poetry," said Matthew. "Perhaps about the bonds of brotherly love."

Kellington gave Matthew an amused look. He had a sharply handsome sort of face, and curling chestnut hair. A gold ring stamped with the words *Beati Bellicosi* flashed on his hand. "I recall the poetry you recited to me once," he said. "Though not as particularly brotherly. However, we're looking for new performers tonight." He glanced at James. "Do you have any talents, besides standing there looking good and saying nothing?"

"I'm quite skilled at throwing knives," James said calmly. He moved to the side, Kellington's gaze following him, as Anna slid onto the settee beside Hypatia and lifted the warlock's hand to her lips for a kiss. Hypatia looked more than a little surprised.

"If a Shadowhunter gets up and starts waving knives around, we're going to have a riot," said Kellington. "Hypatia wants to entertain her guests, not kill them." His gaze slid to Cordelia. It was a gaze like being touched, she thought. Not entirely pleasant, but certainly novel. Kellington seemed to be examining her from head to toe and finding himself not displeased. "What about *you?*"

Matthew and James both stared at her.

"I suppose I could perform," Cordelia said breathlessly.

She heard her own voice as if from a distance. Was she mad? What was she offering? What would she even *do?* She heard Kellington agree and felt James's slender, scarred fingers on her arm. "Cordelia, you don't need to—" he began.

"I can do it," she said.

He met her gaze directly, and she saw that there was no doubt in his expression. He was looking at her with exactly the faith he showed when he looked at Matthew, at Lucie, or at Thomas. With a total belief that she could do anything, if it was required of her to do it.

It was as if she could suddenly get enough air into her lungs: Cordelia inhaled, nodded at James, and turned to Kellington.

"I am ready," she said.

With a bow, the werewolf led her toward the stage.

PART TWO

– ❦ –

You have been in every line I have ever read, since I first came here, the rough common boy whose poor heart you wounded even then. You have been in every prospect I have ever seen since—on the river, on the sails of the ships, on the marshes, in the clouds, in the light, in the darkness, in the wind, in the woods, in the sea, in the streets. You have been the embodiment of every graceful fancy that my mind has ever become acquainted with. The stones of which the strongest London buildings are made, are not more real, or more impossible to be displaced by your hands, than your presence and influence have been to me, there and everywhere, and will be. Estella, to the last hours of my life, you cannot choose but remain part of my character, part of the little good in me, part of the evil.

—Charles Dickens, *Great Expectations*

15

The Whispering Room

Where beauty has no ebb, decay no flood,
But joy is wisdom, Time an endless song.
I kiss you and the world begins to fade.
—William Butler Yeats, *Land of Heart's Desire*

From her window, Lucie could see the steady stream of carriages arriving through the arched entrance to the Institute. She drew back with a frown. Where *were* Thomas and Christopher? She didn't blame either of them for having had difficulty concentrating the day before. Barbara's death was on all their minds. But it *had* meant the three of them had failed to make a proper plan for meeting up tonight.

Well, she thought, if she had to spy on the Enclave meeting alone, then that was what she'd do. She had just gone to fetch her stele from atop the dresser when she heard something rattle against the glass of her window. Assuming Thomas and Christopher were trying to get her attention with pebbles—their usual method—she darted over and threw the window open.

Something that looked like a burning butterfly sailed past her head, and Lucie gave a shriek. She ran toward it as it alighted on her desk and burst into red-orange flames. It was small, no bigger than her hand, and she hastened to put it out with a handy pen wiper.

"Sorry, Luce!" It was Christopher, clambering in through her window. He dropped to the floor and was followed a moment later by Thomas, who had a hole burned into the collar of his shirt and looked cross about it. "It was an experiment—method of sending messages using fire runes—"

Lucie looked skeptically at the charred spot on her desk where the message had sparked its last. It had landed on several manuscript pages of *The Beautiful Cordelia*, and they were now quite ruined. "Well, don't experiment on me!" she said. "You've destroyed a very important scene in which Cordelia is romanced by a pirate king."

"Piracy is unethical," said Thomas.

"Not in this case," said Lucie. "You see, the pirate king is secretly the son of an earl—"

Christopher and Thomas exchanged glances. "We really ought to go," said Christopher, retrieving Lucie's stele and handing it to her. "The Enclave meeting is about to start."

They crept out of Lucie's room and hurried to one of the empty storerooms on the second floor, above the library. It was Lucie's father who had taught her how to draw this particular rune, so she did the honors as they all knelt in a loose circle on the floor: the rune was a large one, covering a good amount of space. When Lucie was done, she finished it off with a flourish and sat back.

The floor between their kneeling legs shimmered and went transparent. Lucie, Thomas, and Christopher were now looking down at the library below them as if through the lens of a telescope. They could see everyone gathered in the room very clearly, down to the colors of their eyes and the details of their clothes.

Extra rows of tables had been set up, and Shadowhunters filled the room. Lucie's father and mother were there, of course, and her uncle Gabriel as well, seated toward the front of the room where Will stood, flanked by Inquisitor Bridgestock and a stiff-looking Charles Fairchild. Lucie could not help but wonder what their relationship had been like since Charles had ended his engagement to Ariadne.

Charles rapped sharply on one of the tables, making Lilian Highsmith jolt in her seat. "To order," he said. "To order. My thanks to the members of the Enclave who could join us here. Though this information has not been made public, as of today there have been a total of six major attacks by an unknown type of demon on Nephilim in London. All except the attack at the Baybrooks' residence took place in daylight."

Lucie turned to Thomas and Christopher. "Six attacks?" she whispered. "I only know of three. Did you know of more?"

Thomas shook his head. "Even I did not know. I imagine the Enclave has become fearful of panicking people. If it makes you feel better, I think a lot of people didn't know."

Lucie looked back down. Many members of the Enclave seemed to be murmuring to each other in agitation. She could see her father standing with his arms crossed over his chest, a frozen expression on his face. He had not known.

"There are now twenty-five very sick Shadowhunters in the Silent City," said Charles. "Due to the gravity of the situation, travel in and out of London has been suspended for the moment by the Clave."

Lucie, Christopher, and Thomas exchanged startled looks. When had this happened? As a murmur swept through the crowd in the library, it seemed clear that many of the adults in attendance were equally surprised.

"What do you mean by 'for the moment'?" called George Penhallow. "How long will we be forbidden to travel?"

Charles clasped his hands behind his back. "Indefinitely."

The murmur in the room became a roar. "What of those in

Idris?" called Ida Rosewain. "Will they be able to return? What of our families there?"

Bridgestock shook his head. "All Portal travel is suspended—"

"Good," muttered Lilian Highsmith. "I've never trusted those newfangled inventions. I heard about a young man who went through a Portal with his *parabatai* and ended up with the other fellow's leg attached to him."

Bridgestock ignored this. "There will be no entering or exiting London, no passing beyond the warded boundaries of the city. Not for now."

Lucie and Christopher looked at Thomas in dismay, but his mouth had only tightened into a sharp line. "Good," he said. "My family will be safe in Idris."

"Henry, though," said Christopher in a worried voice. "He was to return and help us with the antidote."

Lucie had not known that. She patted Christopher's hand as comfortingly as she could. "The Silent Brothers are also looking for a cure," she whispered. "It is not just you, Christopher. Besides, I have every confidence you could do it on your own."

"And I will help you," Thomas added, but Christopher only looked mournfully down at the scene unfolding below.

"What is the meaning of this? Why are we being imprisoned in London?" Martin Wentworth was shouting. He had risen to his feet. "Now is the time we need the Clave's assistance—"

"It's a quarantine, Martin," said Will, in his steady voice. "Let the Inquisitor explain."

But it was Charles who spoke. "All of you," he said loudly. "You know that my—that Barbara Lightwood was stricken down by a demon attack. Poison flooded her system. She could not withstand it and died a few days ago."

Thomas winced, and Martin Wentworth's face turned from red to white as he clearly thought of his son, Piers.

Charles went on. "Oliver Hayward was with her when she died. In the last throes of her agony, not recognizing her friends and loved ones, she attacked him, scratching and hitting him."

Lucie remembered the blood on Oliver's hands, his cuffs. The library was silent. She could not bear to look at Thomas.

"As you may also know," Charles went on, "the Hayward family runs the York Institute, and Oliver understandably wished to return home after losing his beloved."

"As any upstanding young man might well do," muttered Bridgestock.

Charles ignored this. "We received the news yesterday that Oliver had fallen ill. His scratches festered and he was overcome by the same symptoms that have claimed those here in London who have been attacked by these demons." He paused. "Oliver died this morning."

There was an audible gasp. Lucie felt sick.

Laurence Ashdown bolted to his feet. "But Hayward wasn't attacked by a demon! Nor is the poison of demons contagious!"

"The poison causes an ailment," said Will calmly. "It has been determined by the Silent Brothers that this ailment can be transmitted by bite or scratch. While it is not highly contagious, it is contagious nonetheless. Hence the quarantine."

"Is that why all the sick were moved to the Silent City and are not being allowed visitors? Is that what's going on?" demanded Wentworth.

Lucie was again startled: she had not known the sick were not to be visited. Thomas, noting her distress, whispered, "The injunction against visitors was handed down only this morning. Christopher and I heard Uncle Gabriel discussing it."

"The Silent City is the right place for them to be," said Charles. "The Brothers can take the best care of the afflicted, and no demon can enter the place."

"So what is the Clave's plan?" Ida Rosewain's voice rose. "Is their intention to trap us in London—with demons carrying a poison disease we don't know how to treat—so we all simply *die*?"

Even Bridgestock looked taken aback. It was Will who spoke.

"We are Shadowhunters," he said. "We do not wait to be saved by others. We save ourselves. We here in London are as equipped as any member of the Clave to solve this problem, and it will be solved."

Lucie felt a spark of warmth in her chest. Her father was a good leader. It was one of the things she loved about him. He knew when people needed to be calmed and encouraged. Charles, who wanted so badly to be a leader himself, knew only how to frighten and demand.

"Will is correct," Charles said cautiously. "We have the assistance of the Silent Brothers, and I myself will be acting as Consul in my mother's stead, since she cannot return from Idris."

Charles glanced into the crowd and, for a moment, seemed to be looking directly at Alastair Carstairs. Odd that he was there, Lucie thought, but Sona was not. Though Alastair would certainly report on the state of things to his family.

Alastair returned Charles's glance and looked away; Lucie sensed Thomas's shoulder tense beside hers.

"We will be splitting into three groups," said Bridgestock. "One group will be in charge of research, digging up everything in our libraries regarding whether anything like this has happened before—demon disease, demons that can exist in daylight, and so on. Group two will handle night patrols, and group three day patrols. Every Shadowhunter over the age of eighteen and under the age of fifty-five will be given an area of London to patrol."

"I do not see why the demons would remain within the boundary of the city," said Lilian Highsmith darkly. "We may be quarantined, but they are not."

"We have not been abandoned," said Will. "York, too, is under quarantine, though there have been no further cases of illness there yet, but the Shadowhunters of the Cornwall Institute as well as some Shadowhunters from Idris will be patrolling outside London, and patrols will be stepped up through all the British Isles. If the demons flee London, they will be caught."

"These demons didn't just appear out of thin air," said Bridgestock. "They were summoned. We need to interrogate all the magic users in London in order to track down the culprit."

"It's not quite demons, is it?" Lucie whispered. "If it's a Mandikhor, then it's really just one demon. Maybe . . . Ought we to tell them?"

"Not at the moment," said Thomas. "The last thing they need is us falling out of the ceiling to announce that we have a theory that it's a demon that splits into parts."

"In fact, not even so much as a theory as a hypothesis," said Christopher. "We have not proved it yet, or even tested it. And I am not sure how it would change their plans or behavior. It may be one demon, but it acts as many demons, and that is what they are seeking to combat."

In the library, Will frowned. "Maurice, we've been over this. Not only will such an action panic all the magicians and Downworlders in London, we have no assurance that whoever raised these demons is even still in the city. It would be a waste of manpower that we need elsewhere."

"But someone is at fault for this and must pay for it!" snapped Bridgestock.

Will began to say, surprisingly gently, "And that will happen, but we must find this demon first—"

"My daughter is dying!" Bridgestock shouted, suddenly enough to jolt the room. "Ariadne is dying, and I demand to know who is responsible!"

"Well, my niece is already dead." It was Uncle Gabriel, having risen to his feet. He looked furious, his green eyes nearly black. Lucy rather wished her aunt Cecily was there, for she would surely have been cheering him on. "And yet rather than wasting my energy on imagining revenge, I will be patrolling London's streets, hoping to prevent what happened to her from happening to another innocent—"

"Well and good, Lightwood," said Bridgestock, his eyes glittering, "but I am the Inquisitor, and you are not. It is my task to root out evil at its source—"

The view went dark and the library below vanished. Lucie glanced up in surprise to see that Thomas had drawn a line through her rune, closing their window to the library below. His eyes, like his uncle Gabriel's, were glittering with fury.

Christopher put his hand on Thomas's shoulder. "I'm sorry, Tom. About Oliver, and—"

"There's no need to apologize." Thomas spoke in a tight voice. "It is best we know the situation. As soon as we have hold of the Pyxis, we will handle this ourselves, for if we wait for the Enclave to come to a consensus, I expect more will die."

James watched as Cordelia ascended the steps to the raised cherrywood stage in the middle of the room. He was aware of Matthew standing beside him, swearing under his breath. He didn't blame him—he knew how his *parabatai* felt: that somehow they had thrown Cordelia to the wolves of the Hell Ruelle.

Kellington, standing beside her, clapped his hands, and the crowd began to quiet. Not fast enough, James thought. He began to applaud loudly, and beside him, following his lead, Matthew did the same. Anna, snuggled next to Hypatia on the settee, also clapped, causing Kellington to glance toward her and frown. Hypatia looked back at him with wide, starry eyes and shrugged.

Kellington cleared his throat. "Honored guests," he said. "Tonight we have something unusual. A *Shadowhunter* has offered to entertain us."

A murmur ran through the room. James and Matthew kept clapping, and a dark-haired vampire girl with bright combs in her hair joined in the applause. Anna leaned over and whispered in Hypatia's ear.

"Please enjoy the performance of the lovely Cordelia Carstairs," Kellington said, hastily turning to descend the stairs.

Cordelia laid a hand on his arm. "I will require you to accompany me," she said. "On the violin."

Matthew chuckled, almost reluctantly. "She *is* clever," he said, as Kellington, looking annoyed, strode off to retrieve his instrument. As he moved through the crowd, Cordelia, looking far calmer than James suspected she was, reached up and unpinned her hair.

James caught his breath as it fell down around her shoulders, spilled down her back, the deep red of rose petals. It stroked her bare brown skin like silk. Her glowing bronze dress clung to her as she reached back and unsheathed Cortana, drawing it forward. Every glittering light in the Hell Ruelle caught fire along the blade.

"I have always loved stories," she said, and her clear voice carried through the room. "One of my favorite tales is that of the servant girl Tawaddud. After the death of a rich merchant, his son wasted all the inheritance he got until he had nothing left but one servant, a girl known through all the caliphate for her brilliance and her beauty. Her name was Tawaddud. She begged the son to take her to the court of the caliph Harun al-Rashid, and there to sell her for a vast sum of money. The son insisted he could not get such a princely sum for the sale of one servant. Tawaddud insisted she would convince the caliph that there was no wiser or more eloquent or learned woman in all the land but she. Eventually the son was worn down. He brought her to the court, and she came before the caliph, and she told him this."

Cordelia nodded at Kellington, who had come to stand beside the stage. He began to play a haunting tune on the violin, and Cordelia began to move.

It was a dance, but not a dance. She moved fluidly with Cortana. It was gold and she followed that gold in fire. She spoke, and her low, husky voice matched the dance and the music of the violin.

"*Oh my Lord, I am versed in syntax and poetry and jurisprudence and exegesis and philosophy. I am skilled in music and in the knowledge of the divine ordinances, and in arithmetic and geodesy and geometry and the fables of the ancients.*"

Cortana wove with her words, underlining each one with steel. She turned as her sword turned, and her body curved and moved like water or fire, like a river under an infinity of stars. It was beautiful—*she* was beautiful, but it was not a distant beauty. It was a beauty that lived and breathed and reached out with its hands to crush James's chest and make him breathless.

"*I have studied the exact sciences, geometry and philosophy, and medicine and logic and rhetoric and composition.*"

Cordelia sank to her knees. Her sword whipped around her, a narrow circlet of fire. The violin sang, and her body sang, and James could see the court of the caliph, and the brave girl kneeling before Harun al-Rashid and telling him of her worth.

"*I can play the lute and know its gamut and notes and notation and the crescendo and diminuendo.*"

Beside James, Matthew sucked in his breath. James glanced quickly at his *parabatai*. Matthew—Matthew looked as he did sometimes when he thought no one was watching him. There was a haunted loneliness in that look, a desire almost beyond comprehension for something even Matthew himself did not understand.

His gaze was fixed on Cordelia. But then, everyone in the room was looking at her as her body bent backward and her hair swept from side to side, an arc of fire. Her brown skin glowed; perspiration glimmered on her collarbones. James's blood was pounding through his body like a river through a broken dam.

"*If I sing and dance, I seduce.*" Cordelia straightened with a snap. Her eyes met the gaze of her audience, direct and challenging. "*And if I dress and scent myself, I slay.*"

She slammed Cortana into its sheath. Kellington had stopped playing the violin; he, too, was staring at Cordelia like a lovesick sheep. James had an overwhelming urge to kick him.

Cordelia rose to her feet, her chest rising and falling with her quick breath. "And wise men were brought from around the land to test Tawaddud, but she was wiser than them all. So wise and beautiful was she that in the end, the caliph granted her whatever it was she wanted—all the wishes of her heart."

Cordelia bowed.

"And that is the end of the story," she said, and began to descend the steps.

Cordelia had never been stared at by so many people in her life. Escaping the stage, she slithered into the crowd, though it was a different crowd than it had been—everyone seemed to want to smile at her now, or incline their heads, or wink. Several Downworlders said, "Beautifully done," as she passed.

She murmured her thanks and was immensely grateful when she reached James and Matthew. James seemed completely composed; Matthew was looking at her with wide eyes. "Bloody hell," he said admiringly, as soon as she came into range. He looked far more serious than he usually did. "What was *that*?"

"It was a fairy tale," James said briefly. "Well done, Cordelia." He indicated the now-empty jacquard settee. "Anna has disappeared with Hypatia, so I would call your distraction a success."

Cordelia. He had not called her Daisy. She didn't know what to think of that. She put a hand to her chest; her heart was pounding, from nerves and from the dancing. "What do we do now?" she said. "How long does seduction usually last?"

"Depends if you do it properly," said Matthew, with a little of his old grin.

"Well, I hope for Hypatia's sake that Anna does it properly, yet for our sake I hope she hurries it up," said James.

Matthew had gone still. "Both of you," he said. "Listen."

Cordelia listened, and heard at first only the buzz and murmur of the crowd. Then, beneath it, the whisper of a familiar word, spoken low and urgently.

A Shadowhunter. A Shadowhunter is here.

"Do they mean us?" She looked around in puzzlement and saw Kellington gazing toward the door, his mouth flat with irritation. Someone had just come into the chamber—someone with bright red hair, wearing a heavy tweed coat.

"Charles." Matthew's eyes were green slits. "By the Angel. What is he doing here?"

James swore softly. Charles was moving through the crowd, his coat buttoned to the throat, looking around uncomfortably. He looked desperately out of place.

"We should go," James said. "But we can't leave Anna."

"You two run and hide yourselves," said Matthew. "Charles will go off his head if he sees you here."

"But what about you?" said Cordelia.

"He's used to this kind of thing from me," Matthew said, and his whole face seemed to have tightened. His eyes were glittering like chips of glass. "I'll deal with Charles."

James looked at Matthew for a long moment. Cordelia sensed the whisper of unspoken words passing between them, the silent communication of *parabatai*. Perhaps one day she would have that with Lucie; at the moment, it seemed almost like magic.

James nodded at Matthew, turned, and caught hold of Cordelia's hand. "This way," he said, and they plunged into the crowd. Behind her, Cordelia heard Matthew say Charles's name with exaggerated loud surprise. The crowd was shifting and moving as Downworlders flinched away from Charles; James and Cordelia edged around Kellington and into a red-paneled corridor leading away from the main chamber.

There was an open door about halfway down the corridor; a plaque on the door proclaimed it to be THE WHISPERING ROOM. James ducked into it, drawing Cordelia after him. She had time only to see that they were in a dimly lit, deserted room when he slammed the door behind them. She leaned against the wall, catching her breath, as they both looked around.

They were in a sort of parlor, or perhaps an office. The walls were hung with silver paper, decorated with images of golden scales and feathers. There was a tall walnut desk large as a table, with a raised surface piled with neat stacks of writing paper weighted down by a copper bowl of peaches. Hypatia's writing desk, perhaps? A clearly enchanted fire burned in the grate, the flames silver and blue. The smoke that rose from the fire traced delicate patterns on the air in the shape of acanthus leaves. Its smoke smelled sweet, like attar of roses.

"What do you think Charles is doing here?" Cordelia said.

James was studying the books on the walls—a very typically Herondale thing to do. "Where did you learn to dance like that?" he said abruptly.

She turned to look at him in surprise. He was leaning against the bookshelf now, watching her. "I had a dance instructor in Paris," she said. "My mother believed that learning to dance aided in learning grace in battle. *That* dance," she added, "was forbidden to be taught to unmarried ladies, but my dance instructor did not care."

"Well, thank the Angel you were there," he said. "Matthew and I could certainly not have pulled off that dance on our own."

Cordelia smiled wanly. On the stage, dancing, she had imagined that James was watching her, that he found her beautiful, and the power that had flooded through her at the thought had felt like electricity. Now she looked away from him, trailing her hand along the top of the desk, near the stack of papers held down by the copper bowl.

"Be careful," James said, with a quick warning gesture. "I suspect that is faerie fruit. It has no effect on warlocks—no magical effect, at least. But on humans . . ."

She drew back. "Surely it does not harm you if you do not eat it."

"Oh, it does not. But I have met those who have tasted it. They say the more you have of it, the more you want, and the more you ache when you can have no more. And yet . . . I have always thought—is *not* knowing what it tastes like just another form of torture? The torture of wondering?"

His words were light, but there was an oddness to the way he was looking at her, Cordelia thought—a sort of depth to his gaze that seemed unfamiliar. His lips were slightly parted, his eyes a deeper gold than usual.

Beauty could tear at your heart like teeth, she thought, but she did not love James because he was beautiful: he was beautiful to her because she loved him. The thought brought hot blood to her cheeks; she glanced away, just as the door rattled in its frame.

Someone was trying to get in. James whirled, his eyes wild. Cordelia's hand flew to the hilt of Cortana. "We're not meant to be in here—" she began.

She got no further. A moment later James had pulled her toward him. His arms went round her, lifting her up and against him. His mouth was gentle, even as he crushed her against him; she realized what he was doing a beat later as the door opened, and she heard voices on the threshold. She gave a little gasp, and felt James's pulse jump; his right hand slid into her hair, his rune-scarred palm against her cheek as he kissed her.

James was kissing her.

She knew it wasn't real. She knew he was making it look as if they were Downworlders having an assignation in the Whispering Room—but it didn't matter, nothing mattered except the way he was kissing her, gloriously kissing her.

She wrapped her arms around his neck, arching her body up against his. She felt his breath hiss out against her mouth; he was kissing her carefully, even as the movements of his hands and body mimicked passion.

But she didn't want careful. She wanted it shattering and tremendous, wanted the passion to be real, the kissing to be the desperate everything she had always dreamed of.

She opened her lips against James's. His were so soft, and he tasted of barley sugar and spice. She heard nervous laughter at the door of the room and felt James's hand tighten on her waist. His other hand left her cheek and cupped the back of her neck as he deepened the kiss, suddenly, as if he couldn't help himself. He leaned into it, into her, his tongue tracing the shape of her mouth, making her shudder.

"Oh," she whispered softly against him, and heard the door close. Whoever it was had gone. She kept her arms around James's neck. If he wanted this over, he would have to end it.

He broke off the kiss but didn't let her go. He was still holding her against him, his body a hard cradle for hers. She stroked the side of his neck with her fingers; there was a faint white scar just above his collar, in the shape of a star. . . .

His breathing went ragged. "*Daisy* . . . my Daisy . . ."

"I think more people are coming," she whispered.

It wasn't true, and they both knew it. It didn't matter. He pulled her against him with such force she nearly tripped, her heel catching on the rug. Her shoe came off, and she kicked away the second one, going up on tiptoe to reach James's mouth—his lips were firm and sweet, teasing now as he ran them over the seam of her lips, over her cheekbone, down to her jaw. She was swimming in dizziness as she felt him undo the strap of Cortana with one hand, his other hand tracing the bodice of her dress. She had never known her body could feel like this, tense and taut with desire while at the same time she seemed to float.

He kissed her throat as her head fell back. She felt him bend to lay Cortana against the wall; when he straightened, his arms tightened around her. He moved them both away from the bookcase, half-carrying her, his mouth urgent against hers. They stumbled across the carpet, hands and lips frantic as they fetched up against the massive desk. Cordelia arched backward, her hands gripping the desk's edge, her body curving into James's in a way that made him inhale sharply.

His hands shaped the curves of her, sweeping from her hips to her waist, rising to cup her breasts. She gasped, breathing into the new sensation, wanting his hands on her. His fingers curved to hook into the neckline of her gown. He was touching her skin, her bare skin. She shivered in amazement and he looked at her, his eyes wild and hot and golden. He shrugged off his black frock coat, tossing it aside; when he came back to her, she could feel the heat of his body through her thin silk dress.

Even in her dance, even in the training room, she had never felt her body so absolutely right as she did now. He lifted her onto the walnut desk, so she sat on a wooden perch above him. She wrapped her legs around his waist. He cradled her face between his hands. Her hair was a curtain of flames streaming about both of them as they kissed and kissed.

At last she drew him up. Her back met the wood of the desk as he leaned over her, one hand braced above her head. The feel of his body all along hers scorched her blood. She understood now why poets said love was like burning. The heat of it was all through her and in her, and all she wanted was more—more kisses, more touches, to be devoured by this like a forest by wildfire.

And his face—she had never seen him like this, eyes burning and lost to desire, his pupils wide and black. He groaned as she touched him, running her palms over his hard chest, his rigid arms holding him braced over her. She tangled her fingers in the dark riot of his hair as he bent to kiss the swell of each breast, his breath hot against her skin.

The door to the room opened again. James froze, and a moment later scrambled up and off the desk, seizing his coat. He handed it to Cordelia as she sat up hurriedly.

Matthew stood on the threshold, staring at them both. Cordelia clutched the coat to her, though she was still fully dressed. Still, it felt like something of a shield against Matthew's stunned gaze.

"James," he said, and he sounded as if he didn't quite believe the evidence of his own eyes. His expression was tense and sharp as his eyes flicked from James to Cordelia's shoes, discarded on the floor.

"We're not meant to be in here," Cordelia said hurriedly. "James thought if we pretended—I mean, if someone came in and thought—"

"I understand," Matthew said, looking not at her, but at James. And James, Cordelia thought, looked composed—so composed, as if nothing had happened. Only his hair was mussed a little, and his tie askew, but his expression was unremarkable: calm, faintly curious.

"Is Charles still here?" he said.

Languidly, Matthew leaned against the doorframe. His hands moved slowly as he spoke, describing pale arcs in the air. "He left. He gave me quite a dressing-down first, I can assure you, for spending my time in such a swamp of debauchery and ruin. He said he thought I would have at least brought you or Anna to look after me." He grimaced.

"Hard luck, old chap," said James, turning to Cordelia, and reaching out a hand to help her down from the desk. The heat had gone from his golden eyes; they were cool and unreadable. She handed him his coat and he shrugged it on. "Why was he here?"

"The Enclave is looking into what Downworlders know about the situation," said Matthew. "Days after we already had the idea, of course."

"We ought to leave," said James. "Charles may have gone, but nothing prevents other Clave members from making an unwelcome appearance."

"We have to warn Anna," said Cordelia, clearing her throat. She thought she sounded remarkably steady, all things considered.

Matthew's smile was brittle. "Hypatia won't like that."

"Still," Cordelia said stubbornly, retrieving one shoe, and then the other. "We must."

She took Cortana back from where James had leaned it against the wall and followed the boys out into the corridor. She bit her lip as they hurried down the damask-papered hallway in silence. The scent of the smoke in the Whispering Room clung to her hair and clothes, sickly sweet.

"Here," Matthew said, as an ornately carved golden door rose up in front of them, its knob carved in the shape of a dancing nymph. It seemed Hypatia had altered the entrance to her room, just as she had altered the walls in the central chamber. "The bedroom of Hypatia Vex. Cordelia, I assume you wish to knock?"

Cordelia refrained from glaring at Matthew. He stood close to her, nearly shoulder to shoulder, and she could smell alcohol on him—something rich and dark, like brandy or rum. She thought of the too-slow deliberation of his gestures, the way he'd blinked at her and James. Before he had come to fetch them from the Whispering Room, he had gotten drunk, she realized. Probably far more drunk than he was letting on.

Before she could move, the nymph-knob turned, and Anna opened the door in a wash of bronze light and a heavy rush of scent, redolent of white flowers: jasmine and tuberose. Anna's hair was mussed and the collar of her shirt hung open to display a ruby necklace glimmering red as blood against her throat. She held a wooden box, carved with the *ourobouros* and dark with the patina of years, in her left hand.

"*Shhh,*" she whispered, glaring at them. "Hypatia's asleep, but she won't stay that way long. Take it!"

And she tossed the Pyxis to James.

"Then we're done," said Matthew. "Come along with us."

"And make Hypatia suspicious? Don't be ridiculous." Anna rolled her blue eyes. "Off you go, conspirators. I've done my part, and the rest of my evening will not require you."

"Anna?" Hypatia's voice sounded from somewhere inside the bronze-lit room. "Anna, darling, where are you?"

"Take my carriage," Anna whispered. Then she smiled. "And you did very well, Cordelia. They'll be talking about that dance for ages."

She winked and shut the door in their faces.

Sleep eluded Cordelia that night. Long after the boys had dropped her at the house in Kensington, long after she had wearily climbed the steps to her bedroom, long after her new dress had been discarded in a pile of bronze silk on the floor, she lay awake, staring up at the white plaster ceiling of her room. She could still feel James's lips on hers, the touch of his hands and fingers on her body.

He had kissed her with violent desperation, as if he were dying for her. He had said her name: *Daisy, my Daisy*. Hadn't he? Yet when they had reached Kensington, he had helped her down from the carriage and bid her good night casually, as if they were simply the friends they had always been. She tried to hold the memory of what it felt like to kiss him in her mind, but it slipped away and vanished with only the memory of sweetness, like the smoke in the Whispering Room.

16
LEGION

*The sea gave up its dead,
and death and the grave gave up their dead.*
—Revelations 20:13

When Cordelia arrived at the Institute in the late afternoon, she found Lucie and the Merry Thieves in the ballroom, clearly taking advantage of the fact that Will and Tessa had gone on a day patrol. White sheets had been thrown over the furniture and the piano, and the only light came from the arched windows, whose heavy velvet curtains had been pulled back. Even in the short time that had passed since the ball, the floor had grown lightly grained with dust.

Lucie, Christopher, James, Matthew, and Thomas were standing in a circle around an object that had been placed in the middle of the room. As Cordelia drew near them, she recognized it as the Pyxis Anna had handed to James the night before.

In the watery daylight, Cordelia could see it more clearly. It was made of a dark golden wood, with the pattern of the *ouroboros*, the snake swallowing its own tail, burned into four of its sides. A handle protruded from the top.

"Cordelia!" Lucie exclaimed. "We were just exchanging information. We learned a great deal that was important at the Enclave meeting last night, and it sounds as if you did something or other at the Hell Ruelle. Nothing that compelling, no doubt, but we cannot all be spies."

"I heard about the meeting from my brother this morning," said Cordelia, joining the others in their makeshift circle. Like Cordelia, Lucie and the boys were in gear. James wore a Norfolk jacket over his, with the storm collar turned up. Locks of black hair tumbled over his forehead and kissed the tops of his cheekbones. She looked away quickly, before their eyes could meet. "The quarantine and—and all the rest."

Alastair was still angry at her, but to be fair to him he had been gentle in breaking the bad news about Oliver Hayward. She did not know what to say about it now, though. She had not known Oliver, except as a presence at Barbara's side, but the others had. She could not imagine what they felt, especially Thomas, who looked even more tense and strained than he had before.

"It seems even more urgent to find and trap the demon responsible for this contagion now, before it attacks anyone else," she said at last.

Christopher enthusiastically waved an enormous book he was holding, his glasses balanced on the tip of his nose. The words *On the Uses of Pyxides and Other Phylacteries* were stamped across the front in gold. "It appears that this generation of Pyxis is fairly simple. When you wish to trap a demon, you first wound or weaken it. Then you place the Pyxis on the ground nearby and speak the words 'Thaam Tholach Thechembaor,' and the demon will be sucked into the box."

The Pyxis wobbled sharply, nearly tipping onto its side. Everyone jumped about a foot back.

"It's *alive*," Thomas said, staring. "Not the Pyxis, I mean—well, you know what I mean."

"Indeed," said James. "I see a flaw in our plan."

Matthew nodded. "I do as well. What if the Pyxis has an occupant? There was no real reason to assume the box at Hypatia's was *empty*. It could have had a demon in it all these years."

They all stared at each other.

"What would happen if we tried to put *another* demon in there?" Cordelia asked at last. "Could they both fit?"

"It isn't a good idea," said Christopher, consulting the book. "Since we don't know what kind of demon is already in there, we don't know if there will be enough space. Pyxides are bigger inside than they appear, but still finite."

"Well, then we have to empty this Pyxis out," Lucie said practically. "Anything could be in there. It could be a Greater Demon."

"What ho," said Christopher sadly.

"I'm sure it isn't," said James. "Still—let's relocate to the Sanctuary. No matter what happens, we can at least keep it contained until help arrives."

"Why not?" said Matthew. "Surely there's no way this plan can go wrong."

James raised an eyebrow. "Have you got another idea?"

"I think we should do it," said Thomas. "It's ridiculous to come this far and turn back."

Lucie sniffed. "Well, you'd all better hope it works. Especially you, James, because if Mam and Papa find out you released a demon in the Sanctuary, they will feed you to it."

James shot Lucie a dark older-brother glare that almost made Cordelia giggle. She had always been a little jealous of the closeness Lucie and James shared, something she had always wanted with Alastair but never had. It was nice that at some moments they were perfectly ordinary.

They relocated themselves to the Sanctuary, James carrying the Pyxis carefully, as if it were an infernal device that might explode at any moment. Cordelia found herself walking beside James and Lucie. She wondered if she and James would ever discuss what had happened the night before in the Whispering Room or if she would be left to go quietly mad wondering about it.

"Don't worry," Lucie said to her brother. "It won't be like it was with Papa."

"What do you mean?" Cordelia asked.

James said, "When he was a child, my father opened a Pyxis with tragic consequences. My aunt Ella was killed."

Cordelia was horrified. "Maybe we shouldn't—"

"This will be different," Lucie said, and Cordelia wasn't sure if Lucie was reassuring herself or James. "We know what we're getting into. Papa didn't."

They had arrived at the Sanctuary, the only room in the Institute where Downworlders could freely enter without being invited in by a Shadowhunter. It was warded all around with spells preventing them from entering the main body of the Institute. Meetings with prominent Downworlders were often held there, and Downworlders could even seek refuge in a Sanctuary under the Accords.

It was certainly clear that the London Institute had once been a cathedral, and a large one. Massive stone pillars stretched up to a vaulted roof. Thomas had produced a box of vestas and was moving around the room, lighting a dozen enormous candelabras, their sconces stuffed with fat white candles that cast a glimmering light. The tapestries and pillars were all traced with the designs of runes, as were the tiles of the floor. Cordelia had to admit that if one was going to release a demon, this seemed one of the better places to do it.

In the middle of the room was a dry stone fountain, in the center of which stood the statue of an angel with folded wings, its stone face streaked with black lines like tears.

James set the box on the floor, directly on top of a rune of angelic power. He knelt down, studying the Pyxis. After a moment, he took an unlit seraph blade from the inside of his coat.

"Arm yourselves, everyone," he said.

Cordelia unsheathed Cortana; the others drew seraph blades as James had done, save Thomas, who took out his *bolas*. James reached out and took hold of the handle of the Pyxis.

Cordelia's hand tightened on the hilt of her sword.

James twisted the handle sideways, as if turning a corkscrew. There was a loud *click* as the Pyxis popped open. All through the Sanctuary, the white candles spat and guttered. James sprang back, raising his blade.

There was a sound like the whistle of a train at night, and smoke billowed from the open Pyxis, bringing with it a foul, burnt smell. Cordelia coughed, raising Cortana. She heard James call out, *"Barachiel!"* and the light of his seraph blade cut through the smoke, followed by the blades of the others—Matthew, Christopher, and Lucie.

Something was rising through the smoke—something like a massive caterpillar, greenish in color, with a segmented, undulating body and a smooth head slashed across by a lipless mouth. The mouth cracked open, showing row upon row of blackened teeth. Then, to Cordelia's surprise, it spoke.

"At last I am free," it hissed. "I, Agaliarept, am free to recover the domain of my master, stolen from him by a demon of great cunning. I shall retrieve his lost world and flood this one with blood and death." Its blind head turned toward the Shadowhunters. "Those who have freed me, what is thy bidding? Speak! I am commanded to do anything you ask."

"Anything?" said Matthew curiously.

There was a flash of light as James's seraph blade arced through the smoke and plunged into the demon's middle. Black ichor sprayed as the demon shrieked in a high, chittering voice. The candles guttered and went out as James pulled his blade free; he was spattered with black fluid, his jaw set, his eyes glittering.

The demon howled and vanished, leaving only smoke and stink behind. Lucie staggered back, coughing, her face screwed up in disgust.

"But it would have done our bidding!" Matthew protested.

"It seemed untrustworthy," said James, wiping ichor from his face with his sleeve. His seraph blade had gone dark.

"I thought he seemed all right, for a demon," said Christopher. "You know."

"*What* is going on here?" said a loud voice.

They all spun around, Cordelia raising Cortana reflexively. She waved smoke away from her face and stared.

Someone had come in through the door to the street outside. A tall man—very tall, with a shock of black hair. His skin was brown, a shade darker than Cordelia's own, his eyes gold-green and slit-pupilled like a cat's. He was dressed as if for a summer wedding, in a gray frock coat and trousers, with gray suede gloves and boots. The outfit was topped off by a magnificent waistcoat of gray-and-magenta brocade, a walking stick, and bright magenta spats.

"Magnus *Bane*?" said Matthew, with a mixture of amazement and horror.

Magnus Bane walked some distance into the Sanctuary, shaking his head as he studied the scene before him. "I want to know what you're doing, but I must confess I'm afraid to find out," he said. "A spot of demon-summoning, I gather?"

"It's a bit complicated," said James. "Hello, Magnus. It's good to see you."

"Last time I saw *you*, you were facedown in the Serpentine," Magnus said cheerfully. "Now you're fiddling with a Pyxis. I see you have decided to follow in the long Herondale tradition of poor decision-making."

"So have I!" said Lucie, determined not to be left out.

"I came all the way from Jakarta to have a meeting with Tessa and Will about this whole daylight demon plague business," Magnus said. "Yet when I knocked on the front door, no one answered. Thus I was forced to come in through the Sanctuary."

"It's odd they would have asked you to come here now," said Thomas. "Everyone over eighteen is out searching for the demons responsible for the attacks."

Magnus furrowed his brow. He lifted his hand to stare at the expensive-looking watch on his wrist and groaned. "It seems that I forgot to turn my watch backward and therefore have arrived six hours early. Bloody hell."

Matthew looked delighted. "We could have tea. I am a true enthusiast of your work, Mr. Bane. Also, your personal style. Your waistcoats alone . . ."

"Matthew, do shut up," said Thomas. "Mr. Bane doesn't want to talk about waistcoats."

"Untrue," said Magnus. "I always want to talk about waistcoats. But I admit I'm more curious about this Pyxis." He drew closer and poked at the box with his Malacca walking stick. "Am I correct in deducing that you opened the box on purpose and let a Palpis demon out?"

"Yes," said James.

". . . Why?" said Magnus.

"We need to be able to use the Pyxis," Matthew burst out. "To trap a demon. So it had to be empty. We were just—clearing it out."

James sighed. "Matthew, you would be a terrible spy. You might not break under torture, but you'd tell someone anything they wanted to know in exchange for a nice pair of trousers."

"Oh, for goodness' sake," Cordelia said. She turned to Magnus. "You want this demon business over, right? You don't want any more Shadowhunters to die?"

Magnus looked startled to be addressed so forcefully. "I am generally not on the side of murderous demons, no."

"Then perhaps you could help us," James said, and quickly outlined their plan, or at least as much of it as he could tell without breaking faith with Ragnor. Their belief that they were seeking a kind of demon that could only be trapped by a Pyxis. James's vision of the shadow realm and reason to think that the demon would be on Tower Bridge. As he spoke, Magnus looked more and more curious. By the end of the story, Magnus had seated himself on the edge of the fountain, his long legs stretched out in front of him.

"This is quite a collection of suppositions," he said, when James was done. "But I must ask, especially you, Lucie and James—why do you not seek your parents' assistance with this? Why the secrecy?"

"Because we made a promise," said Matthew. "To the person who gave us the key that unlocked a great deal of this information. And we can't break it."

Magnus smiled an odd sideways smile. "Ragnor told me that he trusted you with some information, and it appears that you have not betrayed his trust. Not many Shadowhunters would honor such a vow made to a Downworlder. Since I am Ragnor's best friend, or at least the only person who can tolerate him for long stretches, I will keep your secret." He glanced from James to Lucie. "In days past, when I knew your parents well, they probably would have been spearheading this plan." He stood up. "But now they are no longer children. They are parents, and thus devoted to something they love more than their own lives. So indeed, perhaps they should not be told."

Even Matthew had no response to that.

"Well, good luck," Magnus said, picking up his walking stick. "I suppose I shall go to Hatchards for a few hours. There is no better distraction in this world than losing oneself in books for a while."

Cordelia stepped forward, her hands held out as if to prevent him from leaving. "Mr. Bane," she said. "I know it is a great deal to ask, especially when you have promised to keep our secrets. But would you help us?"

Magnus tapped gloved fingers on the head of his cane. "You're a Carstairs, right? Cordelia Carstairs?"

"Yes, I'm Jem's cousin," Cordelia said. "Look—we know this is a wild plan, but it could save many lives. You needn't help us directly, or get involved in the fighting. I understand you feel loyalty to our parents. But you could help us very much just by casting a spell to keep mundanes off Tower Bridge while we venture onto it. It would be safer for them, too."

Magnus hesitated. It was utterly silent in the Sanctuary. Cordelia imagined she could hear the sound of the blood pounding in her ears as Magnus considered her request.

At last the warlock shrugged a silk-suited shoulder. "Very well," he said. "Even though that green bastard Ragnor has hared off to Capri, I don't think he would have wanted you to put yourselves in danger because of a promise to him. I'll keep an eye on you, but remember—if I see anything I think Will and Tessa need to know, I will tell them about it posthaste."

After gathering what they needed from the weapons room—James was loaded down with more than a dozen of Christopher's specially designed throwing knives—the group made their way down Ludgate Hill and Cannon Street as the sun set over the City. James caught himself stealing glances at Cordelia when he was sure he wouldn't be observed; she was deep in conversation with Lucie, their heads bent together as they walked. Cordelia's flame-dark hair had been pulled back into a smooth chignon, leaving the light brown nape of her neck exposed.

James tried not to think about the fact that he knew what it was like to curl his fingers around the back of that neck while he kissed her mouth. He was sure that if he did think about it, it would drive him mad and he would be no further use to anyone.

Those moments in the Whispering Room with Cordelia had been like nothing else in his life. No other experience was comparable, and certainly no moment with Grace. But what did that say about him? Hadn't he loved Grace, and wasn't love the same as desire? Didn't the one grow from the other? And he couldn't love Cordelia. It wasn't possible for him to have been in love with Grace mere days ago and have transferred his affections so quickly.

He wished to talk to Cordelia, desperately, but what on earth would he say? He couldn't tell her he loved her, but neither could he express regret for what had happened the night before. If he had to choose between a long life of peace and happiness and another five minutes like the ones he'd spent with Cordelia in the Whispering Room, he dared not guess what he would choose.

"Are you all right?" To James's surprise, Magnus had joined him as they passed the church of St. Margaret Pattens. "I have to admit," Magnus added, "I had been hoping to talk to you tonight, so perhaps this development is fortuitous."

"Why would you be hoping to talk to me?" James slid his hands into the pockets of his gear jacket. It buttoned closely to the body, allowing for ease of movement while fighting. "If you are concerned that I have continued my career of shooting chandeliers, you will be relieved to know that according to the Clave, I have moved on to vandalizing greenhouses."

Magnus merely raised an eyebrow. "Henry," he said. "Before he went to Idris, he sent me a vial of dirt to analyze. Said he couldn't make head or tail of it. He also said you gave it to him."

James had nearly forgotten that Magnus and Henry were good friends and had, famously, invented the magic that powered Portals together. "And?" he said cautiously.

"It's strange stuff," Magnus said. "In fact, it isn't from this world."

They had reached the bottom of Great Tower Street and were nearing the Tower of London. Flags waved from the turrets of the White Tower, backlit dimly against the last fitful gleams of the setting sun. Magnus nimbly avoided a group of tourists with box cameras and steered James down Tower Hill, a hand on his shoulder.

James lowered his voice, though the others were a distance away. Matthew, who was carrying the Pyxis, had stopped to point out something about the Tower to Cordelia. "What do you mean?"

"You know that there are other realms," said Magnus. "Other worlds than this."

Think of the universe then as like a honeycomb, each of its chambers a different realm. So some chambers lie next to one another. "Demons come from them, yes. They travel through the dimensions to reach our world and others."

Magnus nodded. "There are some worlds ruled by demons, usually Greater Demons. Those worlds can be imbued with the very essence of those creatures. The dirt you gave Henry comes from one such place. A dimension under the power of the demon Belphegor."

"Belphegor?" The name was immediately familiar. "He's one of the Princes of Hell, isn't he?"

"I know what you're thinking about," said Magnus, tapping his walking stick against the cobblestones. "Jem also contacted me about you. All roads lead to James Herondale these days, it seems."

James rubbed his cold hands together. The wind off the river was sharp. "Jem contacted you?"

"About your grandfather," said Magnus. "He told me that he was a Prince of Hell." He glanced at the darkening sky. "You are wondering now if it might be Belphegor because the realm that you visit belongs to him."

"Wouldn't that make a kind of sense?" said James.

"It might. It might mean nothing at all. I can tell you that there is no record of anyone sighting Belphegor in more than a century." Magnus hesitated. "Jem told me you were desperate to know who your grandfather is. My own father is a Prince of Hell. They are dark angels, James. Intelligent and cunning and manipulative. They bear the knowledge of thousands of years of life. Like angels, they have seen the face of the divine, but they turned away from it. They have chosen darkness, and that choice has reverberated through eternity. They cannot be killed, only wounded, and no good can come from knowing a Prince of Hell. They can never cause you anything but sorrow."

"But wouldn't it be better for me to know—"

"I summoned my father once. It was the worst mistake of my life. James, you are not defined by this—by this blood in you. I have found no trace, no hint of who your grandfather is, and I advised Jem to cease looking. It does not matter. You are who you are, made by the sum of your choices and actions. Not a teaspoon of demon's blood."

"So you *don't* think it's Belphegor?" said James. "What about Sammael?"

Magnus snorted. "Good Lord, you are determined. I recall seeking a demon for your father, once. He was equally stubborn." He pointed with his walking stick. "Look. Here we are."

They were in front of the bridge; though it was quite dark now and the gas lamps were lit, there was still a good amount of traffic—even the occasional motorcar purring along Tower Bridge Approach.

The others had begun to gather around. Reluctantly, James dropped the topic of his grandfather. "So, do you think you can do it?" he asked Magnus. "Create a distraction? Or should we come back later, when there are fewer mundanes about?"

Magnus's eyes glittered. "No need for that," he said. He stepped to the railing along the river's edge, where a high wall dropped down to a stony beach that ran beside and below the bridge. With a flourish, he drew off his gloves and tucked them into his waistcoat pocket. Then he held out his hands. Blue fire sparked at his fingertips.

Light arced over the Thames. Bright as a thousand naphtha beacons, it formed a glimmering path laid from bank to bank of the Thames. James heard Cordelia gasp in wonder as the light rose and twined, forming the ghostly shape of a shimmering Tower Bridge made of light. It was perfect down to the last detail, from the towers to the spiderweb cables and gleaming chains.

Magnus lowered his hands. He was breathing hard.

"It's spectacular," said Thomas, and there was a look of real wonder on his face that James was glad to see. "But—"

"It will not appear to mundanes as it does to you," said Magnus. "They will not see the real bridge. They will see this instead. Look."

He indicated an oncoming hansom cab with a wave of his hand. The small group of Shadowhunters gaped as it swung toward the glimmering illusion of Tower Bridge and onto the bridge deck. The wheels of the hansom rattled over the glimmering tarmac.

"Oh, good, I was afraid the bridge was going to collapse," said Lucie, as more carriages followed the cab.

Magnus seemed to have thrown up a glamour over the entrance to the real bridge, as all the traffic, pedestrian and even omnibuses, seemed to be swerving unconsciously toward Magnus's secondary, shining structure.

"Magnus would never create a bridge that would collapse," said Matthew. His green eyes were shining, and James felt a rush of affection for his *parabatai*; Matthew had always loved magic. It was probably why he seemed so at home in the Hell Ruelle and places like it, surrounded by enchanted fire and starry-eyed warlocks.

"Thank you," said Magnus dryly. "If you're going to capture that demon, you'd better get to it. I can only keep this illusion going for so long."

James inclined his head. "Thank you."

Magnus just shook his head slightly. "Good luck. Don't get killed."

James had already turned and was making his way through the archway that led to the steps up to the bridge, the others close behind and around him. All of them held seraph blades except Cordelia; as always, Cortana glimmered in her hand.

James had thought there seemed a sort of shadow hanging over the bridge, a darkness that he had attributed to the shadow of the glamour Magnus had cast. But as they gained the top of the steps, seraph blades drawn, the world began to darken in front of James's eyes. The gas lamps flickered wildly and went out.

The stone towers cracked and blackened, deep jagged lines spreading across the pavement beneath them. The wind picked up, and the heavy steel suspension chains seemed to sway: the clouds overhead roiled and darkened in the dark gray sky. There was an acid tang to the air, as if a storm was oncoming.

"Jamie." Matthew was still beside him; as James turned to look at his *parabatai*, he realized that Matthew's hair looked white, like an old man's. The color was leaching out of everything, turning the world to a photograph. He sucked in a breath. "Are you all right? You look—"

"I can see the shadow realm." James's own voice sounded hollow to him, distant and echoing. "It's all around me, Math. The bridge is splintering—"

Matthew's hand clasped his arm. His fingers seemed the only warm thing in a world made of ice and ashes. "There's nothing wrong with the bridge. Everything's all right, Jamie."

James wasn't sure that was true. The bridge looked warped and broken. From the cracks in the granite poured a reddish light. The blood-colored light from his vision.

The others were fanning out, looking up and down the bridge. Clouds were scudding back and forth above the bridge like anxious messengers.

James tipped his head back. More clouds were gathering directly overhead. They were heavy and reddish, almost wet-looking, as if they were filled with blood. James narrowed his eyes. He had thought he could see stars through the clouds, a few faint stars hovering above the bridge's upper walkways. They were not stars, he realized, instinctively sliding a throwing knife from the scabbard at his waist. Stars did not have pupils, or scarlet irises. Stars did not blink.

James drew his arm back and flung the blade.

It came screaming out of the air like a diving hawk—a demon the size of an omnibus, its yellowish coat streaked with dried blood. It shot straight for James, a blur of black teeth and red talons—and a haft of gold, where the hilt of James's knife protruded from its shoulder.

James stood upright on the bridge, his right arm outstretched, and flung a second blade. The demon ducked out of the path of the knife and landed on the bridge, taloned feet splayed. It began to move toward the Nephilim.

Cordelia raised Cortana, its golden blade slicing the air. All around her she could hear voices as angel blades were named and blazed up in light: *"Eleleth!" "Adamiel!" "Jophiel!"*

The demon bared its teeth as seraph light illuminated the bridge. Cordelia could see it more clearly now: the body of a mangy lion with elongated legs, each one ending in a massive, taloned paw. Its head was snakelike and scaled, with glittering red eyes and a triple row of serrated jaws. Its scorpion's tail lashed back and forth as it paced toward James, a low growl coming from its throat.

By the Angel, Cordelia thought. *We were right. It is a Mandikhor.*

James caught up a seraph blade as the demon paced toward them. *"Raguel!"*

The blade flared up as the demon lunged, teeth bared. James

flung himself sideways, avoiding its slashing claws. Matthew dropped the Pyxis and ran forward to flank James, seraph blade flashing. The tip sliced across the demon's shoulder as it leaped back, causing it to howl. It reared up, and Cordelia heard Lucie cry out as the demon seemed to tremble all over. A grotesque lump swelled under the skin of its side—swelled and swelled and then burst into a sticky black *thing*. Cordelia tried not to gag as the thing peeled away from the Mandikhor, dropping to the ground. As it rose to its feet, Cordelia recognized it as one of the creatures that had attacked them in Regent's Park. A Khora demon.

It shot toward Matthew, who swore and slashed out at it with his seraph blade. Cordelia charged forward, only to be met with another of the Khora demons. The demon had shed several others: two leaped toward Christopher and Thomas, springing through the air like black spiders. Lucie ran to join them, impaling one of the Khora from behind: it vanished, spattering ash and ichor, as Christopher and Thomas dispatched the other.

Cordelia whipped Cortana forward with a slashing motion, shredding the demon in front of her with such force that the blade passed through the Khora, carried on, and embedded itself in the granite railing of the bridge. She yanked it free as the demon disappeared with a howl. The blade of Cortana was smeared with black, but it was undamaged. *I suppose it really can cut anything*, she thought dazedly, before turning to rejoin the battle.

She pushed forward as James hurled a knife, pinning one of the shadow demons to the cables of the bridge like a hideous butterfly. It struggled and hissed as Matthew and James leaped up onto the bridge's railing, their seraph blades blazing in their hands as they slew shadow after shadow.

But it didn't matter how many of these shadow creatures they killed, Cordelia knew. The Mandikhor could make an infinite number of Khora: it was the source of them, and the source had to be destroyed.

"Christopher!" she heard Thomas shout. She spun and saw that a group of Khora were starting to circle Christopher. Even as Christopher tried to fight his way free, the circle tightened. Lucie and Thomas raced toward him—James and Matthew leaped down from the railing—but Cordelia, raising her sword, raced the other way, toward the Mandikhor.

It had been watching Christopher and the others, licking its lips as the Khora closed in. Now it reared back as Cordelia approached, but too late—she hurled herself forward, Cortana sinking deep into the creature's torso. Hot ichor spilled onto her hand, and the world seemed to tilt around her, the color rushing out of it like blood from a wound. She stood on the bridge among black-and-white shadows and twisted, gnarled trees—the suspension cables hung like rotting vines, blackening in the night air. She yanked Cortana back, gasping, and fell to her knees. Suddenly she felt a hand on her arm. She was wrenched to her feet and looked with surprise at Matthew, staring at her, his face very white. "Cordelia—"

"She's all right!" It was Lucie, spattered with blood and ichor, clutching the Pyxis box. The others had fanned out around Cordelia: James had his blade in one hand, his gaze trained on the roaring, bleeding Mandikhor.

The bridge was empty of Khora. Cordelia had distracted the Mandikhor just long enough for the others to kill the shadow creatures; but the Mandikhor was growling now, another lump already beginning to swell on its back. "*Now!*" Lucie cried. "We must get it into the Pyxis!"

"Put the box on the ground!" It was Thomas, vaulting up onto the railing, his *bolas* in his hand. "Christopher, say the words!"

Christopher stepped closer to the Pyxis. The Mandikhor, realizing what was happening at last, charged.

Christopher shouted, in a voice that cut through the noise of battle: "*Thaam Tholach Thechembaor!*"

The alchemical symbols carved on the Pyxis box lit as if the lines on the wood were burning: they seemed to bloom on the wood, glowing like coals.

A spear of light shot from the Pyxis, and then another, and another. The beams of light arrowed along the bridge, wrapping around the Mandikhor in a bright cage. It gave a howl—the cage of light flared up one last time and was sucked back into the Pyxis, the Mandikhor vanishing with it.

There was a long silence. James mopped at the blood on his face, his golden eyes burning. Matthew's hand was still wrapped around Cordelia's arm.

"I don't mean to put a damper on things," said Thomas at last, "but—did that work? Because it seems rather—"

The Pyxis exploded. The Shadowhunters yelled and dived out of the way as wooden shrapnel blew in all directions. Wind tore across the bridge, flattening Cordelia to her knees, a howling hurricane of fire-scented air.

At last the howling died down. The bridge was empty and silent, only the wind blowing a bit of discarded refuse back and forth across the roadway. Cordelia rose to her feet and reached down a hand to help Lucie up after her. Ahead, she could still see the glimmering light of Magnus's bridge, mundane traffic still making its way across it.

"—too easy," Thomas finished. His face was smeared with soot.

"Bloody hell," said James, reaching for a knife, just as the world seemed to explode around them.

Out of the wind and air, the Mandikhor suddenly appeared, twice as big as it had been before, and clothed in ragged darkness. It rose above them like a shadow drawn in blood, its head thrown back, each of its talons gleaming like a dagger.

James flung his knife just as the Mandikhor sprang toward him, shadows spilling from it and racing across the bridge in all directions. The world had turned gray and black again. James could see London on either side of the river, but it was a ruined London, the Tower shattered and broken, fires burning along the wharves, the blackened spires of churches standing as skeletons against a smoke-stained sky. He could hear his friends all around him, their shouts and cries as they fought back the shadows, but he could no longer see them. He was alone in his nightmare realm.

The Mandikhor leaped toward him and seized hold of him. James had been braced for an attack, but this was something different: the demon was holding him fast, claws sunk into the front of his gear jacket. Its lips curled back from its teeth. *"Come with me,"* the demon hissed. *"Come with me, child of demons, to where you will be honored. You see the same world I do. You see the world as it really is. I know who your mother is, and who your grandfather is. Come with me."*

James went cold.

I know who your mother is, and who your grandfather is. He thought of the demon in the park: *Why destroy your own kind?*

"I am a Shadowhunter," he said. "I will not listen to your lies."

"You know I speak the truth," said the Mandikhor, its hot breath searing James's skin. *"I swear on the names of Asmodeus, of Belial, of Belphegor and Sammael, that I can end this scourge if you will come with me. No more need die."*

James froze. A demon, swearing on the names of the Princes of Hell. A voice in the back of his head screamed, *Do it! Go with him! End the sickening, the dying!* Another voice, quieter but steadier, whispered, *Demons lie. Even when they swear, they lie.*

"No," he said, but his voice shook.

The Mandikhor hissed. *"So ungrateful,"* it said. *"You alone can walk between the world of Earth and the dark kingdom."*

James stared into the demon's blood-red eyes. "Do you mean the kingdom of Belphegor?"

The Mandikhor made an awful noise; after a moment, James realized it was chuckling. *"So like a human,"* it said, *"to know so much, and yet know so little."*

James opened his mouth to speak, just as an arcing golden light seared the air. "Leave him alone!" Cordelia shouted, as Cortana divided the darkness.

James jerked free, rolling away from the demon and up onto his feet as Cordelia threw herself at the Mandikhor. The gold of the sword was the only color in the black-and-white world—the gold and the flame-red of her hair. Cortana whipped back and forth—its blade slashed across the demon's chest, opening a long black wound—the demon howled and struck out, its massive paw slamming into Cordelia and sending her flying. Cortana tumbled from her hand, skidding across the bridge as she hurtled over the railing with a scream.

James heard Lucie scream, "Daisy!" and the sound of a distant splash. The world seemed to go silent as he bent to seize up Cortana. He strode toward the Mandikhor, his blood burning.

The demon had sunk to its forelegs. It was bleeding from the wound Cordelia had dealt it, ichor spreading around it like a shadow. *"You cannot slay me here,"* it snarled as James came near. *"My roots are deep within another realm. As I feed there, I grow stronger. I am a legion who cannot be touched."* With a final hiss, it vanished.

Color sprang back into the world. James spun, Cortana in hand: he could see the bridge as it had always been, dull gold and white in the moonlight, and his friends running toward him. He did not see Lucie. He remembered her calling out Cordelia's name. He remembered the sound of the water. *Cordelia. Cordelia.*

"Where is she?" Matthew gasped as he neared James. "Where's Cordelia?"

"She's in the river," James said, and began to run.

Lucie stared frantically at the river. She could see steps leading down to it from what looked like a passage through a building beside the bridge. She hurtled down the stairs to ground level and found herself in a dimly lit, narrow street lined with tall warehouses, blackened with soot and grime. There was the passage, a dark hole in the nearest building. She ran to it and saw stone stairs descending to a faint gleam at the bottom: the river. She raced to where an old cobbled ramp led into the water, an empty barge moored beside it. The river flowed by, black and silent, under the clouded sky; mist rose from the water.

There was no sign of Cordelia. Panic mounted in Lucie's stomach as she stared out into the black water. She didn't know if Cordelia could swim, and even a strong swimmer could drown in the currents of the Thames. And what if Cordelia had hit her head, or had been knocked out by the long fall from the bridge?

A sob caught in her throat. She dropped her seraph blade, which sputtered against the muddy pebbles of the bank, and began to fumble with the buttons of her gear jacket. The water didn't look very deep. She wasn't a strong swimmer, but she could try.

In the distance, she could see the fog-enshrouded shape of a barge arrowing slowly down the center of the river. "Help!" she shouted. "Help! Someone has fallen in the river!" She raced along the bank, waving frantically at the barge, which was disappearing into the mist. "Bring her out, please!" Lucie screamed. "Help me!"

But the barge had vanished. She could see figures on the bridge above her, the eerie light of seraph blades. The boys were still fighting. She could never reach Magnus in time, nor could he put aside what he was doing: he had to remain utterly focused on the illusion of the false bridge. She would have to go into the river, even if she might drown herself.

She took a step forward, her boot coming down in the shallow, dark water. She shivered as the icy liquid seeped through the leather. She took another step in, and froze.

The river was moving, surging, about ten feet from the bridge. The water had begun to churn, yellowish-gray foam sliding along its dark surface. A bitter smell wafted across the water: rotten fish and old blood and the age-old mud of the riverbed.

Lucie's foot slipped on a loose pebble. She went to her knees as the waters of the Thames began to rise and part like the water of the Red Sea. A shine of white broke the black surface of the water. She stared for an uncomprehending instant until she realized what she was seeing. The shine was moonlight on river-washed bone.

Figures rose from the water, pallid as ash. A woman with long, streaming hair, her face bloated and black. A woman in a wide-skirted gown, her throat cut, her eyes black and empty. A massive man with the marks of a rope still dark around his neck, wearing the arrow-stamped uniform of a prisoner.

He was carrying Cordelia in his arms. Ghosts rose up on either side of him, a veritable army of the drowned and dead. In the center of them all, the ghost prisoner held Cordelia, her body limp, her bright hair soaked and streaming down over her shoulders. Her gear was dark with river water, all of it sluicing off her as the ghosts carried her inexorably forward to the riverbank and laid her down.

"Thank you," Lucie whispered.

The ghost prisoner straightened up. For a long moment, all the ghosts simply stared at Lucie, their eyes empty hollows of darkness. Then they vanished.

"Cordelia?" Lucie tried to rise, to go to Cordelia, but her damp knees gave out under her. In the distance, she was aware that the fight on the bridge had stopped. She knew James and the others would come to her, but every second seemed stretched out to a year. Her energy seemed to have fled her body completely. Every breath was a chore.

"Cordelia," she whispered again, and this time Cordelia stirred. With relief so overwhelming Lucie was almost sick, she saw her friend's lashes flutter against her cheeks. Cordelia rolled to her side and began to cough, her body spasming as she choked up river water.

Lucie sagged back, half-delirious. The boys were coming down the steps of the bridge now, racing toward her and Cordelia, calling out their names. A distance behind them came Magnus, hurrying but looking exhausted. As he came closer, he slowed and gave Lucie a peculiar, searching look. Or maybe she was imagining it. . . . At least there were arms around her, Lucie thought, arms holding her up, wrapping her close.

Only then did it strike her as strange. She looked up and saw a face hovering above hers, white as salt, with jade-green eyes. Behind his dark head the sky seemed to be spinning. Around his neck, his golden locket burned like a star. As she watched, he touched it with two fingers, his lips tightening.

"Jesse Blackthorn," Lucie whispered, as the world swam away and the dim light faded. He was the one, she realized. He had called up the ghosts. He had saved Cordelia. "Why did you do that?"

But the darkness drew her down before he could reply.

DAYS PAST:
CIRENWORTH HALL, 1900

"It's mine!"

"It certainly isn't!" Outraged, Alastair made another grab for the sword. Cordelia stepped nimbly backward, holding Cortana over her head, but Alastair was taller. He stomped on her foot and snatched it away, his black hair falling into his eyes as he scowled.

"Tell her, Father," he said. "Tell her it isn't hers!"

"*Kerm nariz*, Alastair. Enough." Tall and weathered, his blond hair just turning to silver, Elias Carstairs had a lazy voice that matched his lazy and economical gestures. He was in good health today, and Cordelia was glad. There were many days her father was absent from the training room, lying ill in a darkened room, a damp cloth over his eyes.

He peeled himself away from the pillar he'd been leaning against and regarded his offspring with a thoughtful indulgence. Elias had always been their weapons master, the one who had trained them in the physical arts of Shadowhunting since they had been small.

He was the one who had turned the ballroom at Cirenworth into a training area. He had bought the great house from mundanes and seemed to take pleasure in removing evidence of their mundanity. He tore out the parquet floors and put down softer wood from trees in Idris, better for cushioning falls. Chandeliers were replaced with hooks to hang weapons from, and the walls were painted saffron yellow, the color of victory.

Elias had lived in Beijing for many years and favored the weapons and fighting styles of Nephilim there, from the *zhǎn mǎ dāo* to the double-edged *jiàn* to the long-handled *qiāng*. He taught his children *shuāngdāo*, the art of wielding two swords at the same time. He hung rope darts and chain whips from the rafters and built a *lei tai*, a raised fighting platform, at the west end of the room. Alastair and Cordelia stood on the *lei tai* now, glaring at each other.

"Cordelia," said Elias, clasping his hands behind his back. "Why, exactly, do you want Cortana?"

Cordelia paused a moment. She was thirteen, and she rarely bothered to try to get in between Alastair and the things he wanted. There was no one in the world more stubborn or fussy than her brother, in her opinion. But Cortana was different. She'd been dreaming of wielding Cortana since she was a little girl—the heft of its golden hilt, the arc of its blade through the air.

And Alastair, she knew, had never dreamed about that: he was a good fighter, but largely disinterested. He preferred following Shadowhunter politics and scheming to actual demon chasing.

"Cortana was made by Wayland the Smith," she said. "He made swords for all the greatest heroes. Excalibur for Arthur. Durendal for Roland and Hector. Sigurd, who slew the dragon Fafnir, bore a sword named Balmung made by Wayland—"

"Cordelia, we know all this," said Alastair crossly. "No need for a history lesson."

Cordelia glared.

"So you want to be a hero," said Elias, with a gleam of interest.

Cordelia considered. "Cortana has one sharp edge and one dull one," she said. "Because of that, it has often been called a sword of mercy. I want to be a merciful hero."

Elias nodded and turned to his son. "And you?"

Alastair flushed. "It's a Carstairs sword," he said shortly. "I'm Alastair Carstairs and I always will be. When Cordelia gets married and has a passel of brats, one of them will end up with Cortana— and they won't be a Carstairs."

Cordelia made an indignant sound, but Elias held up a silencing hand. "He's right," he said. "Cordelia, let your brother keep the sword."

Alastair smirked, twirled the sword in his hand, and headed for the edge of the *lei tai*. Cordelia stood where she was, rage and indignation prickling up her spine. She thought of all the times she'd come into the training room to gaze at Cortana in its crystal box, the words etched on its blade the first thing she'd learned to read: *I am Cortana, of the same steel and temper as Joyeuse and Durendal.* She thought of the way she'd always gently tapped the box, barely brushing it with her fingers, as if to reassure the sword that someday it would be taken out and wielded again. And when Elias had finally opened the box, declaring that today was the day he would choose Cortana's owner, her heart had soared.

She couldn't bear it. "But Cortana is mine!" she burst out as her brother reached the edge of the platform. "I know it is!"

Alastair opened his mouth to deliver a retort—but only gasped as the sword wrenched itself out of his grasp and flew across the room toward his sister. Cordelia held out a hand as if to ward it off, startled, and the hilt smacked into her palm. She closed her hand around it reflexively and felt a jolt go up her arm.

Cortana.

Alastair looked as if he wanted to sputter, but didn't. He was too clever and too self-conscious to be a sputterer. "Father," he said instead. "Is this some sort of trick?"

Elias only smiled as if he'd known what was going to happen. "Sometimes the sword chooses the bearer," he said. "Cortana will be Cordelia's. Now, Alastair—"

But Alastair had stalked from the room.

Elias turned to his daughter. "Cordelia," he said. "A blade of Wayland the Smith is a great gift, but it is also a great responsibility. One that may one day cause you sorrow."

Cordelia nodded. She was sure her father was right, in some distant way that adults were sometimes. Still, gazing down at Cortana's golden blade, she couldn't imagine ever being anything but happy with it in her hand.

17

THE HOLLOW SEA

"Oh whence do you come, my dear friend, to me,
With your golden hair all fallen below your knee,
And your face as white as snowdrops on the lea,
And your voice as hollow as the hollow sea?"

"From the other world I come back to you:
My locks are uncurled with dripping drenching dew.
You know the old, whilst I know the new:
But to-morrow you shall know this too."
—Christina Rossetti, "The Poor Ghost"

"So," said Will Herondale, a dark edge to his voice, "for some reason, you thought it was a good idea to take on a Mandikhor demon all by yourselves?"

Lucie's eyes fluttered open. For a moment she thought her father was talking to her, and considered flight. She discarded the idea immediately—her body was pinned down by heavy sheets and blankets. She blinked at her familiar surroundings; somehow she had been tucked into her own bed at home. The room smelled comfortingly of tea and of her father's cologne. Not surprisingly, as he was seated in a chair next to the bed. Her mother had her hand on Will's shoulder, and James leaned against a wall nearby. He clearly hadn't changed clothes since the fight on the bridge, though his hands and face had been cleaned of blood and ichor and a new healing rune gleamed against his throat.

Someone had laid the golden blade of Cortana across Lucie's vanity table. She supposed there had been no chance to return it to Cordelia after her recovery from the river.

"Christopher was using one of his new devices," James lied. "It's meant to pick up the traces of dark magic. We didn't think it would really come to anything. That is why we didn't summon you."

Will's eyebrows flew up. "All six of you showed up to Tower Bridge in gear, despite thinking it wouldn't come to anything?"

Lucie squeezed her eyes half-shut. Better by far that they think she was asleep. James could definitely handle this on his own: as he never tired of reminding her, he was older.

"We thought it best to be prepared," said James. "Besides, I know you did much more risky things when you were my age."

"It's dreadful the way you keep throwing that in my face," said Will.

"Well, I think they did very well," said Tessa. "A Mandikhor demon is not easy to defeat."

"And we did not defeat it," James said grimly. "There will continue to be attacks. The Nephilim are still in danger."

"Darling, the responsibility does not lie on you to fix all this," said Tessa, her voice gentle. "Just to know the demon is in fact a Mandikhor will help a great deal."

"Yes, and you should tell Christopher that the Clave wishes to use this new device of his—it seems as if it could be very useful," said Will.

"Ah," said James. "Tragically, the device was eaten by the demon."

Unable to help herself, Lucie giggled.

"You're awake!" Tessa rushed to the bed and hugged her daughter furiously. "Oh, Lucie!"

Will rose and hugged her as well. For a moment Lucie let herself enjoy being surrounded by the love and attention of her parents, even as she could hear Will scolding her for running out onto the riverbank alone.

"But I did it for Cordelia!" she exclaimed, as her parents drew back, her mother seating herself on the bed beside Lucie, where she could hold her hand. "You would have done it for Jem, Papa, when you were *parabatai*."

Will leaned back against a post of the bed. "You aren't *parabatai* with Cordelia yet."

"It isn't just for boys to risk their lives for each other," Lucie said fiercely. "I had to call for help—"

"Yes, and thank the Angel one of the passing boatmen saw Cordelia and brought her to shore," said Tessa. "You did help save her, Lucie."

Lucie glanced at James. She knew he had not seen the ghosts who had taken Cordelia from the water—even Magnus had been too far away to glimpse them. Nevertheless, he looked thoughtful.

"Cordelia was quite all right once she coughed up the river water," he said reassuringly. "Matthew, Christopher, and Thomas took her home in a hansom cab."

"But Cortana is still here," Lucie said, indicating the shining blade. "Daisy will be miserable without it. It's more than just a sword to her." She started to struggle upright. "I must bring it to her immediately."

"Lucie, no," said Tessa. "You need to rest—"

"I will bring it to Kensington," said James. There was a distant look in his eyes. "I wish to check on Cordelia and make sure she is recovering from the river."

Tessa still looked worried. "Take the carriage, James, please," she said. "It will be safer."

Nephilim carriages were reinforced with demon-repelling electrum and runes cleverly woven throughout the wood. James sighed and nodded.

"And take Bridget and her massive spear," said Will, doing a poor job at hiding a smile. "And perhaps change out of your gear first? It never hurts to look your best for a social call."

If only there were a rune for drying clothes, Cordelia thought mournfully. She felt as if she were definitely squelching. She was pressed up against Matthew in the back of the hansom cab on a bench seat that faced Thomas and Christopher. Matthew had kindly thrown his gear jacket over her shoulders since her own was wet; he was in shirtsleeves, one arm around her, holding her steady. It was an odd but not unpleasant feeling.

It was still all something of a blur—she recalled the force with which the demon's paw had struck her, the feeling of weightlessness as her feet left the bridge. The moon turning upside down and the river rushing up with horrifying speed. Bitter black water, the smell of damp and rot, the struggle to free herself from what she thought now might have been river weeds. Her first clear memory was of James leaning down over her with a stele in one hand and Cortana in the other. She had been choking and gasping, her body convulsing as her lungs emptied of water. James had drawn *iratze* after *iratze* onto her arm as the Merry Thieves crowded around.

At some point Matthew had arrived to take over while James hurried to Lucie, who had fainted on the riverbank. Magnus was there too, reassuring them that Lucie was fine and suffering from nothing more than shock. The shining bridge Magnus had summoned had vanished, and traffic had resumed over the real Tower

Bridge, so it had been easy for him to get hold of two hansom cabs and firmly separate the group: Lucie and James to go to the Institute, and the remaining Merry Thieves to accompany Cordelia to Kensington.

He had also told James, in no uncertain terms, that if James didn't pass on the information to Will and Tessa that the demon responsible for the attacks was a Mandikhor, he would do it himself.

Cordelia had managed to squeeze Lucie's hand once before she and James had been bundled into their hansom and driven away. Cordelia found herself on her way home, shivering with cold, her damp hair clammy with river water.

"Are you sure you're all right?" Thomas inquired, not for the first time. He sat opposite Cordelia, his knees knocking into hers. People Thomas's size were not made for ordinary hansom cabs.

"I'm fine," Cordelia insisted. "Utterly fine."

"It was amazing the way you charged at that demon, absolutely capital," said Christopher. "I really thought you had him in your sights, until you fell into the river, that is."

Cordelia felt Matthew's shoulder shake with silent laughter.

"Yes," said Cordelia. "I was under the same misapprehension myself."

"What happened, exactly?" Thomas said. "How did Lucie get you out of the water?"

Startled, Cordelia furrowed her brow. "I don't know," she said slowly. "I don't understand it. I did hear Lucie calling—calling my name—and then I just woke up on the bank, coughing."

"The current could just have brought her ashore," said Christopher. "Thames currents can be quite strong."

Matthew looked at her curiously. "When we were on the bridge, when James was fighting the Mandikhor, it looked as if the demon was speaking to him. Did you hear it?"

Cordelia hesitated. *Come with me, child of demons, to where you will be honored. You see the same world I do. You see the world as it really is. I know who your mother is, and who your grandfather is.*

Come with me.

"No," she said. "Just sort of a growling noise. Not any words."

The cab came to a stop; they had arrived at the Kensington house, gleaming white in the moonlight. The street was quiet and peaceful, a low wind rustling the tops of the plane trees.

Cordelia wasn't exactly sure how it happened, but Thomas and Christopher wound up waiting in the cab as Matthew escorted her to her front door, past the black-and-gold railing that circled the gardens.

"Will your mother be angry?" Matthew said.

"Have you heard of the death of a thousand cuts?" Cordelia replied.

"I always preferred the death of a thousand cats, in which one is buried under kittens," said Matthew.

Cordelia laughed. They had reached the glossy black front door. She began to remove Matthew's jacket to return it to him; he held up a slender hand, scarred as all Shadowhunters' hands were scarred. She could see his *parabatai* rune, printed darkly on the inside of his wrist. "Keep it," he said. "I have at least seventeen, and this is the plainest."

Seventeen coats. He was ridiculous. He was also rich, Cordelia realized. Of course he was. His mother had been Consul longer than they had been alive. His clothes were always a bit outrageous, but they were also expensive-looking and finely made. There was a silk flower, dyed green and secured in the buttonhole of his shirt. She touched the petal lightly with a fingertip.

"What does this mean?"

"The green carnation symbolizes a love of art and artifice, since a green carnation has to be created rather than appearing in nature." Matthew hesitated. "It also celebrates loving anyone you choose, whether that is a man or a woman."

A man or a woman. She looked at Matthew in surprise for a moment: Was he like Alastair? But no, she thought—it seemed to her that Alastair preferred only men romantically, as he had said he would never deceive a woman by pretending he loved her. Matthew was clearly saying he liked women and men both.

Matthew was looking at her hesitantly, as if he could not puzzle out her response or perhaps thought she might be angry. She thought of the hurt look in Alastair's eyes when he'd realized she had spied on him. She thought of the secrets people kept and the way they were like scars or wounds beneath the skin. You could not always see them, but if you touched on them in the wrong way, you could cause great pain.

"I like that," she said. "And I am sure anyone you chose to be in your life, whether it was a man or a woman, would be a good person who I would like very much."

"I wouldn't be so sure of me, Cordelia," Matthew said, "or my choices."

"Matthew," she said. "What could you ever have done that would be so bad?"

He set one hand on the doorframe, above her head, and gazed down at her. The faint glow from the streetlamps illuminated the high arches of Matthew's cheekbones and the soft, disarranged fall of his hair. "You wouldn't believe me if I told you."

"I believe James would not have chosen you as a *parabatai* if there was anything so terrible about you."

He closed his eyes for a moment, as if he felt a flash of pain. When he opened them, he was smiling, though it did not reach his eyes. "You have been quite a surprise since you came into our lives," he said, and she knew by "our" he meant the five of them, the Merry Thieves and Lucie. "I did not feel that our little group was missing anything before you arrived, but now that you are here, I cannot imagine it without you."

Before Cordelia could respond, the door opened and Risa was there. She took one astonished look at Cordelia, then called over her shoulder for Sona. Cordelia's mother appeared, wrapped in a silk robe de chambre. She looked from Matthew to Cordelia, dripping water on the front steps, and her dark eyes widened. "Oh," she said, her voice carrying that mixture of disapproval and concern that only a mother's could. "Oh, Layla. What happened?"

If Cordelia had expected her mother to be angry, she was pleasantly surprised. Like a master artisan of falsehoods, Matthew spun a story for Sona of bravery, intrigue, danger, and hinted romance. Cordelia had been at the Institute, he claimed, and would have remained loyally by James's side—for he was suffering the loss of Barbara with great sorrow—but knew her mother would worry if she did not return home. Matthew had offered to escort her, but they had been set upon by demons on the Thames footpath. Cordelia had fought bravely but was knocked into the river. It had all been very dramatic.

Sona forced a bar of Fry's Chocolate Cream and a thick scarf on Matthew before he was able to make his escape. She then went for Cordelia with an icy will, making sure she stripped off her wet clothes and that Risa drew a hot bath for her. No sooner had Cordelia exited the bath and put on a nightgown and slippers than she found herself reclining on the couch in the library in front of a roaring fire. A cozy dressing gown was wrapped around her shoulders, and Risa placed a fresh cup of tea in her hands while shaking her head with a disapproving air.

Cordelia had never been so hot in her life.

Sona perched on the arm of the sofa. Cordelia watched her mother warily over the edge of her teacup, fairly sure that Sona was settling in for a lengthy scold. Instead her dark eyes were worried. "Cordelia," she said. "Where is Cortana?"

Cordelia started. She knew when she had last seen Cortana—in James's hand, by the riverbank. But in the ensuing chaos, she had forgotten to take it back from him before she climbed into the carriage Magnus had summoned.

"I . . ."

"I don't want you to be worried, Cordelia *joon delam*," said Sona. "I know how your father has always made you feel about that sword. That it was a greater part of the Carstairs destiny than you—than I believe it is." Cordelia stared; this was the closest she'd seen her mother come to criticizing Elias. "A weapon can be lost during a battle. It is always better to lose the weapon than the warrior."

"*Mâdar,*" Cordelia began, struggling up against the mass of pillows. "It is not what you think—"

A knock sounded at the door. A moment later Risa stepped back into the library, James in tow.

He had changed out of the filthy gear he'd been wearing on the bridge and wore a dark chesterfield coat, its velvet collar turned up against the wind outside. He was carrying Cortana carefully, the gold bright and sharp against the dark tweed of his clothes.

Risa dusted off her hands with a satisfied air and headed for the kitchen. Sona was beaming all over her face. "Cordelia! James has brought you back Cortana."

Cordelia was speechless. She had certainly expected to get Cortana back, but not for James to show up in Cornwall Gardens after midnight.

"I will leave you alone to talk," said Sona, and left the room, closing the door behind her.

Cordelia was a little shocked. If Sona was willing to leave her daughter alone with James while Cordelia was wearing her night attire, she must be very convinced of James's marital intentions. *Oh, dear.*

Setting her teacup down on the low table beside the sofa, Cordelia lifted her head to look at James. His deep gold eyes were startling in their intensity; there were several bruises on his skin, and his hair was damp, probably from being recently washed.

The quiet seemed to stretch out between them. Maybe neither of them would ever speak again.

"Did you tell your parents?" asked Cordelia. "About the Mandikhor? And what happened on the bridge?"

"Most of it," James said. "Not about the Pyxis, of course, or Agaliarept, or—well, really I left most of what we've done lately out of it. They do know the Mandikhor is responsible for the attacks now, and that's the important part."

Cordelia wondered for a moment if he had told them what the Mandikhor had said to him on the bridge. *Child of demons.* It was the second time she had heard a demon taunt him about his heritage. It was the way of Greater Demons, to find the weak spots in humans and pierce them. She hoped James was able to dismiss their words, to see that he was no more a child of demons than Lucie, or Tessa, or Magnus Bane.

"Thank you," James said, making her start. "For what you did on the bridge. That was exceedingly brave."

"Which part?"

His smile flashed like heat lightning, transforming his face. "That's true. You did quite a lot of brave things on the bridge."

"That's not what I—" she began to sputter, then reached up as he held Cortana out to her. It was lovely to have it in her arms again. "Cortana, *moosh moosh-am*," she said. "I'm glad you're back."

"Did you just use a term of endearment for your sword?" said James. He had looked exhausted when he'd come into the room, but he seemed greatly cheered up now.

"It means 'mouse,' and yes, it is a term of endearment. Cortana has been with me through many difficult times. It should be appreciated." She leaned the sword against the fireplace grate; the heat would not tarnish the blade. Nothing did.

"I wish I knew more Persian," said James. He sank into one of the armchairs. "I would like to thank you in it, Daisy, for saving my life and risking your own. And for helping us as you have, especially when no one you know is ill. You could all have fled back to Paris or Cirenworth the moment this started."

Cordelia had often dreamed of teaching James Persian herself. English endearments were so limited and bland in comparison, she had always thought: Persians thought nothing of telling someone they loved *fadat besham*, I would die for you, or calling that person *noore cheshmam*, the light of my eyes, or *delbaram*, the thief of my heart. She thought suddenly of the sparking fire in the Whispering Room and the smell of roses. She bit her lower lip.

"You should not thank me," she said. "Or treat me as though I am being entirely unselfish."

James raised his winging black eyebrows. "What do you mean?"

"I have my own reasons for involving myself in the search for a cure. Of course I want to help those who are sick, but I also cannot help believing that if I were able to do such a service to the Clave as aiding in ending this demonic disease, surely they would grant my father leniency in his trial."

"I wouldn't call that selfish," said James. "What you are talking about is undertaking to do good for the sake of your father and your family."

Cordelia smiled weakly. "Well, I'm sure you'll add that to the list of my many qualities when you are helping me find a husband."

James did not smile back. "Daisy," he said. "I cannot—I do not think that I—" He cleared his throat. "Perhaps, after what happened in the Whispering Room, I am not the right person to find you a husband. I can't imagine you would trust me to—"

"I do trust you." Cordelia spoke through numb lips. "I entirely understand. You did not take liberties, James. It was a pretense. It was false, I know—"

"False?" he echoed.

Despite the heat, Cordelia shivered as James rose to his feet. The firelight flickered through his hair, edging the black locks with scarlet, as if he wore a crown of flames.

"I kissed you because I wanted to," he said. "Because I'd never wanted anything so much."

Cordelia felt herself go scarlet.

"I am no longer bound to Grace," he went on. "Yet for so many years I loved her. I know—I *remember*—that I did. That love ruled my life."

Cordelia's fingers tightened on her dressing gown.

"I wonder sometimes now if it was a dream," James said. "I idealized her, I suppose, as children do. Perhaps it was a child's dream of what love should and must be. I believed love was pain, and when I bled, I bled for her."

"It need not be pain," Cordelia whispered. "But James, if you love Grace—"

"I don't know," James said, turning away from the fire. His eyes were dark, as they had been in the Whispering Room, and desperate. "How can I have loved her so much, and feel what I feel now, for—" He broke off. "Maybe I am not who I thought I was."

"James—" The pain in his voice was too much. She started to rise to her feet.

"No." He shook his head, voice rough. "Don't. If you come close to me, Daisy, I will want—"

The library door flew open. Cordelia looked up, expecting to see her mother.

But it was Alastair, fully dressed for the outside in boots and an Inverness cape. He slammed the door behind him and turned to face them both, his gaze raking Cordelia and then James.

"My mother said you were both in here," he said in the drawl that meant he was out of his mind with rage. Cordelia's heart sank. The last time she had seen Alastair, he had been furious. He seemed still furious. She wondered if he had ever stopped being furious, or if he had been in a temper all day. "I didn't credit it at first, but now I see it is true." His black gaze snapped to James. "*She* may feel that it is permissible to leave you alone with my sister, but I don't. You brought her home in the dead of night, injured and looking like a drowned rat."

James crossed his arms over his chest. His eyes were golden slits. "Actually, Matthew brought her back. I've only just arrived."

Alastair shrugged off his heavy coat and threw it angrily over the arm of a chair. "I thought you had better sense, Herondale, than to put yourself in a position to compromise my sister."

"He brought back Cortana," Cordelia protested.

"Your mother welcomed me into this room," said James, his expression like ice. "Hers is the authority here, not yours."

"My mother doesn't understand—" Alastair broke off. He was yanking at the gloves on his hands with shaking fingers, and Cordelia realized with a shock that Alastair was far more upset than she'd realized. "I know you hate me for how I treated you in school, and rightfully so," Alastair said, fixing James with a level gaze. "But however much you hate me, do not take it out on my sister."

Cordelia saw a flicker of surprise in James's eyes. "Alastair, you made my life a living hell at the Academy. But I'd never take it out on Cordelia. That's something you would do, not something I would do."

"I see how it is. In school I had the power, and here you have the power to lord it over me. What's your game? What do you want with my sister?"

"Your sister," James said, speaking with a slow, deliberate

coldness. "Your sister is the only thing keeping me from punching you in the face. Your sister loves you, Angel knows why, and you aren't even the least bit grateful."

Alastair's voice was hoarse. "You have no idea what I've done for my sister. You have no idea about our family. You don't know the first thing—"

He broke off and glowered.

It was as if a jolt went through Cordelia. She had always thought of their family as fairly ordinary, aside from their constant travel. What was Alastair hinting at? "James," she said. The air was crackling with violence; it was only a matter of time before one of the boys took a swing at the other. "James, you'd better go."

James turned to her. "Are you sure?" he said in a low voice. "I won't leave you alone, Cordelia, not unless you wish me to."

"I'll be fine," she whispered back. "Alastair's bark is worse than his bite. I promise."

He raised his hand, as if he meant to cup her cheek, or brush back a lock of her hair. She could feel the energy between them, even now, even with her brother three feet away and mad with rage. It felt like the sparks of a bonfire.

James dropped his hand, and with a last hard look at Alastair, strode from the room. Cordelia went immediately to the door, shut and locked it. She turned to face him.

"What did you mean?" she said. "By 'you have no idea what I've done for my sister'?"

"Nothing," Alastair said, picking up his gloves. "I meant nothing, Cordelia."

"Yes, you did," she said. "I can tell that there is something you're not telling me, something that has to do with Father. All this time you have acted like my attempts to save him, to save *us*, are childish and silly. You haven't stood up for him at all. What are you not telling me?"

Alastair squeezed his eyes shut. "Please stop asking."

"I won't," Cordelia said. "You think Father did something wrong. Don't you?"

The gloves Alastair had been holding fell to the floor. "It doesn't matter what I think, Cordelia—"

"It does matter!" Cordelia said. "It matters when you hide things from me, you and *Mâmân*. I got a letter from the Consul. It said that they couldn't try Father with the Mortal Sword because he didn't remember a thing about the expedition. How could that be? What did he do—"

"He was drunk," Alastair said. "The night of the expedition, he was drunk, so drunk he probably sent those poor bastards into a nest of vampires because he didn't know enough not to. So drunk he doesn't remember a thing. Because he's *always* bloody drunk, Cordelia. The only one of us who didn't know that is you."

Cordelia sank down on the couch. She no longer felt her legs could hold her up. "Why didn't you tell me?" she whispered.

"Because I never wanted you to know!" Alastair burst out. "Because I wanted you to have a childhood, a thing I never had. I wanted you to be able to love and respect your father as I never could. Every time he made a mess, who do you think had to clean it up? Who told you Father was ill or sleeping when he was drunk? Who went out and fetched him when he passed out in a gin palace and smuggled him in through the back door? Who learned at ten years old to refill the brandy bottles with water each morning so no one would notice the levels had sunk—?"

He broke off, breathing hard.

"Alastair," Cordelia whispered. It was all true, she knew. She could not help but recall Father lying day after day in a darkened room, her mother saying he was "sick." Elias's hands shaking. Wine ceasing to appear at the dinner table. Elias never eating. Cordelia coming across bottles of brandy in odd places: a hall closet, a trunk of linens. Alastair never acknowledging any of it, laughing it off, turning her attention in some other direction, always, so she did not dwell. So she would not have to.

"He will never win this trial," said Alastair. He was trembling. "Even though the Mortal Sword is useless, he will indict himself with the way he looks, the way he speaks. The Clave knows a drunk when they see one. That is why Mother wants you married quickly. So you will be safe when the shame of it comes down."

"But what of you?" said Cordelia. "No shame should accrue to you, either—Father's weakness is not your weakness."

The fire in the grate had nearly burned down. Alastair's eyes were luminous in the dark. "I have my own weaknesses, as you well know."

"Love is not a weakness, Alastair *dâdâsh*," she said, and for a moment she saw Alastair hesitate at the use of the Persian word.

Then his mouth tightened. The shadows under his eyes looked like bruises; she wondered where he had been, to return so late at night.

"Isn't it?" he said, turning to leave the room. "Don't give your heart to James Herondale, Cordelia. He is in love with Grace Blackthorn and he always will be."

"You should brush your hair," Jessamine said, pushing the silver-backed hairbrush along the nightstand toward Lucie. "It will get tangled."

"Why must you be such a fussy ghost?" said Lucie, scooting upright against the pillows. She had been firmly ordered to stay in bed, though she was itching to leap up, seize her pen, and write. What was the point of having exciting things happen to you if you couldn't tell a story about them?

"When I was a girl, I brushed my hair one hundred strokes a

day," said Jessamine—who, being a ghost, had hair that floated like fine gossamer and never needed brushing. "Why, I—"

She shrieked and shot up into the air, hovering a foot above the nightstand. A wash of cold went over Lucie. She pulled the blankets up around her, looking about the room anxiously. "Jesse?"

He materialized at the foot of the bed, in the same black trousers and shirtsleeves he always wore. His eyes were green and very serious. "I am here."

Lucie looked up at Jessamine. "Could I have a moment to speak with Jesse alone?"

"Alone?" Jessamine looked horrified. "But he's a gentleman. In your bedroom."

"I am a ghost," said Jesse dryly. "What is it exactly you imagine I might do?"

"Please, Jessamine," said Lucie.

Jessamine sniffed. "Never in my day!" she announced, and vanished in a swirl of petticoats.

"Why are you here?" Lucie said, hugging the blankets to her chest. It was true that Jesse was a ghost, but she still felt awkward about the idea of him seeing her in her nightgown. "I don't remember you leaving. At the bridge."

"Your brother and friends seemed to have the situation well in hand," Jesse said. His gold locket glimmered at his throat. "And your brother can see ghosts. He's never seen me before, but—"

"Humph," Lucie said. "You do realize I just had to be dishonest with my family and pretend as if I didn't know you existed or that you raised the dead to bring Cordelia out of the river."

"*What?*"

"I mean, I'm grateful that you did it. Brought Cordelia out of the river, I mean. Don't think I'm not. It's just—"

"You think I called the dead out of the river?" Jesse demanded. "I *answered* the call."

Despite the blanket, Lucie suddenly felt cold all over. "What do you mean?"

"You called the dead," said Jesse. "You called the dead, and the dead came. I heard you, across the whole city, calling for someone to help you."

"What do you mean? Why would I have any ability to call the dead up? I can see them, but I certainly can't command—"

She broke off. She was suddenly back in Emmanuel Gast's bedroom in that small, terrible flat. *You will,* she had said when the ghost proclaimed he would never tell, and he had given up his secrets. *Leave us,* she had said, and he had winked out of existence.

"You were the only one who could see me in the ballroom," said Jesse. "You have always been the only one who can see me besides my family. There's something unusual about you."

She stared at him. What if she ordered Jesse to do something? Would he have to do it? Would he have to come to her if she called, as he had on the riverbank?

She swallowed. "When we were beside the river, when you were with me, you were holding that locket at your throat. Clutching it."

"And you want me to tell you why?" he said, and she knew he'd had the same thought she had. She didn't like the thought. She didn't want to order him around, or Jessamine. Perhaps she had to be panicked, though, she told herself. She'd been frightened in Gast's flat, and again at the river.

"If you want to," she said.

"This locket was placed around my throat by my mother," he said. "It contains my last breath."

"Your last breath?"

"I ought to tell you how I died, I suppose," he said, perching himself on the windowsill. He seemed to like it there, Lucie thought, just on the threshold. "I was a sickly child. My mother told the Silent Brothers that I wasn't well enough to withstand being given runes, but I begged and begged. She managed to fight me off until I was seventeen. You might understand that by then, I was desperate to be a Shadowhunter like other Shadowhunters. I told her that if she did not let me get the Marks, I would run away to Alicante and get them myself."

"And did you? Run away?"

He shook his head. "My mother relented, and the Silent Brothers came to the manor house. The rune ceremony went off without a hitch, and I thought I had triumphed." He held up his right hand, and she realized what she had thought was a scar was the faint outline of the Voyance rune. "My first rune and my last."

"What happened?"

"When I returned to my room, I collapsed on my bed. Then I woke in the night burning with fever. I remember screaming, and Grace running into my room. She was half-hysterical. Blood was welling from my skin, turning the sheets to scarlet. I writhed and screamed and tore at the bedspread, but I was weakening, nor could they use healing runes on me. I remember realizing I was dying. I had become so weak. Grace held me as I shivered. She was barefoot, and her nightgown and wrapper were soaked with my blood. I remember my mother coming in. She held the locket to my lips, as if she meant me to kiss it. . . ."

"Did you?" Lucie whispered.

"No," said Jesse matter-of-factly. "I died."

For the first time in her life, Lucie felt a pang of pity for Grace. To have her brother die in her arms like that. She could not imagine the agony.

"I came slowly to understand I was a ghost after that," said Jesse. "And it took me months of trying before my mother and sister could hear me and speak to me. Even then, I disappeared every morning when the sun came up, and only came back to consciousness with evening. I spent many nights walking alone in Brocelind Forest, with only the dead to see me. And you. A little girl who'd fallen into a faerie trap."

Lucie blushed.

"I was surprised when you saw me," he said. "And even more when I was able to touch your hand and lift you out of that pit. I thought perhaps it was because you were so young, but no. There is something unusual about you, Lucie. You have a power that is tied to the dead."

Lucie sighed. "If only I could have had a power that was tied to bread-and-butter pudding."

"That would not have helped Cordelia last night," Jesse said. He let his head fall back against the windowpane, and Lucie saw that of course he was not reflected in the dark glass. "My mother believes that once everything is in order, and she has all the ingredients a warlock will need, the last breath in this locket can be used to resurrect me. But on the riverbank, I was holding it because . . ."

Lucie raised her eyebrows.

"I thought at first you might have been in the water. Drowning. The life force in the locket could have emptied your lungs and let you breathe." He hesitated. "I thought, if you were dying, I would use it to bring you back."

Lucie inhaled sharply. "You would do that? For me?"

His eyes were fathomless deep green, the way Lucie imagined the depth of the ocean. His lips parted as if he meant to answer, just as a shaft of dawn light pierced the window glass. He stiffened, his eyes still locked on hers, as if he had been shot through with an arrow.

"Jesse," she whispered, but he had already vanished.

Days Past: London, Grosvenor Square, 1901

On the night of the death of Queen Victoria, the bells of London erupted into clamorous alarm.

Matthew Fairchild also grieved, but not for a dead queen. He grieved for the loss of someone he had never known, for a life that had ended. For a future whose happiness would always be tainted with the shadow of what he had done.

He knelt before the statue of Jonathan Shadowhunter in his family's parlor, his hands covered in ash. "Bless me," he said haltingly, "for I have sinned. I have . . ." He stopped, unable to say the words. "Tonight someone died because of me. Because of my actions. Someone I loved. Someone I didn't know. But I loved them just the same."

He had thought the prayer might help. It did not. He had shared his secret with Jonathan Shadowhunter, but he would never share it with anyone else: not his *parabatai*, not his parents, not a single friend or stranger. From that night on, an impassable chasm opened between Matthew and the whole world. None of them knew it, but he was cut off from them forever in all the ways that mattered.

But that was as it should be, Matthew thought. After all, he had committed murder.

18

Darkness Stirs

The dead are sleeping in their sepulchres:
And, mouldering as they sleep, a thrilling sound,
Half sense, half thought, among the darkness stirs,
Breathed from their wormy beds all living things around,
And, mingling with the still night and mute sky,
Its awful hush is felt inaudibly
—Percy Bysshe Shelley, "A Summer Evening Churchyard,
Lechlade, Gloucestershire"

It was late afternoon by the time James was able to pry himself away from the Institute—it seemed every Enclave member who passed through the gates wanted to interrogate him about Mandikhor demons—and head to Grosvenor Square to meet the rest of the Merry Thieves.

After letting himself into Matthew's house with his key, James paused for a moment on the steps that led to the cellar. He knew his friends were in the laboratory: he could hear their voices rising up toward him like smoke, could hear Christopher chattering, Matthew's low and musical tones. He could *feel* Matthew's presence, this close to his *parabatai*, like one magnet coming within range of another.

He found his friends seated around a high, marble-topped laboratory table. Everywhere were instruments of curious design: a galvanometer for measuring electrical currents, a torsion balance machine, and a clockwork orrery of gold, bronze, and silver—a gift from Charlotte to Henry some years ago. A dozen different microscopes, astrolabes, retorts, and measuring devices were scattered across the table and cabinet tops. On a plinth rested the Colt Single Action army revolver Christopher and Henry had been working on for months before all this had happened. Its river-gray nickel plating was deeply engraved with runes and a curving inscription: LUKE 12:49.

Christopher's brass goggles were pushed up into his hair; he wore a shirt and trousers that had been burned and stained so many times he had been forbidden to wear them outside. Matthew could have been his mirror opposite: in blue-and-gold waistcoat and matching spats, he stood well away from the flames of the Bunsen burners, which had been turned up so high that the room was the temperature of a tropical island. Oscar napped gently at his feet.

"What's going on, Kit?" said James. "Testing to see the temperature at which Shadowhunters melt?"

"My hair is certainly ruined," said Matthew, pushing his hands through the sweat-darkened strands. "I believe Christopher is hard at work on the antidote. I am assisting by providing witty observations and trenchant commentary."

"I'd rather you handed me that beaker," said Christopher, pointing. Matthew shook his head. James grabbed the beaker and passed it to Christopher, who added a few drops of its contents to the liquid simmering in a retort by his elbow. He frowned. "It's not going well, I'm afraid. Without this one ingredient, it doesn't seem likely to work."

"What ingredient?" James asked.

"Malos root, a rare plant. Shadowhunters aren't supposed to cultivate it because doing so violates the Accords. I have been searching, and I asked Anna to try to get me some in Downworld, but we've had no luck."

"Why would anyone be forbidden from growing some silly plant?" said Matthew.

"This plant only grows in soil that has been soaked by the blood of murdered mundanes," said Christopher.

"I stand corrected," Matthew admitted. "Ugh."

"Dark magic plants, is it?" James's eyes narrowed. "Christopher—can you draw me a sketch of the root?"

"Certainly," said Christopher, as if this were not at all an odd request. He took a notebook from the inside pocket of his jacket and began to scribble on the back. The liquid in the retort had begun to turn black. James eyed it warily.

"There were some forbidden plants growing in Tatiana's green-house," James explained. "I told Charles about it at the time, and he didn't seem to feel they were of great concern, but—"

Christopher held up the sketch, of an almost tulip-like plant with sharp-edged white leaves and a black root.

"Yes," James said, his excitement rising. "I remember those—they *were* in the greenhouse at Chiswick. They struck me because those leaves looked like knives. We could go there now—is there a carriage free?"

"Yes." Matthew's excitement matched James's own. "Charles had some sort of meeting, but he left the second carriage in the mews. Put your goggles down, Christopher—time for some field-work."

Christopher grumbled slightly. "All right, all right—but I have to go change. I'm not allowed out in these clothes."

"Just switch off anything that might burn down the house first," said Matthew, catching hold of James's arm. "We'll meet you in the front garden."

James and Matthew fled through the house (pursued by Oscar,

barking in excitement), then paused a moment on the front steps, breathing in the cool air. The sky was heavy with clouds; a bit of weak sunlight peeked through, illuminating the path from the Fairchilds' front steps to the wall of the front garden, and the gate that led to the street. It had been raining earlier, and the stone was still wet.

"Where's Thomas?" James asked, as Matthew tipped his face back to look up at the clouds: though they did not look rain-heavy, they had an energy to them as of an oncoming electrical storm. As did Matthew, James thought.

"Patrolling with Anna," said Matthew. "Remember, Thomas is the most elderly of our group. He is required for day patrol."

"I am not sure just eighteen is precisely elderly," said James. "He should have some years before senility sets in."

"I get the sense sometimes that he rather likes Alastair Carstairs. Which would indicate senility has already set in."

"I am not sure he *likes* him precisely," said James, "but rather feels as if he ought to be given a second chance after his behavior at school." James paused, thinking of Alastair's strained face and panicked eyes in the library at Cornwall Gardens. "And perhaps he is right. Perhaps we all deserve one."

"There are some people who do not deserve one." Matthew's voice was fierce. "If I ever catch you considering befriending Alastair, James—"

"Then what?" James said, arching an eyebrow.

"Then I will have to tell you what Alastair said to me the day we left the Academy," said Matthew. "And I would rather not. Cordelia should never know it, if nothing else. She loves him and she should be allowed that."

Cordelia. There was something about the way Matthew said her name. James turned to him, puzzled. He wanted to say that if Alastair had truly said something so awful it would threaten Cordelia's affection for him, Matthew should not suffer it in silence, but there was no chance. Christopher had burst out the front door, pulling on gloves. He wore a hat, tilted sideways on his head, and a green scarf that matched none of his other clothes.

"Where's the carriage?" he asked, descending the steps.

"We were waiting for you, Christopher, not fetching you a carriage," said James, as the three of them crossed the front garden to the mews, where a large carriage house held the Consul's horses and means of transportation. "Besides, I'm fairly sure Darwin said something about it being healthful for scientists to walk."

Christopher looked indignant. "He certainly didn't—"

The front gate rattled. James turned to see shadows perched atop it. No, not shadows—demons, ragged and black. They leaped soundlessly to the ground, one after another, stalking toward the Shadowhunters.

"Khora demons," James whispered; Matthew already had a shortsword out, and Christopher a seraph blade. It crackled as he named it, like a broken radiometer.

James whipped a throwing knife from his belt, turning to realize that they had been cut off from retreating to the house. The demons were circling them, as they had tried to circle Christopher on the bridge.

"I don't like this," said Matthew. His eyes were burning, his teeth bared. "At all."

The hat had fallen from Christopher's head; it lay sodden on the damp, stony ground. He kicked at it in frustration. "James? What next?"

James heard Cordelia's voice in his head, gentle and certain. *You are the leader.* "We cut through the circle of demons, there"—he pointed, talking fast—"and duck into the carriage house. Lock the doors behind us with a rune."

"Brings new meaning to the saying 'don't frighten the horses,'" Matthew muttered. "All right. Let's go."

They spun toward the area James had indicated, knives flying from James's hands like arrows from a bow. Each met its target, sinking deep into demon flesh. The Khora demons skittered away, howling, and the boys bolted through the gap between them toward the mews, just as the sky crackled with thunder.

They sprang through white tendrils of fog; James reached the gate to the mews first and kicked it open, then nearly doubled over, pain shooting through him.

He turned to see that a Khora had seized hold of Matthew and thrown him. Christopher was battling another of the shadowy creatures, his seraph blade describing a sputtering arc of light as he slashed at it. James choked—Matthew must have had the breath knocked out of him—and turned to race toward his *parabatai* as the Khora reared up over Matthew's body—

A flash of gold sprang between Matthew and the shadow, sending the Khora reeling back.

It was Oscar. The retriever sailed past the demon, missing a savage blow from its claws by barely an inch, and landed near Matthew.

The Khora started back toward the boy and the dog. Matthew threw his arms around Oscar—the puppy James had saved and given to him so long ago—curving his body to protect his dog. James spun, a knife in each hand, and let them fly.

The knives sank to their hilts in the demon's skull. It blew apart; one of the other demons screamed, and Matthew leaped to his feet, seizing up his fallen sword. James could hear him shouting at Oscar to go back into the house, but Oscar clearly felt he had scored a great victory and had no intention of listening. He growled as Christopher paused at the mews gate, shouting for the others to follow him.

James turned. *"Christopher—"*

It rose up behind Christopher, a massive shadow, the biggest

Khora demon James had seen yet. Christopher started to turn, raising his seraph blade, but it was too late. The Khora had reached around Christopher, almost as if it meant to embrace him, pulling his body back toward it. His weapon went flying.

Matthew started to run toward Christopher, skidding across the wet ground. James couldn't move—he was out of knives; he grabbed for the seraph blade in his belt, but there was no time. The demon's great clawed hand raked across Christopher's chest.

Christopher screamed, and the Khora demon shoved him away. He crumpled to the ground.

"No!" James broke into a run, zigzagging toward Christopher's fallen body. Something lunged toward him; he heard Matthew shout, and a *chalikar* sliced an oncoming Khora in half. James jerked his seraph blade free, heading for the demon that had wounded Kit.

It turned to look at him. Its eyes were knowing, almost amused. It bared its teeth—and vanished, just as the Khora demons in the park had.

"Jamie, they've gone," Matthew called. "They've all gone—"

The front gates burst open with a ringing clang of metal, and a carriage rolled into the front garden. The doors flew open, disgorging Charles Fairchild; James dimly realized that Alastair Carstairs was also there, looking around himself with a stunned expression. As James dropped to his knees by Christopher, he could hear Charles demanding to know what was going on.

Matthew shouted back, asking if Charles was blind, couldn't he see Christopher was hurt and needed to go to the Silent City? Charles kept demanding what had happened to the demons, where had they gone, he'd seen one when they'd first crashed through the gates, but where were they now?

I will take him, Alastair was saying. *I will take him to the Silent City.* But the words seemed to echo from some far-off place, someplace where James was not kneeling in the wet and the fog next to a motionless Christopher, whose chest had been scored across by the ragged lines of demon claws. Someplace where Christopher was not still and silent no matter how much James begged him to open his eyes. Someplace where Christopher's blood was not mixing with the rain on the cobblestones, surrounding him in a pool of crimson. Someplace better than this.

Cordelia had been hoping to speak to her brother again, but she rose so late in the day that by the time Risa had helped her dress and sent her downstairs, Alastair had already gone out.

Despite the afternoon sunlight streaming through the windows, the house seemed muffled and dim, the ticking of the clock unnaturally loud as she ate her porridge in the dining room. It tasted like sawdust in her mouth. She kept remembering Alastair's words of the night before: *I wanted you to have a childhood, a thing I never had. I wanted you to be able to love and respect your father as I never could.*

She realized with a chill of shame that she had badly misunderstood her mother and brother. She had thought they would not stand up for her father because of cowardice and social pressure. Now she realized they knew Elias might have been in the wrong— so drunk that he could not properly consider the safety of those he was sending on a dangerous mission.

She had thought her mother wanted her to marry to rid her of the shame of being the daughter of a man on trial in Idris. Now she realized it was far more complicated.

No wonder Sona and Alastair had looked with wariness on her attempts to "save" her father. They had been afraid she would find out the truth. Her blood felt cold in her veins. They really could lose everything, she thought. She had never quite believed it before. She had always thought justice would prevail. But justice was not as simple as she'd thought.

She started when Sona came into the dining room. Her mother eyed Cordelia consideringly before saying, "Is that one of the dresses James sent you?"

Cordelia nodded. She was wearing a deep rose day dress that had been part of the package from Anna.

For a moment, Sona looked wistful. "It is a lovely color," she said. "The dresses are indeed very beautiful and probably much better suited to you than the dresses I have given you."

"No!" Cordelia rose to her feet, stricken. *"Khāk bar saram!"* It was a phrase that literally meant "I should die"—the most extreme form of apology. "I'm an awful daughter. I know you did the best you could."

I know you did, Mâmân. I know you were only trying to protect me.

Sona looked astonished. "By the Angel. They are only dresses, Layla." She smiled. "Perhaps you could make it up to me by helping about the house? As a good daughter should?"

Tricked as usual, Cordelia thought, but she was more than a little glad to have the distraction. More unpacking had been done, and there were decisions to be made as to where certain bits of Isfahan pottery might be set, or where their Tabriz rugs could be placed to best advantage. As Cordelia watched her mother bustle about, clearly in her element, she felt the words roll to the tip of her tongue: *Did you know when you married him, Mâmân? Did you find out one day, or was it a slow realization, a terrible dawning of knowledge? All those times you said he should go to the Basilias, did you think they could cure his drunkenness? Did you weep that he refused to go? Do you still love him?*

Sona stepped back to admire a small collection of framed miniatures by the stairs. "That looks nice there, doesn't it? Or do you think it was better in the other room?"

"Definitely better there," Cordelia said, having no idea what other room her mother meant.

Sona turned, a hand braced against the small of her back. "Have you been paying atten—" she began, and winced suddenly. She leaned back against the wall as Cordelia hurried over to her, worried.

"Are you feeling well? You look tired."

Sona sighed. "I am perfectly all right, Cordelia." She straightened up, her hands hovering as if she couldn't quite decide what she wanted to do with them. It was a gesture she made only when very nervous. "But—I am expecting a baby."

"*What?*"

Sona smiled a shaky smile. "You will have a little brother or sister, Layla. In only a few more months."

Cordelia wanted to throw her arms around her mother but was suddenly terrified. Her mother was forty-two, late for a woman to carry a child. For the first time in her life, her formidable mother looked fragile to her. "How long have you known?"

"Three months," Sona said. "Alastair knows as well. So does your father."

Cordelia swallowed. "But you didn't tell me."

"Layla *joon*." Her mother came closer to her. "I didn't want to worry you more than you were already worried about our family. I know you have been trying—" She broke off, stroking a stray lock of hair back from her daughter's face. "You know you do not have to marry, if you do not want to," she said, almost in a whisper. "We will get by, darling. We always do."

Cordelia placed a kiss in the palm of her mother's thin hand, marked with many ancient scars from the time long ago when she had fought demons. "*Cheshmet roshan, mâdar joon*," she whispered.

Her mother's eyes sparkled with tears. "Thank you, darling."

A heavy knock came at the front door. Cordelia exchanged a surprised look with her mother before heading to the entryway. Risa had answered the door, and on the front step stood the grubby newsboy Matthew had given her satchel to outside Gast's flat. One of the Irregulars, she recalled, the Downworlder boys who worked out of the Devil Tavern and ran errands for James and the others.

"Got a message here for Miss Cordelia Carstairs," he said, clinging to a folded piece of paper.

"That's me," Cordelia said. "Do you, er, require payment?"

"Nope," said the boy, grinning cheerfully. "Been paid already by Mr. Matthew Fairchild. 'Ere you go!"

He handed over the message and scrambled down the steps, whistling. Risa shut the door, sharing a puzzled look with Cordelia. Why would Matthew send her a note like this? Cordelia wondered, unfolding the paper. What could be so urgent?

The note fell open. There were only a few words on the page, but they stood out in shocking black ink.

> *Come at once to the Devil Tavern. There was an attack.*
> *Christopher is badly wounded.*
> *—James*

"Cordelia?" Sona had come into the entryway. "What's going on?"

Her hands shaking, Cordelia handed the note to her mother. Sona read it quickly before pressing the note back into Cordelia's hand. "You must go and be with your friends."

Relief washed over Cordelia. She started to dash upstairs for her things but paused. "I should wear my gear," she said. "But it's still damp from the river."

Sona smiled at her—a weary, worried smile, the smile of so many Shadowhunter parents down through the ages who had watched their children march into the night, carrying blades blessed by angels, knowing they might never return. "Layla, my daughter. You can wear mine."

* * *

Cordelia raced up the steps inside the Devil Tavern and burst into the Merry Thieves' clubrooms. It was quite late in the afternoon now, and sunlight filtered through the east window, laying gold bars of light across the shabby little space and its occupants. Matthew was sprawled on the sofa, Lucie in a ragged armchair. Lucie looked up and smiled when Cordelia came in, but her eyes were red. James alone was standing: he leaned against the wall by the window, the shadows deep under his eyes. All three Shadowhunters were in gear.

"What happened?" Cordelia said, a little breathless. "I—what can I do?"

Matthew looked up at her. His voice was hoarse. "We were at my house, using my father's laboratory," he said. "They—the Khora demons—were waiting for us when we left."

"We ought to have been prepared," said James. He was opening and closing his right hand, as if he wished to crush something in his palm. "We should have remembered. We were hurrying for the carriage—they attacked us in front of the house. One of them tore a gash across Christopher's chest."

Christopher. Cordelia could see his bright smile, his dented spectacles; she could hear his eager and excited voice in her ears, explaining some new aspect of science or Shadowhunting. "I am so—I am so sorry," she whispered. "Is he ill? What can we do?"

"He was already feverish when they took him to the Silent City," said Matthew grimly. "We summoned you and Lucie as soon as we could, and—"

There were footsteps on the stairs. The door flew open, and Thomas burst in. He wore a long Inverness coat, though Cordelia could see that he was in gear beneath.

"Sorry," he said breathlessly. "I was patrolling with Anna—didn't get your message until we returned to Uncle Gabriel's house. They all wanted to go to the Silent City, of course, but Brother Enoch came by—said it was impossible—" Thomas sank down into a chair, burying his face in his hands. "Everyone's frantic. Anna went to ask Magnus for help in putting up extra wards around the house. Aunt Cecily nearly lost her mind at the thought of letting her go, but she went. Uncle Will and Aunt Tessa came, of course, but I couldn't bear to be there too, bothering them all, intruding on them in their fear—"

"You're not an *intrusion*, Thomas," said Matthew. "You're family. There and here."

The door creaked open and Polly came in, carrying a bottle and a few glasses with chipped rims. She set them down on the table, cast Thomas a worried glance, and disappeared.

Matthew rose and took the bottle, pouring out the glasses with the grace of long habit. For the first time in Cordelia's memory, Thomas picked one up and downed the contents.

James spun one of the chairs around and sat down, arms crossed across the chair back, his long legs hooked around the front. "Tom," he said, his eyes flaring intently. "We need to make the antidote to the Mandikhor poison. I think you can do it."

Thomas choked, coughed, and began spluttering as Matthew took the glass from him and set it back down on the table. "I can't," he said, when he caught his breath. "Not without Christopher."

"Yes, you can," said James. "You've done everything with him. You've been in the laboratory with him nearly every moment since Barbara died. You *know* how to do this."

Thomas was silent for a long moment. James didn't move. His gaze was fixed on his friend. It was a look Cordelia couldn't describe— a quiet intensity mixed with immovable conviction. This was James at his best, she thought. His faith in his friends was unwavering: it was strength, and they shared that strength between them.

"Perhaps," Thomas said at last, slowly. "But we're still missing an ingredient. Without it, the antidote won't work, and Kit said it was impossible to find—"

"Malos root," said Matthew. "We know where it is, and where to get it. All we need to do is go to Chiswick House. To the greenhouse."

"My grandfather's house?" Thomas said incredulously. He ran his fingers distractedly through his light brown hair.

"Finally Benedict Lightwood will be responsible for something useful," Matthew said. "If we leave now, we can be there in half an hour—"

"Wait," said Thomas, rising to his feet. "James, I'd nearly forgotten. Neddy gave me this."

He handed over a folded piece of thin vellum paper, with James's name scrawled across the front in a careful hand. James unfolded the note and stood up with a violent swiftness, nearly knocking the chair over.

"What is it?" said Cordelia. "James?"

As he handed her the note, Cordelia saw Matthew's thoughtful gaze flick between the two of them. She glanced down.

> *Come to the Silent City. I shall meet you in the infirmary.*
> *Do not reveal yourself to the other Brothers. I will*
> *explain when you arrive.*
> *Please hurry.*
> *—Jem*

She handed it wordlessly to Lucie. James was pacing the floor, hands in his pockets.

"If Jem says I must go, then I must," he said, as Matthew and Thomas both glanced at the note's contents. "The rest of you go to Chiswick—"

"No," Matthew said. He had reached for the flask in his pocket—a gesture of long-practiced habit—but quickly dropped his hand. His fingers were shaking slightly, but his voice was light. "Whither thou goest, I will go, James. Even unto the tedious suburb of Highgate."

Jem, Cordelia thought. She had to talk to him about her father. There was no one else she could speak to about what Alastair had told her. There was no one else she could tell that she had changed her mind.

Cousin Jem, I have something to tell you about my father. I think he needs to be in the Basilias. I think he should not come back from Idris after all. I think I need your help.

She took a deep breath. "I will also go. I must see Jem. Unless—" She turned to Lucie. "If you'd rather I go with you to Chiswick—"

"Nonsense," Lucie said, sympathy in her eyes. "All we're doing is fetching a plant, and I'm familiar with the house and the grounds—not," she added hastily as James looked dark, "because I've lurked about or spied on that property at all, because of course I haven't."

"You and Thomas can take my carriage," said Matthew. "It is downstairs."

"And the rest of us can take a hansom cab," said Cordelia. "Where is the nearest entrance to the Silent City?"

"In Highgate Cemetery," said James, reaching for his weapons belt as the others caught up gear jackets, belts, and blades. "It's a good distance. We'll have to hurry—there's no time to waste."

There was little to slow Cordelia and the others down until they reached Highgate, where the narrow streets were snarled up with evening traffic. The driver of the hansom cab, refusing to brave the bottleneck, deposited them in front of a pub on Salisbury Road.

James asked Cordelia and Matthew to wait while he went to search for the entrance to the Silent City. It often moved about within the cemetery, he had told Cordelia in the carriage, and could be found in various locations depending on the day.

Matthew gave the pub a longing look, but was soon distracted by a large stone tablet at the junction of Highgate Hill and Salisbury Road. It was caged by iron rails and carved with the words THRICE LORD MAYOR OF LONDON.

"'Turn again, Whittington, thrice Lord Mayor of London Town,'" said Matthew, with a dramatic gesture. "This is where it's meant to have happened—him hearing the Bow Bells, I mean."

Cordelia nodded; she had been told the story often enough when she was a child. Richard Whittington had been a mundane boy who set out from London with his cat, determined to make his fortune elsewhere, only to hear the bells of St. Mary-le-Bow calling him back to a promised glory if he returned. And so he had, and become mayor of London, three times.

Cordelia wasn't sure what had happened to the cat. All the stories might be true, she thought, but it would be awfully nice if such obvious signals were on offer for her own destiny.

Matthew slipped his silver flask from his waistcoat and began to unscrew it. Though he was in gear, he had not sacrificed his blue spats to duty. Cordelia only looked at him as he tipped back his head and swallowed, then screwed the cap back on. "Dutch courage," he said.

"Are the Dutch particularly brave, or just particularly drunk?" she asked, her voice sharper than she'd intended.

"A little of both, I imagine." His tone was light, but he put away the flask. "Did you know Dick Whittington's cat might never have existed? Scandalous fiction, apparently."

"Does it matter if he had a cat or not?"

"The truth always matters," Matthew said.

"Not when it comes to stories," Cordelia said. "The point of stories is not that they are objectively true, but that the soul of the story is truer than reality. Those who mock fiction do so because they fear the truth."

She felt, rather than saw, Matthew turn to look at her in the dimming light. His voice was hoarse. "James is my *parabatai*," he said. "And I love him. The only thing that I have never understood about him is his feelings for Grace Blackthorn. I have wished for a long time for him to place his affections somewhere else, and yet, when I saw him with you in the Whispering Room, I was not happy."

Cordelia had not expected such frankness. "What do you mean?"

"I suppose I question if he knows what he feels," said Matthew. "I suppose I worry that he will hurt you."

"He is your *parabatai*," said Cordelia. "Why should you care if he hurts me?"

Matthew tipped his head back to look at the darkening evening sky. His lashes were several shades darker than his blond hair. "I don't know," he said. "But I find that I do care."

Cordelia wished they were discussing anything else. "Don't worry. Alastair gave me the same warning about James just yesterday. I have been well told."

Matthew's jaw tightened. "I always said that the day I would be in charity with Alastair Carstairs would be the day I burn in Hell."

"Was he really so horrible to James at school?" said Cordelia.

Matthew turned to her, and the look on his face startled her. It was the purest fury. "It was more than that—"

James appeared out of the shadows, his black hair disarrayed, and beckoned to them. "I've found the entrance. We ought to go quickly."

They proceeded to the cemetery and passed through the tall gates. Dark cypress trees soared overhead, their overlapping leaves blocking out the last of the evening light. In their shadow rose elaborate monuments to the dead. Great mausoleums and Egyptian obelisks towered beside broken granite columns, symbolizing life cut short. Headstones were carved into hourglasses with wings, Greek urns, and beautiful women with streaming hair. And everywhere, of course, there were stone angels: chubby and sentimental-looking, sweet-faced as children. How little mundanes understood about angels, Cordelia thought, picking her way along the twig-strewn path after James. How much they did not understand what was terrifying about their power.

James turned off one of the gray avenues then, and they found themselves in an open space that seemed deep in the woods, leaves clustered so thickly above them that the waning light was tinged with green. In the center of the clearing was a statue of an angel, but this was no cherub. It was the marble figure of a beautiful man of great height. Scaled armor had been carved on his body. He held a sword in one outstretched hand, etched with the words QUIS UT DEUS, and his head was thrown back as if he were crying out to heaven.

James stepped forward, raising one hand—the one that bore the Herondale ring with its pattern of birds. *"Quis ut Deus?"* he said. "'Who is like God?' the Angel asks. The answer is 'No one. No one is like God.'"

The stone angel's eyes opened, absolutely black, apertures into a great and silent dark. Then, with a grinding of stone, the angel slid aside, revealing a great empty pit in the earth and stairs leading downward.

James lit his witchlight as they proceeded down the stairs into a shadowed darkness. The Silent Brothers, living as they did with eyes sewn shut, did not see as ordinary Shadowhunters did, and did not require light.

The shimmering white witchlight rayed out between James's fingers, painting the walls with bars of light. As they reached the bottom of the stairs, James caught Cordelia's arm and swung her around into an archway below the steps. Matthew followed a moment later. James closed his hand over the witchlight, dousing its illumination; the three of them watched in silence as a group of Silent Brothers, their parchment robes brushing the ground, swept by and vanished through another archway.

"Jem said not to reveal ourselves to the other Brothers," James whispered. "The infirmary is on the far side of the Speaking Stars. We must move quickly and quietly."

Cordelia and Matthew nodded. A moment later they were passing through an enormous room full of keyhole-shaped stone archways rising overhead. Semiprecious stones alternated with marble: tiger's-eye, jade, malachite. Beneath the arches huddled mausoleums, many with family names etched into them: RAVENSCAR, CROSSKILL, LOVELACE.

They reached a great square whose floor was inlaid with tiles printed in a pattern of shimmering stars. On a wall, high above reach, hung a massive dull-silver sword whose crosspiece was carved in the shape of angel wings.

The Mortal Sword. Cordelia's heart skipped a beat. The sword that her father had held, though it had not been able to make him speak a truth he could not remember.

They passed through the square and into a large space lined with rough flagstones. A pair of wooden doors led one way; a great square arch led another. The doors sported runes of death and peace and silence.

"Get back!" Matthew whispered suddenly; he threw an arm out, pressing James and Cordelia back into the shadows. Cordelia remained motionless as a Silent Brother passed by them and went up a set of nearby stairs. With a nod, James slipped from the shadows, followed by Matthew and Cordelia. They ducked under the square archway and into another massive room with a vaulted stone ceiling, crisscrossed with beams of stone and wood. The walls were bare, and up and down the room marched rows of beds, each with a still figure lying in it: Cordelia guessed there might have been thirty or so sick people there. Young and old, male and female, they lay as soundless and unmoving as if they had already died.

The room was utterly silent. Silent—and empty. Cordelia bit her lip. "Where is Jem?"

But Matthew's eyes had lighted on a familiar figure. "Christopher," he said, and darted over, followed by James. Cordelia came after them more slowly, reluctant to intrude. Matthew was crouching down beside a narrow iron bed; James stood at the head, leaning over Christopher.

Christopher had been stripped of his shirt. Dozens of white bandages encircled his narrow chest; blood had already soaked through some of them, forming a scarlet patch over his heart. His glasses were gone, and his eyes seemed sunk deep into his skull, the shadows below them dark purple. Black veins unfurled like coral beneath his skin. "Matthew," he said with hoarse disbelief. "Jamie."

James reached to touch his friend's shoulder, and Christopher caught at his wrist. His fingers were twitching; he picked restlessly at the cuff of James's jacket. "Tell Thomas," he whispered. "He can finish the antidote without me. He only needs the root. Tell him."

Matthew was silent; he seemed sick with pain. James said, "Thomas knows. He is with Lucie now, collecting the root. He'll finish it, Kit."

Cordelia cleared her throat, knowing her voice would come out as a whisper regardless. It did. "Jem," she whispered. "Has Jem been in here, Christopher?"

He smiled at her sweetly. "James Carstairs," he said. "Jem."

Cordelia looked nervously at James, who gave her an encouraging nod. "Yes," she said. "James Carstairs. My cousin."

"*James*," Christopher whispered, and then the figure in the bed next to his echoed the word.

"*James*," whispered Piers Wentworth. "*James*."

And then the next figure, in the next bed. "*James.*"

Matthew rose to his feet. "What's going on?"

Christopher's lilac eyes flew wide; his grip on James's wrist tightened as he jerked him forward. Face inches from James's, he hissed, "Get out of here—you have to get out of here. You have to leave. James, you don't understand. It's about you. *It's always been about you.*"

"What does that mean?" Matthew demanded, as more and more voices were added to the chant:

"*James. James. James.*"

Matthew took hold of James's sleeve and drew him back from Christopher, who let go of James reluctantly. Cordelia put her hand to the hilt of Cortana. "What's going on?" she demanded. "Christopher—?"

One by one the sick were rising into sitting positions, though it did not look as if they were doing so of their own volition. It seemed they were being dragged upward like puppets on strings; their heads sagged loosely to the side, their arms limp and dangling. Their eyes were wide open, white and shining in the dimness of the room. Cordelia saw with horror that the whites of them were also veined in black.

"James Herondale." It was the voice of Ariadne Bridgestock. She sat at the edge of her own narrow bed, her body slumped forward. Her voice rasped, empty of emotion. "James Herondale, you have been summoned."

"By who?" Matthew shouted. "Who's summoning him?"

"The Prince," said Ariadne, "the Lord of Thieves. Only he can stop the dying. Only he can call off the Mandikhor, the poison bringer. You carry the taint now, Herondale. Your blood can open the gateway." She took a deep, shuddering breath. "*You have no other choice.*"

Drawing away from Matthew, James took a step toward her. "What gateway? Ariadne—"

Cordelia threw out an arm to stop him. "This is not Ariadne."

What is going on here?

They all turned. It was Jem, who had entered the room in a swirl of parchment robes; he carried his oak staff in his hand. Despite the stillness of his face, Cordelia could sense how furious he was. It radiated from the words that exploded into her mind: *What are you three doing here?*

"I got your message," said James. "You told me to come."

I sent no message, said Jem.

"Yes, you did," protested Cordelia indignantly. "We all saw it."

"Our master sent the message," said Ariadne. "He waits in the shadows. Still, he controls all."

Jem shook his head. His hood had fallen back so that Cordelia could see the white streak in his dark hair.

There is foulness at work here, he said. He lifted the oaken staff in his hands, and Cordelia saw the letters WH carved into the grip.

The sick were all chanting James's name now, their voices rising in a hazy murmur.

Jem brought the staff down, and the noise of the wood striking the stone floor echoed in their ears. The chanting stopped; the sick went still.

Jem turned to Cordelia and the boys. *Some evil has brought you here,* Jem said. *Get out. I fear you are in danger.*

They ran.

The flight out of the Silent City was almost a blur to Cordelia. James went first, the witchlight in his hand illuminating their path as they darted out of the way of various Silent Brothers. She and Matthew came after; in seconds they had all reached the last stairway, where it arced up toward the sky.

Suddenly Matthew gasped. He staggered, falling back against

the stone wall as if he'd been pushed. Cordelia caught at his arm. "Matthew! What's happening?"

His face was paper white. "James," he whispered. "There's something very wrong with James."

Cordelia glanced up the stairs. James vanished from her view. He must not have realized they were no longer following. "Matthew, he's fine—he's out of the City—"

Matthew pushed away from the wall. "We must hurry," was all he said, and began to run again.

They tore up the stairs and burst out into the clearing above. James was nowhere to be seen.

Matthew took Cordelia's hand. "He's this way," he said, and drew her through a narrow path between the trees. It was nearly black beneath the canopy of leaves, but Matthew seemed to know exactly where he was going.

They emerged in a shadowy grove ringed with tombs, the sky above them the deep blue of late twilight. James was there, standing still as a statue. A statue of a dark prince, all in black, with hair like crow's feathers. He was in the process of casting aside his jacket, puzzlingly, since it had grown cold now that it was evening.

He was not looking at Matthew or Cordelia, but at something in the distance. His expression was stark, his eyes ringed with darkness. He looked ill, Cordelia realized with dismay. As if, just as Matthew had said, there was something very wrong.

Matthew cupped his hands around his mouth. *"James!"*

James turned slowly, dropping his jacket to the ground. He was moving mechanically, like an automaton.

Cordelia's unease mounted. She went toward James, slowly, as if she were approaching a startled deer in the forest. He watched her with restless gold eyes; there was color in his cheeks, a high consumptive flush. She heard Matthew curse under his breath.

"James," she said. "What's wrong?"

He rolled up the left sleeve of his shirt. On the back of his wrist, just above where the cuff of his shirt would have ended, were four small, bloody crescents, surrounded by a tracery of darkening veins.

Nail marks.

"Christopher," said James, and Cordelia remembered with horror the way Christopher had clutched at James in the sickroom, gripping his wrist. "I know he didn't mean to." His mouth twisted into a painful smile. "No one tell him. He'd be so upset."

Oh, James, no. Please, no. She thought of Oliver Hayward, dead because Barbara had clawed him in her last agonies. *Not James.*

Matthew's voice shook. "We have to go back to the Silent City. We have to get you to Jem—"

"No," Cordelia whispered. "It isn't safe for James there. If we went to the Institute—or brought Jem there—"

"Absolutely not," said James very calmly. "I'm not going anywhere. Not anywhere in London, at least."

"Bloody hell, he's hallucinating," said Matthew with a groan.

But Cordelia didn't think he was. In a low voice, she said, "James. What do you see?"

James raised his hand and pointed. "There. Between those two trees."

And he was right—suddenly Cordelia, and Matthew as well, could see what James had been staring at all this time. Between two cedar trees was a large archway. It seemed to be made of dark light; it curved with Gothic flourishes, as though it were part of the cemetery, but Cordelia knew it was not. Through it, she could glimpse a swirl of dark chaos, as if she were looking through a Portal into the vastness of black space itself.

"A gateway," said Matthew slowly.

"Like Ariadne said," whispered Cordelia. "James—your blood—" She shook her head. "Don't. Don't do it, whatever it is. Everything about this feels wrong."

But James only turned and went over toward the archway. He stretched out his arm toward it—the one with the wounds where Christopher's nails had punctured his skin—and made a fist.

The muscles of his arm swelled, and blood ran from the cuts on his wrist—they looked slight, but fat drops of red rose up along his arm and dripped onto the ground. The view through the archway seemed to solidify and clear itself, and now Cordelia could glimpse the world she'd seen on the bridge: a place with earth and sky like ashes, and trees like protrusions of bone.

"James," Matthew said, closing the gap between himself and his friend. "Stop."

"I have to do this." James lowered his bleeding arm. His eyes were feverish, whether from determination or the poison now in his veins, Cordelia wasn't sure. "Math—you shouldn't touch me. It's not safe."

Matthew, who had been reaching for James, stopped abruptly and flung his arms wide. *"James—"*

"Is that why you're going?" Cordelia demanded. She could taste tears in the back of her throat. She wanted to break something, to take Cortana and smash the blade against the granite sides of the tombs. "Because you think you're going to die? Thomas and Lucie are getting the malos root right now. We could have an antidote in a day. In *hours*."

"It's not that." James shook his head. "Whether I'd been infected or not, I'd have to go, and you would have to let me."

"Why?" Matthew demanded. "Tell us why, Jamie."

"Because Christopher was right," said James. "So was Ariadne. Only my going through the gateway can stop all this. It's about me. It's always been about me. *I have no other choice.*"

19

All Places Hell

When all the world dissolves,
And every creature shall be purified,
All places shall be hell that is not heaven.
—Christopher Marlowe, *Doctor Faustus*

By the time Lucie and Thomas reached Chiswick House, it was near dark. The sun had set, and the mansion was tarnished silver against the dying light. Leaving the carriage at the curb, they made their way in silence up the long road flanked by twisted trees to the main house. Somehow the place looked worse than it had when Lucie had been here with Cordelia.

Lucie could see the humped shadow of the greenhouse in the distance, and the ruined Italian gardens in the other direction. Seeing the manor and its grounds in better light, Lucie wished she had not. She couldn't imagine living in such a house.

"Poor Grace," she said. "This place is a rathole. Actually, I wouldn't wish it on a rat."

"That is because you like rats," said Thomas. "Remember Marie?"

Marie Curie had been a small white rat Christopher had kept in the room at the Devil Tavern and fed on bread and chicken bones. Marie had been friendly enough to rest on Lucie's shoulder and nuzzle at her hair. Eventually Marie had died of natural causes and been buried with pomp and circumstance in Matthew's back garden.

"But I don't know if we ought to feel sorry for Grace," said Lucie. "She broke James's heart."

"For someone with a broken heart, he seems in remarkably fine fettle," said Thomas. "Honestly, he actually seems *more* cheerful."

Lucie could not deny that this was true. "Still," she said. "It is the principle of the thing."

They reached the greenhouse, a long structure of glass and wood. Long ago it had provided the Lightwood family with pineapples and grapes in winter. Now there were holes smashed into the glass walls, and the once-clean windows were smeared and dark.

A massive padlock hung on the door. Lucie started to reach for her stele, but Thomas put a hand on her wrist. "I can go around the back," he said. "There ought to be a small shed there with an entrance into the greenhouse. They would have needed to heat the place by hypocaust."

"I have no idea what you mean," said Lucie. "But I suspect you know this because of all the hours you've spent listening to Christopher in the lab. Certainly, by all means, let us crawl into a dark and spider-infested shed."

"It isn't spiders I'm worried about," said Thomas. "And you won't be doing any crawling. We need you out here as sentry. If you see any unusual activity, send up an alarm."

"I hate being the watchman. Are you certain we need one?"

"Yes," said Thomas, "because if one of us is going to be devoured by demonic tree roots, then the other one had better be around to get help, or at least grab the malos root and run for it."

Lucie had to admit he had a point. "Go on, then."

Thomas headed toward the back of the greenhouse. Lucie

attempted to do as he had suggested for at least five minutes, but it was very dull. There was only so long one could pace back and forth in front of the door to a greenhouse before feeling like a goldfish swimming to and fro in its bowl. She was very nearly relieved to glimpse something out of the corner of her eye.

It looked like a spark of bright light, down toward the Italian gardens. She moved away from the greenhouse, narrowing her eyes. The light was pale in color and wavering against the twilight. A torch, perhaps?

She moved closer, keeping to the shadows. The gardens were a ruin. Once there had been neat hedgerows, but they were overgrown now, a mess of shrubbery leading in all directions. The marble statues of Virgil, Sophocles, and Ovid had been smashed to jagged pieces that protruded upward from broken plinths. In the center of the whole mess was a square brick structure, like an old storage shed.

As she moved toward it, she saw the flicker of light once again. It was stronger now, and seemed to be rising over the walls of the small structure, as if it had no roof, though that was not unusual for old buildings—the roof was often the first thing to go. It certainly had no windows, but the light continued to shine steadily from within.

Consumed by curiosity, Lucie reached the square little building and stared. It appeared to have been built long ago, of large and sturdy stone. There was a door in one side; though it was closed, light gleamed beneath the door.

As Lucie watched, the light moved. Someone, or something, was very definitely inside.

Throwing caution to the wind, Lucie began to climb one of the walls.

She reached the top almost immediately. The structure was indeed roofless: open to the elements despite the four thick walls.

Lucie flattened herself atop the wall she'd climbed and stared down into the space below.

It was a single room, bare of any decoration save a sword hanging upon one wall. It bore a crosspiece carved with thorns, the symbol of the Blackthorn family. In the center of the room was a table, on which rested a coffin. Standing beside the coffin was Grace Blackthorn, a witchlight torch in her right hand. Her left hand lay atop the coffin, her slim fingers outspread as if she could reach through the glass front and touch the body within.

For the coffin was made of glass, like the coffin of Snow White in fairy tales. And lying within it was Jesse Blackthorn—hair as black as ebony, skin as white as snow. His lips were not red as blood, though: they were pale and set, and his eyes were closed. He wore a suit of funeral white—it was jarring to see him in something other than the clothes he had died in—and his hands were crossed over his chest.

Lucie gripped the wall tightly. Jesse's body. It had probably only been in this shed a short time—Tatiana would have kept her son with her in Idris until they came to London. But why hadn't she simply put Jesse inside the main house, rather than in this odd little structure? Somewhere where there would have been a roof over him?

The thought of cold rain falling on his coffin was almost painful. Jesse didn't look dead; he looked as if sleep had found him as he lay at rest in a garden. He looked as if he might rise at any moment and step free of his glass prison. He looked—alive.

"Jesse," Grace said. "Jesse, I'm afraid."

Lucie froze. She had never heard Grace speak like this. Grace sounded afraid, it was true, but more than that, she sounded gentle.

"Jesse, I'm sorry. I hate to leave you out here in the cold, even though I know you don't feel it." Grace sounded as if she were fighting tears. "Charles is always wandering around the inside of the manor.

I suppose he wants to see what kind of property he will inherit when Mama dies." Her voice dropped; Lucie had to lean down to hear her. "Oh, Jesse. I'm afraid that they are going to stop me coming here at night. Charles is constantly saying that I shouldn't be alone in this tumbledown house. He doesn't know that I'm not alone. *You* come to talk to me." She drew her lace-gloved hand back from the coffin. "You asked me why I'm marrying Charles. You asked if it was because I feared what Mama might do to James."

Lucie froze. In the near-darkness, it was impossible to see Grace's expression—it seemed to change as the witchlight flickered: gentle one moment, vicious the next.

"But I am so much more selfish than that," breathed Grace. "I am doing it because it will free me from Mama. I want her to recover, I truly do, but when she does, I must have her realize that I am part of the Consul's family now and can't be touched. As for James . . ."

The shadows thickened in the small room below. Behind Grace, there was only darkness. Lucie knew she should return to the greenhouse, but she was desperate to hear more of what Grace was saying.

"You have asked me so many times what I truly felt for James. And I never told you. I hid so much from you. I always wished to show you my best face, Jesse. You were the only one who ever spoke up for me against Mama. I wish—"

The shadows behind Grace seemed to move.

Lucie gasped. Grace looked up at the noise, just as a crouching shape emerged from the darkness.

It was a demon, half-reptilian and half-human, with leathery bat's wings and a sharply pointed chin like the tip of a knife. It loomed above Grace, massive and scaled, and she shrieked aloud, dropping her witchlight torch. She began to back away, but the demon was too swift. Its leathery claw shot out; it seized Grace by the throat and lifted her off the ground. Her small feet in their heeled boots kicked wildly.

The demon spoke, its voice echoing off the brick walls. "*Grace Blackthorn. You foolish girl.*" In the light from the torch, Lucie could see that its face was flat, snakelike, its ovoid eyes glittering like black stones. It had two mouths, but only the lower one moved as it spoke. Great horns curved up from either side of its head, sheened with black and gray scales. "*You should never have betrayed the oaths your mother swore to those far more powerful than she. Some enchantments are not yours to remove. Do you understand?*"

"It had already begun to fade," Grace gasped. "It was not working—"

She must be talking about the enchantments placed on Jesse, Lucie thought. Maybe something had happened to them when Tatiana had succumbed to the poison?

"*You will do as you are told. Put the enchantment back where it was; I, Namtar, will see to its strengthening.*" Its voice was like gravel. "*Otherwise, when our master finds out it was removed, his wrath will be beyond your imagining. Remember, all you care for can be destroyed with one word from him. With one flick of his wrist.*"

Its free hand shot out toward the coffin containing Jesse. Grace cried out. And Lucie flung herself from the wall, landing hard on the demon's back, her arms about its neck.

With a roar of surprise, the demon staggered back, releasing Grace. She landed hard, her eyes feral, her fair hair straggling about her face. The demon snarled and ducked its head as if to sink its teeth into Lucie's hands; she let go, dropping to the ground, and seized Grace by the wrist.

Grace stared at her in frozen astonishment. "What are *you* doing here?"

This did not seem to Lucie to be the most pressing issue at hand. She gritted her teeth and yanked Grace toward the door. "*Run, Grace!*"

At the sound of her name, Grace snapped free of her paralysis. She began to run, tugging Lucie after her; they burst through the door and into the garden. Grace let go of Lucie and swung around to slam the door shut behind them, but the demon had already seized it from the other side. There was a shriek of metal as the door was torn from its hinges and flung aside.

The demon advanced on the two girls. Lucie had half expected Grace to bolt for the house, but she was standing her ground. Lucie tugged a seraph blade free of her belt just as Grace bent, seized up a rock, and flung it at the demon. Lucie had to give her points for enterprise, at least.

The rock bounced off the demon's leathery chest. It grinned with both mouths and seized Lucie around the torso, sending her seraph blade flying. She was lifted off her feet as the demon's black gaze raked her up and down. Its eyes narrowed. "I know you," it snarled. It sounded almost surprised. "You are the second one."

Lucie kicked out, her feet connecting hard with the demon's torso. It grunted and she shrieked in pain as its grip tightened. Its lower mouth opened; she saw the glint of fangs, and then a flood of black as ichor poured forth. Staggering, it released Lucie; she fell to the ground and rolled aside as the demon's body arched backward. The blade of a sword emerged from its chest, smeared with green-black ichor. It looked down incredulously at the steel protruding from its torso, snarled, and vanished.

Standing just behind where the demon had been was Jesse.

He held the sword that had hung on the wall in the tiny coffin-room. Though there was ichor on the blade and spattered on the ground at his feet, there were no stains on his clothes, or on his bare hands. The sky was black above: his green eyes glittered as he slowly lowered the sword.

"Jesse," Lucie breathed. "I—"

She broke off as Grace took a staggering step forward. Her gaze

darted from Lucie to Jesse and back again, her expression incredulous. "But I don't understand," she said, gripping one hand with the
other. "How can you see Jesse?"

James had thought Matthew and Cordelia still might try to prevent
him, but after he explained—the words echoing in his own ears as
he told them how he had put the pieces of it all together—he knew
that they would not. Both stared at him with drained, pale faces,
but neither made a move to stand between him and the gateway.

Matthew—disheveled, dirty, still with his incongruous spats
on—drew himself up, his chin high. "Then, if you must go, I will
go with you," he said.

James's heart broke. How could he do this to Matthew? How
could he contemplate dying in a place Matthew could never follow
him to?

And yet.

"It won't work," he said softly. "No one can follow me into the
shadows, Math. Not even you."

Matthew walked swiftly toward the archway, even as James
called out to him in sharp alarm. He reached out to touch the
empty space below the arch, where the green ground of the cemetery turned to ash and grayness.

His hand bounced back as if he had slammed it into glass. He
turned back to face his companions, and Cordelia saw that he was
shaking.

"Cordelia, do you have rope?" he said.

Cordelia still had the rope they had used to climb to Gast's window. Matthew took it from her; as James and Cordelia looked on,
mystified, he secured one end of the rope around James's waist.

Despite the shaking of his hands, he tied an excellent knot.

The other end of the rope he secured around his own waist.

When he was done, he looked steadily at James. "Go on, then," he said. "If something happens—if you need us to pull you back through—tug on the rope three times."

"I will," James said. He turned to Cordelia; he was standing so close to the archway that the outline of his left side seemed grayed out, as if he were a sketch that was rapidly being erased. "Cordelia—"

Cordelia leaned over and kissed James swiftly on the cheek. She saw him blink and touch his fingers to the spot in surprise. "Come back," she said.

James nodded. There was nothing more for any of them to say. With a last look behind him, James stepped through the archway and disappeared.

The world beyond the archway was black and gray. James moved first through amorphous shapes, and then into a place where a path wound between dunes of dry sand. The air was thick and acrid and tasted of smoke, and dust seemed to blow ceaselessly through the air, forcing him to shield his eyes with one hand.

Just above him, he could see a hole in gray-black clouds, and strange constellations of stars. They gleamed like the eyes of spiders. Some distance away, clouds had gathered and black rain was falling.

His only comfort was the rope around his waist. Like all Shadowhunter rope, its reach was much longer than it appeared: it unrolled and unrolled behind him with no sign of running out. He kept tight hold of it with his right hand: somewhere on the other end were Matthew and Cordelia.

After some time, the landscape changed. For the first time he saw the ruins of what had once been a civilization. Broken pillars littered the dry ground, along with the crumbling remains of old stone walls. In the far distance he thought he could make out the shape of a watchtower.

The path curved around a dune. When James emerged from the other side, he could see the tower more clearly. It rose like a spear against the torn sky. In front of him was a square surrounded by the ruins of walls, and in the middle of the square stood a man.

He was dressed all in white, like a mourning Shadowhunter. His hair was a pale gray color, though he did not look old: it was the color of doves' feathers, cut unfashionably long. His eyes were a familiar steel gray. James recalled the illustration of the princes in the book he had studied, but those had been monstrous depictions: this was a Prince of Hell showing himself in his most human form. He looked like a statue carved by a divine hand: his features were ageless, handsome, everything in balance. It was possible to see in his face the terrible beauty of the fallen. Even his hands looked as if they had once been shaped for acts of divinity: for prayer and holy war at once.

"Hello, Grandfather," James said.

The demon came toward him, smiling courteously. The acrid wind ruffled his pale hair. "You know who I am, then?"

"You are Belial," said James.

"What a clever boy," said Belial. "I had taken great care to leave no trace behind me." His hand described a graceful parabola in the air; his knuckles were like curved hinges. "But then, you are *my* grandson."

"But this is not your realm," said James. "It was Belphegor's realm, was it not? And you took it from him."

Belial chuckled benignly. "Poor Belphegor," he said. "I wounded him quite gravely when he was not expecting it. No doubt he is still floating about in the space between the worlds, trying to find his way home. Not a nice fellow, Belphegor—I wouldn't waste your sympathy on *him*."

"It isn't sympathy," said James. "I thought at first perhaps Belphegor was my grandfather. But it didn't fit. Not quite. Then Agaliarept said that his master's realm had been taken from him—"

"You met *Agaliarept*?" Belial seemed highly amused. "What a fellow. We spent some good times together before he got himself trapped in that box. You do move in interesting circles, James."

James ignored this. "And I started to think, who would steal a whole world? And why?" He watched Belial's face for any change, but the Prince of Hell betrayed no emotion. "Then I remembered reading a book that mentioned you."

"Many books mention me," said Belial.

"This one called you the thief of realms, of worlds. And I—I thought it was a mistake. That it had meant to say you were the greatest thief in all the worlds, in any world. But it was correct, wasn't it? You *steal realms*. You stole this realm from Belphegor." James felt dizzy; his wrist, where Christopher's nails had scored him, ached and throbbed. "You thought no one would guess you were behind the demon attacks. You thought that if you left traces, they would be ascribed to Belphegor. What I don't understand is that all my life, you have been showing me this place, this realm—" He broke off, fighting for control. "I see this world whether I wish to or not. But why show me a realm that isn't yours?"

Belial grimaced. "You are mortal, and you measure out your lives in days and years. We demons measure our lives in centuries and millennia. When I wrested this place from my brother, there were no Shadowhunters. They were not even a thought in Raziel's stupid pretty little head. Over the centuries I have bent everything in this realm to my will. Every tree, every rock, every grain of sand is under my command, and so, my boy, are you. That is why I brought you here."

"I came here of my own free will," said James. "I *chose* to meet you face-to-face."

"When did you know I was not Belphegor?"

James felt suddenly weary. "Does it matter? I guessed some of it when the Mandikhor on the bridge spoke to me. There was no reason for a Prince of Hell to want to see me so badly unless we shared blood, and no reason for him to be so cagey about which prince he was unless he was playing some sort of trick. Agaliarept said his master's realm had been stolen by a more cunning demon, and I had heard my grandfather called Hell's most cunning prince. When Ariadne spoke, when she called her master the Lord of Thieves, I *knew* it. The Mandikhor's master, the thief, the cunning prince, my grandfather—they were one and the same."

"And who do you think spoke to you through Ariadne, and the others?" said Belial. He waved a lazy hand in the air, and for a moment, James glimpsed the infirmary in the Silent City. The sick were lying motionless in their beds, Jem guarding the archway, his staff in his hand. The room was silent. James could not help but gaze at Christopher, still and bruised-looking. "I had grown tired of your dawdling," Belial said, lowering his hand. The vision blinked out of existence. "You needed to understand that if you did not come to me, the dying would never stop."

James thought of Matthew and Cordelia. How they had stared at him in disbelief when he had told them why he had to go through the gateway, why he had no choice. *I must meet my grandfather in his realm, whether it is a trap or not. Some traps must be sprung. For if I do not meet him and bargain with him, there will never be an end to this death.*

"You are the reason there have been so few demons all these years in London," said James. *Too scared to show their faces,* Polly had said. "They stayed away because they were afraid of *you.* But why?"

"To make you all soft," Belial said. "The Mandikhor has cut through you like a knife through bread, and why not? You remember nothing of what it means to be warriors."

"And then you started to let the demons back in," James said slowly. "To keep us anxious and distracted. Not paying attention."

Belial flicked sand from his sleeve. "You and your friends seem to have been paying quite a bit of attention."

James spoke coldly. "We humans are not such fools as you think."

Belial's smile widened. "You have me all wrong, child, if you think I feel that humans are foolish," he said. "They are Heaven's most beloved creation. 'In action how like an angel, in apprehension how like a god,'" he quoted softly. "'The beauty of the world. The paragon of animals.'"

"Shakespeare," said James, "was being sarcastic."

"You are not truly human, regardless, are you?" said Belial. "No Nephilim is. You walk among humans, you look like them, but the powers of even the lowest among you exceed the strongest human being."

James wasn't sure what he had been expecting of Belial. This attitude toward human beings was not it. But demons were tricky creatures, like faeries in that way: they twisted and shaped truth to their own purposes. And demons, unlike faeries, could lie.

"Why did you want to meet me so badly?" James said, keeping his voice neutral. "And why not come to me? Why did you insist I come to you?"

Belial threw his head back, but if he laughed, it made no sound. "You are a surprise," he said.

"Did you expect more fear?" said James. "Then you do not know my father. You do not know my mother. You do not know my family, or me."

"I expected more anger," said Belial. "But perhaps you have moved past such things. You do seem to know about me already. You Nephilim and all your little books. What have you learned about your grandfather, then?"

"'You made Belial for the pit, angel of enmity; in darkness is his domain, his counsel is to bring about wickedness and guilt. All the spirits of his lot are angels of destruction, they walk in the laws of darkness; towards it goes their only desire,'" James quoted.

Belial seemed amused. "Did you not also learn the meaning of my name? *Beli ya'al* in the original Aramaic—or is it Hebrew? It means 'never to rise.' I alone among the Princes of Hell cannot walk on Earth in my own form. I must possess a body in order to exist in your realm."

"You possessed Ariadne," James said. "In the sickroom."

"Only for a moment," Belial said bitterly. "When my spirit possesses a human body, it is like a bonfire burning within a fragile casing of paper. The body will be destroyed within hours. Lilith, Sammael, all the others—they can walk upon Earth, even in their own forms. Only I am thus restricted, for Heaven punishes us all according to its lights. I of all the princes loved human beings most, so I alone am separated from walking among them." As he spoke, he gestured. His hands were as beautiful and ageless as the rest of him, with slim, long fingers. His nails were matte black. "And then there is you."

The burning had intensified in James's veins. He could feel fever-sweat trickling between his shoulder blades, dampening his hair. He did not dare look down at his arm.

"The only host body I can use," said Belial, "is one of my own blood. I tried with your mother, but that clockwork angel she wore prevented me from getting near her. Even when it was gone, Ithuriel protected her. She is too poisoned with angel blood to make a home for me." His lip curled. "But *you*. We could share your body, James. My presence would cure the Mandikhor venom in your veins. You would live, and the power you would have would be immense. For are you not my heir, my own flesh and blood?"

James shook his head. "The demon attacks, the sickness—you

caused all of it because you need me to be *willing*." The last piece of the puzzle fell into place. James's whole body throbbed with pain. "This is why you wanted Belphegor to be blamed for what you've been trying to do. For all of this. You've been trying to get around the law that says you cannot rise. You were never trying to fool *us*, the Shadowhunters, about who my grandfather was. You were trying to fool the others like you."

"Angels above and demons of the Pit," said Belial, examining his black nails. "Indeed. I don't deny that."

"You need me to *volunteer* myself for possession. To allow you to become me."

"Quite," said Belial. He looked bored.

"You took my grandmother's happiness from her. You took my cousin Barbara's life. And you want me to—"

"To give me your body for my rising," said Belial impatiently. "Yes, yes. Because I can make it all *stop*. My creature on the bridge told you as much."

"The Mandikhor," said James. "You possessed someone and sent them to Emmanuel Gast. Had him raise the demon."

"Gast was a useful idiot," said Belial. "He somehow thought that after he raised the demon, I would let him live, though the trail would have led to him eventually and he's hardly the sort who could withstand torture or interrogation." He yawned. "It's really too bad—Gast was quite talented at dimensional magic. He managed to raise the Mandikhor in such a way that it exists partly in your world, and partly here, where it thrives."

"That's why it can withstand sunlight in our world," James said.

"Precisely. Worlds are layered upon one another: the Mandikhor and its children are shielded in your realm by this one. And here it serves me completely. When I order it to cease attacking Nephilim, the attacks will stop. The deaths will stop. But if you refuse me, they will continue. And you, my boy, will die."

"Stop the demon first," James rasped. "Bring him forth and destroy him, and you can—you can possess me. I'll let you."

"No," purred Belial. "That is not how these things work, James Herondale. This is *my* realm, and there will be no tricks. First you become my host. Then—"

James shook his head. "No. The demon first. And you cannot just rescind your orders to the creature. You must destroy it."

Belial's icy gaze hardened. *His eyes are so much like my mother's,* James thought. It was strange to see those eyes filled with so much evil. So much hate.

"It is not your place to give me orders," said Belial. "Come here, boy."

James didn't move. Belial's eyes narrowed, then flicked over him, taking in his face, his gear, his bleeding wrist.

"You refuse me," he said slowly, almost as if he could not quite believe it. James would have said he seemed aghast, if Princes of Hell could be aghast.

"As I said before," said James. "I came here of my own free will."

"I see," Belial said. "You are not as tractable as I had been led to believe. But you will realize the wisdom of my plans soon enough. I would prefer an adult male body," he added, almost as an aside. "In fact, I would prefer you were a bit older, but needs must as the devil drives. As they say." He grinned. "Recall that you are not the only one I could approach."

He waved a black-nailed hand, and multicolored light streaked across the dark air. It resolved into the shape of Lucie—Lucie in gear, her hair up in a determinedly tight chignon. She looked exactly herself, down to the ink stains on her hands. James's stomach clenched.

"Don't you dare touch her," he said. "Besides—Lucie would never agree."

Belial laughed. "Don't be so sure. Consider it, James. Despite the strength in your blood, the body you occupy is frail. Look what you are dying of now. Four small nail marks in your arm. So very little to end so much. You reside in a flimsy shell that can age, and die, and feel terrible pain. But if you joined with me, you would become immortal. Would you not want that for your sister? For yourself?"

"No," said James. "It would not be worth it."

"Ah, the foolish confidence of Nephilim." Belial's eyes narrowed. "Perhaps it is time for me to remind you, boy, just how fragile you truly are."

There was a silence. Jesse stood, not breathing hard—not breathing at all—the sword in his hand. He looked from Grace to where Lucie crouched, still on the ground. He inclined his head toward Lucie, then, in the smallest of nods.

She turned to Grace.

"Yes," Lucie said. "I can see Jesse."

Grace's hand flew to her mouth. "But how?" she whispered. "James is a Herondale too but can't see him—James could never see him—"

"Lucie is unusual," said Jesse. "She seems to be able to see more than ordinary ghosts."

He propped the sword against the side of the shed and went over to his sister. "Grace," he said, gently putting his arms around her. Grace laid her head against his shoulder. "That demon. Was that Grandfather's work, still lingering about?"

Grace drew back slightly. "No," she said, "It was—" She shook her head. "It isn't safe. We can't speak in front of her, not about anything. She's the daughter of Will Herondale, Jesse; she's practically the Consul's niece—"

Lucie rose silently, brushing grass from her clothes. She felt very awkward. She thought of the demon, its hissing whisper: *the oaths your mother swore to those far more powerful than she.* The demon had been Tatiana's doing, she knew, and she suspected from the look on his face that Jesse guessed it too.

"I know Lucie," Jesse said, looking at Lucie over the top of Grace's blond head. "I trust her. Just as you trust James."

Grace drew back and frowned. "I've never told him about you—"

"Lucie!" A voice called her name; she looked up to see Thomas racing toward her. He cleared the low hedge easily and approached, looking puzzled but ready for a fight, *bolas* in his hand.

Grace stepped back hastily from Jesse, wiping at her face. She turned to glare at Thomas. "Why have you invaded my home?" she demanded. "What is going on here?"

"We didn't think you'd be home," Thomas said.

"Not helpful," said Lucie. "Tell her about the antidote, Thomas."

"Ah," said Thomas, looking nervously at Grace. "Christopher and I have been trying to work out an antidote for the demonic poison."

"And?" said Grace in a clipped tone. She was watching Jesse out of the corner of her eye; he had retreated several feet and was looking at them silently. It seemed clear Thomas could not see him.

"We needed something from your greenhouse," said Thomas. "A particular plant. I retrieved it and I suspect it will not be missed, given the state of the conservatory."

Jesse raised his eyebrows.

"Do you make a habit of breaking into people's houses and insulting their gardening?" demanded Grace. "And why was Miss Herondale in the Italian gardens?"

"I—" Lucie began.

The world went white. White, then gray. Lucie gasped as the garden in front of her vanished, replaced with a vast desert and a night sky blooming with unfamiliar stars. In front of her, she could see James, his clothes spattered in blood. He looked ill, sick and feverish. As she stared in shock, he lunged forward with a blade in his hand.

The vision disappeared. She was back on the grounds of the manor in Chiswick, her body doubled up, fighting for breath. What she had seen was real; she knew it.

"James," she choked. *James is in some sort of trouble. We have to help him.* But she could not say that in front of Thomas; he had to concentrate on the antidote, and besides, he would think she was mad. She tried to steady her voice. "I should join him."

Thomas looked puzzled. So did Grace. Only Jesse seemed to understand.

"Where is he now?" said Jesse. "I'll go check on him. You know how quickly I travel."

Lucie and Grace exchanged a quick, almost conspiratorial look. "Where *is* James, by the by?" Grace asked loudly. "Is he not with you?"

"He is in Highgate Cemetery," said Lucie. "He went to the Silent City."

Jesse gave a short nod and vanished.

"What on earth, Lucie?" said Thomas. "What's this about James?"

"I should join him in Highgate," said Lucie. "I will be more help to our friends there than I will be to you in the laboratory. Now that we have the last ingredient, time is of the essence in creating this antidote, is it not?"

"Yes, but must you go to Highgate now?"

"I just feel I ought to be with him, and with Cordelia. We've done what we came for here—I'll only be a distraction to you in the lab."

"Lucie may borrow our pony trap," Grace said quickly. "It should suffice to get her to the Silent City if she wishes."

Surprised, Lucie shot her a grateful look. Thomas looked torn. "I ought to go with you, Lucie."

"No," Lucie protested. "Tom, you *must* go to the Consul's house. I could not live with myself if the antidote was delayed on my account."

Which, Lucie thought, was certainly true. Thomas was persuaded at last to bid farewell and headed back toward the manor's long drive.

As soon as he was out of earshot, Grace bent a hard gaze on Lucie. "What are you planning? I know you sent him away for a reason. A real one."

"I sent him away because of Jesse," Lucie said. "And because— I heard you talking to that demon, Grace. It was threatening you about some spell. The Clave—"

Grace had gone an awful sort of color. In books, when people went pale, it was dramatic. In this moment, the sight made Lucie feel a little sick. "Do not even say their name," she said. "Yes, my mother invoked black magic to try to bring my brother back, and with black magic came demons—demons with whom she made bargains, demons with demands, exacting promises. I wish to the Angel she had not done any of it. I tried to keep the worst of it from Jesse, but I—he is all I have, and I cannot lose him. If the Clave learned of my mother's doings —"

"I know," Lucie said, trying for a calming tone. "I understand that no one can know Jesse is here, that you're hiding him because if the Nephilim found his body, they'd destroy it. But he must be hidden, protected? The Enclave didn't find him when they searched the grounds here—"

"Mama kept Jesse's coffin in her bedroom, and the Enclave did not enter there," said Grace in a near-whisper. "I moved him, after she became ill. I couldn't bear to go in there. And I couldn't bear for him to have to wake there every sunset."

"That's awful—" Lucie began, then she gave a cry of surprise as Jesse reappeared. Grace, clearly more used to Jesse's ghostly comings and goings, looked unruffled.

"Did you find him?" Lucie asked immediately. "Did you see James?"

Jesse hesitated. "I did not see him, but I did see Matthew and Cordelia. James was—missing."

"That's all? James was *missing*?" Lucie demanded. "Matthew and Cordelia would not leave him."

"I think he left them, if he even chose to go," said Jesse slowly. "There were . . . remnants of dark magic there."

Lucie's stomach clenched. "We must get to them. Now."

"You could take our trap, as I suggested," Grace said, though Lucie noticed she did not offer to come with her.

"No. Thank you, but—" Lucie turned to Jesse. "Please, can you take me with you? The way you travel?"

Jesse was taken aback. "The way *ghosts* travel?" he said. "I've no idea if it would work, Lucie. I've never brought anyone with me."

Lucie put her hand out. Jesse was standing close to her, and she could rest her palm upon his chest. He was solid, his skin soft where her fingers brushed against his collarbone. But there was no heartbeat beneath her hand.

She looked into his eyes. He might never forgive her for this, she knew, but she had no choice.

"Jesse Blackthorn," she said. "I command you to bring me with you to my brother. Take me to Highgate Cemetery."

He stiffened. "Lucie. No."

Grace took a step toward them, looking puzzled. She began to reach out her hand toward Jesse.

"I *command* it," Lucie said fiercely. With a look of fury on his face, Jesse pulled her into his arms, and the ground disappeared beneath her feet.

20
LESS THAN GODS

Desperate revenge, and battle dangerous
To less than gods. On the other side up rose
Belial, in act more graceful and humane.
A fairer person lost not Heaven; he seemed
For dignity composed, and high exploit.
—John Milton, *Paradise Lost*

"The rope is still slack," Matthew said, after some interminable amount of time had gone by in the graveyard. He was very pale; Cordelia was worried about him. James's passage into the other world seemed to be sapping his strength.

Cordelia had come as close to the archway as she could. She'd thought perhaps she could glimpse James through it, but she saw only a view of dead ground and broken trees, and a red moon rising.

"What if something's happened to him?" Matthew asked.

"You told James to yank on the rope if he needed to get out," said Cordelia. "He knows what to do." She glanced down; she could see where his faint footprints led up to the archway and abruptly vanished. She reached out to touch the space below the arch, experimentally— maybe there was a weak spot in the barrier?

There was not. It was as unyielding as granite. Through it, she could see individual grains of sand stirred by the wind of another world. It seemed so close.

There was a crack as the rope pulled taut. Cordelia whirled as Matthew shouted out, the rope whiplashing forward, yanking him off his feet. He hit the ground hard on his back, struggling as he was dragged toward the archway.

He scrabbled at the earth, trying to slow his progress, his clothes catching and ripping on roots protruding from the ground. He slammed into the archway, hard, just before the rope went slack—he rolled away, groaning, as Cordelia ran toward him, unsheathing Cortana.

She dropped to her knees beside Matthew. There was dirt and blood in his hair. She caught at the rope, raising her blade.

"No," Matthew rasped. "James—"

He didn't want her to cut the connection to James, she knew. But being repeatedly slammed into the barrier between this world and the next would kill Matthew. Cordelia knew that, too; even if Matthew didn't care, she did.

She brought Cortana down, cutting the rope around Matthew's waist. Matthew rolled onto his stomach, struggling to his knees, just as Cordelia seized the severed end of the rope, wrapping a loose coil around her wrist and gripping as tightly as she could.

"*Cordelia*—" Matthew reached for her.

The rope jerked taut again. The force was incredible—it yanked Cordelia sideways, nearly impaling her on her own sword. She cried out as she was dragged toward the archway. She saw the barrier getting close as the rope was pulled through it. The space below the arch shimmered. She rolled, twisting her body around, raising Cortana in her hand; she was moving faster and faster.

She remembered the way the sword had embedded itself in the granite of Tower Bridge. And she heard her father's voice, a painful sound, in her ears. *This is a blade that can cut through anything.*

She felt the hilt pulse against her palm—she heard Matthew shout—and she whipped Cortana forward, angled toward the archway as if it were so much paper she could slice through.

There was the sound of something shattering as Cortana drove through the barrier between this world and the next. Cordelia screamed as shards like plates of glass flew past her, each containing an image—she saw a beach and a bleeding moon, an underground cave, a citadel on a hill, a demon rising up before a watchtower.

The shards skimmed past and vanished. The rope went slack, leaving Cordelia's wrist and hand burning. She rolled over, choking and gasping.

She was in the shadow realm: the sky above her was riven with gray clouds, hanging heavy like blocks of granite. Everywhere stretched dunes of ash and sand. The whitened bones of strange animals, long dead, protruded from the earth.

"Daisy?" said a familiar voice.

The rope fell from her hand as she struggled to sit up. Kneeling in the sand beside her was James. He was white-faced, the shadows under his eyes like bruises, his cheekbones streaked with dirt. "How are you here?" he whispered. "How are you possibly here?"

"Cortana. The blade—it cut through the archway—"

"Daisy," he breathed, and caught her in his arms.

She had not expected it, and she let go of the hilt of Cortana in surprise—which was fortunate, as she might otherwise have stabbed one or both of them. His cheek pressed against hers; she could feel his heart pounding. "I thought I would never see you again," he murmured. "Daisy, angel—"

She wrapped her arms around his neck. "James."

It was likely only a few seconds that she was in James's arms, but it felt like all time and no time at all. She pressed her lips against his soft hair, just as a sound like a crack of thunder echoed overhead. James bolted to his feet, drawing Cordelia up with him.

"Go back, Daisy," he said, gazing down into her face. "You've got to cut your way back. Get out of here."

The sound like thunder came again, closer now. "James, no. I won't leave you."

James turned her loose with a groan. He caught up Cortana, pressing the hilt into her hand. Her fingers closed automatically around the grip. "I know what Belial wants now. I promise, there's nothing you can do—"

Her hand tightened on Cortana. "Only if you come back with me," she said stubbornly. The sound came again; it was not thunder, but it seemed to echo through the earth.

"I can't," he said. The wind from the desert had risen, blowing his black-silk hair across his forehead. "I must destroy it. It is the only way to end this." He touched her face. "Go back, my Daisy. Tell Matthew—"

A roar split the night, shaking the earth beneath them. Cordelia gasped as the dunes all around them suddenly blew apart. Sand exploded upward, blotting out the stars; the earth broke open, and *something* clawed its way free, roaring like thunder.

Cordelia raised her hand to cover her face. When she lowered it, her skin and hair gritty with sand, she blinked and stared. Where before there had been empty desert, the Mandikhor demon, three times the size it had appeared on the bridge, loomed above her and James, its bulk dividing the sky.

The Consul's mansion in Grosvenor Square had been built in the style of Georgian times, pale stucco swathing brick to create a pillared facade reminiscent of ancient Rome. It was a big house: the tops of trees brushed against the windows on the fourth floor. For Thomas, it had been a place he had played with his friends since he was very young, long devoid of the ability to impress or alarm.

Or so he'd thought. As he descended from the carriage and began to climb the broad steps to the front door, anxiety settled in the pit of his stomach. He and Lucie had broken every rule in the *Codex*, and now he had fled straight to the Consul's house. He must be mad.

He thought of James, of Lucie and Matthew. Of Cordelia. None of them would have a moment's hesitation about walking straight up to the front door. He thought of Christopher, dying in the Silent City. Alone in the darkness, without his friends, the poison burning through his veins. Christopher, Thomas's cousin, and the brother of his heart.

Thomas bolted up the stairs and hammered at the front door. "Charles!" he called. "Charles, it's Thomas Lightwood, let me in!"

As if Charles had been waiting by the entryway, the door opened immediately.

Charles wore a crisp black suit, his red hair slicked back. Thomas felt a mix of hurt and anger, as he always did in Charles's presence these days. Once Charles had only been Matthew's annoying older brother, rarely thought about. Now Thomas saw the way Alastair looked at Charles, and felt a dull pain.

"If this is about Christopher, I know no more than you do," said Charles, looking impatient. "He's at the Silent City. I believe Matthew has gone to the Institute to be with James. I suggest you do the same."

He started to shut the door. Without thinking, Thomas jammed his considerable shoulder in the gap between the door and the frame. "I already know about Christopher," he said. "I need to use the laboratory downstairs. Christopher can't, so I will."

"No," said Charles. "Don't be ridiculous. People are dying. This isn't the time for playing about—"

"Charles." Alastair appeared in the entryway. He was in trousers and shirtsleeves, and was jacketless. His bare forearms were lightly muscled, his chin lifted in that arrogant tilt he affected, even when no one was looking at him. "Let Thomas in."

Charles rolled his eyes but stepped back from the door. Thomas half stumbled into the entryway.

"What is it that you want to do?" Alastair said. He was looking at Thomas, his dark brows knotted.

Thomas explained Christopher's idea for an antidote quickly, skipping, of course, all the bits that involved illegal visits to greenhouses. "I just need the laboratory to see if it will work," he finished. "Alastair—"

"Thomas, honestly," said Charles. "Perhaps you mean well, but this isn't the time to be doing rash and silly experiments. I'm on my way to meet with the Enclave. I don't have time to stay here and make sure you don't blow up the house."

Thomas thought of Christopher—shy, clever Christopher— and the years and years of quiet determination that had made him an expert at what he did, respected by Henry, far more capable than he was ever given credit for.

Thomas clutched the box that held the malos root to his chest with determination.

"My sister and my cousin have both been struck down by this thing—this demon poison," Thomas said. "My sister is dead. Christopher is dying. How can you think I am not being serious about this? That this is rash or silly? Creating an antidote is the *only* way that we can save those who are still living."

"The Enclave—" Charles began, buttoning his jacket.

"Even if the Enclave locates and kills the Mandikhor demon, that won't help those who are ill," said Thomas. "It won't help Ariadne."

Charles's mouth flattened into an irritated line, and for a moment Thomas had the bizarre feeling that he was going to say that he didn't care about Ariadne. He saw Alastair give Charles a dark sort of look—almost as if the same thought had occurred to him.

Thomas cleared his throat. "Someone once told me that we need to stand back and let people do what they're good at, and Christopher is good at this. I have faith in him. This antidote will *work*."

Charles merely looked puzzled, but Thomas hadn't said it for Charles. He looked at Alastair, who had been putting on a pair of gloves. Alastair glanced up casually, without looking at Thomas, and said, "Charles, let him use the lab. I will remain and make sure he doesn't burn down the house."

Charles looked flabbergasted. "You'd do that?"

"It seems the best course of action, and you know I have no interest in another Enclave meeting."

"I suppose not," said Charles, a little reluctantly. "All right. Come when you can, then." He reached out a hand toward Alastair, as if it were habit, then dropped it quickly. He and Alastair regarded each other with an awkwardness that felt like a pinch at Thomas's heart.

Charles started down the steps. Halfway to the bottom, he turned and glared. "Destroy *nothing*," he said to Thomas, stalked to the foot of the steps, and vanished round the corner.

"We had best get to the lab—" Thomas began, starting toward the main part of the house.

"Stop," Alastair said. Thomas froze, more surprised than anything else. Alastair's eyes were chips of black ice. "I don't care a whit about the lab," he said. "I want to know where my sister is in all this madness. Where's she gone?"

"Highgate Cemetery," said Thomas. "Entrance to the Silent City."

"Bloody hell," said Alastair. "Why? You know what, never mind why. It'll only make me angry."

"I'm sorry," Thomas said. "Not that she's there—if there were danger, and I don't think there will be, Cordelia could defend herself admirably—but that all of this is happening. It's none of our fault, but I'm just—sorry."

Alastair's gaze softened, and for a moment, Thomas felt himself back in Paris, hands in his pockets, talking in a low voice to Alastair Carstairs as if it were only the two of them in all the world. "I am sorry as well," he said. "About your sister. I had not gotten a chance to tell you before."

Thomas's breath caught. "Thank you."

"Do you really think this antidote will work?" Alastair asked.

"I know it will."

Alastair held Thomas's gaze for a long moment, then nodded. "And how long will it take to make it?"

"Twenty minutes, if everything goes right."

Alastair exhaled. "All right," he said. "Twenty minutes it is. After that, I'm going to find Cordelia." At Thomas's puzzled look, he gestured impatiently toward the steps that went down to the laboratory. "I'll help you," he said. "Let's get to work."

The Mandikhor was massive. It rose over them like the smoke of a bonfire. There was no mistaking it: though it had grown tremendously in size, it had the same scaled, lion-shaped body, the same triple row of fanged jaws. There was something else about it that was new too—here in the shadow realm, its body was marked with a thousand kinds of disease. As it moved toward them, its claws tearing the sand, Cordelia felt herself gag. Demons as a group were often disgusting; one trained oneself to cope with the horror. But there was something visceral about the markers of death that covered this creature—the ugly buboes of the Black Death decorated its arms, while its torso was bumped with smallpox, its chest cracked and runnelled with leprosy. Patches of its skin were eaten away with acidic rot, while others were red with scarlet fever. Black ichor dripped from its ears and mouth.

James backed up, pulling Cordelia with him, but sand and dirt had piled up all around them in sheer-sided dunes. There was no real way to retreat.

A sharp laugh rang out. Standing atop one of the dunes of sand was a man with pale gray hair and eyes. He looked young, and startlingly beautiful, but there was a dark edge to his beauty—it was like the loveliness of blood in snow, or the gleam of white bone through shadow.

He resembled James. Not in any specific way, but the shape of his eyes, perhaps, the bones in his face, the curve of his mouth. She had to remind herself: *This is Belial, Prince of Hell. If he reminds you of James, that is deliberate on his part. In his true form, he may look nothing like this.*

As the dust settled around them, he held out a hand toward the Mandikhor demon. The demon seemed to freeze in place as Belial turned to regard Cordelia with a cold gaze. "Tsk-tsk, James," he said. "Bringing in reinforcements like this is cheating. What of the rules of fair play?"

James drew a gleaming shortsword from his weapons belt. He was breathing hard, and very pale: streaked with dirt and sand, he no longer looked like a young Edwardian gentleman, but something more primal than that. "Let her go back to our world," he said. "Just leave her be. I'm the one you have business with—"

"No," Cordelia said sharply. "I won't abandon you!"

Belial made a bored gesture, a lazy flick of the wrist. Cordelia gasped as black vines exploded from the earth, twining around her feet and legs, pinning her in place. James took a step toward her; she raised Cortana and brought it down, intending to slice through the vines—

The blade vanished from her hand. She overbalanced, falling to her knees; the vines twisted tighter around her legs and she choked down a scream. The pain was agonizing, turning her vision red. She heard James shout something and looked up through blurred eyes to see Belial, smiling a terrible smile, Cortana gripped in his hand.

He laughed at her expression. "In this realm, all things obey me," he said. "Even a blade of Wayland the Smith." He snapped his fingers, the sound loud as a gunshot.

The Mandikhor demon reared back and sprang at James.

James rolled to the side as the Mandikhor demon sprang. He heard it hit the ground beside him, sending shock waves through the sand and dirt. He rolled onto his back as it rose up over him, stabbing upward with his sword. He heard a grunt, and burning ichor spattered his arm.

The demon reared back, giving him just enough room to spring to his feet. He could see Cordelia, struggling desperately against the vines. James somersaulted forward, rolling over and over until he shot to his feet and spun around: the Mandikhor was behind him, swinging a mace-like clubbed paw. James ducked as it whistled overhead, just missing him.

His head ached and throbbed. His skin felt hot and tight, his wrist a burning agony. He backed up, trying to center his vision on the Mandikhor. It was a shadow moving against a brighter light that hurt his eyes. Belial watched intently as the Mandikhor circled, growling.

Cordelia screamed a warning. The Mandikhor had leaped into the air—it was peculiarly swift, despite its sores and wounds—claws outstretched. One raked James's arm; he spun sideways, blade whipping overhead, slashing across the demon's torso. More ichor splashed him, mixing with his own blood now. He tasted metal in his mouth and rolled into a crouch that spun into a lunge: the Mandikhor threw up a clawed fist, catching at the blade of his sword.

It howled, its skin sliced open, as it gripped the blade and shoved, hurling James backward.

He hit the ground with enough force to knock his breath out of him. His sword skidded from his hand. He reached for it just as one of the Mandikhor's feet slammed down on the blade. He rolled to the side as a racking cough seized him; crawling to his knees, he spit up blood. He could hear Belial laughing.

He wiped the blood from his mouth. The demon had reared up over him to its full height: it looked down through slitted red eyes.

"Give up, James," Belial said. "Concede defeat. Or I will order the Mandikhor to strike you down."

James rose painfully to his knees. He saw Cordelia, her hands bloody from tearing at the vines. He wanted to apologize to her, to tell her he was sorry for dragging her into this hopeless mess.

She looked at him—it was as if she was trying to tell him something, trying to speak to him with her eyes. Her hands still gripped the vines. She hadn't given up, despite the blood, despite the pain. She was Cordelia; she would never give up.

Fight on, he told himself, but he couldn't rise: his body was shutting down. Shadows had begun to creep in at the edge of his vision. The Mandikhor hovered above him, waiting for a word, a gesture from Belial. Belial, who ruled over all this place, who bent this realm to his will.

James stretched out his right arm. The slash made by the Mandikhor's claw was still bleeding freely: drops struck the ground, and the sand drank them up. He thought he could hear the sand whispering, a soft murmur of sound, but perhaps it was only the poison in his body.

Shadows, the sand whispered, and James thought of all the things Jem had ever taught him. Focus. Clarity. Breathing. *You must build a fortress of control around yourself. You must come to know this power so that you may master it.*

Belial had mastered this world. He had bent everything in it to his will—*every tree, every rock, every grain of sand is under my command.* Each part of this realm responded to that which made Belial himself.

Are you not my heir, my own flesh and blood?

James focused. He drew all his concentration down like light drawn through a magnifying glass. He bore down with his will, with his resolve, with the blood in his veins. He felt the ground shift and change beneath him; he reached out for the substance of this realm itself: the petrified wood of the gnarled trees, the teetering piles of bones, the dunes of sand, the shadow of the Mandikhor.

Belial cried out: the Mandikhor demon surged upward. James bolted to his feet. He was funneling his own strength into the realm around him, and it responded with alacrity: the earth roared under his feet; the air exploded like dark fire from his hands, his fingers. The Mandikhor staggered toward James, but the wind was full of swirling sand, creating a dark tornado.

Belial shouted, but the Mandikhor could no longer hear him: his voice was lost in the tearing wind. James stood with his arms flung wide to either side, wind and sand tearing around him like a storm in the desert. The Mandikhor was howling and howling now: the whole substance of the realm had turned against it. Branches sheared free of trees, flying through the air like knives; bones became missiles. The demon gave one last howl as the dark, churning air rose up in a circle around it before plunging inward, crushing and tearing.

The Mandikhor vanished. Instantly James let go: the wind quieted, the earth stilling under his feet. Debris pattered softly to the ground. He wiped sand and blood from his eyes, casting around desperately. The whole landscape had changed: the dunes had shifted, the sand had flattened out in front of him. He saw Cordelia then: she was lying motionless, her red hair like a splash of blood against the sand.

"*Daisy,*" James said hoarsely, and started forward.

He barely took a single step. Belial appeared in front of him, though he had not been there a moment ago. There were no tracks in the sand to show that he had crossed it to get to James. In his left hand, he clutched Cortana, its deep golden blade shining against his gray skin.

"*Well,*" Belial said, his face twisting into an approximation of a smile. "How very, very clever you are."

James only stared. He could feel the exhaustion, the poison in his veins, waiting to rush back, to claim him. He was desperate to get to Cordelia before he collapsed. "Get out of my way," he snarled, his voice rasping out of his dry throat.

Belial chuckled. "'*Resist the devil, and he will flee from you.*' It's a nice thought, isn't it? From the book of James, too." He leaned toward James, and James could smell the burnt-chalk scent of him. "I see that you begin to understand a fraction of the power you could have if you embraced your true heritage," he whispered. "The blood you share with me is far more powerful than the blood you share with Raziel. What power do you think you will have, if you remain what you are now?"

"Let me be," James said hoarsely. "I won't let you—"

"*Enough!*" Belial roared. It was as if the demon had lost control of the features of his face: his eyes appeared strangely elongated, as did his mouth, stretching and stretching across his chin in a snarl of terrible rage. "You think I would allow you to let this body die? You have no choice, you—"

Belial's left arm jerked backward. James's eyes widened as Cortana flew from Belial's hand, ripping free of his clawed fingers. Belial cried out, twisting around to see what James himself had only just seen: Cordelia standing behind them, her gear shredded from the knees down. Cortana flew to her like a bird: she reached out for her blade, and it thumped home against her bloody palm.

"It's very rude to take someone else's sword without asking," she said.

Belial's eyes narrowed; he raised his hand, and the ground under Cordelia's feet began to crack open. James staggered forward blindly, meaning to catch her before she fell—but Cordelia was steady on her feet. She sprang toward Belial, driving Cortana into the demon's chest in a single, smooth motion.

Belial threw back his head and roared in agony.

"Daisy!" James darted forward as Cordelia wrenched the sword back; Belial was still howling. Blood spilled from the wound, the color of dark rubies, a shimmering red-black. James seized hold of Cordelia, who was gasping and shaking; her eyes were fixed on Belial.

"*Fools,*" Belial hissed. "You have no idea what you've done."

He raised a hand as if he meant to strike one of them, but it crumbled away like sand. Belial gaped as his body shuddered into pieces, like a child's puzzle tossed haphazardly in the air. He opened his mouth as if to roar or scream, but his face caved in before he could make a sound—he crumbled, dissolving against the air as James stared in horror.

Cordelia cried out. The ground heaved under them. The sky began to crack, red-black light pouring from the fissures like the blood from Belial's wound. The realm was crumbling around them. James pulled Cordelia toward him as the bottom fell out of the world.

It was not like traveling by Portal, Lucie thought, a whirlwind of sound and sight. The path the dead traveled was utterly silent and utterly dark. She could neither see nor hear anything at all. If it were not for Jesse's arms around her, the solid feel of his body, she might have thought she had lost the living world forever—that she had died, or been spun away into a terrible featureless void.

The feeling of relief when the world opened back up again was immense. Solid ground struck her feet; she stumbled, and was steadied by the arms around her. She blinked the dizziness out of her eyes and looked around.

She saw Jesse first. He held her close, but the expression in his green eyes was absolutely furious.

"God damn you, Lucie Herondale," he said, and turned her loose.

"Jesse—" she began, and realized she had no idea where she was. She looked around wildly. They were in a clearing in the middle of Highgate Cemetery, under a canopy of cedar trees. It was dark, the gaps between the leaves overhead letting in little starlight.

Lucie took a witchlight out of her pocket with shaking hands. Light blazed up: now she could see tombs standing around them in a ring. The earth here was torn, churned up as if there had been a recent fight. Lying in the grass some distance away was a crumpled figure.

Lucie gasped. *"Matthew!"*

She tore across the clearing and threw herself down next to James's *parabatai*. In the glow of the witchlight, she could see the bruises on his face. His jacket and shirt were ripped and spattered with blood. She fumbled her stele out of her belt, reaching for his hand.

His *parabatai* rune stood out stark and black on the inside of his wrist. Lucie bit back tears.

"Lucie." Jesse stood over her. Wind was rattling the leaves overhead, but neither his clothes nor hair moved in the breeze. "He's all right. Unconscious, but not in danger."

She pressed the tip of the stele to Matthew's palm and drew a quick *iratze*. "How do you know?"

"If he were dying, I would see it," Jesse said quietly. "And he would see me."

Lucie finished the *iratze* and saw it burn to life on Matthew's skin. He moaned and stirred, his eyes fluttering open. "Matthew," she said, leaning over him. She slipped the stele back into her belt and laid her hand against his cheek, where the bruises and scratches were beginning to fade. His eyes fastened on her, pupils wide and unfocused.

"Cordelia?" he whispered.

She blinked. "Math, no," she said. "It's Lucie." She took his hand. "Where is Cordelia? And James? Matthew, where are they?"

He started to struggle into a sitting position. "The archway," he said, and Lucie stared at him in puzzlement. "They went through. James first, and then Cordelia. She used Cortana." His dark green gaze darted around the clearing. "The archway," he said again, a note of panic in his voice. "Where is it?"

Worried, Lucie glanced at Jesse. His jaw was still set with anger, but he hadn't walked away, at least. He hadn't disappeared on her. He shrugged—clearly he hadn't seen an archway either.

"Matthew, try to remember—" she began, and then the sky tore, silently and unbelievably, down the middle. For a moment there was a gap in the center of the sky, and through it Lucie could see the constellations of another world. She saw shadows that rose into the air like towers of star-fire, darkly blazing. For a moment, she glimpsed a pair of silver eyes.

Then James and Cordelia hurtled out of the sky.

Cordelia fell first. She sprang into existence like a falling star, appearing between one moment and the next ten feet above the ground. She struck the earth hard, Cortana flying from her hand. James followed a moment later, his body limp. He hit the ground beside Cordelia and lay motionless.

"Get me up," Matthew said, gripping Lucie's hand. As Jesse watched, Lucie helped Matthew to his feet. James and Cordelia were lying a few yards away; Lucie and Matthew ran to kneel down beside them.

Cordelia was already struggling to get up. She was filthy with sand and dirt. Her hair had come out of its fastenings and spilled down over her shoulders like fire. "James," she gasped, her dark eyes wide with fear. "See to him, please, not me—the demon poison—"

Demon poison? Cold all over, Lucie bent over her brother. He lay unmoving, his hands black with ichor, perfectly pale and still. His wild black hair was stiff with blood.

Cordelia tried to rise to her feet but screamed out in pain and collapsed back to her knees. Lucie, kneeling over James, looked at her with sudden panic. "Daisy—"

"It's nothing," Cordelia said. "Please, there must be something we can do for James—" She drew in a shuddering breath. "He killed the Mandikhor. He destroyed it. He *can't* die. It's not fair."

Matthew was kneeling by James's side, his stele already in his hand. Runes given by one's *parabatai* were always the most powerful: Matthew's hands were steady as he scrolled healing runes over James's hands, his wrists, the base of his throat.

They all froze, holding their breath. Cordelia, painfully, pulled herself closer, her scarlet hair hanging down to touch the green leaves on the ground. Her gaze was fixed on James.

The *iratzes* on his skin shimmered—and vanished.

"They won't work." It was Jesse. The anger had left his face now; he stood near Cordelia, unseen by anyone but Lucie, and there was a terrible sorrow in his eyes. "He is too close to death."

Matthew gasped. His hand flew to his chest: he pressed there, hard, as if a knife had gone into his heart and he was trying to stop the bleeding. His face was utterly white. "He's dying," he said, his voice cracking. "I can feel it."

Lucie caught at her brother's hands. They were cold in hers, unmoving. Tears spilled from her eyes, and onto his face, tracing tracks in the grime. "Please, Jamie," she whispered. "Please don't die. Please take another breath. For Mam and Papa. For me."

"Give him mine," said Jesse.

Lucie's head jerked up. She stared at Jesse. There was an odd look on his face: a strange, almost luminous resignation. "What do you mean?"

Cordelia stared. "Who are you talking to? Lucie?"

Jesse moved toward them. He knelt down, and the grass did not bend under the weight of his body. He drew the gold chain of his locket over his head and held it out to Lucie.

She remembered what he had said after the fight on Tower Bridge. That he would have given his last breath to her. That it would have had enough life force to empty her lungs of water if she had been drowning. As James was drowning in poison now.

"But what will happen to you?" she whispered. She was aware that Cordelia was staring at her; Matthew was doubled up in agony, his breaths coming in ragged gasps.

"Does it matter?" said Jesse. "This is his life. Not a shadow of a life. Not years of waiting in the dark."

Lucie reached out her hand. It closed around the locket, and she felt it tumble into her palm, cool and solid. For a moment she hesitated—just for a moment, her eyes fixed on Jesse, kneeling in the grass.

Then she looked down at her brother. His lips were blue, his eyes sunken into his head. He was barely breathing. Carefully, as if she were holding a glass containing the last drop of water in the world, Lucie opened the little locket and pressed the curve of the metal against his lips.

There was a pause, enough time for a sigh.

Then her brother's chest lifted with Jesse Blackthorn's last breath. His eyes opened, bright gold, and from the four crescent wounds in his wrist, black fluid spilled—his body was ridding itself of the Mandikhor's poison.

Lucie's hand closed tightly around the locket, so tightly the edge of the metal cut into her palm. Cordelia cried out; Matthew lifted his head, the color returning to his face. He scrambled to James's side and pulled James into his lap.

James, slumped against Matthew's chest, struggled to focus. Lucie knew what he was seeing. A boy leaning over him: a boy with hair as black as his own, a boy with green eyes the color of hawthorn leaves, a boy who was already beginning to fade around the edges, like a figure seen in a cloud that disappears when the wind changes.

"*Who are you?*" James whispered, his voice ragged.

But Jesse was already gone.

"What do you mean, 'Who are you?'" Matthew demanded. "I'm your *parabatai*, you nitwit."

He was busy drawing healing runes on whatever parts of James he could reach, which Cordelia could only applaud. She had no idea what Lucie had done to heal her brother, but that was not what mattered now.

"I didn't mean you, Matthew," James said. His eyes were closed, his dark lashes feathered against the tops of his cheekbones. "Obviously."

Matthew ran a ringed hand through James's wild hair and smiled. "Are you going to tell us what happened yet? It isn't every day a fellow goes into a demon realm and then falls out of the sky. I'd think you'd want to share this experience with your friends."

"Believe me when I say it is a long story," said James. "I promise you we are in no danger now—"

"Did you really kill the Mandikhor?" asked Lucie.

"Yes," said James, "and Cordelia destroyed the one who raised it." He held out a hand, scarred with cuts and filthy with dirt.

"Daisy? Would you come here?" He smiled crookedly. "I would come to you, but I do not think I have the strength to walk."

Cordelia tried to rise, but a hot white pain shot up her leg. She bit down on a whimper. "My leg is broken, I think. Very vexing, but I'm quite all right."

"Oh! *Daisy!* Your leg!" Lucie leaped to her feet and raced over to Cordelia, dropping down and pressing her stele against Cordelia's arm. She began to draw an *iratze*. "I am the worst," she moaned. "The most dreadful would-be *parabatai* who ever lived. Please forgive me, Daisy."

As the healing rune took effect, Cordelia could feel the bone in her leg beginning to knit back together. It was not an entirely pleasant feeling. She gasped and said, "Lucie, it's nothing—I would have done it myself, but I dropped my stele in—in that other place."

Lucie pushed Cordelia's hair out of her eyes and smiled at her. "There is no need ever to do it yourself," she said. "Runes given to you by your *parabatai* are best."

"Ghastly," said Matthew. "Look at them, affirming their eternal bond of friendship. In public."

"I would question your definition of 'public,'" said James. Lucie and Cordelia exchanged a smile: if James was capable of mocking Matthew, he was certainly on the mend. "This is a mostly deserted graveyard."

"Hmmm," said Matthew, in a surprisingly serious tone, his eyes narrowed. He rose to his feet, helping James to sit up against a tree. As Matthew paced to the edge of the clearing, James said:

"Luce. Let me talk to Cordelia for a moment."

Lucie exchanged a glance with Cordelia, who nodded and stood up—it still hurt to put weight on her leg, but Lucie's *iratzes* had mostly done their job. Lucie went to join Matthew as Cordelia limped over to James and sank down beside him under the shadow of a cypress tree.

For a moment, as James's breaths had faded, Cordelia had seen life fork into two paths. One path in which James was dead—in which there was no meaning in the world, in which Lucie was heartbroken and Matthew destroyed, in which Thomas and Christopher were crushed and the Herondale family never smiled again. And a second path in which life continued as it was now—imperfect, confusing, but full of hope.

They were on the second path. That was what mattered—that James *was* breathing, that his lips were no longer blue, that he was looking at her with steady gold eyes. Despite the fact that her whole body ached, she found herself smiling.

"You saved my life," he said. "Just as you saved my sister's all those years ago. We should have given you a more warrior-like nickname. Not Daisy, but Artemis, or Boadicea."

She laughed softly. "I like Daisy."

"So do I," he said, and reached up to lightly brush back a strand of her hair. She felt her heart nearly stop. In a low voice, he said, "'*And when her cheek the moon revealed, a thousand hearts were won: no pride, no shield, could check her power. Layla, she was called.*'"

"*Layla and Majnun,*" she whispered. "You—remember?"

"You read to me," he said. "Perhaps, now all this is over, we could read it again, together?"

Reading together. Never had Cordelia heard of anything so romantic. She started to nod, just as Matthew called out sharply:

"Someone's coming! I see witchlight."

Cordelia turned to look. Lights had appeared between the trees: as they came nearer, she saw the glimmer of torchlight. She tried to rise, but the *iratzes* were already fading: her leg hurt too much. She sat back down.

"Oh, dear," said Lucie. "The Silent Brothers aren't going to be at all pleased, are they? Nor the Enclave. We're probably going to be in awful trouble."

"Maybe we could leg it," suggested Matthew.

"I am not going anywhere," said James. "I will remain here and take whatever punishment is given out. The rack, the iron maiden, death by spiders. Anything but getting up."

"I don't think I *can* stand up," said Cordelia apologetically.

"'*Shades of the prison-house begin to close upon the growing Boy,*'" Matthew intoned. "Coleridge."

"Wordsworth," James corrected.

The lights swung closer. A sharp voice cut through the clearing. A *familiar* voice. "What on earth is going on?"

Cordelia twisted around, trying not to move her leg. Alastair strode into the clearing. He looked disarmingly normal in an old tweed coat of her father's, as if he'd been out for a stroll. His unnaturally pale hair gleamed under the faint starlight. Beside him was Thomas, his hair mussed, carrying what looked like an apothecary's case.

"*Why* are you all on the ground?" said Thomas, and then waved his case in the air. "The antidote—it's ready—what's the quickest way to Christopher?"

There was a babble of voices. Matthew got to his feet and hugged Thomas hard, being careful not to knock the case out of his hand. "Let's go alert the Brothers," he said, and began to pull his friend toward the path leading to the Silent City.

"You needn't come with me," Thomas protested, amused.

"Just in case there's chanting," Matthew said. "I don't think there will be, mind, but you never know."

Alastair had been watching as Thomas and Matthew disappeared into the shadows between the trees. He shook his head, and turned his attention back to Cordelia. "*Biyâ,*" he said, bending down to swing her up in his arms. "Come along home."

In surprise, she looped an arm around his neck. "But, Alastair. I can't leave my friends—"

"Layla," Alastair said, in an unusually gentle voice. "They're not going to be alone. Thomas and I took care of sending a message to the Institute. Look."

She looked, and saw that the broad path behind the tombs was full of the glow of witchlight torches borne by a crowd of Shadow-hunters. She recognized a dozen familiar faces: Will Herondale, his torch casting bright illumination over his black-and-silver hair. Tessa, a sword in her hand, her brown hair loose over her shoulders. Gabriel, Cecily, and Anna Lightwood, Anna smiling, her hair as black as the gear she wore.

She heard Lucie give a short cry. *"Papa!"*

Will broke into a run. He caught hold of his daughter and swept her into his arms. Tessa ran to James, dropping down to kneel beside him and fuss over his bruises and cuts. Gabriel and Cecily followed, and soon Lucie and James were surrounded, being embraced and scolded in equal measure.

Cordelia closed her eyes in relief. James and Lucie were all right. Everywhere Cordelia could hear chatter: Gabriel and Cecily were asking after Thomas, and the others were saying that he was being taken to the Silent City now, where the antidote would be administered. Someone else—one of the Rosewains—was saying that there was still a present danger, that the demons might attack again, whether there was an antidote or not.

"The Mandikhor has been defeated," Cordelia said. "It will not return."

"And how do you know that, young lady?" said George Penhallow.

"BECAUSE JAMES KILLED IT," Cordelia said, as loudly as she could. "James killed the Mandikhor demon. I *saw* it die."

At that point, several people crowded toward her; it was Will who blocked their way, his hand out, protesting that they should not be bothering an injured girl. Alastair took the opportunity to slip from the clearing and into the shadows, still carrying Cordelia in his arms.

"I beg you not to get involved, *khahare azizam*," said Alastair. "It will all be sorted out soon enough, but there's going to be a great deal of nonsense first. And you need to rest."

"But they need to know it was James," Cordelia said. It was oddly comfortable to be carried like this, with her head against her brother's shoulder. The way her father had carried her once, when she was very small. "They need to know what he did, because—because they do."

Because Belial is his grandfather. Because when the Enclave finds that out, who knows what they will think. Because people can be foolish and cruel.

"They will," Alastair said, sounding utterly confident. "The truth is the truth. It will always come out."

She craned her head back to look up at him. "How do you know the antidote works?"

Alastair grinned in the dark. "I have faith in Thomas."

"You *do*?" said Cordelia. "I didn't think you even knew him that well."

Alastair hesitated. "I watched him make it," he said finally. They had reached the Carstairs carriage now, with its design of castle towers on the door. Many more carriages lined the curb beside it. "Because he had such faith in Christopher, he had faith in himself. I never quite thought of friendship like that—as something that makes you more than you are."

"But, Alastair—"

"No more questions," said Alastair, placing Cordelia inside the carriage and swinging himself up after her. He smiled, that rare charming smile of his that was all the better for its rarity. "You were very brave, Layla, but you need healing, too. Time to go home."

DAYS PAST:
CIRENWORTH HALL, 1898

Cordelia often felt alone when it was just her and her parents,
but never as much as when Alastair went away to the Academy.
While he was gone, the rest of the Carstairs family traveled to India,
to Paris, to Cape Town and Canada, but they were at Cirenworth for
the holidays when he finally returned.

She had waited months for his return, but when he stepped out
of the carriage—taller, more angular, and sharper than ever—he
seemed like a different person. He'd always been short-tempered
and prickly, but now he would barely speak to her. When he did, it
was mostly to tell her not to bother him.

Her parents ignored the transformation. When Cordelia asked
her father why Alastair wouldn't spend time with her, he smiled at
her and told her that teenage boys went through "times like this"
and she would "understand when she was older." "He's been having fun with boys his own age all year and now he's got to be back
in the countryside with the likes of us," Elias said with a chuckle.
"He'll get over it."

This was not a satisfying answer. Cordelia tried to put herself in

Alastair's path as much as she could, to force him to acknowledge her. Often, though, she couldn't even find him. He spent hours locked in his bedroom, and when she knocked on the door, he didn't even bother to tell her to go away. He just ignored her. The only way she knew he'd been in there was when he emerged to eat, or to announce he was going out for a long walk by himself.

This went on for a few weeks. Cordelia's feelings changed from disappointment, to sorrow, to blaming herself, to annoyance, and then to anger. At dinner one night she threw a spoon at him and shouted, "Why won't you talk to me?" Alastair caught the spoon out of the air, put it down on the table, and glared at her in silence.

"Don't throw things, Cordelia," her mother said.

"*Mâmân!*" Cordelia protested in a tone of betrayal. Her father ignored the entire business and went on eating as though nothing had happened. Risa glided by and set a new spoon down at Cordelia's place, which Cordelia found extremely irritating.

Alastair's refusal to engage with Cordelia was, she understood, meant to cause her to give up and stop trying. So she redoubled her efforts. "Well," she would announce, if she found herself in the same room with him, "I'm going to collect wild blackberries down the lane." (Alastair loved blackberries.) Or, "I think I'll do some tumbling in the training room after lunch." (Alastair was always on her to practice how to fall safely, and she'd need a partner for that.)

One day when he went out for one of his walks, Cordelia waited a minute and then followed. It was good practice, she told herself— stealthy movement, awareness of her surroundings, honing her senses. She made it a game: How long could she track her brother before he noticed? Could she remain undetected long enough to find out where he went?

It turned out Alastair didn't go anywhere. He just walked and walked, knowing these woods well enough not to get lost. Cordelia began to get tired after a couple of hours. Then she began to get hungry.

Then she got distracted, and hooked her foot into a protruding tree root, and fell in a thud on the hard-packed dirt. Ahead, Alastair turned at the noise and spotted her as she, annoyed, scrambled to her feet. She folded her arms and held up her chin, stubborn and determined to retain her pride in the face of whatever unpleasant reaction he was preparing: his contempt, his rage, his dismissal.

Instead, he let out a sigh and walked over to her. Without preamble he said gruffly, "Are you hurt?"

Cordelia lifted her foot and wiggled it experimentally. "I'll be okay. Just bruised, I think."

"Come on," he said. "Let's go home."

They walked in silence, Alastair a few steps ahead, not speaking. Eventually, driven mad by the silence, Cordelia burst out, "Don't you want to know why I was following you?"

He turned and considered her. "I assume you thought I was coming out here to do something exciting."

"I'm sorry," she said, growing—as always—more agitated in the face of Alastair's imperturbable calm. "I'm sorry that since you went away to the Academy you've become all grown-up and mature and you have fancy new friends. I'm sorry I'm just your stupid little sister."

Alastair stared at her a moment, and then let out a bark of laughter. There was no humor in it. "You have no idea what you're talking about."

"I'm sorry you're too good for your family now! I'm sorry you're too good to train with me!"

He shook his head, dismissive. "Don't be daft, Cordelia."

"Just talk to me!" she said. "I don't know why you're so grumpy. You're the lucky one who got to go away. Who got to have fun in Idris. You know how alone I've been all year?"

For a moment, Alastair looked lost, hesitant. It had been a long time since Cordelia had seen an expression so open on his face. Then he slammed shut like an iron gate. "We're all of us alone," he said. "In the end."

"What does that mean?" she demanded, but he'd turned to walk away. After a moment, wiping the wetness from her face with her sleeve, she followed.

When they got back to the house, she left him in the entryway while she retrieved the entire stock of throwing knives from the china cabinet that served as the house's armory. She walked past her brother on the way from cabinet to training room, glaring at him, barely able to carry the pile. He watched her in silence.

In the training room she set up and went through her paces. *Thunk. Thunk.* Throwing knives were not her strongest weapon, but she needed the sense of impact, of getting to hurt something, even just a target on a backstop. As usual, the rhythm of training soothed her. Her breathing became more calm and even. The repetition grounded her: five throws, then the walk to retrieve the knives from the target and the walk back to try again. Five throws. Walk. Retrieve. Walk. Five throws.

After twenty minutes or so of this she realized that Alastair was standing in the doorway of the training room. She ignored him.

Someone else might have said that she'd gotten better since he saw her last, or asked if he could take a turn. Alastair, though, eventually cleared his throat and said, "You're turning your left foot on the release. That's why you're so inconsistent."

She glared and went back to throwing. But she paid more attention to her footwork.

After a while Alastair said, "It's stupid to say I'm lucky. I'm not lucky."

"You weren't stuck here all year."

"Oh?" Alastair sneered. "How many people came here this year to mock you? How many asked what was wrong with you that you didn't have a private tutor? Or suggested your family was some kind of ne'er-do-wells because we've moved around a lot?"

Cordelia looked over at him, expecting to see vulnerability and sadness there, but Alastair's eyes were hard, his mouth a thin line. "They treated you badly?"

Alastair let out another mirthless laugh. "For a while. I realized I had a choice. There were only two kinds of people at the Academy. The bullies and the bullied."

"And you . . . ?"

Alastair said tightly, "Which would you have chosen?"

"If those were my only two choices," Cordelia said, "I would have left and come home."

"Yes, well," he said. "I chose the one where I wasn't made to feel like a laughingstock."

Cordelia was very still and silent. Alastair's face was impassive. "And how has that worked out?" she said, as mildly as she dared.

"Awful," he said. "It's awful."

Cordelia did not know what to say or what to do. She wanted to go and throw her arms around her brother, to tell him that she loved him, but he stood rigid, with his arms crossed in front of him, and she didn't dare. Finally she held out the knife in her hand. "Do you want to have a throw? You're much better than I am."

When he looked suspicious, she said, "I could use some help, Alastair. You see how careless my form is."

Alastair came and took the knife from her. "Very careless," he agreed. "I know swordplay comes naturally to you, but not everything will. You must slow down. Pay attention to your feet. Now, follow my gestures. That's it, Layla. Stay with me."

And she would.

21

BURN

My heart is bound by beauty's spell.
My love is indestructible.
Although I like a candle burn,
And almost to a shadow turn,
I envy not the heart that's free:
Love's soul-encircling chains for me.
—Nizami Ganjavi, *Layla and Majnun*

James lay on the bed in his room, atop the covers, his arm flung behind his head. He was gazing at a familiar crack in the ceiling that was shaped a bit like a duck. His father would be horrified.

Matthew sat beside him, wearing a velvet jacket and matching trousers. James had wavered in and out of consciousness for the first two days after his visit to Belial's realm. Sometimes he dreamed of the demon world and woke up yelling, reaching for a weapon that wasn't there. His knives might not have been beside him, but Matthew always was.

If there was anyone in the world who understood about *parabatai*, it was James's parents. On the first night of their return from Highgate, Matthew had dragged a pile of bedding into James's room, rolled himself up in it, and gone to sleep. No one tried to make him leave—when Tessa brought soup and tea to James, she brought some for Matthew, too. When Will came and brought card games to while away the time, Matthew played as well, and usually lost.

Not that others weren't kind as well. When Anna brought James a stylish new necktie to cheer him, she brought one for Matthew. When Lucie smuggled in midnight tarts from the kitchen, there were extras for Matthew. It was possible, as a result, that Matthew was never going home. James could hardly blame him: Charles had certainly been a pill lately. Everyone was hailing Christopher as a hero for having created the antidote to the Mandikhor poison—a tale made even more romantic by the fact that Christopher had been stricken down and healed himself. Few knew Charles almost hadn't let Thomas use the lab to make it. The words "If it hadn't been for Alastair Carstairs, everything would have been ruined," had actually passed Thomas's lips, causing James to wonder if he'd wandered back into the demon realm.

Thomas and Christopher visited every day, carrying stories of the aftermath of the sickness. None of those who had been ill remembered chanting James's name, nor did Ariadne recall her brief possession. The quarantine had been lifted and Charlotte and Henry were returning shortly; Christopher and James were currently both heroes, which angered James greatly as, he pointed out, Cordelia had been with him in the demon realm and had it not been for her, he would have died. Lucie had also saved the day, as had Matthew. Thomas had helped retrieve the malos root from Chiswick House and had made the antidote with his own hands. Anna had taken them to the Hell Ruelle. They were all heroes, in his opinion.

It was Matthew who asked him, when they were alone, if he thought he might be missing Cordelia. She alone hadn't come to visit him: the break in her leg was a bad one, it turned out, and would take several days to heal. Lucie had been to see her and reported her in good spirits. "I read to her from *The Beautiful Cordelia* and she went right to sleep," Lucie said with delight, "so she must have been very tired."

Thomas and Christopher had gone to see her as well, and brought her chocolates. They asked James if he had anything he wanted them to bring to her with his compliments. He shook his head without speaking, afraid what might pour out if he opened his mouth. He didn't want to discuss Cordelia with anyone. He just wanted to see her. If he saw her, he would know.

"So," Matthew said, folding his own arms behind his head. "With your new status as hero of the Clave, do you plan to make any demands?" He regarded the crack in the ceiling plaster. "I would ask for my own personal valet, and Oscar Wilde to be brought to me for conversation."

"Isn't he dead?" said James.

"Nothing wrong with the undead." Matthew chuckled. "Wait until our next visit to the Hell Ruelle."

James was silent for a moment. He preferred to avoid the Clave, in truth; there was too much they didn't know. All they had been told—by Lucie, Matthew, and Cordelia—was that he had found and slain the Mandikhor in Highgate Cemetery with the help of his friends. He saw no reason for them to know more.

The situation had been different with his parents, however. When he had finally been coherent enough to tell the story, he had explained it to them, and to Lucie. He had told them the truth about his encounter with Belial, and the way Belial, having been wounded by Cortana, had crumbled to dust. Lastly, he told them of the blood relationship that existed between the Herondales and the Prince of Hell.

They had all reacted characteristically. Tessa had been practical and said that she'd been trying to find out who her father was for years, and at least now they knew. Lucie had looked shaken but said she would turn the story into a novel. Will had been angry at the world, and then gone to see Jem.

Jem, who had promised to keep the secret of Tessa's parentage, had told Will that while a Prince of Hell could not be killed, such a serious wound would keep Belial weak and disembodied for at least a century.

James had told Christopher and Thomas as well, but everyone had agreed that it was best to keep the details regarding Belial a secret for now, especially as the Prince of Hell was not a current threat. His realm had crumbled away, Jem had explained, signifying a true loss of power for the Lord of Thieves. It was unlikely that James would ever feel the pull to the demon realm again, or ever see it at all.

"James?" His door cracked open and his mother stood on the threshold. She smiled when she saw him and Matthew, but there was a line of concern between her brows. She tucked a strand of hair behind her ear and said, "Someone is here to see you. A young lady."

James sat upright. "Cordelia?"

He saw Matthew give him a sideways look, but Tessa was already shaking her head.

"Not Cordelia," she said. "It is Grace Blackthorn."

It was Matthew's turn to bolt into a sitting position. "Oh no," he said. "No, no. Send her away. Tell her there's a rat infestation. Tell her that vague, insidious behavior has been made illegal in the Institute and she's not allowed in."

Tessa merely raised her eyebrows. "She said it was regarding an important matter."

Matthew turned to James imploringly. "Jamie. Don't. After what she did . . ."

James glared at his *parabatai*. Even now, Tessa and Will knew little of the understanding he had once shared with Grace, and he preferred to keep it that way.

"Is it about her mother?" he said. "Isn't Tatiana well again?"

"She is quite well," said Tessa. The antidote had been incredibly effective; as far as James knew, not a single poisoned Shadowhunter had not recovered. "James, if you don't want to see her—"

"I'll see her," James said, rising to his feet. "Send her in."

As Tessa went to fetch Grace, Matthew rolled off the bed and toed on his shoes. He turned at the door to give James a sharp look. "Be careful," he said, and departed, leaving the door open.

A moment later, as if she had been waiting for Matthew to leave, Grace came into the room.

She looked beautiful, as always. Her white-blond hair was pulled smoothly back from her oval face. Her cheeks were flushed with pale pink color, like the inside of a seashell. She wore a green dress, its hem wet and a bit draggled—it had been raining on and off for most of the day, and it was now late afternoon.

Once her beauty had shaken him like a storm. Now, seeing her, he felt only a great weariness—a bleary exhaustion, as if he had drunk too much the night before. He wished she were not here. Not because it hurt him to look at her, but because it didn't.

He had thought of himself as someone who loved more deeply than that. "You wanted to talk to me alone," he said. "Are you sure that's a good idea? Your mother—"

"Would go mad if she knew I was here," Grace said. "Yes. But I had to talk to you."

"You had better close the door, then," he said. He had never been so short with Grace. It felt odd and awkward, but then, it felt odd and awkward for her to be here at all.

Grace's hands shook as she closed the door. She turned back and, to James's immense surprise, knelt down on the floor in front of him.

He took a step back. "Grace. Don't."

"I must," she said. Her hands were in fists. "I understand why you don't want to listen to me. You have every reason. But I must beg you to do just that." She exhaled a shuddering breath. "I engaged myself to Charles because I believed that by the time my mother recovered, she would be unable to hurt me. She would find me protected by the Consul's family."

"Yes," said James. "I know. They will indeed protect you. The Fairchilds are good people." He exhaled. "Grace, get up, please."

She got to her feet, her chin raised. "I returned to Chiswick House with Charles yesterday, to fetch some of my belongings," she said. "I intend to remain away from home until my marriage. I saw my mother there, and at first I thought I had been successful. She seemed pleased I had made a powerful match. Then I realized she had lost interest in what I had done because she had larger plans."

James frowned. Under her eyes he could see the tracks of recent tears. Worry stirred, despite himself. "What kind of plans?"

"You know she hates you and your father," Grace said rapidly. "She hates her brothers as well. She has always believed that one day they would kill her to get Chiswick House back."

"In the state it's in, she'd be lucky if anyone wanted it," said James, but Grace didn't seem to hear him.

"When she woke from her sickness, she found out somehow—I do not know how—that you had nearly died, and she believes . . ." Grace seemed to be struggling for words. "She has always believed that Jesse might be brought back from the dead if she used necromancy. She called upon warlocks, hoping they would do dark magic for her. She begged demons to help her—"

James was appalled. "But that is madness. To dabble in such things is a near-certain death sentence."

"She did not dabble. She *dedicated* herself to the idea, collecting books of necromancy, scouring Shadow Markets for Hands of Glory—"

"But the Enclave searched Chiswick House. They found no trace of dark magic."

"She keeps it all at the manor in Idris."

"And you never told me of any of this?" said James.

"How could I? And implicate you, too? She is mad where you are concerned. Since she awoke from her poisoned sleep, she has been raging and ranting. She says she knows now there is no chance Jesse will ever return. She says it is as if you stole his last breath by surviving the Mandikhor."

"*What?*" James's head was spinning. "How would that be possible?"

"I would tell you if I knew. James, she is *dangerous*," said Grace. "She has built herself a palace of dreams and lies, and when those lies are threatened, she lashes out. Do you remember the automaton in the hallway of the manor in Idris?"

"Yes, though I don't see what that has to do with anything—"

"It was enspelled by a warlock years ago," said Grace. "In the event of her death, it is enchanted to rise up and kill Shadowhunters. Now she has decided that Jesse will never rise and that she has nothing to live for. She plans to end her life tonight, and when she does, it will wreak havoc. It will go to Alicante—"

James's heart had begun to pound. "I understand what it will do," he said. "Grace, we must go to my parents with this information."

"No! No one must know, James. If the Clave arrests my mother, if they search Blackthorn Manor, they will see how deeply my mother has sunk into necromancy and black magic, and I will be at fault as well, and Jesse—" She broke off, her hands fluttering like panicked moths. "If she knew I had given away her secrets, Mama would want me to be blamed, James. I could be locked in the Silent City."

"That need not happen. This is Tatiana's sin, not yours. And she is clearly mad—there can be mercy for the mad—"

She raised her face to his. Her eyes gleamed; tears or determination, he could not tell. "James," she said. "I'm so sorry."

"Sorry?" he echoed. "For what?"

"I never wanted to do this to you," she said. "But she insisted. And *he* insisted. It had to be you. My mother made me her blade, to cut every barrier raised against her. But your blood, *his* blood, is a barrier I cannot cut. I cannot bind you without his chain."

Something silver flashed in her hand. She caught at his arm; he tried to pull away, but she held fast. He felt something cold against his skin, and heard a click like a lock turning as the metal circle closed about his wrist. A spark of pain traveled up his arm, like a sudden shock of electricity.

He tried to step back. Shadowy images rose before his eyes. In the last moment before it all changed, he saw Cordelia—she stood some distance away from him, at the edge of the Institute roof. When he tried to turn, to look at her, she covered her face with her hands and moved back, out of his reach. He saw the moon behind her, or perhaps it was not the moon. It was a silver, spinning thing, a wheel in the night, so bright it blinded him to every other star.

It had been raining in London, but the weather in Idris, even at the edge of sunset, was warm. Lucie had followed Uncle Jem along the path from the spot where they had Portaled in, just outside Alicante. One could not Portal directly into the walled city; it was warded against such things. Lucie didn't mind. Her destination was not within the city limits.

Jem—she never could think of him as Brother Zachariah, no matter how hard she tried—walked along beside her as they skirted the Imperishable Fields. His hood was down, and the wind ruffled his black hair. Though his face was scarred, she realized for the first time that it was a young face—much more like her mother's than her father's. Was it strange for Will, she wondered, to be aging and have Jem remain in appearance still a boy? Or when you loved someone, did you not notice these things, just as her parents saw no difference between themselves?

It is there. Jem gestured toward what looked like a miniature city of white houses. It was the necropolis of Alicante, where families of Idris were buried. Narrow lanes threaded among the mausoleums, paved with crushed white stone. Lucie had always loved the way the tombs looked like small houses, with doors or gates and sloping roofs. Unlike mundanes, Shadowhunters did not tend to decorate their graves with statues of angels. The names of the families who owned the tombs were carved over the doors, or etched on metal plates: BELLEFLEUR, CARTWRIGHT, CROSSKILL, LOVELACE, even BRIDGESTOCK. Death made unlikely neighbors. She found what she was looking for at last, a large tomb under a shaded tree, bearing the name BLACKTHORN.

She stopped and looked. It was a tomb like any other, save for the design of thorns that ran around the plinth. The names of those who had died marched up and down the tomb's left side like orderly soldiers. It was easy to find the newest. JESSE BLACKTHORN, BORN 1879, DIED 1896.

It had only been 1897 when she had met him in the woods, Lucie realized. He had been a ghost for such a short time. He had seemed so much older than her then; she had never given thought to how frightened he must have been himself.

Everybody thought Jesse had died long ago. Nobody knew what he had sacrificed since.

She touched the locket hanging around her throat and turned to Jem. "Can I have a moment alone here, please?"

Jem glanced down at her, clearly worried. It was hard to read his face, his closed eyes, but he had hesitated when she first asked him to bring her to Idris to pay respects in the graveyard and not to tell her parents. He had only agreed when she'd said that if he didn't do it, she'd find a warlock who would take her.

He touched her hair lightly. *Do not dwell too much on death. Lucie means light. Look to the day, not the night.*

"I know, Uncle Jem," she said. "It will only be a moment."

He nodded and vanished into the shadows, the way Silent Brothers always did.

Lucie turned back to the tomb. She knew it did not contain any part of Jesse, yet it comforted her to be there all the same. "I have told no one what I saw at Chiswick House, and I never shall," she said aloud. "I haven't kept silence to protect Grace, or your mother. Only to protect you. I did not expect you to be such a true friend as you were, Jesse. I did not expect you to give your life for my brother's. I knew you had been angry at me only moments before, and more than anything I regret not being able to tell you I was sorry. I should not have used my power like that. It is still hard to imagine I have a power, and even now I do not quite understand it." She touched his name with her fingertips, letters cut evenly into smooth marble. "Without you, I am not sure I will ever understand it."

"You will."

She looked up, and there he was. Jesse, leaning against the side of the tomb like a farmer's boy against a gate. Smiling his odd little smile, straight black hair in his eyes. Lucie dropped the flowers she was holding and reached out, without pausing to think, to grasp his hand.

Her fingers brushed through emptiness. Aside from a path of colder air, there was no solidity to him, as there had been before.

She drew her hand back, pressing it against her chest. "Jesse."

"I find my strength is fading," he said. "Perhaps there was more to this last breath business than I thought."

"I am so sorry," Lucie whispered. "This is my fault."

"Lucie, no." Jesse stepped forward; she felt the cold emanating from his body, and stared up at him. He seemed less human, and ironically more oddly beautiful, than he had before: his skin was smooth as glass, his lashes black and startling. "You let me be something I had never been before, even when I was living. A Shadowhunter. You let me be part of what you did. I never thought I would again be given the chance to make a difference."

"You made every difference," Lucie said. "Without your help, we could not have done what we did, even if the others don't know it. And you saved James's life. I will always owe you."

Jesse's eyes were nearly black. "You need not owe the dead, Lucie."

"I do," she whispered. "Is your body still at Chiswick House? Is Grace watching over you?"

"Yes. She will come whenever she can, on the pretense of looking after the house, now that we cannot trust—" He broke off. "You have taught me to see things very differently, Lucie," he said after a moment. "I had thought my mother's madness harmless. I did not realize she had dealings with demons until I saw that creature attack Grace."

"I am sorry," Lucie whispered. "For all of it."

His voice gentled. "It was never your fault. My mother needs help. Grace plans to make sure she gets it. Do not be sorry, Lucie. You brought light into my lightless world, and for that I am grateful."

"I am the one who is grateful," she said. "And I will find a way to help you, Jesse. I swear to bring you back if I can, or lay you to rest if I cannot."

He shook his head. "You cannot promise something so grave."

"I can promise it. I do promise it. I am a Herondale, and we keep our promises."

"Lucie—" Jesse began. His brow furrowed. "I hear something. Who is with you?"

"Je—Brother Zachariah," Lucie said. She supposed she should not be surprised ghosts could hear the Silent Brothers.

Late afternoon was sliding into dusk. The demon towers sparkled with sunset, turning the colors of a tree in autumn: red and gold, copper and flame.

"I must go," Jesse said. "James Carstairs is a Silent Brother. He might be able to see me. I would not want to bring you trouble." He gave her a long, last look. "Promise you will not try to help me."

"Jesse," Lucie whispered, and reached out her hand; she felt the slightest pressure on her fingers, and it was gone. Jesse had faded into nothingness, like mist dissolving in rain.

Grace was standing by the window. The sun had set, but the glow of streetlamps was visible through the glass. It outlined Grace's hair, the curve of her cheekbones, the hollows at her temples. Had she always been standing there? She must have been—of course she had been. James's arm was braced against the back of the armchair. He felt dizzy. Maybe he was not as recovered as he had thought.

"James?" Grace came closer to him, the rustle of her green dress loud in the quiet room. "Will you help me? Will you destroy the automaton?"

James looked at her in astonishment. She was Grace—his Grace, who he loved and always had loved. "Loyalty binds me, Grace," he said in a low voice. "And even if it did not, I am yours and you are mine. I would do anything for you."

Something like pain flashed in her eyes; she glanced away. "You know I must still marry Charles."

James's mouth felt dry. He had forgotten. Grace marrying

Charles. Had she mentioned that when she'd come into the room? He no longer recalled.

"If I were to marry you—" She shook her head. "My mother would find ways to torment you and your family forever. She would never stop. I could not bring that down upon you."

"You don't love Charles."

She looked up at him. "Oh, James," she said. "No. No, I don't."

His father had always told him there was no higher emotion than love: that it trumped all doubt and all distrust.

He loved Grace.

He knew he did.

Grace slipped her hand into his. "We have no more time," she murmured. "Kiss me, James. Just once before you go."

She was so much smaller than he that he had to lift her into his arms to kiss her. She wrapped her arms around his neck, and for a flash as his lips touched hers he remembered soft lips that had fastened hungrily on his, a body arced against him, soft curves and tumbling hair. The maddening, shattering desire that had blinded him to everything but how Cordelia felt in his arms, to the sweet, soft heat of her.

Grace drew back. She kissed him lightly on the cheek. She was not in the least mussed as he set her down; Cordelia had been barefoot, her bodice tugged sideways, her hair come completely out of its pins. But that had all been pretense, he understood now. He and Cordelia had been performing for the sake of strangers who had come into the room. And if he had wanted Cordelia in that moment, then that was natural: physical desire was not love, and he was sure she had felt nothing for him. Cordelia was his friend; she had even asked him to help her find a husband.

"We will have to tell the Clave," he said. "Your mother cannot be left to practice black magic in freedom. Even if this automaton is destroyed, she will still have plotted to kill Shadowhunters. She might do so again."

Grace's smile faded. "But, James—" She searched his face for a moment, then nodded her head. "Wait until my engagement to Charles is formally announced. As soon as I am truly and safely away from my mother, the Clave can be told."

He felt a dull relief. He was about to kiss her again when there was a knock on the door. Grace withdrew her hand from James's, as he said, "Just a moment."

He was too late—the door had been flung wide, and Matthew stood on the threshold. Beside him was Cordelia, pretty in a kingfisher-blue gown and matching jacket, looking from James to Grace with wide, surprised eyes.

"I should go," Grace said. Her cheeks were flushed, but otherwise she looked perfectly composed. Cordelia couldn't help staring at her—she knew Lucie had encountered her on the grounds of Chiswick House, and that Lucie would not say more than that Grace had been eager for Thomas and Lucie to be gone.

Cordelia had not seen Grace together with James since the fight at Battersea Bridge. She had not thought it would hurt like this.

She had prepared carefully for this long-awaited visit. She had picked out one of her favorite new dresses in bright blue; she had worn her nicest gold earbobs, and she had brought with her a translated copy of *Layla and Majnun*. It was not as beautiful in English as it was in the original Persian, but it would be perfect for reading with James.

Now, as she stared at James and Grace, she was glad the book was hidden inside her jacket.

"Miss Blackthorn," Cordelia said, inclining her head politely. Beside her, Matthew stood stiffly. He said nothing as Grace murmured a goodbye and left the room, a cloud of tuberose scent trailing in her wake.

Cordelia told herself not to be foolish. Everyone else had apparently paid James a visit to see how he was, why not Grace?

"James," Matthew said, the moment Grace was gone. "Are you all right?"

James seemed a little stunned to see them. He was in shirtsleeves and a pair of pin-striped trousers; Cordelia could see the marks of fading bruises on his face and arms. A healing cut ran along his collarbone. His hair, a wild dark mess as always, tumbled into his eyes, and as always Cordelia fought the urge to push it back.

"I'm fine. Better even than fine," James said, rolling his sleeves down and fastening the cuffs. Cordelia caught a glimpse of silver gleaming on his wrist.

Grace's bracelet. Cordelia felt as if she were burning inside.

Matthew stared. "Has Grace ended things with my brother?"

"No." James's quick smile faded. "They are still marrying."

"Then perhaps she is planning to kill Charles?" said Matthew.

"Matthew, cease sounding hopeful at the prospect of homicide." Throwing open his wardrobe, James took out a gear jacket and flung it on. "She is not marrying Charles because she loves him. She is marrying him to free herself from her mother. She believes Charles's influence and power will protect her."

"But surely *you* could protect her," Cordelia said, in a low voice, unable to help herself.

If the remark made an impression on James, she could not tell. The Mask seemed back in full force. She could not read his face. "Tatiana wants Grace to make a powerful alliance," said James. "She may not be entirely pleased, but if Grace were to marry me, it would be war. Grace will not brook that." He did up the buttons on the jacket. "She has made me understand that everything she has done, she has done because she loves me. Now I must do something for her."

In the back of her head, Cordelia heard Alastair's voice. *Everything he does is so he and I can be together.*

Since they had returned home from Highgate, Alastair hadn't mentioned Charles or anything connected to him. He had spent most of his time at home, often in Cordelia's room as her leg healed, reading out loud to her from the day's newspapers. He did not go out at night. She and Alastair were certainly a pair, weren't they, Cordelia thought. Miserable in love.

"James," Matthew said tensely, "after what she did to you—you owe her nothing."

"It is not a debt," James said. "It is because I love her."

It was as if someone had taken a small, sharp knife to Cordelia's heart and sliced it into pieces that formed the shape of James's name. She could barely breathe; she heard his voice in her head, low and sweet:

Daisy, my angel.

Shaking his head, James stalked out of the room. After exchanging a single glance, Cordelia and Matthew followed. They hurried down the corridor after James, through the Institute, occasionally weaving to avoid colliding with furniture.

"What's going on?" Matthew demanded, avoiding a decorative suit of armor. "What did she ask you to do?"

"There is an object in Blackthorn Manor that must be destroyed," said James, and quickly told them the tale of Tatiana's madness, the clockwork automaton and the warlock spell that waited to animate it. That he must destroy it, while Grace did all she could to stay her mother's hand.

There was something different, not just in James's expression, but in the way he spoke. He had not said Grace's name with that intonation since she had become engaged to Charles. Cordelia's nails bit into her palm. She wanted to be sick; she wanted to scream. She knew she would do none of those things. *She did not yell out—no! she would have scorned to do it.*

"I am sure I am not the only one who fails to be astonished that

Tatiana Blackthorn has been dabbling in necromancy," said Matthew. "But we must tell the Clave."

James, taking the stairs two at a time, shook his head. "Not yet. I must do this first. I will explain more later, but we cannot destroy Grace's life."

They had reached the top of a set of stone steps, leading downward into deep shadow. Cordelia was half-relieved to see the same expression on Matthew's face that she was sure was on hers. Surprise and distress.

"So you're going to go to *Idris*?" Cordelia said. "How?"

"There's a Portal in the crypt," Matthew said tightly as the stairs ended with an entrance into an enormous stone room. It was not as dark as Cordelia had imagined: dim brass lamps gleamed on the walls, illuminating smooth stone walls and floors. "My father used to tinker with his experiments down here when he and my mother ran the Institute. Most of his work was moved to the laboratory in our home, but—"

He gestured toward a glowing square the size of a pier glass that adorned the far wall. Its surface rippled like water, alight with strange gleams.

"The Portal is still here," said James. "It was locked down during the quarantine, but no longer."

"It's still forbidden to Portal to Idris without permission from the Clave," said Matthew.

"And you've become fascinated with the Laws suddenly?" James smiled. "I'll be the one breaking the rules, anyway. It is a simple thing for me to do: go through, destroy the object, and return."

"You must be mad if you think that we're not coming with you," said Matthew.

James shook his head. "I need you to remain here to open the Portal for me so that I can return. Give me twenty minutes. I know my way around the house, and I know exactly where the thing is. Then open the Portal and I will come back through."

"I don't know if this is a wise idea," Cordelia said. "We've already stood and watched you disappear through one Portal, and look how that turned out—"

"We survived," James said. "We killed the Mandikhor and wounded Belial. Many would say it turned out very well." He moved to stand before the Portal. For a moment he was only a silhouette, a black shadow against the silvery surface behind him. "Wait for me," he said, and for the second time in a week, Cordelia watched as James Herondale vanished through a Portal in front of her eyes.

She glanced at Matthew. He gleamed like one of the brass fixtures on the wall in a bronze velvet jacket and trousers. He looked as if he was ready to return to the Hell Ruelle, not to stand watch in a crypt.

"You didn't try to stop him," she said.

Matthew shook his head. "Not this time," he said. "There seemed no point." He glanced at her. "I truly thought it was over. Even when Grace came by today, I thought he would send her away. That perhaps you had cured him of that particular disease."

The words landed like arrows. *I thought you had cured him.* She had thought the same thing, somehow—had let herself believe it, let herself hope that James offering to read a book with her was something more than an offer of friendship. She had read his eyes, his expressions, all wrong—how could she have been so mistaken? How could she have believed he felt anything like she felt when she *knew better?*

"Because of the Whispering Room? That truly was just pretense." The words sounded brittle to her own ears. It was not the truth—not for her, at least—but she would not be considered pitiable, not by Matthew or anyone else. "It was nothing else."

"I find that I am glad to hear that," Matthew said. His eyes were very dark, the green just a rim around the pupil as he looked at her. "Glad that you are not hurt. And glad—"

"I am not hurt. It's just that I don't understand," Cordelia said. Her voice seemed to echo off the walls. "James seems an entirely different person."

Matthew's mouth twisted in a bitter half smile. "He has been like this for years. Sometimes he is the James of my heart, the friend I have always loved. Sometimes he is behind a wall of glass and I cannot reach him no matter how I pound my fists against it."

The Mask, Cordelia thought. So Matthew saw it too.

"You must find me ridiculous," Matthew said. "*Parabatai* ought to be close, and in truth, I would not want to live in this world without James. Yet he tells me nothing of what he feels."

"I do not find you ridiculous, and I wish you would not say such things," Cordelia said. "Matthew, you may speak however badly of yourself as you like, but it does not make it true. *You* decide the truth about yourself. No one else. And the choice about what kind of person you will be is yours alone."

Matthew stared at her—for once, it seemed, speechless.

Cordelia stalked over to the Portal. "Do you know what Blackthorn Manor looks like?"

Matthew seemed to snap back to reality. "Of course," he said. "But it has been only ten minutes."

"I do not see why we must do as he says," said Cordelia. "Open the Portal, Matthew."

He looked at her for a long moment, and finally the corner of his mouth twitched up in a smile. "You are quite bossy for a girl whose nickname is Daisy," he said, and went over to the Portal. He placed his palm against the surface, and it shimmered like disturbed water. An image evolved slowly from the center: a great old stone pile of a manor house, set far back from a spreading green lawn.

The lawn was overgrown, the black iron gates before the manor thick with twisting briars. They were thrown open, and through the gap Cordelia could see the blank stone face of the house, inset with a dozen windows.

As she stared, one of the windows went up in orange flames. Then another. The sky above the manor house turned a dark, foreboding red.

Matthew swore.

"He's burning the house down, isn't he?" said Cordelia.

"Bloody Herondales," said Matthew, with a sort of epic despair. "I'll go through—"

"Not alone, you won't," said Cordelia, and picking up the skirts of her blue frock, she leaped through the open Portal.

Though Grace and Tatiana had left it only recently, Blackthorn Manor had the air of a place long abandoned. One of the side doors was unlocked, and James found himself in an empty front hall, lit only by the moonlight pouring in through the great windows. The floor was covered in a thick, feathery dust, and above him hung a chandelier, so roped about with spiderwebs it resembled a ball of gray yarn.

He passed through the empty hall in the quiet of the moonlight and up the sweeping curve of the staircase. As he reached the second floor an oily film of blackness dropped before him: the upstairs windows had been covered with thick black curtains, and no light escaped around their edges.

He lit his witchlight rune-stone; it illuminated the long-dusty passage stretching before him. As he made his way down it, his boots crunched unpleasantly on the floor, and he imagined himself crushing the dried bones of tiny animals as he walked.

At the end of the corridor, in front of a curved wall of covered windows, stood the metal creature: a towering monster of steel and copper. On the wall beside it, as he had recalled, hung a knight's sword with a wheel pommel, a rusty antique.

James took the sword down and, without a moment's hesitation, swung it.

It sheared through the torso of the clockwork monster, slicing it in half. The upper part of the body clanged to the ground. James drove down with the sword again, decapitating the creature; he felt half ridiculous, as if he were hacking an enormous tin can to pieces. But the other half of him was full of rage: rage against the meaningless bitterness that had consumed Tatiana Blackthorn, that had turned this house into a prison for Grace, that had turned Tatiana viciously against her own family and all the world.

He broke off, breathing heavily. The clockwork suit was a pile of scrap metal at his feet.

Stop, he told himself, and oddly, he saw Cordelia in his mind, felt her hand on his arm, steadying him. *Stop.*

He tossed the sword to the ground and turned to go; as he did, he heard a soft explosion.

The pile of shredded metal had caught fire and gone up as if it were tinder. James took a step back, staring, as the fire leaped up to catch at the spiderwebs stretched across the walls: they caught alight like burning lace. James jammed his witchlight back into his pocket; the corridor was already alive with gold and crimson, strange shadows shuddering against the walls. The smoke that rose from the smoldering drapes was thick and choking, emitting an acrid and terrible scent.

There was something hypnotic about the flames as they leaped from one set of drapes to another, like a bouquet being tossed down the corridor. If James stayed here, he would die on his knees, choking on the ashes of Tatiana Blackthorn's bitterness. He spun and made for the stairs.

* * *

Matthew didn't bother with an Open rune, just kicked the front door in and raced inside, Cordelia on his heels. The entryway was full of seething smoke.

Cordelia looked around in horror. She could see into a parlor with a high chimneypiece: it had probably once been a grand room but now was covered in dust and mold. A table hung with spiderwebs stood in the middle, still with plates set out: they were covered in rotted food, and mice and blackbeetles ran freely over the surface.

The floor was thickly coated in gray dust; a set of footprints wound up the stairs. Cordelia pointed and jostled Matthew's shoulder: "That way."

They started toward the steps: at the top they could see a roaring inferno. Cordelia gasped as James appeared from the heart of the flames, racing down the stairs. He flung himself over the banister as the top steps caught alight, landing in the center of the entryway. He stared incredulously at Cordelia and Matthew.

"What are you *doing* here?" he demanded over the roar of the fire.

"We came for you, idiot!" Matthew shouted.

"And how were you expecting to get *back*?"

"There's a Portal in the greenhouse here that connects to the greenhouse in Chiswick," Cordelia said. Grace had told her that; it felt like a million years ago. "We can return that way."

From somewhere deep within the manor came a deep, grinding noise, as of the bones of a giant crumbling to dust. Matthew's eyes rounded. "The house—"

"Is on fire! Yes, I *know!*" James shouted. "To the door, quickly!"

It was a short way back to the front entrance. They ran, their feet sending up puffs of dust. They had nearly reached the door— Matthew was over the threshold—when the nearest wall caved in.

Cordelia staggered back as a wave of hot air struck her; she saw a plaster-covered wooden beam break free of the wall and sweep toward her, heard Matthew shout her name, and then something struck her from the side. She rolled over in the dust, tangled up with James, as the beam hit the floor with immense force, shattering the parquet.

She choked, gasped, and looked up: James had knocked her out of the way of the falling timber. His body pinned hers to the floor. The color of his eyes matched the flames all around them; she felt his breath, short and sharp, as they stared almost blindly at each other.

"*James!*" Matthew shouted, and James blinked and got to his feet, reaching down to clasp Cordelia's hand. The blue of her dress glimmered as she rose, dotted with a thousand tiny glowing points of fire where sparks had landed.

It was not just her dress: everything was fire. In a daze, they raced for the front door, where Matthew stood; he had taken off his velvet jacket and was using it to beat out the flames consuming the threshold. James turned to lift Cordelia in his arms as if they were in some strange, fiery ballet, carrying her over the last burst of flames as they soared up and consumed the front doors of the manor.

The three of them staggered a good distance from the house into the weeds and scraggly grass of the gardens. At last they stopped, and James raised his head to stare at the manor house. It was burning merrily, sending up gouts of black smoke, turning the sky above it to the color of blood.

"You can put Cordelia down now," Matthew said, a touch of acid in his tone. He was panting, his hair full of soot, his velvet jacket abandoned.

James set Cordelia carefully on the ground. "Your leg . . . ?" he began.

She tried to push back a lock of her hair and found it full of ash. "It's all right. It's quite healed," she said. "Did you, ah . . ."

"Burn the house down? Not purposely," said James. His already black lashes were clogged with soot, his face streaked with black.

"It coincidentally burned down while you were in it?" grumbled Matthew.

"If I could explain—"

"You cannot." Matthew shook his head, scattering ash. "I am completely out of patience. The bank of patience is exhausted! I am not even being extended any patience on credit! You and I and Cordelia are going home, and once home, I will berate you at enormous length. Prepare yourself."

James hid a smile. "I shall do exactly that. Meanwhile, the greenhouse. We should not linger here."

Cordelia and Matthew fervently agreed. The three made their way to the greenhouse, which was empty save for a fallen-down grapevine, some bottles, and the Portal itself, which shone like a mirror, reflecting back the glaring red light of the fire.

James placed his hand on its surface. It shimmered, and Cordelia saw, as if at a distance, the Blackthorn house in Chiswick, and beyond that, the glittering skyline of London.

She stepped through.

The room at the Devil Tavern was cozy, a low fire burning in the grate—Cordelia had thought she might never want to see fire again, but she was pleased to have this one. The Merry Thieves were sprawled all about on the battered furniture: Christopher and Thomas on the old chesterfield sofa, James in an armchair, and Matthew in a seat at the round wooden table.

James had taken off his jacket, which had several burn holes in it, and his shirtsleeves were rolled up. They had all done what they could to clean up when they arrived at the tavern, but there was still soot on his collar, and in Matthew's and Cordelia's hair, and the kingfisher-blue dress was, Cordelia suspected, utterly ruined.

Matthew was turning a glass in his hand, looking thoughtfully at the pale amber contents.

"Matthew, you should really drink some water," said Christopher. "Alcohol won't help with the dehydration after you inhaled all that smoke."

Matthew raised an eyebrow. Christopher seemed undeterred—Cordelia had noticed when Christopher first came in that he seemed a little different: less shy and owlish, more assured.

"Water is the devil's brew," said Matthew.

Cordelia glanced at James, but he only said, "That is why you are always dyspeptic, Math." His expression was unreadable. The Mask had slipped briefly at Blackthorn Manor, she thought, when he had saved her life. It was back now.

She wondered if he was thinking of Grace. The pain in her chest had gone from a sharp pain to a dull throb that ached with every heartbeat.

Footsteps sounded on the steps and Lucie burst in, nearly staggering under the weight of a pile of clothes: two suits for James and Matthew, and a plain cotton dress for Cordelia.

She was greeted with a round of applause. When Cordelia, James, and Matthew had first stumbled out of the greenhouse in Chiswick, they had realized that not a one of them could return home in their singed state. Even Will would be apoplectic, James had to admit. "We have got to start keeping spare clothes at the Devil for such occurrences as this," James had said.

"There had better not be any more occurrences such as this," Matthew had glowered.

They had flagged down a hansom cab to Fleet Street, where they had been the recipients of many curious stares from patrons of the Devil Tavern. Matthew and Cordelia had taken refuge in the upstairs room, while James had tracked down a few of the Irregulars and sent them to Thomas and Christopher with messages saying to come immediately and bring new outfits for all three. Thomas and Christopher, unfortunately, had been unable to lay hands on anything: they had come running, but without any extra clothes. An Irregular had been dispatched immediately to Lucie, which, Cordelia pointed out, was what should have been undertaken in the first place. Lucie knew how to get things done.

Lucie dumped the clothes into her brother's lap and glared at him. "I cannot believe," she said, "that you burned down Blackthorn Manor without me!"

"But you weren't around, Luce," James protested. "You went to see Uncle Jem."

"It's true," Lucie said. "I just wish I had been with you. I never liked the manor when we were growing up. Besides, I've always wanted to burn down a house."

"I assure you," said James, "that it is overrated."

Lucie plucked the dress from James's lap and gestured for Cordelia to follow her into the adjoining bedroom. She set about helping Cordelia undo the hooks at the back of her blue dress. "I will mourn this one," said Lucie, as it crumpled to the floor in a charred heap, leaving Cordelia standing in her petticoat and combination. "It was so pretty."

"Do I smell like burnt toast?" Cordelia inquired.

"A bit, yes," Lucie said, handing Cordelia the cotton dress. "Try this. I borrowed it from my mother's wardrobe. A tea gown, so it ought to fit." She regarded Cordelia thoughtfully. "So. What happened? How did James come to burn down Blackthorn Manor?"

Cordelia told her the story as Lucie deftly helped brush the ash out of her hair and pin it back up in something resembling a passable style. When she was done with the tale, Lucie sighed.

"So it was at Grace's request," she said. "I thought—I hoped—well, never mind." She set the brush down on the vanity table.

"Grace is still marrying Charles, so it can only be hoped James will forget her."

"Yes," Cordelia said. She, too, had thought and hoped. She, too, had been wrong. The dull ache in her chest increased, as if she were missing a piece of herself, some vital organ she could barely breathe without. She could feel the hard shape of *Layla and Majnun* still secured under her jacket. Perhaps she should have thrown it into the flames of the manor.

They went back into the main room, where the Merry Thieves appeared to be arguing among themselves. Thomas had joined Matthew in brandy drinking; the other two had not.

"I still cannot believe you burned down a house," Thomas said, toasting James.

"Most of you never saw inside that house," said Lucie, perching herself on the edge of the sofa, near James. "I peeked in the windows when I was a little girl. All the rooms full of dry rot and blackbeetles, and the clocks all stopped at twenty to nine. No one will think it burned down for any reason save neglect."

"Is that what we're claiming?" asked Christopher. "To the Enclave, I mean. There is the meeting tomorrow to consider."

James templed his fingers under his chin. The bracelet on his right wrist gleamed. "I should be willing to confess to what I did, but I wish to leave Matthew and Cordelia out of it, and I cannot speak of the reason I went in the first place. It would be breaking my promise to Grace."

Christopher looked puzzled. "Then are we meant to invent a reason?"

"You could always say you burned it down to improve the view from Herondale Manor," said Matthew. "Or perhaps to raise the property value."

"Or you could claim to be an incorrigible pyromaniac," said Lucie cheerfully.

Thomas cleared his throat. "It seems to me," he said, "that many people will be harmed if you tell the story of what happened tonight. Whereas if you keep the story to yourselves, an evil old house full of dark magic items will have been destroyed, along with a dangerous automaton. I would strongly urge you not to say anything."

Matthew looked startled. "Really? Our True Thomas, who so often counsels honesty?"

Thomas shrugged. "Not in every situation. I do think the Clave will need to be told of Tatiana's dangerous proclivities eventually. But it seems the loss of Blackthorn Manor will leave her harmless for a while."

"Once Grace and Charles formally announce their engagement," said James quietly. "We can do it then."

"I am happy to keep silent for now," said Cordelia. "It was, after all, Grace's request, and we ought to protect her."

James shot her a grateful look. She glanced down, twisting the fabric of her gown between her fingers.

"It is a pity, actually, that no one will ever know how James, Cordelia, and Matthew are heroes for foiling a demonic plan to attack Idris," said Lucie.

"We will always know," said Thomas, and raised his glass. "To being secret heroes."

"To standing by each other no matter what," said Matthew, raising his own, and as they all cheered and toasted, Cordelia felt the iron band around her heart loosen, just a little.

22

THE RULES OF
ENGAGEMENT

"O 'Melia, my dear, this does everything crown!
Who could have supposed I should meet you in Town?
And whence such fair garments, such prosperity?"—
"O didn't you know I'd been ruined?" said she. . . .

—"I wish I had feathers, a fine sweeping gown,
And a delicate face, and could strut about Town!"—
"My dear—a raw country girl, such as you be,
Cannot quite expect that. You ain't ruined," said she.
—Thomas Hardy, "The Ruined Maid"

Cordelia had never attended a meeting of the entire Enclave
before. Her family had moved so frequently until this summer, and
she was still underage. Luckily, as many young Shadowhunters had
been directly involved with the incidents under discussion, the age
limit had been waived for the meeting. They had all jumped at the
chance to attend; Lucie had even brought her writing materials
with her, in case she was inspired.

The Sanctuary had been set up to be a meeting place, with rows
of chairs facing a lectern. Golden statues of Raziel were set in each

alcove, and Tessa had hung tapestries showing the crests of every London Shadowhunter family on the walls. James and Christopher had both been seated at the front of the room. Every chair was filled and many were standing; the room was stuffed to bursting. Cordelia had come with her family, but had split off from Alastair and Sona so she could sit with Lucie and Matthew.

Will Herondale stood up at the lectern, handsome in a gray coat and waistcoat with pin-striped trousers; he appeared to be having a friendly argument with Gabriel Lightwood as Tessa looked on. Inquisitor Bridgestock was not far away, glowering.

Lucie was quick to point out to Cordelia all those in attendance who had recovered from the poison: Ariadne Bridgestock was there, looking calm and very beautiful in a deep aubergine dress, with a matching bow in her dark hair. Cordelia could not help but remember Anna reaching for Ariadne's hand as Ariadne lay deathly still, her eyes swollen shut.

Please don't die.

Rosamund Wentworth was also there, as were Anna and Cecily Lightwood, who were playing with little Alexander at the edge of the dry fountain. Alexander appeared to be tossing something shiny and likely breakable into the air.

Sophie and Gideon Lightwood, freshly back from Idris, were smiling over at Cecily and little Alex, but Sophie's eyes were sad. Thomas and his sister Eugenia sat close by. Eugenia resembled a sharper version of Barbara: she was small but angular, with dusky hair upswept in a Gibson girl pompadour.

Seated at the very edge of the group of Shadowhunters, near Mrs. Bridgestock, was Tatiana Blackthorn, rigidly upright in her chair; she had not removed her hat, and the ornate stuffed bird atop it glared menacingly. She was thinner than ever, her hands tightly clenched in her lap, her face rigid with fury.

Grace sat some distance from her mother, beside Charles, who was chattering away in her ear. She and Tatiana did not look at each other. Cordelia knew from James that Grace had gone to stop her mother from taking desperate action the night before: it seemed to have worked, but she could not help but wonder what had happened between them—not to mention whether they knew yet of the fate of Blackthorn Manor.

The most surprising guest was Magnus Bane, sitting across the room with his legs elegantly crossed. He seemed to sense Cordelia looking at him and glanced over with a wink.

"I idolize him," said Matthew sorrowfully.

Lucie patted his hand. "I know."

Matthew looked amused; Cordelia sensed something had changed in his interactions with Lucie. She couldn't quite put a finger on it. It was as if a certain tension had gone out of them.

"Welcome, everyone." Will's voice echoed through the room; the lectern had been carved with runes to amplify his voice. "I've just received word that the Consul has been delayed but is on her way. It would be ideal if everyone could be patient a bit longer and refrain from breaking any of the valuable objects in the Sanctuary."

He shot a meaning glance at Cecily, who made a sisterly face at him.

"In the meantime—"

Will broke off in surprise as Charles joined him at the lectern. He wore a stiffly formal frock coat, his red hair slicked back and gleaming. "I'd just like to thank everyone for placing their trust in me as acting Consul," he said, his voice echoing off the walls. "As you all know, the antidote to this awful disease was developed in my father's laboratory at Grosvenor Square."

Cordelia glanced over at Alastair. To her pleased surprise, Alastair rolled his eyes. In fact, if Charles had been hoping for a round of applause, it did not come: the room was silent.

Charles cleared his throat. "But of course there are many

brave Shadowhunters who should be acknowledged, in addition to myself. Christopher Lightwood, of course, as well as Cordelia Carstairs and James Herondale."

Tatiana Blackthorn shot to her feet. The bird on her hat trembled, but in that moment she did not seem ridiculous, as she often did. She seemed menacing. "James Herondale is a fraud!" she cried in a hoarse voice. "He has ties to demons! No doubt he worked in concert with them to orchestrate these attacks!"

Lucie made a choking sound. A murmur of astonishment raced around the room. Inquisitor Bridgestock looked absolutely flabbergasted. Cordelia looked over at James: he sat frozen, utterly expressionless. Christopher had his hand on James's shoulder, but James had not moved.

Matthew's hands closed into fists. "How dare she—"

Tatiana seemed to tower over the crowd. "Deny it, boy!" she shouted at James. "Your grandfather was a demon."

Cordelia tried not to look at any of the Merry Thieves, or Lucie, either. Surely Tatiana couldn't know about Belial? Surely she was only repeating what the whole Clave was already aware of—that Tessa was a warlock, and therefore, James had demon blood.

James kicked his chair back and stood, turning to face the room. Behind him, Will and Tessa stood stunned; Tessa was gripping Will's shoulder, as if entreating him not to move. "I will not deny it," he said, in a voice that dripped contempt. "Everyone knows it. It is true, it has always been true, and no one here has tried to hide it."

"Don't you see?" Tatiana raged. "He conspired with the enemy! I have been collecting evidence of his plots—"

"Then where is that evidence?" demanded Will. He was flushed with anger. "Damn it, Tatiana—"

"It was in my house," she hissed. "In my house in Idris, I gathered it all, but then this boy, this demon's spawn, burned my house to the ground! Why else would he do that, save to protect his secret?"

Cordelia felt as if her heart had stopped. She dared not look at any of the others—not Lucie, or Matthew, or Thomas. She could not even look at James.

"Tatiana," Gabriel Lightwood said, rising to his feet, and Cordelia thought, *Of course, he is her brother*. "Tatiana, this makes no sense. Why have we heard nothing about this fire if it transpired? In fact, how do you know about it?"

Tatiana's face twisted with rage. "You've never believed in me, Gabriel. Even when we were children, you didn't believe anything I said. You know as well as I do that there is a Portal between Blackthorn Manor and Chiswick House. I went through this morning to get some papers and found the manor a smoldering heap of ash!"

It was Gideon's turn to rise up. Recent grief had cut deep lines into his face; the look he turned on his sister was flinty. "That bloody house was a firetrap because you refused to look after it. It was going to burn down eventually. It is very ill done for you to try to drag James into this, very ill done!"

"Enough! All of you!" shouted Bridgestock. He had moved to the lectern, and his voice echoed loudly through the room. "James Herondale, is there any truth to what Mrs. Blackthorn says?"

"Of course there isn't—" Will began.

Tatiana's voice rose to a scream. "He told Grace he did it. Ask *her* what James said!"

"Oh God," whispered Matthew. His hands gripped the arms of his chair, his fingers white. Lucie had dropped her pen and notebook: her hands were shaking.

Grace began to get to her feet. Her eyes were cast down. Someone in the crowd shouted that a trial by the Mortal Sword would clear things up; Tessa was still clutching Will, but looked sick to her stomach.

Cordelia chanced a look at James. He was the color of old ashes, his eyes blazing, his head thrown back. He would not defend himself, she thought. He would never explain.

And then there was Grace. What if Grace intended to tell the truth? Charles would throw her over just as he had done to Ariadne. He had no loyalty. She would be easy prey for her mother, then. She had so very much to lose.

"The fact is," Grace began, in a voice barely above a whisper, "the—the truth is that James—"

Cordelia bolted to her feet. "The truth is that James Herondale did *not* burn down Blackthorn Manor last night," she said, in a voice so loud she thought they could probably hear her on Fleet Street. "James cannot have been in Idris. He was with me. In my bedroom. *All night.*"

The gasp of shock that went around the room would almost have been satisfying, under other circumstances. Sona slumped against Alastair, burying her head in his chest. Heads whipped around; curious eyes fixed on Cordelia. Her heart beat like a trip-hammer. Anna gazed at her with a dumbfounded look. Will and Tessa seemed thunderstruck.

Matthew put his face in his hands.

Bridgestock was staring at Cordelia in amazement. "Are you quite sure about this, Miss Carstairs?"

Cordelia lifted her chin. She knew that she was compromised now, in the eyes of all the Enclave. More than compromised, she was ruined. She would never be married. She would be lucky if she was received at parties. Shadowhunters were less strict than mundanes about such matters, but a young woman who spent the night alone with a young man, in her bedroom no less, was not marriage material.

"Obviously, I am sure," she said. "Which aspect do you think I am confused about?"

Bridgestock flushed. Rosamund Wentworth looked as if today

had turned out to be her birthday. Cordelia did not dare glance at James.

Tatiana was spluttering. "Grace, tell them—"

In a clear voice, Grace said, "I'm sure Cordelia is correct. James must be innocent."

Tatiana screamed. It was a horrible sound, as if she had been stabbed. "No!" she wailed. "If it wasn't James, it was one of you!" She stabbed her finger at the crowd, identifying the Thieves. "Matthew Fairchild, Thomas Lightwood, Christopher Lightwood! One of them, one of them is responsible, I know it!"

Murmurs of speculation swept through the crowd. Bridgestock was calling out for order. As the chaos mounted, the front doors of the Sanctuary opened, and Charlotte Fairchild, the Consul, marched into the room.

She was a small woman, her dark brown hair gathered into a simple knot. There was gray at her temples. She wore a high-necked white blouse and a dark skirt; everything about her was neat and small, from her boots to her gold-rimmed spectacles. "I'm sorry to arrive late," she said, in the practiced tone of someone used to pitching her voice loudly to be heard over a room full of men. "I was planning to be here earlier, but I was required to remain in Idris in order to investigate a fire that claimed Blackthorn Manor last night."

"I told you! I told you they did it!" Tatiana cried.

Charlotte pressed her lips together. "Mrs. Blackthorn, I spent several hours with a group of Alicante guards, picking through the wreckage of your home. There were many items present that were associated with and imbued with necromantic magic and demonic magic, both of which are forbidden to Shadowhunters."

Tatiana's face folded up like old paper. "I had to have those things!" she wailed, in a voice like a broken child's. "I had to use those things, I had to have them, for Jesse—my son died and none of you would help me! He died, and none of you would help me bring him back!" She gazed around the room with wet, hateful eyes. "Grace, why won't you help me?" she shrieked, and crumpled to the floor.

Grace picked her way across the room to Tatiana. She laid a hand on her adoptive mother's shoulder, but her face was stony. Cordelia could see no sympathy in it for Tatiana's plight.

"I can confirm what Charlotte says." It was Magnus Bane, who had gotten gracefully to his feet. "In January Mrs. Blackthorn attempted to hire me to help bring her son back from the dead. I declined, but saw much evidence of her dedication to the study of the necromantic arts. What many would call *black magic*. I should have said something then, but my heart was wrung with pity. Many wish to bring back their beloved dead. Few ever get very far." He sighed. "When such objects fall into the hands of the untutored, it can be dangerous. Certainly that explains the tragic and entirely accidental fire that destroyed Mrs. Blackthorn's manor house."

There were yet more exclamations among the crowd. "Laying it on a bit thick, isn't he?" Lucie murmured.

"Hardly matters—as long as the Clave believes it," Matthew said.

Will inclined his head to Magnus; Cordelia had the feeling that there was a friendship there that went back a long way. Amid the uproar, Charlotte gestured at Inquisitor Bridgestock to take Tatiana into custody.

A hand fell on Cordelia's shoulder. She looked up and saw James. Everything inside her chest seemed to tighten up, as if her heart were contracting. He was pale, two spots of color burning on his cheeks.

"Cordelia," he said. "I need to talk to you. Right now."

* * *

James slammed the door of the drawing room shut behind him and spun to face Cordelia. His hair actually seemed to have exploded, she thought, with a sort of bleak amusement. It was sticking out darkly in all directions.

"You cannot do this to yourself, Daisy," he said, with a cold desperation. "You must take it back."

"There is no taking it back," she said, as James paced in front of the fireplace. There was no fire lit, but the room was not chilly: outside the sun shone brightly, and the world went about its business on a bright London day.

"Cordelia," James said. "You will be ruined."

"I know that." A cold calm had descended upon her. "That is why I said what I said, James. I needed to be believed, and no one would believe that I would say such a terrible thing about myself unless it was true."

He stopped pacing. The look he bent on her was agonized, as if he were being pierced by a thousand small daggers. "Is this because I saved your life?" he whispered.

"You mean last night? At the manor?"

He nodded.

"Oh, James." She felt suddenly very weary. "No. It was not that. Do you think I could sit by and watch myself acclaimed a hero while you were made a villain? I don't care what they think of my honor. I know you, and your friends, and what you would do for each other. I am also your friend, and I know what I think honor is. Let me do this."

"Daisy," he said, and she realized with a sort of shock that the Mask was off—his expression was starkly vulnerable. "I can't bear it. To have your life ruined by this? Let's go back now and tell them I did it—I burned down the house—and you were lying to shield me."

Cordelia set her hand against a chair, upholstered in pale blue and the back carved with crossed swords, to hold herself steady.

"Nobody will believe it," she said, dropping each word into the silence between them like stones into a pond. She saw him flinch. "When it comes to a woman's reputation, if she is suspected, she is guilty. That is the way the world works. I knew they would believe I was guilty, and now, no matter what we say, they'll never believe I was innocent. It's done, James. It doesn't matter so very much. I needn't stay in London. I can go back to the country."

As she spoke, she knew that was how it must be. She was not Anna, able to live a wild bohemian lifestyle with her family's support. She must go back to Cirenworth, where she talked to mirrors for companionship. She would drown slowly in loneliness, and there would be no dream of London to live on: no Devil Tavern, no battling demons alongside Lucie, no laughing late into the night with the Thieves.

James's eyes blazed. "Absolutely not," he said. "And let Lucie's heart be broken because she's lost her *parabatai*? Let you live a secluded life of disgrace? I will not accept that."

"I cannot regret my choice," Cordelia said softly. "I would do the same again. And there is nothing either of us can do about it now, James."

He could not make the world fair, any more than she could. It was only in stories that heroes were rewarded; in real life, acts of heroism went unrewarded, or were punished, and the world turned on as it always had.

He might be angry, but he was safe. She wasn't sorry.

"I can ask one last thing of you," he said. "One last sacrifice for me."

Since it might be the last time she ever saw him, Cordelia let her eyes linger on James's face. The curve of his mouth, the arch of his high cheekbones, the long lashes that shadowed his pale gold eyes. That faint mark of the white star on his neck, just where his dark hair nearly touched his collar. "What?" Cordelia said. "If it is in my power, I will do it."

He took a step toward her. She could see that his hands were shaking slightly. A moment later he was kneeling on the rug in front of her, his head tipped back, his eyes fixed on her face. She realized what he was about to do and lifted her hands to protest, but it was already too late.

"Daisy," he said. "Will you marry me?"

The world seemed to stop. She thought of the clocks in Blackthorn Manor, all frozen at twenty to nine. She thought of the thousand times she had imagined James saying these words, but never under these circumstances. Never like this.

"James," she said. "You don't love me."

He rose to his feet. He was no longer kneeling, and she was glad for it, but he was still close to her—so close to her she could have reached out and set her palm against his chest.

"No," he said. "I don't."

She knew that. Hearing him say it still felt like a blow, unexpected and shocking, like the moment when you were stabbed. The surprise was how much it hurt.

Distantly, she could still hear him talking.

"Not in that way, and you don't love me that way either," James continued.

Oh, James. So brilliantly clever and so blind.

"But we are friends, aren't we?" he said. "You are one of the best friends I've ever had. I will not leave you in trouble alone."

"You love Grace," Cordelia whispered. "Don't you?"

She saw him flinch then. It was her turn to hurt him. They were only talking, but it was as if their words were blades.

"Grace is marrying someone else," James said. "I am perfectly free to marry you." He caught her hand, and she let him: she felt dizzy, as if she were clinging to the mast of a storm-tossed ship.

"I also do not want a situation in which my husband is unfaithful to me," Cordelia said. "I will not marry you and turn some blind eye to whatever you do, James. I would rather be alone and scorned, and you would rather be free—"

"Daisy," James said. "I would never, ever do that to you. When I make a promise, I keep it."

She shook her head. "I don't understand what you're proposing—"

"A year," he said rapidly. "Give me a year to make things right. Let us be married and live together as friends. We are exceptionally compatible, Daisy. It might well be a great deal of fun. I promise I will be better breakfast-table company than Alastair."

Cordelia blinked. "A *mariage blanc*?" she said slowly. "White marriages" usually took place when one partner needed to marry to claim an inheritance, or to protect a woman against a dangerous situation in her home. There were other reasons too. Charles was seeking something very like this with Grace, she thought; it was hard to miss the irony.

"Divorce is far more accepted among Shadowhunters than among mundanes," said James. "In a year, you may divorce me for any reason you like. Claim I cannot give you children. Say anything you want about how we are not compatible and I will go along with it. Then you will be a desirable divorcée with your honor intact. You could marry again."

The relief and hope in his eyes were agony to see. And yet—

Cordelia could not say she did not want it. If they were married, they would live together. They would have their own house. An untold level of intimacy. They would go to sleep in the same place and wake in the same place. It would be a life lived in the guise of everything she had ever desired.

"But what about our friends?" she whispered. "We cannot hide the truth from them for a year. Besides, they know I was lying. They know you burned down the manor."

"We will tell them the truth," said James. "They will keep our secret. They may even find it a great prank on the Clave. And they'll be delighted to have a whole house to disport themselves in. We shall have to guard our china."

"Lucie as well," Cordelia said. "I cannot lie to my *parabatai*."

"Of course," James said, beginning to smile. "Our friends love us and will keep our secrets. Are we agreed? Or shall I go back on my knees?"

"No!" Cordelia said sharply. "Do not go on your knees, James. I will marry you, but don't go on your knees."

"Of course," he said, and the understanding in his eyes cracked what was left of her heart. "You wish to save such things for the true marriage you will find after this. Love *will* find you, Daisy. It is only a year."

"Yes," she said. "Only a year."

He drew off the Herondale ring, with its pattern of soaring birds. She held out her hand, and James slid it onto her finger without hesitation. Cordelia watched as he did it, watched the fall of his long lashes against his cheek, like black ink against a white page.

Love will find you.

Love had found her years ago, and now, and every day since she had first seen James in London. *You don't love me,* he'd said to her. He had no idea. He never would.

The door opened. Cordelia started, and Will came through the door, his face like thunder. Tessa followed him, more sedately, and Sona came after her. All wore expressions of grim fury. Well, perhaps not Tessa—she looked more worried, Cordelia thought, and more resigned.

"Tatiana has been taken into custody by Bridgestock and the Consul," Will announced, his blue eyes icy. "Under other circumstances, this would be a great relief, considering her false accusations against you, James."

James held up a hand. "Father, I understand why you are angry, but—"

"James." Will snapped the word like a whip. There was more than anger in his eyes, though—there was a deep hurt that made Cordelia want to cringe. She could only imagine the pain James was feeling. "I can't express how disappointed Tessa and I are in you. We have taught you better than this, both in how you treat women, and in how you own up to your mistakes."

"Oh, Layla," Sona said. Her gaze was bleak. *"Che kar kardi?"*
What have you done?

"Enough!" James moved protectively in front of Cordelia, but Cordelia stepped forward to stand next to him. They should face trouble side by side. If their agreement meant nothing else, it should mean that.

"Father," said James. "Mother. Mrs. Carstairs. I will hear anything you have to say, and apologize for all that I have done wrong, but first let me present to you my promised wife."

The three adults exchanged surprised glances. "You mean . . ." Tessa began.

James smiled. He actually looked quite happy, Cordelia thought, but she could sense the Mask going up again, like a sheet of glass. She saw the way Tessa looked at James and wondered if she sensed it too. "Cordelia has done me the honor of agreeing to marry me."

Cordelia held out her hand, on which the Herondale ring gleamed. "We are both," she said, "very happy, and we hope you will be happy too."

She glanced at her mother. To her surprise, Sona's eyes were troubled. *But I did as you wished,* Mâmân, she cried out silently. *I made a good marriage.*

Both Will and Tessa were looking at Sona, as if waiting for her reaction.

Cordelia's mother exhaled slowly and straightened, her dark eyes passing from Cordelia to James. *"Cheshmet roshan,"* she said, and inclined her head toward Will and Tessa. "I have given my blessing."

A broad smile spread across Will's face. "Then we have no choice but to give our blessing too. Cordelia Carstairs," he said, "the Carstairs and the Herondales will be bonded even more closely now. If James could have chosen his wife from all the women in all the worlds that are or ever were, I would wish for no other."

Tessa laughed. "Will! You cannot compliment our new daughter only on the chance of her last name!"

Will was grinning like a boy. "Wait until I tell Jem—"

The door burst open, and Lucie spilled in. "I was just listening at the door," she announced, with no shame whatsoever. "Daisy! You are to be my sister!"

She raced to Cordelia and embraced her. Alastair came into the room, too—quiet, but smiling when Cordelia looked at him. It was so close to the joyous scene Cordelia had always dreamed of. She had only to try to forget that Will might have wished for her to join his family, but if James had been free to choose, he would have chosen someone else.

It was only later that night that Cordelia learned what had happened to Tatiana, from Alastair—who, she assumed, had heard the story from Charles.

Tatiana had been shown relative leniency. It was the general opinion of the Enclave that the death of her son had broken her mind, and that though what she had done in response—sought out the help of dark warlocks to engage with her in necromancy and dark magic—was reprehensible, she had been maddened by grief. They all recalled the loss of Jesse and pitied her; rather than be locked up in the Silent City, or have her Marks stripped, Tatiana would be sent to live with the Iron Sisters in the Adamant Citadel.

Almost prison, but not quite, as Alastair described it.

Grace would move in with the Bridgestocks. Apparently Ariadne had insisted; Alastair theorized that it was also a way for the Bridge-stocks to save face and make it look as if Ariadne and Charles's engagement had been dissolved amicably.

"How odd," said Cordelia. She wondered why Ariadne had made such a demand. Even if she didn't want to marry Charles, why would she want to live with Grace? Then again, Cordelia suspected there was more to pretty Ariadne Bridgestock than met the eye.

"There is more," Alastair said. He was sitting at the foot of his sister's bed. Cordelia was propped against her pillows, brushing out her long hair. "Our father is to be released."

"*Released?*" Cordelia sat bolt upright, her heart pounding. "What do you mean?"

"The charges against him have been resolved," said Alastair, "the whole messy business deemed an accident. He will be return-ing to London in a fortnight."

"Why would they let him go free, Alastair?"

He smiled at her, though his eyes did not light up. "Because of you, just as you wanted. You did it, Cordelia—you are a hero now. That changes things. For them to try your father for a crime of negligence he no longer remembers—it would be an unpopular gesture. People want to see things set right, after so much loss and horror. They want to see families reunited. Even more so because of the baby."

"How do they know about the baby?"

Alastair's eyes darted away from hers—his tell, the small sign that he was lying, which he had displayed since he was a small child. "I don't know. Someone must have told them."

Cordelia could not speak. It was all she had wanted, for so long. Free her father, save her family. It had been her mantra, the words she had chanted over and over to herself as she fell asleep at night. Now she did not know how she felt.

"Alastair," she whispered, "the reason I went to the Silent City with Matthew and James was to talk to Cousin Jem. I know *Mâmân* wanted Father to go to the Basilias as a patient. I thought perhaps if we told the Clave of his sickness—and it is a sickness—they might let him be treated there instead of imprisoned."

"Ah, by the Angel, Cordelia." Alastair covered his eyes with his hands for a long moment. When he dropped them, his dark eyes were troubled. "You would have been all right with that? With everyone knowing about his drinking?"

"As I said to you before, Alastair. It is not our shame. It is his."

Alastair sighed. "I don't know. Father always refused to go to the Basilias. He said he disliked the Silent Brothers, but I think he was always worried they would see through him to the truth. I imagine that is why he always kept Cousin Jem away from our family." He took a deep breath. "If what you want is for him to go to the Basilias, you should write to him and tell him so. You were the last of the family who did not know his secret. That you do now might well make a difference."

Cordelia set her hairbrush down, relief coursing through her at last. "That is a good idea. Alastair—"

"Are you happy, Layla?" he said. He pointed to the Herondale ring on her hand. "I know that is what you wanted."

"I thought you might be angry," she said. "You were so furious with James when you thought he was trying to compromise me."

"I did not think at the time that he would be willing to marry you," Alastair said apologetically. "But he has stood up and claimed you in front of the world. That is a gesture that is meaningful. Don't let anyone tell you otherwise."

She almost wanted to tell Alastair the truth—that James was sacrificing more than he guessed—but she could not, any more than she could tell her mother. He would be angry; Sona would be crushed. "I have what I wanted," she said, unable to bring herself to say that she was happy, "but what of you, Alastair? What of your happiness?"

He glanced down at his hands. When he looked back up at her, his smile was crooked. "Love is complicated," he said. "Isn't it?"

"I know I love you, Alastair," Cordelia said. "I should not have eavesdropped on you and Charles. I have only ever wanted you to talk to me, not to overhear you."

Alastair flushed and rose to his feet, avoiding her eyes. "You should sleep, Layla," he said. "You've had an eventful day. And I have an important matter to attend to."

Cordelia leaned forward to glimpse him as he left the room. "What kind of important matter?"

He ducked his head back into the room with a rare grin. "My hair," he said, and vanished before she could ask him anything else.

23

No One Who Loves

Let no one who loves be called altogether unhappy.
Even love unreturned has its rainbow.
—J. M. Barrie, *The Little Minister*

Lucie could not help but be impressed, despite her conviction that it was wrong to be impressed by one's parents. Her mother had thrown together the traditional engagement party for James and Cordelia at a moment's notice, but it was so lovely one would have guessed she had spent weeks planning it. The ballroom was bright with festive witchlights and candles, the walls hung about with ribbons in wedding gilt. Lace-draped tables bore plates of sweets, all in the theme of yellow and gold: iced lemon pastries stuffed with cream, cut-glass dishes of crystallized fruit, bonbons in fancy gold wrappings on an epergne, yellow plum and apricot tartlets. There were tumbling arrangements of flowers in urns on pillars around the ballroom: peonies, creamy camellias, sheaves of tall yellow gladioli, sprays of mimosa, pale gold roses and daffodils. The room was full of happy people—the quarantine was over, and everyone wanted to gather and gossip and congratulate Will and Tessa on the happiness of their offspring.

Yet Tessa, even as she slipped an arm around Will's waist and smiled at Ida Rosewain, who had arrived in a simply enormous hat, looked worried. Lucie guessed most people wouldn't see it, but she was a trained observer of her mother's moods, and besides—she was worried herself.

She should have been filled with delight. Her brother and her closest friend were to be married. This was a moment to be happy ever after. But she knew the truth—both James and Cordelia had told her—that the marriage was a sham, a formality to save Cordelia's reputation. Tessa and Will did not know, nor did anyone want to tell them. Let them think James would be happy with Cordelia. Let them think it was all real. Lucie wished she thought it was real herself, and if that could not be the case, she wished she had someone to talk to about it. The Merry Thieves had all decided to treat the marriage as if it were a lark on James's part, and she could hardly voice her worries to Cordelia and make her feel even worse than she surely did already.

Perhaps life was not like books. Perhaps life was never going to be like that. Her brother, elegant in black and white, had joined her parents in greeting guests. Gabriel and Cecily had just arrived with Anna, Alexander, and Christopher and distributed embraces and congratulations; Thomas had already come with his family. The Fairchilds had also arrived earlier, Matthew breaking away immediately from his family to make a beeline for the games room. Meanwhile, Charles was wandering around shaking hands and generally taking credit for the end of the attacks. The sound of carriages rattling into the courtyard made its own sort of odd music as the room began to fill up: the Bridgestocks arrived, Ariadne thin but bright-eyed—and with them, Grace Blackthorn.

Lucie tugged anxiously at the locket around her throat. Grace was lovely as new spring in a pale green dress, her silver-blond hair caught up in a waterfall of curls. Having seen Chiswick House up close, Lucie wondered again that Grace always seemed so splendidly turned out when she lived in a large pile of dirty bricks.

Well, she *had* lived there. She lived with the Bridgestocks now, and would until her marriage to Charles. This was not a celebration for Grace, Lucie thought, looking at the other girl's pale face as she greeted Will and Tessa. James was perfectly composed, both he and Grace almost painfully polite as he received her congratulations. Did Grace *mind*? Lucie wondered. She was the one who had broken it off with James—she was marrying Charles—and Lucie did not want to forgive her for breaking James's heart.

And yet. She watched Grace excuse herself and walk stiffly across the room toward Charles. They greeted each other like strangers or business partners, she thought. Oh, how she wished she could talk to Jesse. Perhaps he would be able to tell her how his sister was really feeling. Perhaps he would be able to tell her more than that—

"She's here," whispered a voice in Lucie's ear. "The guest of honor."

"Cordelia, you mean?" Lucie turned to see Jessamine hovering just beside her near the tall French doors that led out onto the stone balcony. Through them, she could see an electric streetlight in the distance, casting a strange halo on the glass. Jessamine, though, cast no reflection.

"She looks lovely," Jessamine said. She gave a mysterious smile and vanished in the direction of the dessert table. Ghosts could not eat, but Jessamine still enjoyed looking at cakes.

Cordelia did look lovely. She came in with her mother and brother, Sona looking darkly regal in a green dress and black velvet *roosari*, Alastair—well, Lucie hardly noticed Alastair until he handed his hat to the maid and she realized he'd dyed his hair back to its natural black. It stood out strikingly against the brown of his skin.

And then there was Cordelia, arrayed in a tapering gown of

deep blue silk and golden tulle, sleeves ruched and an opalescent brooch gathering together silk and gauze in a rosette between her breasts. Risa had dressed her hair with pearls winking among the dark red strands.

James took her hands and kissed her cheek. Both he and Cordelia looked aware of how many people were staring at them and probably whispering. Cordelia's announcement at the Enclave meeting, though it had led to marriage, remained the shock of the season.

Annoyed on their behalf, Lucie began to make her way across the room toward her family. She was headed off by Thomas, carrying their little cousin Alexander. Aunt Cecily and Uncle Gabriel had clearly palmed Alexander off on Thomas while they devoted themselves to party preparation. It was rather sweet to see tall, muscular Thomas carefully carrying a child, though Lucie would never tell him so lest he get a swelled head.

"Luce," Thomas said. "I must go greet Cordelia and Alastair. Could you take this awful brat?"

"Not a brat," said Alexander, who was sucking a piece of licorice.

"I *could*," Lucie acknowledged. "I don't particularly want to, though."

"Matthew," demanded Alexander darkly. Matthew was his favorite pseudo-relative. "*Oscar.*"

"I don't think Oscar was invited, old chap," said Thomas. "What with him being a dog."

"I think you'd better go look for Matthew," said Lucie, as Alexander appeared to be about to slump into despair. Thomas gave her a wry salute and headed into the crowd, which had only grown. Lucie saw with some delight that Magnus Bane had appeared, dressed rather like a pirate, with ruby buttons on his waistcoat and ruby jewels in his ears. He definitely raised the tone of the party.

She was halfway across the room when Charles, wobbling a bit as if he'd had too much to drink, climbed up onto a low bench and tapped his family ring against his glass. "Excuse me!" he called, as the noise in the room began to quiet. "I've something I'd like to say."

The Herondales had been so immediately kind, welcoming Cordelia to their family. She did not know how to look them in the face, knowing it was all a lie. She was not Will and Tessa's new daughter. She and James would be divorced in a year.

James was being horrifically kind too. In the time since the engagement, Cordelia had convinced herself she had somehow trapped him into marriage. She knew perfectly well that if she hadn't thrown her reputation away to protect him, he'd be in the prisons of the Silent City. He'd been obliged to propose after that.

He did smile at her whenever he looked at her—that lovely smile that seemed to say she was a miracle or a revelation. But it didn't help; James had a good heart, that was all. He didn't love her, and that would not change.

To her immense shock, Alastair had been a great support through the past few days. He'd brought her tea, told her jokes, played chess with her, and generally kept her mind off things. They had talked very little about Elias's return. She didn't think he'd left her alone in the house at all—not even to go see Charles.

Speaking of which, Charles had climbed on a bench and was calling out that he had something to say, creating a racket that quickly got the attention of the room. Everyone looked immensely surprised, including Tessa and Will. Sona frowned, clearly thinking Charles was very rude. She didn't know the half of it, Cordelia thought darkly.

"Let me be the first to raise a glass to the happy couple!" said Charles, doing just that. "To James Herondale and Cordelia Carstairs. I wish to add personally that James, my brother's *parabatai*, has always been like a younger brother to me."

"A younger brother he accused of vandalizing greenhouses across our fair nation," muttered Will.

"As for Cordelia Carstairs—how to describe her?" Charles went on.

"Especially when one has not bothered to get to know her at all," murmured James.

"She is both beautiful *and* fair," said Charles, leaving Cordelia to wonder what the difference was, "as well as being brave. I am sure she will make James as happy as my lovely Grace makes me." He smiled at Grace, who stood quietly near him, her face a mask. "That's right. I am formally announcing my intention to wed Grace Blackthorn. You will all be invited, of course."

Cordelia glanced over at Alastair; he was expressionless, but his hands, jammed into his pockets, were fists. James had narrowed his eyes.

Charles went on merrily. "And lastly, my thanks go out to the folk of the Enclave, who supported my actions as acting Consul through our recent troubles. I am young to have borne so much responsibility, but what could I say when duty called? Only this. I am honored by the trust of my mother, the love of my bride-to-be, and the belief of my people—"

"Thank you, Charles!" James had appeared at Charles's side and done something rather ingenious with his feet that caused the bench Charles had been standing on to tip over. He caught Charles around the shoulder as he slid to the floor, clapping him on the back. Cordelia doubted most people in the room had noticed anything amiss. "What an excellent speech!"

Magnus Bane, looking fiendishly amused, snapped his fingers. The loops of golden ribbons dangling from the chandeliers formed the shapes of soaring herons while "For He's a Jolly Good Fellow" began to play in ghostly fashion on the unmanned piano. James hustled Charles away from the bench he had clambered onto and into a crowd of well-wishers. The room, as a whole, seemed relieved.

"We have raised a fine son, my darling," Will said, kissing Tessa on the cheek. He glanced over at Cordelia and smiled. "And we could ask for no lovelier girl to be his wife."

Alastair looked as if he wished to edge away. Cordelia didn't blame him. "Thank you, Mr. Herondale," she said. "I hope to live up to your expectations."

Tessa looked surprised. "Why would you ever worry about that?"

"Cordelia worries," Alastair said unexpectedly, "because of the idiots who mutter about our father, and our family. She should not let them bother her."

Tessa laid a gentle hand on Cordelia's shoulder. "The cruel will always spread rumors," she said. "And others who take pleasure in that cruelty will believe them and spread them. But I believe that in the end, truth wins out. Besides," she added with a smile, "the most interesting women are always the most whispered about."

"Very true!" said Charles, appearing suddenly in their midst. Alastair started violently. "Might I speak to Alastair for a moment? It's a private matter."

He took hold of Alastair by the elbow and began to lead him toward one of the more shadowy nooks in the ballroom. Alastair's hand shot out and seized hold of Cordelia's wrist. To her immense surprise, she found herself dragged along after the two of them.

When Charles stopped and turned to face Alastair, he looked as surprised as Cordelia felt. "Ah, Cordelia," he said, looking puzzled. "I had hoped to speak to your brother alone."

"No," Alastair said, startling Cordelia. "She will remain."

"*Che kar mikoni?*" Cordelia hissed. "Alastair, *what* are you doing? I should go—"

"I do not wish to speak to you alone, Charles," Alastair went on. "Surely you got my letter."

Charles flushed. "I did not think you meant it."

"I did," said Alastair. "Anything further you have to say can be said in front of my sister. She will tell no one your secrets."

Charles seemed to resign himself. "Very well," he said tightly. "I haven't seen you since the meeting. I came by your house, but Risa indicated that you weren't at home."

"I do not plan to be at home to you ever again," said Alastair evenly.

Cordelia attempted another break for freedom, but Alastair was still clamped firmly onto her wrist. "I should have left you when you became engaged to Ariadne," he said to Charles, color flaming in his cheeks. "I should have left when you abandoned her in such a terrible way. Now you are engaged yet again, and I have realized that you will never care half as much for me—or for anyone—as for your career."

His grip on Cordelia had loosened. She could have left, had she wanted to, but in that moment she realized Alastair needed her there. She stayed, even as Charles went a grayish color.

"Alastair," he said. "That is not true. There is no other way."

"There are other ways," said Alastair. "Look at Anna. Look at Magnus Bane."

"I am not a bohemian, willing to be exiled to the fringes of society. I wish to be the Consul. To be part of the Clave. To *matter*."

The sound Alastair made was half pain, half exhaustion. "And you can have whatever you wish, Charles. You just cannot also have me. I wish to live my life, not to hide in the shadows as you engage yourself to a series of women in an attempt to conceal who you really are. If you choose that for yourself, it is your choice, but you cannot choose for me."

"That is all you have to say to me, then? After these years? Surely that cannot be all," Charles said, and in that moment he was not ridiculous, as he had been when he was toasting himself. There was genuine grief in his eyes, Cordelia thought. In his way, he loved Alastair.

But it was not enough. Some kinds of love weren't.

"Good luck, Charles," Alastair said. His dark eyes shone. "I am sure you will have a very successful life."

He walked away. Cordelia, left suddenly and awkwardly alone with Charles, hastened to follow her brother.

"You must not know what to make of that conversation," Charles said, his voice stiff and overbright, as she turned to go.

She hesitated, not looking at him. "I know you hurt my brother," she said at last. "I know you will not do it again."

"I will not," Charles said very quietly. He said nothing more as she made her escape.

James stood on the balcony outside the ballroom. It was a long stone affair, with chest-high railings; it had not existed when his father was a young man but had been added during the refurbishments to the Institute. Both his parents had a fondness for balconies.

It was almost like being up on the roof and far away, but being outside was not having its usual calming effect on him. The air tasted like London, as it always did, and he could see, in the distance, the shapes of houses rising up against the gap of the Thames. He thought of its deep brown-black waters, the color of the smoke in Belial's realm. His stiff white shirtfront scratched against the stone of the balcony as he leaned forward, wishing he could ease the pressure on his chest.

It was not that he was dreading marrying Cordelia. He was not dreading it, and he wondered if he ought to be. When he thought of marriage to her, he imagined a warm room, a fire in the grate, a chessboard or a pack of cards laid out. Fog pressing against the windows, but the light inside the room gleaming off rows of books in English and Persian. He thought of her soft voice as he fell asleep, reading to him in a language he did not yet know.

He told himself he was being a fool. It would be awkward and strange, a peculiar dance they would do for each other's sakes to last out the year until they would be free. Still, when he closed his eyes—

"James."

He knew who she was before he turned around; he always knew her voice. Grace stood behind him, half in shadow, the French doors closing behind her. Through them he could see golden banners and hear music.

"Magnus Bane has got the piano working somehow," Grace said in her low voice, "and people are dancing."

James gripped the stone railing of the balcony, staring out toward the city. He had not seen Grace since the Enclave meeting, nor had he sent her any kind of message. It would have felt disloyal to Cordelia. "It is probably better if we don't speak to each other, you know."

"This may be our only chance to speak alone again," Grace said. When he did not reply, she said, with a catch in her voice, "It seems the Angel does not want us to be together, doesn't it? First I could not break things off with Charles because of my mother. Then, the moment I was free of her, you became engaged to Cordelia."

"Do not say her name," James said, startling even himself with his vehemence. He bowed his head, tasting rain and metal. "She is the kindest person—"

"I know what she did for you, James," said Grace quietly. "I know you weren't with her that night. You were in Idris, burning down Blackthorn Manor. I know she told that lie to shield you. I wouldn't have thought she had such cunning in her, really."

"It is not cunning. It is generosity," said James. "A waste of a year of her life on a marriage she cannot want, just to protect me."

"A year?" said Grace. "Is that the arrangement between you?"

"I will not discuss this with you," James said. His chest hurt as if it were being compressed. He could barely get enough air.

"You must hate me," Grace said, "if all this is to protect you from the consequences of what *I* asked you to do."

"I do not blame you, Grace. But we cannot be friends. It will make it harder than it already is."

There was a pause. She was in shadow, but he had seen her in the ballroom, in her green dress with emeralds in her ears. He had recognized the earrings. They had been Charlotte's. She must have given them to Charles as a gift for Grace.

"I am glad you will have Cordelia," Grace said.

"I wish I could say the same to you about Charles," said James. "Cordelia deserves better than this; I will do everything I can in this next year to make her happy. I hope Charles does the same for you."

"I could be with you in a year," she said, her voice almost a whisper. "A long engagement with Charles, you divorce Cordelia— it could be done."

James said nothing. The tightness in his chest had become pain. He felt as if he were being torn in two, brutally and literally.

"James?" Grace said.

He fought back the words: *Yes, wait for me, I will wait for you. Grace. I remember the forest, the shadows, your ivory dress.*

Grace.

He could taste blood in his mouth. He was gripping the railing so hard he thought his fingers might break.

A moment later James heard the soft click of the French door opening and closing. He held himself still for a long minute, and then another. When he turned at last, he was alone on the balcony. There was no sign of Grace.

Instead, through the glass, he saw Cordelia. She was dancing with Matthew. Her glorious hair was spilling free of its bandeau, defying all attempts to confine it. They were both laughing.

* * *

Expertly skirting the couples on the dance floor, Anna sighed: she wanted to be enjoying herself much more than she was. Though she had long ago given up believing in romantic love, she still enjoyed an engagement party, especially when she liked the people who were getting engaged, which admittedly didn't happen all that often.

Tonight was different. Many of her favorite people in the Enclave were here: the Merry Thieves, various aunts and uncles and extended family members, and—like an especially gaudy bonbon atop an already gilded cake—Magnus Bane. He had been very helpful in setting up wards around her family's house the day Christopher had been attacked. She owed him a favor, but she didn't mind that: she was sure it would be very entertaining when he came to collect. Still, there were two things nagging at her. Although James was one of her favorite cousins, and she very much liked Cordelia, there was something suspicious about this sudden engagement.

Anna had known since the ball welcoming the Carstairs family to London that Cordelia was hopelessly in love with James, and James was hopelessly in love with Grace Blackthorn. She had observed it, noted it, and determined that she would invite Cordelia to tea. Hopeless love was a dreadful state. Perhaps she could talk the girl out of it.

She had realized soon enough that Cordelia was tough and stubborn—and that she, Anna, liked her very much. Enough to fervently wish that James would wake up and see what was standing right in front of him. She had thought the dresses might help—and been quite gratified by the stunned look on James's face when he'd seen Cordelia dance at the Hell Ruelle. In fact, Anna might almost have *believed* James had realized Cordelia was the girl for him—after all, Grace had become engaged to Charles, so that was off the table—had it not been for Cordelia's sudden announcement at the Enclave meeting.

There were many things Anna knew she excelled at, and one

of them was being a judge of character. Cordelia Carstairs, who blushed at the sight of a seductive gown, was not going to spend the night with a man she was not married to, even if he was the love of her life. Nor would James compromise an unmarried girl. Anna would bet her flat on Percy Street on it.

As she slipped through the door at the end of the room, Anna glanced back to see Matthew and Cordelia dancing together. Cordelia looked amused, which was not surprising: Matthew made everyone laugh. She could not see Matthew's face, though there was something in the way he leaned over Cordelia that unsettled Anna. She could not have put a name to it.

Will had come out onto the dance floor; everyone was all smiles as he cut in to dance with Cordelia. Poor Cordelia, Anna thought: it was a Shadowhunter tradition to dance with a prospective bride for good luck. Cordelia wouldn't get a moment to herself. She looked happy enough to be dancing with her future father-in-law, at least, as Matthew went off to talk to Thomas.

Matthew had also seemed happy as he'd danced, Anna thought, making her way down the hall to the games room. Hopefully he was coming out of the years-long funk he'd been in—she had been worried. The Merry Thieves were like little brothers to her, and Matthew had always been her companion in scrapes and adventures.

The games room was in shadow. Anna liked it here: it was an unfussy room, without ribbons or rosettes or gilt. The chess set her father had given Will gleamed in the moonlight streaming through the window. It spilled like pale fire over the polished floor and the young woman standing in the middle of the room.

Ariadne Bridgestock.

Ariadne was the second thing that had been nagging at Anna all night. A dozen times now, she had wanted to ask Ariadne if she was well, if she had recovered, and a dozen times she had held herself back. If beauty were a measure of wellness, Ariadne would be the healthiest person at the party. Her dark hair gleamed, her soft brown skin looked like silk, and her lips were full and red. The first lips Anna had ever kissed. The first she had loved.

"I am sorry," Anna said, with a slight, formal bow. "I didn't realize you were here."

She turned to go, but Ariadne hastened across the room to her, holding out a hand. "Anna, please. I want to talk to you."

Anna paused, staring at the door. Her heart beat loudly in her ears. She cursed herself quietly; she should be long past feeling this way. So foolish. So young. *I am Anna Lightwood,* she told herself. *Nothing touches me.*

"I heard you," Ariadne said softly.

Anna turned to stare at her. "What?"

"I heard you when you came to the infirmary," Ariadne said, "and asked me not to die."

Shocked, Anna said, "So—you heard about Charles's betrayal from *me?*"

Ariadne waved that away, her slim gold bracelets chiming like bells. "It barely mattered to me at all. The only thing that mattered was the realization that you still have love in your heart for me."

Anna put her hand to the pendant at her throat. Her mother had given it to her when she had been mourning Ariadne's loss. The first and last time Anna had let anyone break her heart.

"I've realized that I was wrong," said Ariadne.

"To become engaged to Charles?" Anna said. She remembered, two years ago, finding Charles at the Bridgestocks' house when she had come with flowers in her hand for Ariadne. How the Bridgestocks had smiled when he kissed Ariadne's hand, even as Anna was ushered out of the room. "There are better men, if marriage is what you insist on."

"No," said Ariadne. "I was wrong about myself and you. Wrong about what I wanted." She clasped her hands together. "What I said years ago, some of it is still true. I do not wish to hurt my parents. I do want to have children. But none of that matters if I do not have love in my life." She smiled wistfully. "You have made quite a name for yourself, Anna, as someone who does not believe in love."

Anna spoke coldly. "Indeed. I think that romantic love is the cause of all the pain and suffering in this world."

The silk of Ariadne's dress rustled as she moved. A moment later she was beside Anna, leaning up on her toes to brush her lips against Anna's cheek. When she drew back, her dark eyes were shining. "I know you are strong-willed, Anna Lightwood, but I am just as strong-willed. I will change your mind. I will win you back."

She gathered her skirts and strode from the room, the scent of her orange-blossom perfume lingering behind her like smoke on the air.

"You don't mind dancing with an old man like myself?" Will said, expertly turning Cordelia about the floor.

She smiled. Will did not have the air of an old man about him— there was something of a boy's mischief in the way he smiled. Strange that neither Jem nor Tessa had aged since the Clockwork War, yet both seemed older and more serious than Will Herondale did. "Not at all," she said. "For many years, when we were growing up, both Alastair and I wished we saw more of you and Mrs. Herondale. We thought of you as an aunt and uncle of sorts."

"Now that you will be so close, and we will in truth be family, many opportunities present themselves," said Will. "A celebration party, perhaps, when your father comes home."

Cordelia blanched. She was sure her father would want nothing of the kind; he would want to forget he had ever been away, because he would not wish to remember why.

Will ducked his head to look at her more closely. "Or we can always arrange nothing, if you prefer. Nothing is my favorite thing to arrange. It takes so little effort."

Cordelia smiled wanly.

Will sighed. "I joke around a great deal," he said. "It is one way in which I manage life in a complex world. But I sense you are not entirely happy about your father coming home."

"It is, as you say, complex," said Cordelia. She was faintly aware that the other dancers were looking at them, probably wondering what they were discussing so intently.

"I loved my father when I was a child," said Will. "I thought he was the best man I'd ever known. Then when I discovered he had squandered all our money at the gaming tables, I thought he was the worst man I'd ever known. Now that I am myself a father, I know that he was simply a man."

Cordelia looked up at him. "Thank you," she said. She wanted to tell Will Herondale that she appreciated his honesty. She wondered how much he knew, or guessed, about her father: surely there were rumors. She wished she could be honest in return about her marriage to James. Surely Will must have noticed that James had hardly spoken to her tonight—at this, their engagement party?

"Daisy?"

Cordelia and Will stopped dancing; she saw with surprise that James had come up to them on the parquet dance floor. The jet and ivory of evening wear perfectly suited his sort of looks, she thought, already a beauty of contrasts, black and white and gold.

"Daisy?" he said, again, shyly, and Cordelia barely noticed Will step away from her. She only saw James's outstretched hand. "Would you like to dance?"

They looked remarkably happy, Lucie thought. She would not have found it odd, save that she knew the truth: still, James and Cordelia *were* good friends. As she watched, Cordelia laughed at something James said, and he reached to tuck a loose bit of hair back under her bandeau. Perhaps the Merry Thieves had been right—perhaps the two of them, her best friend and her brother, would find a way to make it all a sort of frolic?

"What are you thinking, Luce?" said Thomas, who was leaning against the wall of the ballroom, tie loosened. He had nobly danced several dances with Esme Hardcastle before retreating to the safety of the corner near the refreshments table. Matthew had joined him there, as had Lucie. "You're gazing very thoughtfully at Jamie and Cordelia."

"I was thinking she makes him a better dancer," said Lucie.

Matthew cocked his head to the side. "By the Angel," he said. "Marriage. Did you know James asked me to be his *suggenes*?"

In Shadowhunter marriage ceremonies, your *suggenes* was the one who escorted you down the aisle. You could pick anyone in your life—mother, father, brother, best friend. "Well, that's not odd," Lucie said. "*Parabatai* almost always pick each other."

"It does make one feel very grown-up," said Matthew. He was drinking from the flask in his hand, which to Lucie was not a good sign. Usually at parties where spirits were provided, Matthew would be seen with a wineglass in hand. If he were getting his "drain of pale" from his flask, he must be very determined indeed to be as drunk as possible. His eyes were glittering too, rather dangerously. Perhaps he was angry at Charles? Angry at his parents for accepting Charles's marriage to Grace so easily? Though how could they know? Lucie wondered, glancing at Henry and Charlotte where they sat at a table at the far end of the room. Henry's Bath chair stood sentry against the wall and the Consul and her husband leaned together, talking softly, their hands entwined. "Although," he added, his eyes narrowing as he gazed past Thomas, "not grown-up enough to put up with *that*."

Lucie looked over and saw Alastair Carstairs moving through

the crowd toward them. His shoulders were slightly hunched, and his once-again dark hair made him look like a different person.

"Be polite to him, Matthew," said Thomas, straightening. "He was a great help to me when I needed to make the antidote."

"Has anyone tried the lemon tarts?" said Alastair lightly, as he arrived among their group. "You have an excellent cook, Lucie."

Lucie blinked. Matthew set his jaw. "Do not try to make small talk, Alastair," he said. "It gives me a headache."

"Matthew," said Thomas severely. "Do you need to go sit down?"

Matthew shoved his flask back into his jacket with shaking hands. "I do not," he said. "I need Carstairs to leave us alone. Tonight is difficult enough—"

There was no chance for Lucie to ask why tonight might be difficult, for Alastair had already cut in. He seemed half-annoyed and half-abashed, his voice even but tense. "Can we not put our schooldays behind us?" he said. "If I admit I was a cad, is that enough? How can I apologize?"

"You cannot," said Matthew, his voice very strange, and they all looked at him. Lucie had the odd sense she was watching someone balanced on a knife's edge; Matthew seemed all sharp angles in that moment, as if he were made of daggers beneath the skin. "Do not think you are our friend now, or welcome among us, regardless of all that has happened."

Thomas frowned. "Matthew," he said, his usually gentle voice remonstrative, "that was the past. It is time for us to be adults and forget childish slights."

"Thomas, you are kind," said Matthew. "Too kind, and you wish to forget. But I am not kind, and I cannot help but remember."

The light had gone from Alastair's eyes. Yet he did not, to Lucie's surprise, look angry. He looked almost resigned. "Let him say what he wants to say, Thomas."

"You have no right to talk to Thomas in that familiar way," said

Matthew. "I never told this to you, Thomas. I couldn't bear to. But better that you know the truth than that you allow this snake to befriend you."

"Matthew—" Thomas began impatiently.

"Do you know what he used to say at school?" Matthew said. "That my mother and your father were lovers. That I was your father's bastard. He told me that Henry was only half a man and couldn't father children, and therefore Gideon had stepped into the breach. He said that your mother was so hideously ugly because of her scarred face that no one could blame your father for looking elsewhere. And that you were a sickly, ugly little thing because you had inherited her weakness of constitution—because she had been a mundane, but not just a mundane. A servant and a whore."

Matthew stopped on a sort of gasp, as if even he could not quite believe what he had just said. Thomas stood stock-still, the color draining from his face. Alastair had not moved either. It was Lucie who said, to her own surprise, "*He* was the source of that awful rumor? Alastair?"

"Not—not the source," Alastair said, his voice sounding as if he were forcing it through a tight throat. "And I did not say all of those things to Matthew—"

"But you did say them to others," Matthew said icily. "I have heard all about it in the years since."

"Yes," Alastair admitted flatly. "I did spread the story. I repeated—those words. I did do that." He turned to Thomas. "I am—"

"Don't say you are sorry." Thomas's lips were gray. "You think I have not heard that tale? Of course I have, though Matthew may have tried to protect me. I have heard my mother weep over it, my father incoherent with rage and sorrow, my sisters crushed with shame over *lies*—" He broke off, breathless. "You repeated those words without knowing or caring if they were true. How could you?"

"They were just words," said Alastair. "I did not think—"

"You are not who I thought you were," Thomas said, each word cold and sharp. "Matthew is right. This is your sister's engagement party, and for Cordelia's sake, we will mind our manners toward you, Carstairs. But if you come near me or speak to me at any point after this, I will knock you into the Thames."

Lucie had never in her life heard Thomas speak so icily. Alastair backed away, his expression stunned. Then he turned on his heel and darted into the crowd.

Lucie heard Matthew murmur something to Thomas, but she did not stay to hear what: she was already racing after Alastair. He ran like there were wings on his feet, and she bolted after him: through the ballroom doors, down the stone steps, finally catching up to him in the entryway. "Alastair, wait!" she cried.

He spun around to look at her and she realized to her shock that he had been crying. In a strange way, she was reminded of the first time she had ever seen a man cry: the day her father had found out his parents were dead.

Alastair dashed the tears furiously from his eyes. "What do you want?"

Lucie was almost relieved to hear him sound so much himself. "You can't leave."

"What?" he sneered. "Don't you hate me too?"

"It doesn't matter what I think. This is Cordelia's engagement party. You are her brother. It will break her heart if you vanish, and so I say you will not go."

He swallowed hard. "Tell Layla—tell Cordelia that I have a bad headache and am resting in our carriage. There is no need for her to rush or spoil her evening."

"Alastair—"

But he was gone, out into the night. Lucie turned back toward the stairs, dispirited. At least Alastair wasn't leaving the Institute, but she would have preferred—

She jumped. Standing in a niche among the shadows was Grace, her pale green dress almost luminous in the dimness. She grimaced when she saw Lucie. "I suppose it looks as if I have been eavesdropping," she said. "I assure you, however, I had no desire to overhear any of *that*."

Lucie put her fists on her hips. "Then why were you here?"

"I was already on the steps," said Grace. "I heard you galumphing down and decided it would be preferable to hide than to engage in conversation."

"You were leaving," said Lucie. "Weren't you?"

Grace said nothing. She was standing very upright, not leaning against the wall. Lucie recalled something that James had said to her once, about Tatiana forcing Grace to walk back and forth in the parlor of Blackthorn Manor with a book balanced on her head to perfect her posture.

"You know," Lucie said, feeling very weary, "you don't *have* to marry Charles."

Grace rolled her eyes. "Please don't worry yourself. I am not impatient to be gone because of some excess of hurt feelings. And don't bother telling me James doesn't really want to marry Cordelia; I know that, too."

Lucie froze. "I would never have said that."

"No," said Grace. "I suppose *you* wouldn't."

Lucie blew out an exasperated breath. "I know you think we have nothing in common," she said. "But I am the only other person in the world who knows about your brother. Who knows the secret you're protecting."

Grace went still. "You saw Jesse in Idris," she said. "I spoke with him. I know that he told you not to help him, and I know that you Herondales are *honorable*." She practically spat the word. "If he asked you not to help him, you won't. What use do you imagine I have for yet another person who won't help my family?"

Lucie raised her chin. "That shows how well you know me, Miss Blackthorn. I have every intention of doing all I can to help Jesse—whether he wants me to or not."

Grace stepped forward, out of the shadows. Her green earbobs danced in the light, like the jeweled eyes of cats. "In that case," she said, "do tell me more."

It did not take Magnus long to find Matthew Fairchild, leaning against the wall near the door to the withdrawing room, his necktie entirely undone.

Magnus stood a moment, looking at him: Matthew was exactly the sort of person Magnus always wanted to help, and later scolded himself roundly for having tried to help. In Magnus's life there had been a hundred Matthew Fairchilds: young men and women as self-destructive as they were beautiful, who despite all the gifts that had been given to them, seemed to wish for no more than to burn down their own lives. He told himself over and over that the Matthew Fairchilds of this world could not be saved, and yet he could not stop himself from trying.

He leaned against the wall next to Matthew. He wondered why Matthew had chosen to stand here, half-hidden from the rest of the room by a pillar. He seemed to be staring rather blankly at the dance floor.

"I have always heard," Magnus said, "that it was rude for a gentleman to be a wallflower."

"Then you must also have heard that I am generally considered to be very rude," said Matthew. There was a flask in his right hand, and a ring with the insignia of the Fairchilds sparkled on his finger.

Magnus had long observed to himself that a man who brought his own drink to a party where drinks were provided was indeed in a sorry state. But the real question was, he thought, why no one else seemed to notice that Matthew was only standing up because the wall was holding him.

Ordinarily, it would not have struck Magnus as particularly strange—getting tipsy at a party was nothing unusual for a boy of seventeen—but Matthew had been drunk when they were at Tower Bridge as well, though a less expert eye than Magnus's might never have spotted it. A less expert eye might not spot it now. It wasn't the drinking, Magnus thought, so much as the fact that Matthew was clearly practiced at pretending he had *not* been drinking.

Magnus said mildly, "I had thought that I might be an exception, since you said you admired my waistcoats."

Matthew did not answer. He was still looking at the dance floor—though not just the crowd of dancers themselves, but rather a specific couple. Cordelia Carstairs and James Herondale.

Another Carstairs binding themselves to another Herondale. Magnus had been amused when he'd heard about the engagement. He thought he recalled James having muttered about some other girl to him the first time they'd met, but Romeo himself had once thought himself in love with a girl named Rosalind. It was clear from the way James and Cordelia looked at each other that this was a love match. It was also clear why Matthew was standing where he was—from this vantage point, there was a perfect view of James and Cordelia, his dark head bent over her fiery one, their faces close together.

Magnus cleared his throat. "I see why my waistcoats cannot hold your attention, Fairchild. I've been where you are. Wanting what you can't have will only rip your heart apart."

Matthew spoke in a low voice. "It would be one thing if James loved her. I would go into the quiet dark like Jem did and never speak of her again. But he doesn't love her."

"What?" Magnus was unpleasantly startled.

"This is a false marriage," said Matthew. "It's only for a year."

Magnus tucked the information away as a mystery to be solved: it did not go along with what he knew of the Herondales, father or son. "And yet," Magnus said, "during that year, they are man and wife."

Matthew looked up, his green eyes flashing. "And during that year, I will do nothing. What kind of person do you think I am?"

"I think," said Magnus, very slowly, "that you are a person who is incredibly sad, although I don't know why. And I think that, as an immortal, I can tell you that a great deal can happen in a year."

Matthew did not reply. He was watching Cordelia and James. Everyone in the room was. They were dancing close together, and Magnus would have cheerfully bet a thousand pounds that they were in love.

A bet, it seemed, he would have lost. And yet.

Oh, dear, Magnus thought. *I may need to linger in London a bit longer.*

Perhaps I should send for my cat.

It was as if no time had passed since Cordelia's first ball in London, and yet everything had changed.

She felt a million miles from the anxious girl who had come to London desperate to make friends and allies, who had seen in every face a stranger. Now she had friends—a richness of friends: she could see Anna, at the entrance to the ballroom, speaking cheerfully to Christopher. There was Thomas, seated with his sister, and Matthew, beside Magnus Bane. And Lucie, her Lucie, who would one day stand with her in the blazing circles of the *parabatai* ceremony.

"Daisy," said James, with a smile. It was a real smile, though she could not quite tell if he was happy or sad or something in between. "What are you thinking?"

One thing had not changed: her heart still beat too fast when she danced with James.

"I was thinking," she said, "it must be strange to you, that Belial's realm was destroyed."

One dark eyebrow flicked upward, a flourish of ink across a page. "What do you mean?"

"It was a place only you could see," she said. "That only you could go. Now it is gone. It is like an enemy that you have known a long time. Even if you hated it, it must be strange to think of never seeing it again."

"No one else has understood that." James was looking at her with a gentle, puzzling tenderness, the Mask entirely gone now. He drew her closer to him. "We must think of this as an adventure, Daisy."

She could feel his heart beat against her own. "Think of what as an adventure?"

"Being married," James said fiercely. "I know you gave up a great deal for me, and I never want you to regret it. We will live together as the best of friends. I will help you train for your *parabatai* ceremony. I will defend and support you, always. You need never be lonely. I will always be there."

His lips brushed her cheek.

"Remember how well we did in the Whispering Room," James whispered, and she shivered at the feeling of his warm breath against her skin. "We fooled them all."

We fooled them. So it had been as she feared, despite what he had said—and perhaps believed—at the time: it had been real to her, but not to him. A strange and bitter pleasure.

"I suppose," James said, "I am saying that I know this is an odd experience—but I hope you can be at least a little bit happy, Daisy."

His hair was tumbling over his forehead. Cordelia recalled the thousand times she had wanted to push it back from his face. This time, she did, reaching up to brush it away from his eyes.

She smiled a smile as false as it was bright. "I am," she said, "a little bit happy."

The dimple flashed in his cheek. "I'm glad to hear it," he said, and drew her closer for the next step in the dance.

She remembered the ball, when he had left her on the floor and walked to Grace. He would not do that now; he was too honorable. She had him, for this year—a year of bitter joy. She would have her father back as well. She would stay in London and be *parabatai* with Lucie. She had everything she had wanted, and yet none of it the way she had imagined.

She thought of what James had said about faerie fruit: that the more you had of it, the more you wanted, and the more you ached when it was gone. And yet, was not knowing what it was like to taste it not also a form of torment?

She loved James; she always would. So many people loved without hope of return, without the dream of a touch or a glance from the object of their affection. They pined away in silence and misery like mortals starving for faerie fruit.

What fate was offering her now was a year of such fruit for her table. A year of living with James and loving him might ruin her for any other love, but oh, at least she would blaze up in glory. For a year she would share his life. They would walk together, read together, eat together, and live together. They would laugh together. For a year, she would stand close to the fire and know what it was like to burn.

Epilogue
CHISWICK HOUSE,
LONDON

Not far from the lights of London, Nephilim guards had escorted
Tatiana to Chiswick House, its gates and lanes choked and rendered
almost impassable with thorns. Briars clawed sunlight from every
window, preventing the guards—who included her brothers, Gabriel
and Gideon—from seeing inside as Tatiana gathered her things and
reappeared at the front door of the house, a small brown valise in hand.

She looked down at them from the top of the stairs. "I would
like to be allowed to go one more time to the garden," she said. She
did not think the hatred she felt for them showed on her face. They
did not seem to know it; they never had understood how much they
deserved her loathing. "To bid goodbye to the memories of my husband and my father."

A sort of spasm seemed to cross Gabriel's face. Gideon put a
hand on his brother's shoulder. They never had respected their
father properly. Never had mourned him after they let Will Herondale and Jem Carstairs murder him.

Gideon nodded. "Go ahead," he said, with a short nod. "We will
await you here."

Herondales, Tatiana thought as she made her way to the Italian gardens. Tainted blood ran in their veins. In her opinion, their name dominated the history books more than it should. There should be far more instances of the name "Lightwood" and less of the name "Herondale." After all, she wouldn't be surprised if Will Herondale's warlock wife wasn't the first time they'd sullied the line with Downworlder blood.

She had reached the small, walled structure in the center of the garden. The door was unlocked—she cursed Grace silently: *stupid, lazy girl*—and she hurried inside to see if any damage had been done. To her relief, Jesse's coffin was pristine: the wood glowing, the glass untouched by dust. The ancient Blackthorn sword that would one day be her son's hung gleaming on the wall.

She laid a hand on the surface. There lay her boy, her sleeping prince. He resembled her husband, in her opinion. Rupert had possessed such fine bones, such delicacy and perfection of feature and form. The day he had been torn from this world had been a tragedy. She had stopped every clock in this house and the country manor at the time they had taken his body away, for then her world had ended.

Save for Jesse. She lived for Jesse now, and for revenge.

"Worry not," said a silken voice.

Tatiana knew who had spoken before she glanced up.

He was a swirl of dust at first, a handful of glittering sand that re-formed into the shape of a beautiful man clothed in gray, with eyes like shards of mirrors.

"Grace will look after him," Tatiana said. "She cares for her brother like you care for no one."

"I will let no harm come to Jesse," said the Prince of Hell. "What he carries is too precious."

Tatiana knew he was not truly there, that Belial could not walk upon the earth save as an illusion of himself. Still, he was bright as broken glass, bright as cities burning. They said Lucifer was the most beautiful angel who had ever lost Heaven, but Tatiana did not believe that. There could be no angel more beautiful than Belial, for he was ever-changing. He had a thousand shapes.

"Why should I believe that?" she demanded. "You let me sicken from that poison, and I could have died. You promised me that only my enemies would be harmed. And look"—she threw her arm out in the direction of the courtyard where Gideon and Gabriel waited for her—"they *still live!*"

"I would never have let you die," said Belial. "It was necessary to keep suspicion from falling upon you. What I did, I did in order to save you."

Bitterness roughened her voice. "Save me for what? That I may languish in prison while my enemies flourish?"

Belial laid his hands on Jesse's coffin. His fingers were long, like a spider's legs. "We have discussed this before, Tatiana. The death of Barbara was my gift to you, but it was only the beginning. What we have in mind for the Herondales and Lightwoods and Carstairs is so much greater and more terrible than simple death."

"But your plan to raise James Herondale up in darkness seems to have failed. Even after I prepared him for you—"

For just a moment, Belial's expression lost its composure, and in that space Tatiana seemed able to see down through the abyss into the visible darkness of the Pit. "You *prepared* him?" he sneered. "When he came to me in my realm, there was no bracelet on his wrist. He was *protected*."

Tatiana blanched. "That's not possible. It was on his wrist at the meeting today. I saw it!"

A smirk passed over Belial's face, but vanished quickly. "That was not all. You did not tell me that the Carstairs girl bears one of the blades of Wayland the Smith."

He opened his jacket. There on his chest was a wound, a bloody tear in the fabric of his shirt through which dark red blood seeped. A wound that seemed fresh and unhealed. Though Tatiana knew he was not really here in a solid form, not really bleeding, the sight was still disturbing. One should not be able to wound a Prince of Hell.

She took a step back. "I—I didn't think it important. The girl seems like nothing—"

"Then you do not understand what Cortana is. As long as she bears that sword, and protects James, I will not be able to come near him." Belial snapped his jacket closed. "Those fools believe that since I have been wounded by that blade, I will not be able to return to their world for a century's time. They do not know I have an anchor here. Nor do they understand the power of my wrath." He bared his teeth, and each was a sharp, filed point. "They will see my return sooner than they think."

Tatiana knew she should dread the rage of a Prince of Hell, but there could be no fear when you had already lost everything that mattered. Her lip curled back. "I suppose you will be facing that return alone, as I will be imprisoned in the Adamant Citadel." She touched Jesse's coffin, a sob rising in her throat. "And my beautiful boy will languish without me."

"Oh Tatiana, my dark swan," Belial murmured, and now he was smiling. "Don't you see this is the culmination of my plan? The Herondales, the Lightwoods, the Enclave, all of them have blocked you from their seats of power. But where does the heart of the Nephilim lie? It lies in their gift from the angel, the *adamas*. The steles that draw their runes, the seraph blades that protect them."

She looked up at him, realization dawning. "You mean—"

"No one can break into the Adamant Citadel," he said. "But you will be escorted in, my dear. And then you will strike at the Clave from its very heart. We will strike together."

With her hand braced upon the coffin of her son, Tatiana began to smile.

Notes on the Text

Most of the places in the London of *Chain of Gold* are real: there *was* a Devil Tavern on Fleet Street and Chancery, where Samuel Pepys and Dr. Samuel Johnson drank. Though it was demolished in 1787, I like to think it lived on as a Downworlder haunt, invisible to mundanes. The poem Cordelia recites when she is dancing in the Hell Ruelle is from Sir Richard Francis Burton's *The Book of the Thousand Nights and a Night*, published in 1885. The Dick Whittington stone is real, and located at the foot of Highgate Hill. *Layla and Majnun* (ليلى و مجنون) is an epic poem in Persian/Farsi, written in 1188 by the poet Nizami Ganjavi. I have used the exonym "Persian" to refer to the language Cordelia and her family speak throughout, as Cordelia and Alastair did not grow up in Iran and "Persian" was the way anyone speaking or thinking in English in 1903 would have thought of the language. I'd also like to take this moment to thank Tomedes Translation and Fariba Kooklan for help with the Persian in this book. The excerpts of *Layla and Majnun* are taken from James Atkinson's 1836 translation, which is the one most likely for Cordelia to have owned.

Turn the page to read

Fairy Tale of London,

A BONUS STORY FEATURING

WILL AND TESSA.

———◆———

Will Herondale sat in the window of his new bedroom and looked out at a London frozen under a chilly winter sky. Snow dusted the tops of houses reaching away toward the pale ribbon of the Thames, giving the view the feeling of a fairy tale.

Though, at the moment, Will was not feeling very friendly toward fairy tales.

He ought to be happy, he knew that much—after all, it was his wedding day. And he had been happy, since the moment he'd woken up, even through having Henry, Gabriel, and Gideon troop into his room and bother him with advice and jokes while he was getting dressed, all the way up to the end of the ceremony. That was when it had happened. That was why he was sitting on a window seat staring at winter-bitten London instead of downstairs by the fire kissing his wife. His brand-new wife.

Tessa.

Everything had started out perfectly well. It wasn't strictly a Shadow-hunter wedding, because Tessa wasn't strictly a Shadowhunter. But Will had decided to wear wedding gear anyway, because he was going to be the head of the London Institute, and his children would be Shadowhunters, and Tessa would run the Institute by his side and be part of all of his Shadowhunter life and they should begin as they meant to go on, in his opinion.

Henry, wielding a stele from his Bath chair, helped Will with the runes of Love and Luck that decorated his hands and arms before Will put his shirt and gear jacket on. Gideon and Gabriel joked about what a terrible bargain Tessa was getting in Will, and how they would happily take his place, though the Lightwood broth-ers were both engaged, and Henry was delightedly married with a small and loudly screaming son, Charles Buford, currently taking up much of his parents' time and attention.

And Will smiled and laughed, and looked in the mirror to make sure his hair didn't look disgraceful, and he thought of Jem, and his heart ached.

It was tradition for Shadowhunters to have a *suggenes*, someone who walked alongside them up the aisle to the marriage ceremony. Usually a sibling or a close friend—and if you had a *parabatai*, the choice of *suggenes* was made for you. But Will's *parabatai* was a Silent Brother now, and Silent Brothers could not be *suggenes*. So that place beside Will would remain empty as he walked the floor of the cathedral.

Or at least it would look empty to everyone else. To Will, it would be filled with the memory of Jem: Jem's smile, Jem's hand on his arm, Jem's unwavering loyalty.

In the mirror, he saw a Will Herondale, nineteen years old, in deep blue gear—a nod to Tessa's warlock heritage—with a gold lining. The gear was cut like a frock coat, the cuffs and hem finely woven with a pattern of gold runes. Golden links sparkled at his wrists. His wild black hair had been tamed for the moment; he looked composed and calm, though inside, his soul breathed grief and love. Until this last year, he had never thought that the heart could hold a full measure of sorrow and happiness at the same time, and yet as he mourned Jem and loved Tessa, he felt both in equal parts. He knew she did too, and it was a comfort to the two of them to be together and share what few others had ever felt, for though Will believed profound grief and profound joy *could* happen at the same time, as equal love did, he could not believe it was common.

"Don't forget the cane, Will," said Henry, snapping Will out of his reverie, and he handed Will the dragon-headed cane that had been Jem's. Will bowed to Henry, his heart full, then made his way downstairs and into the heart of the church.

The room had been decorated with banners bearing gold runes of Love, Marriage, and Loyalty. The sun was bright outside, illuminating the path through the pews that led to the altar. It was decorated with heaps of white flowers that had come from Idris. They filled the room with a scent that reminded him of Herondale Manor in the Idris countryside, a great pile of golden stone that he had inherited upon turning eighteen. His heart lifted at the thought: he and Tessa had visited the manor in the summer of the last year, when Brocelind Forest's trees had draped themselves in greenery and the fields were alive with color. It had reminded him of his childhood home in Wales; he hoped he and Tessa would spend all summer months there from now on.

His heart lifted further as he leaned Jem's cane against the altar and turned to face the room: he had been afraid that the Enclave of London, in their prejudice and bigotry, would avoid the wedding; feelings about the fact that Tessa was half-warlock ranged from indifference to outright coldness. But the pews were filled, and he saw beaming faces throughout: Henry beside Charlotte (who had left baby Charles in the care of Bridget), who wore a hat trembling with a mass of flowers; the recently married Baybrooks; the Townsends and Wentworths and Bridgestocks; George Penhallow, who was currently serving as interim head of the Institute; Will's sister, Cecily, sitting by the large gold harp that had been brought down from the music room; Gideon and Gabriel Lightwood together; and even Tatiana Blackthorn, holding the blanket-wrapped bundle of her son, Jesse, and wearing an oddly familiar pink dress.

A part of Will wished that his parents could have been here. He had gone to see them several times in secret since Charlotte had given him permission to use the Portal in the crypt to visit his family. But they were very far from the world of Shadowhunters now and had no wish to return to it. He and Tessa would be going to visit them a few days after the wedding, to receive their congratulations and their blessing.

Charlotte rose to her feet. She had removed her hat, and was wearing the full regalia of the Consul she now was, her robes stamped with silver and gold runes, the Consul's staff in her hands. She, like Will, moved slowly between the pews and up the steps to the altar; she took her place behind it and smiled down at Will. To him, she looked just as she had when he'd first arrived at the London Institute, terrified and alone, and she'd taken him in.

A single soft note sounded through the room. Will recalled the harp lessons Cecily had had in Wales; his mother had known how to play it too. Will wished—

And all his wishes fell away, because the doors at the back of the church opened, and Tessa came in.

She had chosen to dress all in gold, defying those who might say that she was not a full Shadowhunter and was not entitled to the color. Her dress was silk, with a seamed basque cut close to her body and a full skirt overlaid with a layer of ivory tulle. Her gloves were silk and delicate, as were the beaded slippers that peeked from the hem of her gown. Her hair had been dressed with small golden flowers of twisted silk.

He had never seen anyone, or anything, so lovely.

She walked with her chin up, proudly, her eyes on Will. Those gray eyes: the first time he had ever looked into them, they had struck through and through him with the sharpness of the metal they resembled. Her cheeks were flushed; she held tightly to Sophie's arm as Sophie sedately walked her down the aisle. Will had not been at all surprised when Tessa had chosen Sophie as her *suggenes*. He liked Sophie too, but at the moment he could look at nothing but Tessa.

She joined him at the altar, Sophie melting away to stand behind her. Will could feel his heart beating out of his chest. Tessa was looking down; he could only see the top of her head and the gold silk flowers among the loops of her hair.

He had never thought this would happen. Not really, in the depths of his heart, where the darkest of his fears were hidden. For so long he had accepted that he would never stop loving Tessa, but that love would never come to anything. It would be hidden, perhaps to burn always with the same terrible agony, perhaps to live on as a choking vine slowly destroying his capacity to feel joy. She would be his only in dreams; the memory of having kissed her the only kisses he would ever know.

Herondales loved but once, and he had given his heart to Tessa. But she could not take it.

When everything changed, it had been a very slow dawning of joy. A light breaking through the clouds of loss that carried his *parabatai*'s name. He would wake up crying out for Jem, and sometimes Tessa would come from her own room and sit with him, holding his hand until he slept again. Then sometimes she would be the one to grieve and he the one to comfort her.

And then he worried that love could not grow out of such bitter soil. But grow it did, and richer and deeper than before. By the time he asked Tessa to marry him, they had become gold that had been forged in fire. The time since that day, anticipating their wedding, had been a delirium of happiness, a daze of plans and laughter.

But Tessa was not looking at him, and for a moment he was assailed by the old doubts: he said in a voice so low he doubted Charlotte or Sophie could hear it, "Tess, *cariad?*" *Tess, darling?*

She looked up at that. She was smiling, her eyes dancing. He wondered how he could ever have thought their color like metal: they were like the clouds that gathered over Cadair Idris. She put her hand over her mouth as if she were trying to stop herself laughing out loud. "Oh, Will," she said. "I'm *so* happy."

He reached out to catch at her hands, and Charlotte cleared her throat. Her eyes were brimming over with love and fondness as she gazed down at Tessa and Will.

"Let us begin," Charlotte said.

The Institute went silent; Cecily had stopped strumming the harp. Will stood looking at Tessa as his life opened out before him.

"I stand here in two capacities," said Charlotte. "As the Consul, it is my duty to join together two of the Nephilim." She stared fiercely into the crowd, daring anyone to disagree with her assessment of Tessa as a Shadowhunter. "As a friend of these two, it is a joy to seal their happiness in the covenant of marriage."

Will thought for a moment he heard someone laugh; he glanced out into the rows of pews but saw only friendly faces looking back. Even Gabriel Lightwood making a face at him was more par for the course than hostile.

"Theresa Gray," said Charlotte. "Hast thou found the one thy soul loves?"

I will rise now, and go about the city in the streets, and in the broad ways I will seek him whom my soul loveth: I sought him, but I found him not. Will knew the words; all Shadowhunters did.

Tessa's whole face seemed to glow. "I have found him," she said. "And I will not let him go."

"William Owen Herondale." Charlotte turned to Will. "Hast thou gone among the watchmen, and in the cities of the world? Hast thou found the one thy soul loves?"

Will thought of the many restless nights he had passed wandering the streets of London, following no particular direction, seeking no particular goal. Perhaps all those nights he had truly been looking for Tessa, without ever knowing she was what he sought.

"I have found her," Will said. "And I will *never* let her go."

Charlotte smiled. "Now is the time for the exchange of rings."

There was a certain murmur of interest among those gathered in the room: Tessa, though her mother had been a Shadowhunter, could not wear the Angel's runes. The audience had no doubt wondered how they would choose to handle the runes that were traditionally exchanged at a wedding—one on the arm and the other over the heart—with the bride and groom Marking each other with steles. They would be disappointed, Will thought; he and Tessa had decided to manage the placing of runes after the ceremony—the rune over the heart was often done in private as it was.

Sophie stepped forward, holding out a shallow velvet box in which had been placed two rings, both with the Herondale design. Inside each ring had been etched a single image of lightning, a nod to Tessa's Starkweather heritage, and six words: *the last dream of my soul.*

Will didn't care if the quote wouldn't mean anything to other people. It meant everything to him and Tessa.

Tessa took the larger ring first and slid it onto Will's finger. He had always worn his family ring, but it felt different now, weighted with new import. She fumbled with her glove, and by the time he was holding her bare hand in his, slipping the Herondale ring onto her left hand, she was bouncing on her toes with impatience.

The ring went on. Tessa looked at her hand and then at Will, her face solemn with joy.

"Theresa Gray Herondale and William Owen Herondale," said Charlotte. "You are now married. Let us rejoice."

A cheer went up from the pews; Cecily began to strum a loud and probably inappropriate marching song on the harp. Will caught Tessa into his arms: she was a bundle of soft silk, slippery tulle, and warm lips turned up to his for a quick kiss. He breathed in her scent of lavender and wished they could be away from all this, alone in the room that had been set up and furnished for their private use. The room they would occupy as a married couple for the rest of his life.

But there was still the lavish banquet dinner to get through. Will tucked Tessa's arm through his and began to lead her down the altar steps.

Charlotte had outdone herself decorating the ballroom. Banners of gold silk hung over the windows, doorways, and fireplaces. A single massive table had been set up, running down the middle of the room. It had been covered in a damask cloth, and the plates, dishes, candlesticks, and cutlery were all gold.

Tessa's eyes were huge. "Charlotte shouldn't have spent so much *money*," she whispered as she and Will inspected the flower arrangements—bushels of hothouse roses dripping from every available surface in shades of gold, cream, and pink.

"Hopefully she raided the Clave's treasury," said Will equably, helping himself to a queen's cake. Tessa laughed and pointed at a matched pair of chairs, massive wooden throne-like objects with pointed backs and gilt inlay. After a whispered conversation, Will and Tessa seated themselves regally just as the ballroom doors were opened to the wedding party.

There were oohs and aahs as everyone poured in, dressed in their finery. Cecily, in a blue dress that matched her eyes, came dancing over to hug and kiss and congratulate them both. Gabriel trailed behind her, gazing at her like a lovesick deer in the forest. Gideon and Sophie, happily engaged, were off giggling together in a corner, and Charlotte and Henry were fussing over baby Charles, who had colic and wished everyone to know about it.

Cecily clapped her hands as two of the servants Charlotte had hired especially for the wedding approached the table, carrying two tiered cakes.

"Why *two*?" Tessa whispered in Will's ear.

"One for the wedding guests and one for the bride," he explained. "The one for the guests will be cut up, and everyone will be sent home with a piece for good luck. Yours is meant to be eaten save one piece, which we will save for our twenty-fifth anniversary."

"You're pulling my leg, Will Herondale," Tessa said. "No one wants to eat a piece of twenty-five-year-old cake."

"Hopefully you will feel differently when we are both ancient and hideous," said Will. He remembered then, just for a moment, that Tessa never would be ancient or hideous. Only he would age and die. It was an odd, intrusive thought: he looked away quickly and caught the eye of Tatiana Blackthorn, who had taken a seat at the end of the table. She was clutching Jesse to her, her green eyes roving suspiciously around the room. He knew she was only nineteen or so, but she looked years older.

She gave Will an unfathomable look and glanced away.

Will shivered and laid his hand over Tessa's, just as Henry began good-naturedly rapping his glass with something that looked very like a test tube. It likely *was* a test tube; Henry had already set up a laboratory in the cellar of the Consul's house in Grosvenor Square. "A toast," he began. "To the happy couple . . ."

Tessa had threaded her fingers through Will's, but he still felt cold, as if Tatiana's gaze had spilled ice water through his veins. Cecily had gone back to Gabriel, and he could tell by the glint in her eye that she was planning something.

As it turned out, all their friends were. After Henry's toast came Charlotte's, then Gideon and Sophie's, Cecily and Gabriel's. They praised Tessa and gently mocked Will, but it was the kind of mockery born out of love, and Will laughed as much as anyone—well, anyone save perhaps Jessamine. She was present in ghostly form, and Will could see her rocking from side to side with amusement, her blond hair drifting in an invisible breeze.

As the dinner came to a close, the silences between Will and Tessa drew out more and more. They were not uncomfortable silences; far from it. There was something else, something between them that crackled like firelight. Every time Tessa glanced at Will, her cheeks turned pink and she bit her lip. Will wondered if it would be considered rude if he leaped onto the table and ordered everyone out of the Institute as he urgently needed to have a private conversation with his wife.

He decided it would be. Nevertheless, he was tapping his polished shoes against the floor impatiently by the time guests began to come up to Will and Tessa and excuse themselves.

"How absolutely delightful," Will said to Lilian Highsmith. *To see you go*, he thought.

"Oh, yes, very wise to leave before the roads are too icy," Tessa said to Martin Wentworth. "We completely understand."

"Ah, absolutely," Will began, turning, "and many thanks to you for coming—"

He broke off abruptly. Tatiana Blackthorn stood directly in front of him. Her face was scoured of all expression, like a pan that had been overcleaned. Her thin hands worked together restlessly. "I have something to say to you," she told him.

He saw Cecily looking over at him a bit anxiously. She was holding baby Jesse—Tatiana must have taken a momentary opportunity to foist the child on Cecily while she came to speak to Will. His uneasiness deepened. "Yes?" he said.

She leaned closer to him. Around her neck hung a gold locket, etched with the thorn pattern of the Blackthorn family. He realized with a sudden sick dizziness that her dress was the same gown she'd worn the day her father and husband had died. The stains on it were surely old blood.

"Today, Will Herondale," she said, speaking very low and very clearly, almost directly into his ear, "will be the happiest day of your life."

He could not have said why, but a shiver passed through him. He did not reply to her, nor did she seem to want him to—she only drew back and went over to Cecily, plucking the swaddled child back from her with a satisfied look.

As soon as Tatiana had left the ballroom, Cecily hurried over. Tessa, at his side, was in conversation with Charlotte, and Will did not think she'd noticed anything, thank the Angel.

"What was that awful Tatiana saying to you?" Cecily demanded. "She gives me the horrors, Will, she really does. Only think, when I am married to Gabriel I will be related to her."

"She said today would be the happiest day of my life," Will said. He felt as if a cold stone had settled in his stomach.

"Oh." Cecily frowned. "Well—that's not so bad, is it? It's the sort of thing people say at weddings."

"Cecy." Gabriel had appeared at Will's sister's side. "It's started to snow. Look."

They all looked: snow in March was unusual, and when it did come, it was usually freezing, spitting sleet. Not the fat white flakes currently falling outside the windows, ready to blanket the dirty city in a cloud of pure silver.

Guests were hurrying to depart now, before the roads became impassable. Cecily had gone to hug Tessa and wish her happy. Will rose to his feet as Charlotte approached him, smiling.

"Tell Tessa I have gone up to make sure there is a fire in our rooms," he said mechanically. He felt as if he were a great distance away from his own body. "She should not be cold on her wedding night."

Charlotte looked puzzled but did not try to stop Will as he hurried from the room.

Today will be the happiest day of your life.

If Tatiana hadn't said that to him, Will thought, would he still be sitting here by the window, staring out at the snow and cold? The city was turning white before his eyes, St. Paul's a ghost before the dichromatic sky.

It was as if Tatiana's words were a key that had unlocked something inside him, and all his fears had come pouring out. There had been no family for Tessa at the wedding, and he worried still that the Clave would never truly accept her, that her part-warlock status would always prevent them from looking upon her as a suitable Shadowhunter. What if they spoke to her cruelly, and he was not there to stop it? What if they made her life a misery, and she grew to resent him for trapping her in the Enclave of London? What if they both missed Jem too much to let go of their grief and live?

What if he could not make Tessa happy?

The thoughts whirled in his mind like snow. He had lit the fire, and the room was warm—there was a great four-poster bed in the center, and someone, Charlotte most likely, had put vases of ivory flowers on both nightstands. They filled the air with their perfume.

Snow rustled softly against the windowpanes as the door opened and Tessa put her head into the room. She was all smiles, glowing like a candle.

What if today is the happiest day of her life? What if every day from this one forward is sadder and more empty?

Will took a shuddering breath and tried to smile. "Tess."

"Oh, good, you're decent," she said. "I was half-worried you'd be dressed as Sydney Carton just to shock me. Can Sophie come in? She needs to help me with my dress."

Will only nodded. Tessa narrowed her eyes; she knew him better than almost anyone in the world, Will thought. She would see his fears and doubts.

What if she thought they were about her?

Tessa gestured, and she and Sophie passed through the bedroom and into the dressing room as Will looked numbly at his hands. Bloody hell, he hadn't had a single fear or second thought leading up to his wedding. He had woken up every morning wondering if it was possible to be so happy, so full of expectation.

Then he would want to tell Jem about it, and Jem would not be there. Grief and love, twinned like dark and light in his soul. But he had never doubted his love for Tessa.

He could hear movement and soft laughter in the dressing room, and then Sophie emerged, winked at Will, and departed, closing the bedroom door firmly behind her. A moment later Tessa stepped out. She was wrapped in a blue velvet dressing gown that covered her from neck to ankles. Her hair was down, spilling over her shoulders in a riot of soft brown waves.

She crossed the room on bare feet and sank down onto the window seat beside him. "Now, Will," she said gently. "Tell me what is bothering you, for I know something is."

He ached to take her into his arms. If he kissed her, he knew he would forget: forget Tatiana's words, the holes in his own soul, every fear he harbored. He never lost himself so thoroughly as he did in Tessa's arms. He remembered the night they had spent together in Cadair Idris, the feel of her under his body, the unbelievable softness of her skin. How grief and regret had dissolved in that moment, and there had only been a happiness he had never thought he would know.

But memory had come in the morning, and he feared it would now, too. He owed her better than that. He owed her more than trying to find forgetfulness in her kisses.

"It is foolishness," he said. "And yet it preys on me. Before she left the ballroom, Tatiana said to me, 'Today will be the happiest day of your life.'"

Tessa raised her eyebrows. "So you think she means each successive day after this one will be unhappier? I'm sure she does. She hates you, Will. She hates me, too. If she could ruin this day for us, she would gladly do it. It does not mean she has the powers of the evil fairy at the christening of Sleeping Beauty."

"I do know that," he said. "But I have worried all this time I will not be able to make you happy, Tessa. Not as Jem could have made you happy."

She looked startled. "Will."

"I have never blamed you for loving him," he said, watching her face closely. "Everything in his life he has done with honor and purity and strength—and who would not want to be loved like that? Whereas when I love you, I know, it is desperate." He almost winced at the word. "You cannot understand, I think, how I love you. Perhaps I have better hidden it than I thought. It is a shattering thing, Tessa. It threatens to break me in pieces and I am terrified to be so . . . changed." He looked away from her. He could see his own reflection in the darkness of the window, his face very pale beneath the fall of his dark hair. He wondered dully if he would frighten her away.

"Will," she said softly. "Will, look at me."

He glanced at her; even in her thick dressing gown, she was adorable and desirable enough to make him feel dizzy. They had done nothing but kiss, and that rarely, since that night in Cadair Idris. They had held themselves back, waiting for this night.

Tessa pressed a folded bit of paper into Will's hand. "Jem was here tonight," she said. "I did not see him either, any more than you did. He gave a letter to Sophie, though, and she passed it to me. I think you should read it."

Will took the letter slowly. How long had it been now since he had seen the familiar loops and lines of his *parabatai's* handwriting?

> *Will,*
>
> *I know that you must be happy today, because how could you help but be happy? Yet the fear that you would not accept your happiness has kept me pacing the floors of the Silent City. You have never believed yourself worthy of love, Will, you who love with all your heart and soul. I fear the results of such doubts, for Tessa does love you, and you must have faith in one another, as I have faith in you.*
>
> *I stopped outside the Institute today to pay my respects. I glanced in through the window and saw you and Tessa sitting by each other. I have never seen you look so happy. I know you will only be happier for each day of your lives together.*
>
> *Wo men shi sheng si ji jiao.*
>
> *Jem*

Will took a struggling breath and handed the note to Tessa. It was as if Jem had reached through the dark and icy night and taken his hand. The place over his heart where his *parabatai* rune had been seemed to spark and burn. He remembered suddenly the last time he and Jem had stood in the Institute together, and Will had said Tessa might not want to marry him. Jem had smiled and said, "Well, that part is up to you."

It was still up to him. He wanted to be married to Tessa more than he had ever wanted anything, and he would not let his own fears destroy that.

Tessa had set the note aside and was looking at Will, her gray eyes very serious. "Well," she said. "That is that, then—who are you going to listen to, Will? Tatiana or Jem?"

He met her gaze with his own. "I am going to listen to my own heart," he said. "For it brought me to you."

She smiled a luminous smile, and then gasped a laugh as he reached for her and pulled her into his lap. "Wait," she said, standing up, which Will did not like at all—they were meant to be getting closer to each other, not farther apart.

She tugged at the sash holding her dressing gown closed. Will sat up straight, his back against the cold window. The blue velvet material slipped from her shoulders, revealing her dressed in a half-transparent peignoir of white lace, held together at the front with a row of blue satin ribbons tied in bows.

She was clearly not wearing anything else. The curves and hollows of her body were outlined by the ivory material, skimming her like gossamer. Will understood now why Sophie had winked at him.

"Tess," he said hoarsely, and reached out his arms: she climbed back into them, giggling softly.

"Do you like it?" she said, nuzzling his ear. "Charlotte took me to the most scandalous place on Bond Street. . . ."

"I love it," he said, capturing her mouth in a soft kiss. "I love you—though I don't want to think about Charlotte in a nightgown." He let his head fall back against the window glass. "Take my shirt off, Tess."

She blushed and reached for the mother-of-pearl buttons. Everything in Cadair Idris had been fast, a blur of heat and contact. This was slow, her fingers trailing over one button to the next slowly, her lips pressing gently against the skin as it was uncovered inch by inch. By the time the shirt drifted to the floor, he wanted nothing more than to pick her up and carry her to the bed.

But they were not quite ready yet. Will fumbled his stele out of his pocket and handed it to Tessa, who looked puzzled.

"The last wedding runes," he said. "I want you to put them on me."

"But . . ."

He placed his hand over hers and brought the stele to his arm, where he traced the first wedding rune. The stele sparked against his skin, mixing pleasure and pain. Tessa's face was flushed as they moved the stele to the place over his heart—beside the faded scar where his *parabatai* rune had once rested. "'Set me as a seal upon thine heart, as a seal upon thine arm,'" he whispered, as they drew the next Mark together. "'For love is strong as death; the coals thereof are coals of fire, which hath a most vehement flame.'"

Tessa leaned back. She stared at the rune, standing out strong and dark against the skin of Will's chest. She laid her hand over it, and he wondered if she could feel the hammering of his heart. "'Many waters cannot quench love; neither can the floods drown it.' I will never stop loving you, Will—"

His stele tumbled to the carpet. She was still sitting in his lap: he took hold of her hips and leaned up to kiss her. He was utterly lost the moment their mouths touched. He was lost in Tessa, in the desperate need to kiss her harder, hold her tighter, have her closer yet. His hands slipped and slid over the silk and lace of her peignoir, the material bunching under the grip of his hands.

As their kissing turned wilder, Will found himself reaching to undo the silk bow at the neck of her peignoir. She gave a little gasp as the material fell away, baring the tops of her breasts. Her skin was soft and pale as cream. Will could not stop himself from kissing her throat, her collarbones, tracing his lips softly over the gentle slope of her shoulders. She moaned softly and squirmed in his lap, her hands braced against his shoulders, her nails digging in lightly.

If he didn't do something quickly, Will realized, they were going to spill themselves onto the carpet and never get back up. With a groan deep in his throat, he slid an arm under Tessa's knees and another around her shoulders: she laughed in delighted surprise as he carried her to the bed. They tumbled among the soft pillows and the down coverlet, reaching for each other, the long starvation of their wait for this moment finally ended.

Will kicked off his shoes, dispatching with the remainder of the peignoir's satin bows as Tessa stretched over him, her long hair forming a curtain about the two of them. In the cave, it had been dark: now he could see all of Tessa, and she was all exquisite.

She touched his face with wondering fingers, then let her hand trail farther down his body, exploring the softness and hardness of his chest, the new rune over his heart. "My beautiful Will," she said, her voice husky with desire.

He drew Tessa down against him, and they rolled together across the bed, skin against skin; kneeling, he began to kiss every inch of her body. As he had known he would, he forgot everything else as she arched and trembled under his touch. There was only this moment, only this night, only the two of them—only Will and Tessa Herondale and the beginning of their life together.

Many hours later, Will was woken by Tessa's gentle touch on his shoulder. He was sleeping with his arm around her, her hair fanned out across his chest. He glanced down at his wife; she was smiling at him.

"What is it?" he whispered, brushing a lock of hair away from her eyes.

"Do you hear the bells?" she asked.

Will nodded; in the distance, the bells of St. Paul's were chiming one in the morning.

"It is the day after our wedding," Tessa said. "Are you not happier than you were yesterday? For I am. I think I will be happier every day of our lives."

Will knew a grin was spreading over his face. "You are shameless, my wife. Did you really wake me in the middle of the night just to make a point?"

Tessa rolled against him under the blankets. He felt her light touch against his skin. "Maybe not *just* to make a point, my love."

He laughed softly and drew her into his arms.

CASSANDRA CLARE is the #1 *New York Times* bestselling author of *The Mortal Instruments*, *The Infernal Devices*, *The Dark Artifices* and *The Shadowhunter's Codex*. She is the co-author of *The Bane Chronicles* with Sarah Rees Brennan and Maureen Johnson, *Tales from the Shadowhunter Academy* with Sarah Rees Brennan, Maureen Johnson and Robin Wasserman, and *Ghosts of the Shadow Market* with Sarah Rees Brennan, Maureen Johnson, Robin Wasserman and Kelly Link. She also co-wrote *The Red Scrolls of Magic* with Wesley Chu. Her books have more than 50 million copies in print worldwide. They have been translated into over thirty-five languages and made into a feature film and a TV show. Cassandra lives in Massachusetts, USA. Visit her online at CassandraClare.com. Learn more about the world of the Shadowhunters at UKShadowhunters.com.